CAROUSEL SUMMER

MORE BOOKS BY KATHLEEN GROS

JO: AN ADAPTATION OF LITTLE WOMEN (SORT OF)
ANNE: AN ADAPTATION OF ANNE OF GREEN GABLES (SORT OF)

CAROUSEL SUMMER

KATHLEEN GROS

Quill Tree Books
Imprints of HarperCollinsPublishers

FOR ROO

Quill Tree Books is an imprint of HarperCollins Publishers.
HarperAlley is an imprint of HarperCollins Publishers.

Carousel Summer
Copyright © 2025 by Kathleen Gros
Photos courtesy of the author.
All rights reserved. Manufactured in Johor, Malaysia.
No part of this book may be used or reproduced in any manner whatsoever without written permission except in the case of brief quotations embodied in critical articles and reviews. For information address HarperCollins Children's Books, a division of HarperCollins Publishers, 195 Broadway, New York, NY 10007.
www.harperalley.com

Library of Congress Control Number: 2024942799
ISBN 978-0-06-305768-5 — ISBN 978-0-06-305769-2 (hardcover)

The artist used Photoshop to create the
digital illustrations for this book.
Lettering by Kathleen Gros
Design by Andrea Vandergrift
24 25 26 27 28   COS   10 9 8 7 6 5 4 3 2 1

First Edition

CHAPTER 1

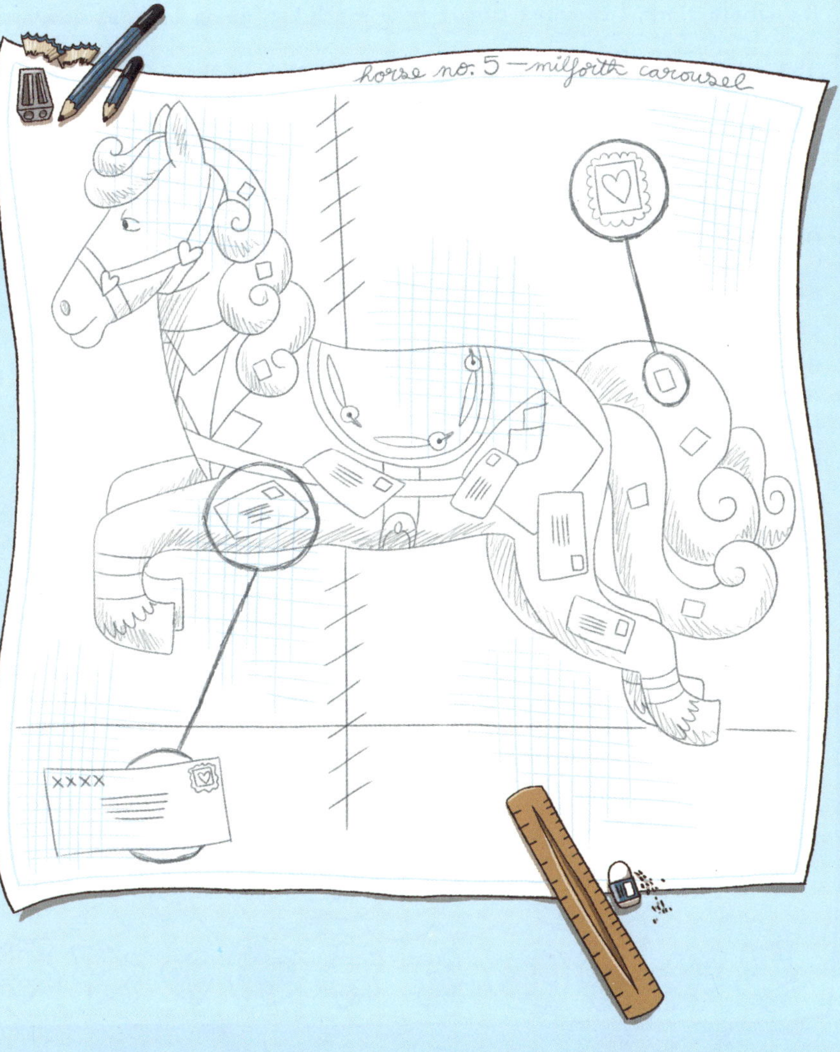
horse no. 5—milforth carousel
XXXX

ONTARIO
MXM XMX

To: LUCY STULLIGROSS

Dear LUCY,

As promised, here is my first dispatch from camp. I'm writing this during breakfast on the very first day. Mom and Dad dropped me off yesterday afternoon. It was a two-hour drive to get here, and the whole time, I thought about how much I'm going to miss you.

The other girls in my cabin seem nice. We're in the Trillium Cabin. All the cabins here are named after plants. Our counselor's name is Beth and she has a nose piercing! I think she even has a tattoo on her arm, but I couldn't totally tell what it was because her sleeve was mostly covering it. I think one day (when we're allowed) we should get matching tattoos.

Today we've got swimming, arts and crafts, a hike, and a campfire after dinner. I'm kind of excited to get to know the girls in my cabin. Don't totally hate me for this but I think camp might actually end up being kind of fun?? It's a coed camp, and honestly . . . the boys are pretty cute. I wonder if I'll get my first kiss this summer!

AH okay I wanted to write more but they're already telling me it's time to head to the lake!!!

Missing you loads and can't wait to see you again. Don't forget to tell me every little thing that happens in Milforth while I'm gone.

Lots and lots of love from your Best Friend Forever (and ever and ever and ever),

KATIA

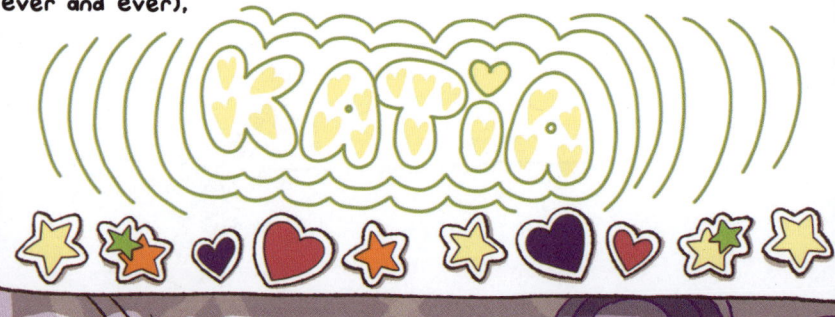

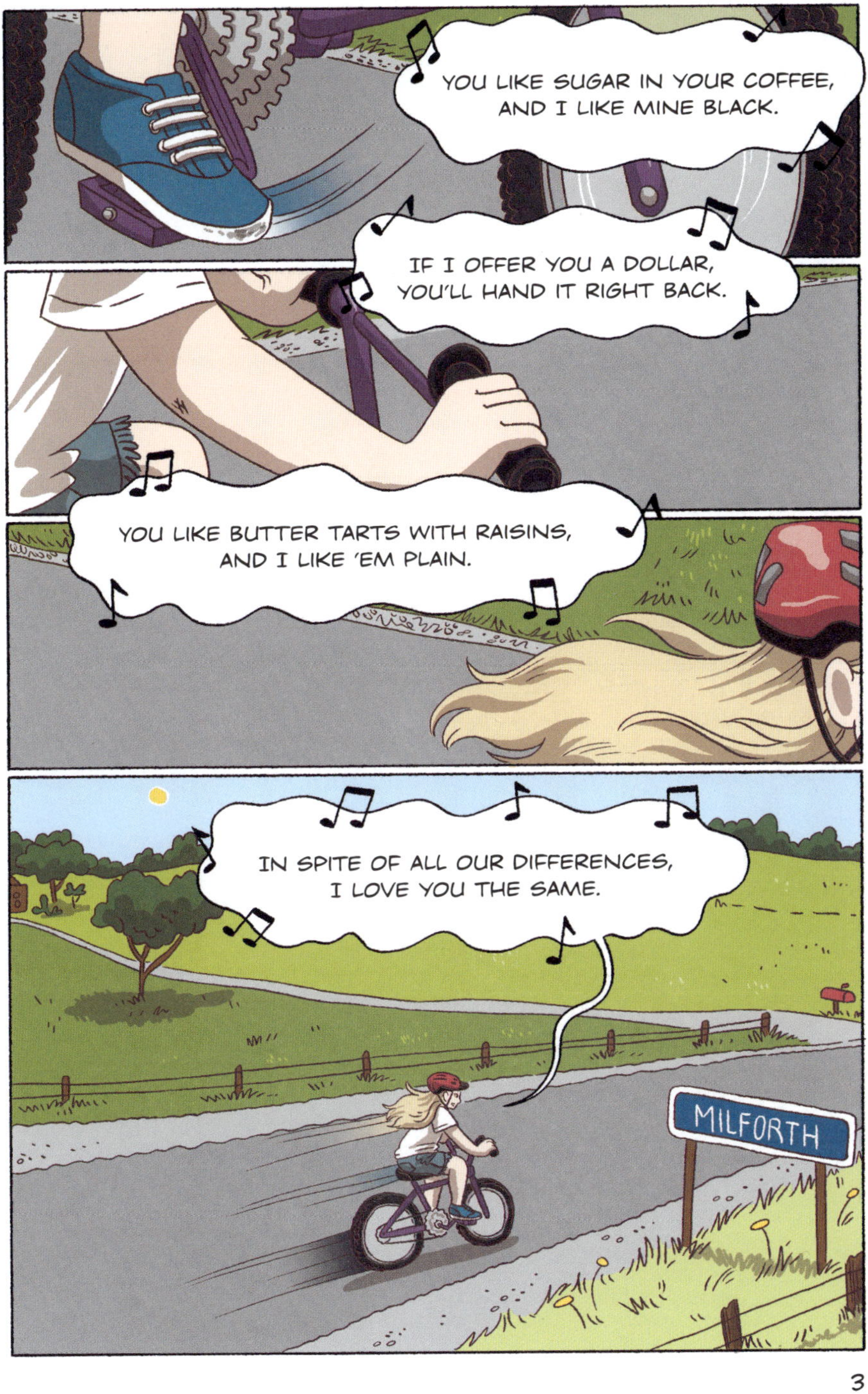
YOU LIKE SUGAR IN YOUR COFFEE, AND I LIKE MINE BLACK.
IF I OFFER YOU A DOLLAR, YOU'LL HAND IT RIGHT BACK.
YOU LIKE BUTTER TARTS WITH RAISINS, AND I LIKE 'EM PLAIN.
IN SPITE OF ALL OUR DIFFERENCES, I LOVE YOU THE SAME.
MILFORTH

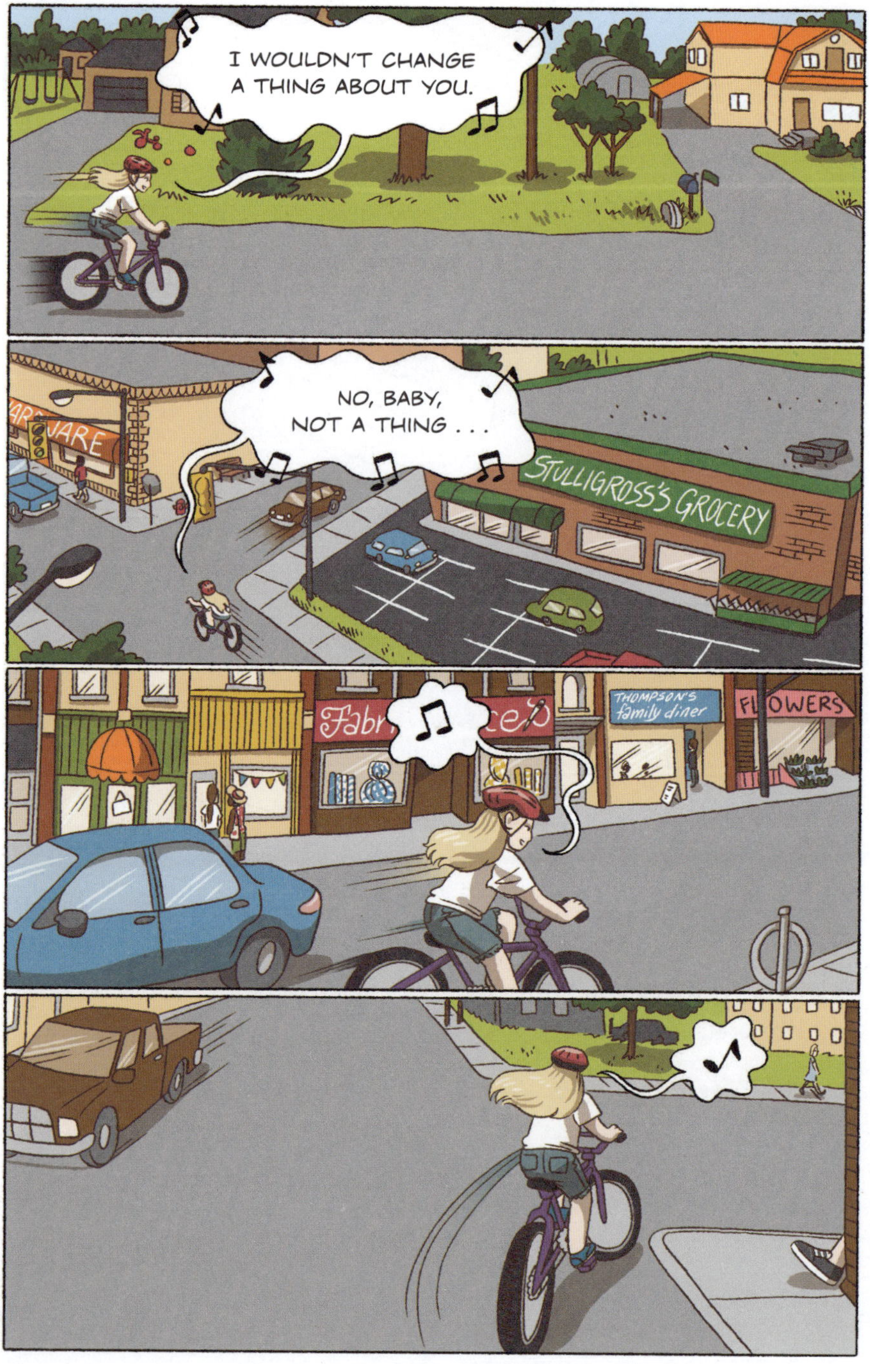
I WOULDN'T CHANGE A THING ABOUT YOU.
NO, BABY, NOT A THING . . .
STULLIGROSS'S GROCERY
THOMPSON'S family diner
FLOWERS

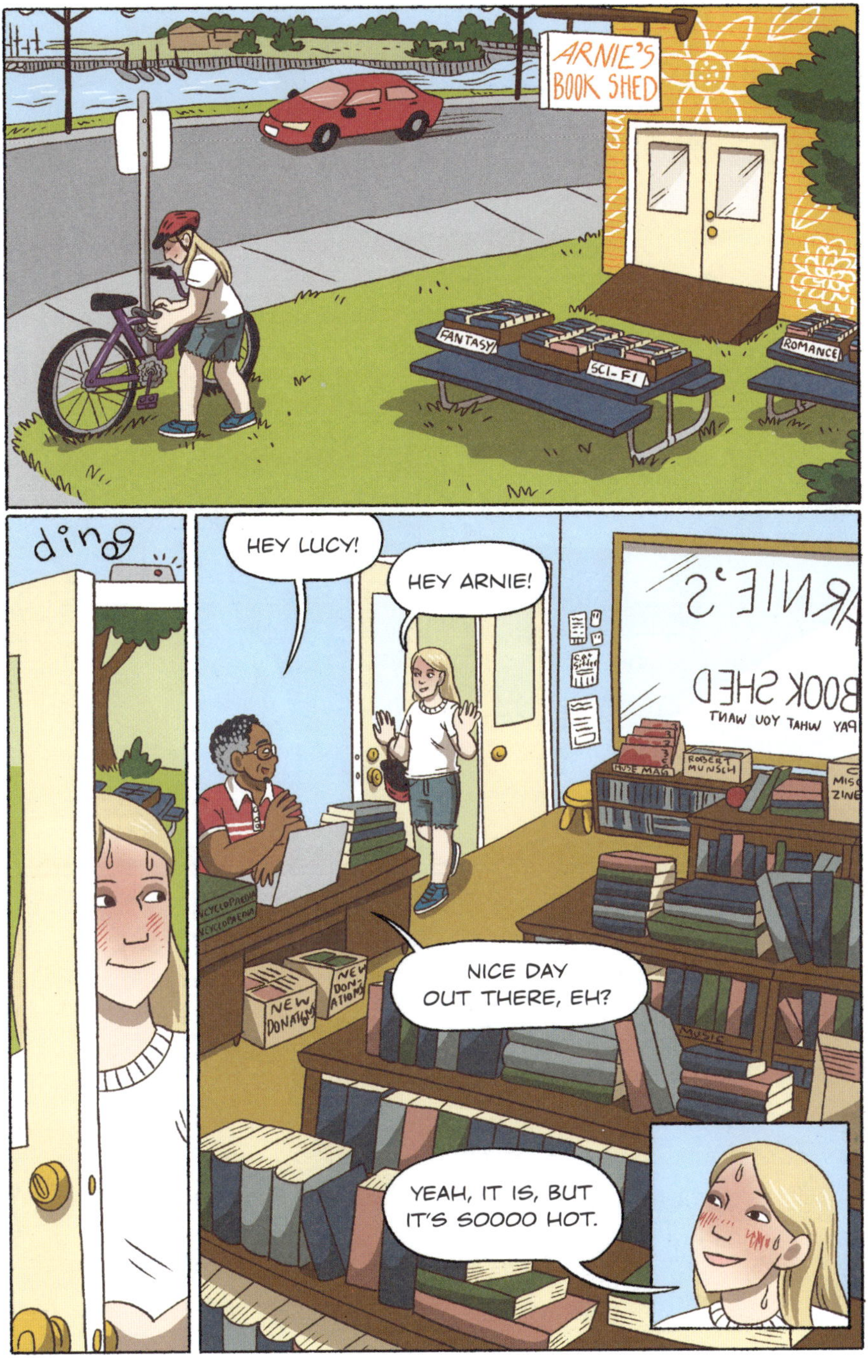
ARNIE'S BOOK SHED
FANTASY
SCI-FI
ROMANCE
ding
HEY LUCY!
HEY ARNIE!
ROBERT MUNSCH
NEW DONATIONS
NEW DONATIONS
NICE DAY OUT THERE, EH?
YEAH, IT IS, BUT IT'S SOOOO HOT.

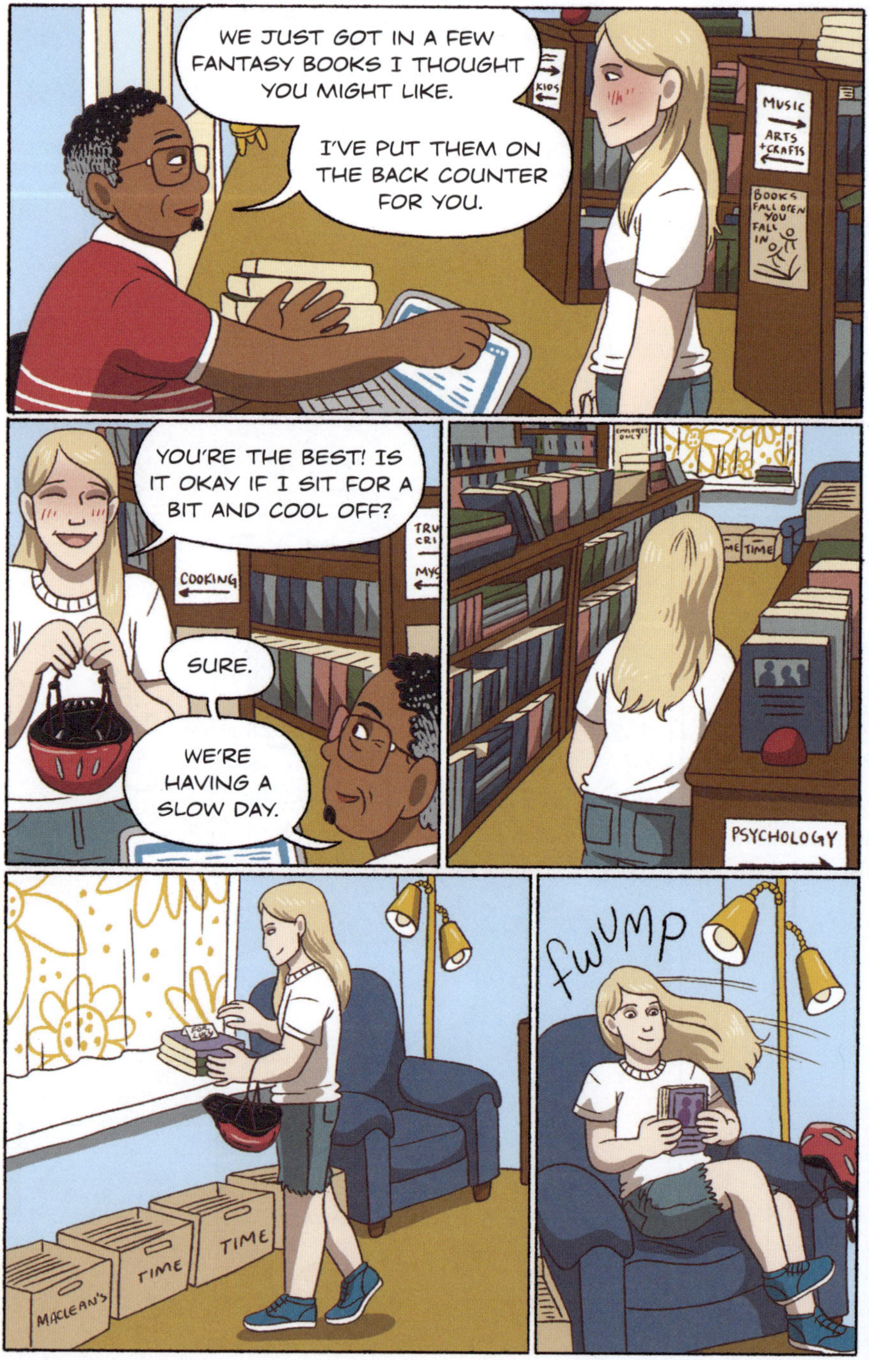
WE JUST GOT IN A FEW FANTASY BOOKS I THOUGHT YOU MIGHT LIKE.
I'VE PUT THEM ON THE BACK COUNTER FOR YOU.
KIDS
MUSIC
ARTS +CRAFTS
BOOKS FALL OPEN YOU FALL IN
YOU'RE THE BEST! IS IT OKAY IF I SIT FOR A BIT AND COOL OFF?
COOKING
SURE.
WE'RE HAVING A SLOW DAY.
PSYCHOLOGY
MACLEAN'S
TIME
TIME
FWUMP

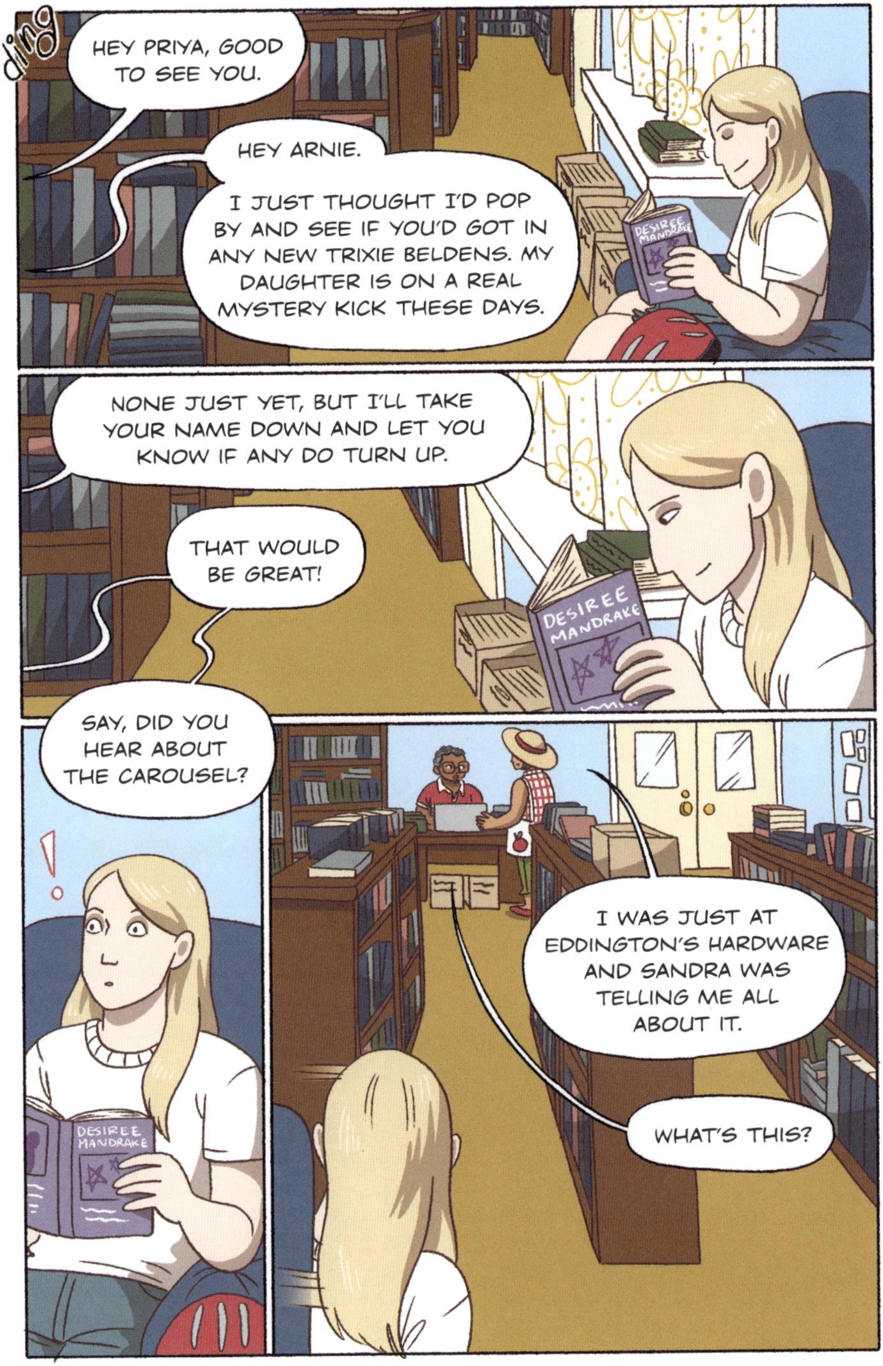
ding
HEY PRIYA, GOOD TO SEE YOU.
HEY ARNIE.
I JUST THOUGHT I'D POP BY AND SEE IF YOU'D GOT IN ANY NEW TRIXIE BELDENS. MY DAUGHTER IS ON A REAL MYSTERY KICK THESE DAYS.
DESIREE MANDRAKE
NONE JUST YET, BUT I'LL TAKE YOUR NAME DOWN AND LET YOU KNOW IF ANY DO TURN UP.
THAT WOULD BE GREAT!
DESIREE MANDRAKE
SAY, DID YOU HEAR ABOUT THE CAROUSEL?
!
DESIREE MANDRAKE
I WAS JUST AT EDDINGTON'S HARDWARE AND SANDRA WAS TELLING ME ALL ABOUT IT.
WHAT'S THIS?

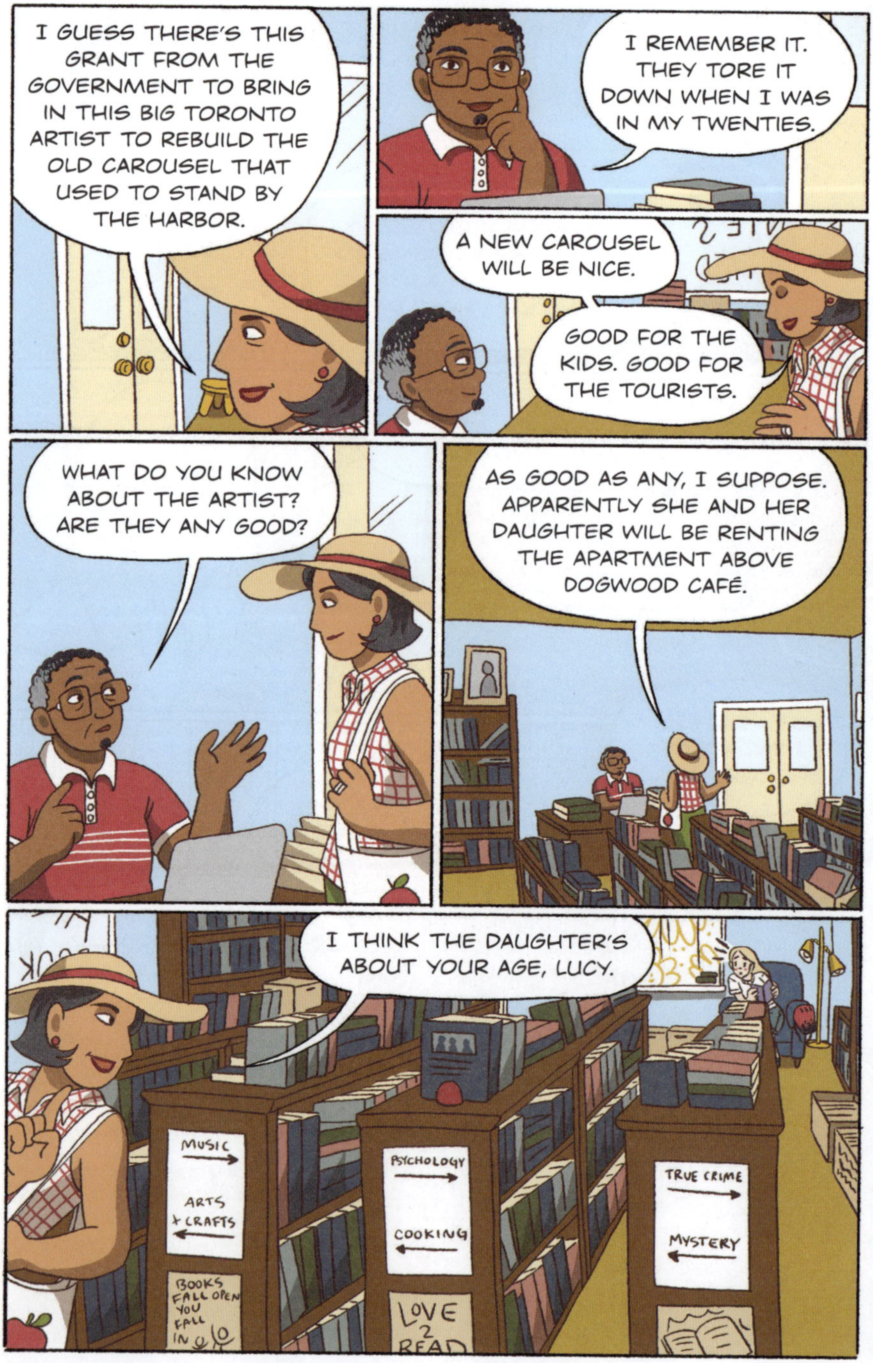
I GUESS THERE'S THIS GRANT FROM THE GOVERNMENT TO BRING IN THIS BIG TORONTO ARTIST TO REBUILD THE OLD CAROUSEL THAT USED TO STAND BY THE HARBOR.
I REMEMBER IT. THEY TORE IT DOWN WHEN I WAS IN MY TWENTIES.
A NEW CAROUSEL WILL BE NICE.
GOOD FOR THE KIDS. GOOD FOR THE TOURISTS.
WHAT DO YOU KNOW ABOUT THE ARTIST? ARE THEY ANY GOOD?
AS GOOD AS ANY, I SUPPOSE. APPARENTLY SHE AND HER DAUGHTER WILL BE RENTING THE APARTMENT ABOVE DOGWOOD CAFÉ.
I THINK THE DAUGHTER'S ABOUT YOUR AGE, LUCY.
MUSIC
ARTS + CRAFTS
PSYCHOLOGY
COOKING
TRUE CRIME
MYSTERY
BOOKS FALL OPEN YOU FALL IN
LOVE 2 READ

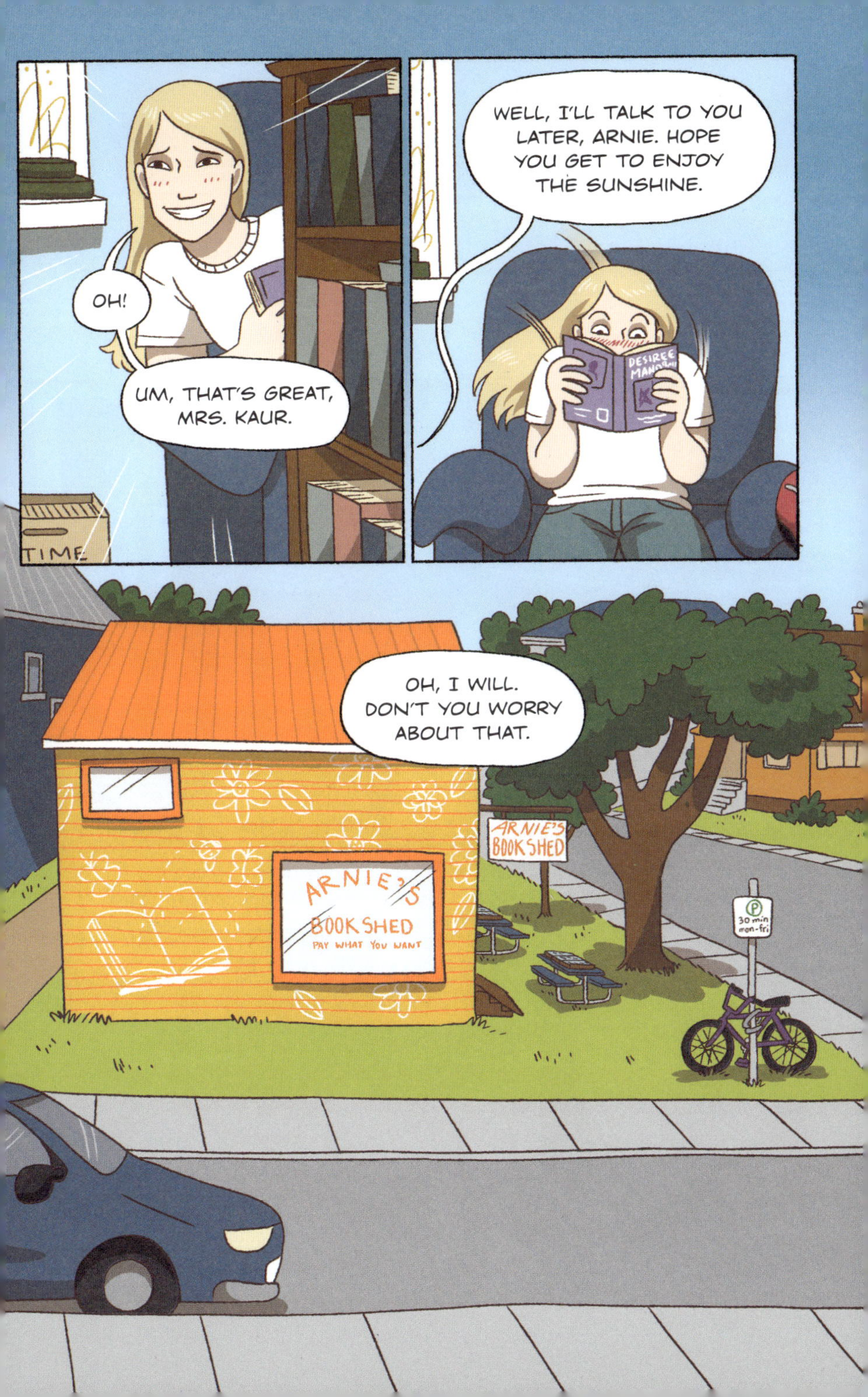
OH!
UM, THAT'S GREAT, MRS. KAUR.
WELL, I'LL TALK TO YOU LATER, ARNIE. HOPE YOU GET TO ENJOY THE SUNSHINE.
DESIREE MANOR
OH, I WILL. DON'T YOU WORRY ABOUT THAT.
ARNIE'S BOOKSHED
ARNIE'S BOOKSHED PAY WHAT YOU WANT
30 min mon-fri

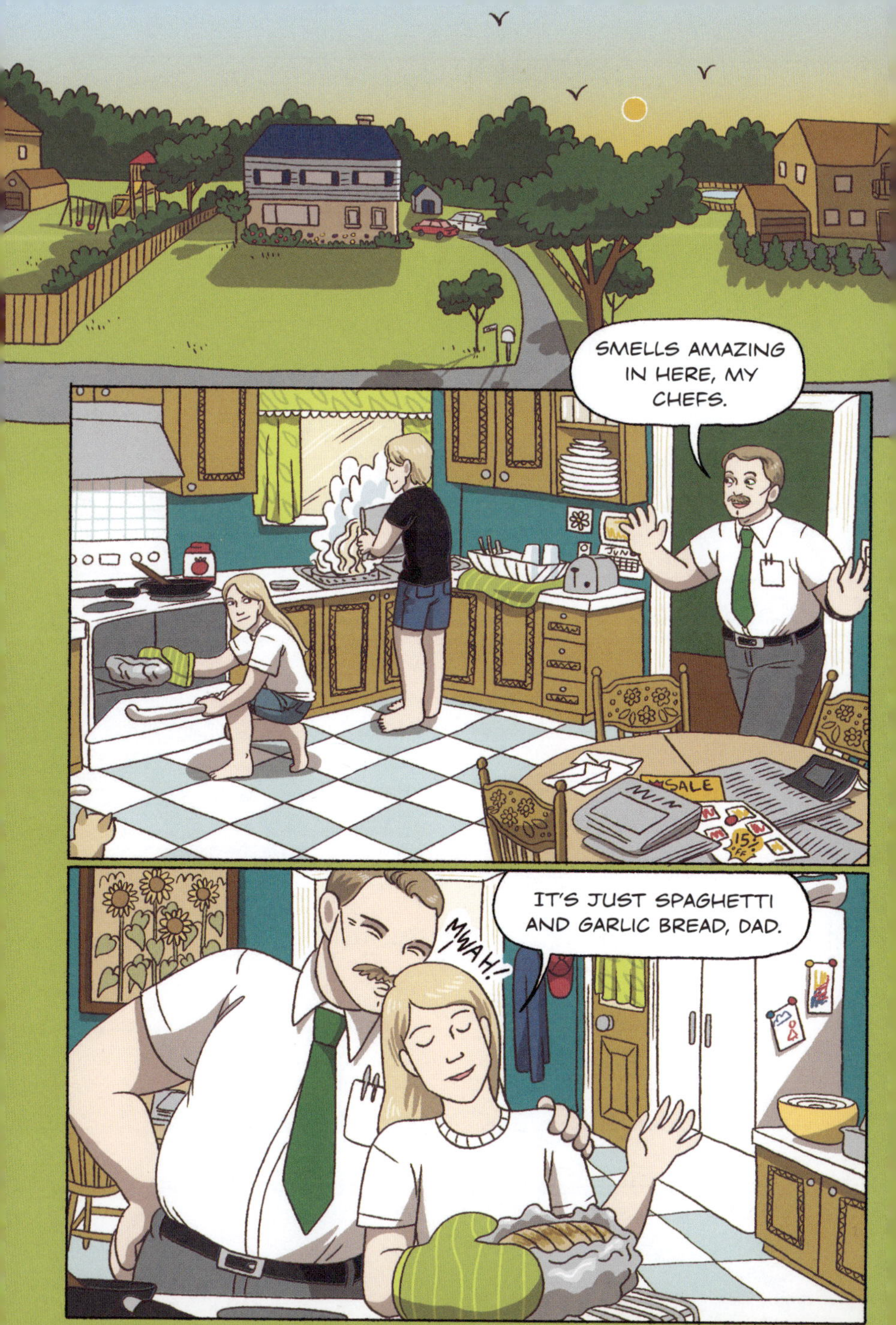
SMELLS AMAZING IN HERE, MY CHEFS.
IT'S JUST SPAGHETTI AND GARLIC BREAD, DAD.
MWAH!

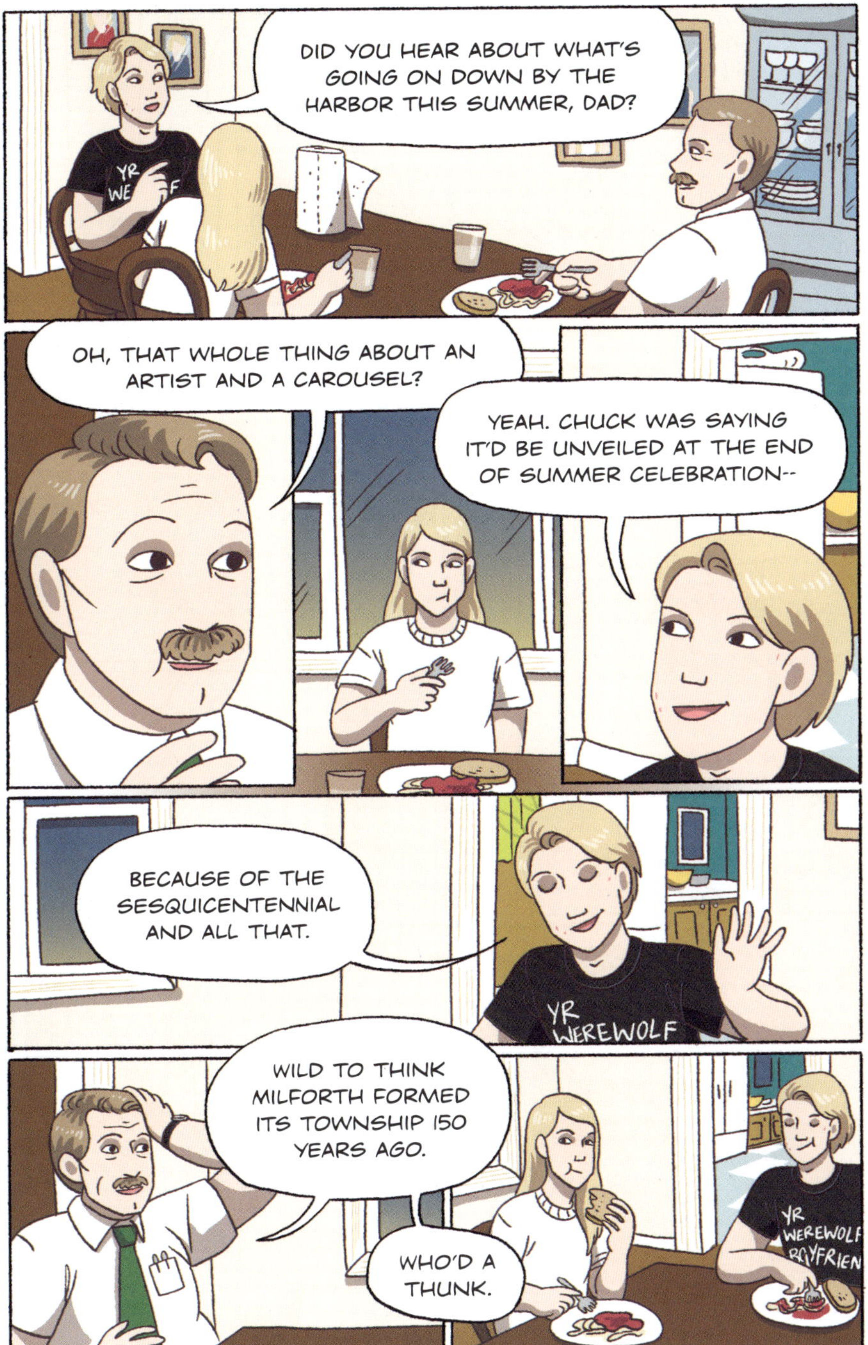
DID YOU HEAR ABOUT WHAT'S GOING ON DOWN BY THE HARBOR THIS SUMMER, DAD?
YR WEREWOLF
OH, THAT WHOLE THING ABOUT AN ARTIST AND A CAROUSEL?
YEAH. CHUCK WAS SAYING IT'D BE UNVEILED AT THE END OF SUMMER CELEBRATION--
BECAUSE OF THE SESQUICENTENNIAL AND ALL THAT.
YR WEREWOLF
WILD TO THINK MILFORTH FORMED ITS TOWNSHIP 150 YEARS AGO.
WHO'D A THUNK.

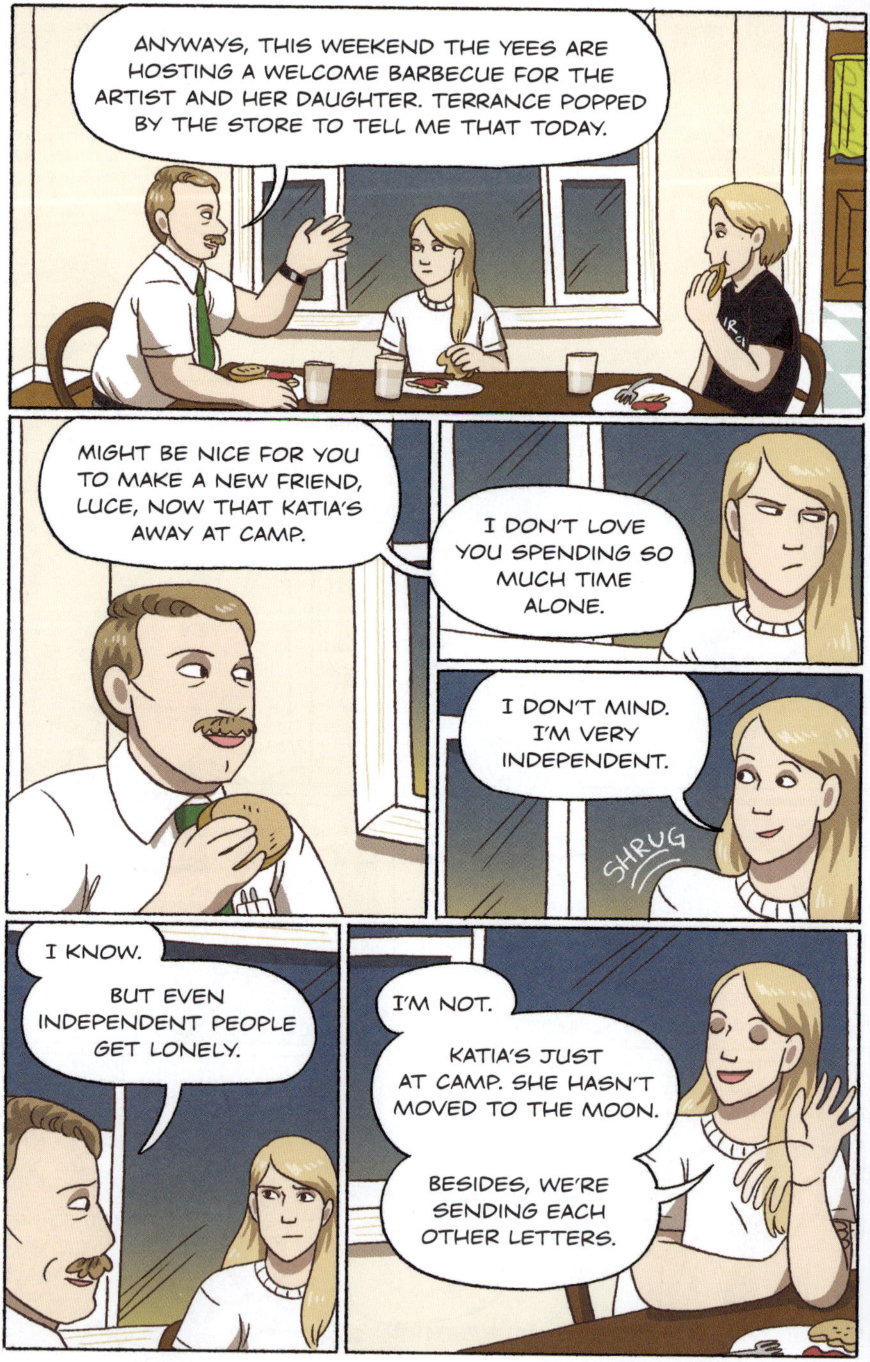
ANYWAYS, THIS WEEKEND THE YEES ARE HOSTING A WELCOME BARBECUE FOR THE ARTIST AND HER DAUGHTER. TERRANCE POPPED BY THE STORE TO TELL ME THAT TODAY.
MIGHT BE NICE FOR YOU TO MAKE A NEW FRIEND, LUCE, NOW THAT KATIA'S AWAY AT CAMP.
I DON'T LOVE YOU SPENDING SO MUCH TIME ALONE.
I DON'T MIND. I'M VERY INDEPENDENT.
SHRUG
I KNOW.
BUT EVEN INDEPENDENT PEOPLE GET LONELY.
I'M NOT.
KATIA'S JUST AT CAMP. SHE HASN'T MOVED TO THE MOON.
BESIDES, WE'RE SENDING EACH OTHER LETTERS.

Dear Katia,

I'm glad the girls in your cabin seem nice. It's cool that there are cute boys. You know there's no one cute in Milforth to kiss... :'(

I miss you, too, obviously. Summer in Milforth is BORING. Dad's working all the time and Daniel's picking up as many shifts as he can at Chuck's Convenience. Dad's only kind of annoyed that Daniel's not working at our store. Daniel gets to work with his best friend at Chuck's, though. I'd pick that over working with Dad for sure. Since I'm the only one with nothing to do, it's my job to clean the house and get dinner started. If I can finish all my chores by noon, then I either watch TV or I bike down to the harbor and see if Arnie needs a hand with anything at the Book Shed. He usually lets me help shelve new donations and says I can sit in the back and read if no one's around.

Maybe I'll do something wild just so I have something to tell you about. Something you'd never expect. ~~Something like~~

It'll be a surprise. Stay tuned!

Your BFF (ae ae ae)

Lucy

xoxo

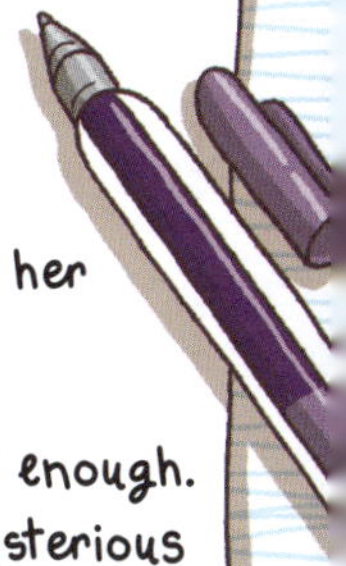

P.S. People keep making a HUGE deal about an artist and her daughter visiting from Toronto... idk though...

P.P.S. Yes 100% to getting matching tattoos when we're old enough. What kind of design should we get? Something cool but mysterious so that only WE understand its meaning?

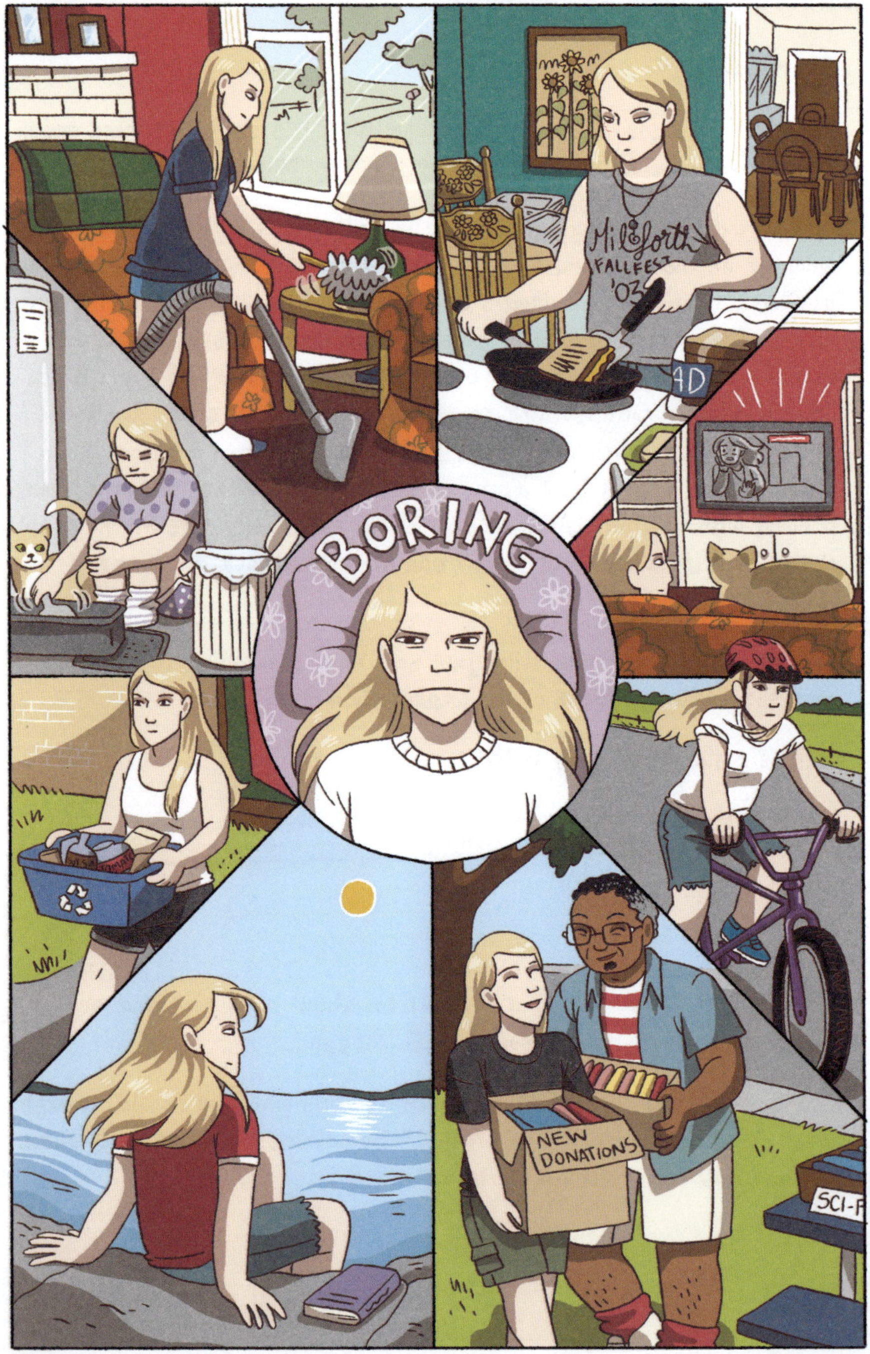
BORING
Milforth FALLFEST '03
NEW DONATIONS
SCI-F

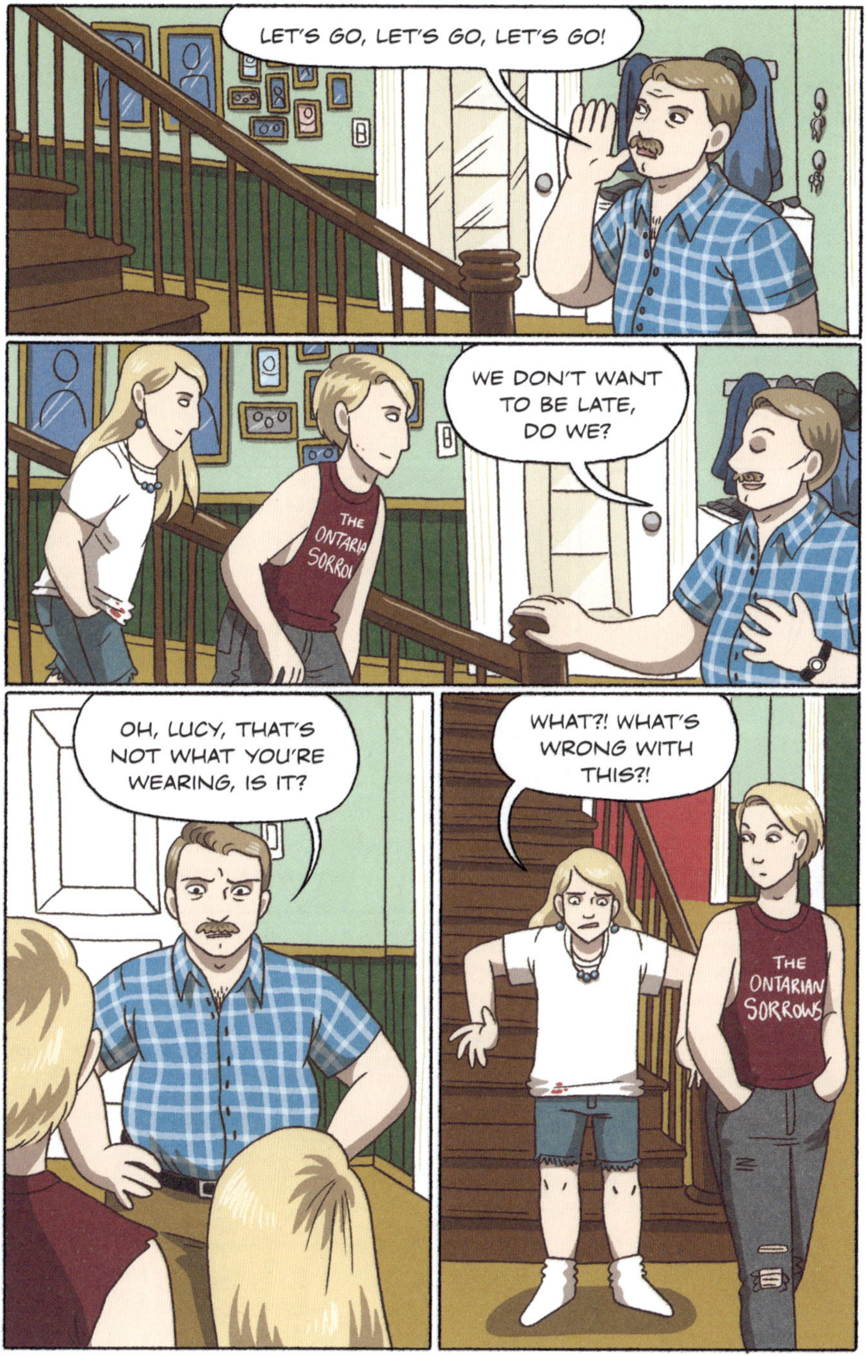
LET'S GO, LET'S GO, LET'S GO!
WE DON'T WANT TO BE LATE, DO WE?
THE ONTARIAN SORROWS
OH, LUCY, THAT'S NOT WHAT YOU'RE WEARING, IS IT?
WHAT?! WHAT'S WRONG WITH THIS?!
THE ONTARIAN SORROWS

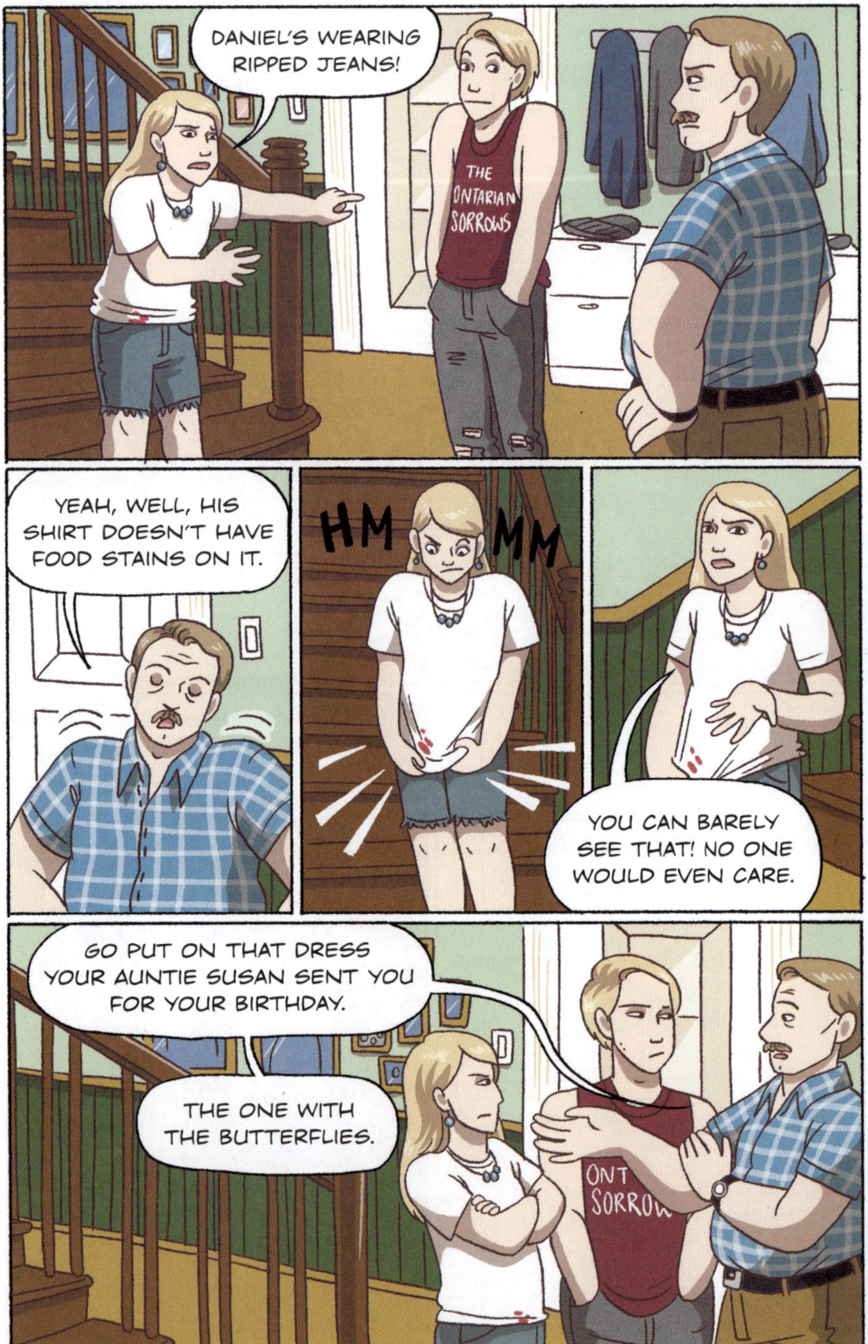
DANIEL'S WEARING RIPPED JEANS!
THE ONTARIAN SORROWS
YEAH, WELL, HIS SHIRT DOESN'T HAVE FOOD STAINS ON IT.
HMMM
YOU CAN BARELY SEE THAT! NO ONE WOULD EVEN CARE.
GO PUT ON THAT DRESS YOUR AUNTIE SUSAN SENT YOU FOR YOUR BIRTHDAY.
THE ONE WITH THE BUTTERFLIES.
ONT SORROW

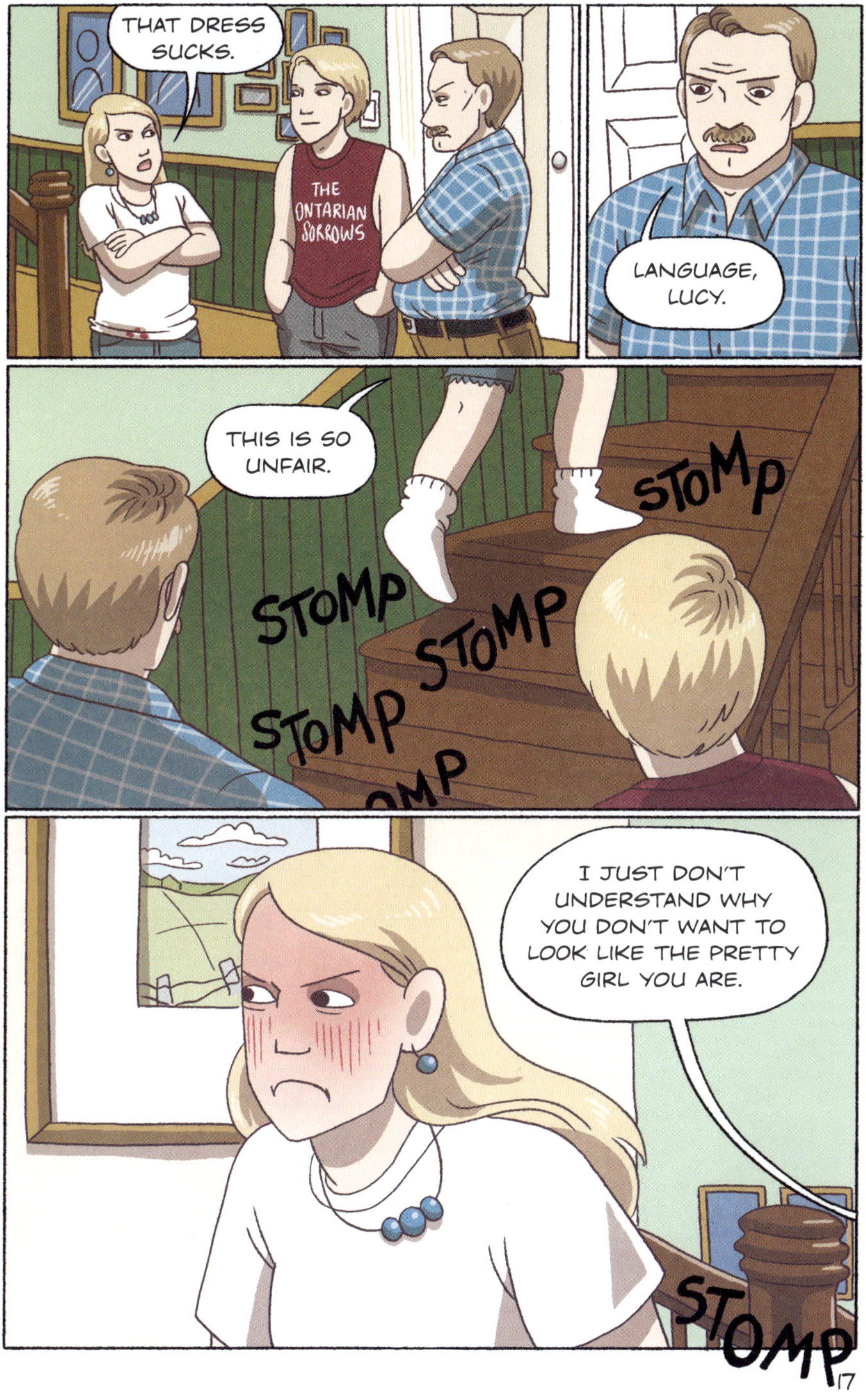
THAT DRESS SUCKS.
THE ONTARIAN SORROWS
LANGUAGE, LUCY.
THIS IS SO UNFAIR.
STOMP
STOMP
STOMP
STOMP
OMP
I JUST DON'T UNDERSTAND WHY YOU DON'T WANT TO LOOK LIKE THE PRETTY GIRL YOU ARE.
STOMP

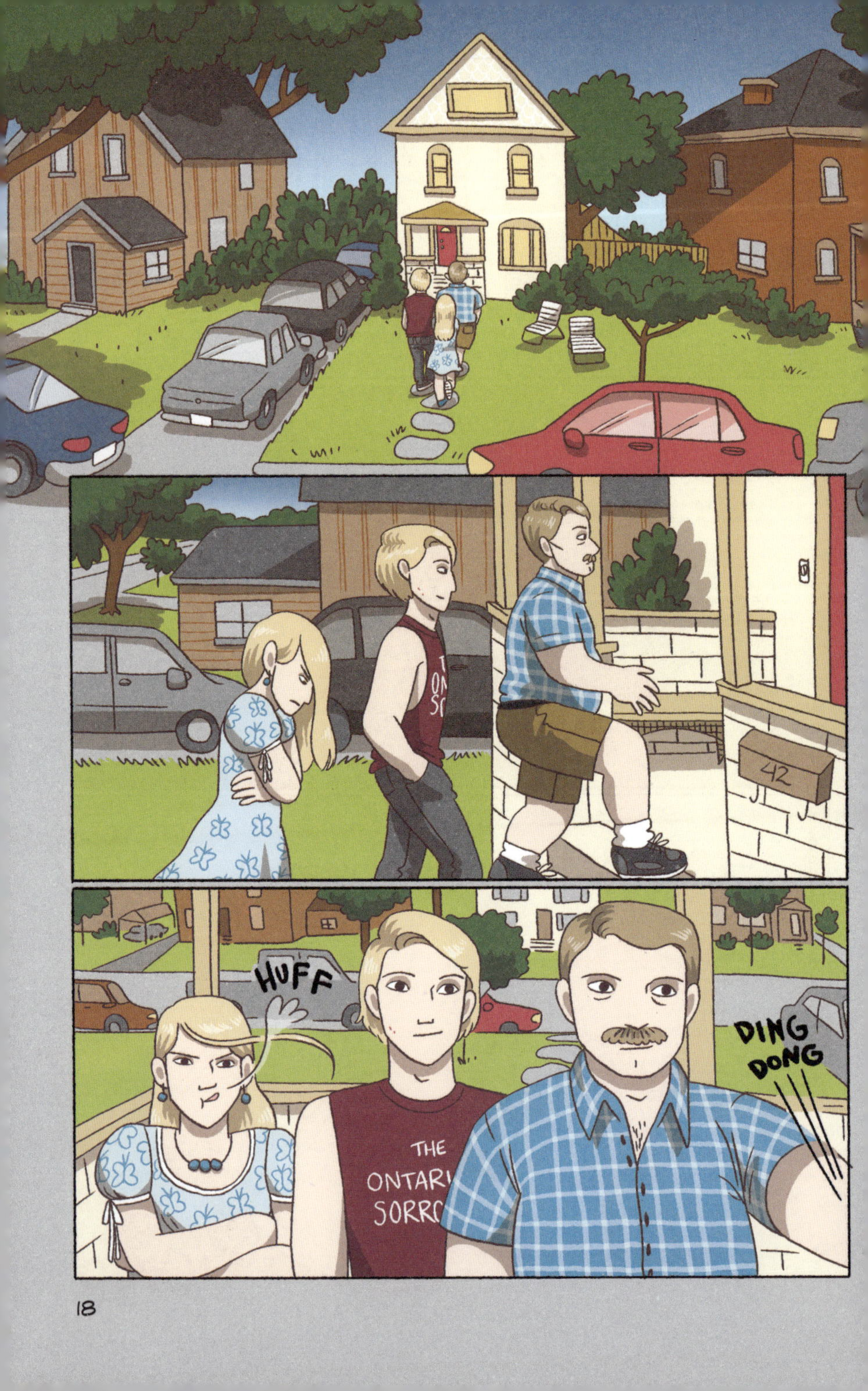
42
HUFF
DING DONG
THE
ONTARI
SORRO

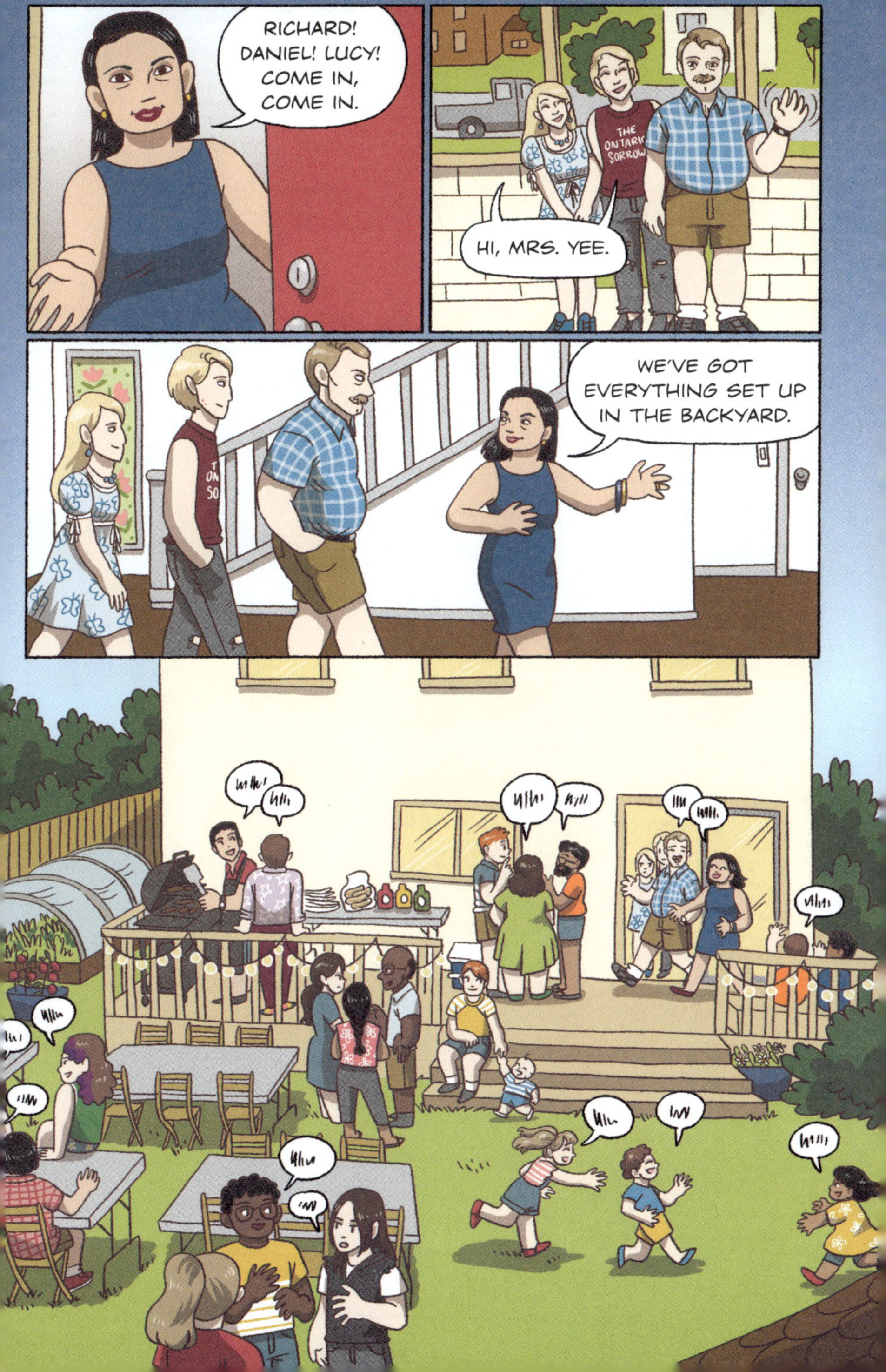
RICHARD! DANIEL! LUCY! COME IN, COME IN.
THE ONTARIO SORROW
HI, MRS. YEE.
WE'VE GOT EVERYTHING SET UP IN THE BACKYARD.

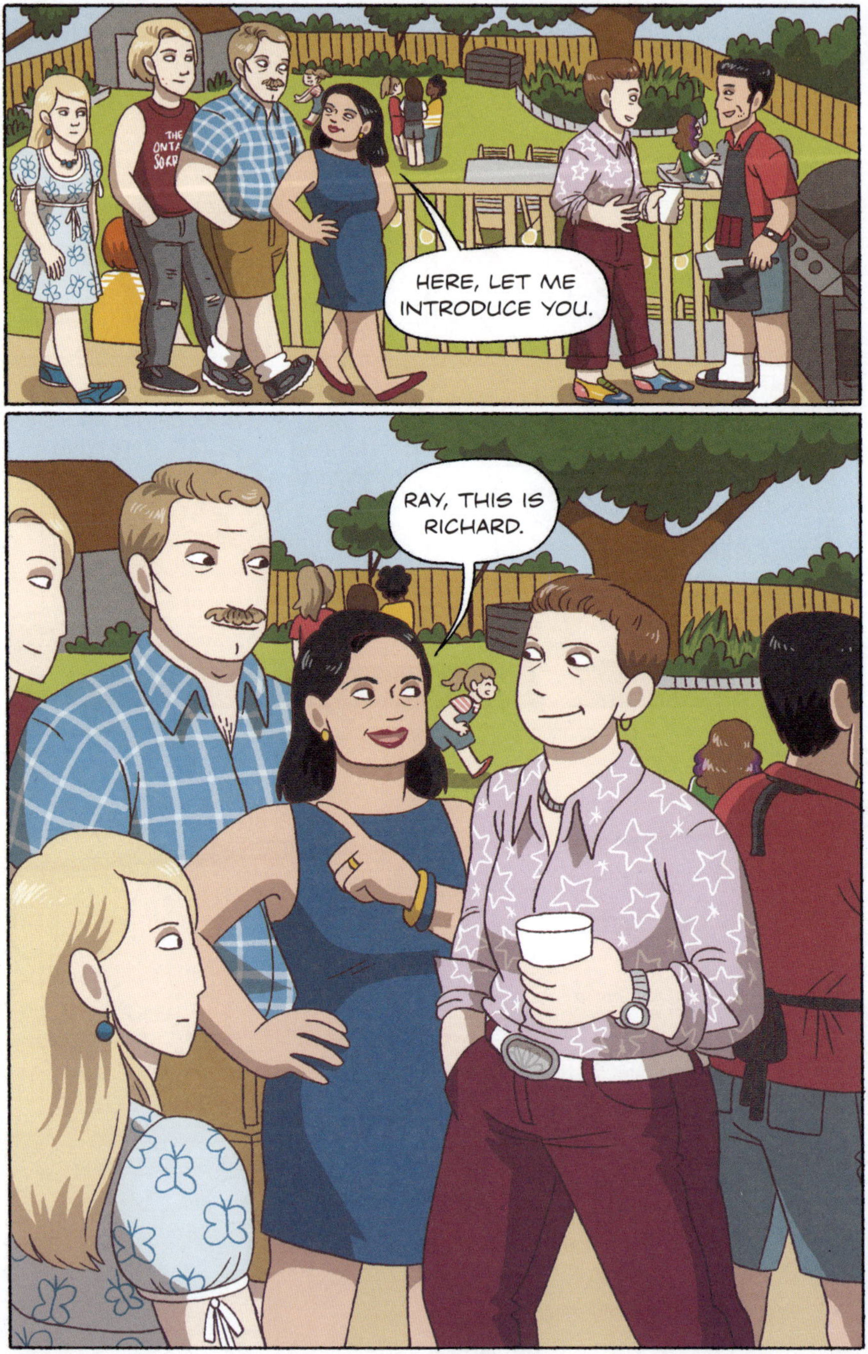
HERE, LET ME INTRODUCE YOU.
RAY, THIS IS RICHARD.

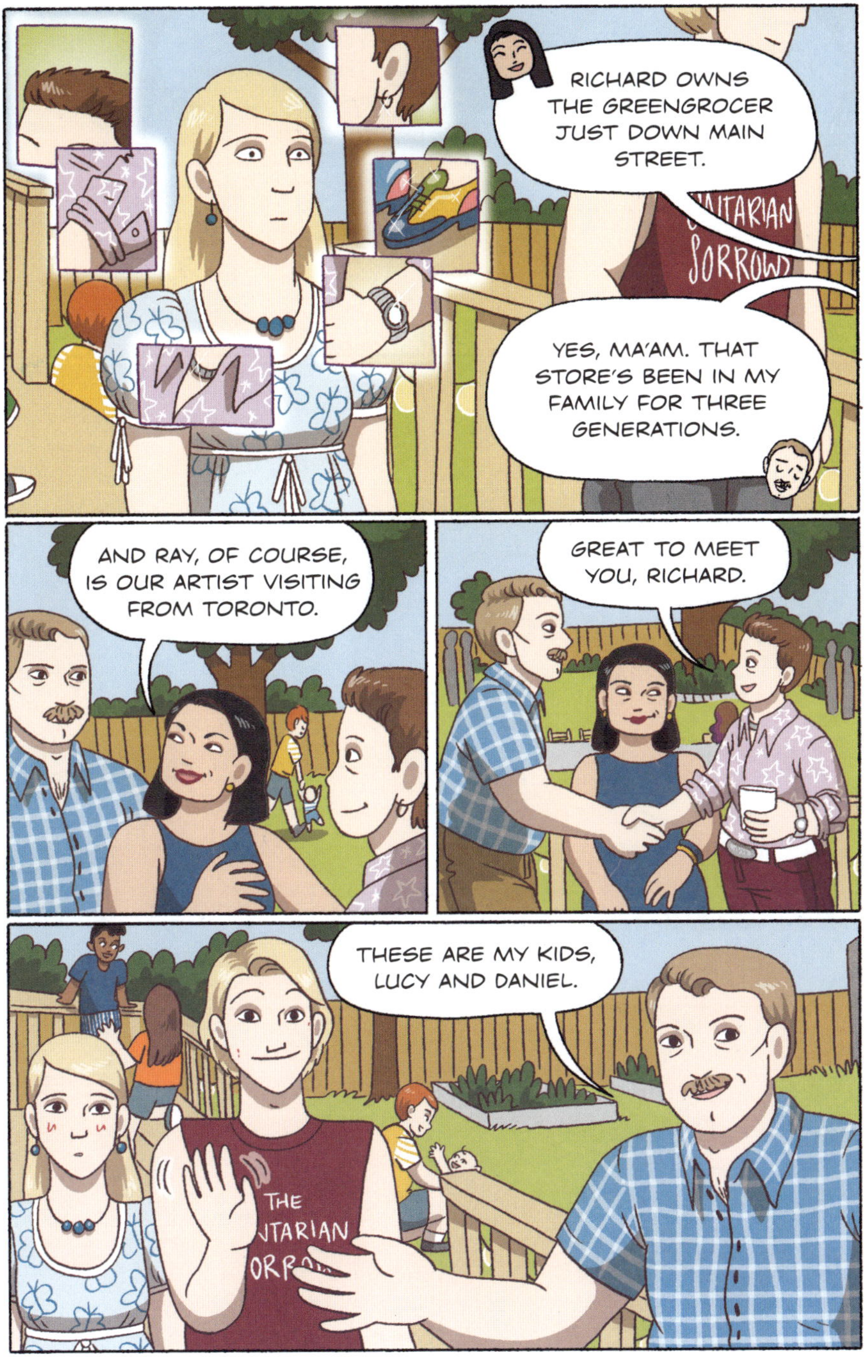
RICHARD OWNS THE GREENGROCER JUST DOWN MAIN STREET.
YES, MA'AM. THAT STORE'S BEEN IN MY FAMILY FOR THREE GENERATIONS.
AND RAY, OF COURSE, IS OUR ARTIST VISITING FROM TORONTO.
GREAT TO MEET YOU, RICHARD.
THESE ARE MY KIDS, LUCY AND DANIEL.

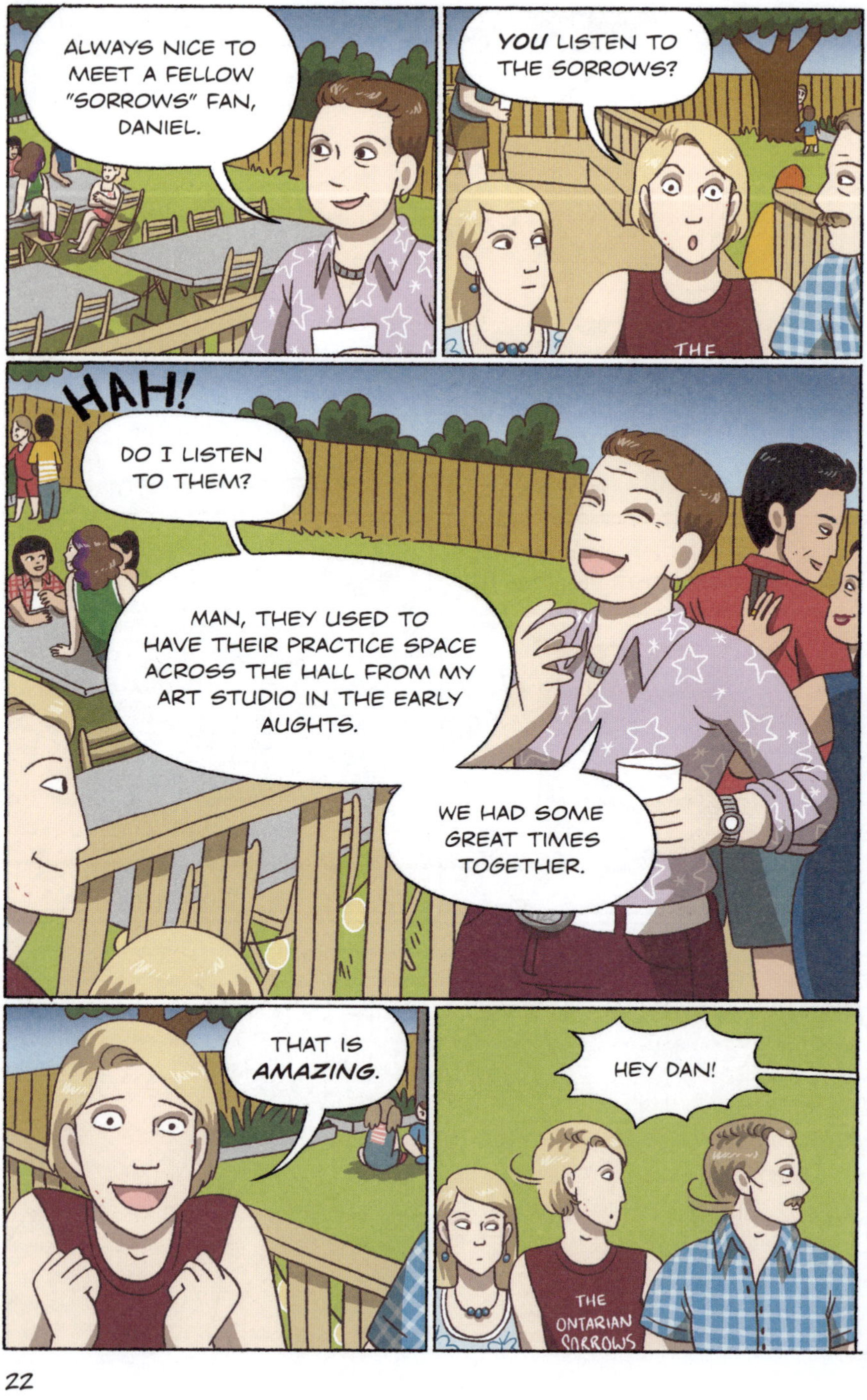
ALWAYS NICE TO MEET A FELLOW "SORROWS" FAN, DANIEL.
YOU LISTEN TO THE SORROWS?
THE
HAH!
DO I LISTEN TO THEM?
MAN, THEY USED TO HAVE THEIR PRACTICE SPACE ACROSS THE HALL FROM MY ART STUDIO IN THE EARLY AUGHTS.
WE HAD SOME GREAT TIMES TOGETHER.
THAT IS AMAZING.
HEY DAN!
THE ONTARIAN SORROWS

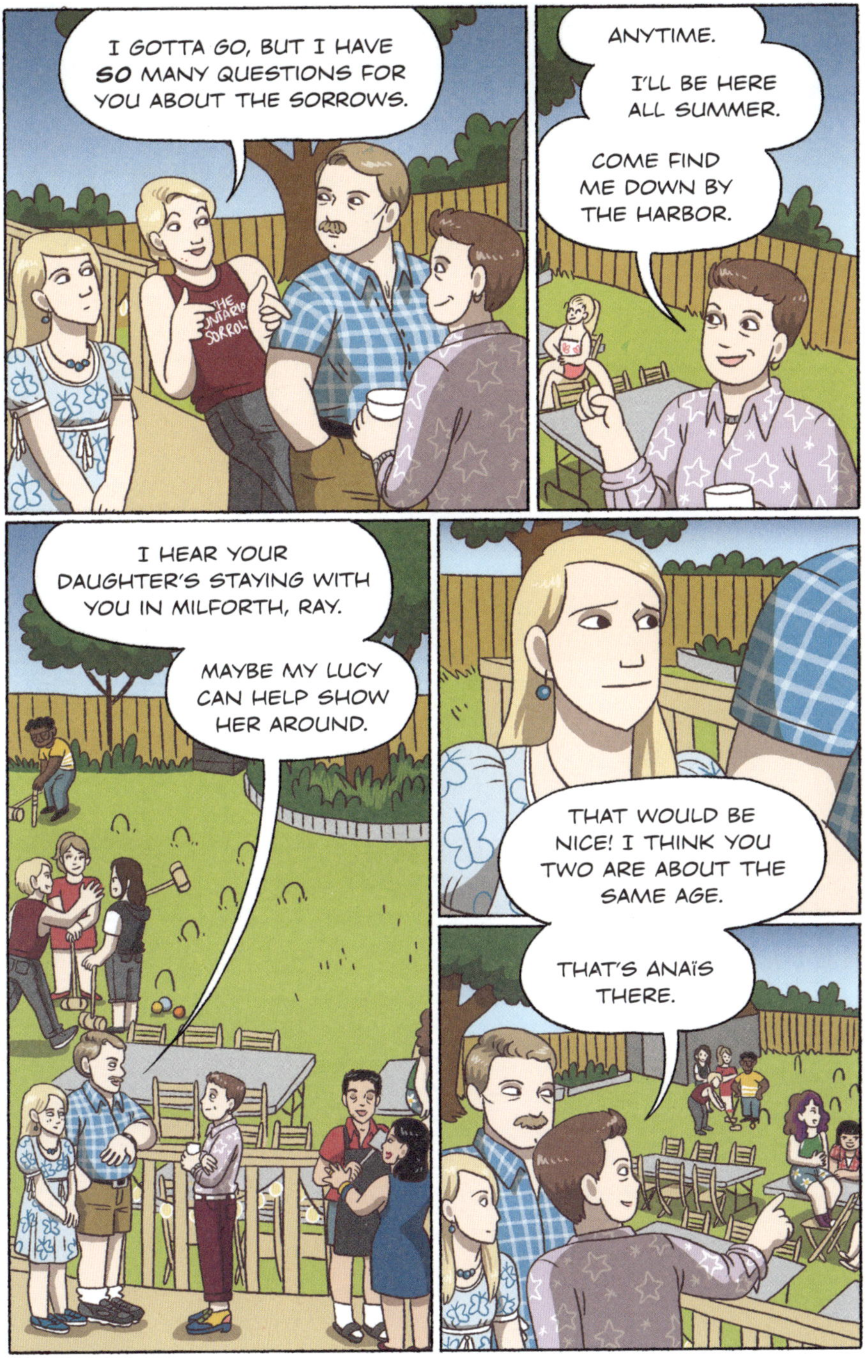
I GOTTA GO, BUT I HAVE **SO** MANY QUESTIONS FOR YOU ABOUT THE SORROWS.
ANYTIME.
I'LL BE HERE ALL SUMMER.
COME FIND ME DOWN BY THE HARBOR.
I HEAR YOUR DAUGHTER'S STAYING WITH YOU IN MILFORTH, RAY.
MAYBE MY LUCY CAN HELP SHOW HER AROUND.
THAT WOULD BE NICE! I THINK YOU TWO ARE ABOUT THE SAME AGE.
THAT'S ANAÏS THERE.

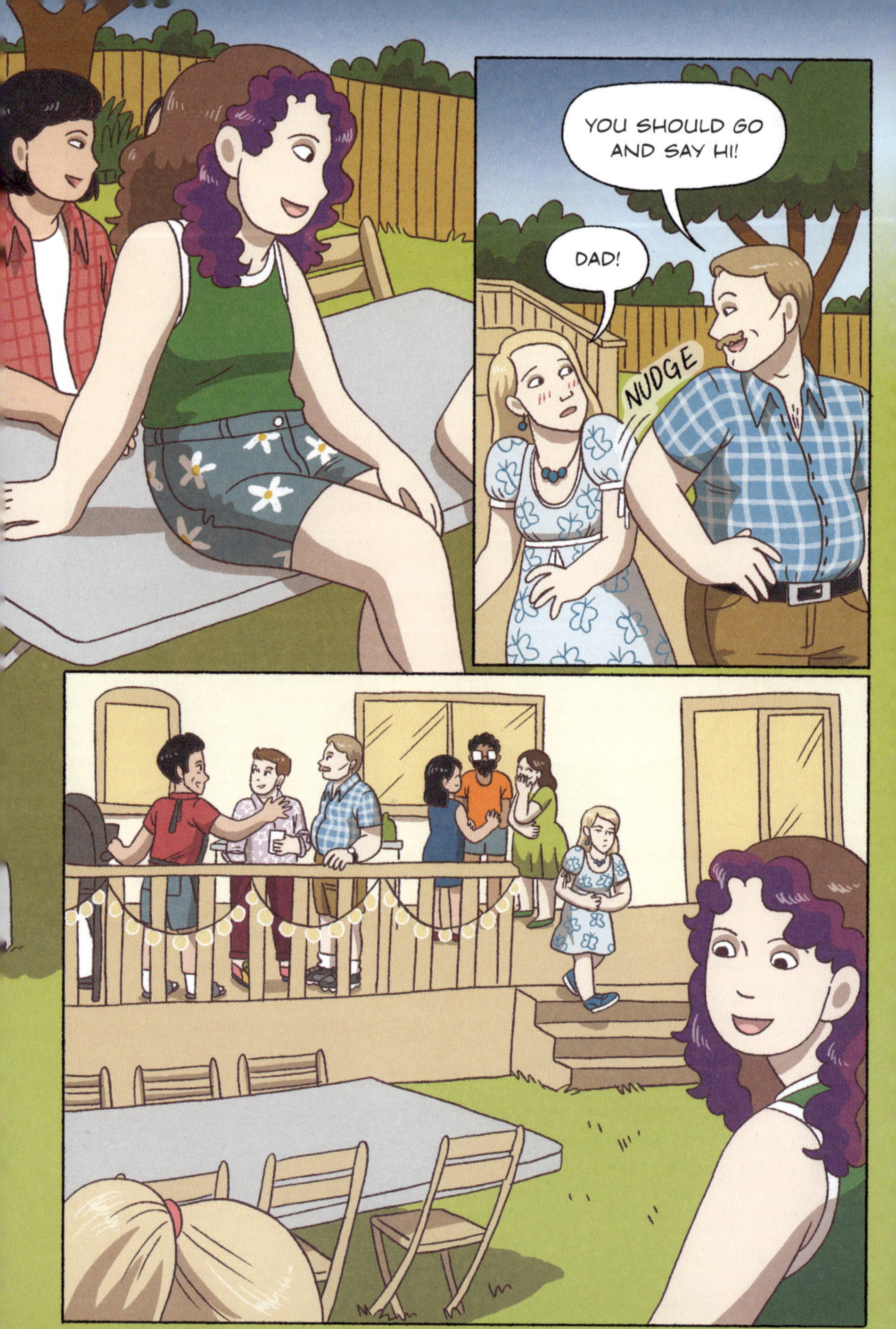
YOU SHOULD GO AND SAY HI!
DAD!
NUDGE

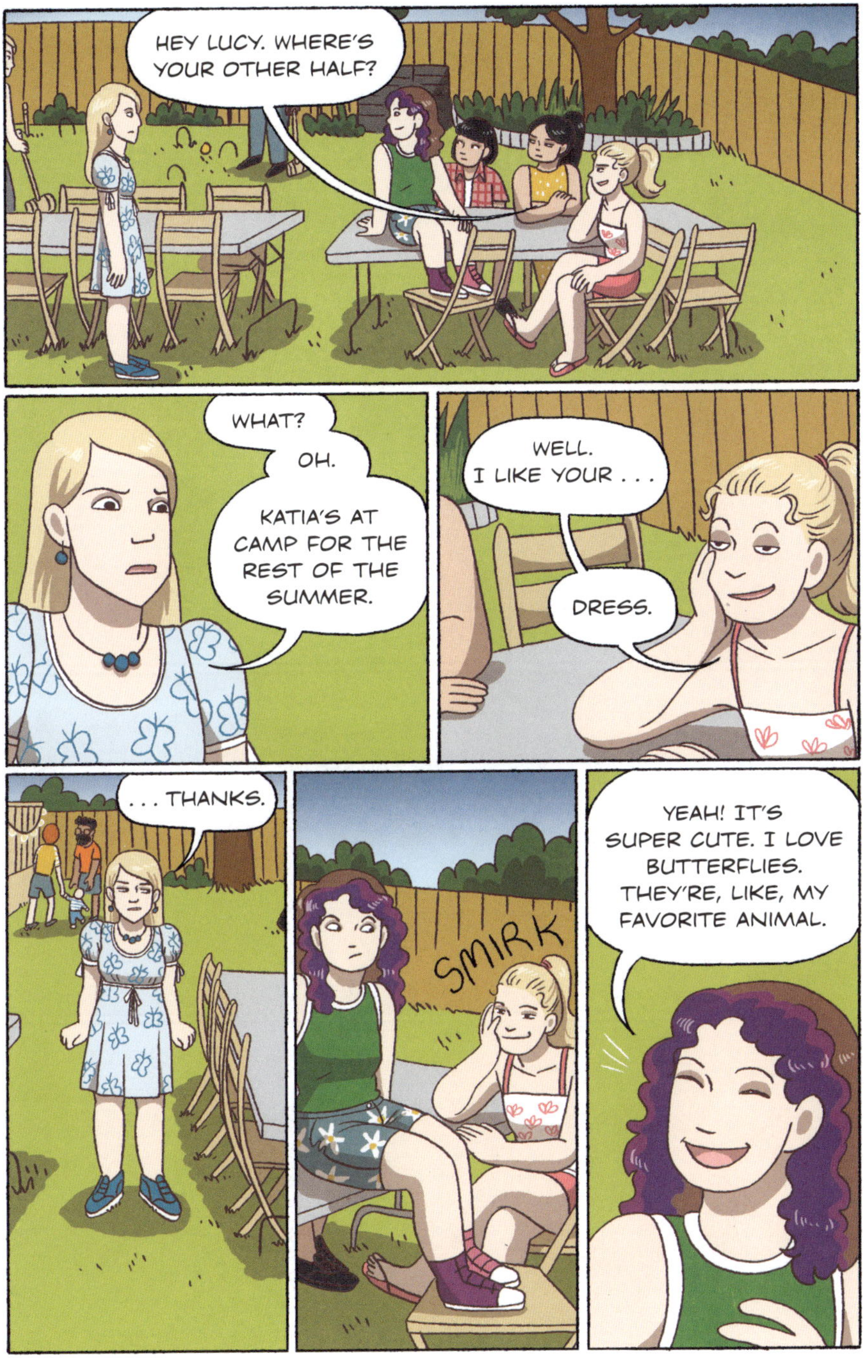
HEY LUCY. WHERE'S YOUR OTHER HALF?
WHAT?
OH.
KATIA'S AT CAMP FOR THE REST OF THE SUMMER.
WELL. I LIKE YOUR . . .
DRESS.
. . . THANKS.
SMIRK
YEAH! IT'S SUPER CUTE. I LOVE BUTTERFLIES. THEY'RE, LIKE, MY FAVORITE ANIMAL.

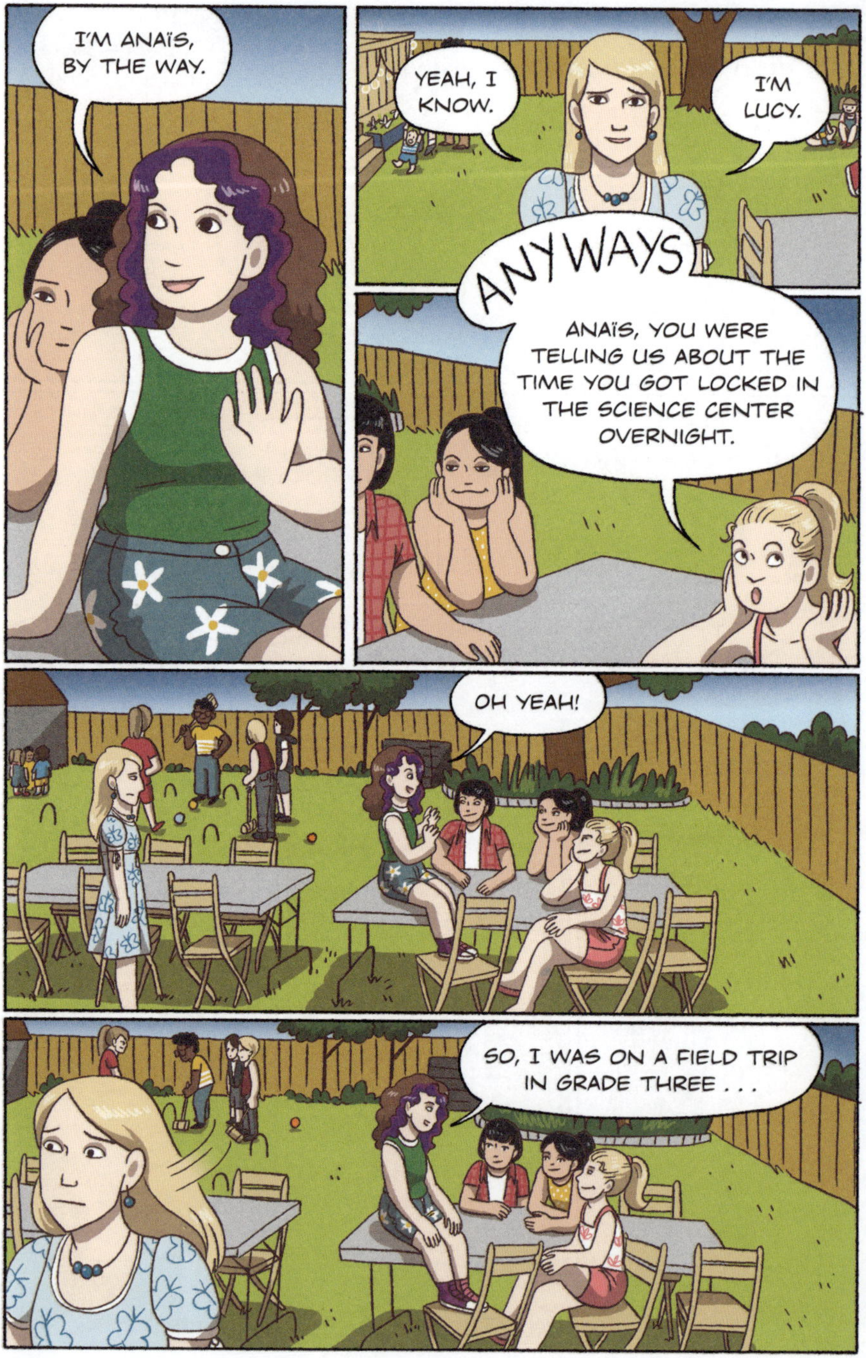
I'M ANAÏS, BY THE WAY.
YEAH, I KNOW.
I'M LUCY.
ANYWAYS
ANAÏS, YOU WERE TELLING US ABOUT THE TIME YOU GOT LOCKED IN THE SCIENCE CENTER OVERNIGHT.
OH YEAH!
SO, I WAS ON A FIELD TRIP IN GRADE THREE . . .

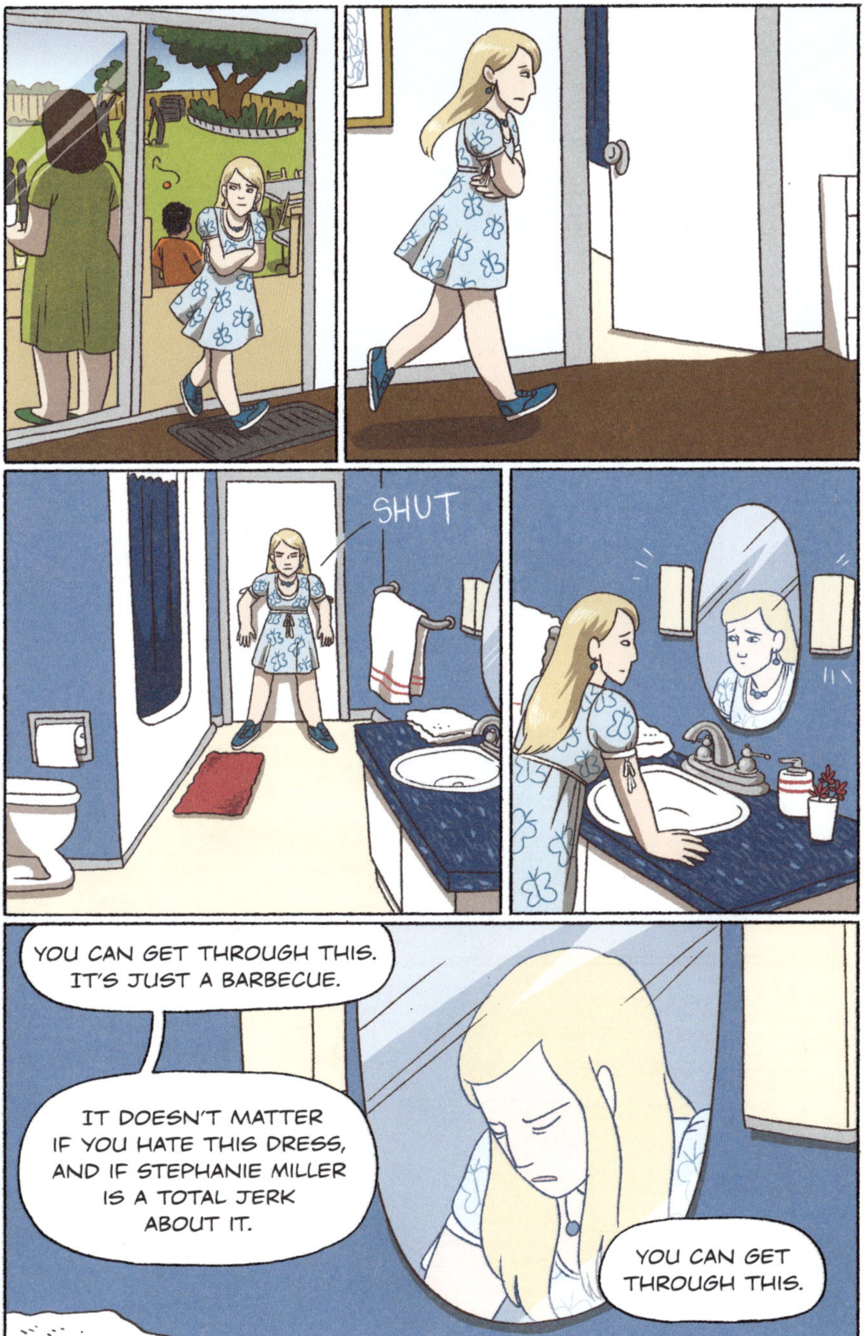
SHUT
YOU CAN GET THROUGH THIS. IT'S JUST A BARBECUE.
IT DOESN'T MATTER IF YOU HATE THIS DRESS, AND IF STEPHANIE MILLER IS A TOTAL JERK ABOUT IT.
YOU CAN GET THROUGH THIS.

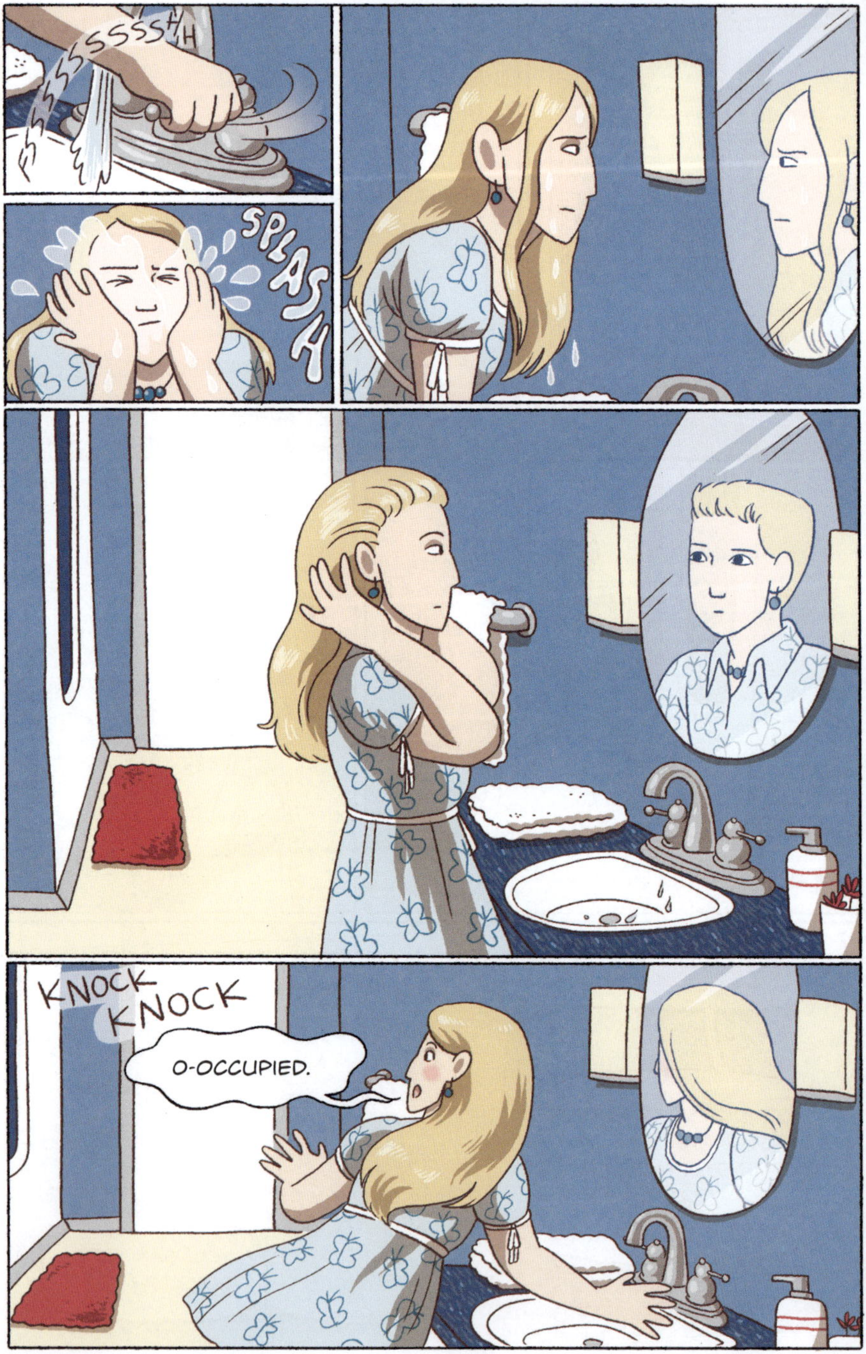
SSSSSSSSHH
SPLASH
KNOCK KNOCK
O-OCCUPIED.

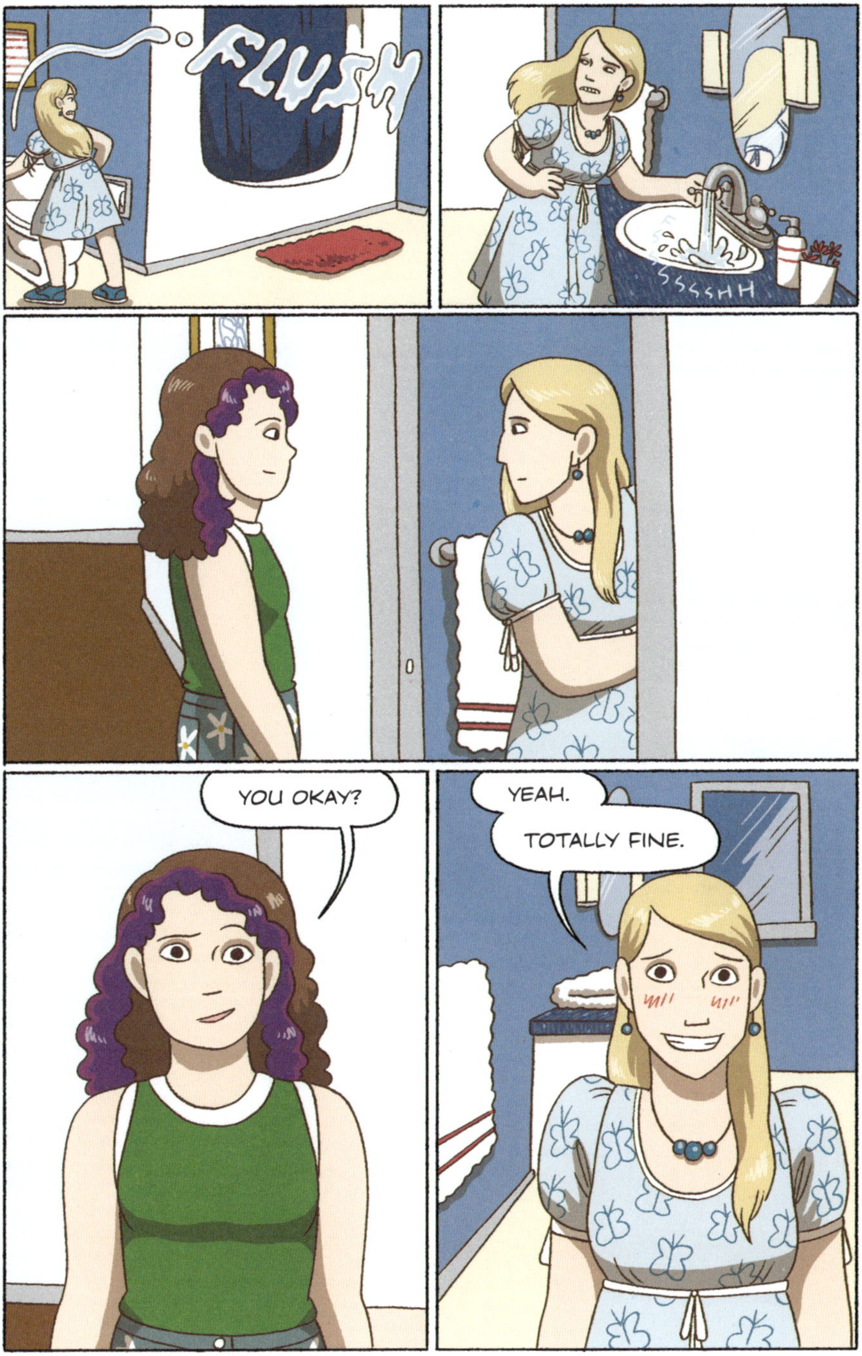
FLUSH
SSSSHH
YOU OKAY?
YEAH.
TOTALLY FINE.

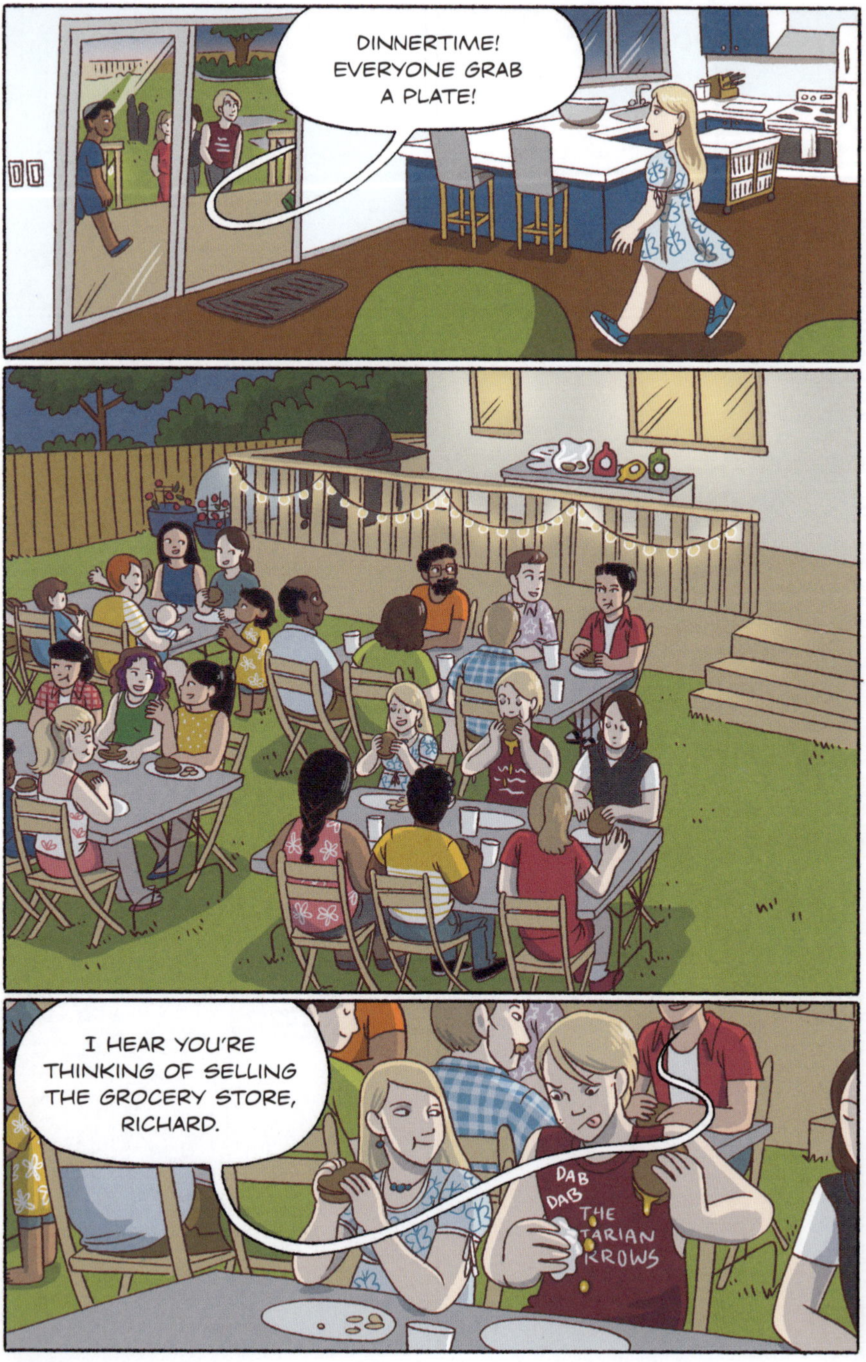
DINNERTIME! EVERYONE GRAB A PLATE!
I HEAR YOU'RE THINKING OF SELLING THE GROCERY STORE, RICHARD.
DAB DAB THE TARIAN KROWS

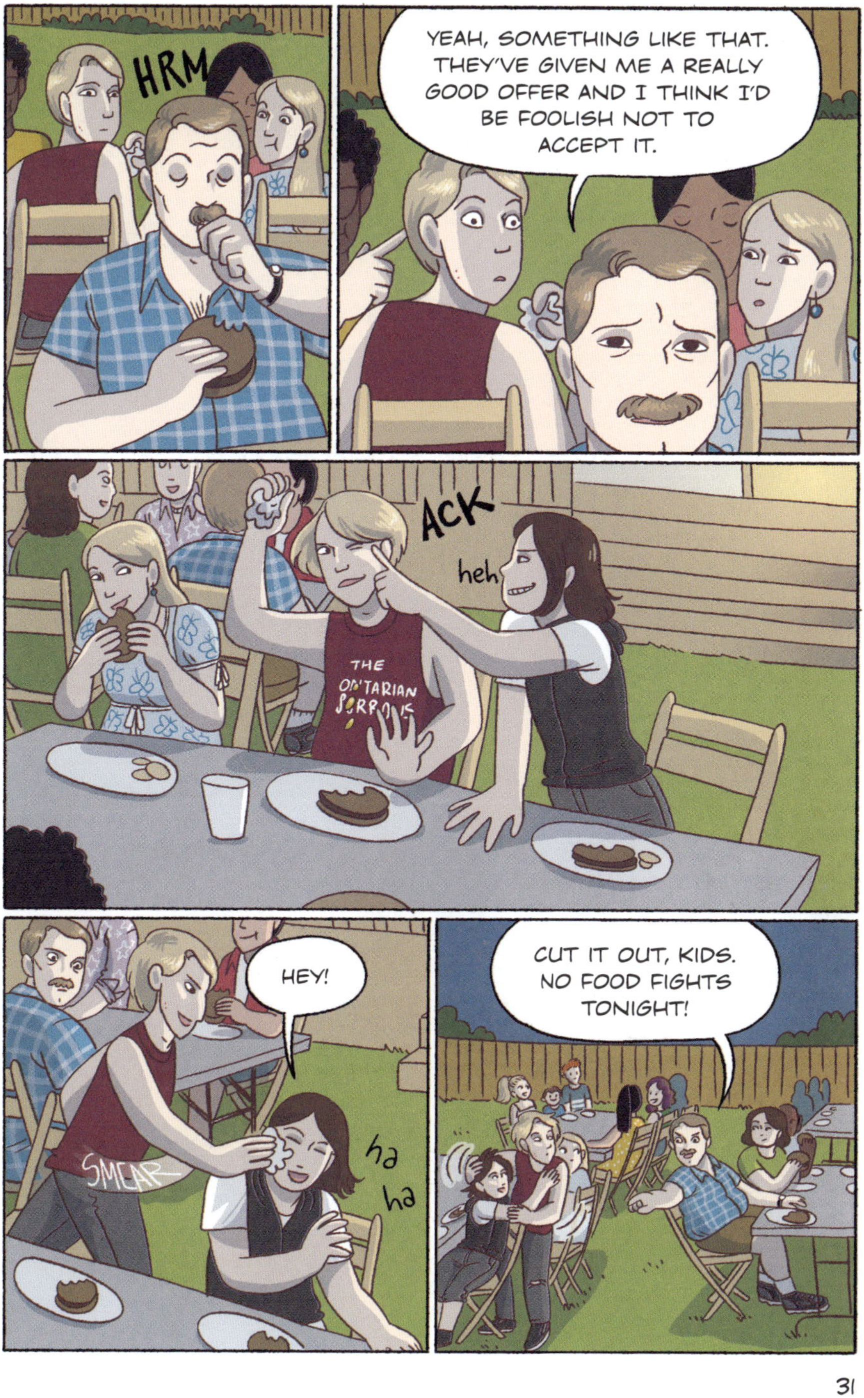
HRM
YEAH, SOMETHING LIKE THAT. THEY'VE GIVEN ME A REALLY GOOD OFFER AND I THINK I'D BE FOOLISH NOT TO ACCEPT IT.
ACK
heh
HEY!
SMEAR
ha ha
CUT IT OUT, KIDS. NO FOOD FIGHTS TONIGHT!

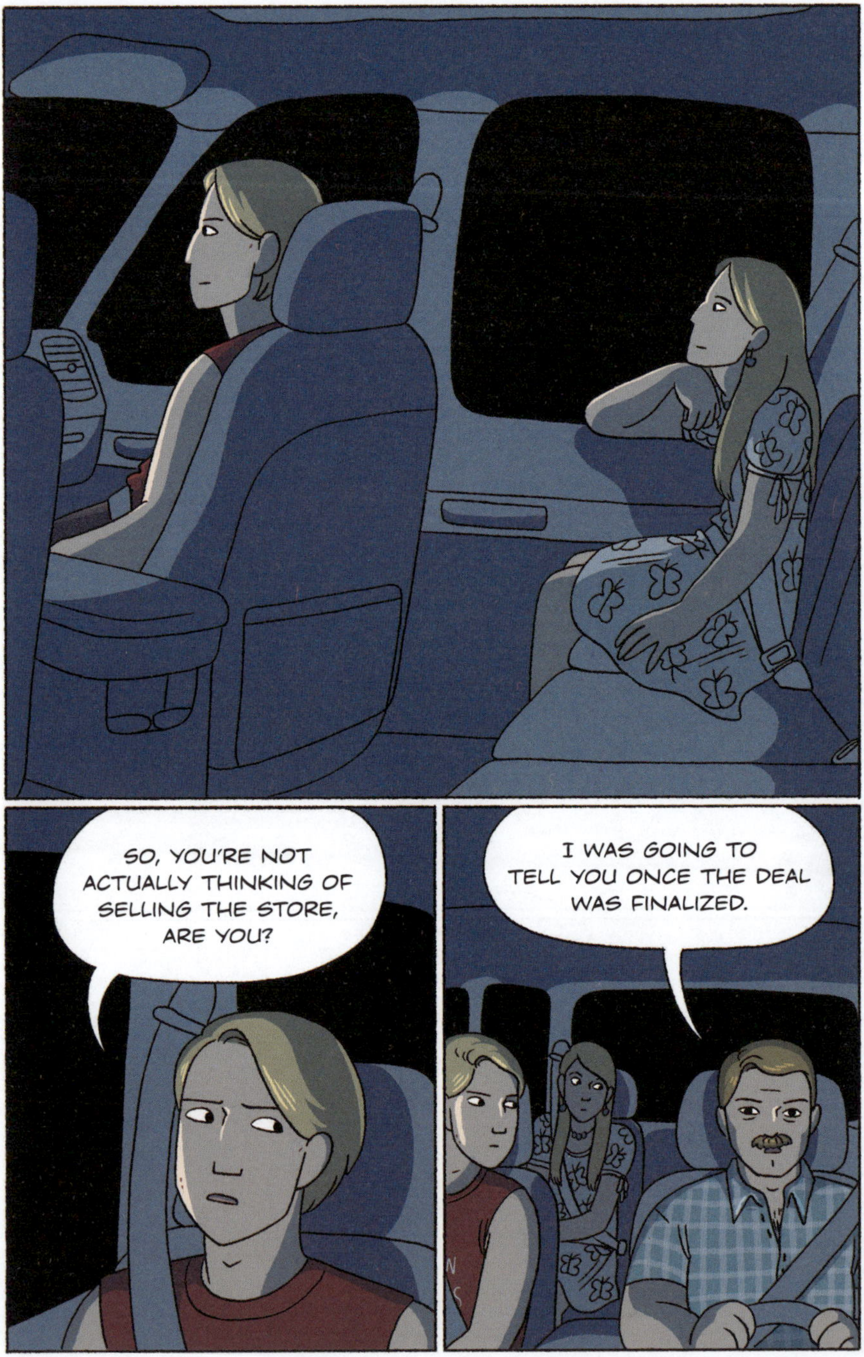
SO, YOU'RE NOT ACTUALLY THINKING OF SELLING THE STORE, ARE YOU?
I WAS GOING TO TELL YOU ONCE THE DEAL WAS FINALIZED.

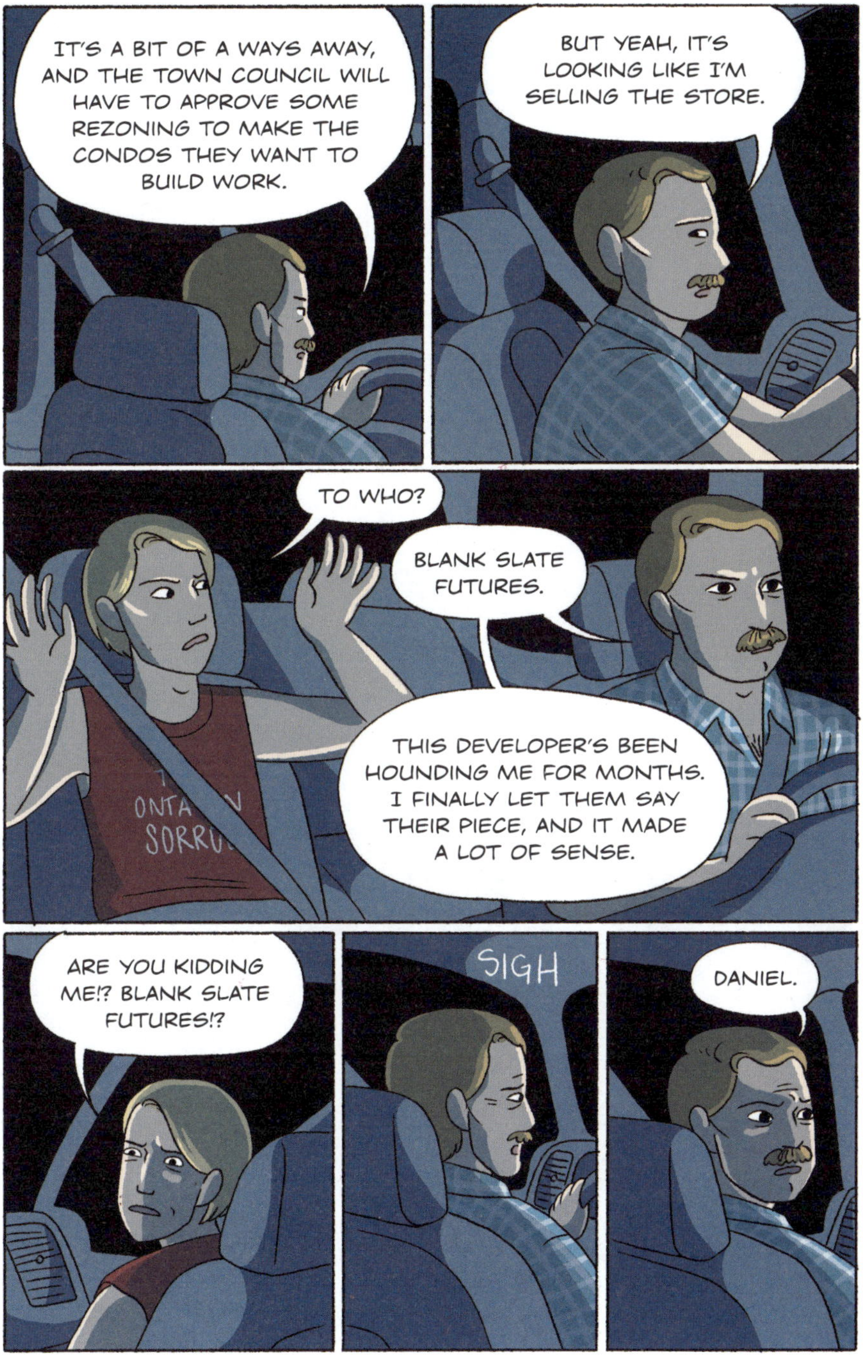
IT'S A BIT OF A WAYS AWAY, AND THE TOWN COUNCIL WILL HAVE TO APPROVE SOME REZONING TO MAKE THE CONDOS THEY WANT TO BUILD WORK.
BUT YEAH, IT'S LOOKING LIKE I'M SELLING THE STORE.
TO WHO?
BLANK SLATE FUTURES.
THIS DEVELOPER'S BEEN HOUNDING ME FOR MONTHS. I FINALLY LET THEM SAY THEIR PIECE, AND IT MADE A LOT OF SENSE.
ARE YOU KIDDING ME!? BLANK SLATE FUTURES!?
SIGH
DANIEL.

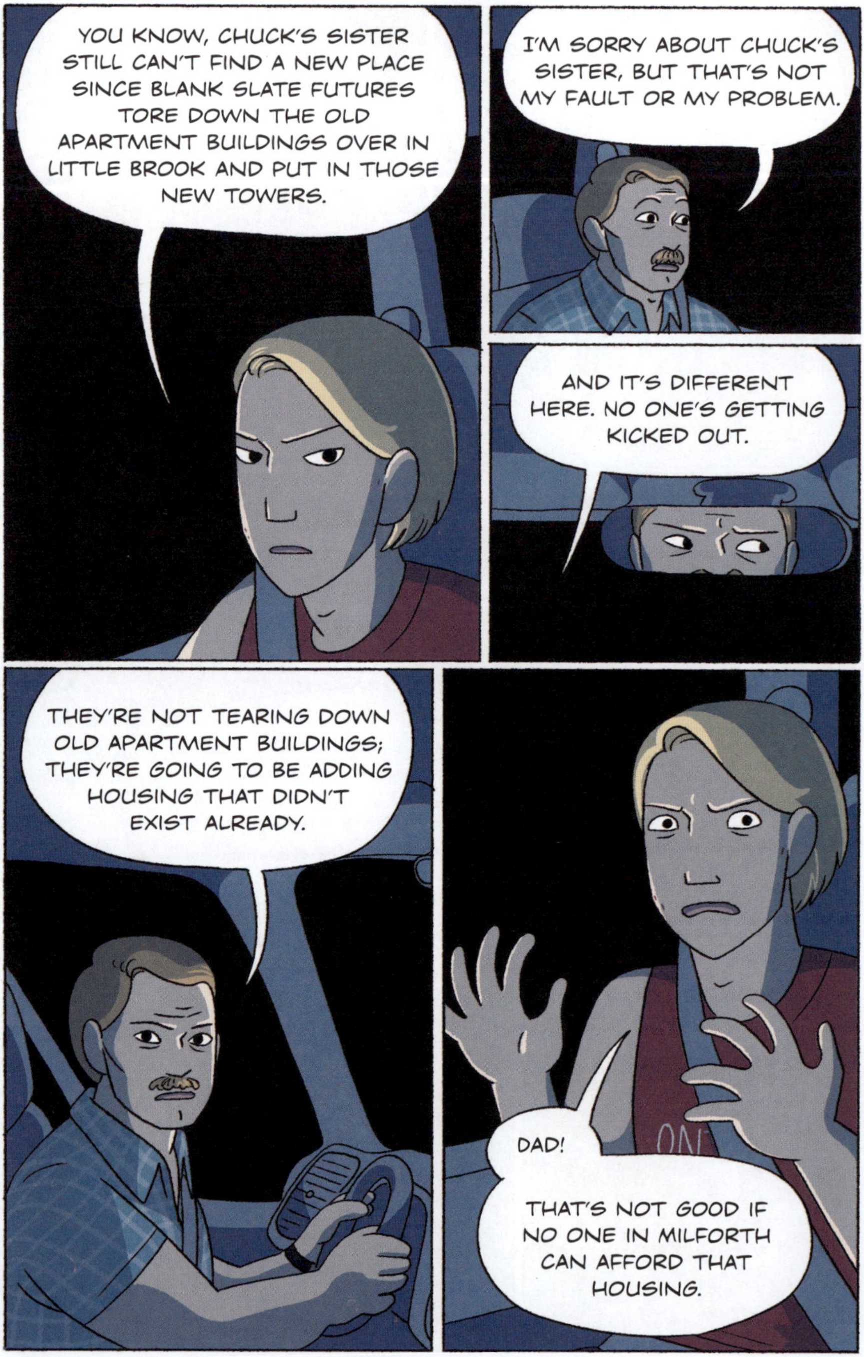
YOU KNOW, CHUCK'S SISTER STILL CAN'T FIND A NEW PLACE SINCE BLANK SLATE FUTURES TORE DOWN THE OLD APARTMENT BUILDINGS OVER IN LITTLE BROOK AND PUT IN THOSE NEW TOWERS.
I'M SORRY ABOUT CHUCK'S SISTER, BUT THAT'S NOT MY FAULT OR MY PROBLEM.
AND IT'S DIFFERENT HERE. NO ONE'S GETTING KICKED OUT.
THEY'RE NOT TEARING DOWN OLD APARTMENT BUILDINGS; THEY'RE GOING TO BE ADDING HOUSING THAT DIDN'T EXIST ALREADY.
DAD!
THAT'S NOT GOOD IF NO ONE IN MILFORTH CAN AFFORD THAT HOUSING.

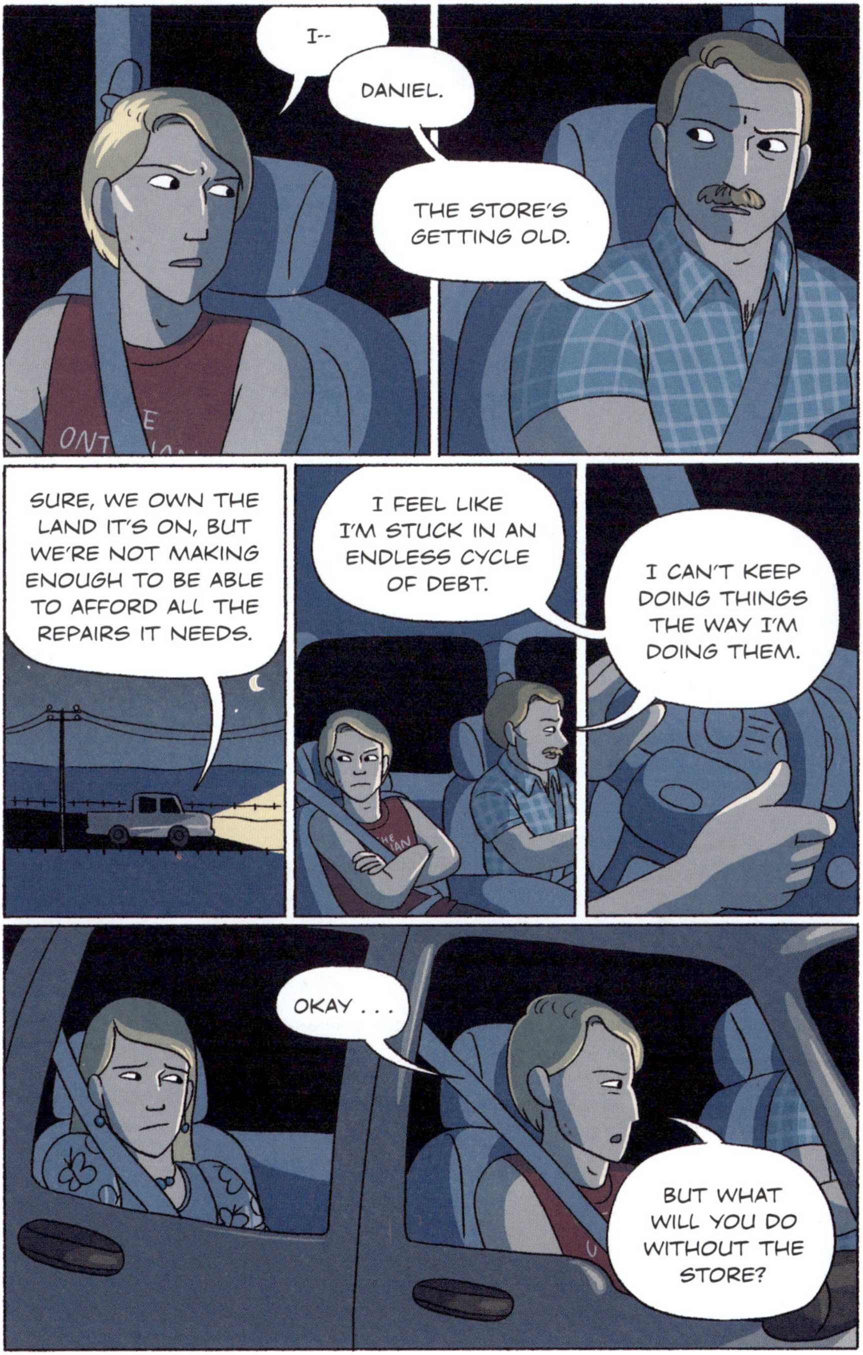
I--
DANIEL.
THE STORE'S GETTING OLD.
SURE, WE OWN THE LAND IT'S ON, BUT WE'RE NOT MAKING ENOUGH TO BE ABLE TO AFFORD ALL THE REPAIRS IT NEEDS.
I FEEL LIKE I'M STUCK IN AN ENDLESS CYCLE OF DEBT.
I CAN'T KEEP DOING THINGS THE WAY I'M DOING THEM.
OKAY . . .
BUT WHAT WILL YOU DO WITHOUT THE STORE?

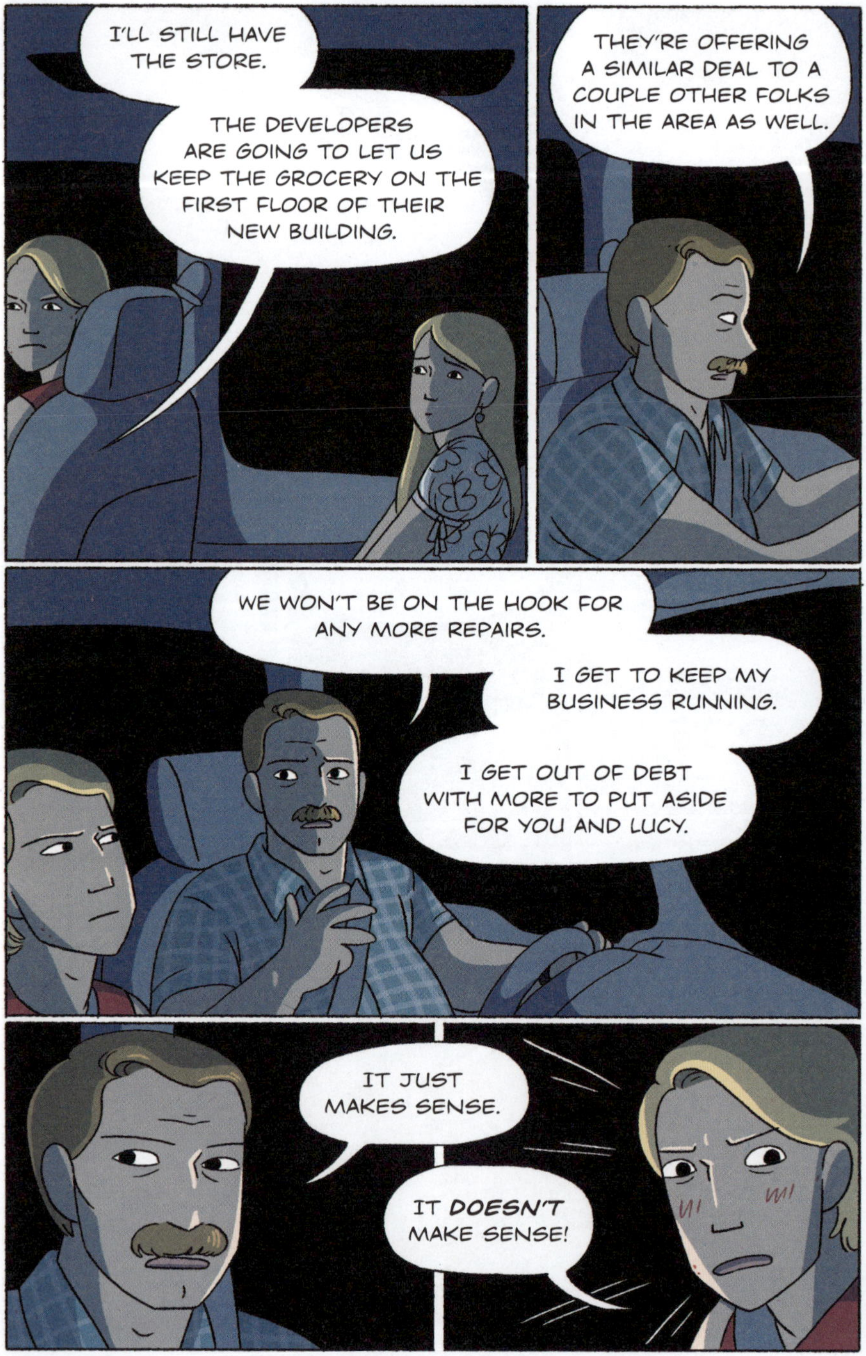
I'LL STILL HAVE THE STORE.
THE DEVELOPERS ARE GOING TO LET US KEEP THE GROCERY ON THE FIRST FLOOR OF THEIR NEW BUILDING.
THEY'RE OFFERING A SIMILAR DEAL TO A COUPLE OTHER FOLKS IN THE AREA AS WELL.
WE WON'T BE ON THE HOOK FOR ANY MORE REPAIRS.
I GET TO KEEP MY BUSINESS RUNNING.
I GET OUT OF DEBT WITH MORE TO PUT ASIDE FOR YOU AND LUCY.
IT JUST MAKES SENSE.
IT ***DOESN'T*** MAKE SENSE!

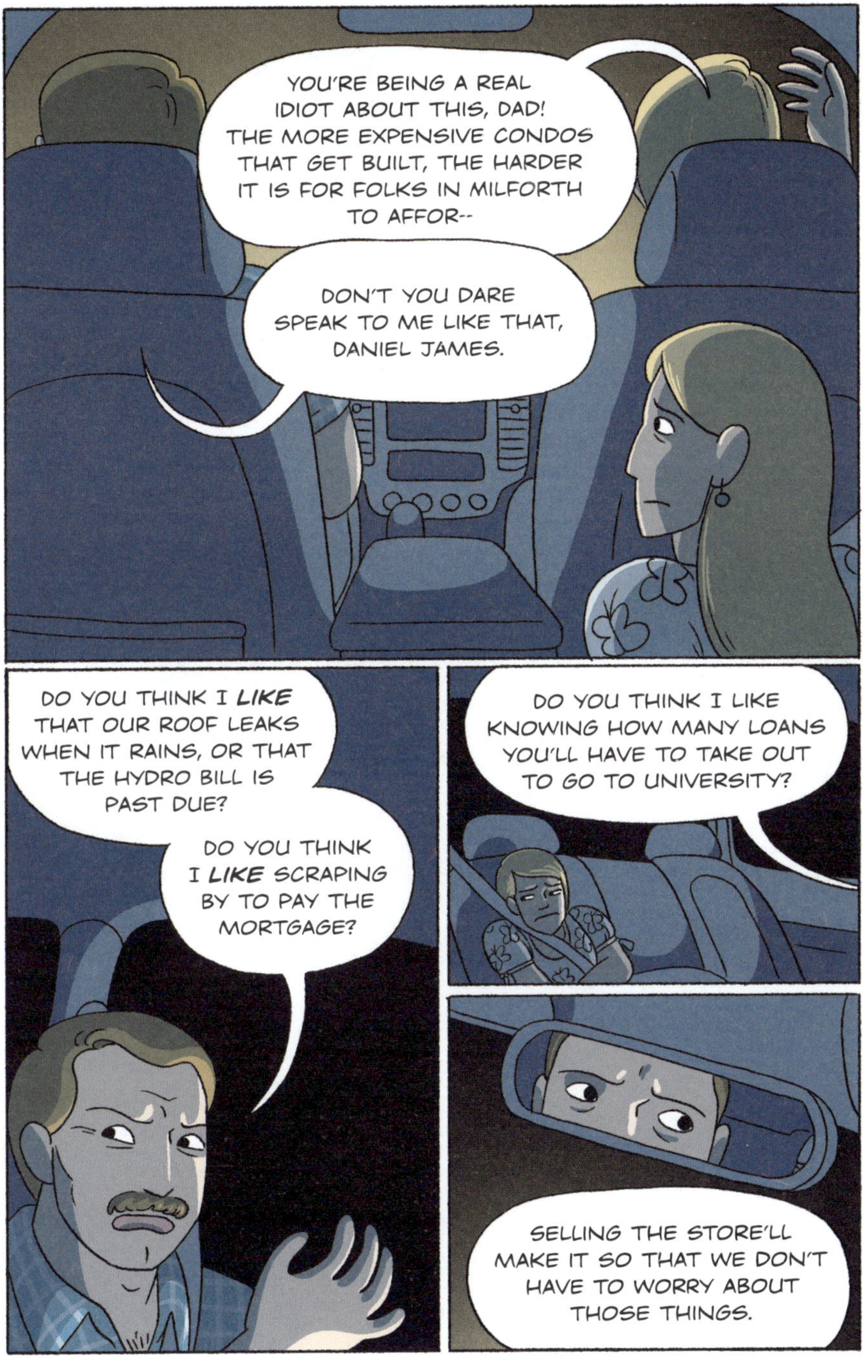
YOU'RE BEING A REAL IDIOT ABOUT THIS, DAD! THE MORE EXPENSIVE CONDOS THAT GET BUILT, THE HARDER IT IS FOR FOLKS IN MILFORTH TO AFFOR--
DON'T YOU DARE SPEAK TO ME LIKE THAT, DANIEL JAMES.
DO YOU THINK I *LIKE* THAT OUR ROOF LEAKS WHEN IT RAINS, OR THAT THE HYDRO BILL IS PAST DUE?
DO YOU THINK I *LIKE* SCRAPING BY TO PAY THE MORTGAGE?
DO YOU THINK I LIKE KNOWING HOW MANY LOANS YOU'LL HAVE TO TAKE OUT TO GO TO UNIVERSITY?
SELLING THE STORE'LL MAKE IT SO THAT WE DON'T HAVE TO WORRY ABOUT THOSE THINGS.

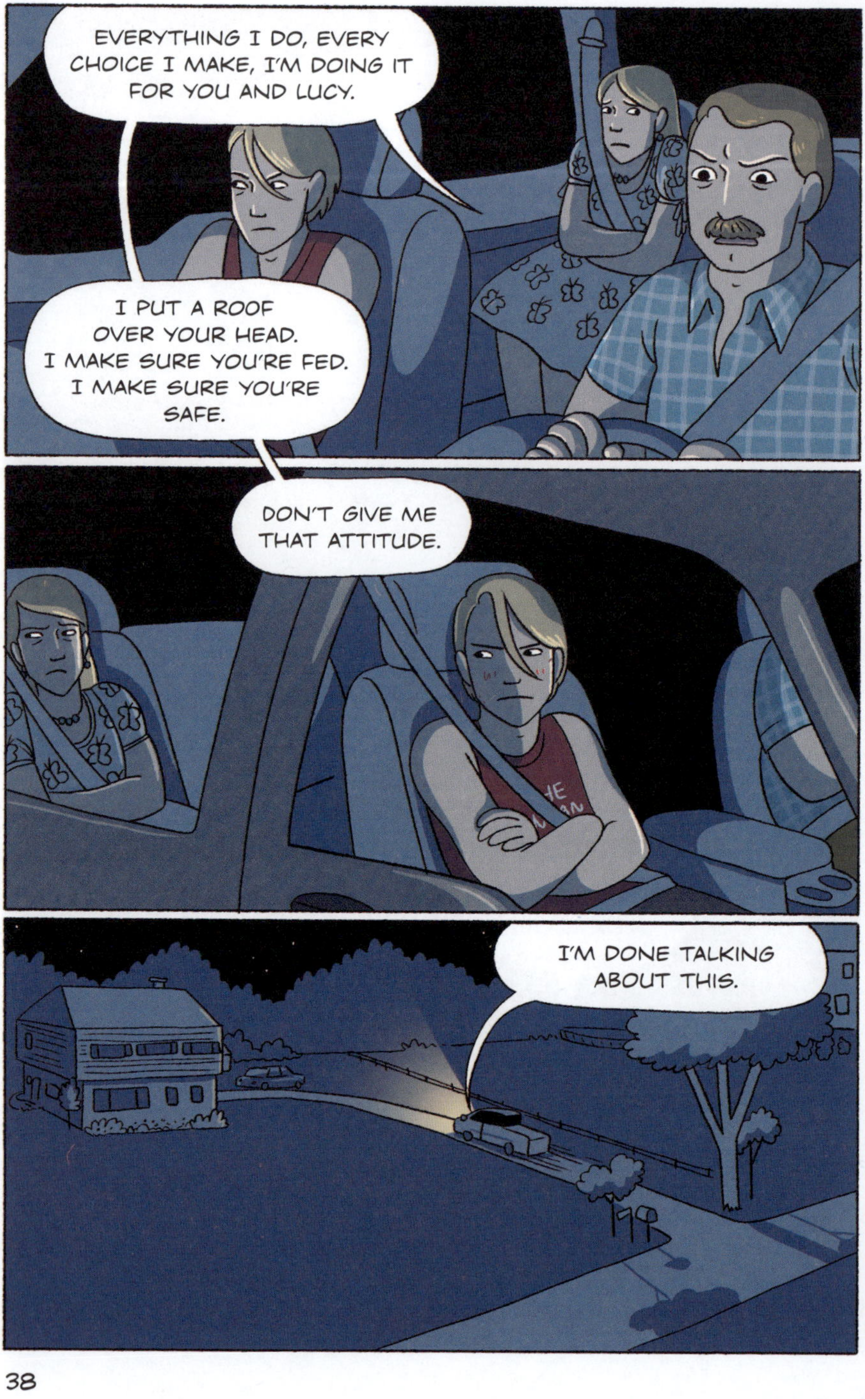
EVERYTHING I DO, EVERY CHOICE I MAKE, I'M DOING IT FOR YOU AND LUCY.
I PUT A ROOF OVER YOUR HEAD. I MAKE SURE YOU'RE FED. I MAKE SURE YOU'RE SAFE.
DON'T GIVE ME THAT ATTITUDE.
I'M DONE TALKING ABOUT THIS.

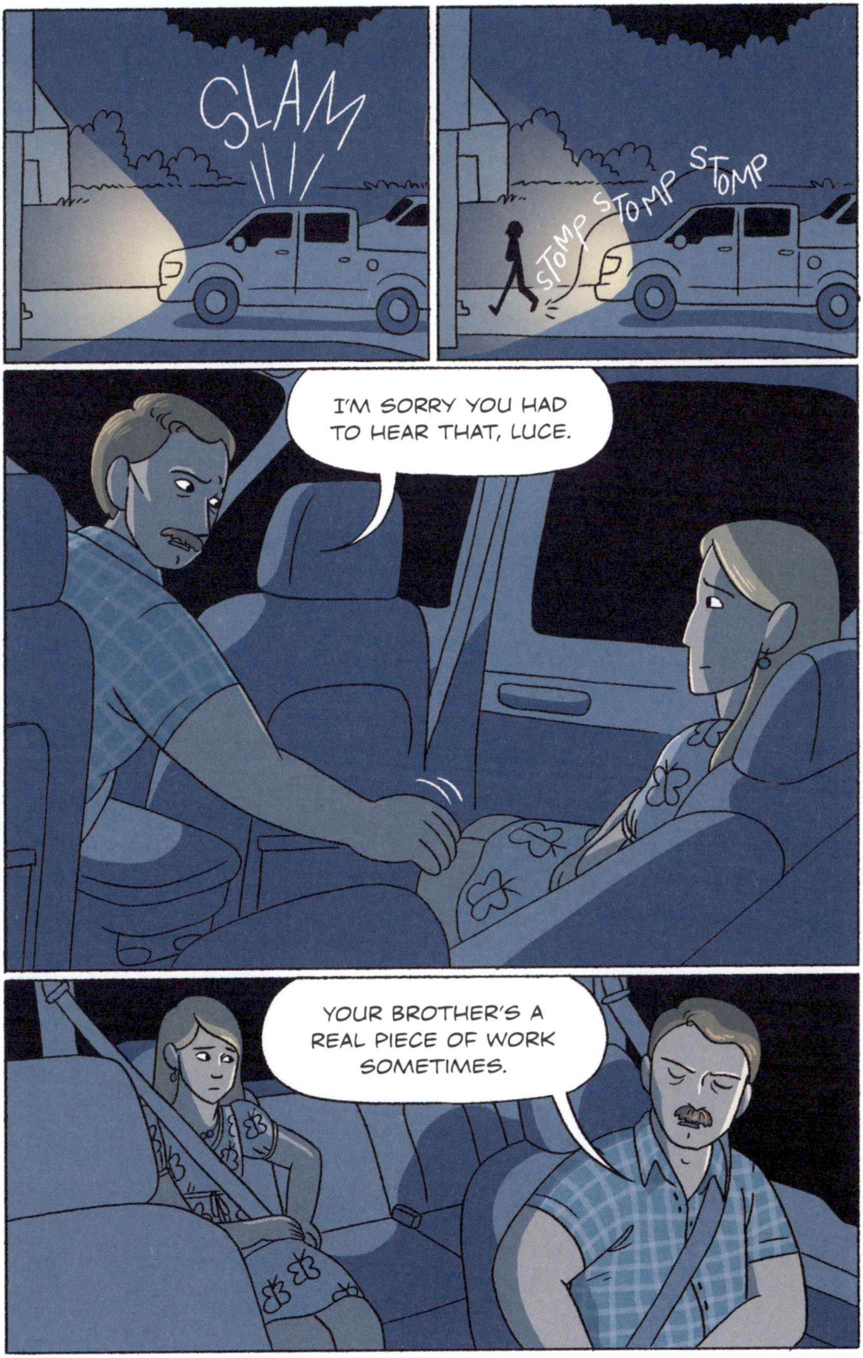
SLAM
STOMP STOMP STOMP
I'M SORRY YOU HAD TO HEAR THAT, LUCE.
YOUR BROTHER'S A REAL PIECE OF WORK SOMETIMES.

Dear Lucy,

Camp is WILD! Last night, my cabin snuck out after curfew to prank the boys in the Oak Cabin. Mike (one of the guys) spilled milk down the back of Tessa's shirt during dinner, and we're CERTAIN it wasn't an accident like he claimed. So, of course, we had to get him back.

While we were on dish duty after dinner, we formed our plan.... At night, everyone always leaves their shoes just inside the door to their cabin, and that gave Min-Ji an idea. We had to wait until after midnight so everyone would be asleep. When the time came, we headed across camp over to the Oak Cabin.

We managed to open the boys' door without waking anyone up (it creaked a little and for a second, we were SO sure we were going to get found out). We stole each boy's left shoe and ran as quickly and quietly as we could to the flagpole in the middle of camp. We tied their shoes together and hoisted them up the flagpole.

The look on the boys' faces in the morning when they realized where their missing shoes were: priceless. It was SO hard not to laugh.

The boys say there's going to be major payback when they find out who did it... but they still don't know it was us!

Anyways, here's a photo of the Trillium girls (although Rachel says we should call ourselves the THRILL-ium girls haha).

Love Ya,

Katia

P.S. Can't wait to hear what you've been up to!

P.P.S. What's this about an artist?? You should totally make friends with the daughter!

THE TRILLIUM CAB
xoxo KATIA

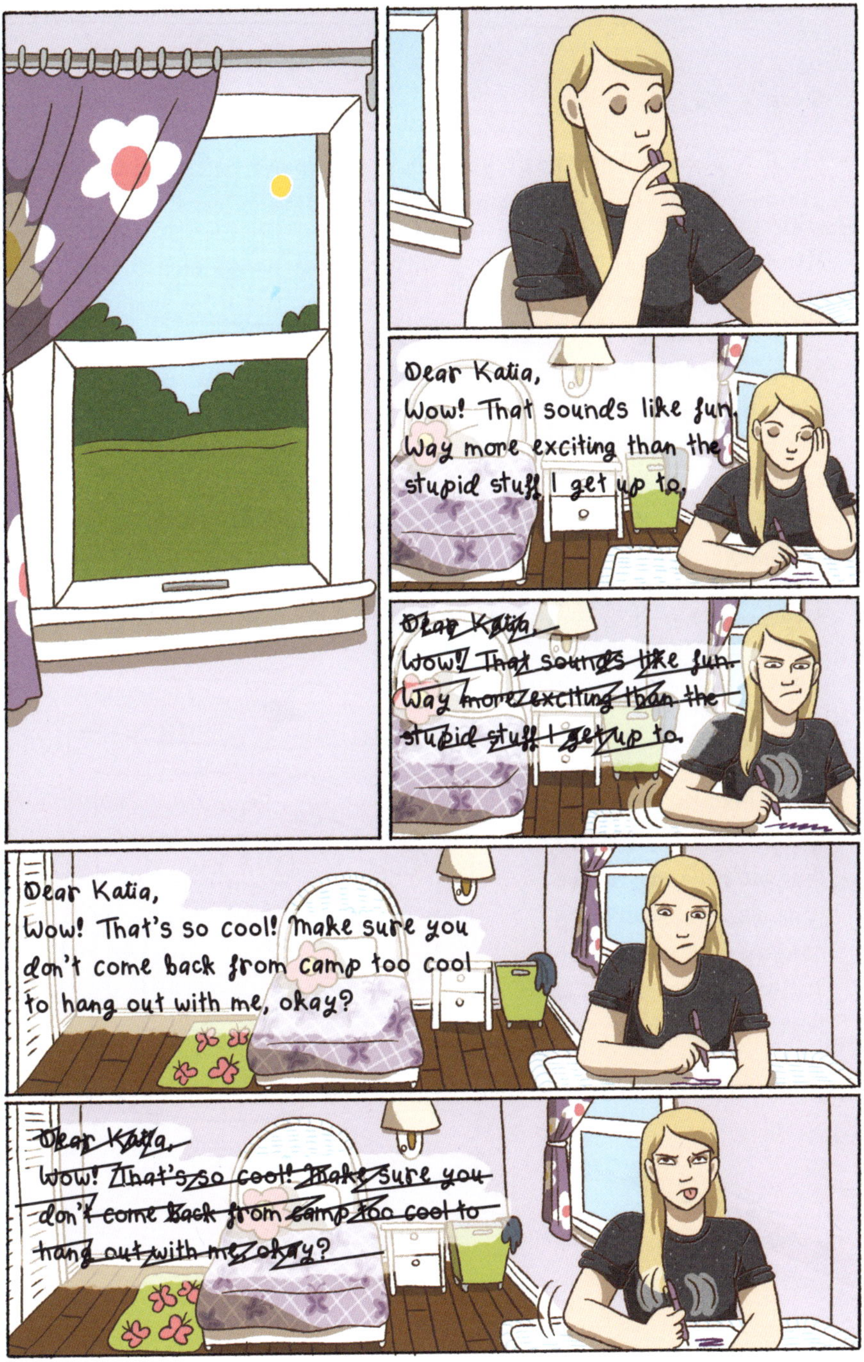
Dear Katia,
Wow! That sounds like fun. Way more exciting than the stupid stuff I get up to.
Dear Katia,
Wow! That sounds like fun. Way more exciting than the stupid stuff I get up to.
Dear Katia,
Wow! That's so cool! Make sure you don't come back from camp too cool to hang out with me, okay?
Dear Katia,
Wow! That's so cool! Make sure you don't come back from camp too cool to hang out with me, okay?

Dear Katia,

Wow! A prank war! I hope you don't get found out. I'd be jealous, but I've got my own cool thing going on here.

Remember that flock of turkey vultures that hangs out at the back of our property? There's this one who's a little smaller than the other birds, and I think some of the other guys bully him a little. I'm calling him Tim, and I'm going to see if I can tame him. When I offer him bits of meat, he comes and hangs out on the back porch with me. He doesn't smell great, but he's pretty cute. The other day he cawed in a way that sounded like "Thanks, Lucy." I'll have him speaking English in no time.

Anyways, here's a photo of Tim.

Love Ya,

Lucy xoxo

P.S. I met the artist's daughter, but I don't know that we're going to be friends. She's already hanging out with Stephanie Miller, and we know what that means...

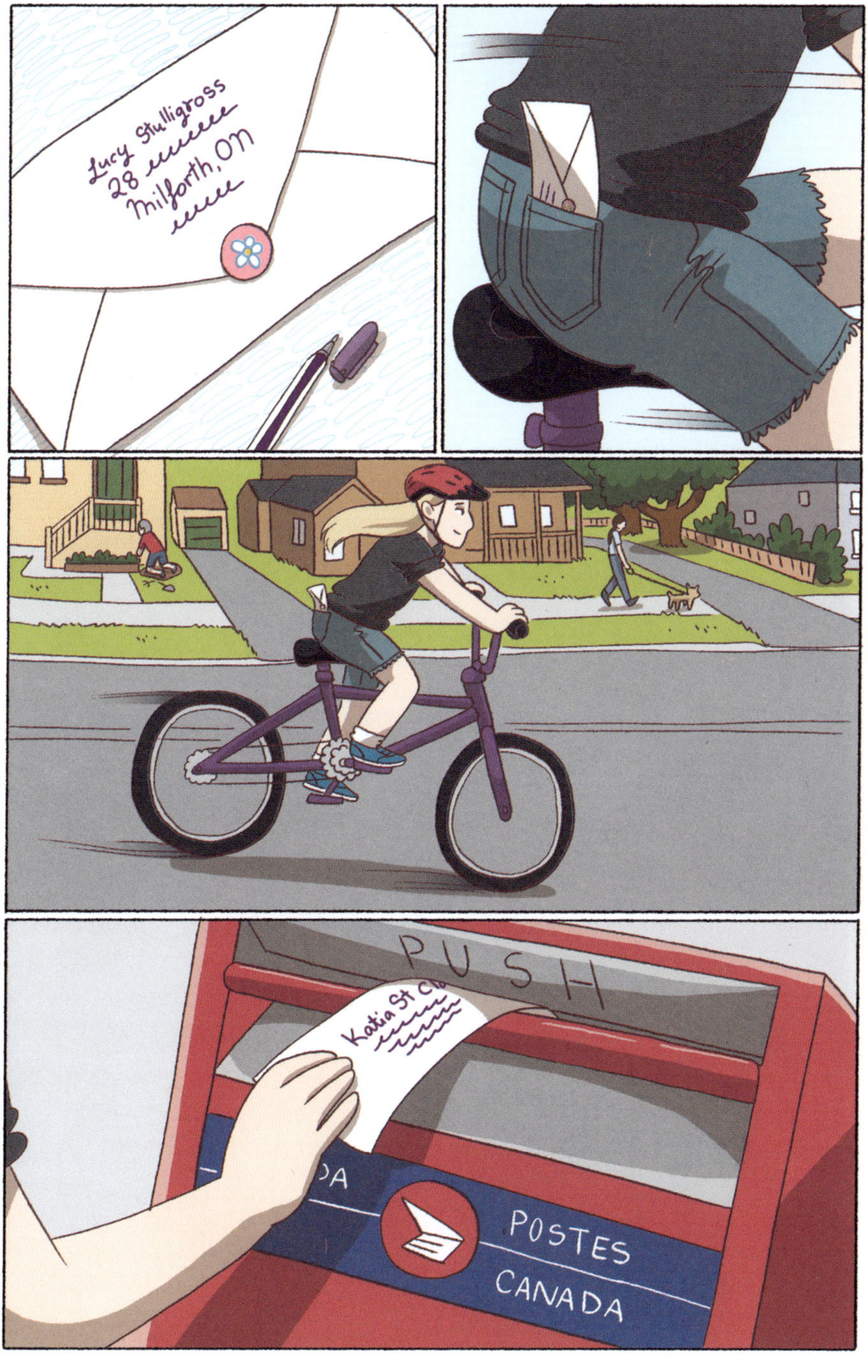
Lucy Stulligross
28
Milforth, ON
PUSH
Katia St Cl
POSTES
CANADA

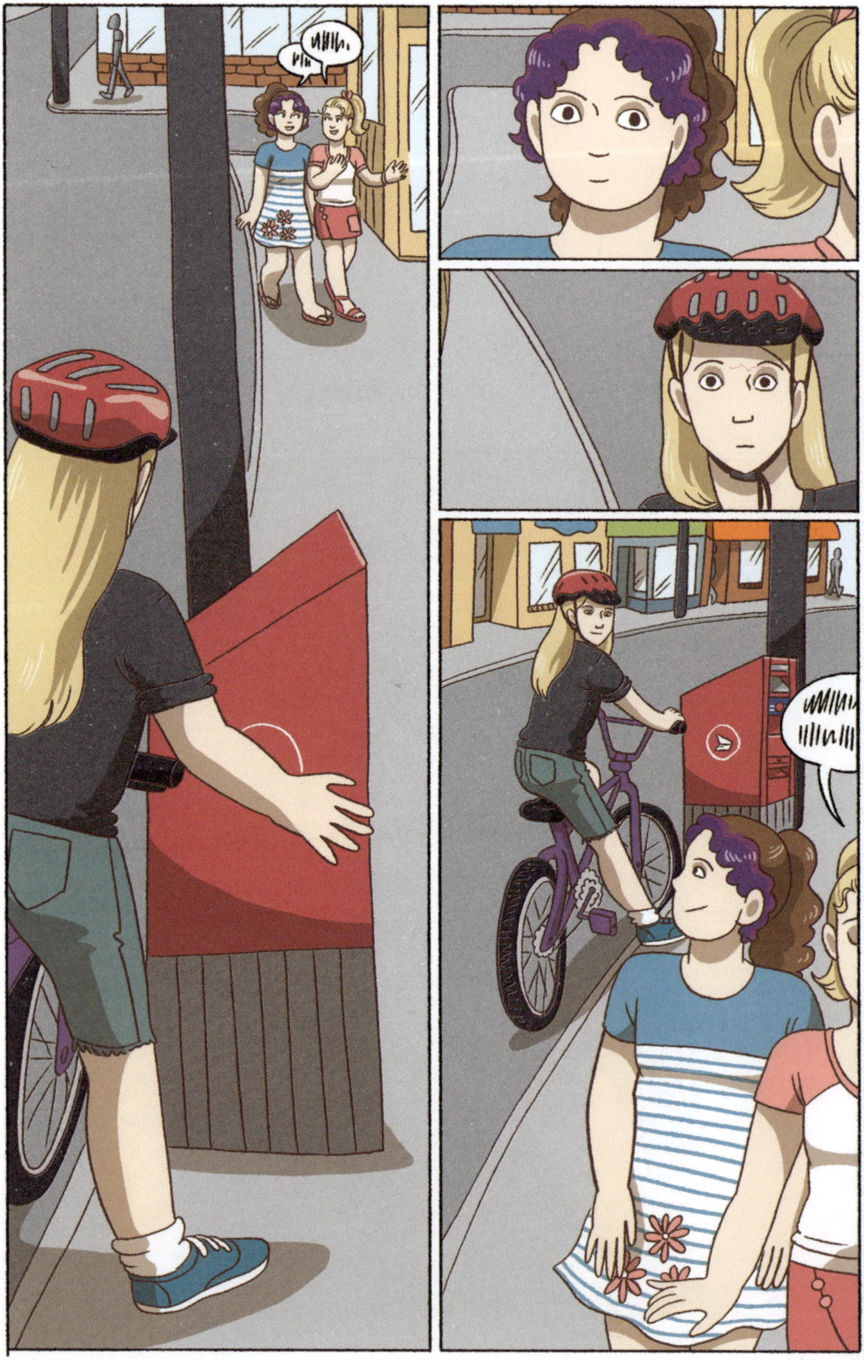

CHAPTER 2

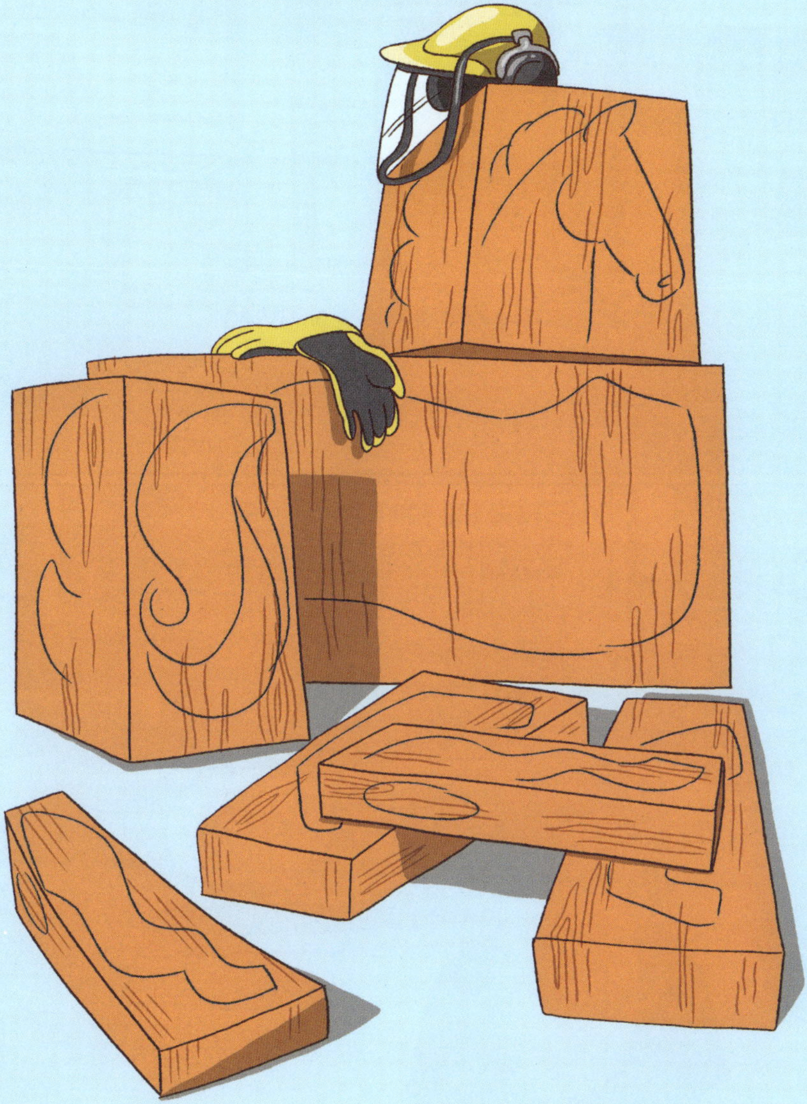

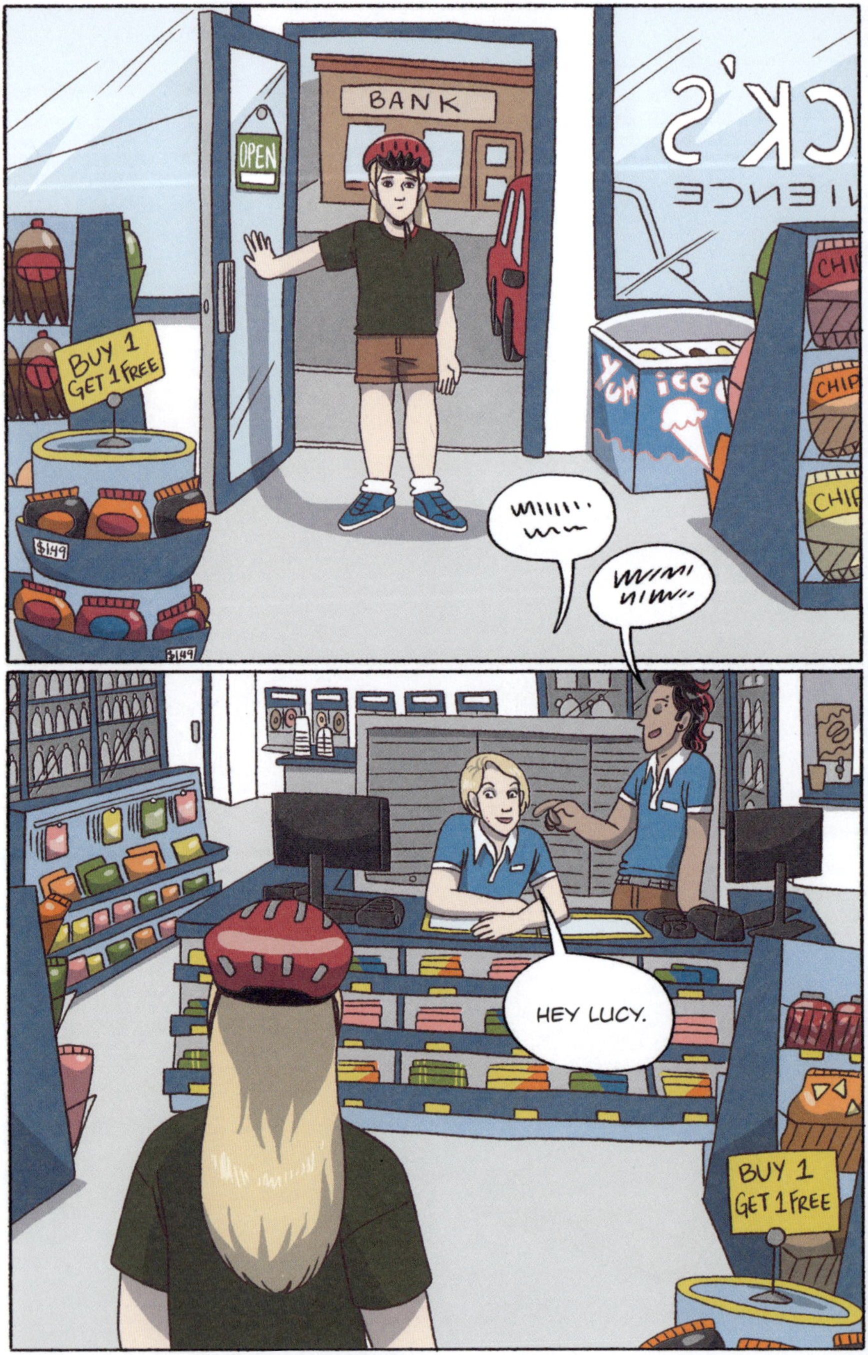
BANK
OPEN
BUY 1 GET 1 FREE
$1.49
YUM ice
CHIP
HEY LUCY.
BUY 1 GET 1 FREE

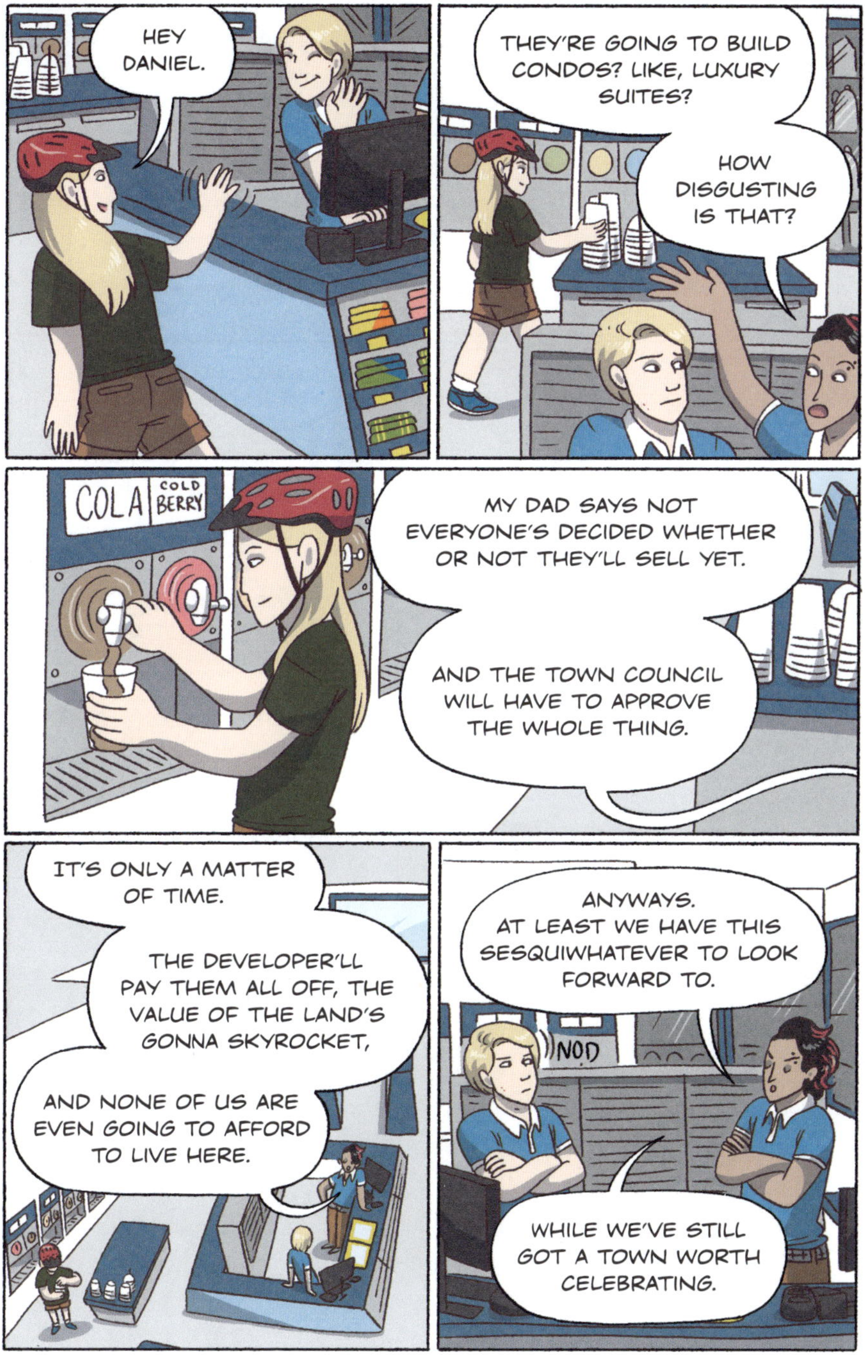
HEY DANIEL.
THEY'RE GOING TO BUILD CONDOS? LIKE, LUXURY SUITES?
HOW DISGUSTING IS THAT?
COLA
COLD BERRY
MY DAD SAYS NOT EVERYONE'S DECIDED WHETHER OR NOT THEY'LL SELL YET.
AND THE TOWN COUNCIL WILL HAVE TO APPROVE THE WHOLE THING.
IT'S ONLY A MATTER OF TIME.
THE DEVELOPER'LL PAY THEM ALL OFF, THE VALUE OF THE LAND'S GONNA SKYROCKET,
AND NONE OF US ARE EVEN GOING TO AFFORD TO LIVE HERE.
ANYWAYS. AT LEAST WE HAVE THIS SESQUIWHATEVER TO LOOK FORWARD TO.
NOD
WHILE WE'VE STILL GOT A TOWN WORTH CELEBRATING.

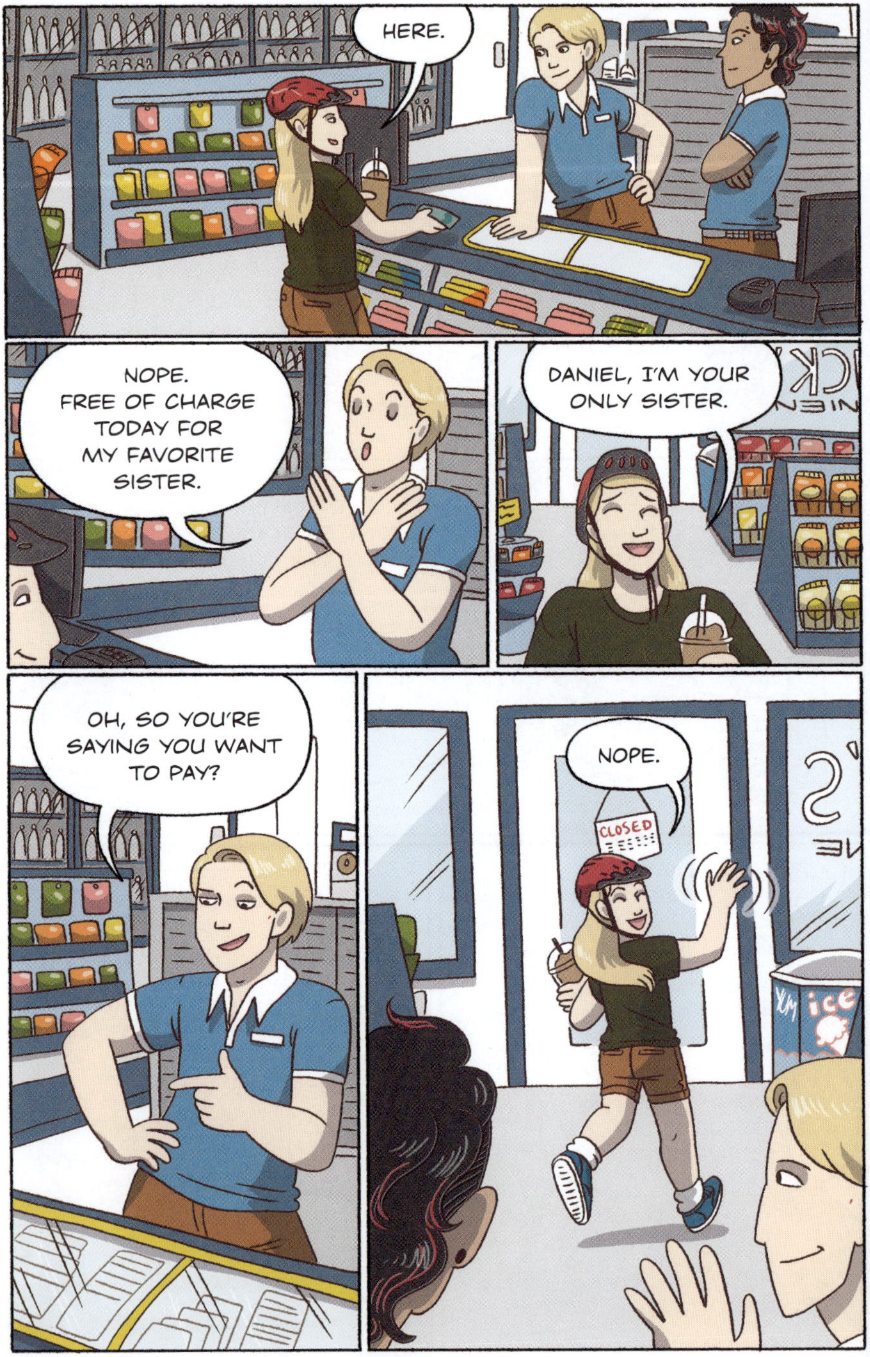
HERE.
NOPE. FREE OF CHARGE TODAY FOR MY FAVORITE SISTER.
DANIEL, I'M YOUR ONLY SISTER.
OH, SO YOU'RE SAYING YOU WANT TO PAY?
NOPE.
CLOSED

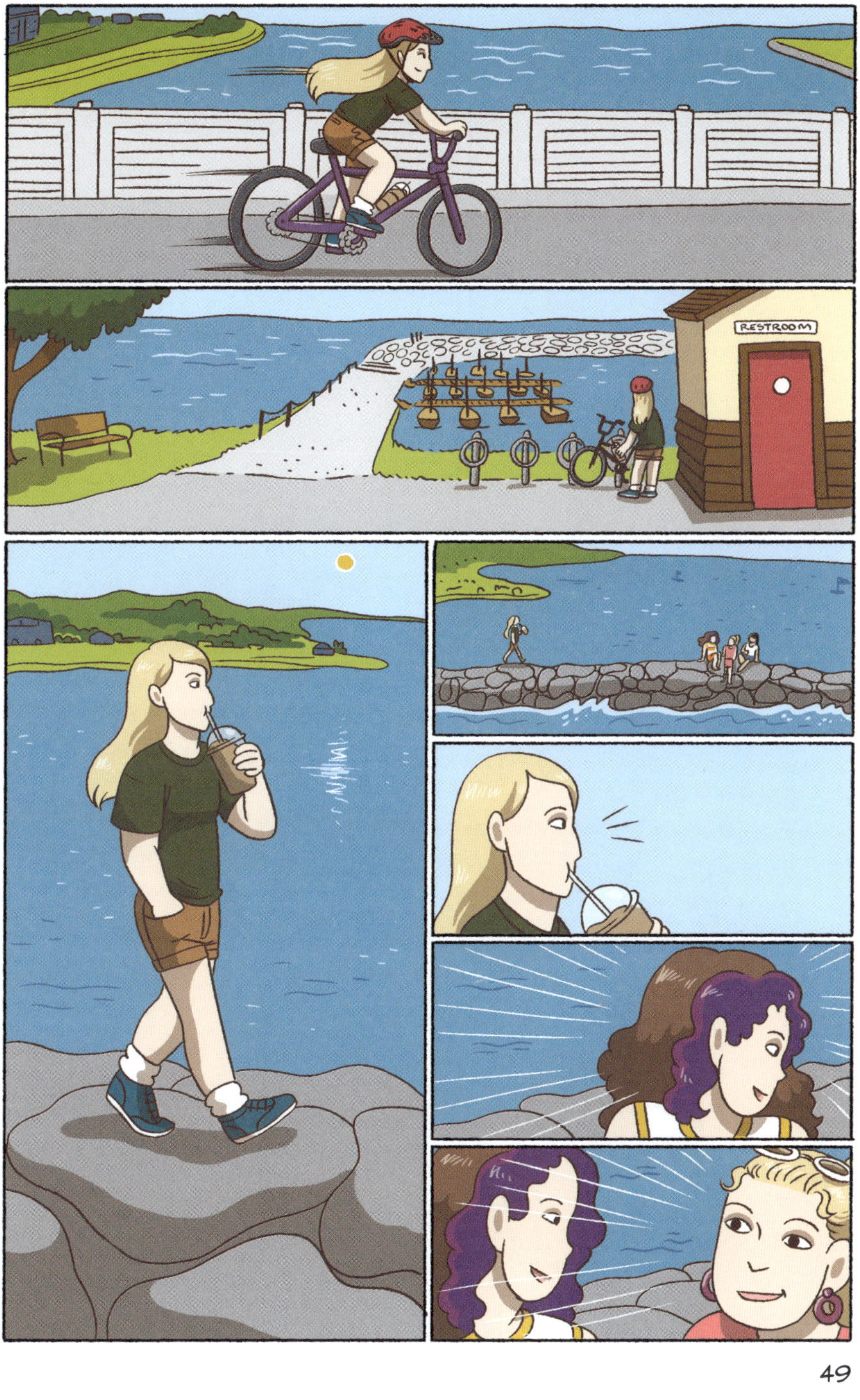
RESTROOM

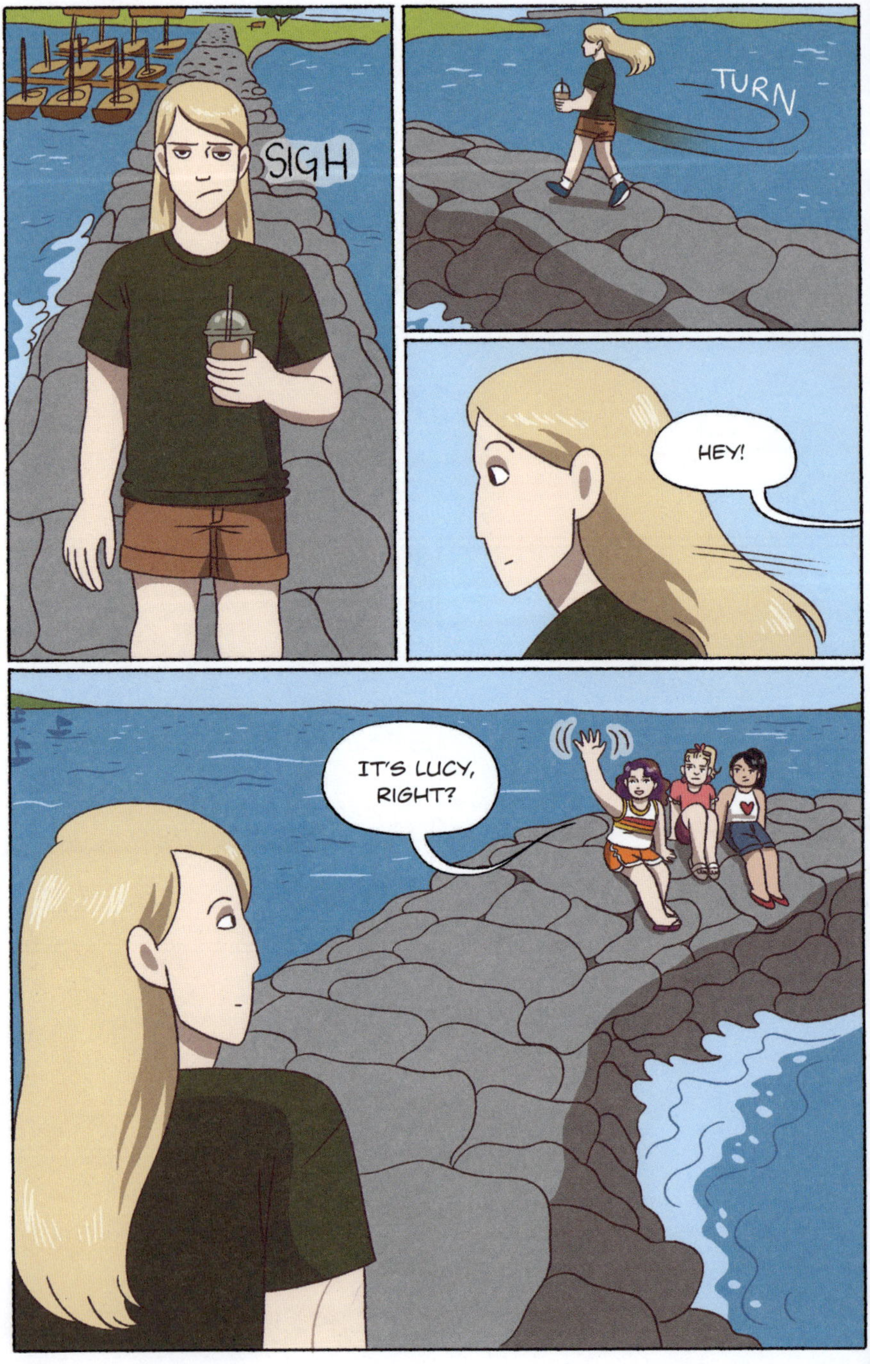
SIGH
TURN
HEY!
IT'S LUCY, RIGHT?

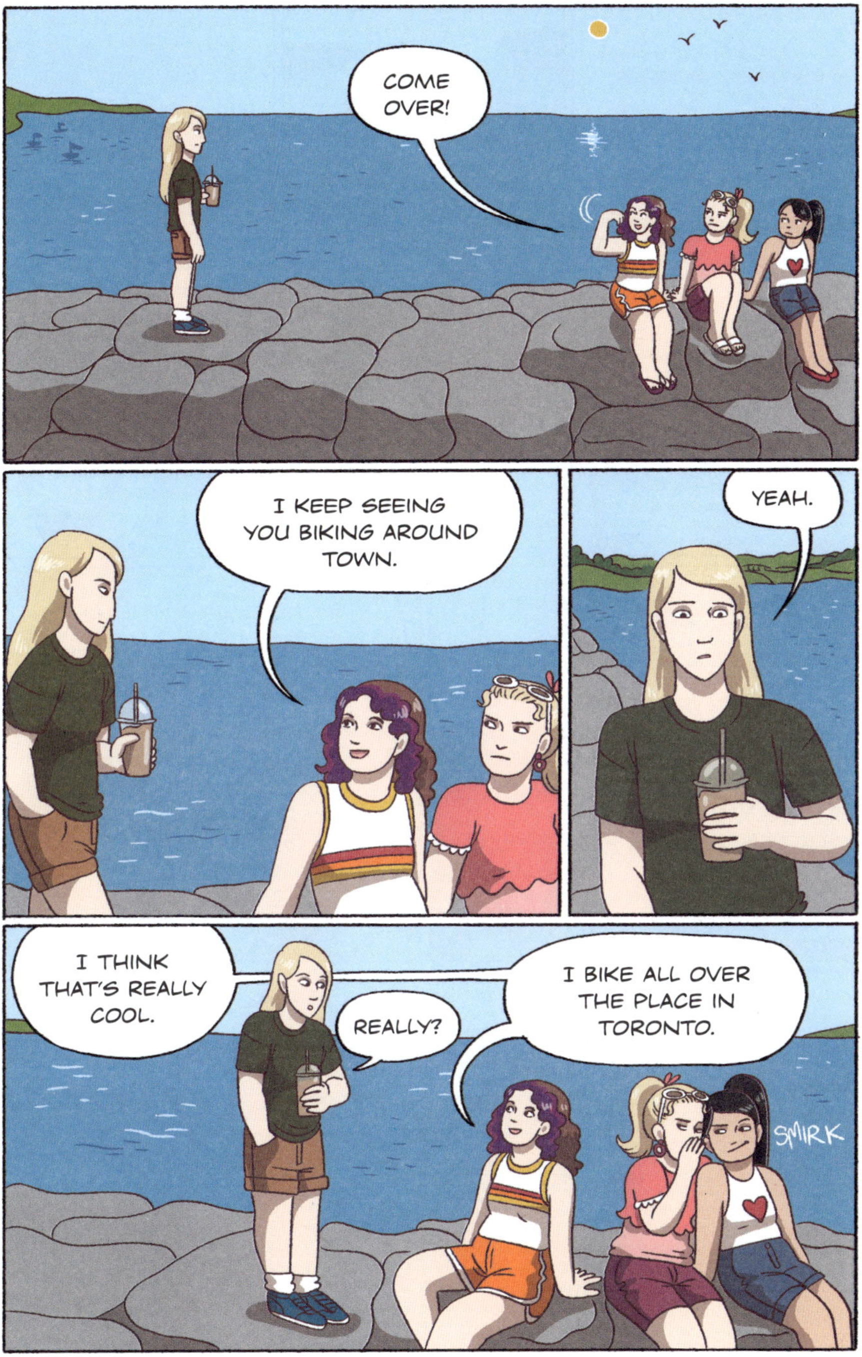
COME OVER!
I KEEP SEEING YOU BIKING AROUND TOWN.
YEAH.
I THINK THAT'S REALLY COOL.
REALLY?
I BIKE ALL OVER THE PLACE IN TORONTO.
SMIRK

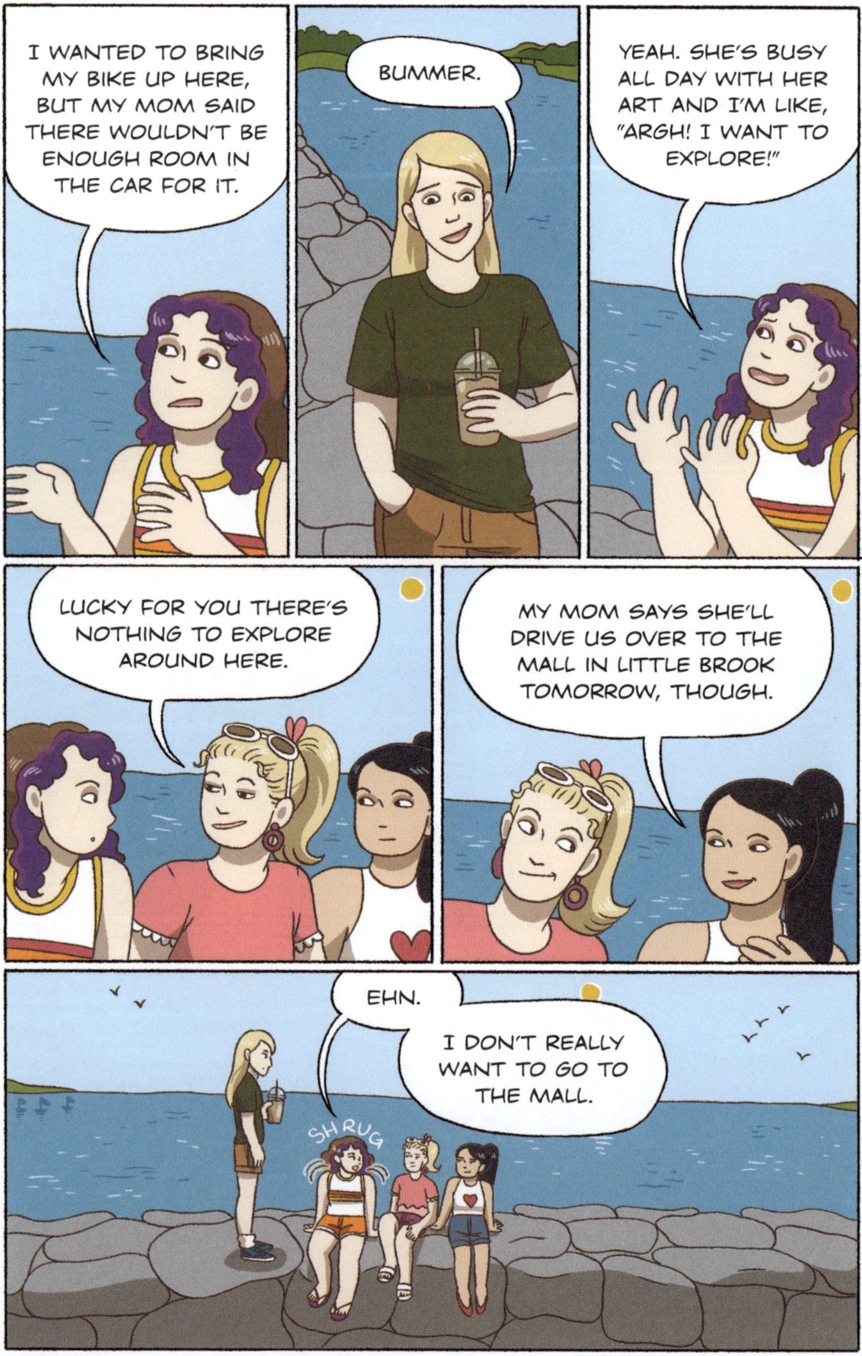
I WANTED TO BRING MY BIKE UP HERE, BUT MY MOM SAID THERE WOULDN'T BE ENOUGH ROOM IN THE CAR FOR IT.
BUMMER.
YEAH. SHE'S BUSY ALL DAY WITH HER ART AND I'M LIKE, "ARGH! I WANT TO EXPLORE!"
LUCKY FOR YOU THERE'S NOTHING TO EXPLORE AROUND HERE.
MY MOM SAYS SHE'LL DRIVE US OVER TO THE MALL IN LITTLE BROOK TOMORROW, THOUGH.
EHN.
I DON'T REALLY WANT TO GO TO THE MALL.
SHRUG

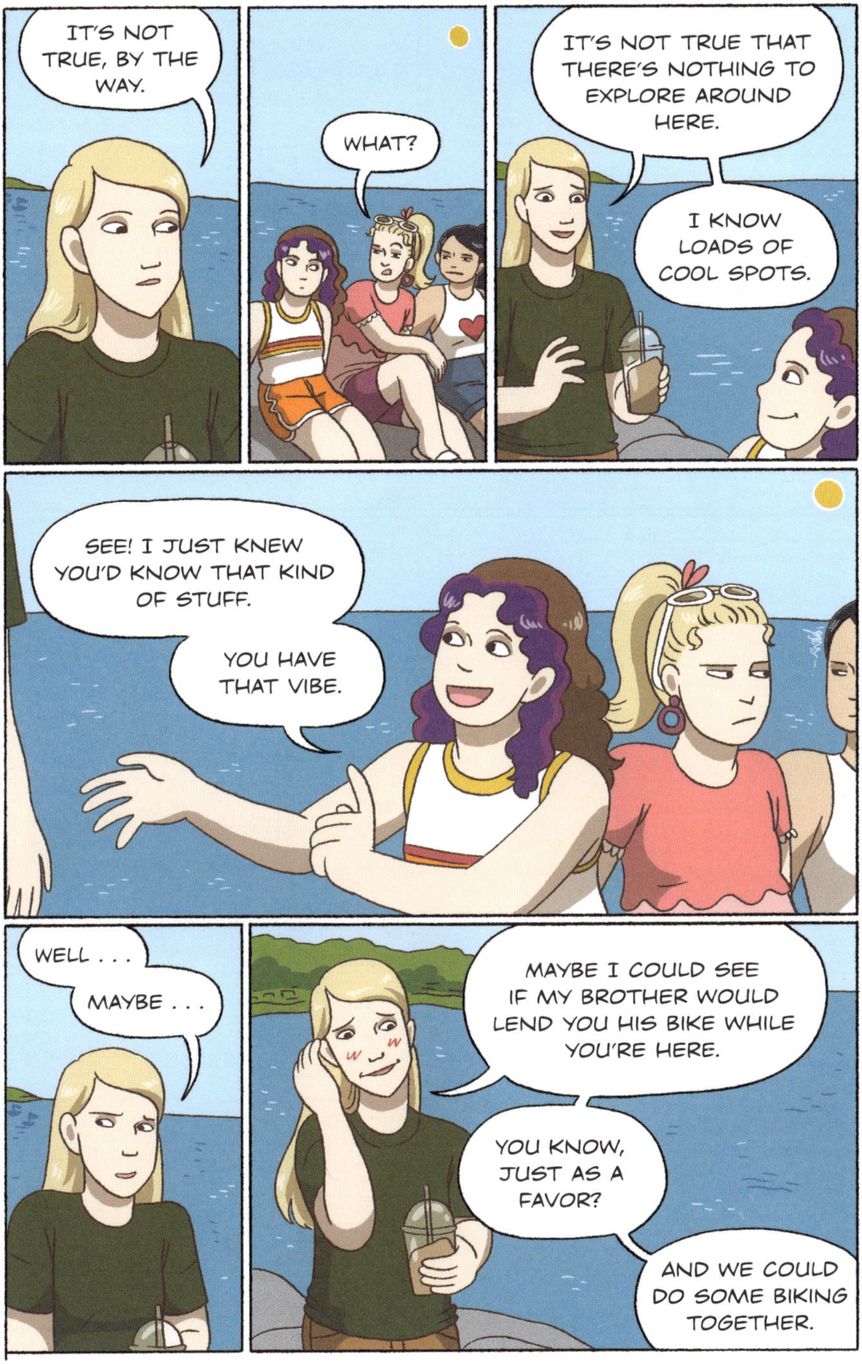
IT'S NOT TRUE, BY THE WAY.
WHAT?
IT'S NOT TRUE THAT THERE'S NOTHING TO EXPLORE AROUND HERE.
I KNOW LOADS OF COOL SPOTS.
SEE! I JUST KNEW YOU'D KNOW THAT KIND OF STUFF.
YOU HAVE THAT VIBE.
WELL . . .
MAYBE . . .
MAYBE I COULD SEE IF MY BROTHER WOULD LEND YOU HIS BIKE WHILE YOU'RE HERE.
YOU KNOW, JUST AS A FAVOR?
AND WE COULD DO SOME BIKING TOGETHER.

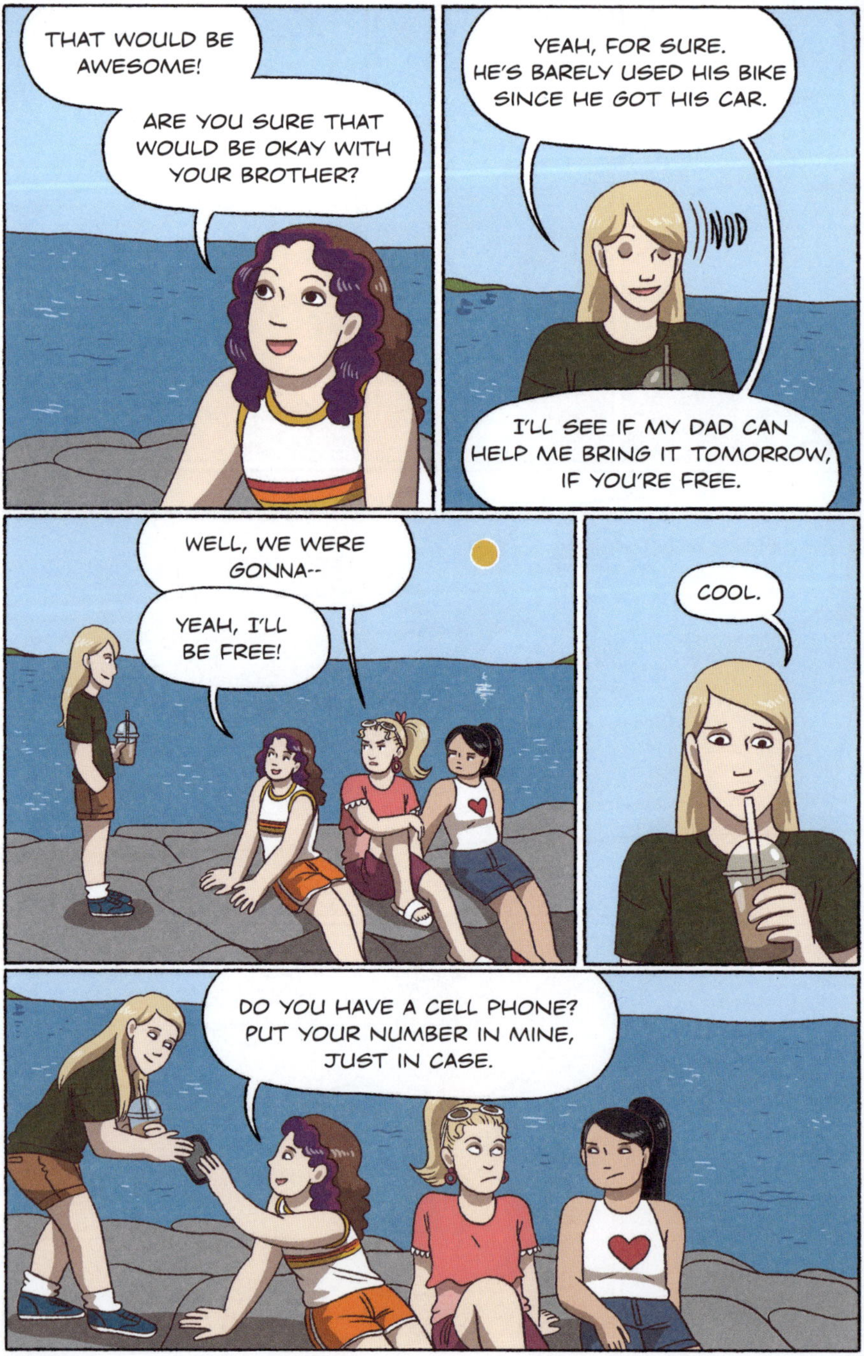
THAT WOULD BE AWESOME!
ARE YOU SURE THAT WOULD BE OKAY WITH YOUR BROTHER?
YEAH, FOR SURE. HE'S BARELY USED HIS BIKE SINCE HE GOT HIS CAR.
NOD
I'LL SEE IF MY DAD CAN HELP ME BRING IT TOMORROW, IF YOU'RE FREE.
WELL, WE WERE GONNA--
YEAH, I'LL BE FREE!
COOL.
DO YOU HAVE A CELL PHONE? PUT YOUR NUMBER IN MINE, JUST IN CASE.

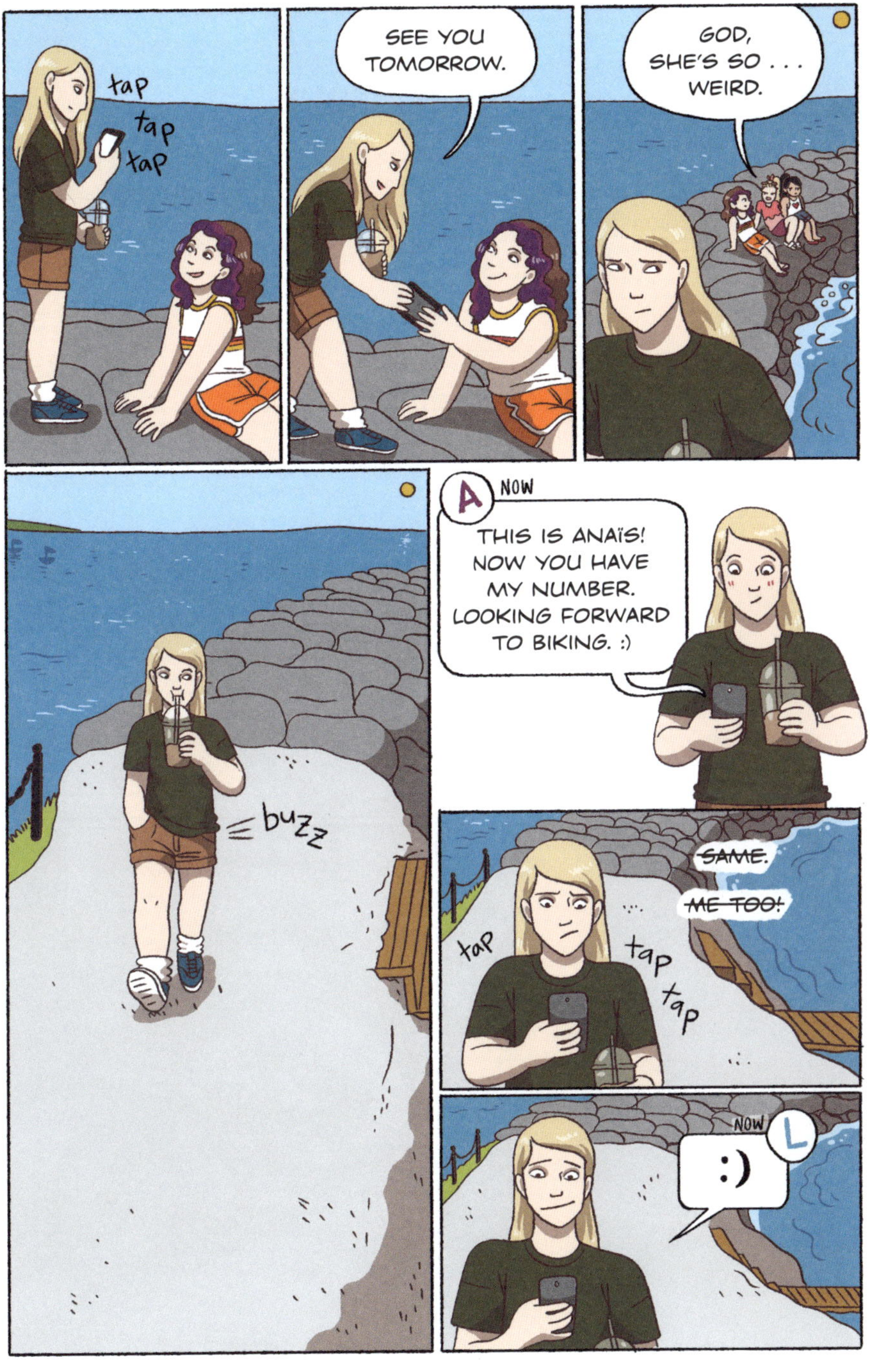
tap
tap
tap
SEE YOU TOMORROW.
GOD, SHE'S SO . . . WEIRD.
buzz
A NOW
THIS IS ANAÏS! NOW YOU HAVE MY NUMBER. LOOKING FORWARD TO BIKING. :)
SAME.
ME TOO!
tap
tap
tap
NOW L
:)

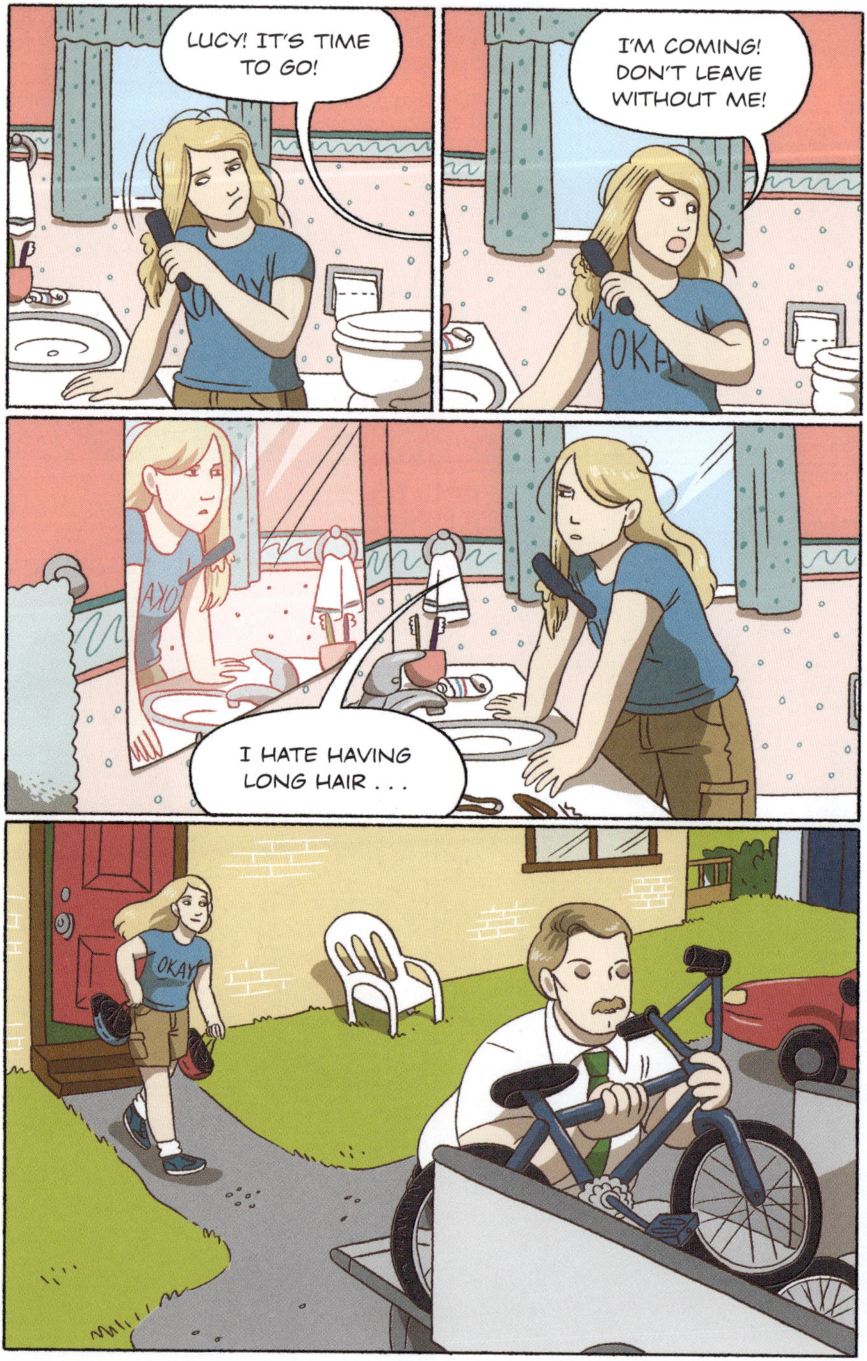
LUCY! IT'S TIME TO GO!
I'M COMING! DON'T LEAVE WITHOUT ME!
OKAY
I HATE HAVING LONG HAIR . . .

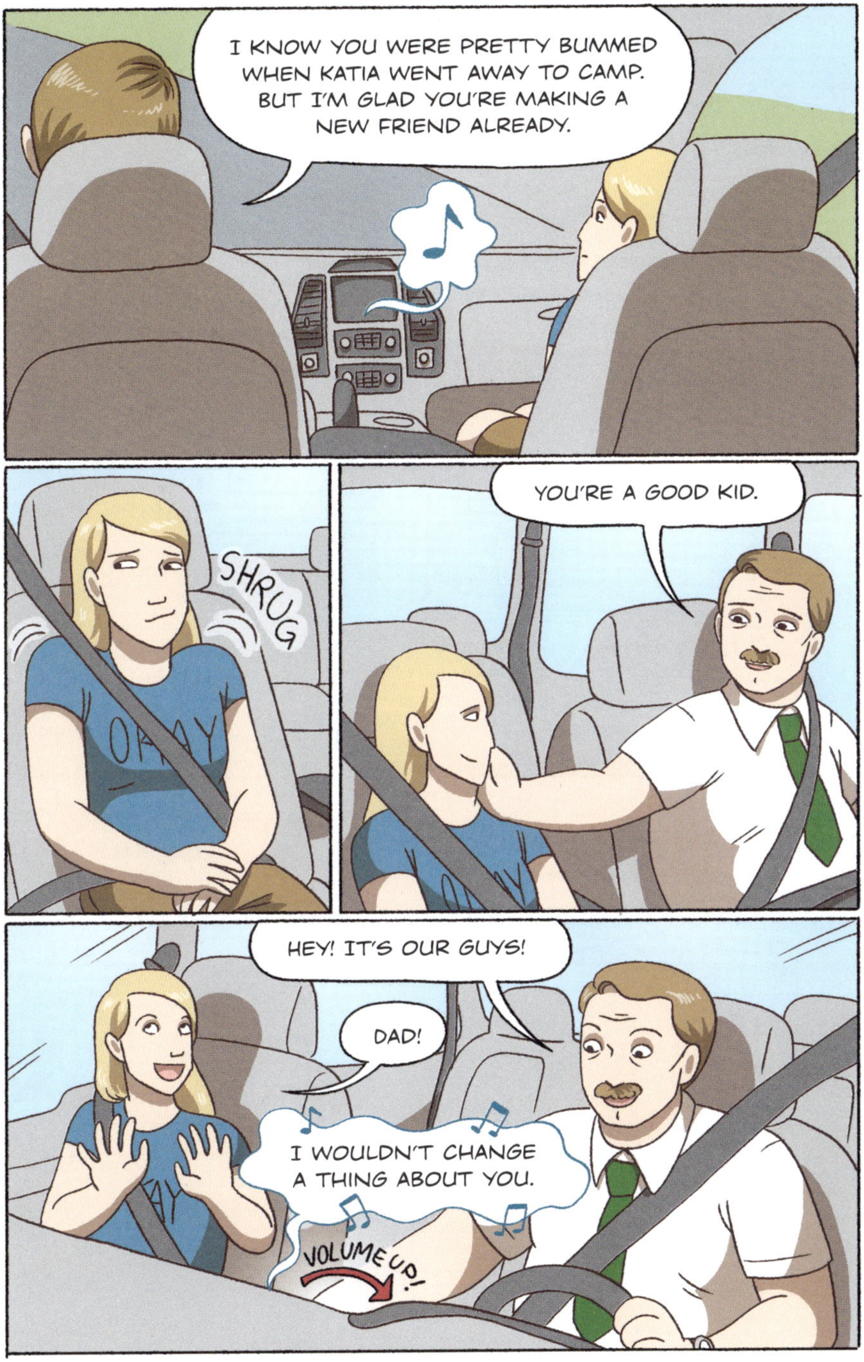
I KNOW YOU WERE PRETTY BUMMED WHEN KATIA WENT AWAY TO CAMP. BUT I'M GLAD YOU'RE MAKING A NEW FRIEND ALREADY.
SHRUG
OKAY
YOU'RE A GOOD KID.
HEY! IT'S OUR GUYS!
DAD!
I WOULDN'T CHANGE A THING ABOUT YOU.
VOLUME UP!

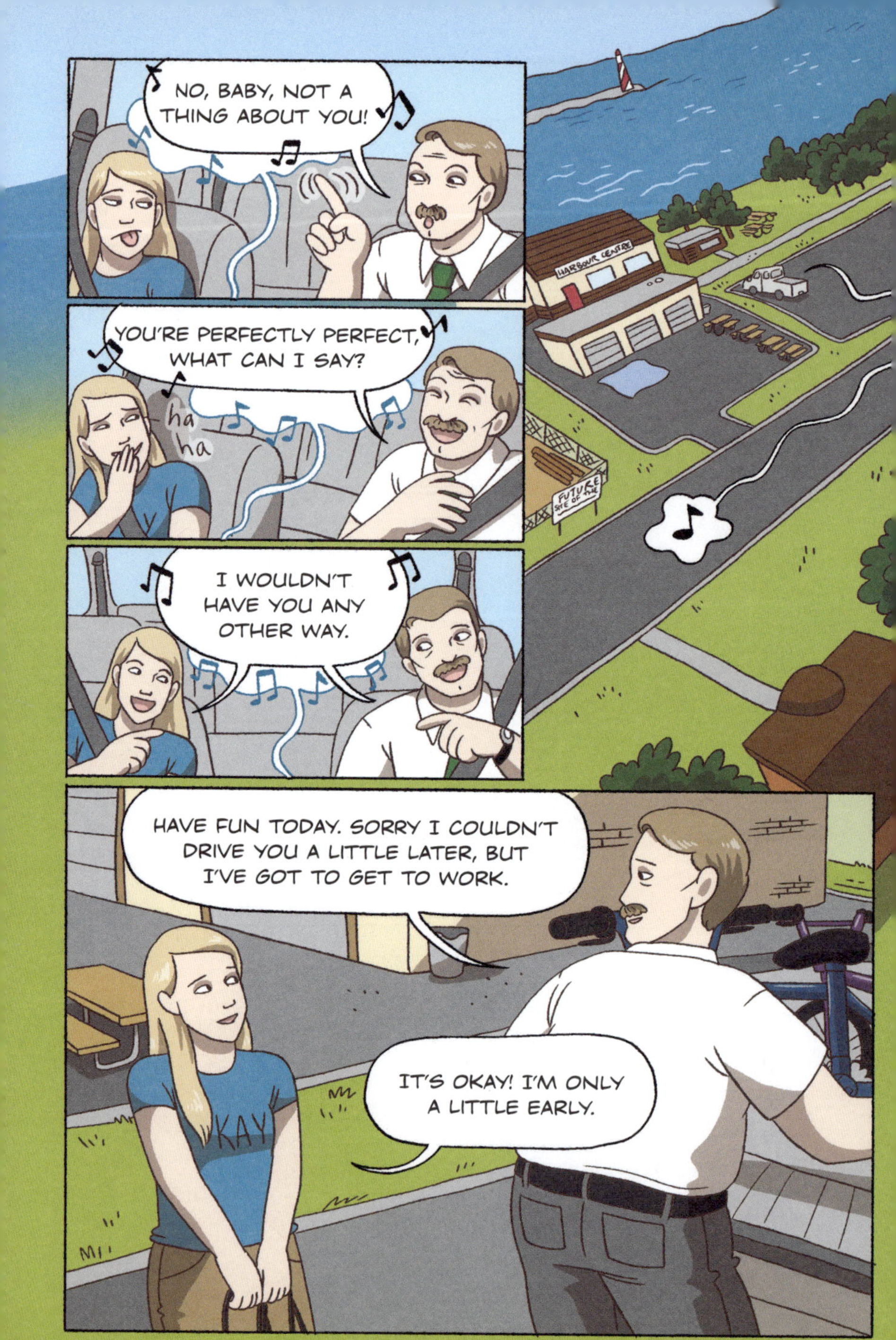
NO, BABY, NOT A THING ABOUT YOU!
YOU'RE PERFECTLY PERFECT, WHAT CAN I SAY?
ha ha
I WOULDN'T HAVE YOU ANY OTHER WAY.
HARBOUR CENTRE
FUTURE SITE OF THE
HAVE FUN TODAY. SORRY I COULDN'T DRIVE YOU A LITTLE LATER, BUT I'VE GOT TO GET TO WORK.
KAY
IT'S OKAY! I'M ONLY A LITTLE EARLY.

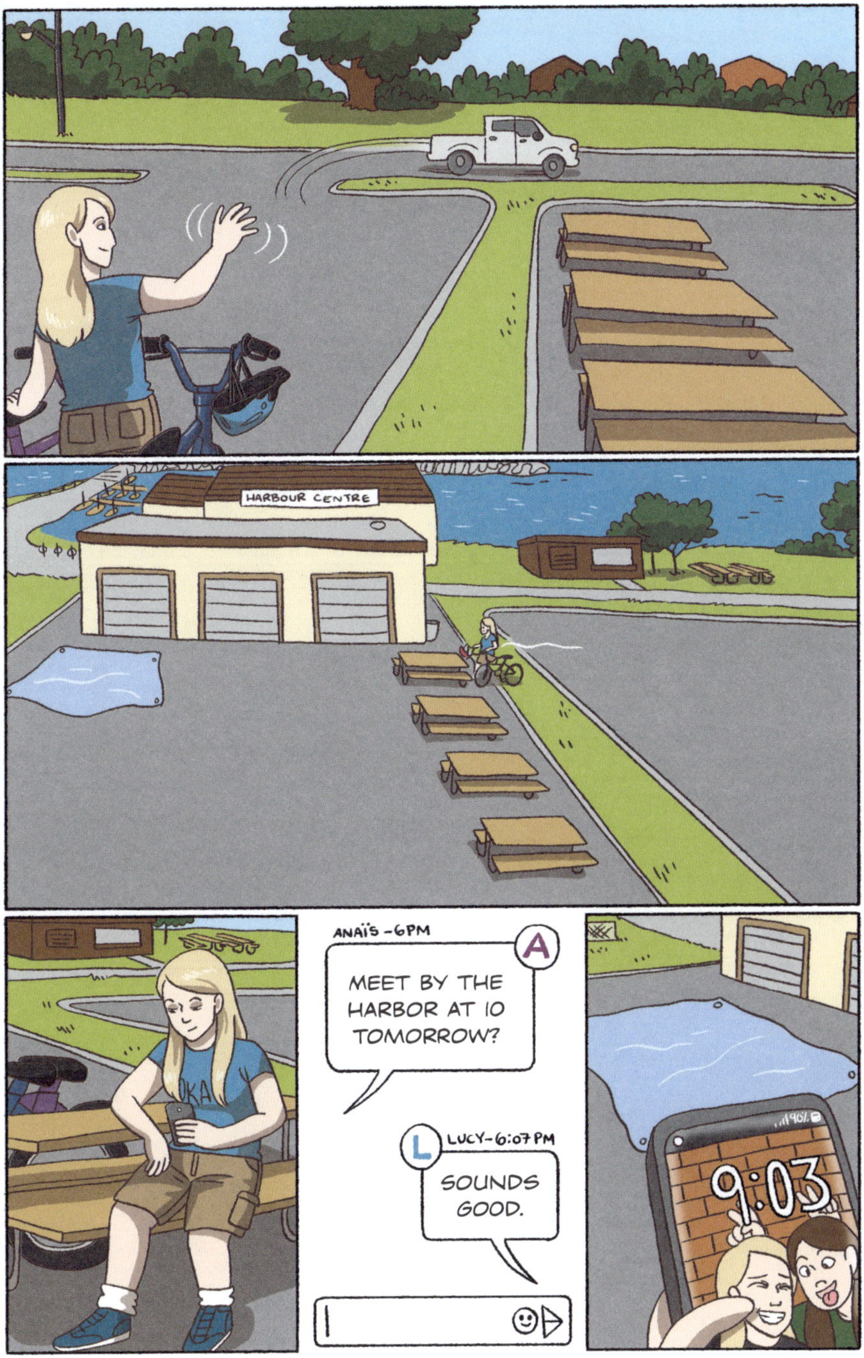
HARBOUR CENTRE
OKA
ANAÏS -6PM
A
MEET BY THE HARBOR AT 10 TOMORROW?
L
LUCY-6:07 PM
SOUNDS GOOD.
9:03

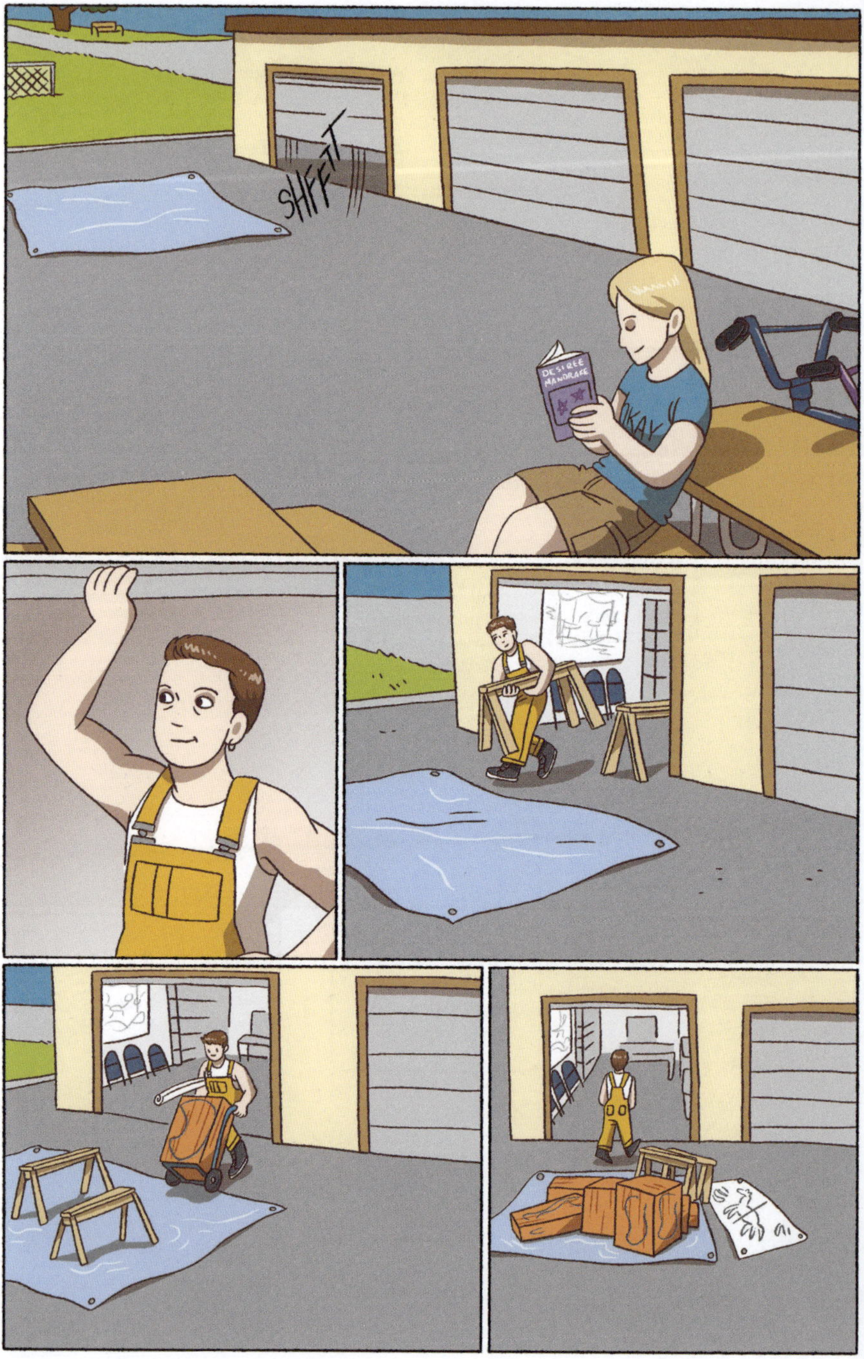
SHFFTT
DESIREE MANDRAKE
OKAY

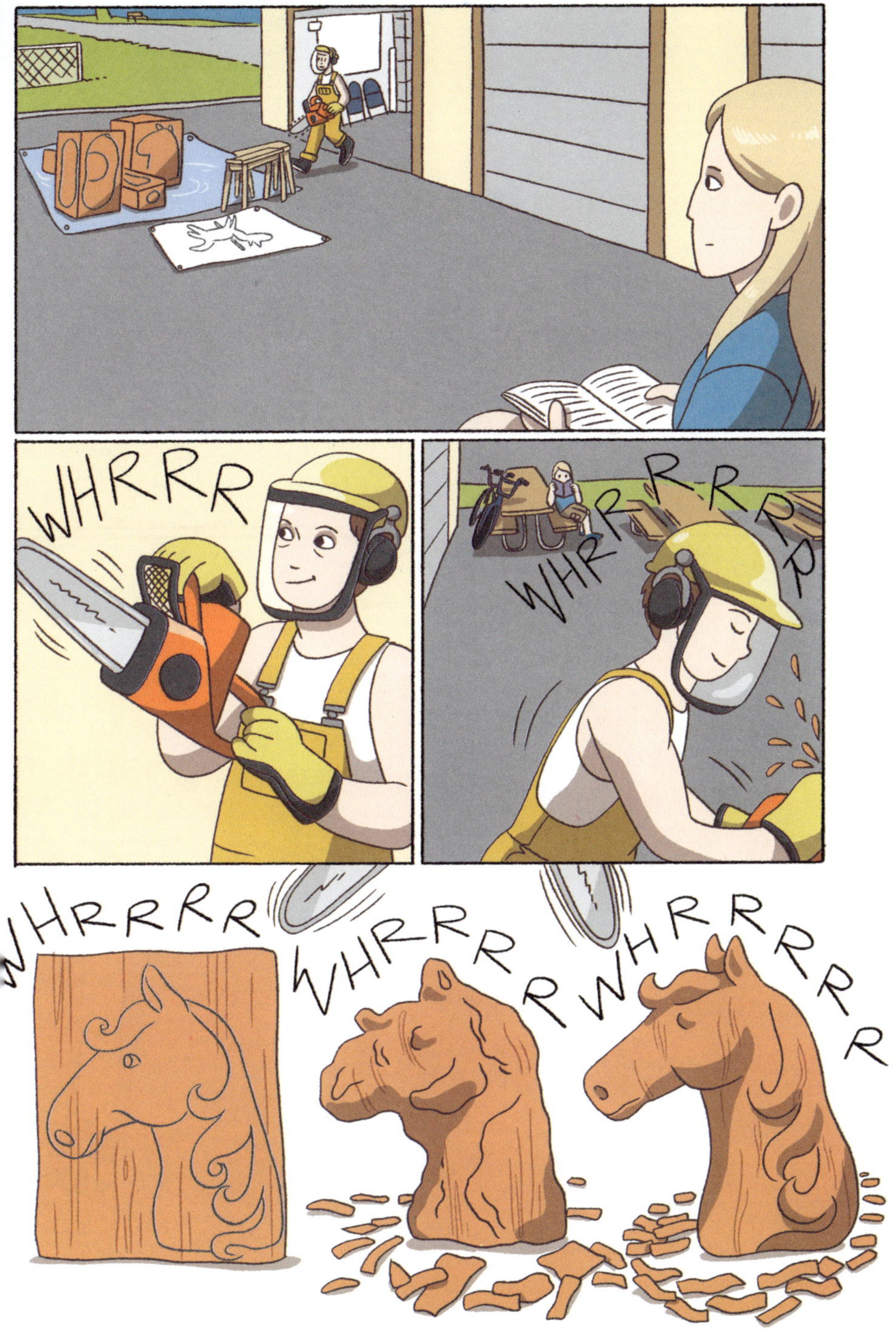
WHRRRR
WHRRRRRR
WHRRRR
WHRRRR
WHRRRRR

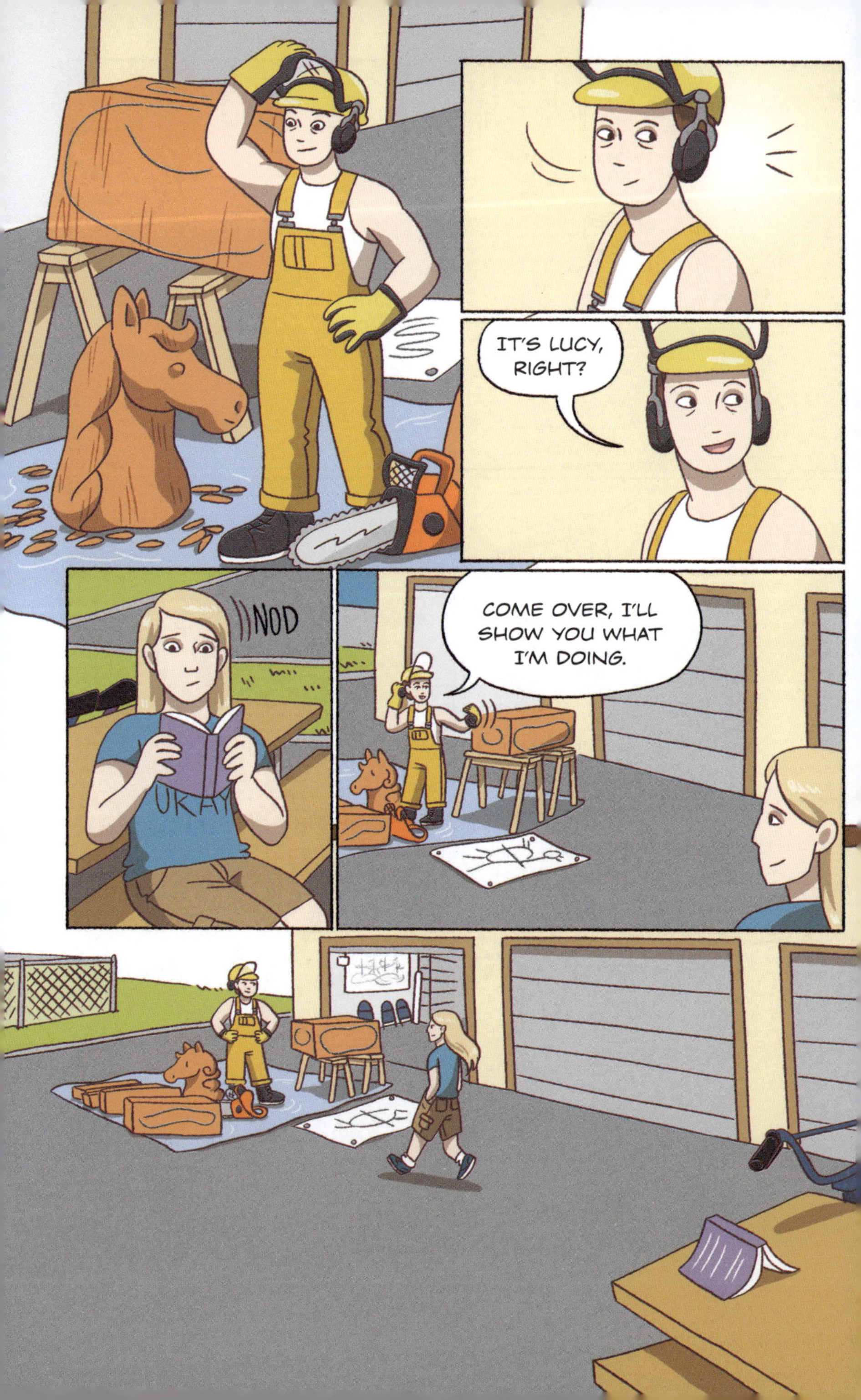
IT'S LUCY, RIGHT?
NOD
UKAY
COME OVER, I'LL SHOW YOU WHAT I'M DOING.

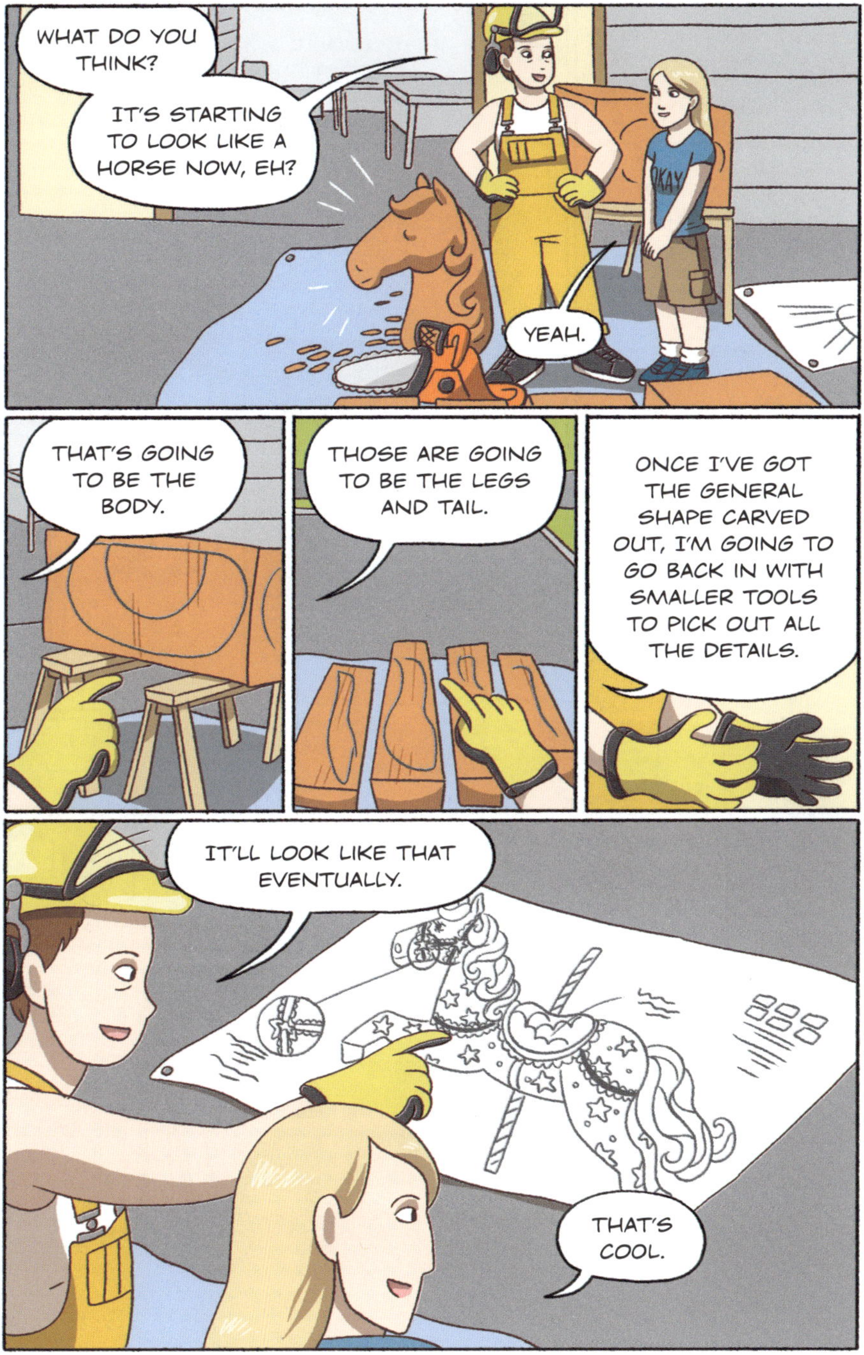
WHAT DO YOU THINK?
IT'S STARTING TO LOOK LIKE A HORSE NOW, EH?
YEAH.
OKAY
THAT'S GOING TO BE THE BODY.
THOSE ARE GOING TO BE THE LEGS AND TAIL.
ONCE I'VE GOT THE GENERAL SHAPE CARVED OUT, I'M GOING TO GO BACK IN WITH SMALLER TOOLS TO PICK OUT ALL THE DETAILS.
IT'LL LOOK LIKE THAT EVENTUALLY.
THAT'S COOL.

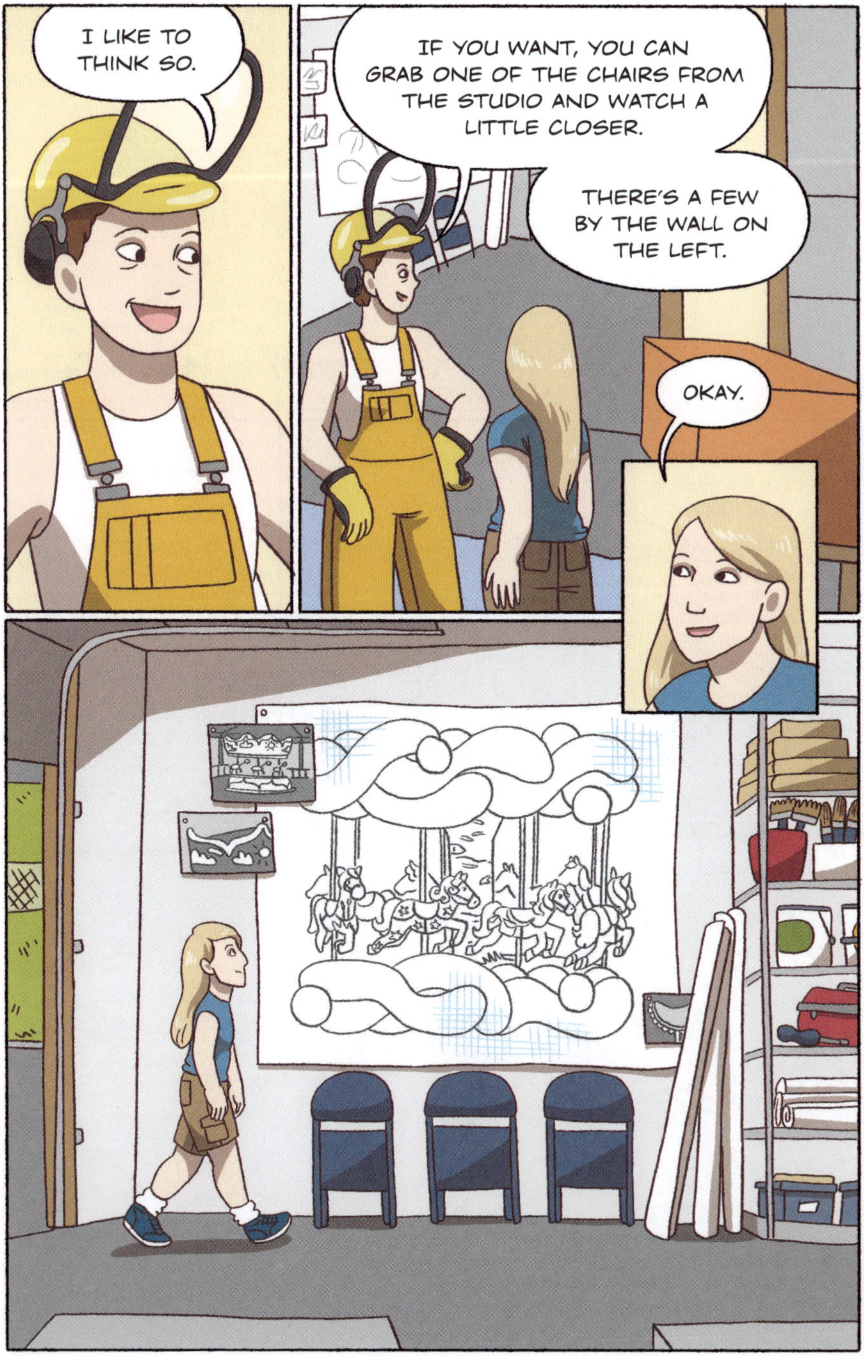
I LIKE TO THINK SO.
IF YOU WANT, YOU CAN GRAB ONE OF THE CHAIRS FROM THE STUDIO AND WATCH A LITTLE CLOSER.
THERE'S A FEW BY THE WALL ON THE LEFT.
OKAY.

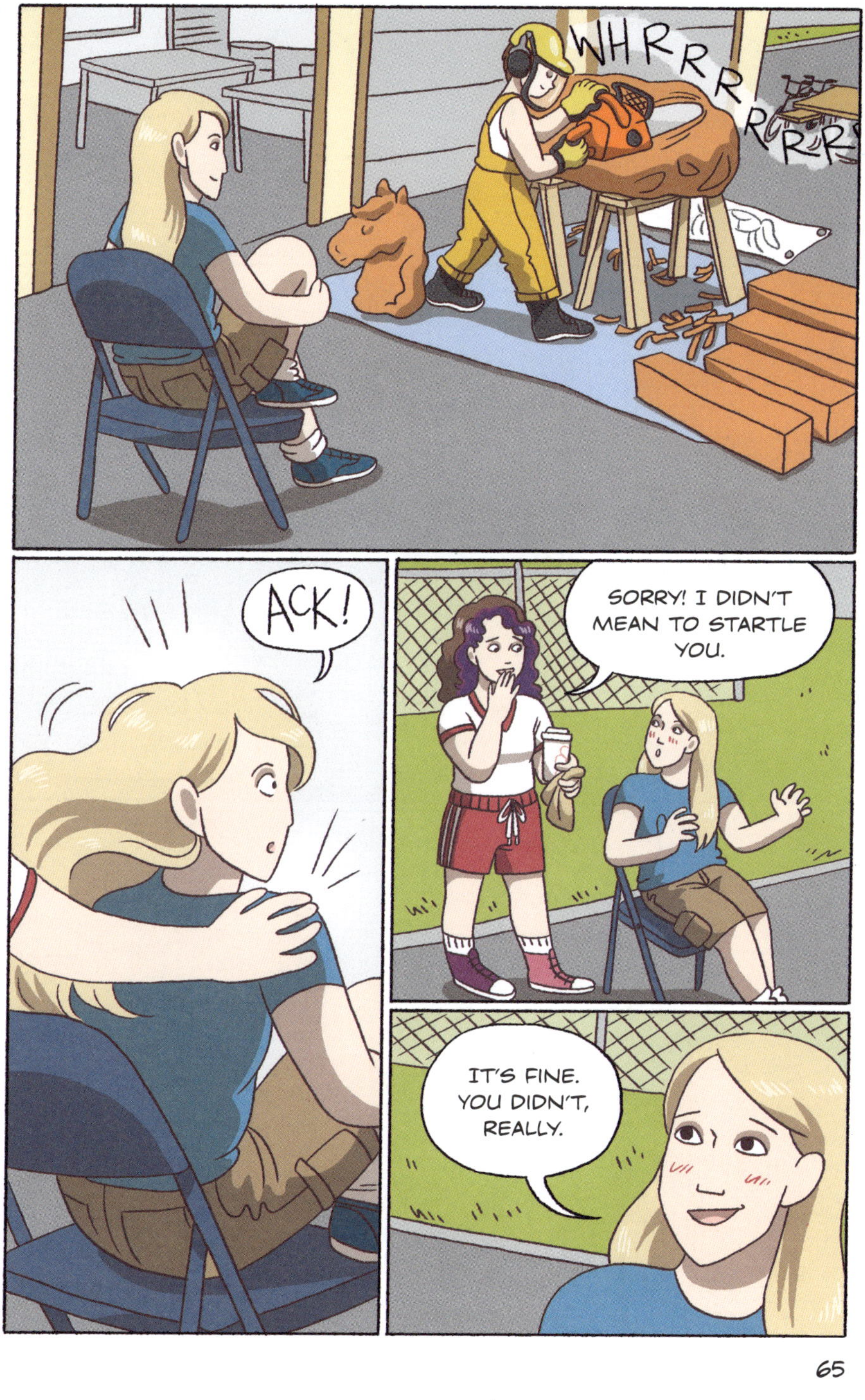

WHRRRRRRRR
ACK!
SORRY! I DIDN'T MEAN TO STARTLE YOU.
IT'S FINE. YOU DIDN'T, REALLY.

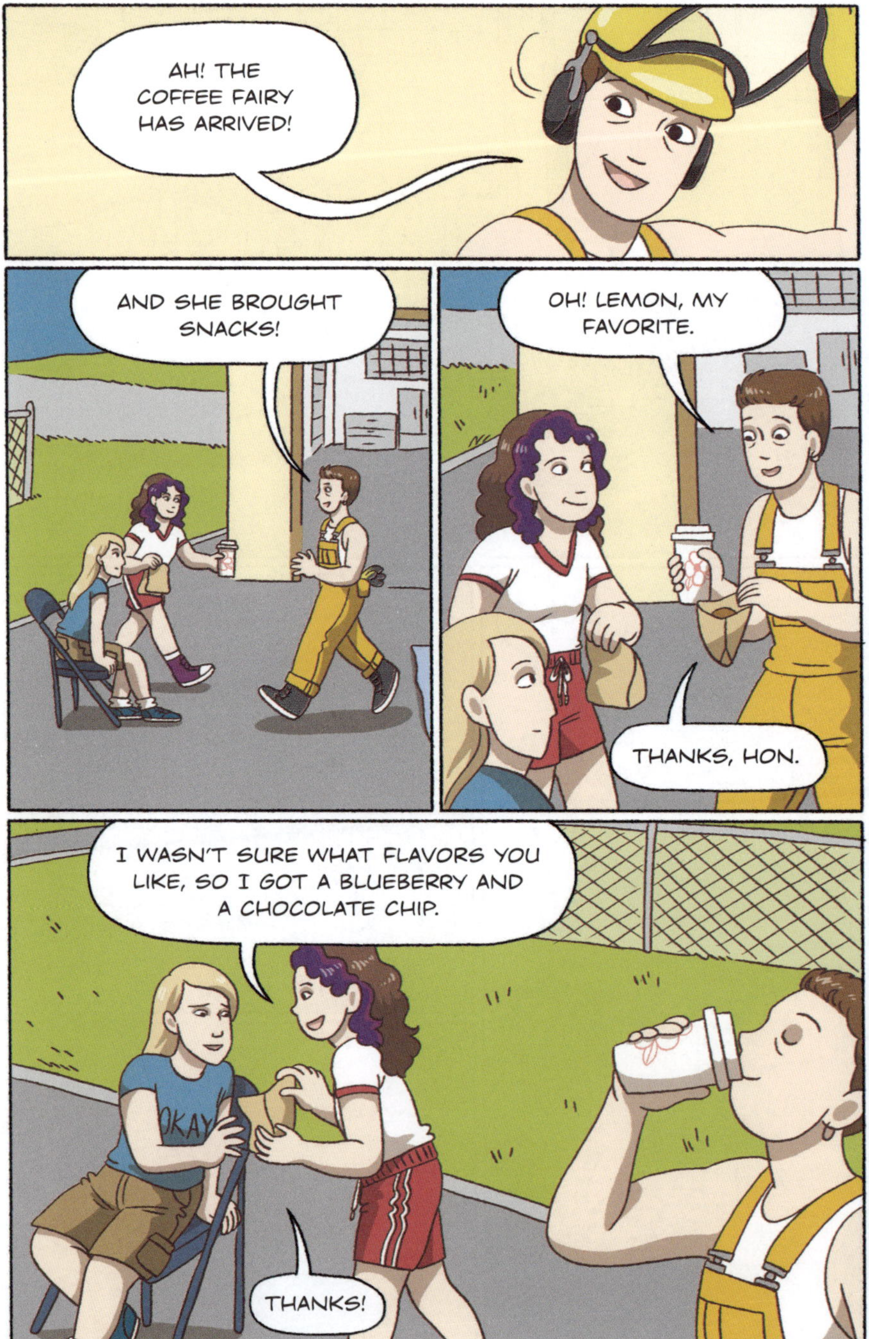
AH! THE COFFEE FAIRY HAS ARRIVED!
AND SHE BROUGHT SNACKS!
OH! LEMON, MY FAVORITE.
THANKS, HON.
I WASN'T SURE WHAT FLAVORS YOU LIKE, SO I GOT A BLUEBERRY AND A CHOCOLATE CHIP.
OKAY
THANKS!

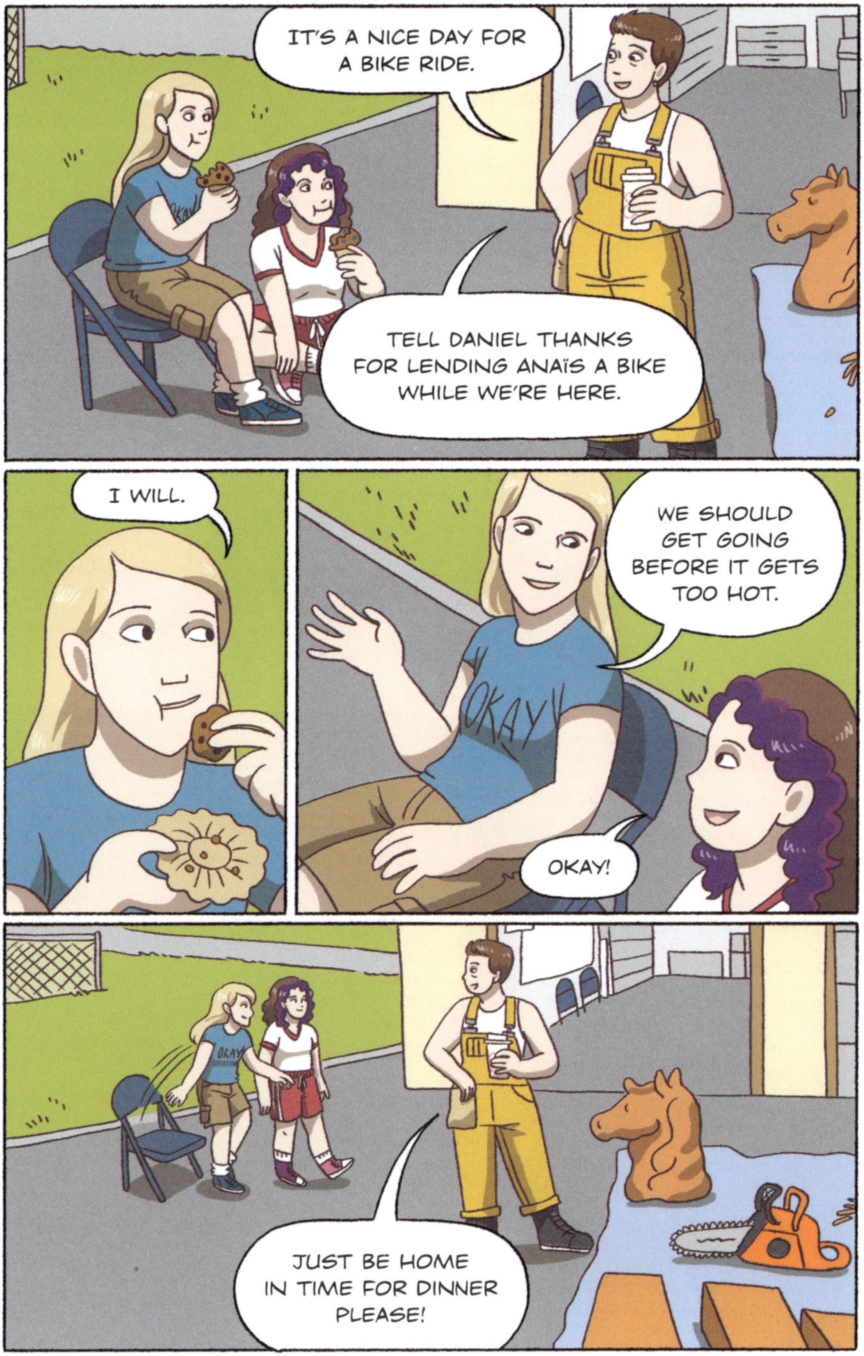
IT'S A NICE DAY FOR A BIKE RIDE.
TELL DANIEL THANKS FOR LENDING ANAÏS A BIKE WHILE WE'RE HERE.
OKAY!
I WILL.
WE SHOULD GET GOING BEFORE IT GETS TOO HOT.
OKAY!
OKAY
JUST BE HOME IN TIME FOR DINNER PLEASE!

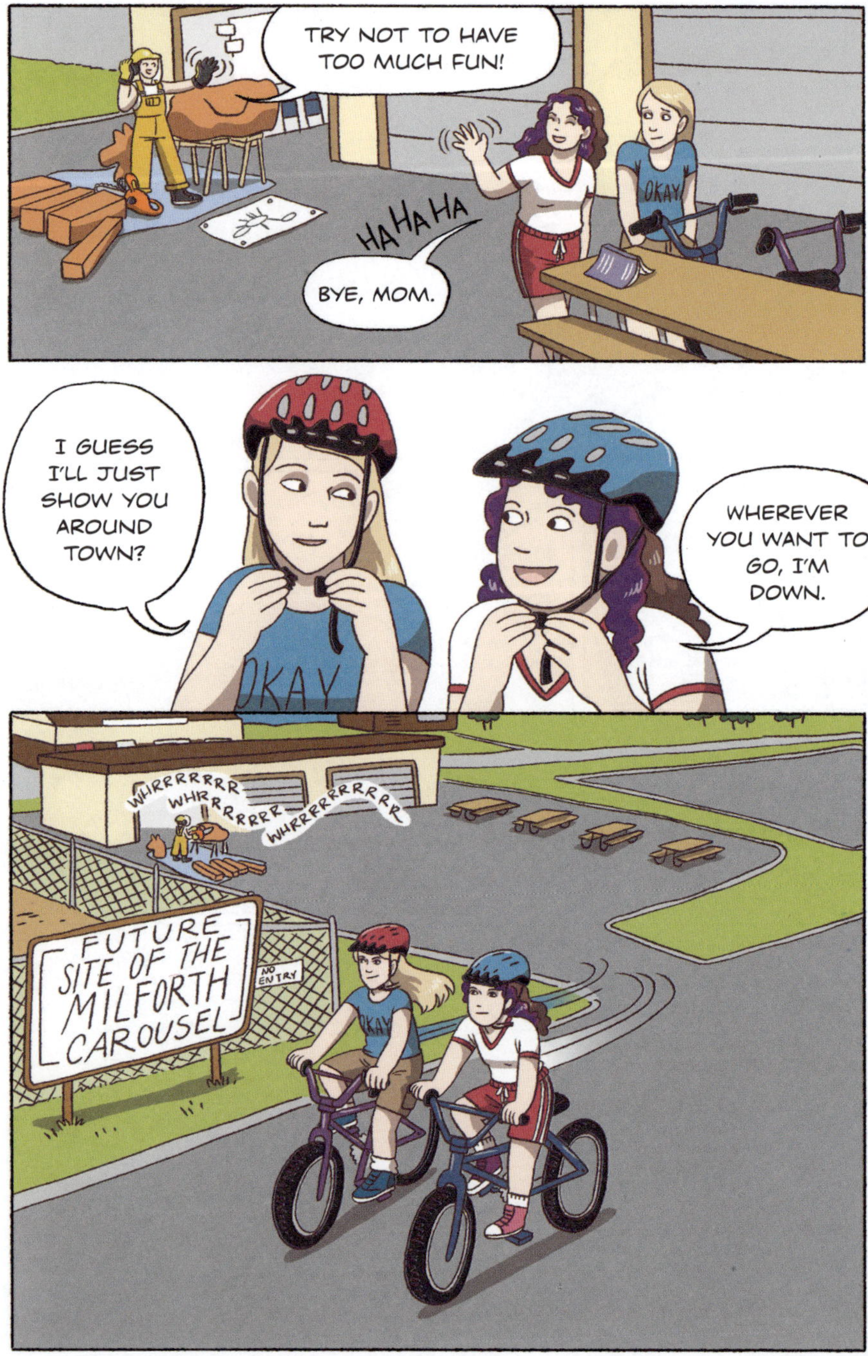
TRY NOT TO HAVE TOO MUCH FUN!
HAHAHA
BYE, MOM.
I GUESS I'LL JUST SHOW YOU AROUND TOWN?
WHEREVER YOU WANT TO GO, I'M DOWN.
WHRRRRRRR WHRRRRRR WHRRRRRRRRR
FUTURE SITE OF THE MILFORTH CAROUSEL
NO ENTRY

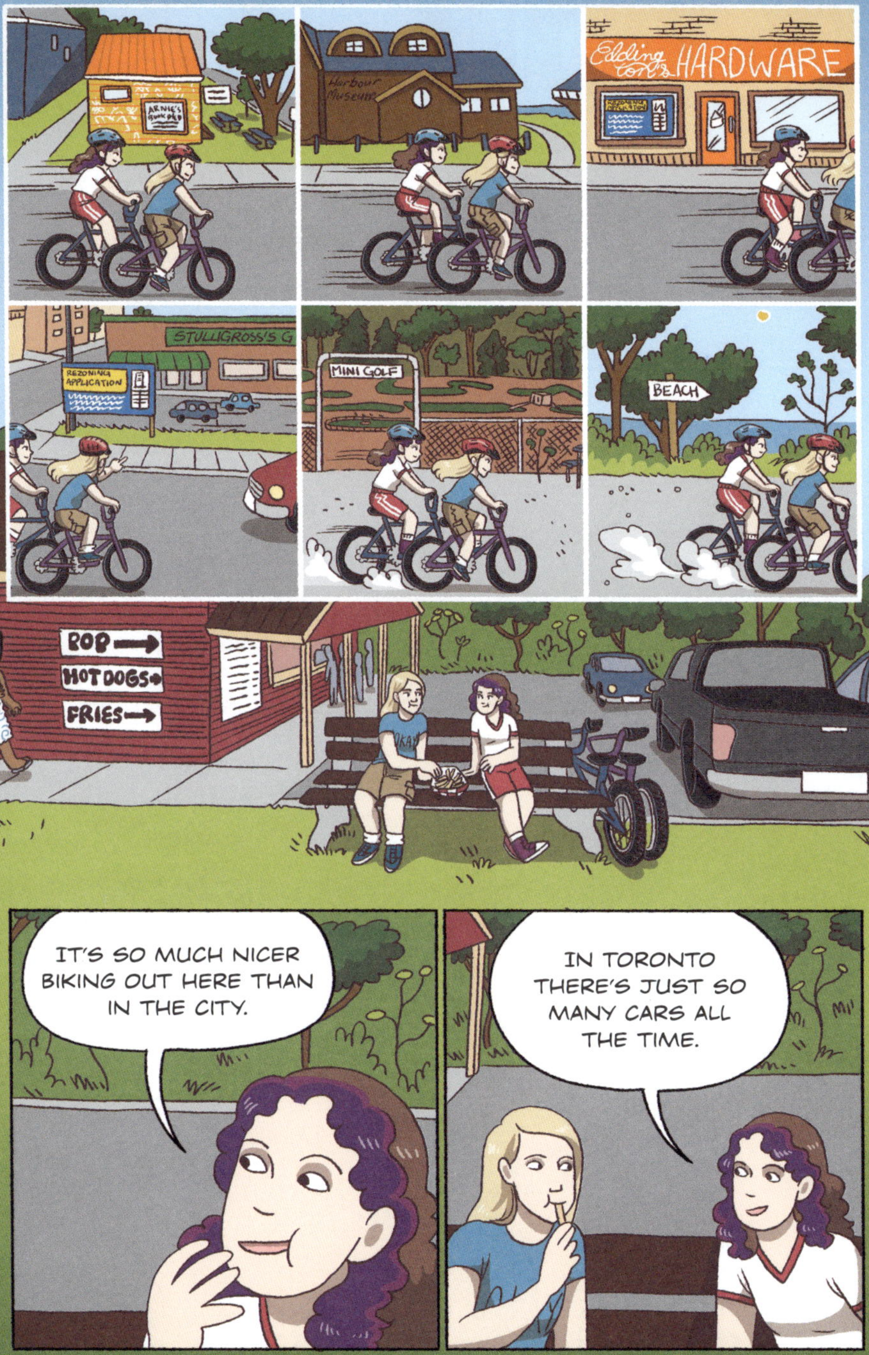
Harbour Museum
HARDWARE
REZONING APPLICATION
STULLGROSS'S G
MINI GOLF
BEACH
POP
HOT DOGS
FRIES
OKAY
IT'S SO MUCH NICER BIKING OUT HERE THAN IN THE CITY.
IN TORONTO THERE'S JUST SO MANY CARS ALL THE TIME.

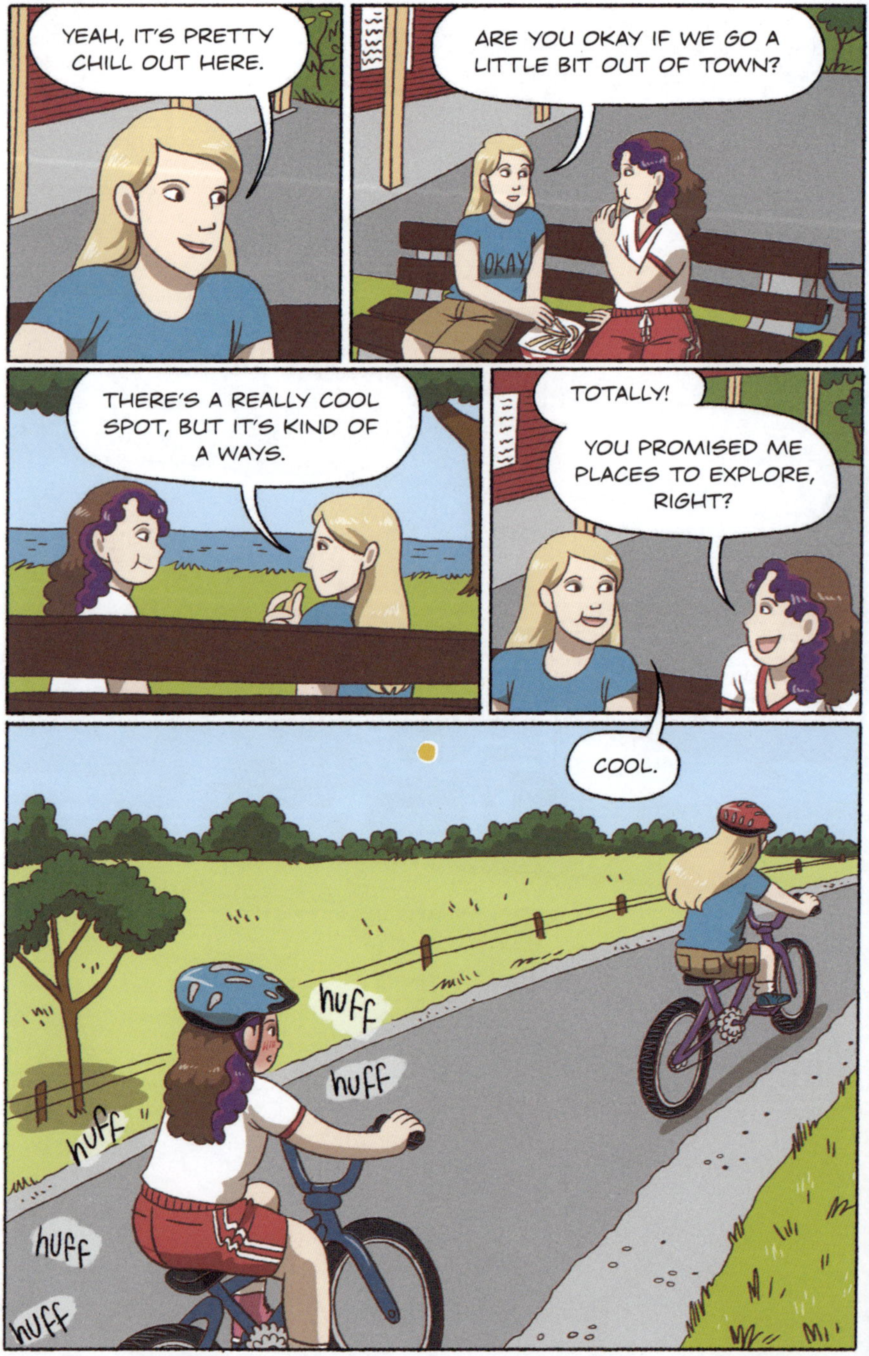
YEAH, IT'S PRETTY CHILL OUT HERE.
ARE YOU OKAY IF WE GO A LITTLE BIT OUT OF TOWN?
OKAY
THERE'S A REALLY COOL SPOT, BUT IT'S KIND OF A WAYS.
TOTALLY!
YOU PROMISED ME PLACES TO EXPLORE, RIGHT?
COOL.
huff
huff
huff
huff
huff

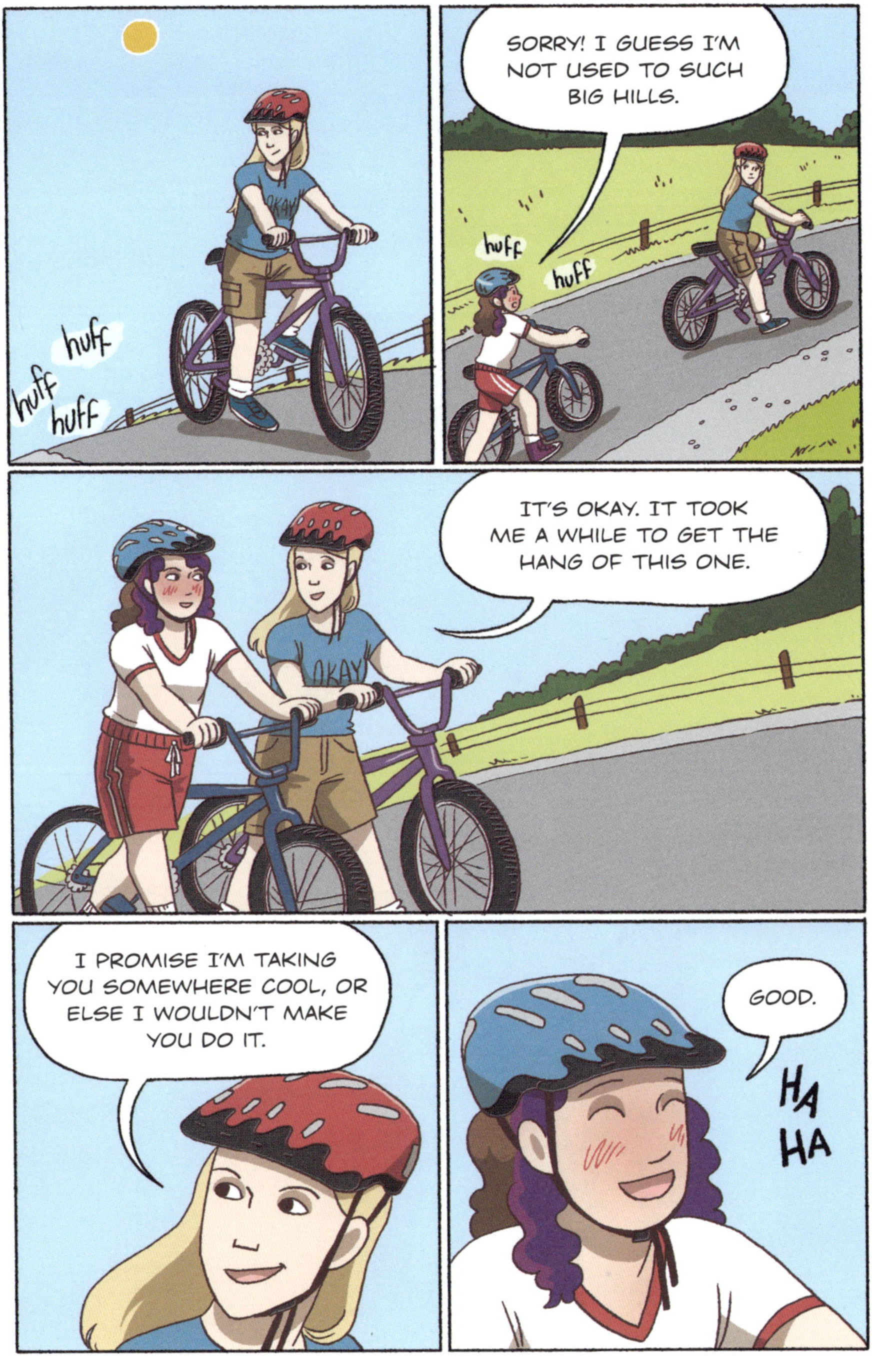
huff
huff
huff
SORRY! I GUESS I'M NOT USED TO SUCH BIG HILLS.
huff
huff
IT'S OKAY. IT TOOK ME A WHILE TO GET THE HANG OF THIS ONE.
I PROMISE I'M TAKING YOU SOMEWHERE COOL, OR ELSE I WOULDN'T MAKE YOU DO IT.
GOOD.
HA HA

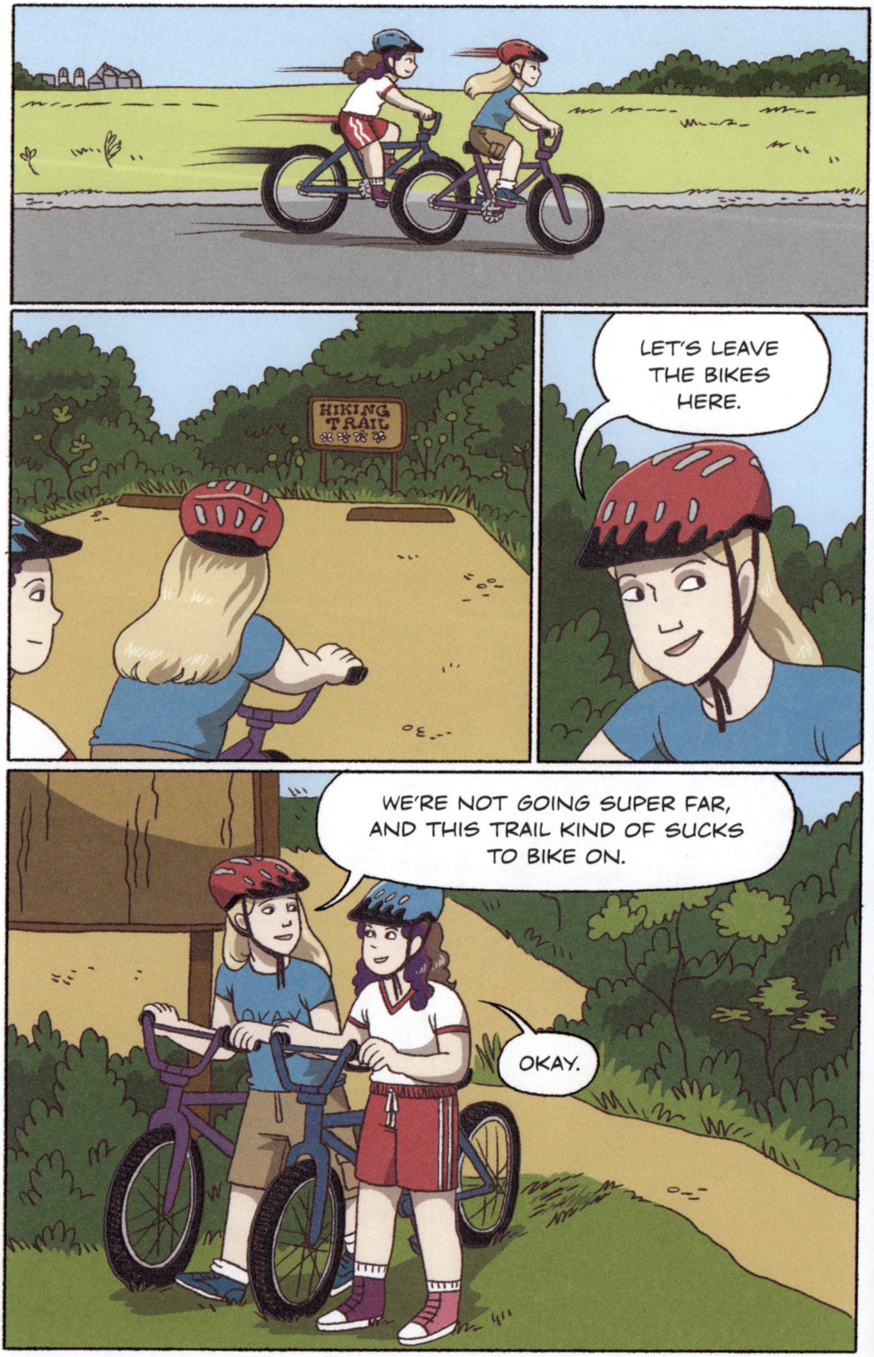
HIKING TRAIL
LET'S LEAVE THE BIKES HERE.
WE'RE NOT GOING SUPER FAR, AND THIS TRAIL KIND OF SUCKS TO BIKE ON.
OKAY.

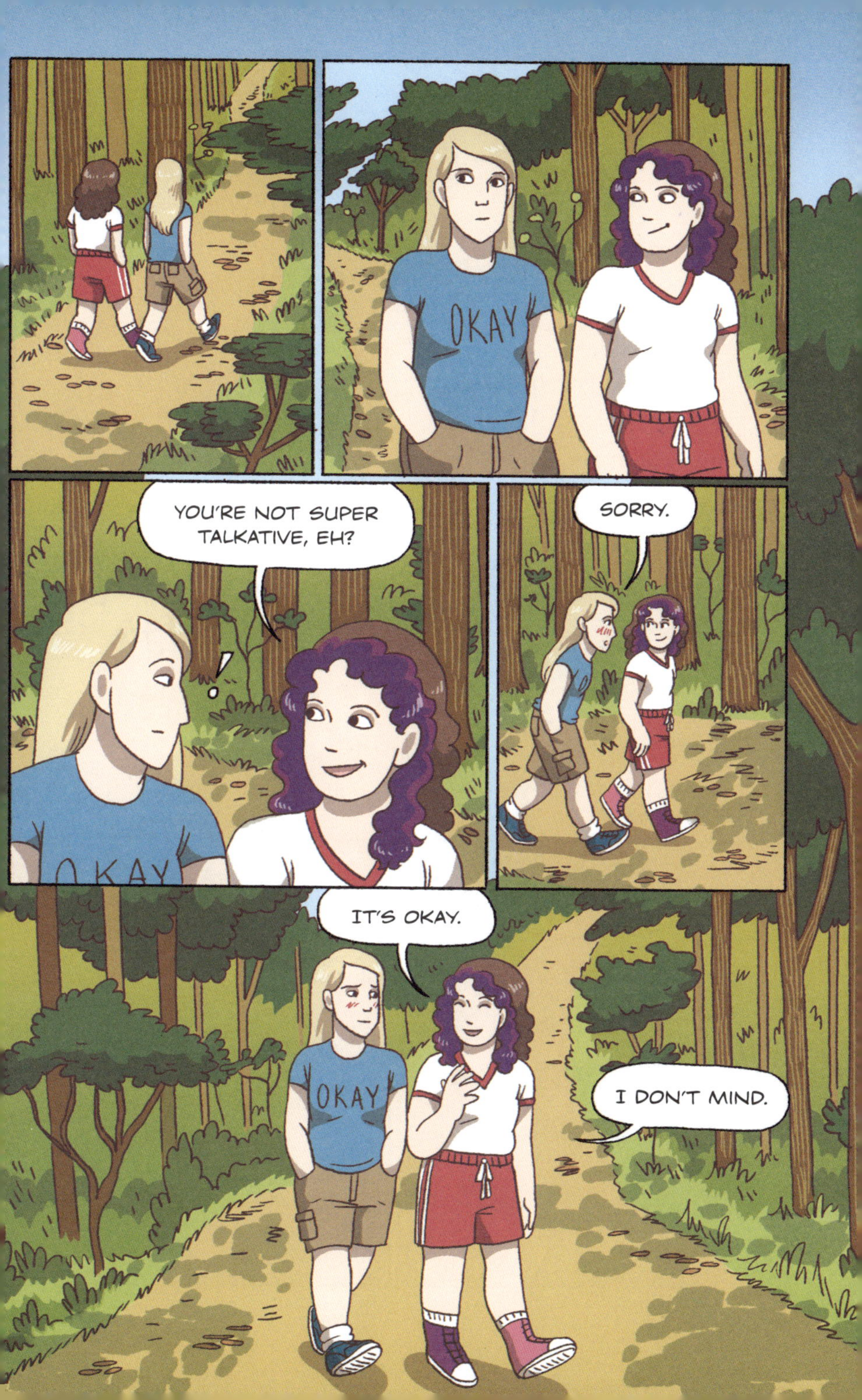
YOU'RE NOT SUPER TALKATIVE, EH?
SORRY.
IT'S OKAY.
I DON'T MIND.

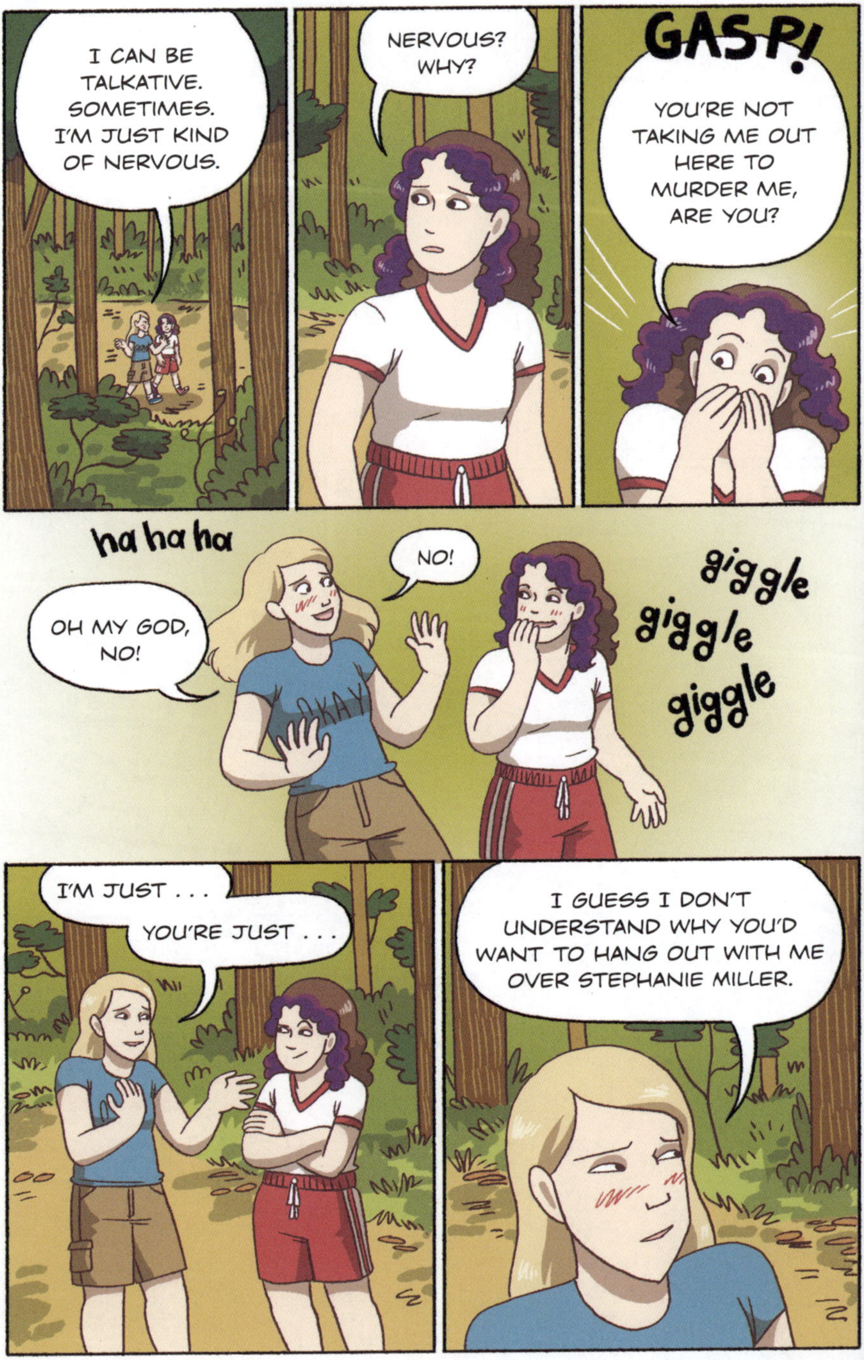
I CAN BE TALKATIVE. SOMETIMES. I'M JUST KIND OF NERVOUS.
NERVOUS? WHY?
GASP!
YOU'RE NOT TAKING ME OUT HERE TO MURDER ME, ARE YOU?
ha ha ha
NO!
OH MY GOD, NO!
giggle
giggle
giggle
OKAY
I'M JUST . . .
YOU'RE JUST . . .
I GUESS I DON'T UNDERSTAND WHY YOU'D WANT TO HANG OUT WITH ME OVER STEPHANIE MILLER.

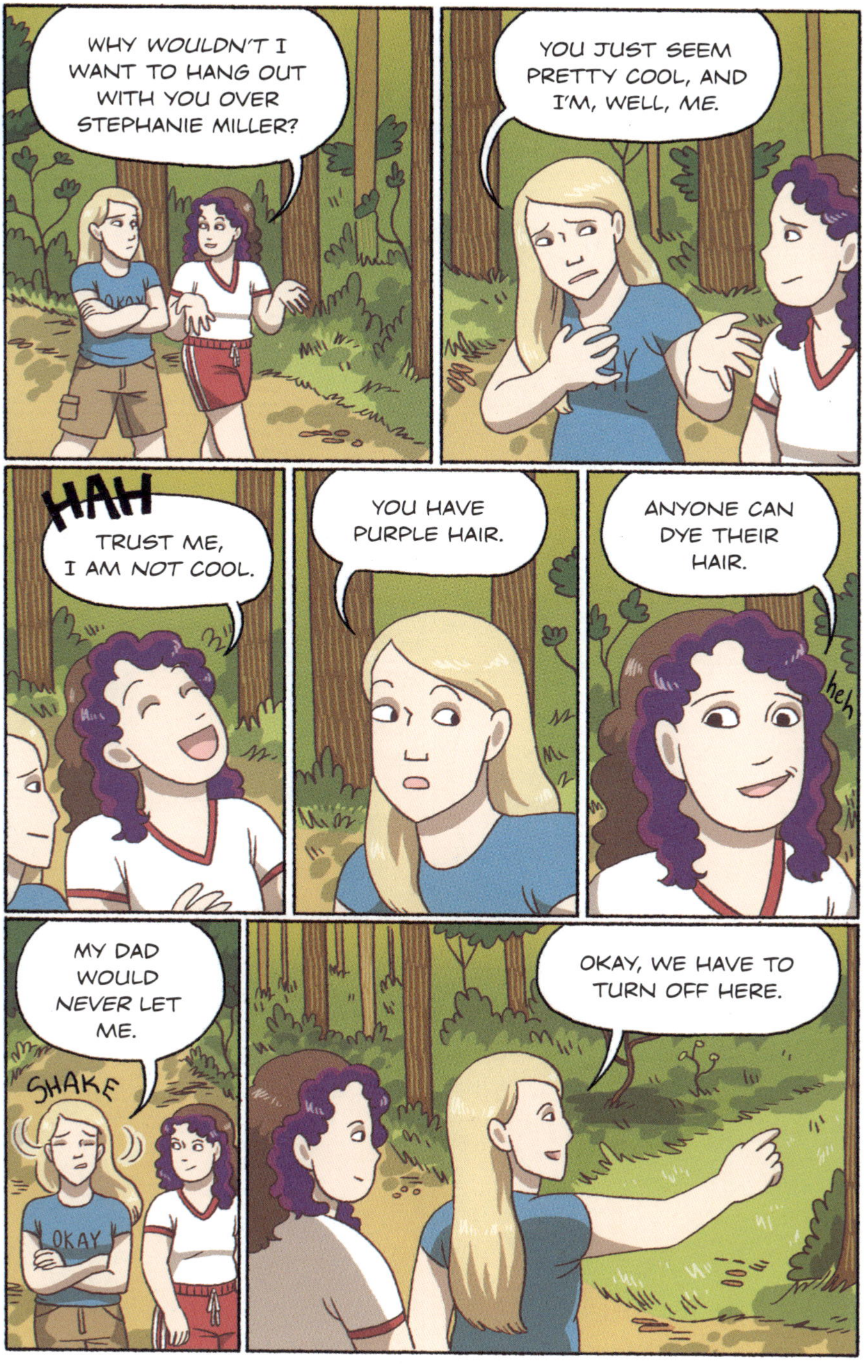
WHY WOULDN'T I WANT TO HANG OUT WITH YOU OVER STEPHANIE MILLER?
YOU JUST SEEM PRETTY COOL, AND I'M, WELL, ME.
HAH
TRUST ME, I AM NOT COOL.
YOU HAVE PURPLE HAIR.
ANYONE CAN DYE THEIR HAIR.
heh
MY DAD WOULD NEVER LET ME.
SHAKE
OKAY
OKAY, WE HAVE TO TURN OFF HERE.

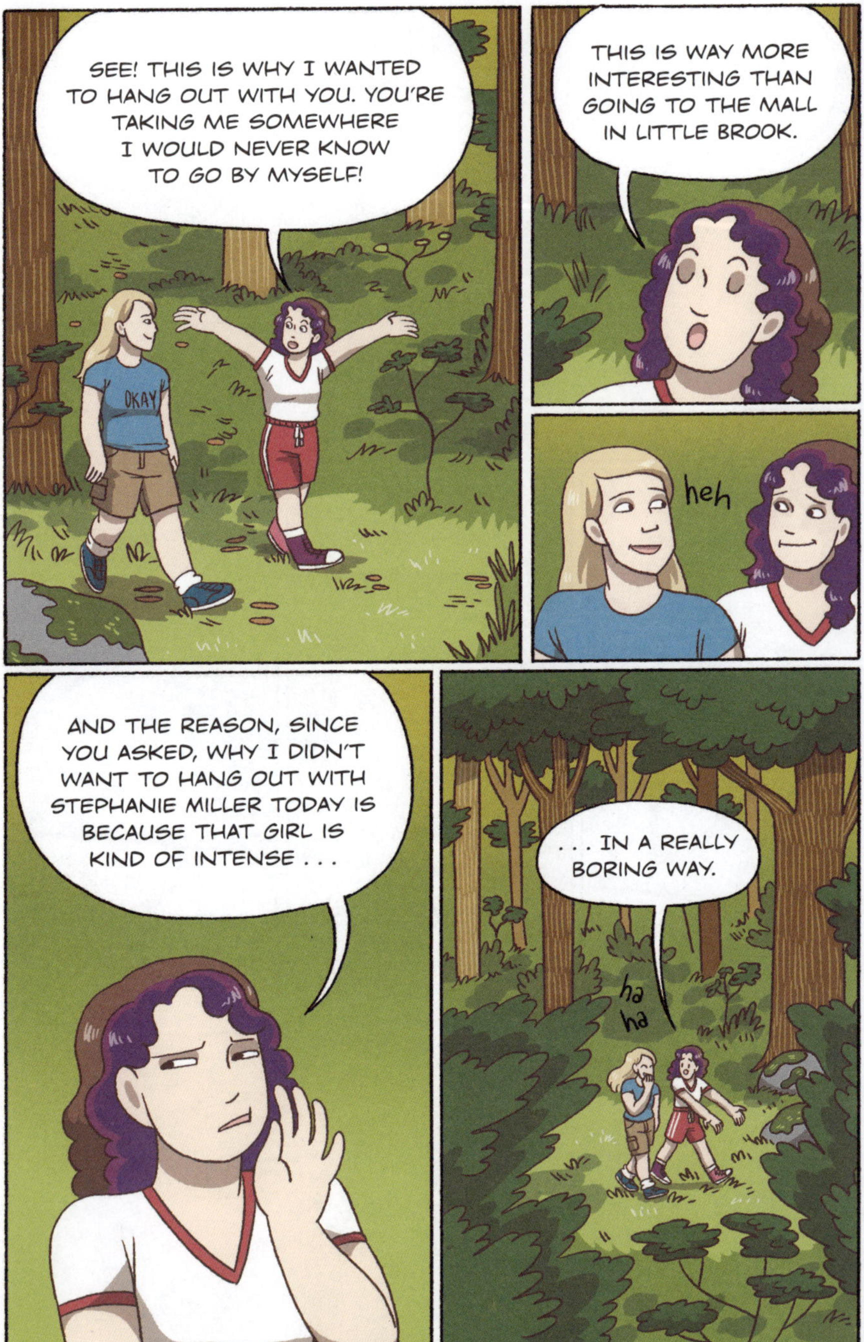

SEE! THIS IS WHY I WANTED TO HANG OUT WITH YOU. YOU'RE TAKING ME SOMEWHERE I WOULD NEVER KNOW TO GO BY MYSELF!
OKAY
THIS IS WAY MORE INTERESTING THAN GOING TO THE MALL IN LITTLE BROOK.
heh
AND THE REASON, SINCE YOU ASKED, WHY I DIDN'T WANT TO HANG OUT WITH STEPHANIE MILLER TODAY IS BECAUSE THAT GIRL IS KIND OF INTENSE . . .
. . . IN A REALLY BORING WAY.
ha ha

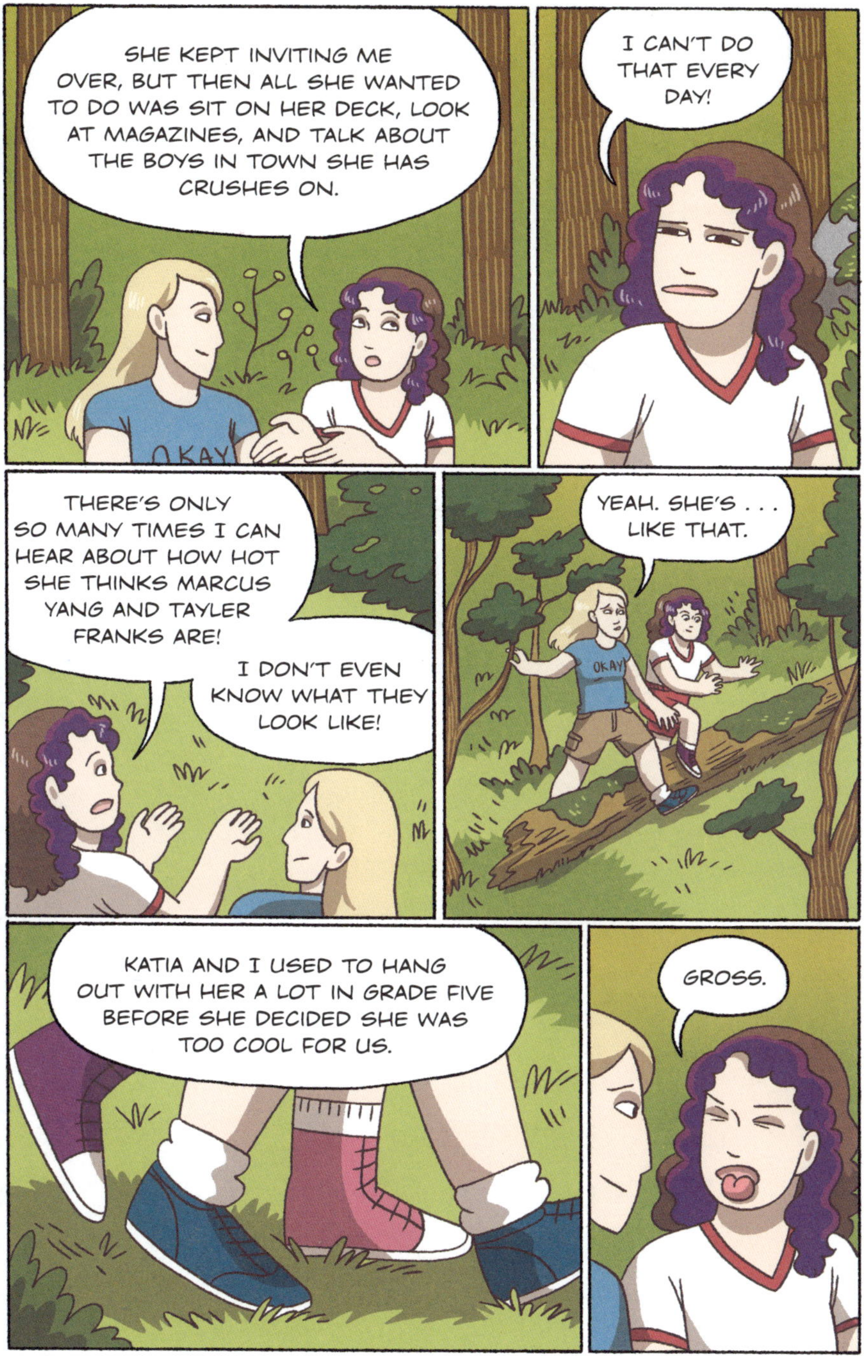
SHE KEPT INVITING ME OVER, BUT THEN ALL SHE WANTED TO DO WAS SIT ON HER DECK, LOOK AT MAGAZINES, AND TALK ABOUT THE BOYS IN TOWN SHE HAS CRUSHES ON.
OKAY
I CAN'T DO THAT EVERY DAY!
THERE'S ONLY SO MANY TIMES I CAN HEAR ABOUT HOW HOT SHE THINKS MARCUS YANG AND TAYLER FRANKS ARE!
I DON'T EVEN KNOW WHAT THEY LOOK LIKE!
YEAH. SHE'S . . . LIKE THAT.
OKAY
KATIA AND I USED TO HANG OUT WITH HER A LOT IN GRADE FIVE BEFORE SHE DECIDED SHE WAS TOO COOL FOR US.
GROSS.

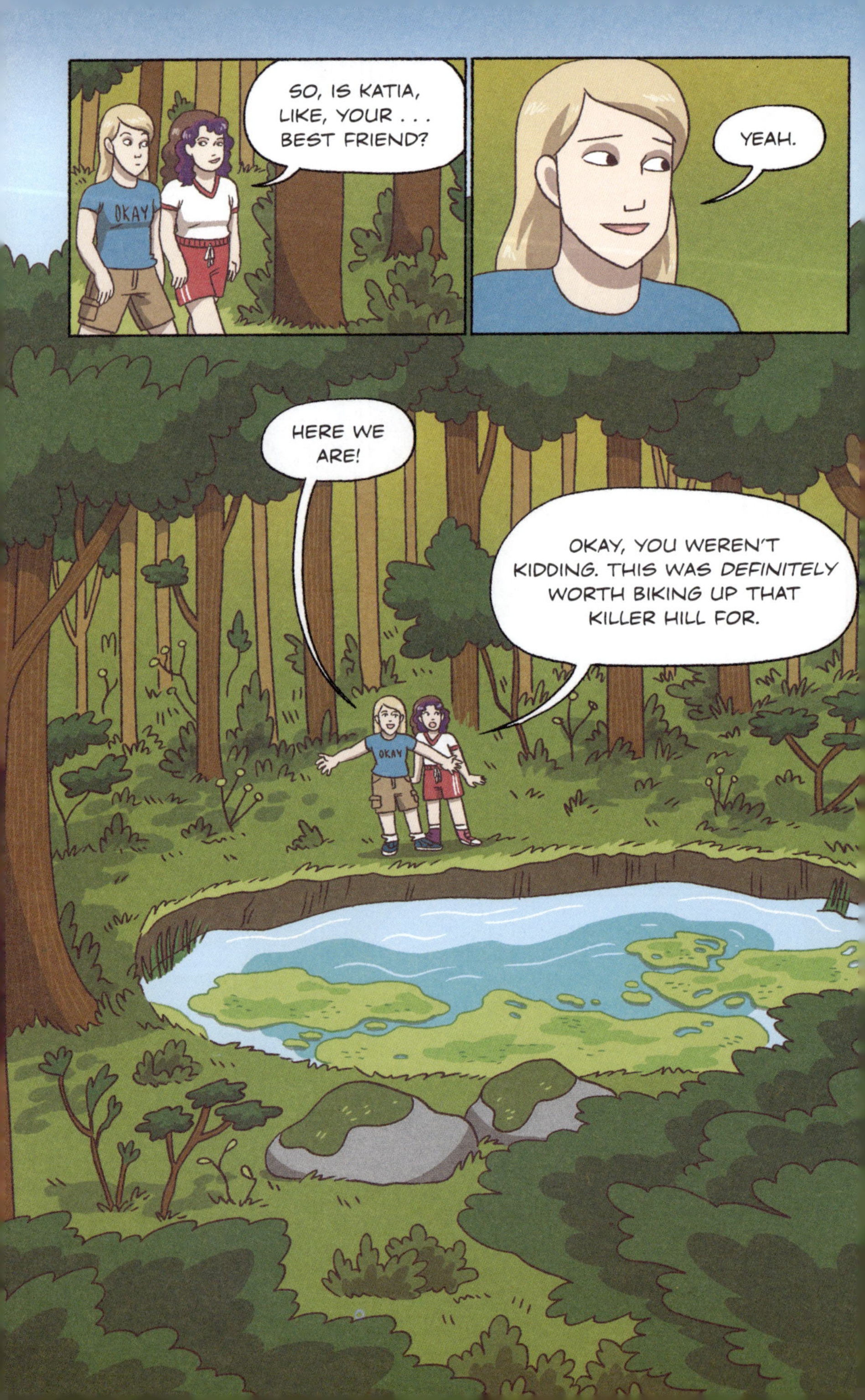
SO, IS KATIA, LIKE, YOUR . . . BEST FRIEND?
OKAY
YEAH.
HERE WE ARE!
OKAY
OKAY, YOU WEREN'T KIDDING. THIS WAS DEFINITELY WORTH BIKING UP THAT KILLER HILL FOR.

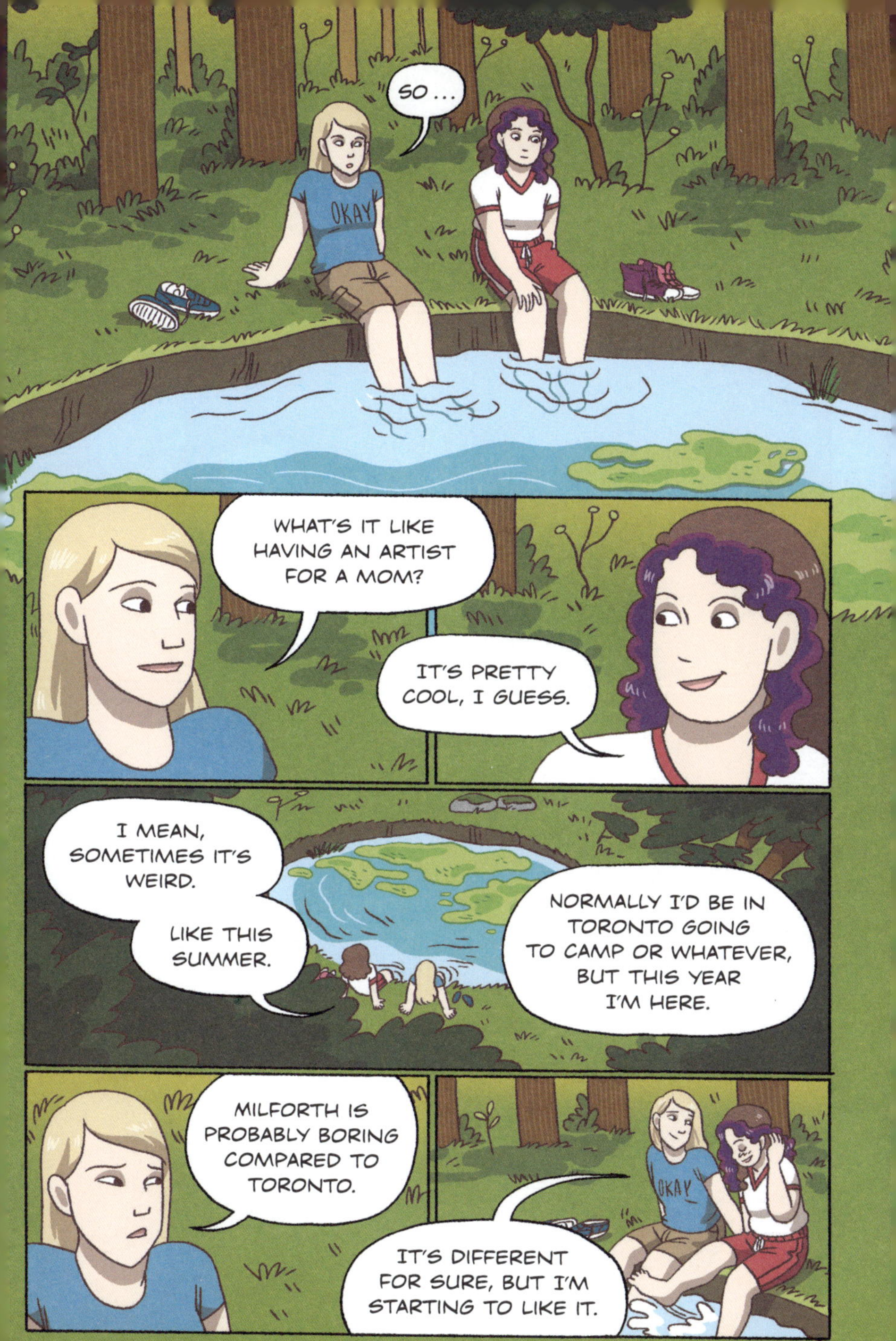
SO ...
WHAT'S IT LIKE HAVING AN ARTIST FOR A MOM?
IT'S PRETTY COOL, I GUESS.
I MEAN, SOMETIMES IT'S WEIRD.
LIKE THIS SUMMER.
NORMALLY I'D BE IN TORONTO GOING TO CAMP OR WHATEVER, BUT THIS YEAR I'M HERE.
MILFORTH IS PROBABLY BORING COMPARED TO TORONTO.
IT'S DIFFERENT FOR SURE, BUT I'M STARTING TO LIKE IT.
OKAY

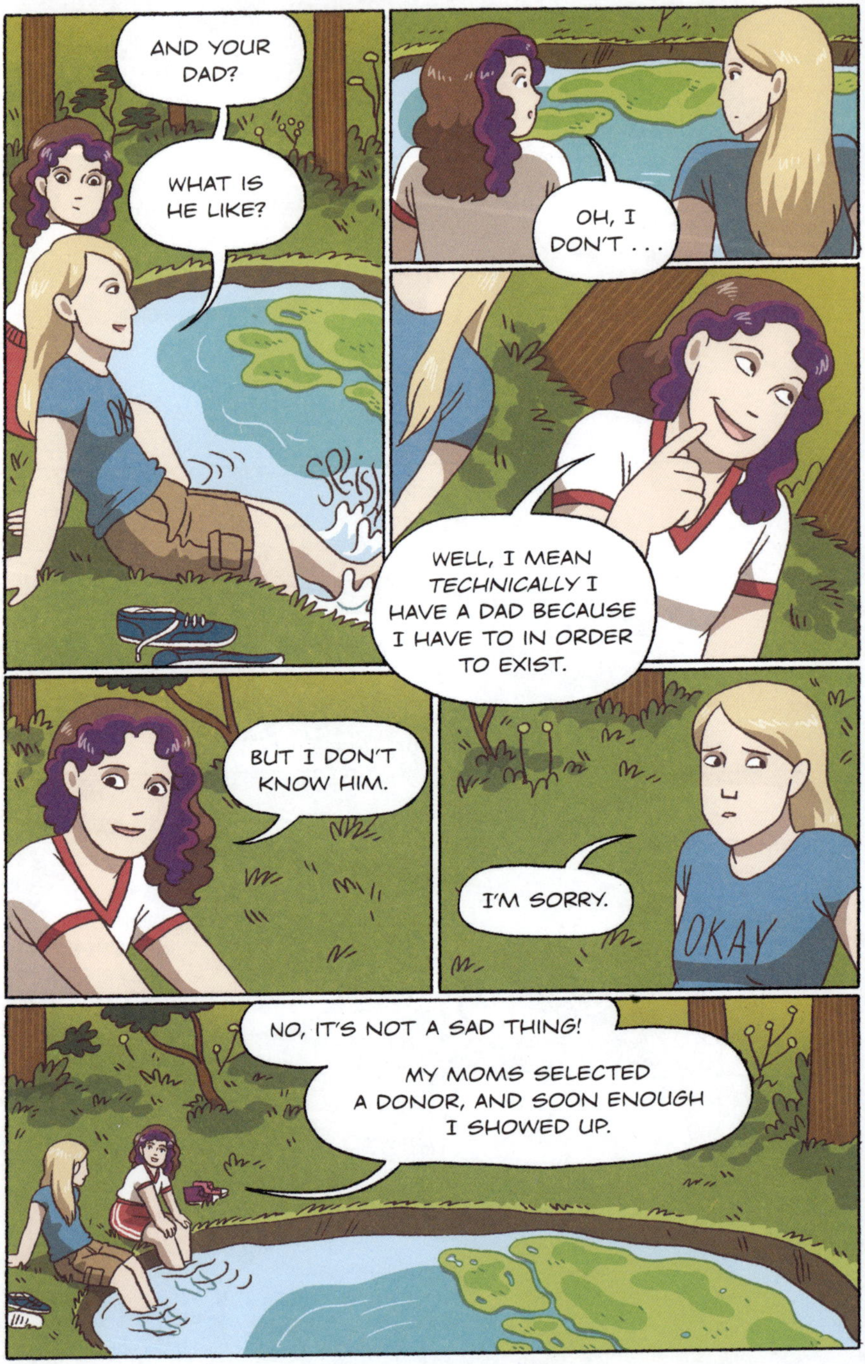
AND YOUR DAD?
WHAT IS HE LIKE?
SPLISH
OH, I DON'T . . .
WELL, I MEAN TECHNICALLY I HAVE A DAD BECAUSE I HAVE TO IN ORDER TO EXIST.
BUT I DON'T KNOW HIM.
I'M SORRY.
OKAY
NO, IT'S NOT A SAD THING!
MY MOMS SELECTED A DONOR, AND SOON ENOUGH I SHOWED UP.

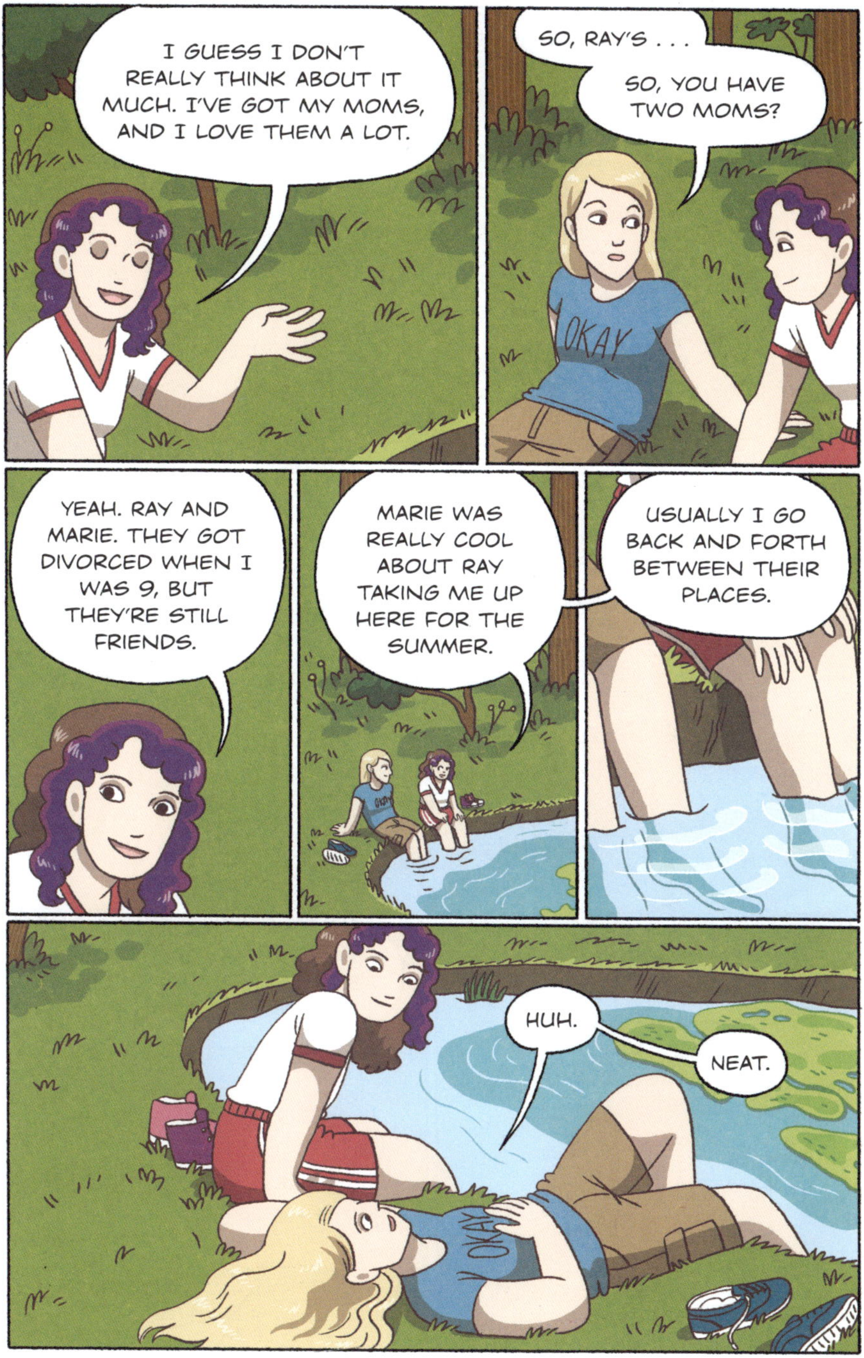
I GUESS I DON'T REALLY THINK ABOUT IT MUCH. I'VE GOT MY MOMS, AND I LOVE THEM A LOT.
SO, RAY'S . . .
SO, YOU HAVE TWO MOMS?
OKAY
YEAH. RAY AND MARIE. THEY GOT DIVORCED WHEN I WAS 9, BUT THEY'RE STILL FRIENDS.
MARIE WAS REALLY COOL ABOUT RAY TAKING ME UP HERE FOR THE SUMMER.
USUALLY I GO BACK AND FORTH BETWEEN THEIR PLACES.
HUH.
NEAT.
OKAY

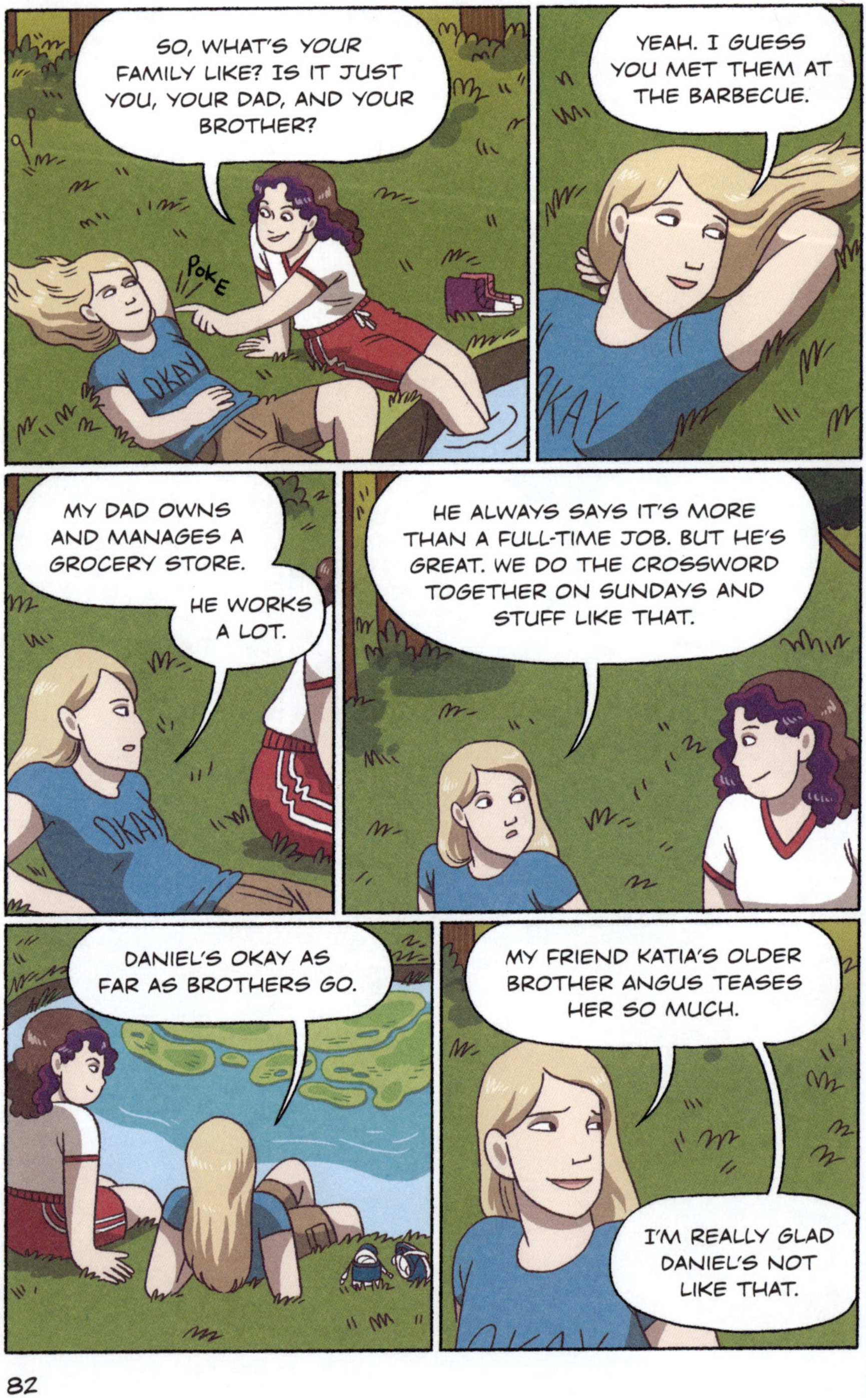
SO, WHAT'S YOUR FAMILY LIKE? IS IT JUST YOU, YOUR DAD, AND YOUR BROTHER?
POKE
OKAY
YEAH. I GUESS YOU MET THEM AT THE BARBECUE.
MY DAD OWNS AND MANAGES A GROCERY STORE.
HE WORKS A LOT.
HE ALWAYS SAYS IT'S MORE THAN A FULL-TIME JOB. BUT HE'S GREAT. WE DO THE CROSSWORD TOGETHER ON SUNDAYS AND STUFF LIKE THAT.
DANIEL'S OKAY AS FAR AS BROTHERS GO.
MY FRIEND KATIA'S OLDER BROTHER ANGUS TEASES HER SO MUCH.
I'M REALLY GLAD DANIEL'S NOT LIKE THAT.

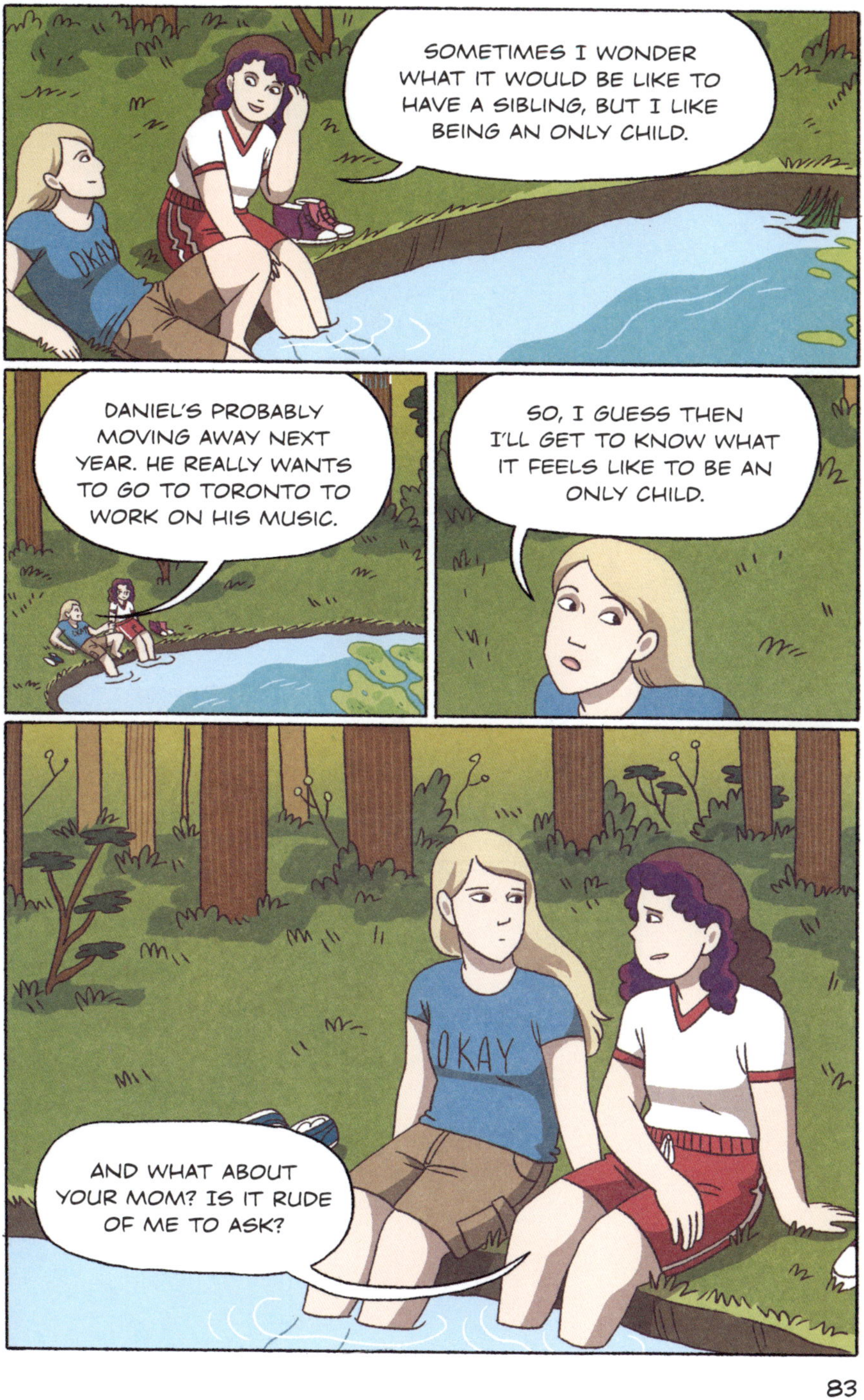
SOMETIMES I WONDER WHAT IT WOULD BE LIKE TO HAVE A SIBLING, BUT I LIKE BEING AN ONLY CHILD.
OKAY
DANIEL'S PROBABLY MOVING AWAY NEXT YEAR. HE REALLY WANTS TO GO TO TORONTO TO WORK ON HIS MUSIC.
SO, I GUESS THEN I'LL GET TO KNOW WHAT IT FEELS LIKE TO BE AN ONLY CHILD.
OKAY
AND WHAT ABOUT YOUR MOM? IS IT RUDE OF ME TO ASK?

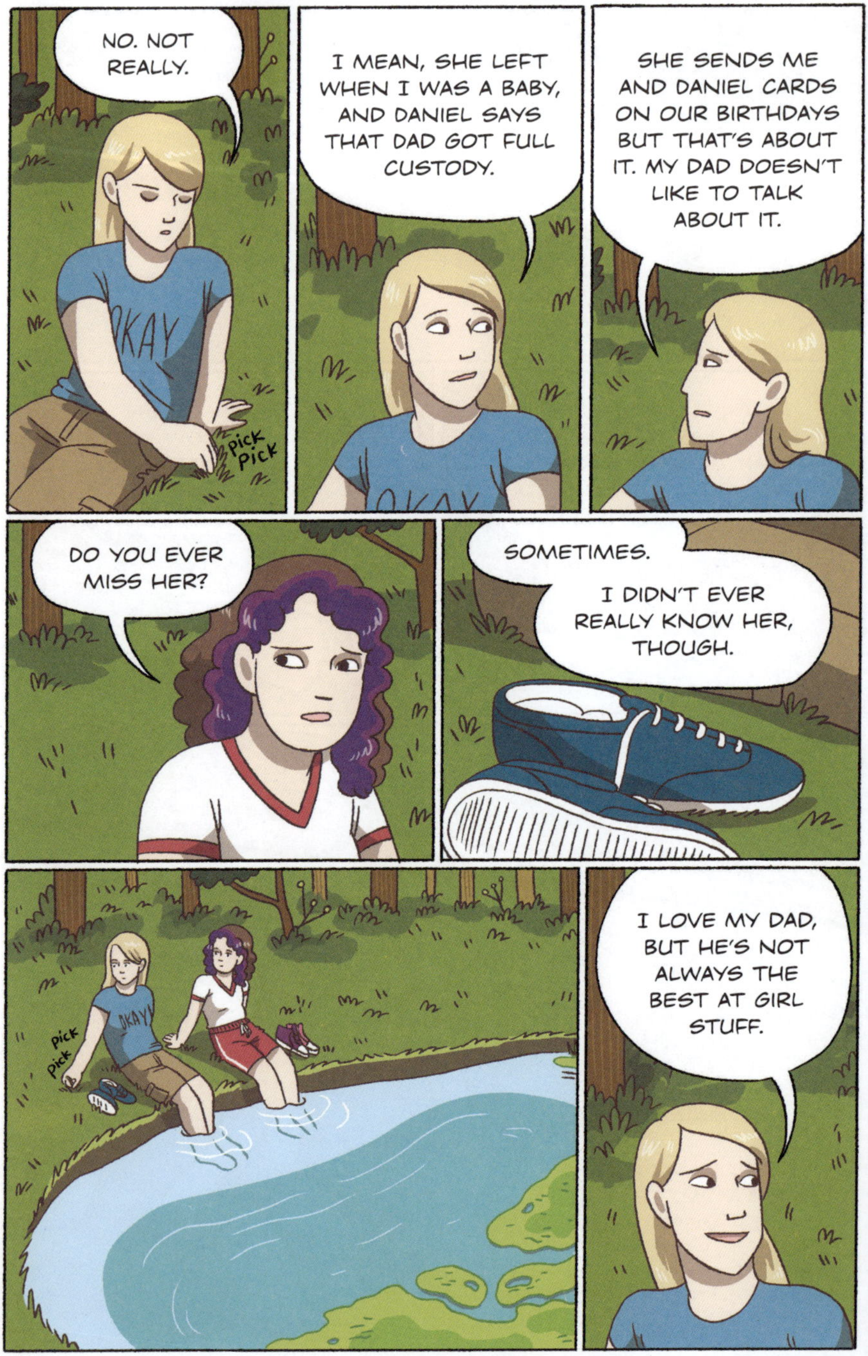
NO. NOT REALLY.
PICK PICK
I MEAN, SHE LEFT WHEN I WAS A BABY, AND DANIEL SAYS THAT DAD GOT FULL CUSTODY.
SHE SENDS ME AND DANIEL CARDS ON OUR BIRTHDAYS BUT THAT'S ABOUT IT. MY DAD DOESN'T LIKE TO TALK ABOUT IT.
DO YOU EVER MISS HER?
SOMETIMES.
I DIDN'T EVER REALLY KNOW HER, THOUGH.
PICK PICK
I LOVE MY DAD, BUT HE'S NOT ALWAYS THE BEST AT GIRL STUFF.

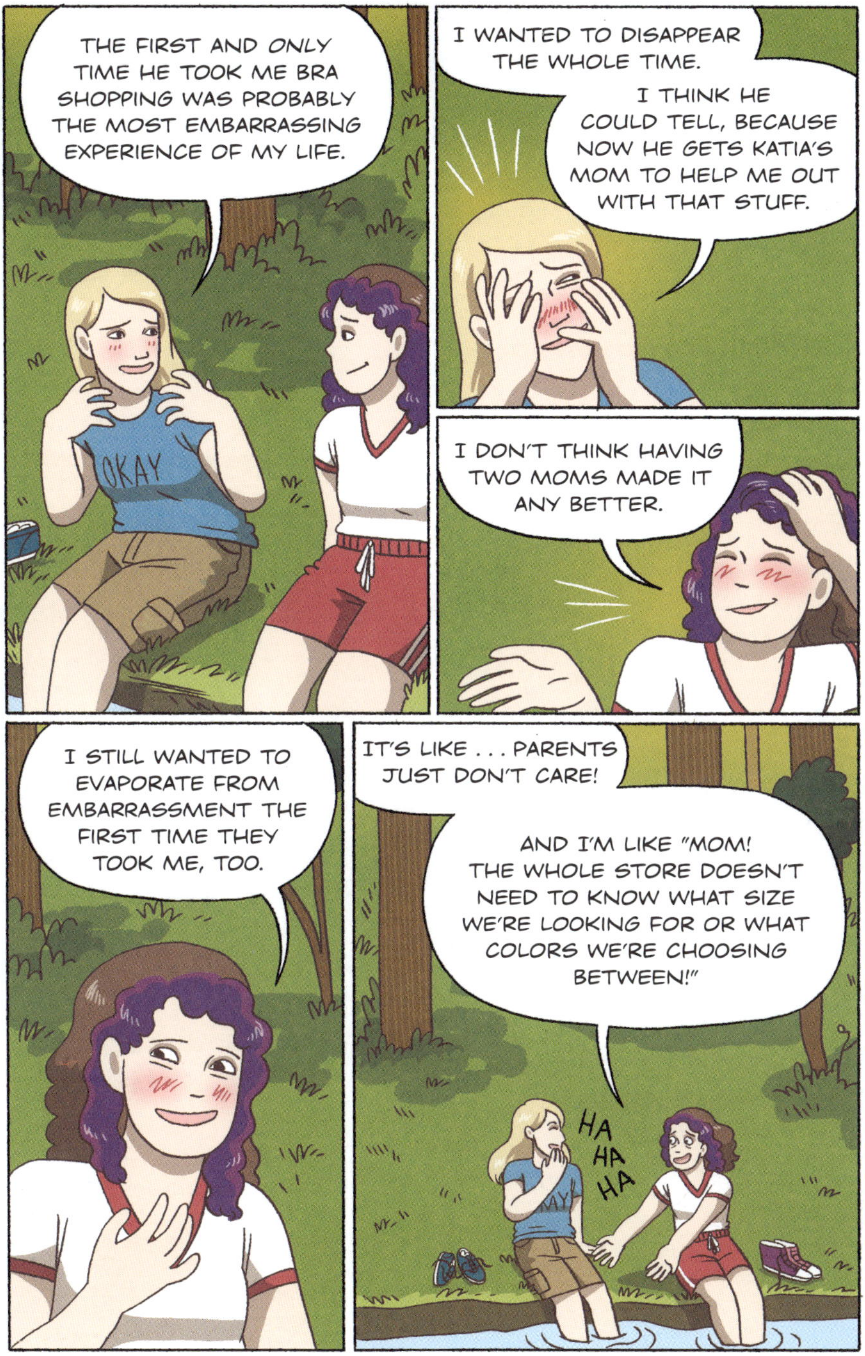
THE FIRST AND ONLY TIME HE TOOK ME BRA SHOPPING WAS PROBABLY THE MOST EMBARRASSING EXPERIENCE OF MY LIFE.
OKAY
I WANTED TO DISAPPEAR THE WHOLE TIME.
I THINK HE COULD TELL, BECAUSE NOW HE GETS KATIA'S MOM TO HELP ME OUT WITH THAT STUFF.
I DON'T THINK HAVING TWO MOMS MADE IT ANY BETTER.
I STILL WANTED TO EVAPORATE FROM EMBARRASSMENT THE FIRST TIME THEY TOOK ME, TOO.
IT'S LIKE . . . PARENTS JUST DON'T CARE!
AND I'M LIKE "MOM! THE WHOLE STORE DOESN'T NEED TO KNOW WHAT SIZE WE'RE LOOKING FOR OR WHAT COLORS WE'RE CHOOSING BETWEEN!"
HA HA HA

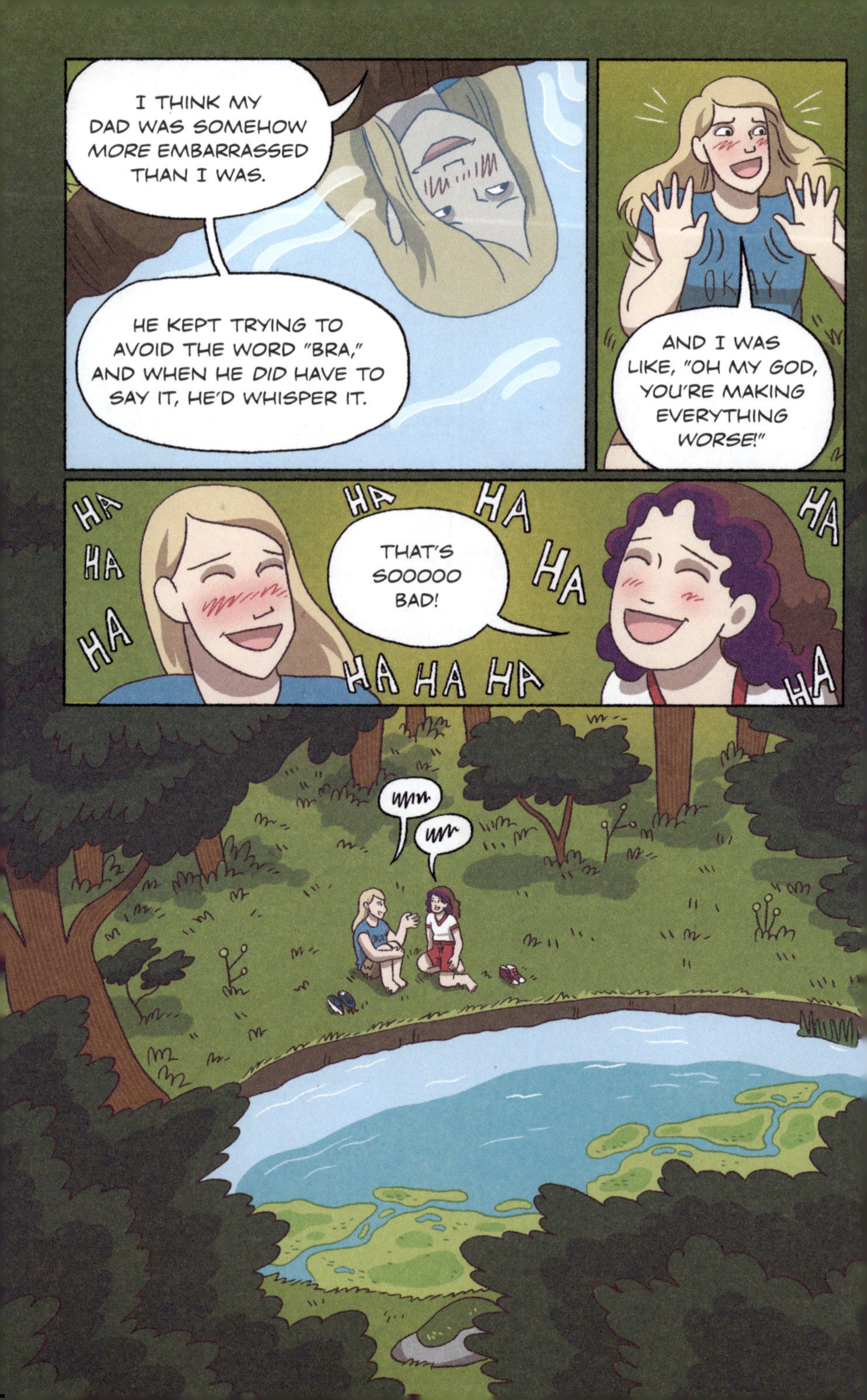
I THINK MY DAD WAS SOMEHOW MORE EMBARRASSED THAN I WAS.
HE KEPT TRYING TO AVOID THE WORD "BRA," AND WHEN HE *DID* HAVE TO SAY IT, HE'D WHISPER IT.
OKAY
AND I WAS LIKE, "OH MY GOD, YOU'RE MAKING EVERYTHING WORSE!"
HA HA HA
HA HA HA
THAT'S SOOOOO BAD!
HA HA HA HA HA HA HA HA

Dear Lucy,

We just got back from a three-day camping trip (which is why this letter is taking longer to get to you). Our cabin canoed across the lake to one of the islands down river. We had to pack everything we needed for the three days, and we had to take all our garbage with us. Even our toilet paper! How gross is that!?

On the first day, we canoed until we found the camp's usual rest spot. There's an old cabin that used to belong to a woodsman out there, but the counselors said it needed a lot of fixing up so we couldn't go inside. We slept outside in our tents in the clearing around it. Jessica told me that the real reason we couldn't go in the cabin was because it's haunted. I mostly don't believe her, but I barely slept because every time I closed my eyes, I imagined the woodsman's ghost and felt super creeped out.

The rest of the trip was less spooky. We saw 5 loons, 2 herons, and 1 deer. It was fun, but I'm glad it's over. Next week we're having a camp-wide dance!

Love ya & miss ya,

Katia

P.S. Boo. That sucks that Stephanie Miller absorbed the new girl into her posse.

P.P.S. I forgot to mention I found out what Beth's tattoo is: a turtle!

Dear Katia,

Ew! Ew! Ew! I definitely couldn't handle the toilet paper situation. I have never felt more grateful for the miracle of modern plumbing than when I read that sentence in your letter. Nothing interesting to report on the toilet front here.

I've been hanging out with Anaïs a bit (her mom is the artist). She said Stephanie Miller was boring LOL. I couldn't agree more. Anaïs is borrowing Daniel's bike while she's in town.

Miss ya & love ya,

Lucy

P.S. Turtle Tattoo = CUTE!

CHAPTER 3

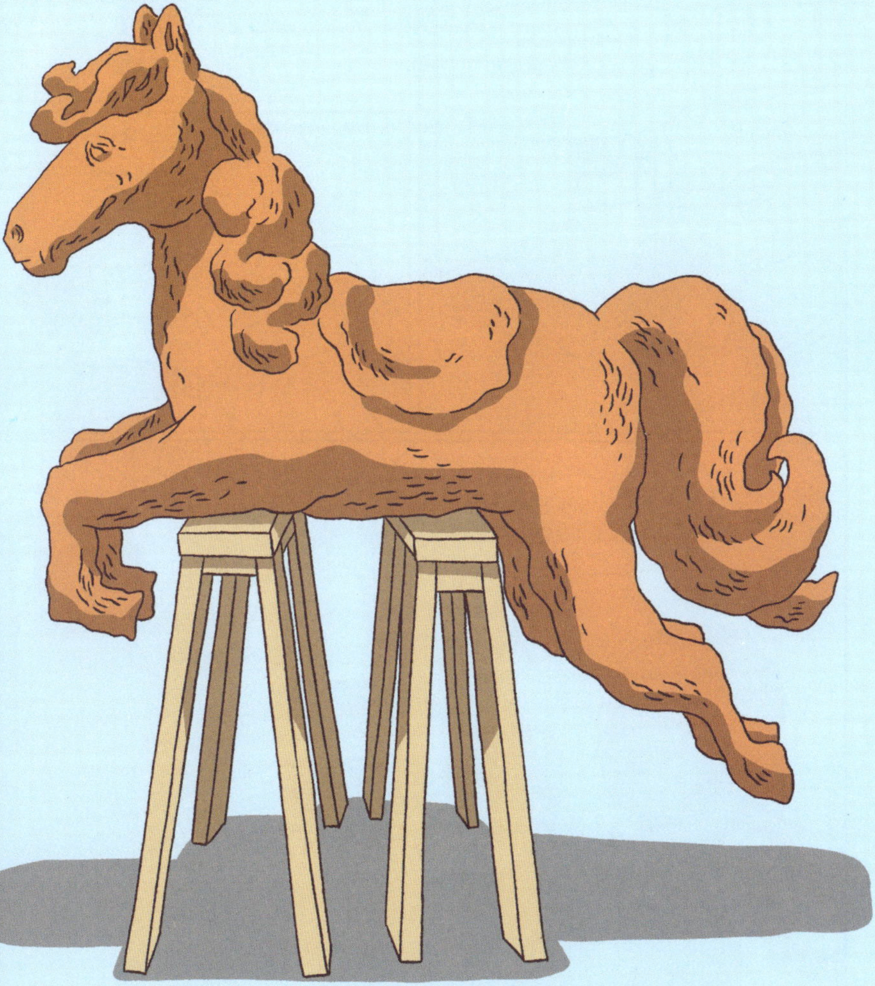

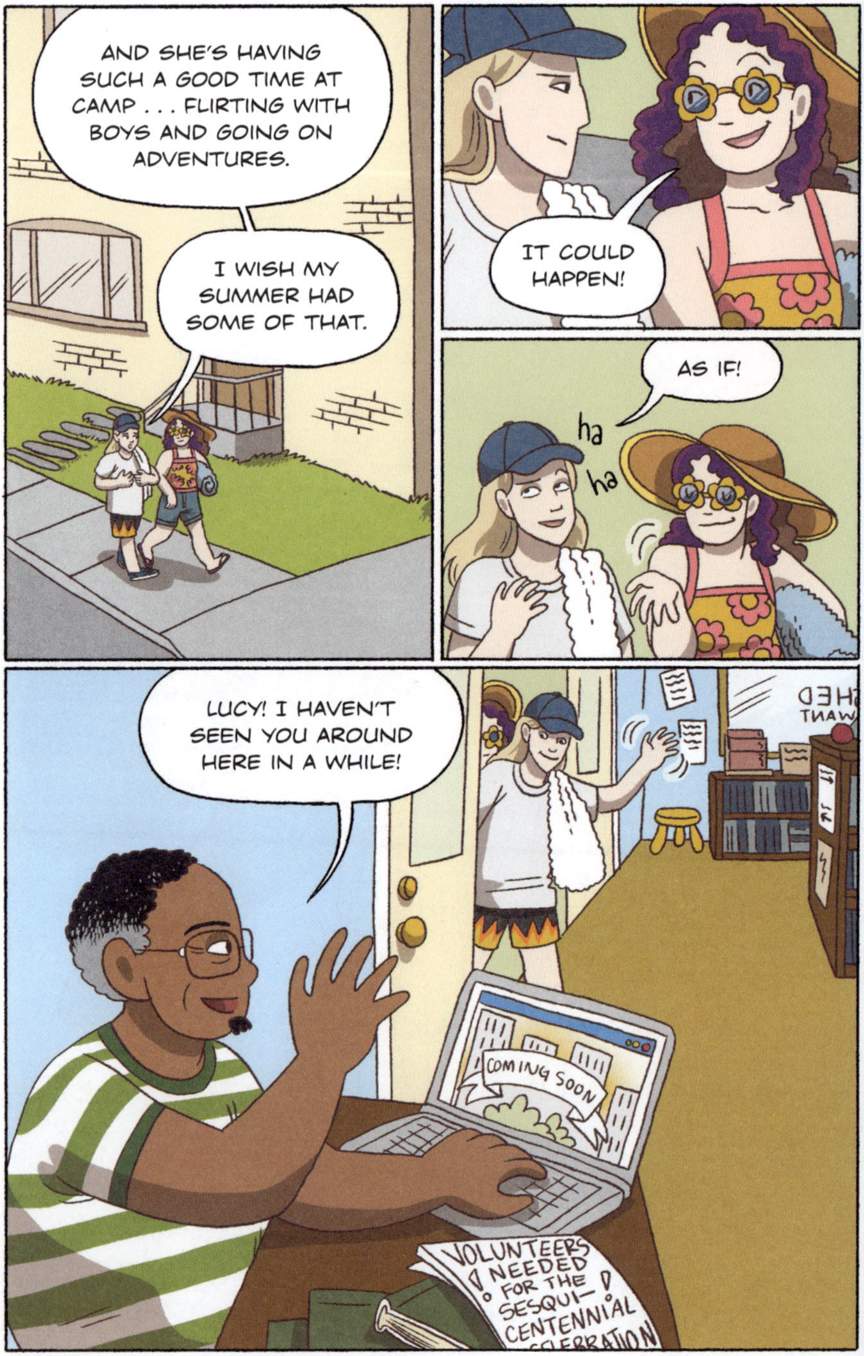
AND SHE'S HAVING SUCH A GOOD TIME AT CAMP . . . FLIRTING WITH BOYS AND GOING ON ADVENTURES.
I WISH MY SUMMER HAD SOME OF THAT.
IT COULD HAPPEN!
AS IF!
ha
ha
LUCY! I HAVEN'T SEEN YOU AROUND HERE IN A WHILE!
COMING SOON
VOLUNTEERS NEEDED FOR THE SESQUI-CENTENNIAL CELEBRATION

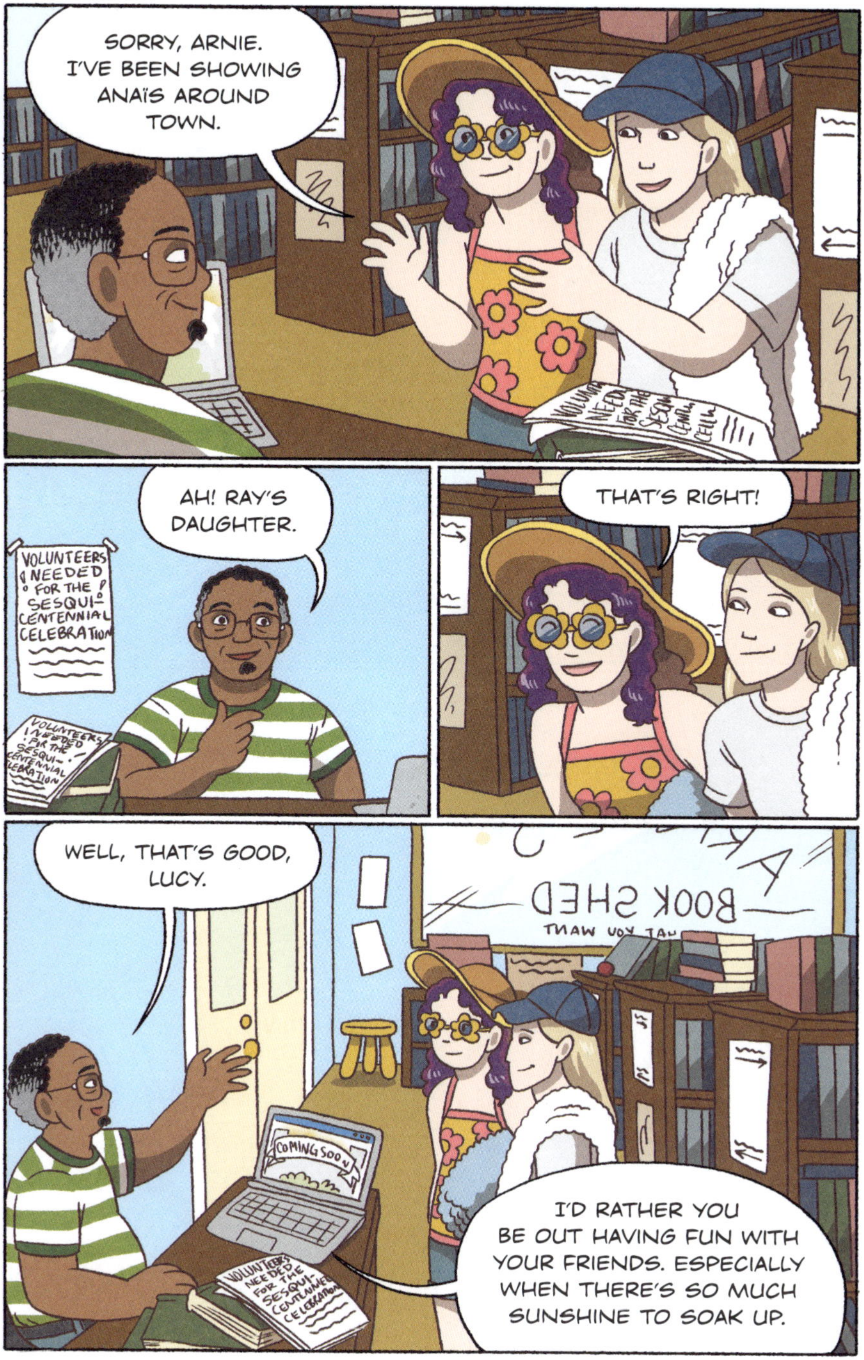
SORRY, ARNIE. I'VE BEEN SHOWING ANAÏS AROUND TOWN.
AH! RAY'S DAUGHTER.
VOLUNTEERS NEEDED FOR THE SESQUI-CENTENNIAL CELEBRATION
THAT'S RIGHT!
WELL, THAT'S GOOD, LUCY.
COMING SOON
I'D RATHER YOU BE OUT HAVING FUN WITH YOUR FRIENDS. ESPECIALLY WHEN THERE'S SO MUCH SUNSHINE TO SOAK UP.

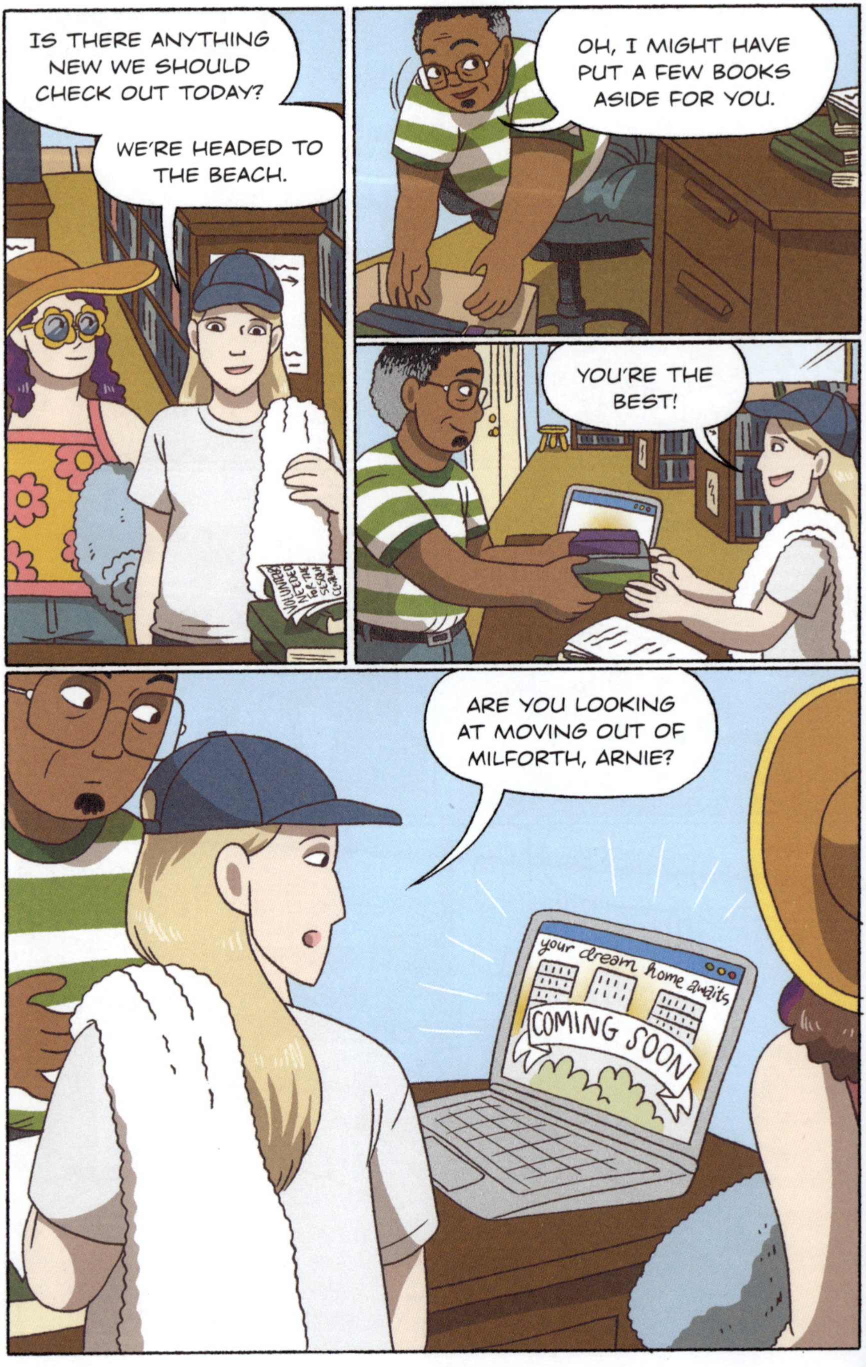
IS THERE ANYTHING NEW WE SHOULD CHECK OUT TODAY?
WE'RE HEADED TO THE BEACH.
OH, I MIGHT HAVE PUT A FEW BOOKS ASIDE FOR YOU.
YOU'RE THE BEST!
ARE YOU LOOKING AT MOVING OUT OF MILFORTH, ARNIE?
your dream home awaits
COMING SOON

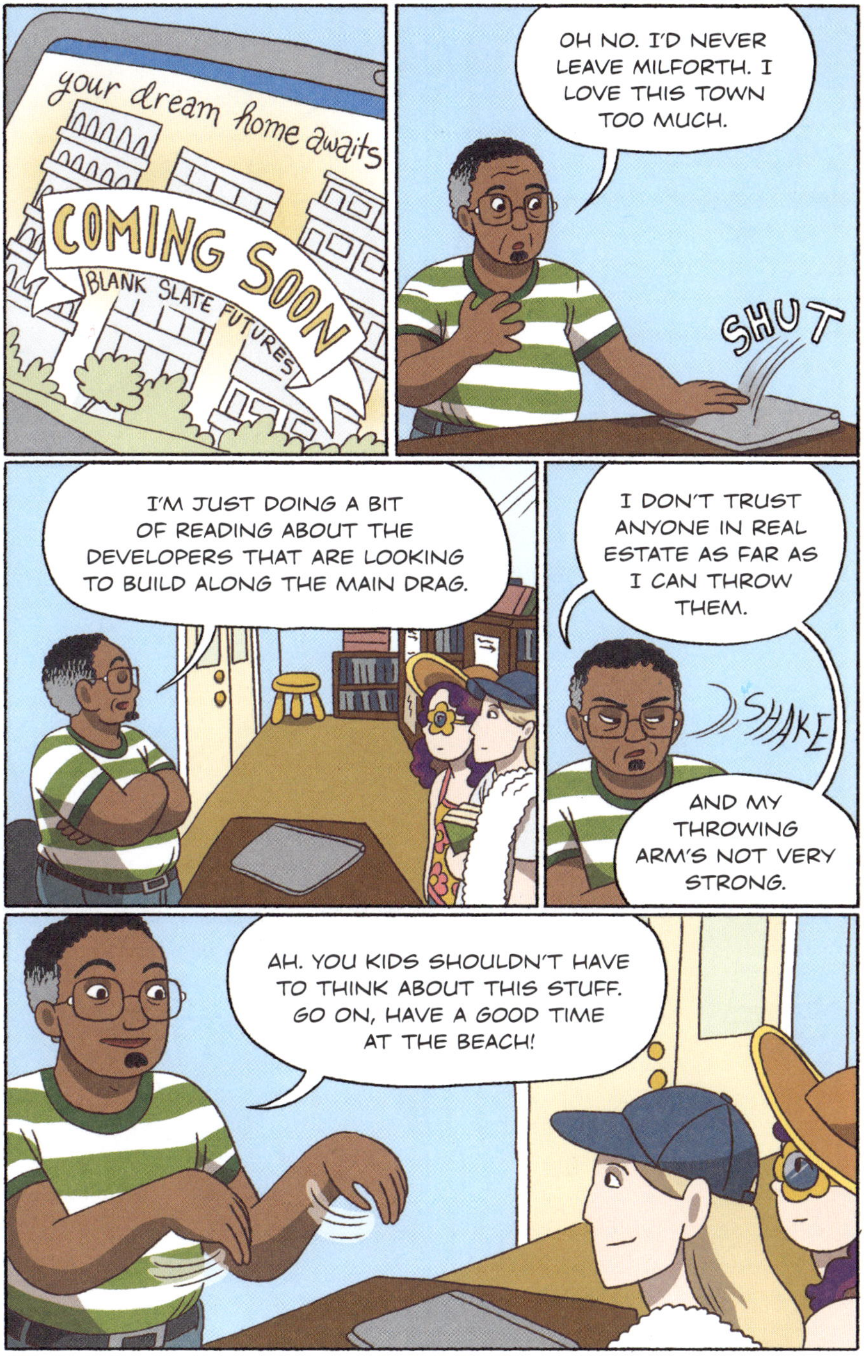
your dream home awaits
COMING SOON
BLANK SLATE FUTURES
OH NO. I'D NEVER LEAVE MILFORTH. I LOVE THIS TOWN TOO MUCH.
SHUT
I'M JUST DOING A BIT OF READING ABOUT THE DEVELOPERS THAT ARE LOOKING TO BUILD ALONG THE MAIN DRAG.
I DON'T TRUST ANYONE IN REAL ESTATE AS FAR AS I CAN THROW THEM.
SHAKE
AND MY THROWING ARM'S NOT VERY STRONG.
AH. YOU KIDS SHOULDN'T HAVE TO THINK ABOUT THIS STUFF. GO ON, HAVE A GOOD TIME AT THE BEACH!

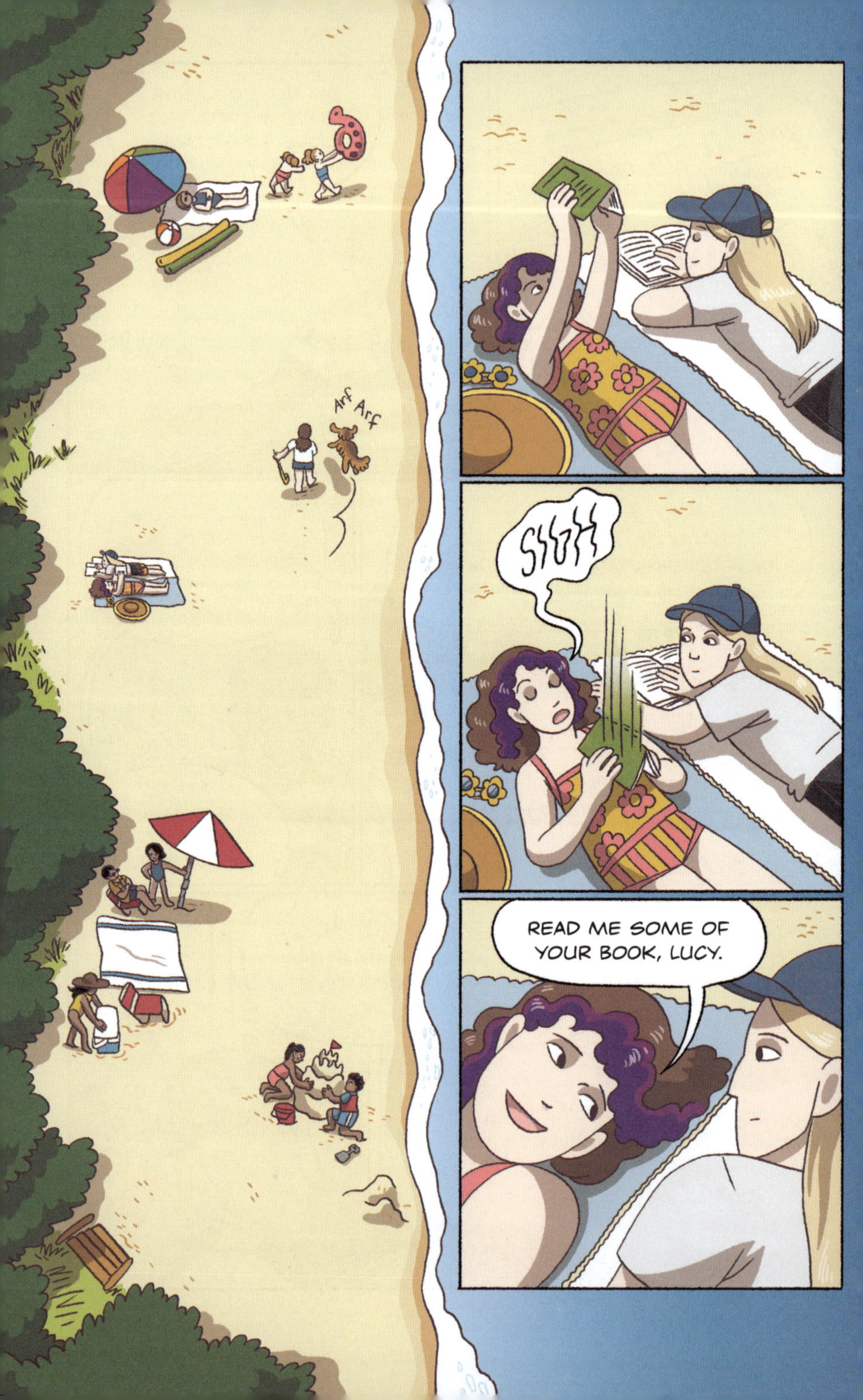
Arf Arf
Shhh
READ ME SOME OF YOUR BOOK, LUCY.

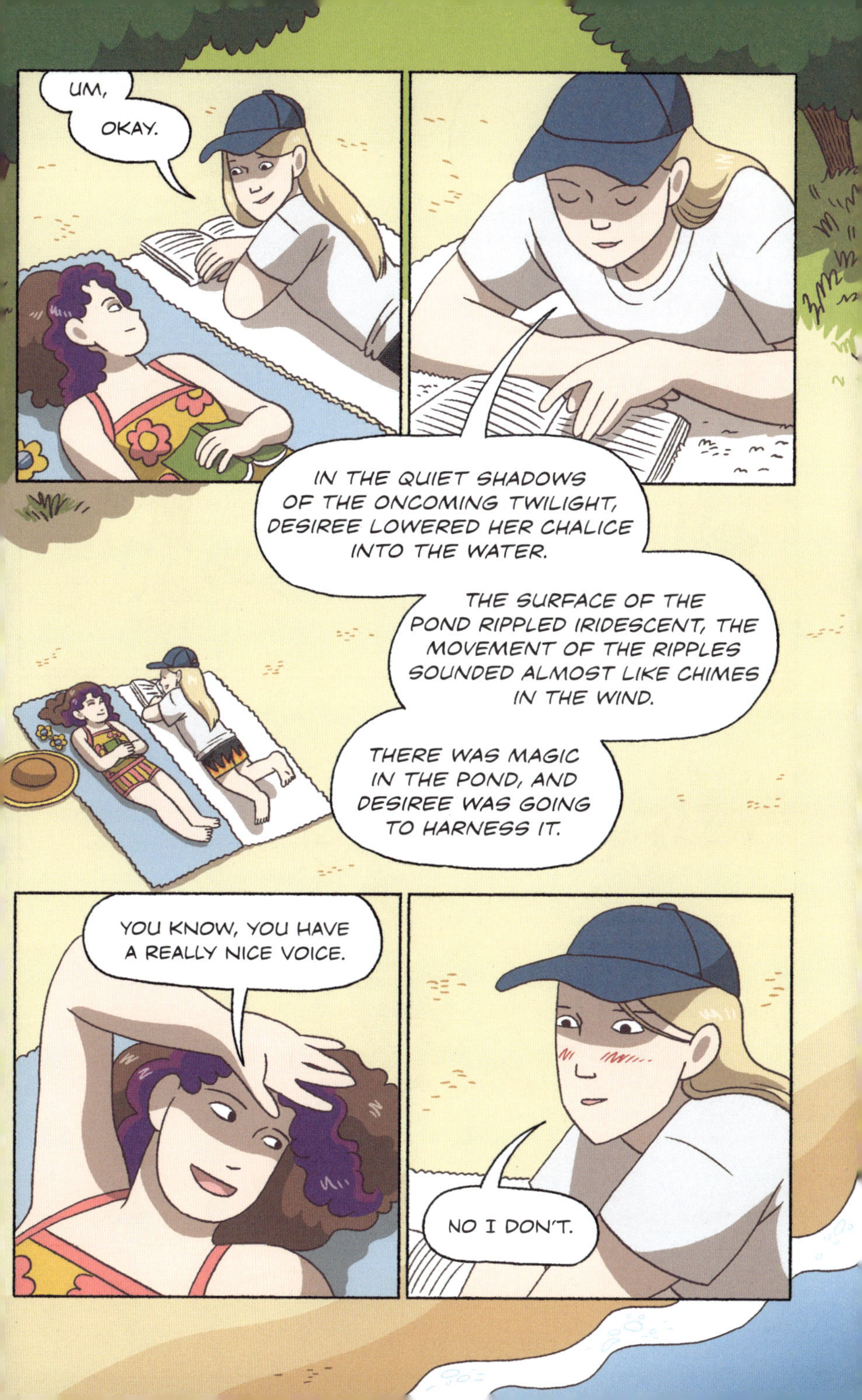
UM, OKAY.
IN THE QUIET SHADOWS OF THE ONCOMING TWILIGHT, DESIREE LOWERED HER CHALICE INTO THE WATER.
THE SURFACE OF THE POND RIPPLED IRIDESCENT, THE MOVEMENT OF THE RIPPLES SOUNDED ALMOST LIKE CHIMES IN THE WIND.
THERE WAS MAGIC IN THE POND, AND DESIREE WAS GOING TO HARNESS IT.
YOU KNOW, YOU HAVE A REALLY NICE VOICE.
NO I DON'T.

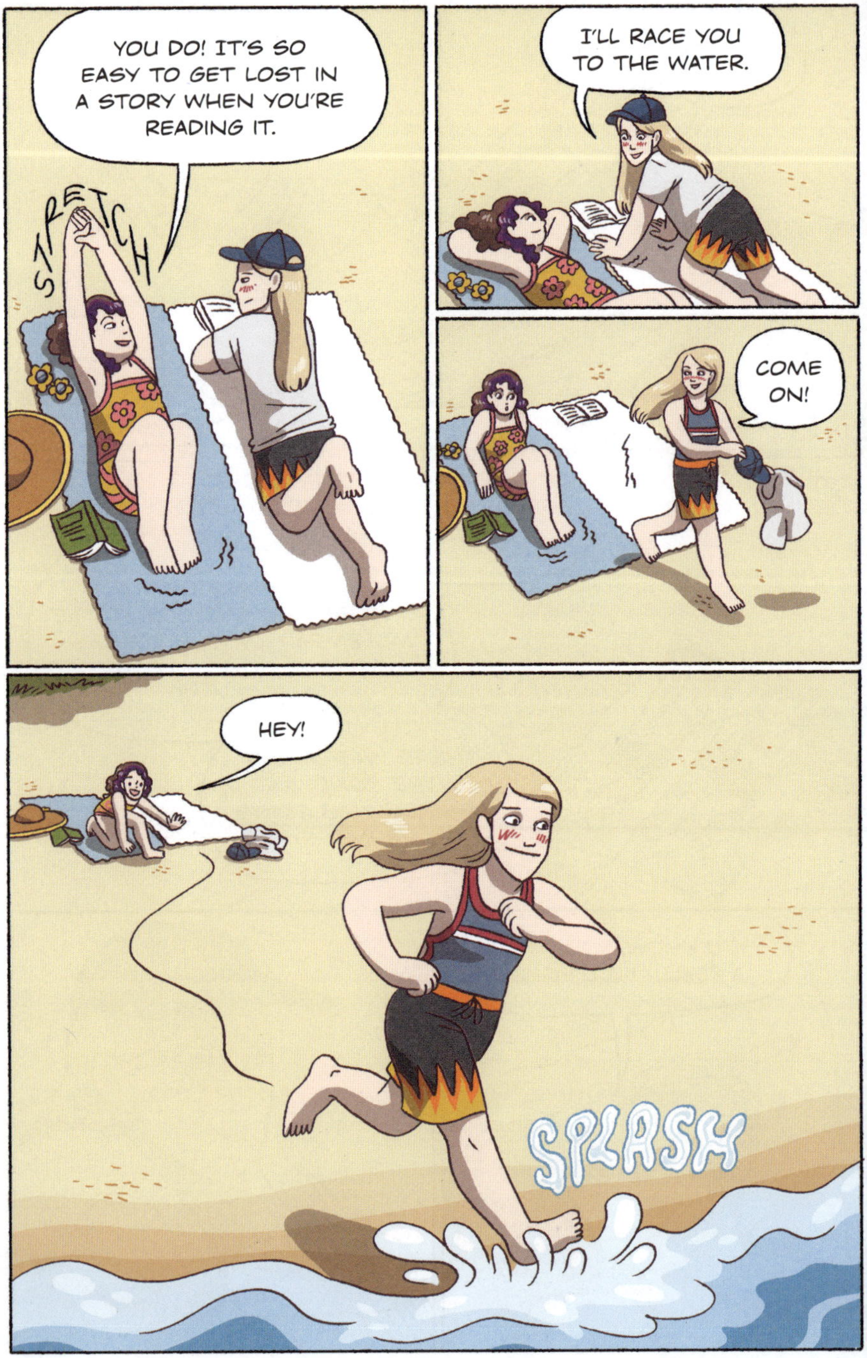
YOU DO! IT'S SO EASY TO GET LOST IN A STORY WHEN YOU'RE READING IT.
STRETCH
I'LL RACE YOU TO THE WATER.
COME ON!
HEY!
SPLASH

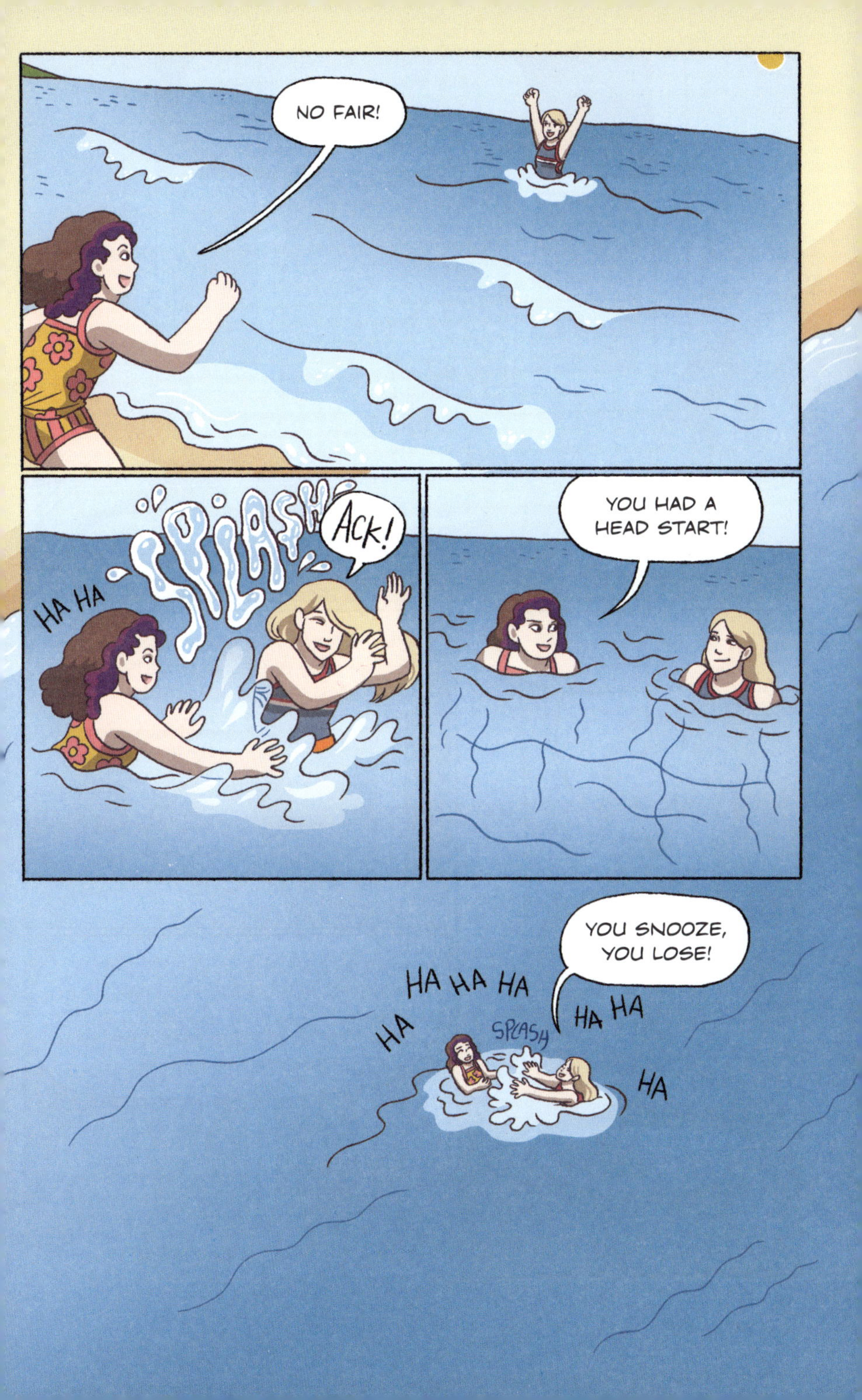
NO FAIR!
HA HA
SPLASH
ACK!
YOU HAD A HEAD START!
HA
HA HA HA HA
SPLASH
YOU SNOOZE, YOU LOSE!
HA HA
HA

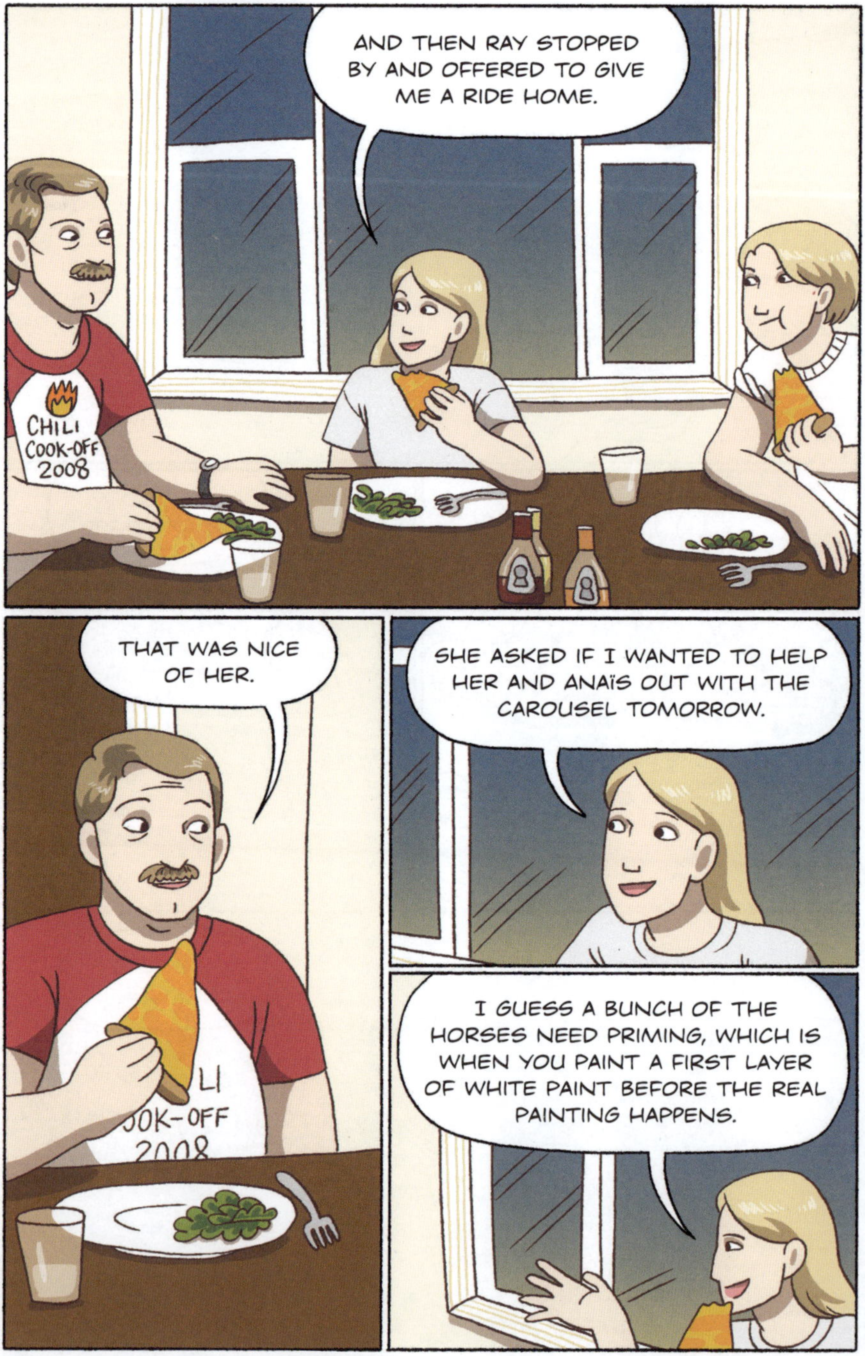
AND THEN RAY STOPPED BY AND OFFERED TO GIVE ME A RIDE HOME.
CHILI COOK-OFF 2008
THAT WAS NICE OF HER.
SHE ASKED IF I WANTED TO HELP HER AND ANAÏS OUT WITH THE CAROUSEL TOMORROW.
I GUESS A BUNCH OF THE HORSES NEED PRIMING, WHICH IS WHEN YOU PAINT A FIRST LAYER OF WHITE PAINT BEFORE THE REAL PAINTING HAPPENS.

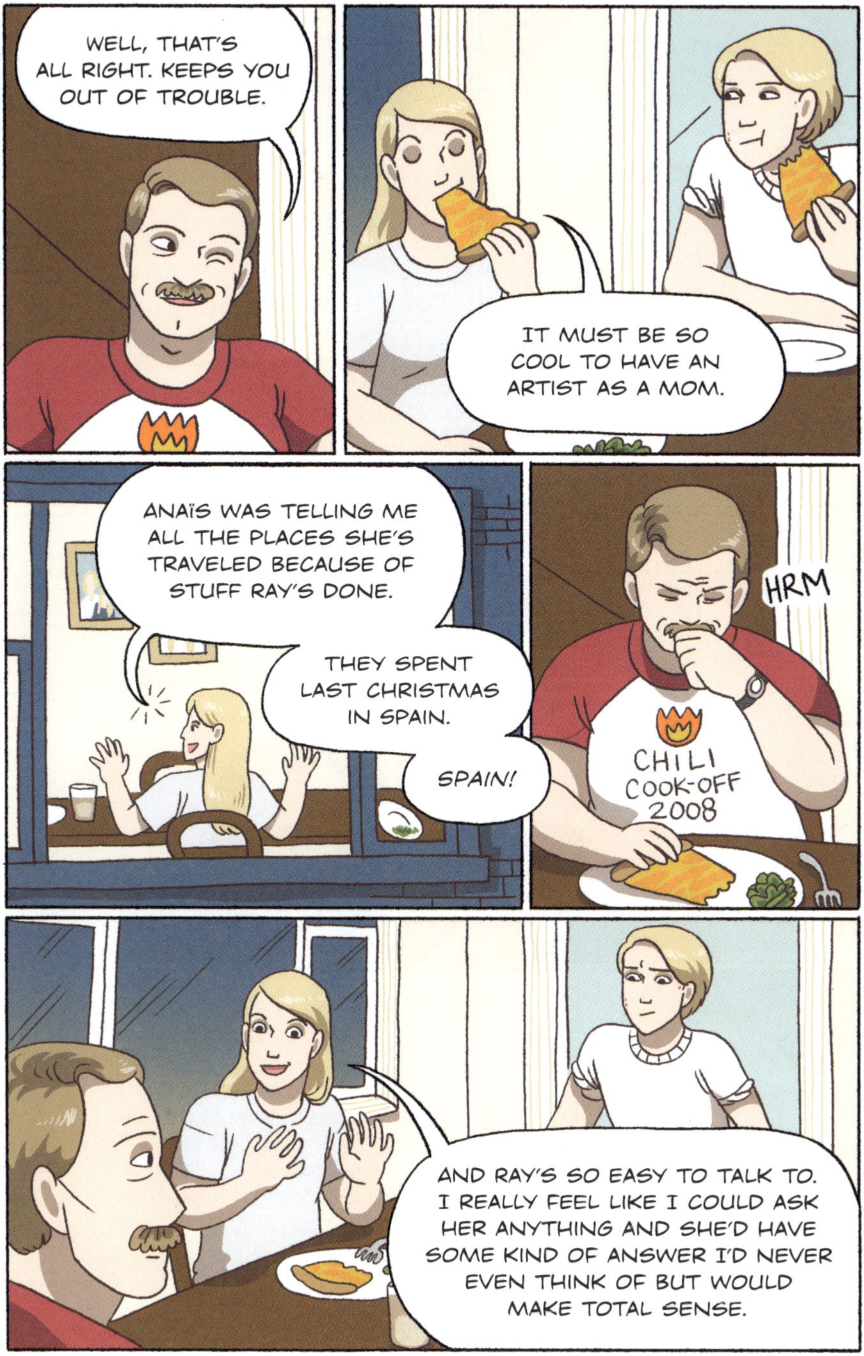
WELL, THAT'S ALL RIGHT. KEEPS YOU OUT OF TROUBLE.
IT MUST BE SO COOL TO HAVE AN ARTIST AS A MOM.
ANAÏS WAS TELLING ME ALL THE PLACES SHE'S TRAVELED BECAUSE OF STUFF RAY'S DONE.
THEY SPENT LAST CHRISTMAS IN SPAIN.
SPAIN!
HRM
CHILI COOK-OFF 2008
AND RAY'S SO EASY TO TALK TO. I REALLY FEEL LIKE I COULD ASK HER ANYTHING AND SHE'D HAVE SOME KIND OF ANSWER I'D NEVER EVEN THINK OF BUT WOULD MAKE TOTAL SENSE.

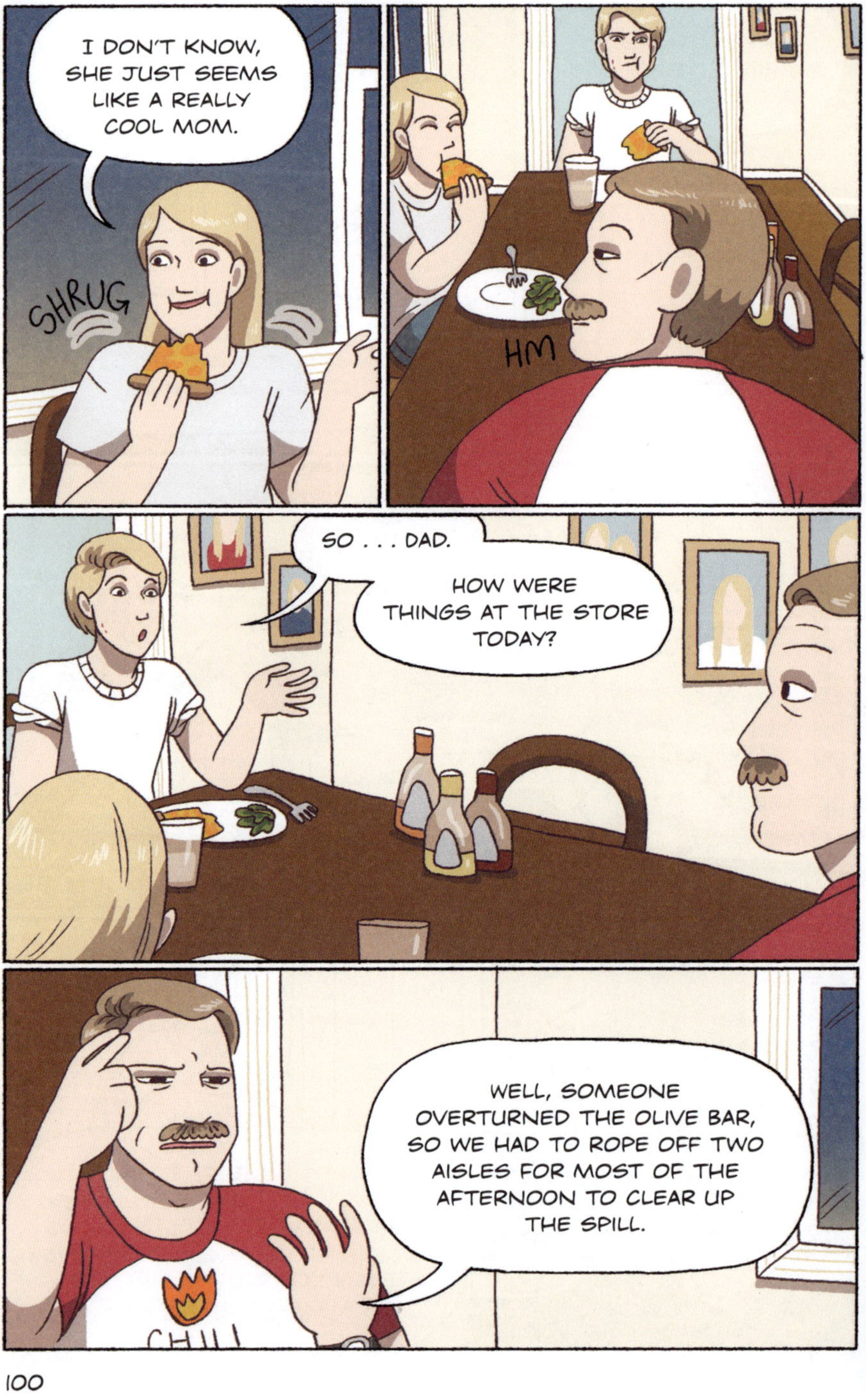
I DON'T KNOW, SHE JUST SEEMS LIKE A REALLY COOL MOM.
SHRUG
HM
SO . . . DAD.
HOW WERE THINGS AT THE STORE TODAY?
WELL, SOMEONE OVERTURNED THE OLIVE BAR, SO WE HAD TO ROPE OFF TWO AISLES FOR MOST OF THE AFTERNOON TO CLEAR UP THE SPILL.

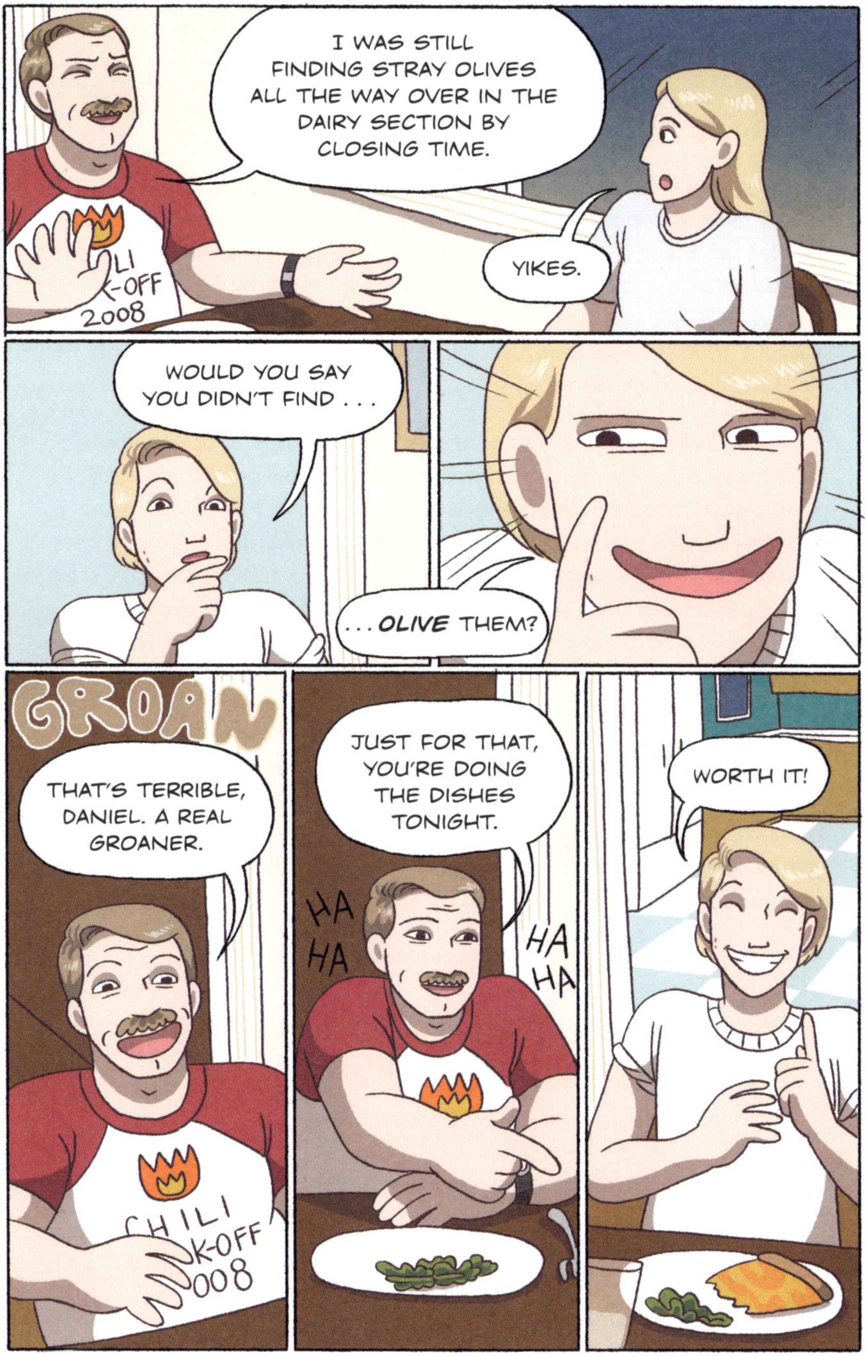
I WAS STILL FINDING STRAY OLIVES ALL THE WAY OVER IN THE DAIRY SECTION BY CLOSING TIME.
YIKES.
CHILI COOK-OFF 2008
WOULD YOU SAY YOU DIDN'T FIND . . .
. . . *OLIVE* THEM?
GROAN
THAT'S TERRIBLE, DANIEL. A REAL GROANER.
CHILI COOK-OFF 2008
JUST FOR THAT, YOU'RE DOING THE DISHES TONIGHT.
HA HA
HA HA
WORTH IT!

Dear Lucy,

A truce was called in our prank war with the Oak Cabin. The first night we were back, after our canoe trip, we woke up in the middle of the night hearing creepy tapping noises around the windows of our cabin. We were all lying there terrified. It didn't sound like normal nature noises, there was a rhythm to it. All I could think about was the ghost of that woodsman. Maybe he followed us back to camp?

Jessica went to the window, trying to see what was out there. Suddenly a white, ghostly face appeared and we all started screaming! Jessica was sure it was real, but Min-Ji and I were suspicious. We ran out into the night and saw more ghosts dancing in the moonlight. I recognized them right away: it was the Oak Cabin boys dressed in torn sheets trying to scare us. I started yelling at them, and Mike yelled back, "That's for the shoes!" And the boys ran back toward their cabin.

In the morning we were summoned before the camp director. She told us we weren't allowed to prank each other anymore and that we needed to call a truce. She made us shake hands with all the boys. It's really too bad, because Min-Ji said she had a bunch of great ideas to get back at them and now we won't be able to use them.

In other news: the dance is tomorrow! I can't wait.

P.S. Even if things are super boring in Milforth, I still want to hear about them! Miss you.

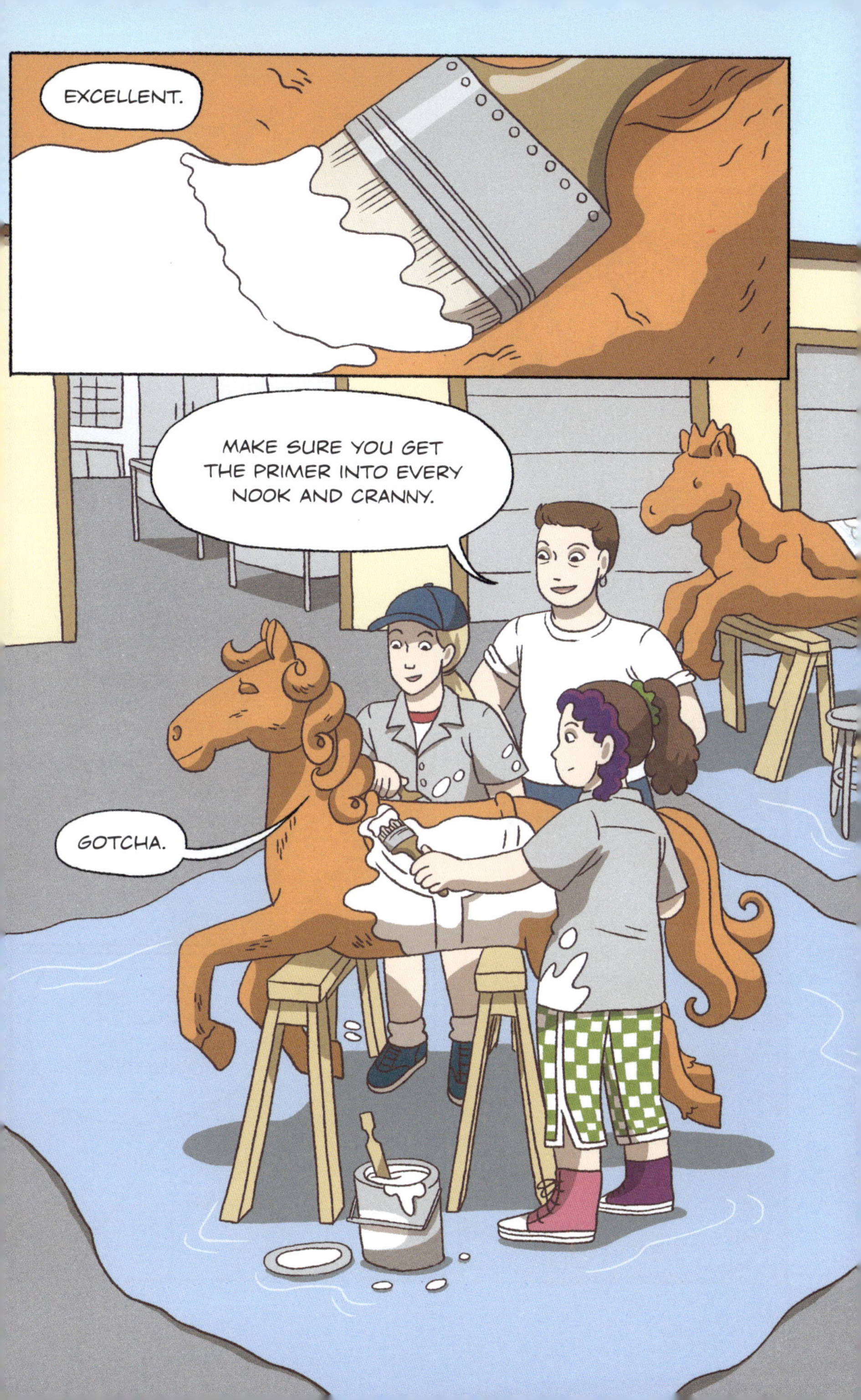
EXCELLENT.
MAKE SURE YOU GET THE PRIMER INTO EVERY NOOK AND CRANNY.
GOTCHA.

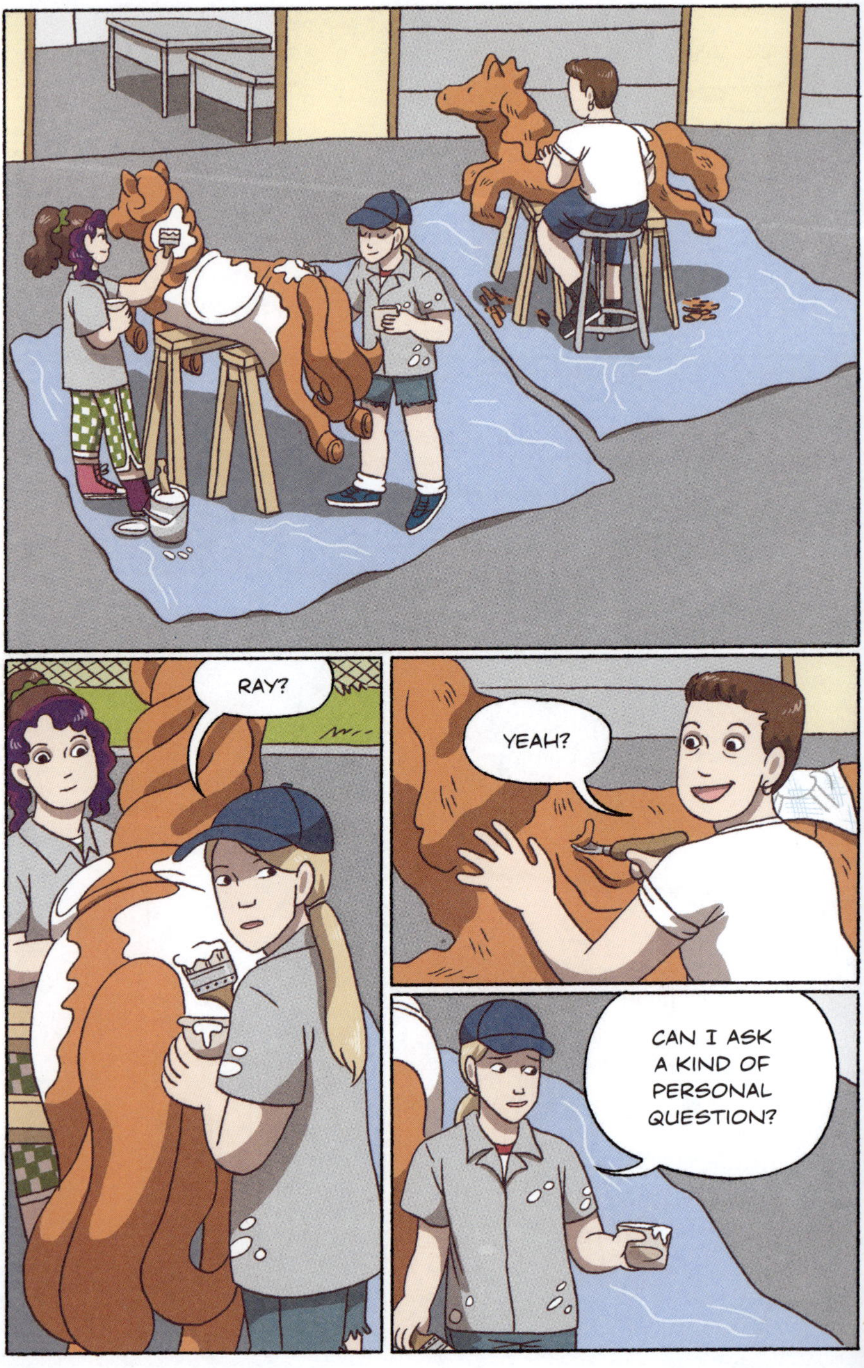
RAY?
YEAH?
CAN I ASK A KIND OF PERSONAL QUESTION?

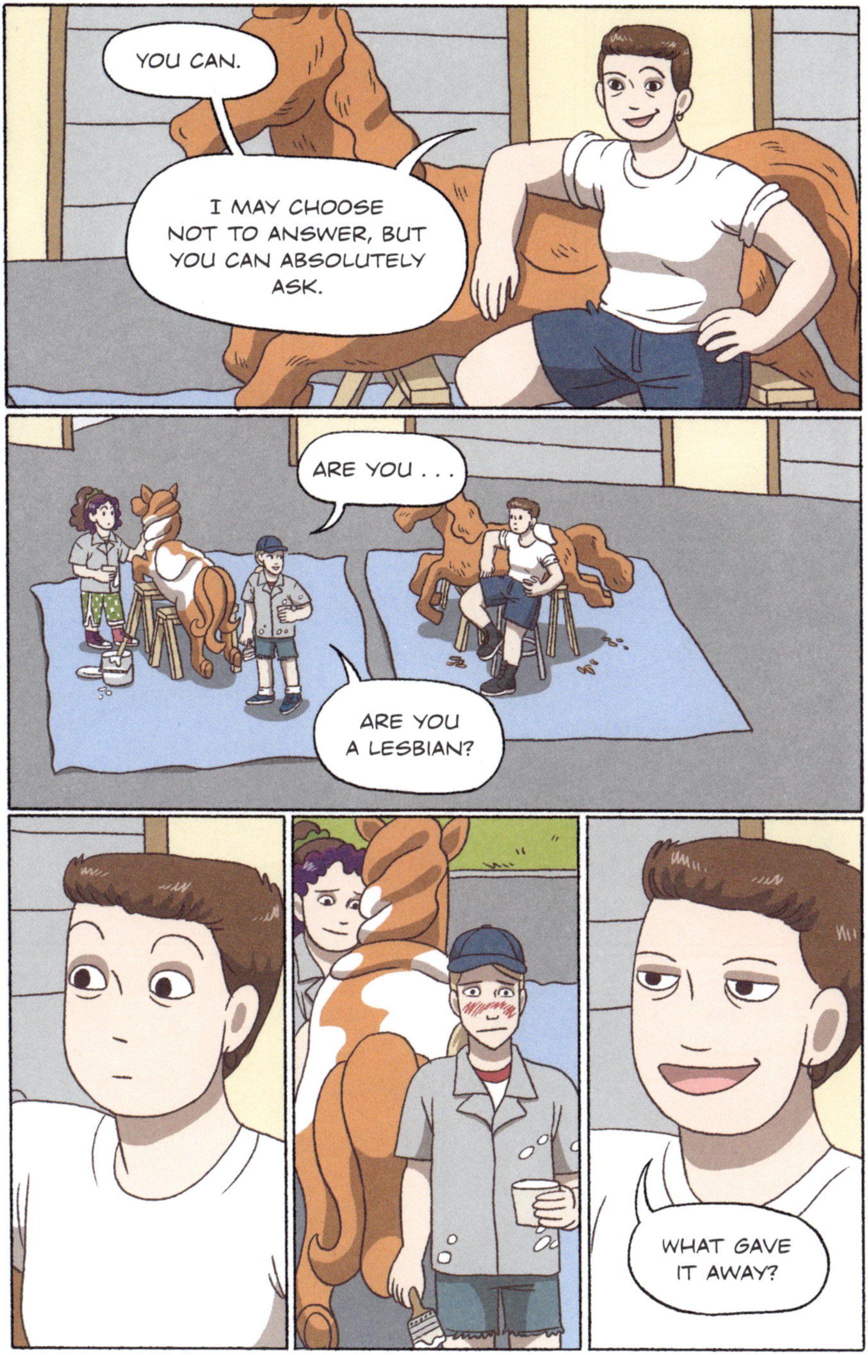
YOU CAN.
I MAY CHOOSE NOT TO ANSWER, BUT YOU CAN ABSOLUTELY ASK.
ARE YOU . . .
ARE YOU A LESBIAN?
WHAT GAVE IT AWAY?

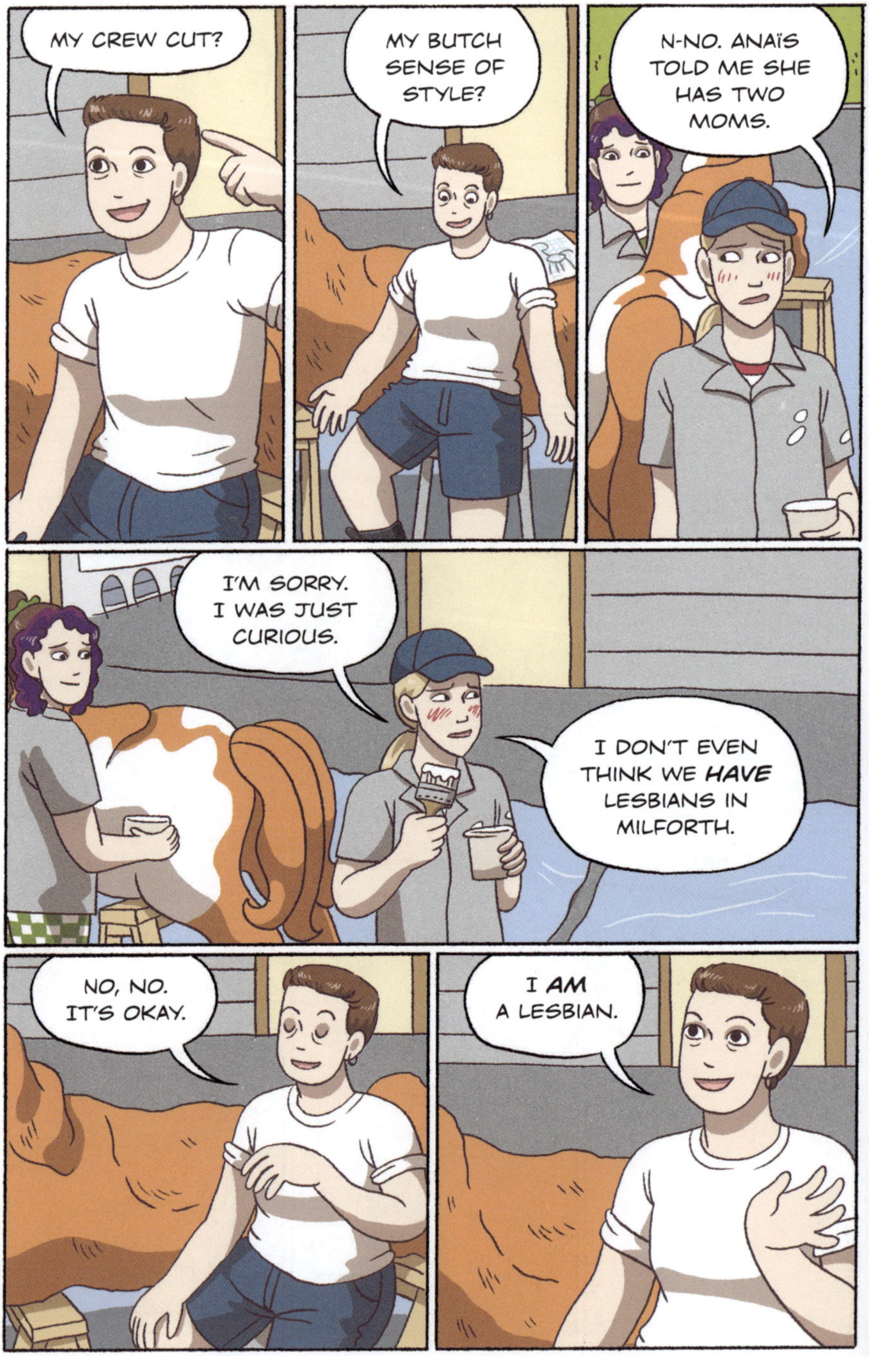
MY CREW CUT?
MY BUTCH SENSE OF STYLE?
N-NO. ANAÏS TOLD ME SHE HAS TWO MOMS.
I'M SORRY. I WAS JUST CURIOUS.
I DON'T EVEN THINK WE **HAVE** LESBIANS IN MILFORTH.
NO, NO. IT'S OKAY.
I **AM** A LESBIAN.

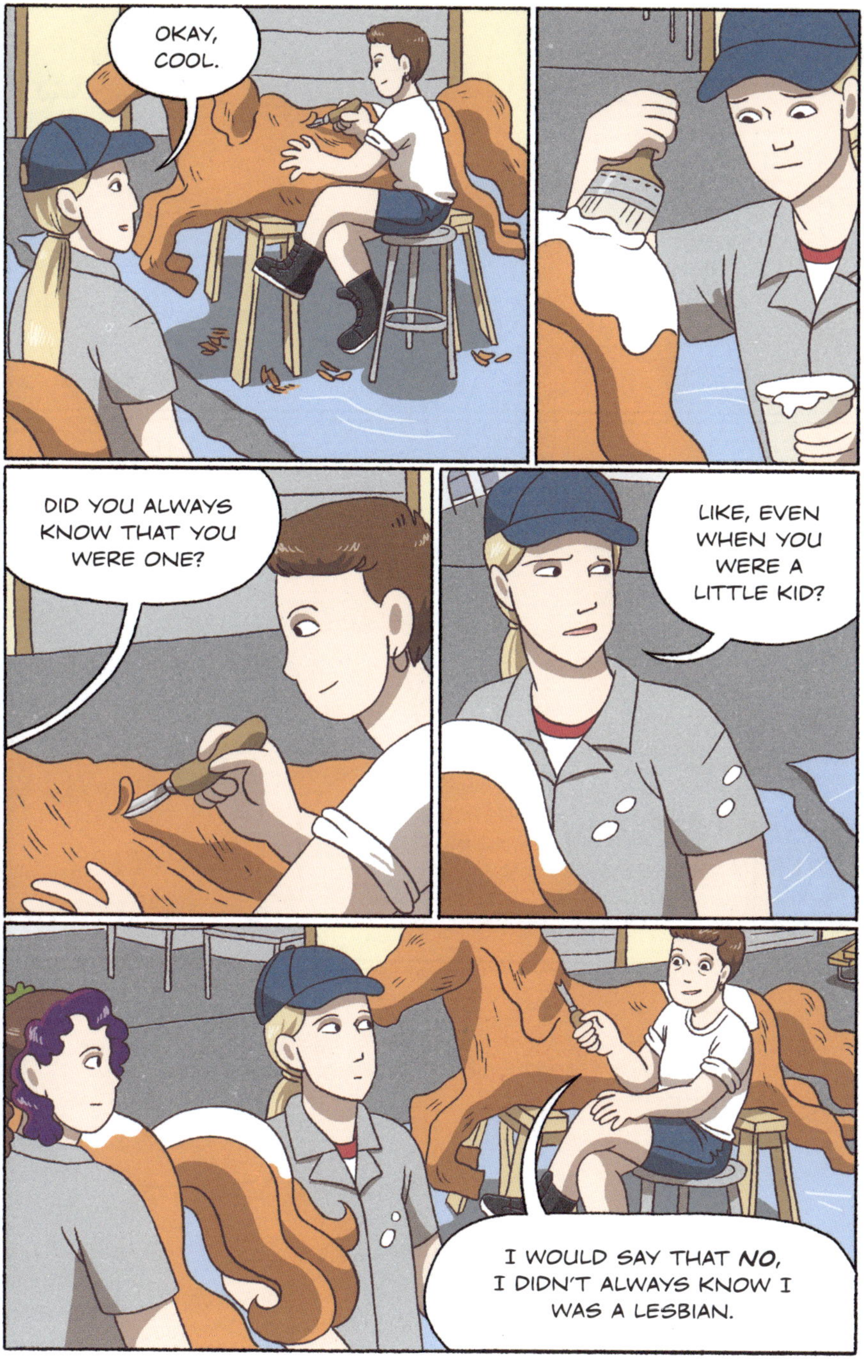
OKAY, COOL.
DID YOU ALWAYS KNOW THAT YOU WERE ONE?
LIKE, EVEN WHEN YOU WERE A LITTLE KID?
I WOULD SAY THAT NO, I DIDN'T ALWAYS KNOW I WAS A LESBIAN.

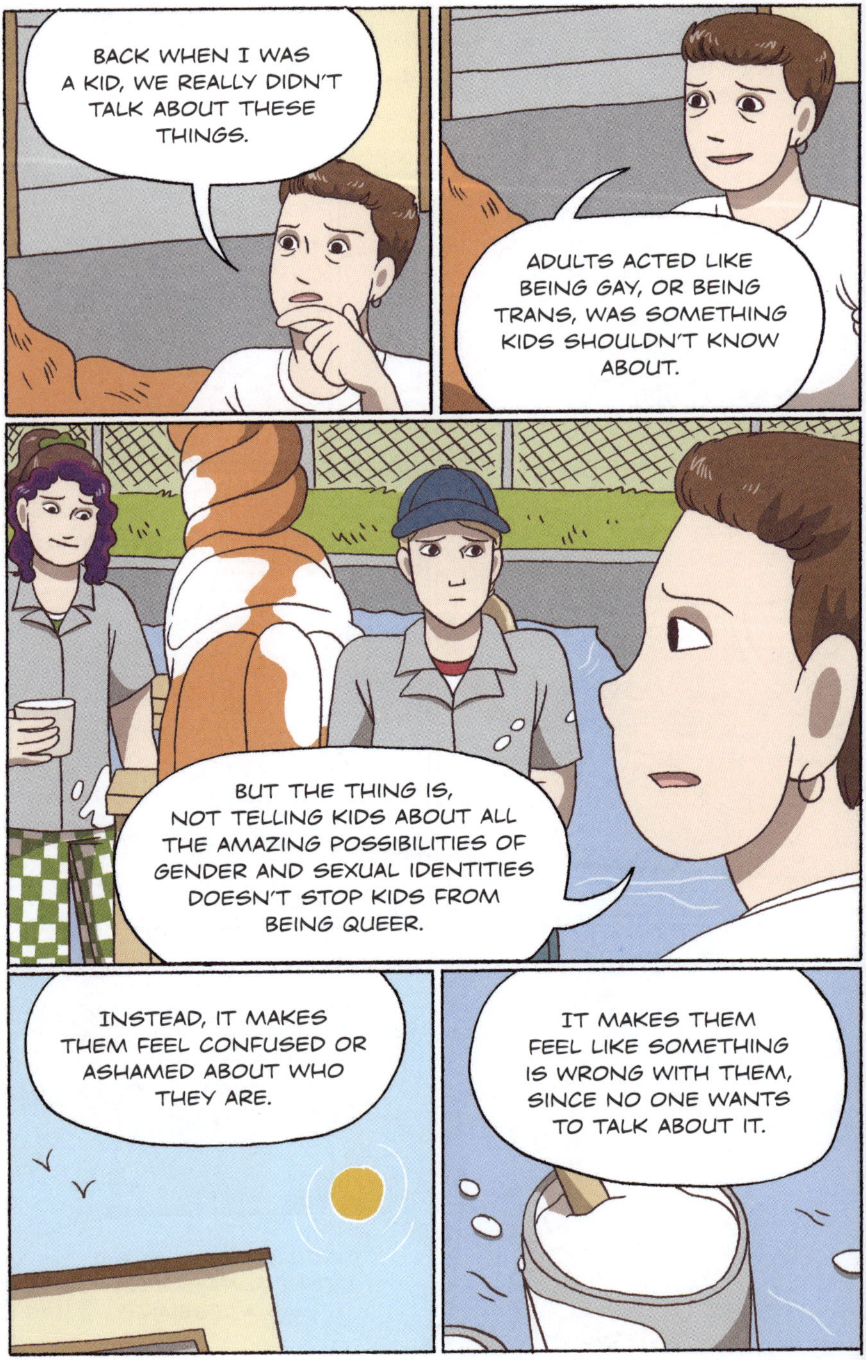
BACK WHEN I WAS A KID, WE REALLY DIDN'T TALK ABOUT THESE THINGS.
ADULTS ACTED LIKE BEING GAY, OR BEING TRANS, WAS SOMETHING KIDS SHOULDN'T KNOW ABOUT.
BUT THE THING IS, NOT TELLING KIDS ABOUT ALL THE AMAZING POSSIBILITIES OF GENDER AND SEXUAL IDENTITIES DOESN'T STOP KIDS FROM BEING QUEER.
INSTEAD, IT MAKES THEM FEEL CONFUSED OR ASHAMED ABOUT WHO THEY ARE.
IT MAKES THEM FEEL LIKE SOMETHING IS WRONG WITH THEM, SINCE NO ONE WANTS TO TALK ABOUT IT.

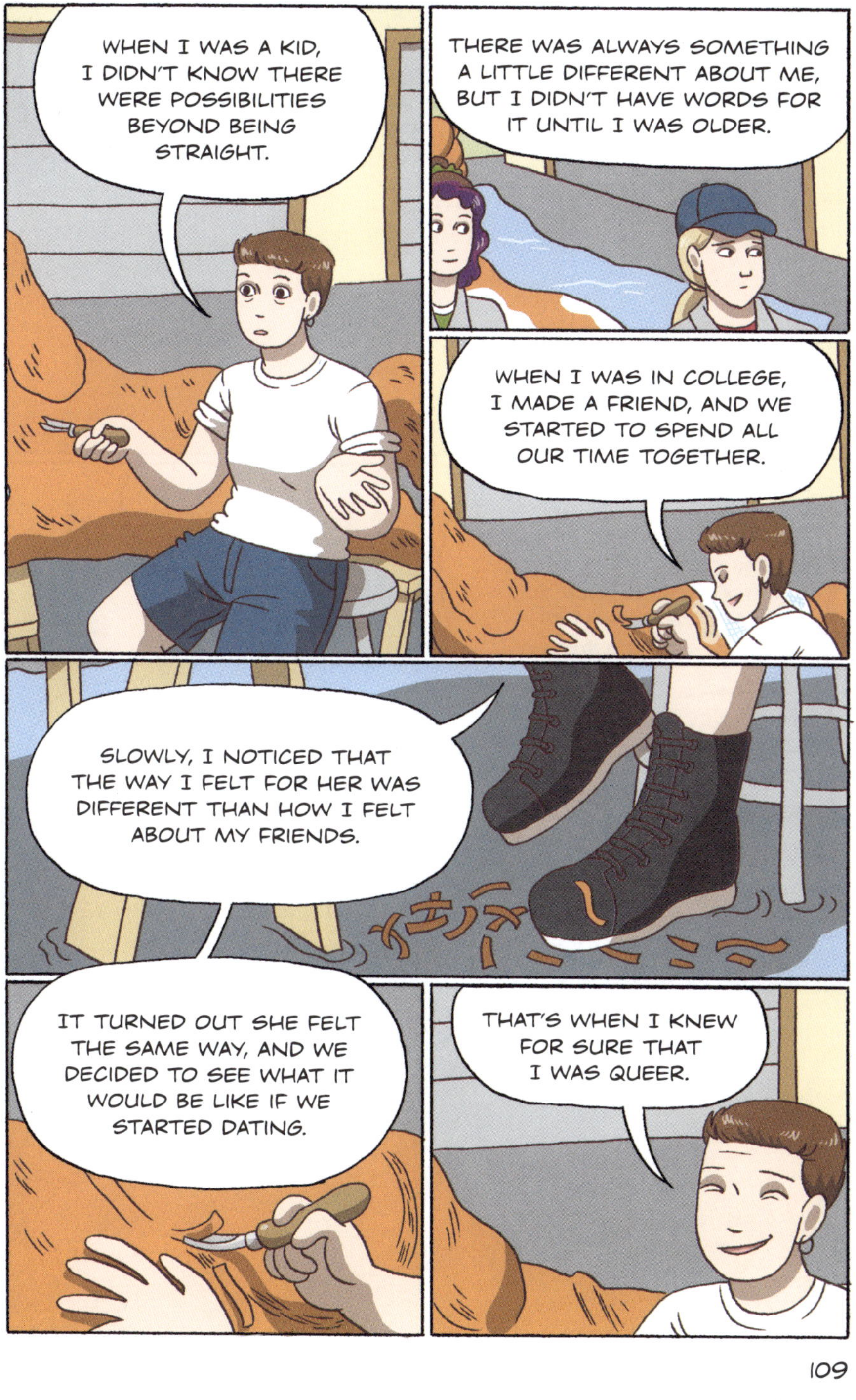
WHEN I WAS A KID, I DIDN'T KNOW THERE WERE POSSIBILITIES BEYOND BEING STRAIGHT.
THERE WAS ALWAYS SOMETHING A LITTLE DIFFERENT ABOUT ME, BUT I DIDN'T HAVE WORDS FOR IT UNTIL I WAS OLDER.
WHEN I WAS IN COLLEGE, I MADE A FRIEND, AND WE STARTED TO SPEND ALL OUR TIME TOGETHER.
SLOWLY, I NOTICED THAT THE WAY I FELT FOR HER WAS DIFFERENT THAN HOW I FELT ABOUT MY FRIENDS.
IT TURNED OUT SHE FELT THE SAME WAY, AND WE DECIDED TO SEE WHAT IT WOULD BE LIKE IF WE STARTED DATING.
THAT'S WHEN I KNEW FOR SURE THAT I WAS QUEER.

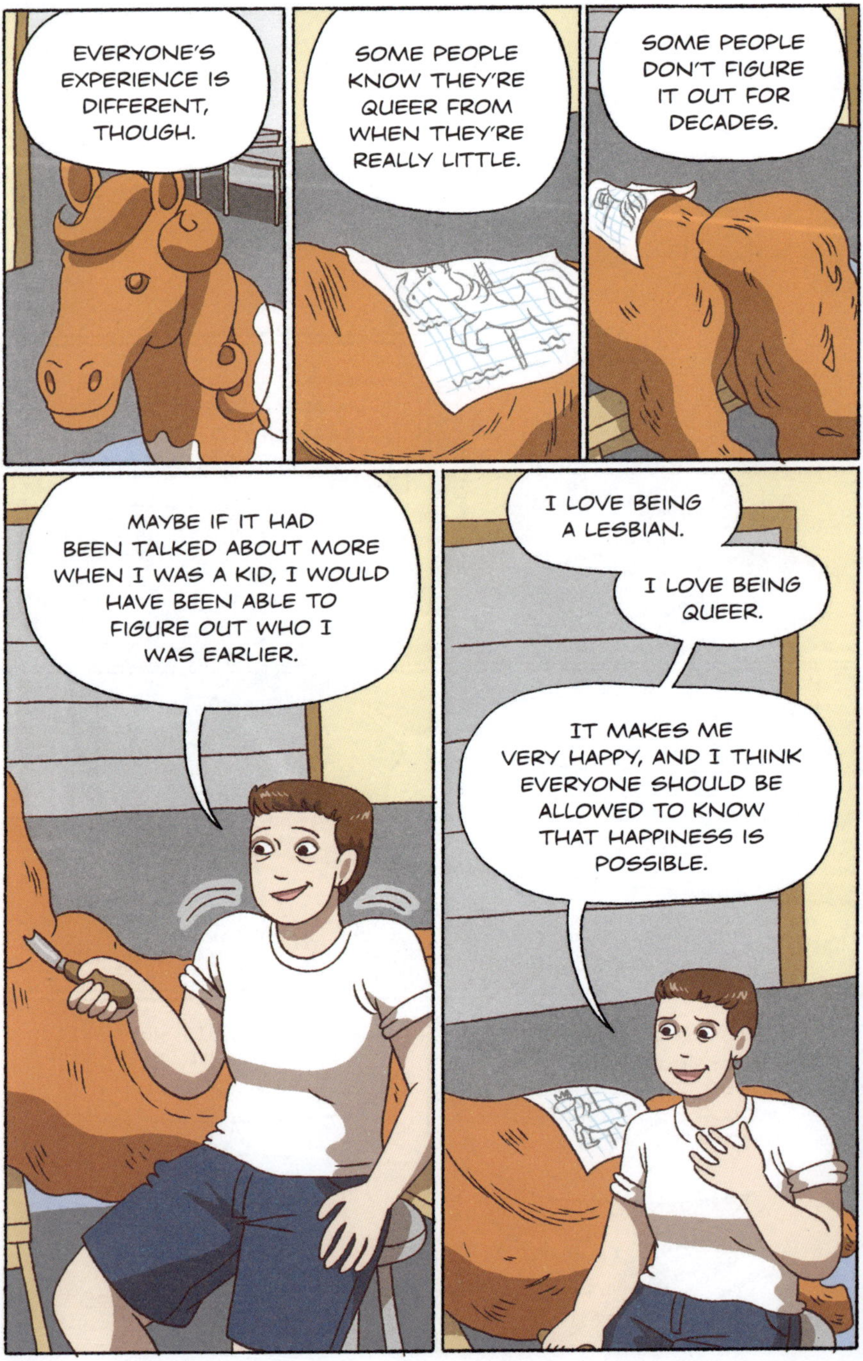
EVERYONE'S EXPERIENCE IS DIFFERENT, THOUGH.
SOME PEOPLE KNOW THEY'RE QUEER FROM WHEN THEY'RE REALLY LITTLE.
SOME PEOPLE DON'T FIGURE IT OUT FOR DECADES.
MAYBE IF IT HAD BEEN TALKED ABOUT MORE WHEN I WAS A KID, I WOULD HAVE BEEN ABLE TO FIGURE OUT WHO I WAS EARLIER.
I LOVE BEING A LESBIAN.
I LOVE BEING QUEER.
IT MAKES ME VERY HAPPY, AND I THINK EVERYONE SHOULD BE ALLOWED TO KNOW THAT HAPPINESS IS POSSIBLE.

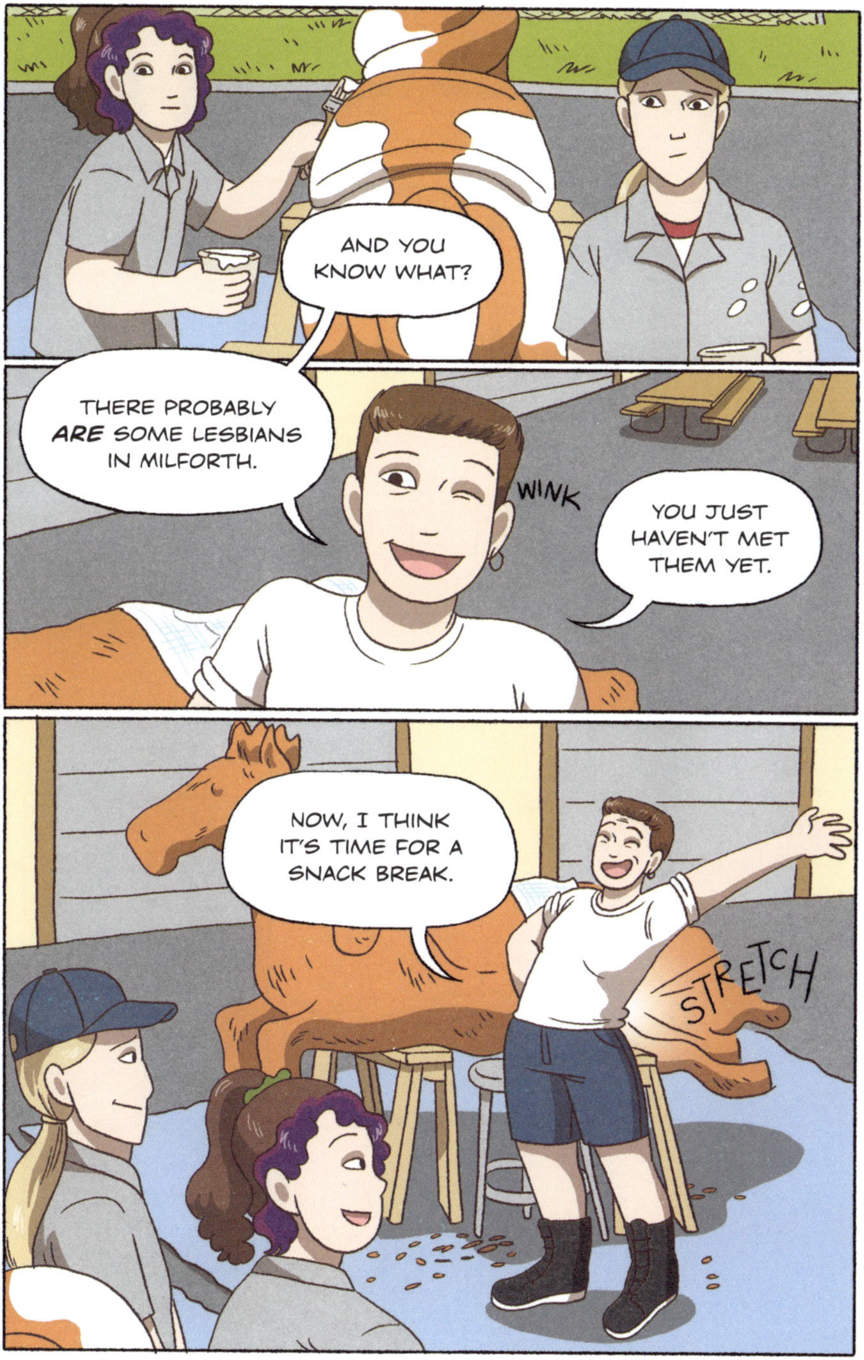
AND YOU KNOW WHAT?
THERE PROBABLY **ARE** SOME LESBIANS IN MILFORTH.
WINK
YOU JUST HAVEN'T MET THEM YET.
NOW, I THINK IT'S TIME FOR A SNACK BREAK.
STRETCH

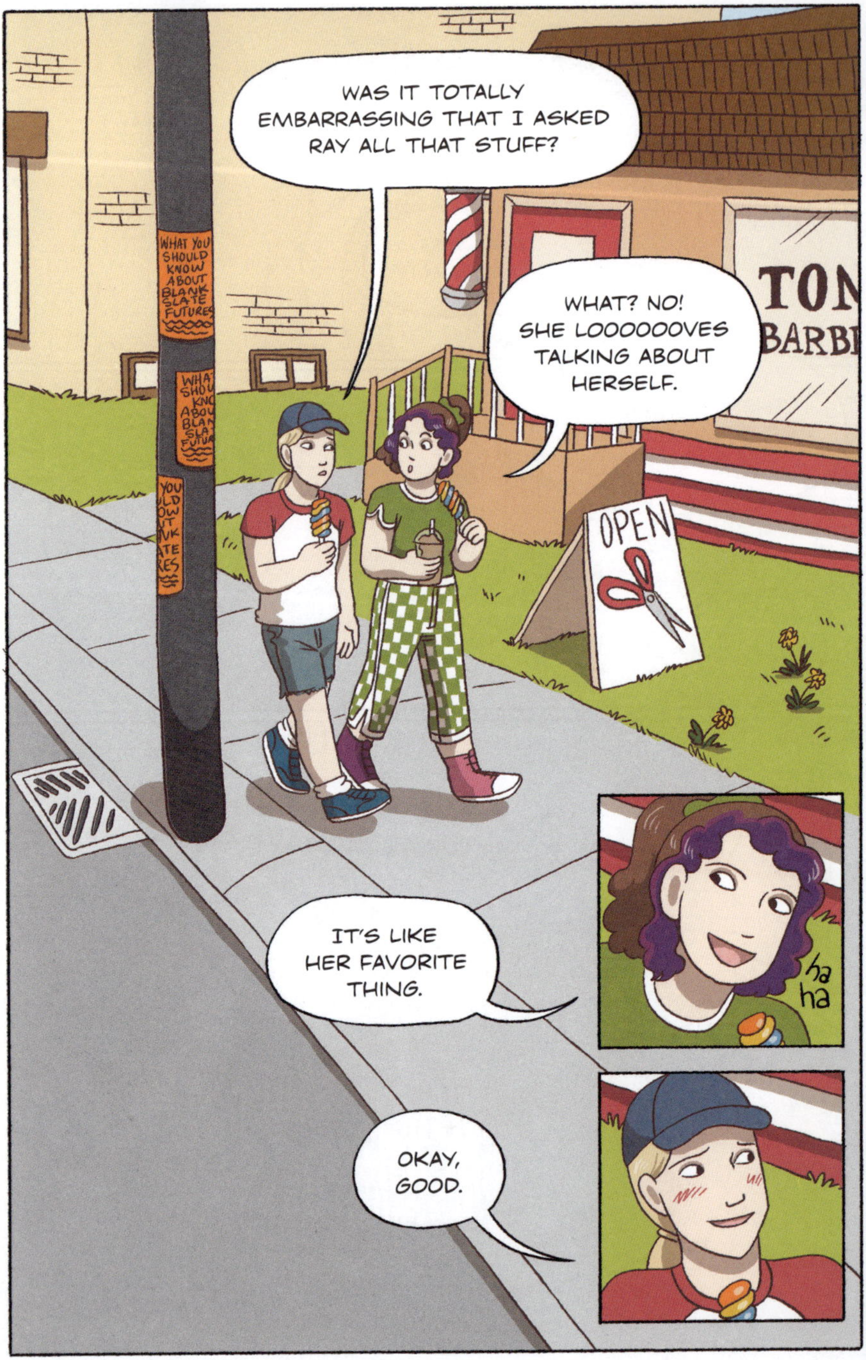
WHAT YOU SHOULD KNOW ABOUT BLANK SLATE FUTURES
WAS IT TOTALLY EMBARRASSING THAT I ASKED RAY ALL THAT STUFF?
WHAT? NO! SHE LOOOOOOVES TALKING ABOUT HERSELF.
OPEN
IT'S LIKE HER FAVORITE THING.
ha ha
OKAY, GOOD.

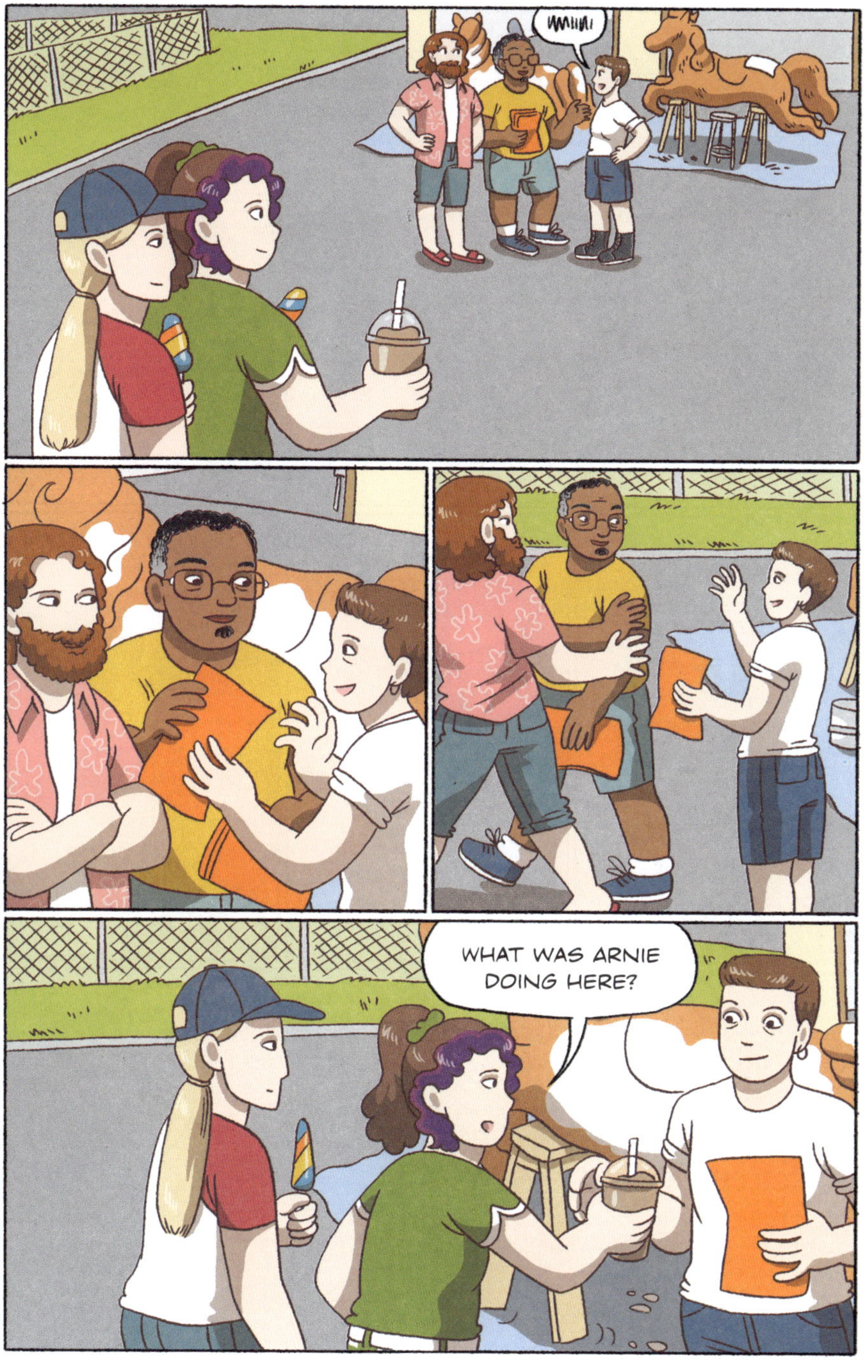
WHAT WAS ARNIE DOING HERE?

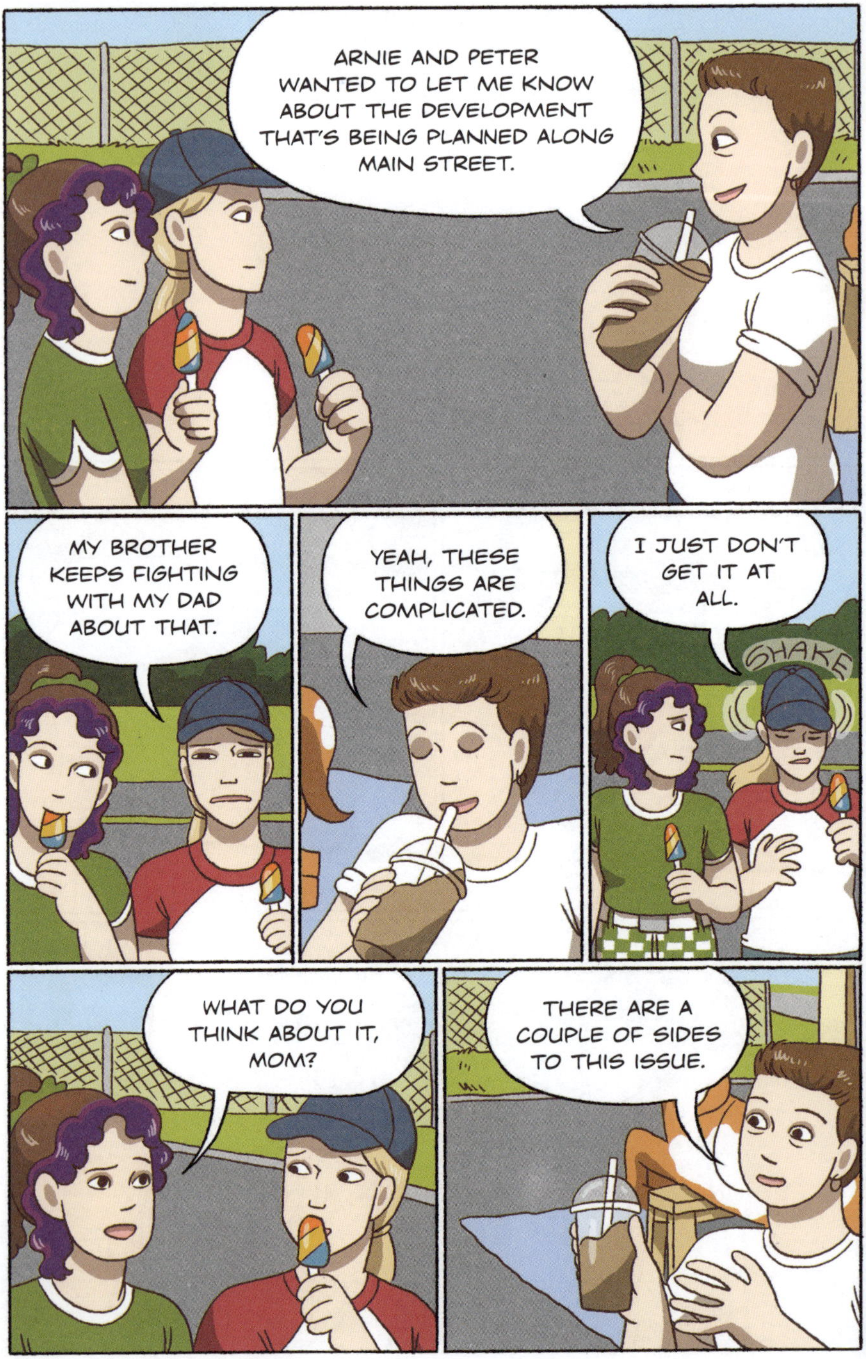
ARNIE AND PETER WANTED TO LET ME KNOW ABOUT THE DEVELOPMENT THAT'S BEING PLANNED ALONG MAIN STREET.
MY BROTHER KEEPS FIGHTING WITH MY DAD ABOUT THAT.
YEAH, THESE THINGS ARE COMPLICATED.
I JUST DON'T GET IT AT ALL.
SHAKE
WHAT DO YOU THINK ABOUT IT, MOM?
THERE ARE A COUPLE OF SIDES TO THIS ISSUE.

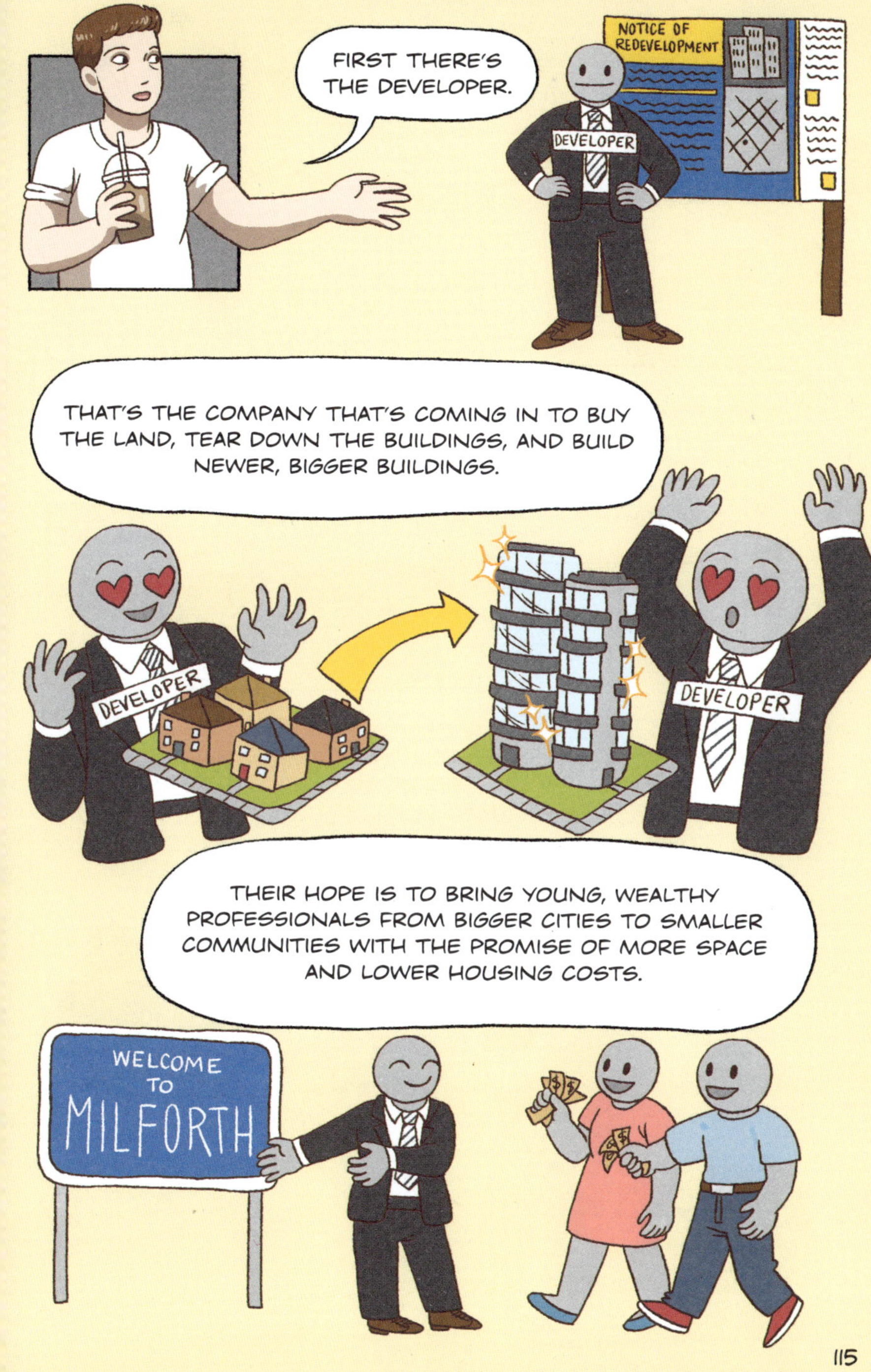
FIRST THERE'S THE DEVELOPER.
NOTICE OF REDEVELOPMENT
DEVELOPER
THAT'S THE COMPANY THAT'S COMING IN TO BUY THE LAND, TEAR DOWN THE BUILDINGS, AND BUILD NEWER, BIGGER BUILDINGS.
DEVELOPER
DEVELOPER
THEIR HOPE IS TO BRING YOUNG, WEALTHY PROFESSIONALS FROM BIGGER CITIES TO SMALLER COMMUNITIES WITH THE PROMISE OF MORE SPACE AND LOWER HOUSING COSTS.
WELCOME TO MILFORTH

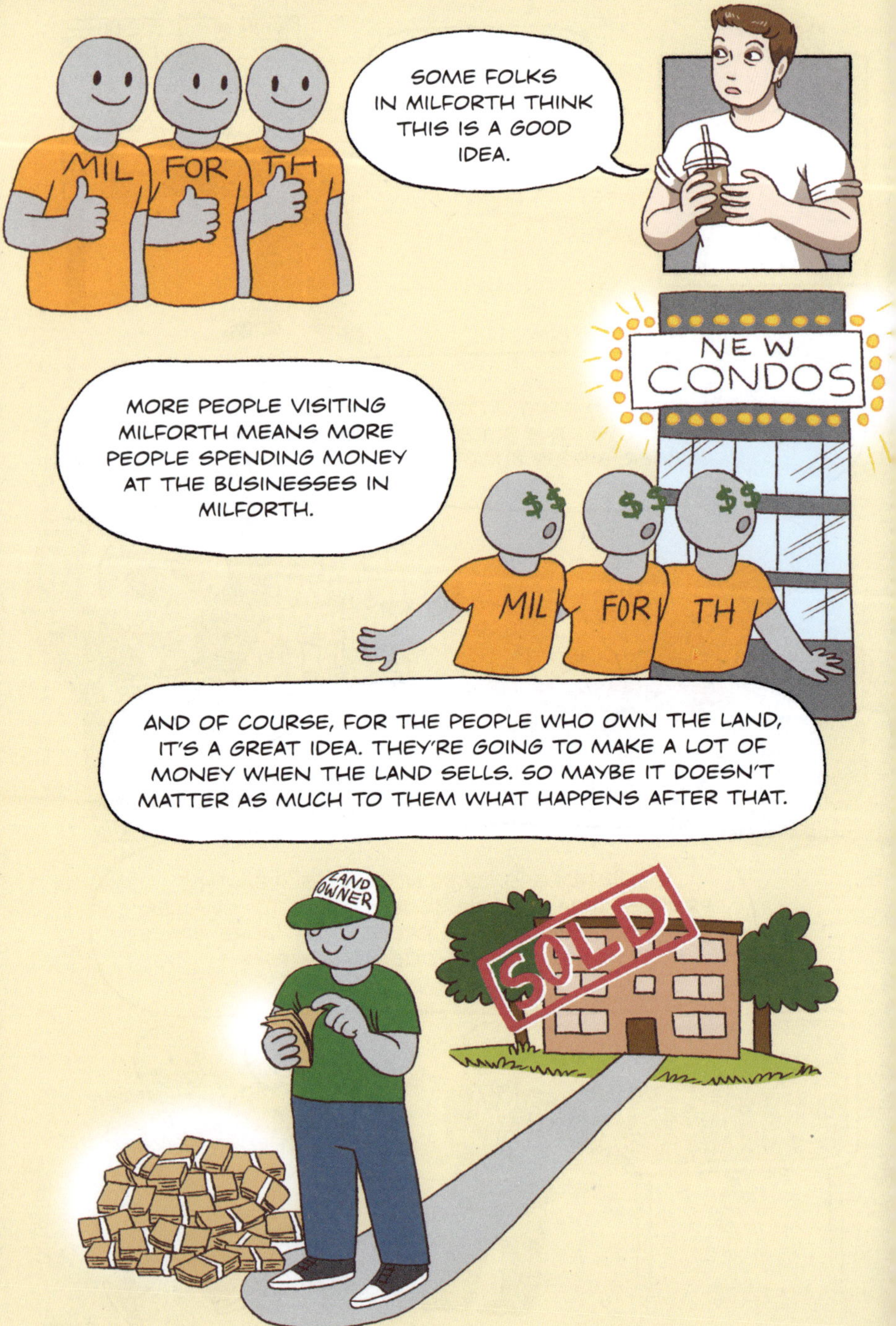
MIL FOR TH
SOME FOLKS IN MILFORTH THINK THIS IS A GOOD IDEA.
NEW CONDOS
MORE PEOPLE VISITING MILFORTH MEANS MORE PEOPLE SPENDING MONEY AT THE BUSINESSES IN MILFORTH.
$$
MIL FOR TH
AND OF COURSE, FOR THE PEOPLE WHO OWN THE LAND, IT'S A GREAT IDEA. THEY'RE GOING TO MAKE A LOT OF MONEY WHEN THE LAND SELLS. SO MAYBE IT DOESN'T MATTER AS MUCH TO THEM WHAT HAPPENS AFTER THAT.
LAND OWNER
SOLD

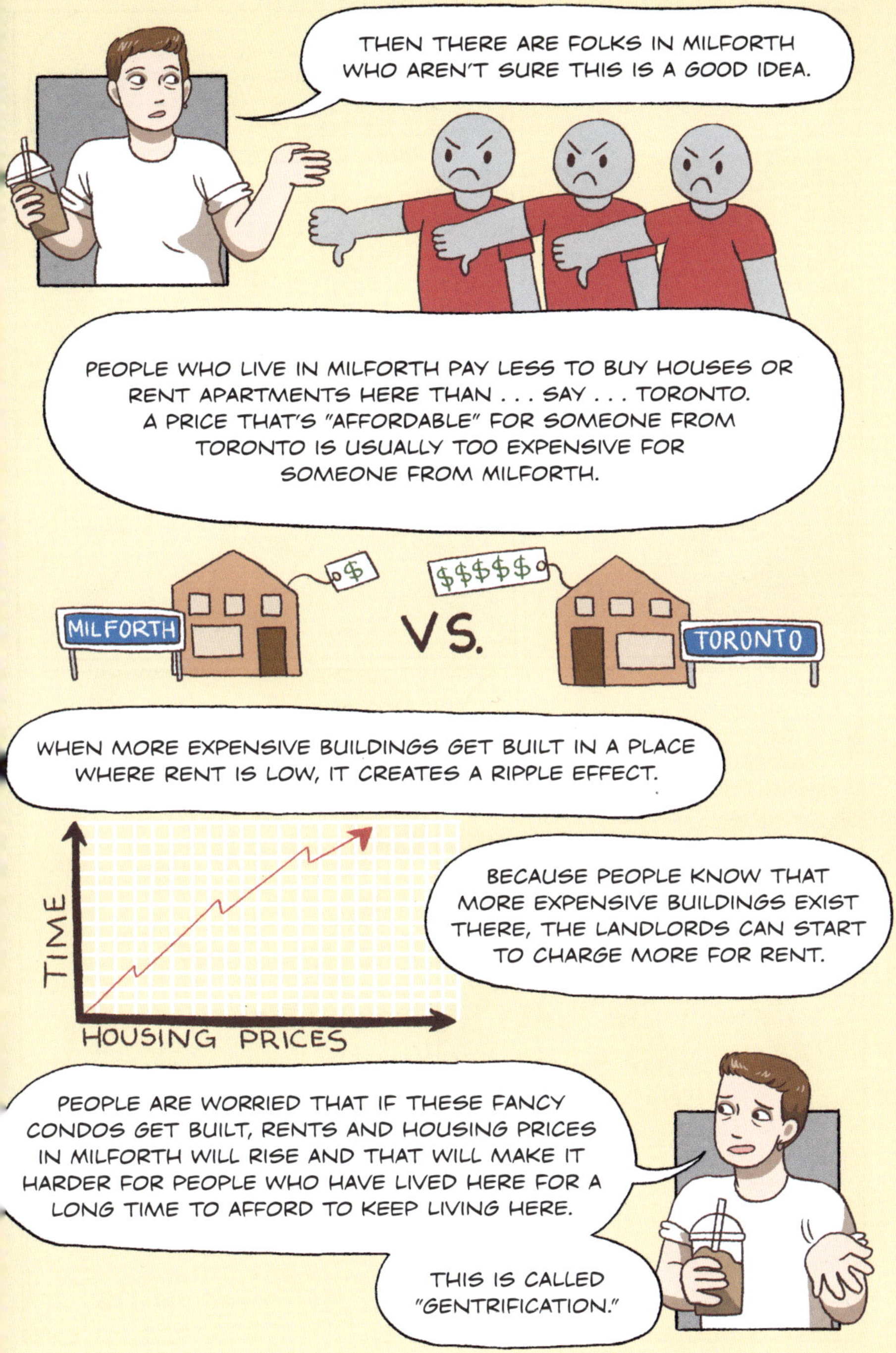
THEN THERE ARE FOLKS IN MILFORTH WHO AREN'T SURE THIS IS A GOOD IDEA.
PEOPLE WHO LIVE IN MILFORTH PAY LESS TO BUY HOUSES OR RENT APARTMENTS HERE THAN . . . SAY . . . TORONTO. A PRICE THAT'S "AFFORDABLE" FOR SOMEONE FROM TORONTO IS USUALLY TOO EXPENSIVE FOR SOMEONE FROM MILFORTH.
$
$$$$$
MILFORTH
VS.
TORONTO
WHEN MORE EXPENSIVE BUILDINGS GET BUILT IN A PLACE WHERE RENT IS LOW, IT CREATES A RIPPLE EFFECT.
TIME
HOUSING PRICES
BECAUSE PEOPLE KNOW THAT MORE EXPENSIVE BUILDINGS EXIST THERE, THE LANDLORDS CAN START TO CHARGE MORE FOR RENT.
PEOPLE ARE WORRIED THAT IF THESE FANCY CONDOS GET BUILT, RENTS AND HOUSING PRICES IN MILFORTH WILL RISE AND THAT WILL MAKE IT HARDER FOR PEOPLE WHO HAVE LIVED HERE FOR A LONG TIME TO AFFORD TO KEEP LIVING HERE.
THIS IS CALLED "GENTRIFICATION."

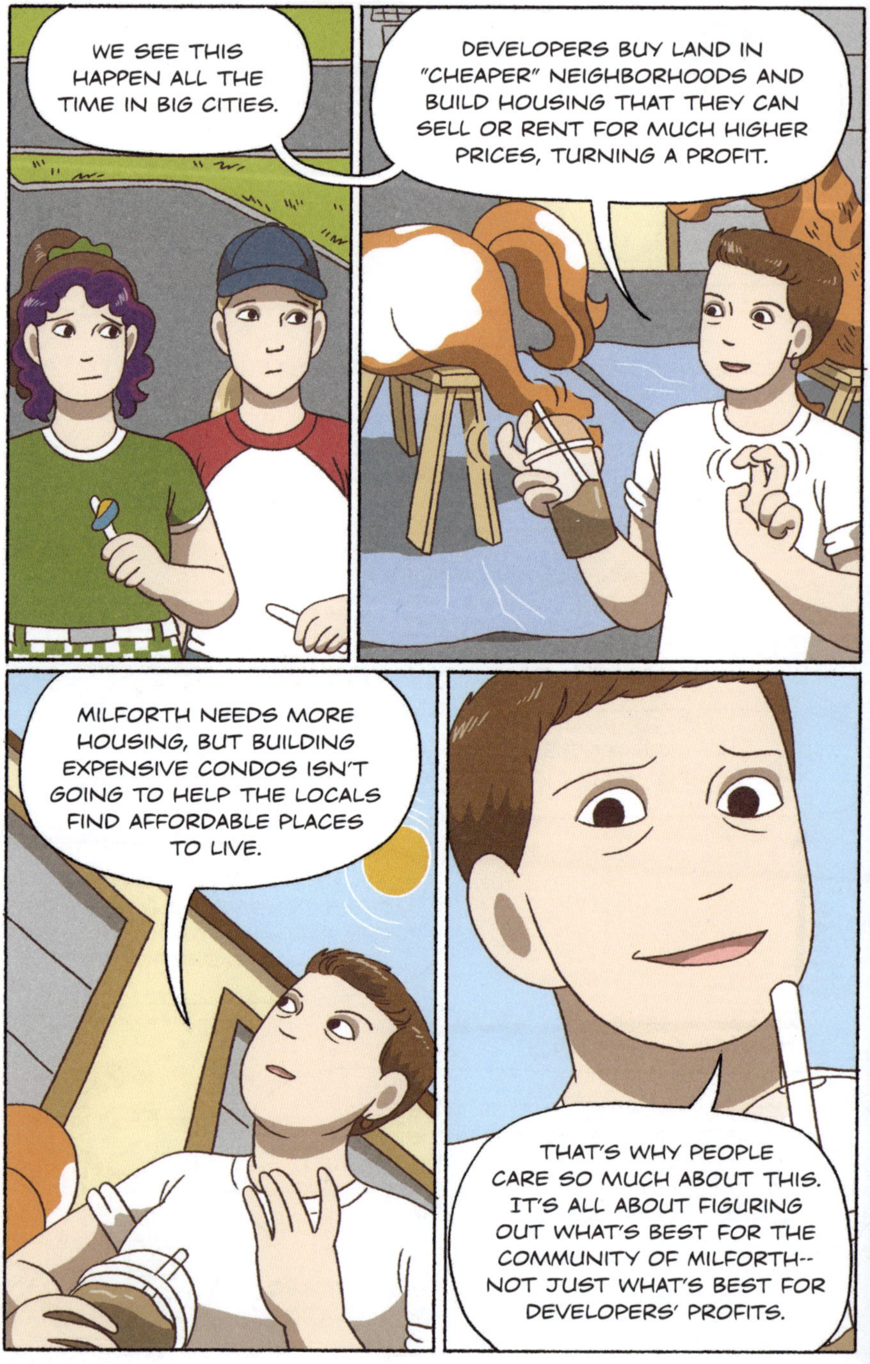
WE SEE THIS HAPPEN ALL THE TIME IN BIG CITIES.
DEVELOPERS BUY LAND IN "CHEAPER" NEIGHBORHOODS AND BUILD HOUSING THAT THEY CAN SELL OR RENT FOR MUCH HIGHER PRICES, TURNING A PROFIT.
MILFORTH NEEDS MORE HOUSING, BUT BUILDING EXPENSIVE CONDOS ISN'T GOING TO HELP THE LOCALS FIND AFFORDABLE PLACES TO LIVE.
THAT'S WHY PEOPLE CARE SO MUCH ABOUT THIS. IT'S ALL ABOUT FIGURING OUT WHAT'S BEST FOR THE COMMUNITY OF MILFORTH--NOT JUST WHAT'S BEST FOR DEVELOPERS' PROFITS.

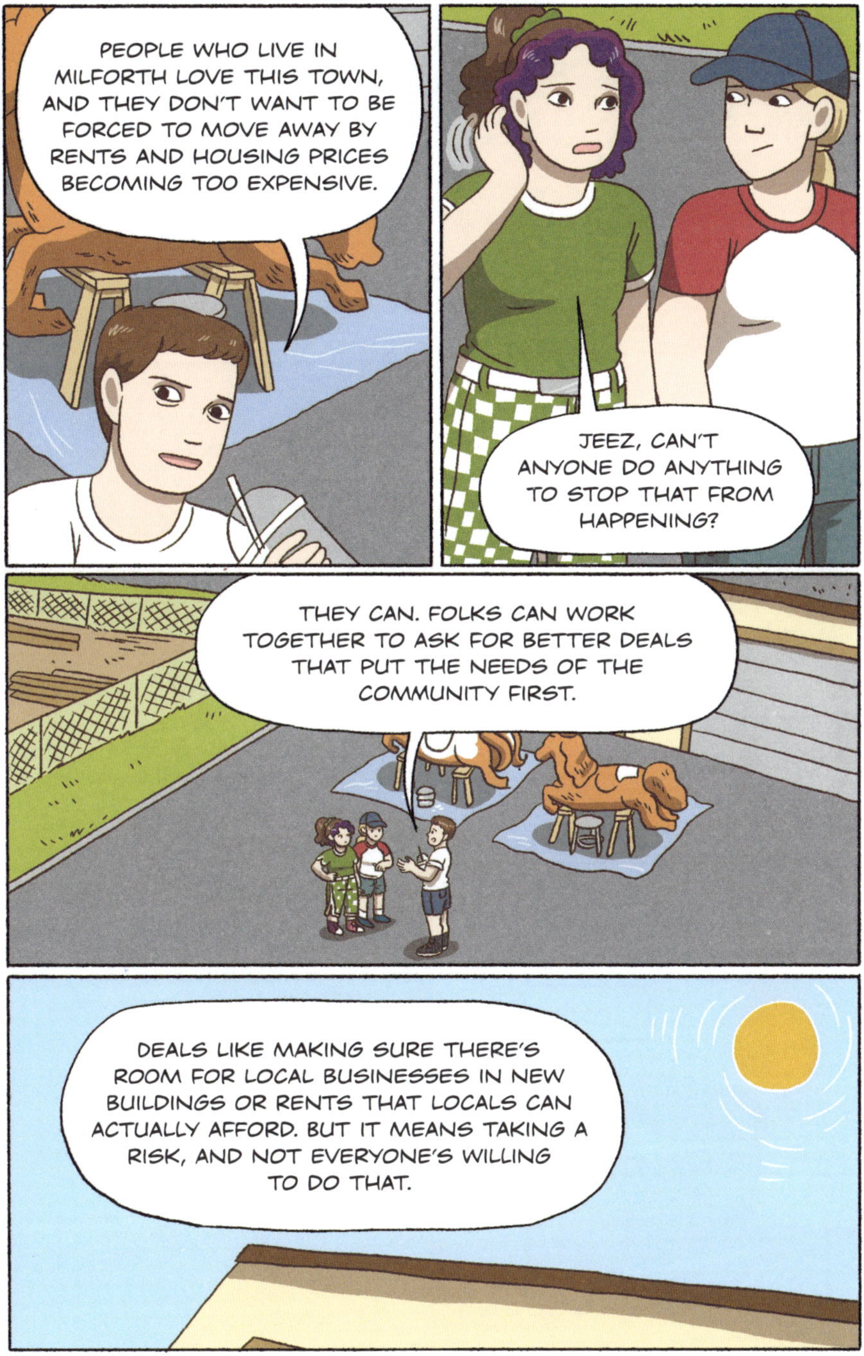
PEOPLE WHO LIVE IN MILFORTH LOVE THIS TOWN, AND THEY DON'T WANT TO BE FORCED TO MOVE AWAY BY RENTS AND HOUSING PRICES BECOMING TOO EXPENSIVE.
JEEZ, CAN'T ANYONE DO ANYTHING TO STOP THAT FROM HAPPENING?
THEY CAN. FOLKS CAN WORK TOGETHER TO ASK FOR BETTER DEALS THAT PUT THE NEEDS OF THE COMMUNITY FIRST.
DEALS LIKE MAKING SURE THERE'S ROOM FOR LOCAL BUSINESSES IN NEW BUILDINGS OR RENTS THAT LOCALS CAN ACTUALLY AFFORD. BUT IT MEANS TAKING A RISK, AND NOT EVERYONE'S WILLING TO DO THAT.

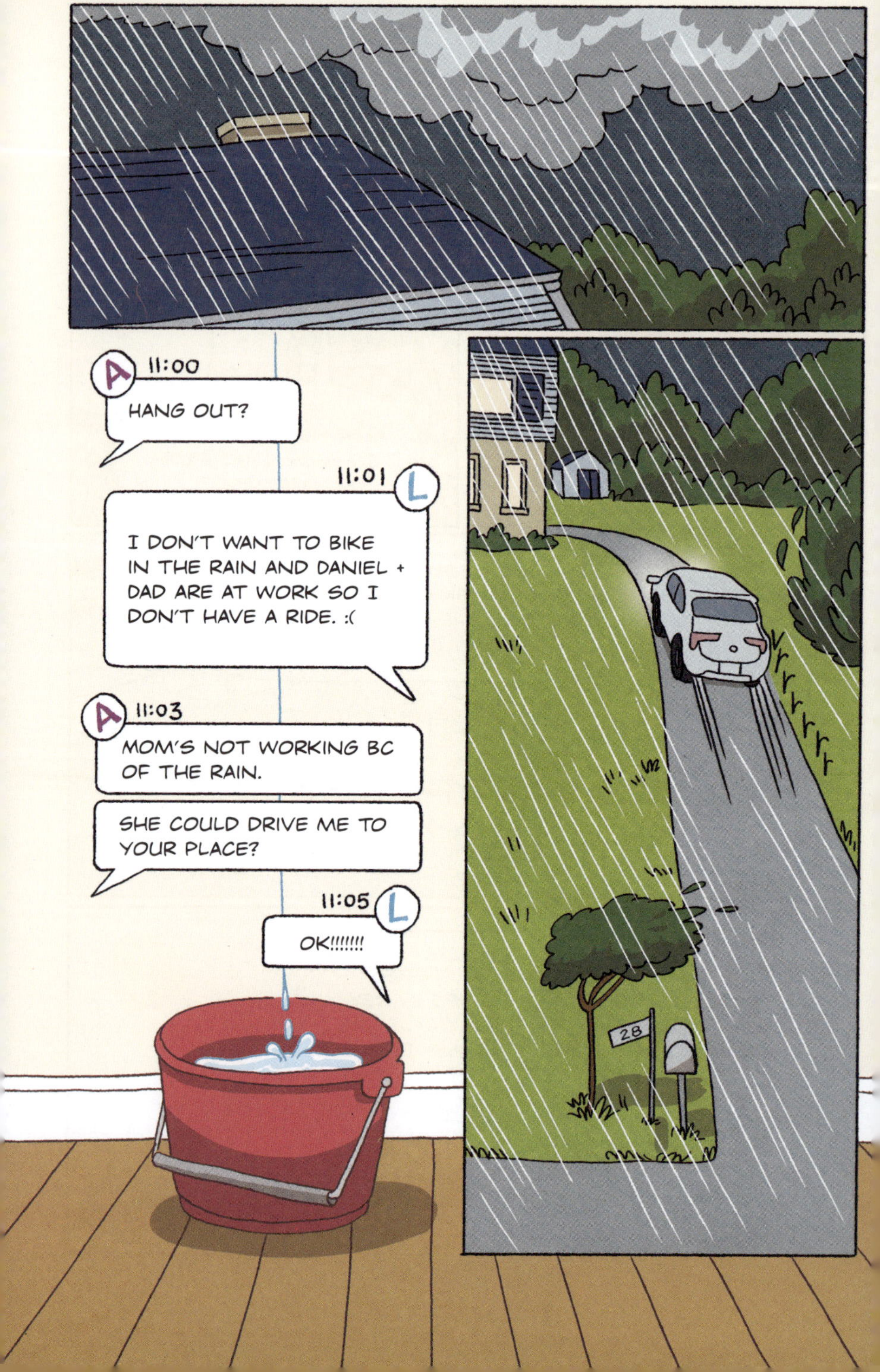

11:00
HANG OUT?
11:01
I DON'T WANT TO BIKE IN THE RAIN AND DANIEL + DAD ARE AT WORK SO I DON'T HAVE A RIDE. :(
11:03
MOM'S NOT WORKING BC OF THE RAIN.
SHE COULD DRIVE ME TO YOUR PLACE?
11:05
OK!!!!!!!
28

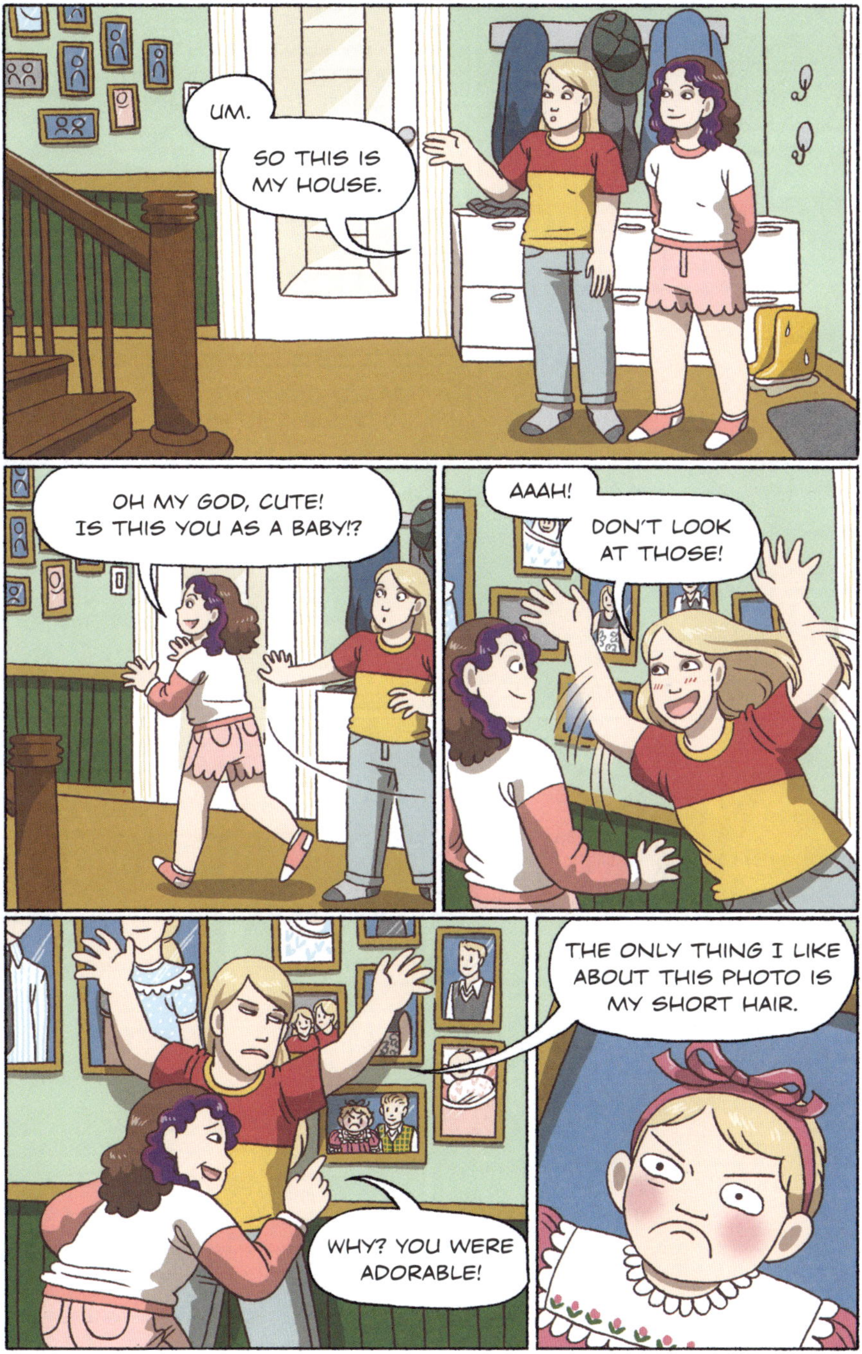
UM.
SO THIS IS MY HOUSE.
OH MY GOD, CUTE! IS THIS YOU AS A BABY!?
AAAH!
DON'T LOOK AT THOSE!
WHY? YOU WERE ADORABLE!
THE ONLY THING I LIKE ABOUT THIS PHOTO IS MY SHORT HAIR.

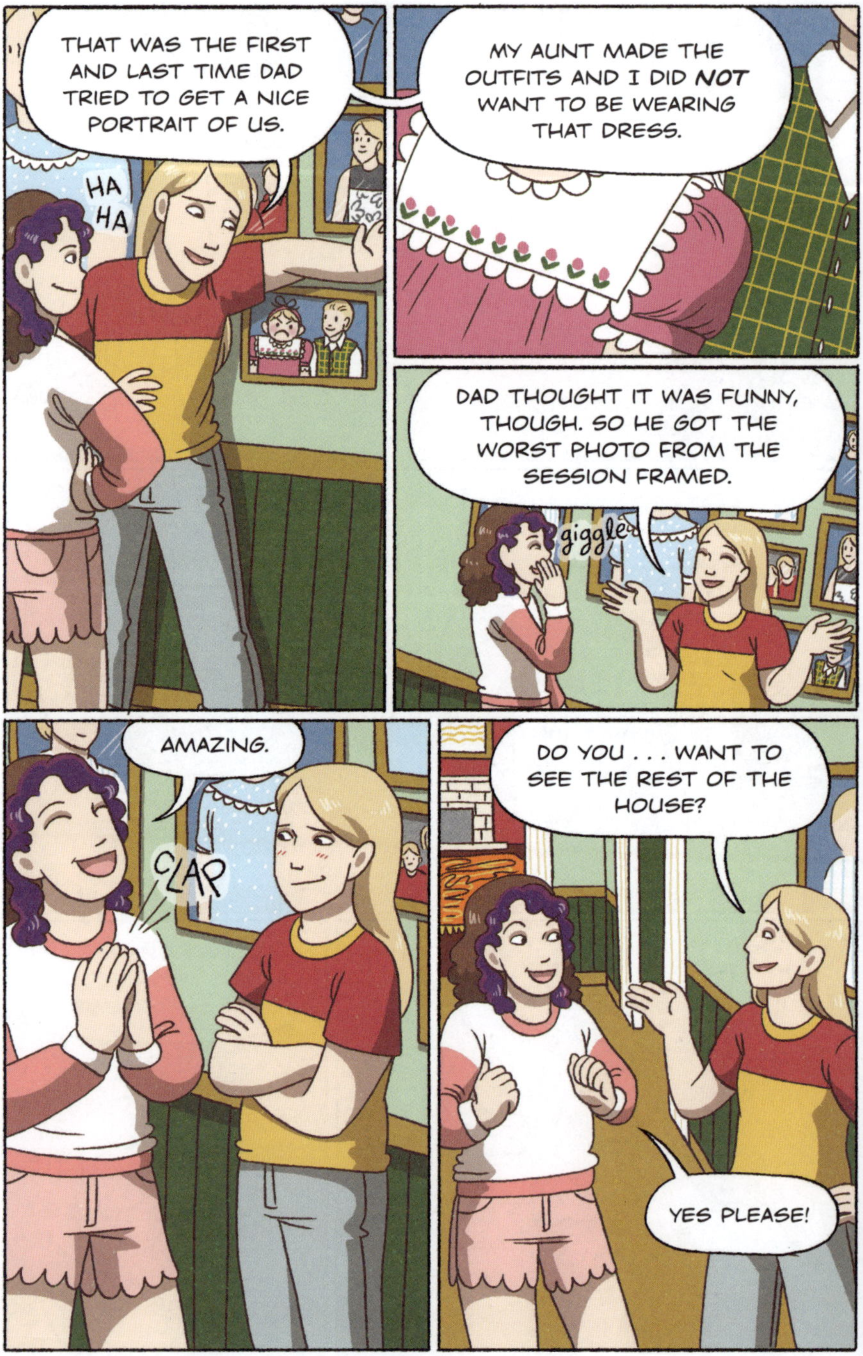
THAT WAS THE FIRST AND LAST TIME DAD TRIED TO GET A NICE PORTRAIT OF US.
HA HA
MY AUNT MADE THE OUTFITS AND I DID **NOT** WANT TO BE WEARING THAT DRESS.
DAD THOUGHT IT WAS FUNNY, THOUGH. SO HE GOT THE WORST PHOTO FROM THE SESSION FRAMED.
giggle
AMAZING.
CLAP
DO YOU . . . WANT TO SEE THE REST OF THE HOUSE?
YES PLEASE!

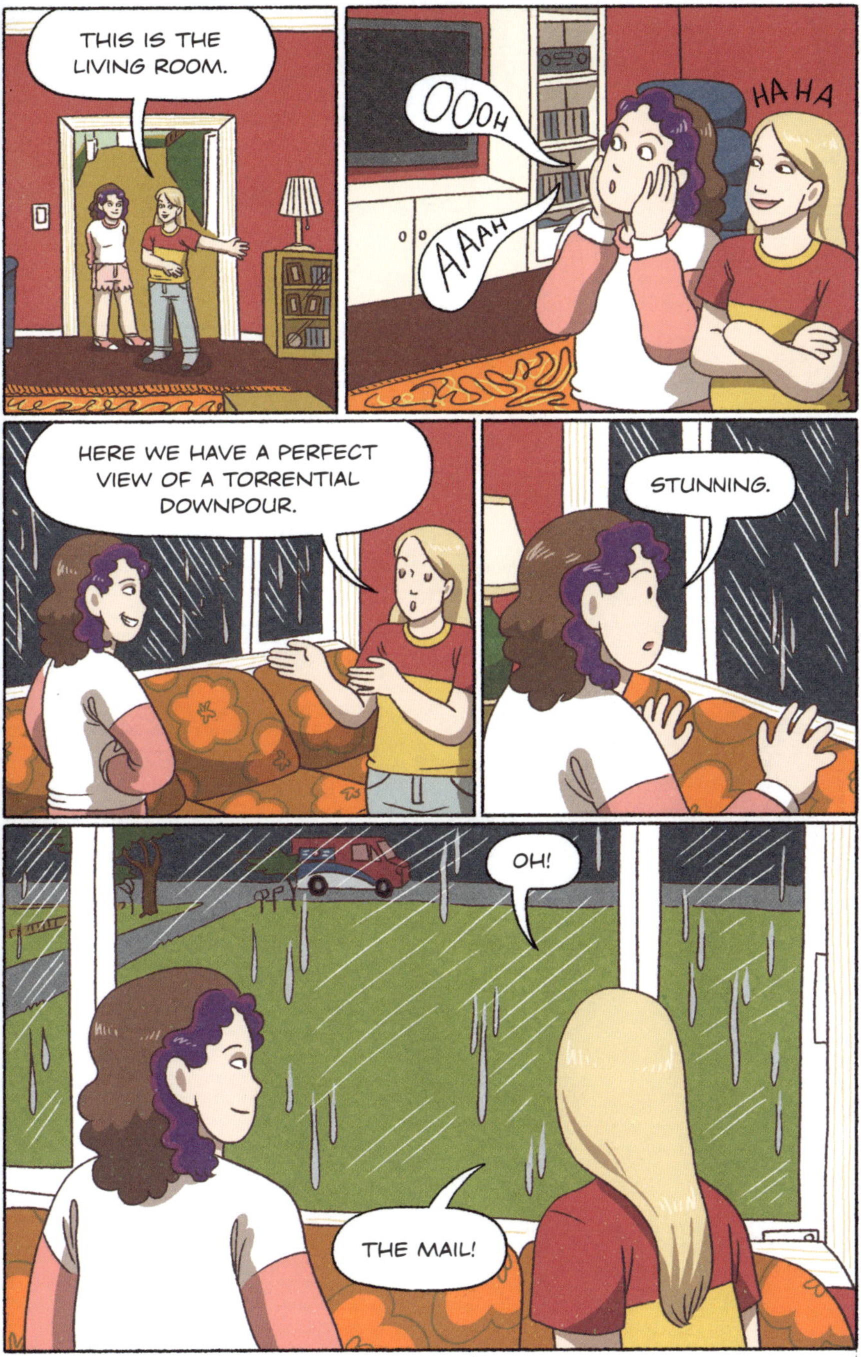
THIS IS THE LIVING ROOM.
OOOH
AAAH
HA HA
HERE WE HAVE A PERFECT VIEW OF A TORRENTIAL DOWNPOUR.
STUNNING.
OH!
THE MAIL!

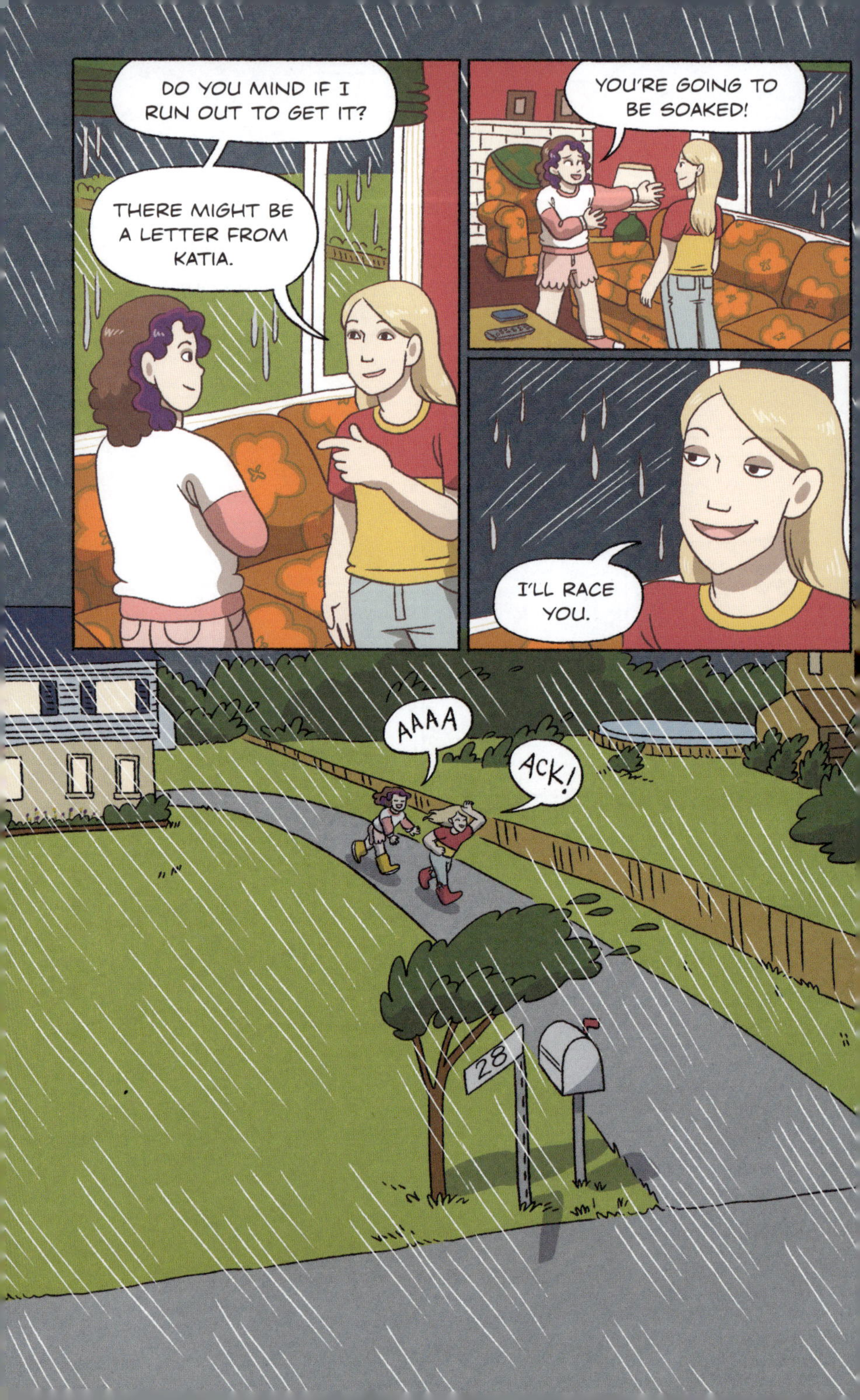
DO YOU MIND IF I RUN OUT TO GET IT?
THERE MIGHT BE A LETTER FROM KATIA.
YOU'RE GOING TO BE SOAKED!
I'LL RACE YOU.
AAAA
ACK!
28

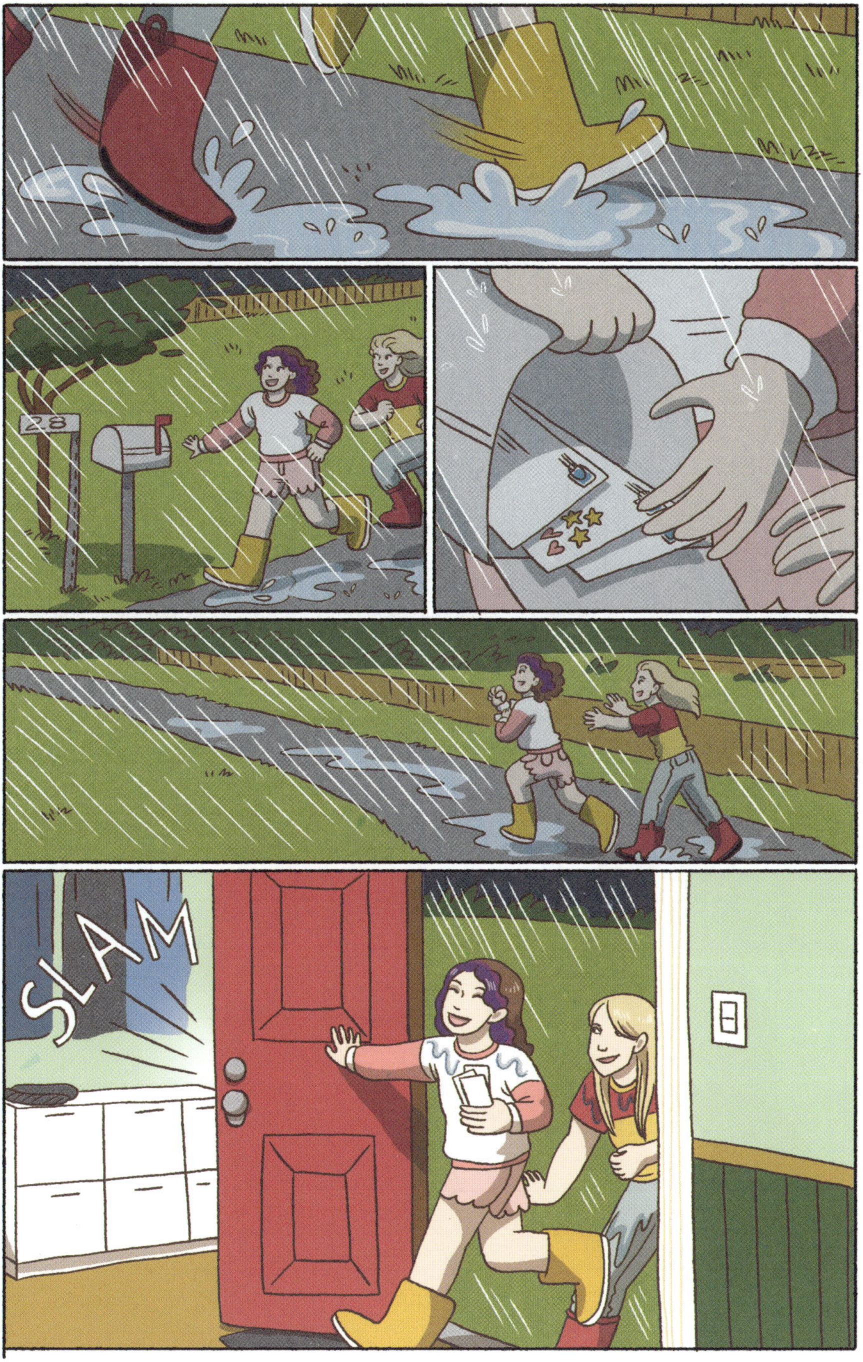
28
SLAM

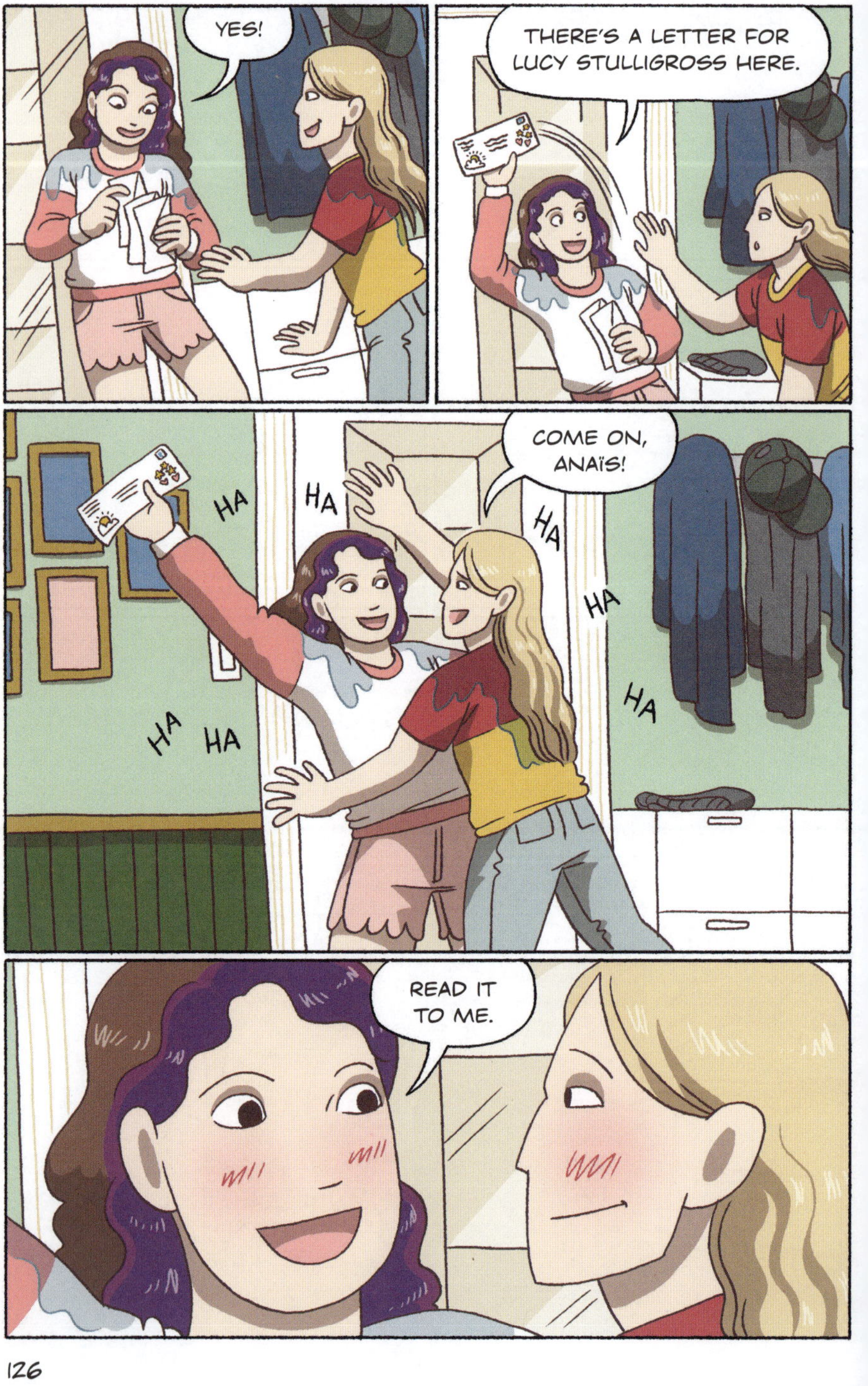
YES!
THERE'S A LETTER FOR LUCY STULLIGROSS HERE.
COME ON, ANAÏS!
HA HA HA HA HA HA HA
READ IT TO ME.

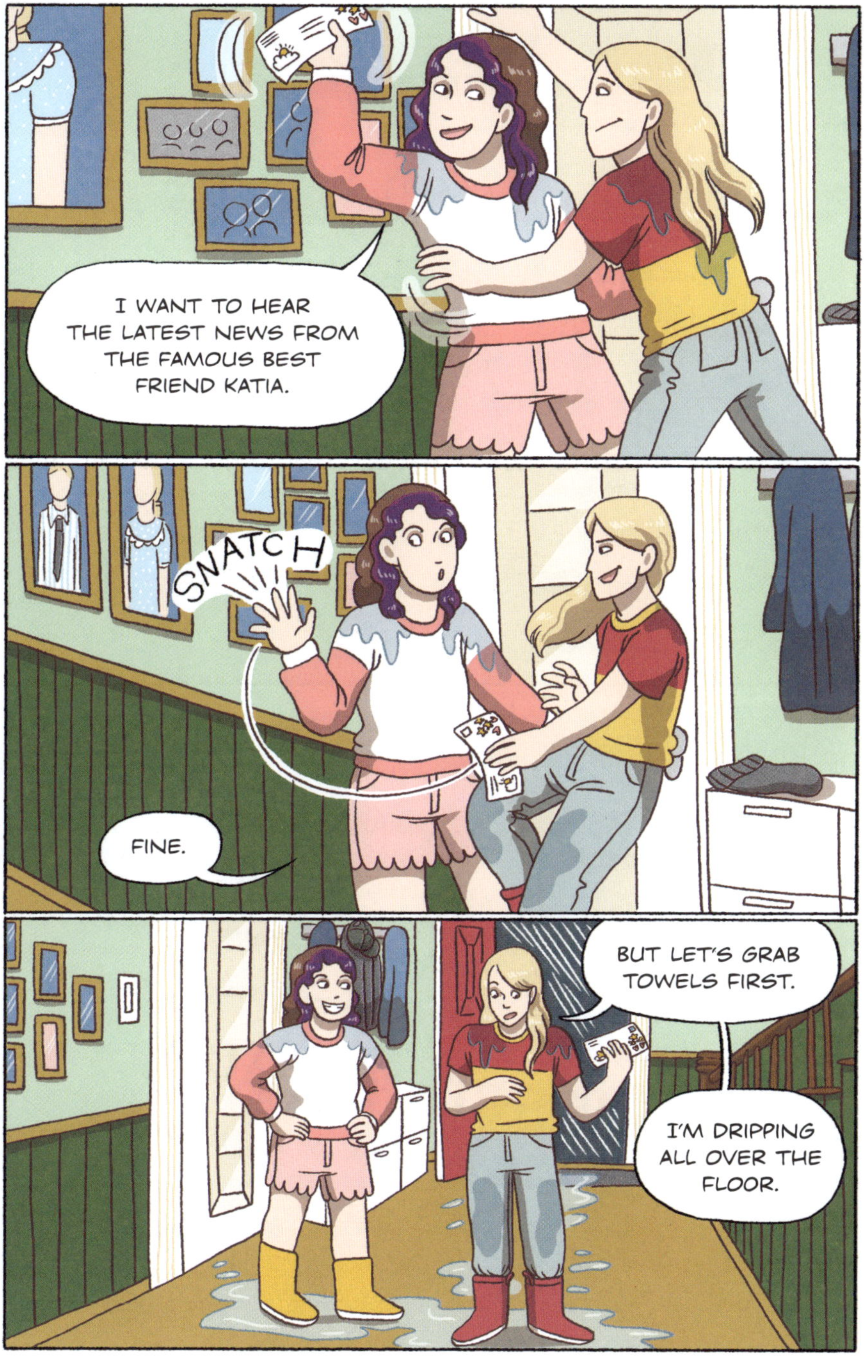
I WANT TO HEAR THE LATEST NEWS FROM THE FAMOUS BEST FRIEND KATIA.
SNATCH
FINE.
BUT LET'S GRAB TOWELS FIRST.
I'M DRIPPING ALL OVER THE FLOOR.

"DEAR LUCY..."

Dear Lucy,

IT FINALLY HAPPENED. AAAAAAAAAAAA

Your dear friend Katia is now wiser, and more mature, than when we said goodbye at the beginning of the summer. Will you even recognize me when I come back to Milforth in August?

Lucy, I am a changed woman. For I, Katia St. Claire, have finally

KISSED. A. BOY.

Ok ok ok. Enough drama: let me tell you how it happened.

that the camp usually uses as an indoor
 the month it gets transforme
 excited. All of

There's a big barn that the camp usually uses as an indoor gym, but on the last Friday of the month it gets transformed into a dance hall. I'll admit it: I was kind of excited. All of us girls in the Trillium Cabin got dressed up for the dance. I wore the yellow dress with the daisies on it that you helped me pick out. Beth even helped us with our makeup. We looked sooooo good.

We were all dancing together when the boys from the Oak Cabin showed up. Even though we had a truce, we were kind of expecting trouble.

Callum (who's usually pretty nice when he's not around Mike) came up just as a slow song started. I can't believe I'm even writing this, but: he asked me if I would dance with him!!!!!! I was like, "Is this a prank?" And he was like, "No, for real. I want to dance with you." He was a good dancer (or at least we never stepped on each other's feet). Every time a slow song came on, he'd ask if he could dance with me, and every time I said, "Yes."

At the end of the night, we had to go back to our cabins. Just before I turned to follow Beth down the path toward the Trillium Cabin, Callum asked if I could wait for a second. He held my hand and asked if he could KISS ME.

I nodded,

and he leaned in,

and it HAPPENED.

It was nice. His lips were
ginger ale

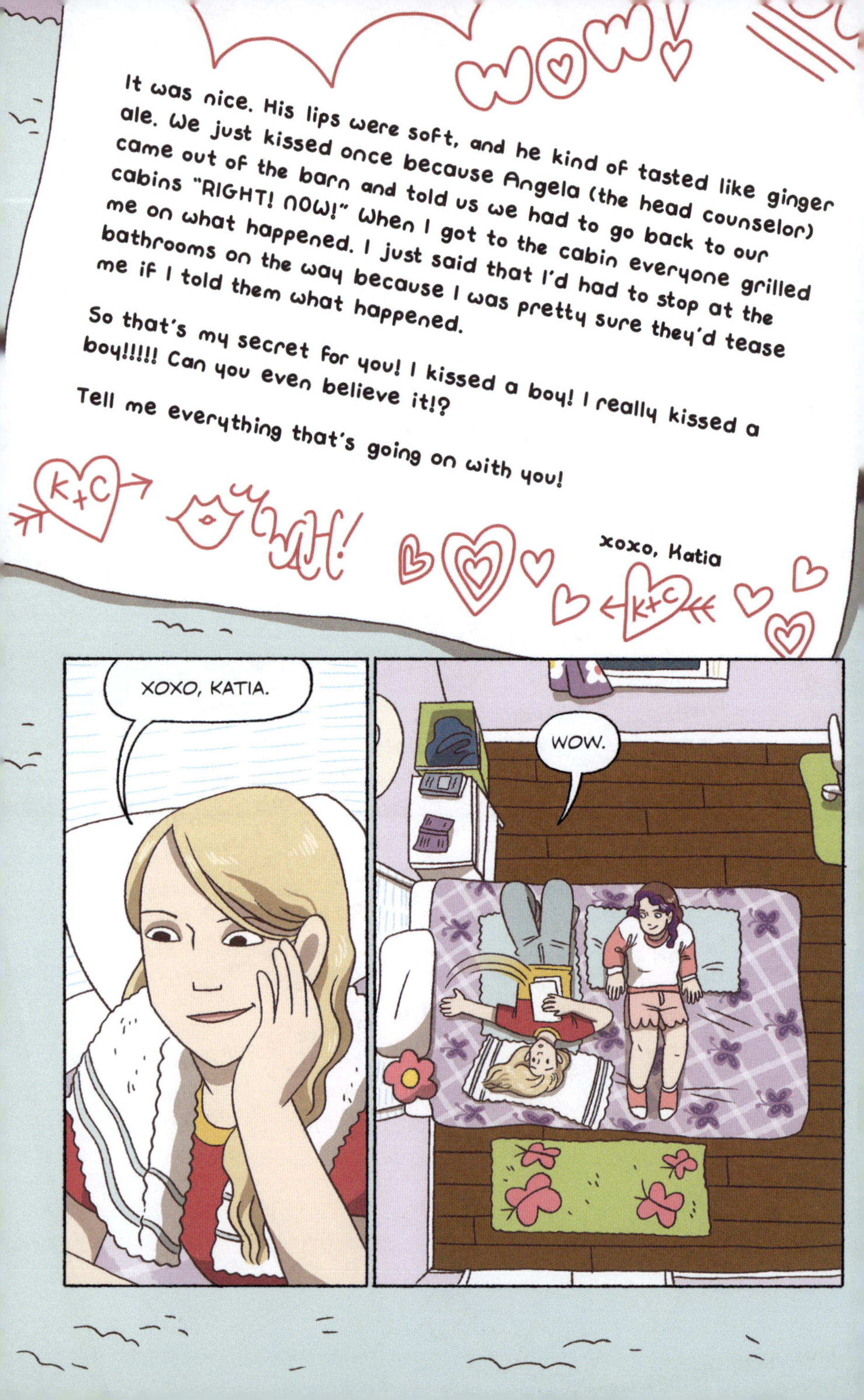

WOW!
It was nice. His lips were soft, and he kind of tasted like ginger ale. We just kissed once because Angela (the head counselor) came out of the barn and told us we had to go back to our cabins "RIGHT! NOW!" When I got to the cabin everyone grilled me on what happened. I just said that I'd had to stop at the bathrooms on the way because I was pretty sure they'd tease me if I told them what happened.
So that's my secret for you! I kissed a boy! I really kissed a boy!!!!! Can you even believe it!?
Tell me everything that's going on with you!
K+C
MWAH!
xoxo, Katia
K+C
XOXO, KATIA.
WOW.

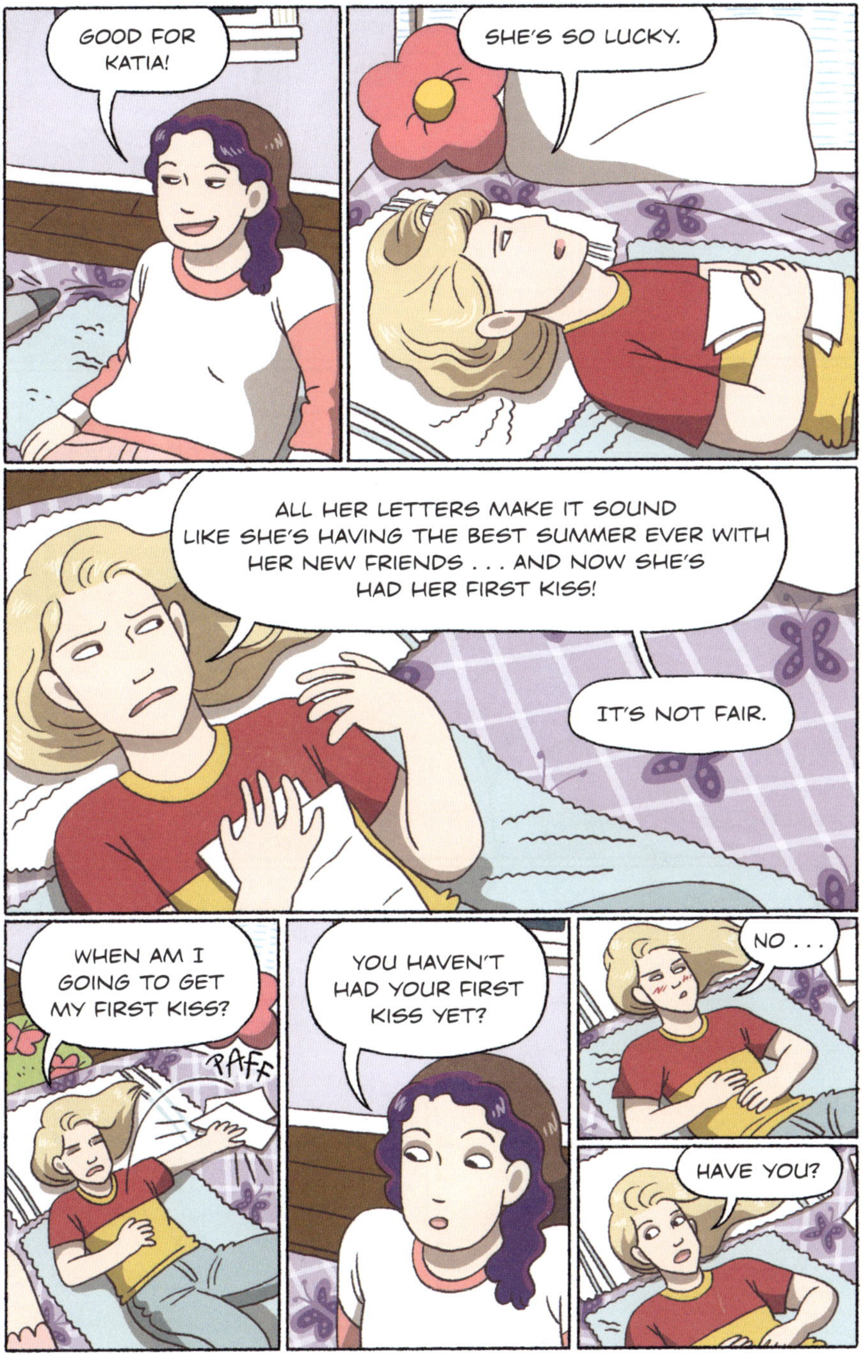
GOOD FOR KATIA!
SHE'S SO LUCKY.
ALL HER LETTERS MAKE IT SOUND LIKE SHE'S HAVING THE BEST SUMMER EVER WITH HER NEW FRIENDS . . . AND NOW SHE'S HAD HER FIRST KISS!
IT'S NOT FAIR.
WHEN AM I GOING TO GET MY FIRST KISS?
PAFF
YOU HAVEN'T HAD YOUR FIRST KISS YET?
NO . . .
HAVE YOU?

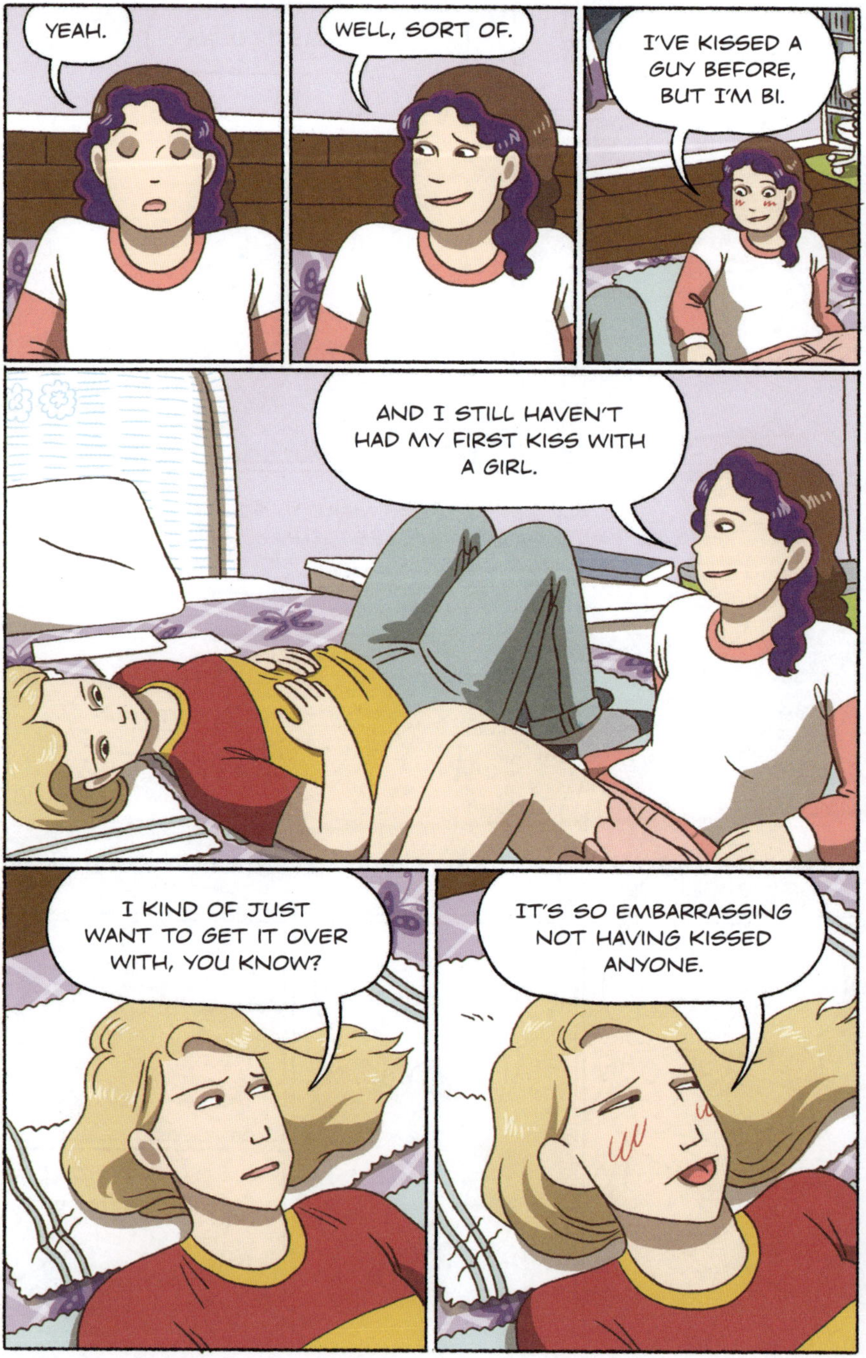
YEAH.
WELL, SORT OF.
I'VE KISSED A GUY BEFORE, BUT I'M BI.
AND I STILL HAVEN'T HAD MY FIRST KISS WITH A GIRL.
I KIND OF JUST WANT TO GET IT OVER WITH, YOU KNOW?
IT'S SO EMBARRASSING NOT HAVING KISSED ANYONE.

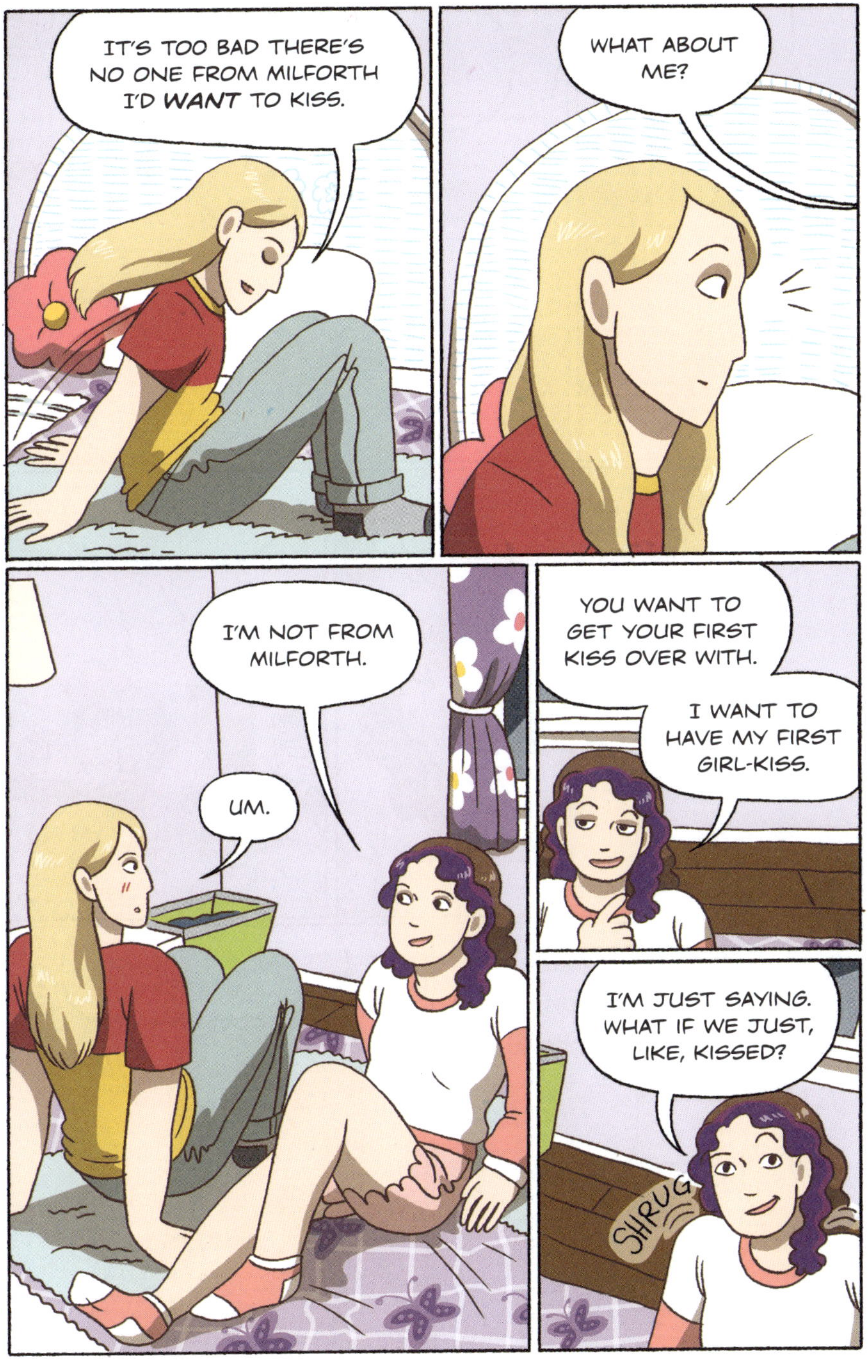
IT'S TOO BAD THERE'S NO ONE FROM MILFORTH I'D **WANT** TO KISS.
WHAT ABOUT ME?
I'M NOT FROM MILFORTH.
UM.
YOU WANT TO GET YOUR FIRST KISS OVER WITH.
I WANT TO HAVE MY FIRST GIRL-KISS.
I'M JUST SAYING. WHAT IF WE JUST, LIKE, KISSED?
SHRUG

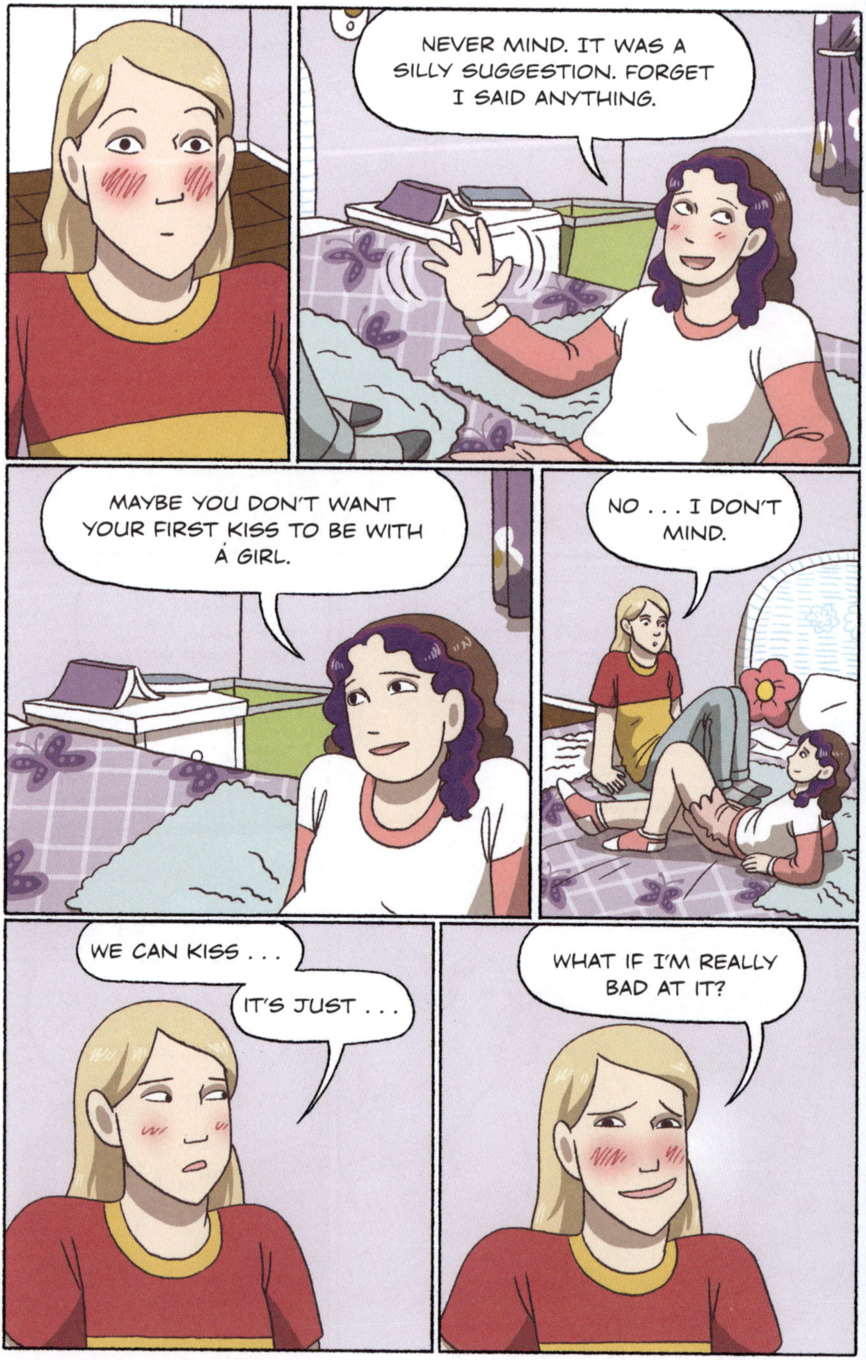
NEVER MIND. IT WAS A SILLY SUGGESTION. FORGET I SAID ANYTHING.
MAYBE YOU DON'T WANT YOUR FIRST KISS TO BE WITH A GIRL.
NO . . . I DON'T MIND.
WE CAN KISS . . .
IT'S JUST . . .
WHAT IF I'M REALLY BAD AT IT?

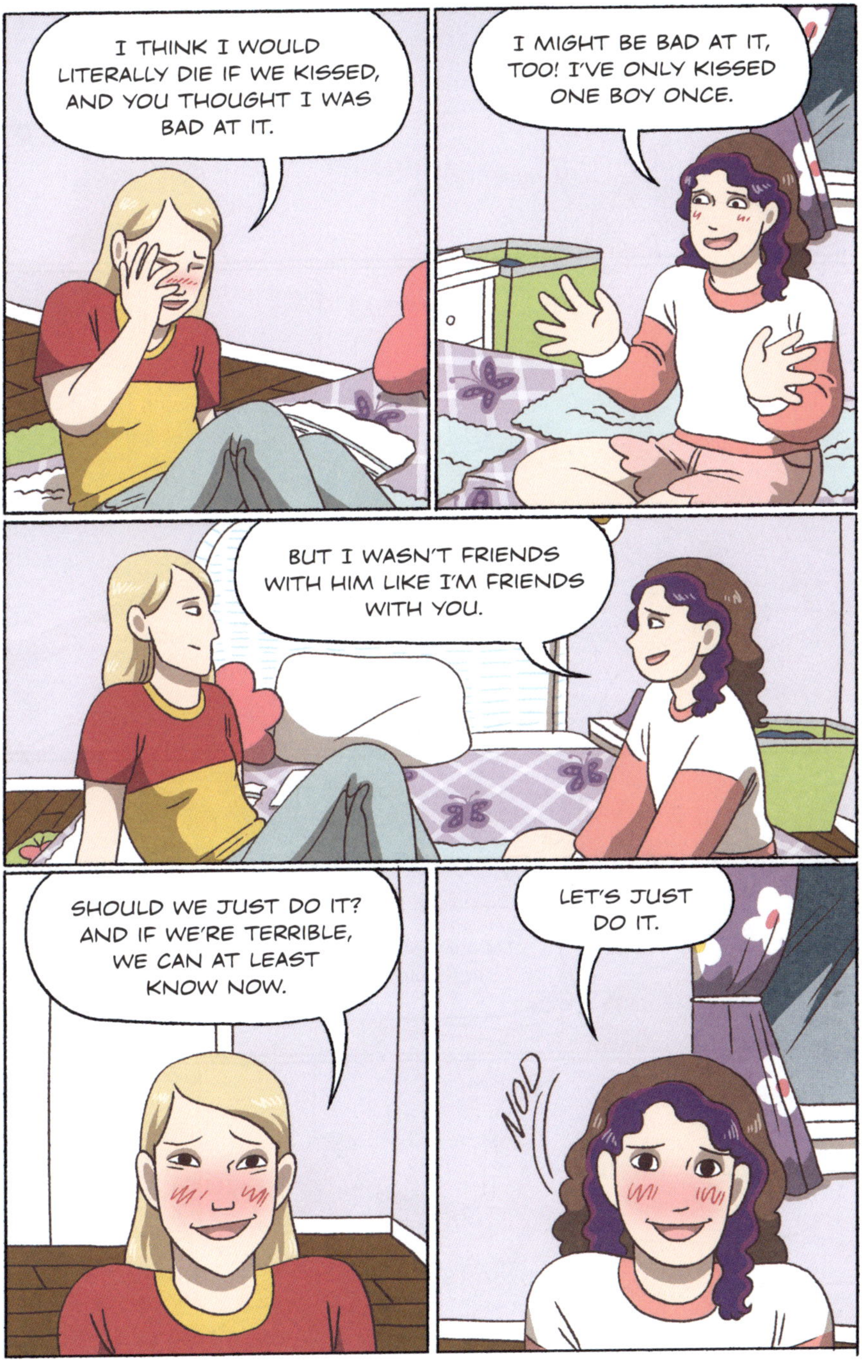
I THINK I WOULD LITERALLY DIE IF WE KISSED, AND YOU THOUGHT I WAS BAD AT IT.
I MIGHT BE BAD AT IT, TOO! I'VE ONLY KISSED ONE BOY ONCE.
BUT I WASN'T FRIENDS WITH HIM LIKE I'M FRIENDS WITH YOU.
SHOULD WE JUST DO IT? AND IF WE'RE TERRIBLE, WE CAN AT LEAST KNOW NOW.
LET'S JUST DO IT.
NOD

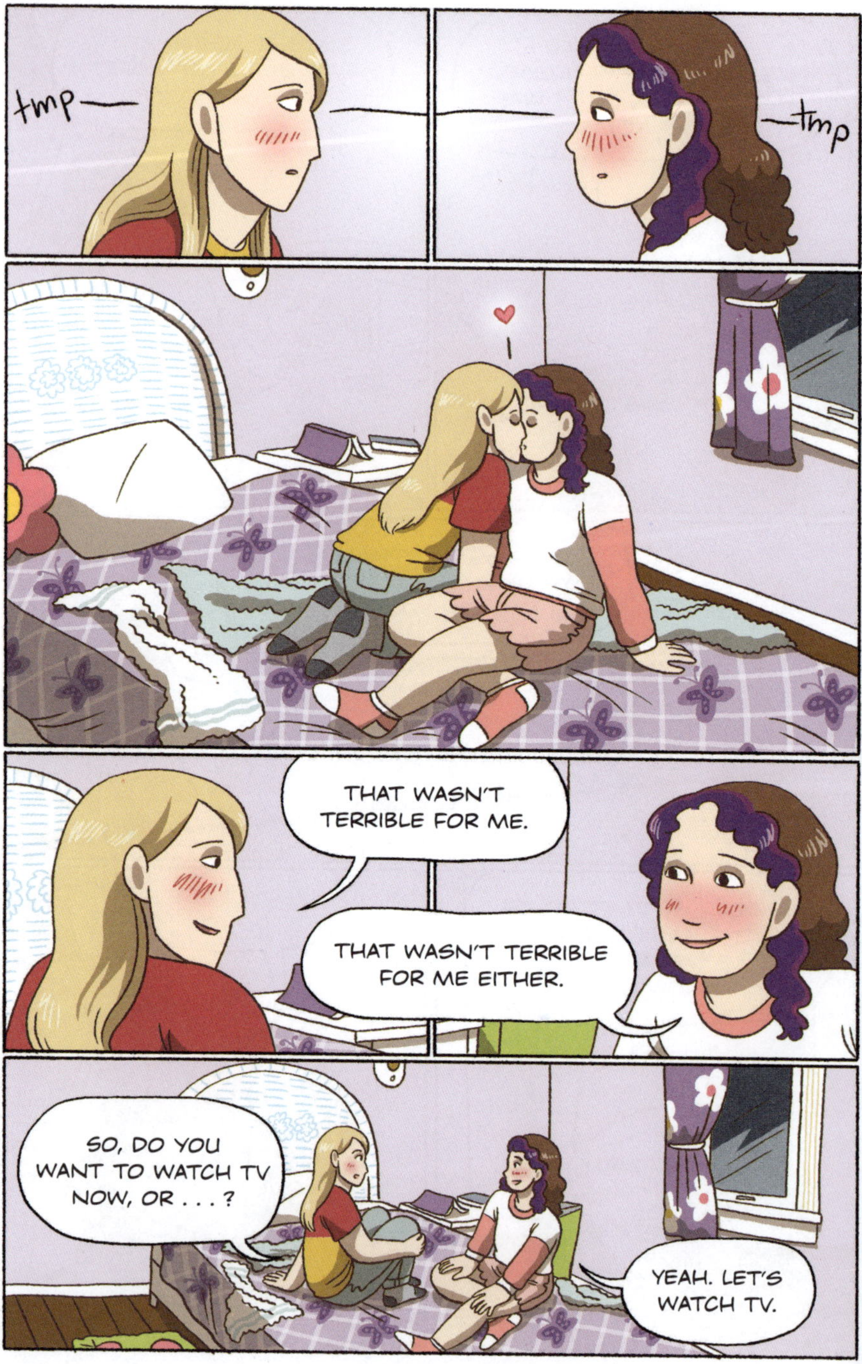
tmp—
—tmp
THAT WASN'T TERRIBLE FOR ME.
THAT WASN'T TERRIBLE FOR ME EITHER.
SO, DO YOU WANT TO WATCH TV NOW, OR . . . ?
YEAH. LET'S WATCH TV.

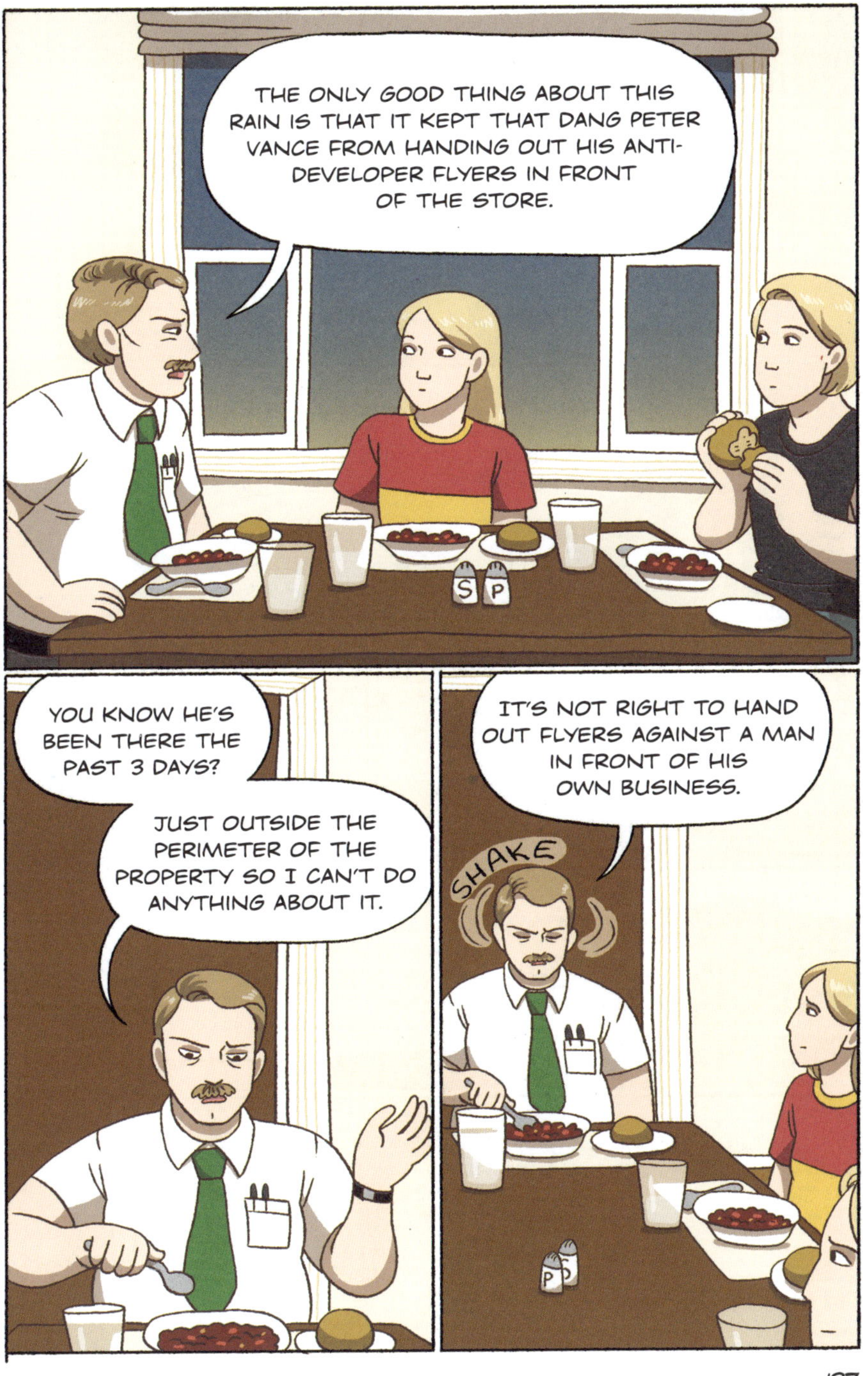
THE ONLY GOOD THING ABOUT THIS RAIN IS THAT IT KEPT THAT DANG PETER VANCE FROM HANDING OUT HIS ANTI-DEVELOPER FLYERS IN FRONT OF THE STORE.
YOU KNOW HE'S BEEN THERE THE PAST 3 DAYS?
JUST OUTSIDE THE PERIMETER OF THE PROPERTY SO I CAN'T DO ANYTHING ABOUT IT.
SHAKE
IT'S NOT RIGHT TO HAND OUT FLYERS AGAINST A MAN IN FRONT OF HIS OWN BUSINESS.

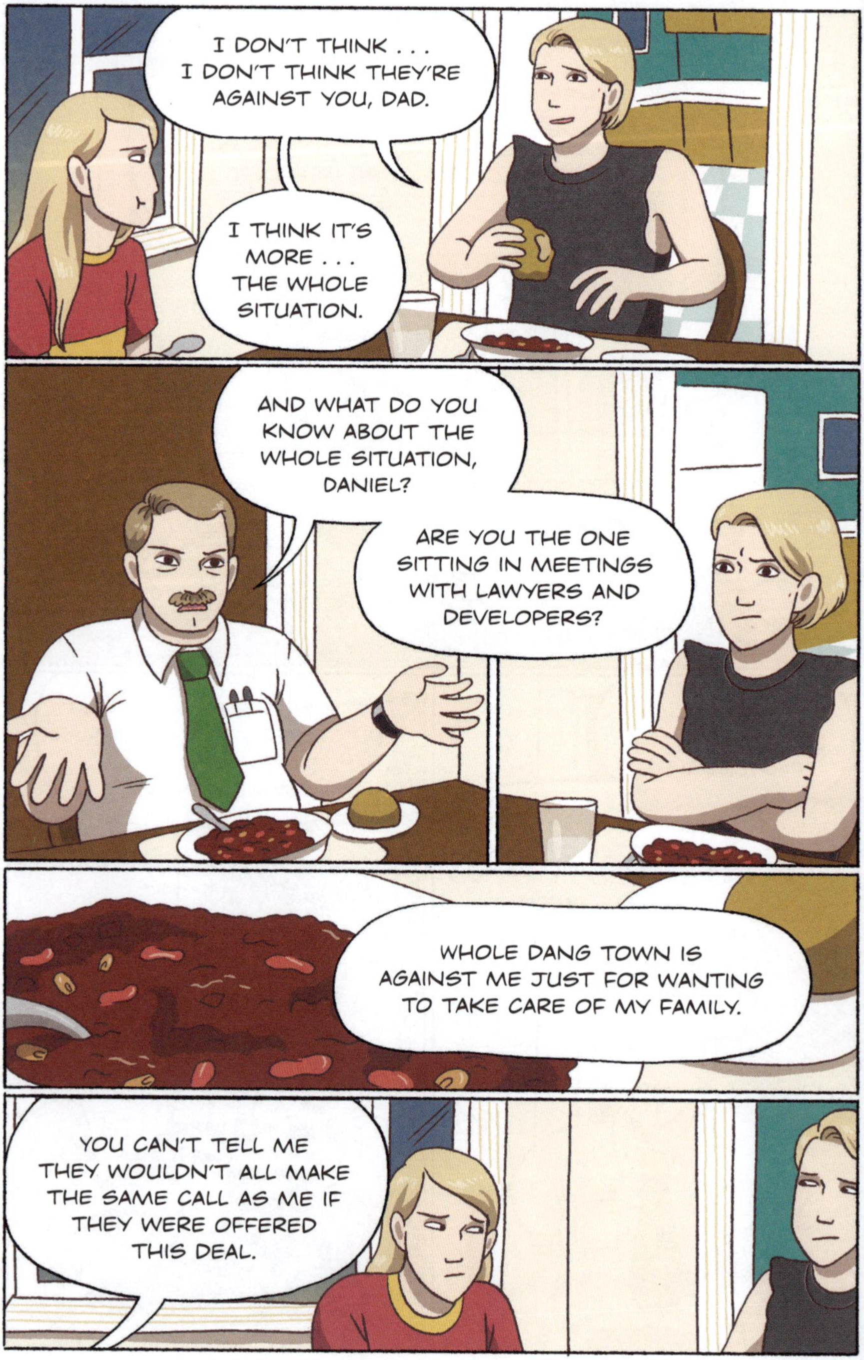
I DON'T THINK . . . I DON'T THINK THEY'RE AGAINST YOU, DAD.
I THINK IT'S MORE . . . THE WHOLE SITUATION.
AND WHAT DO YOU KNOW ABOUT THE WHOLE SITUATION, DANIEL?
ARE YOU THE ONE SITTING IN MEETINGS WITH LAWYERS AND DEVELOPERS?
WHOLE DANG TOWN IS AGAINST ME JUST FOR WANTING TO TAKE CARE OF MY FAMILY.
YOU CAN'T TELL ME THEY WOULDN'T ALL MAKE THE SAME CALL AS ME IF THEY WERE OFFERED THIS DEAL.

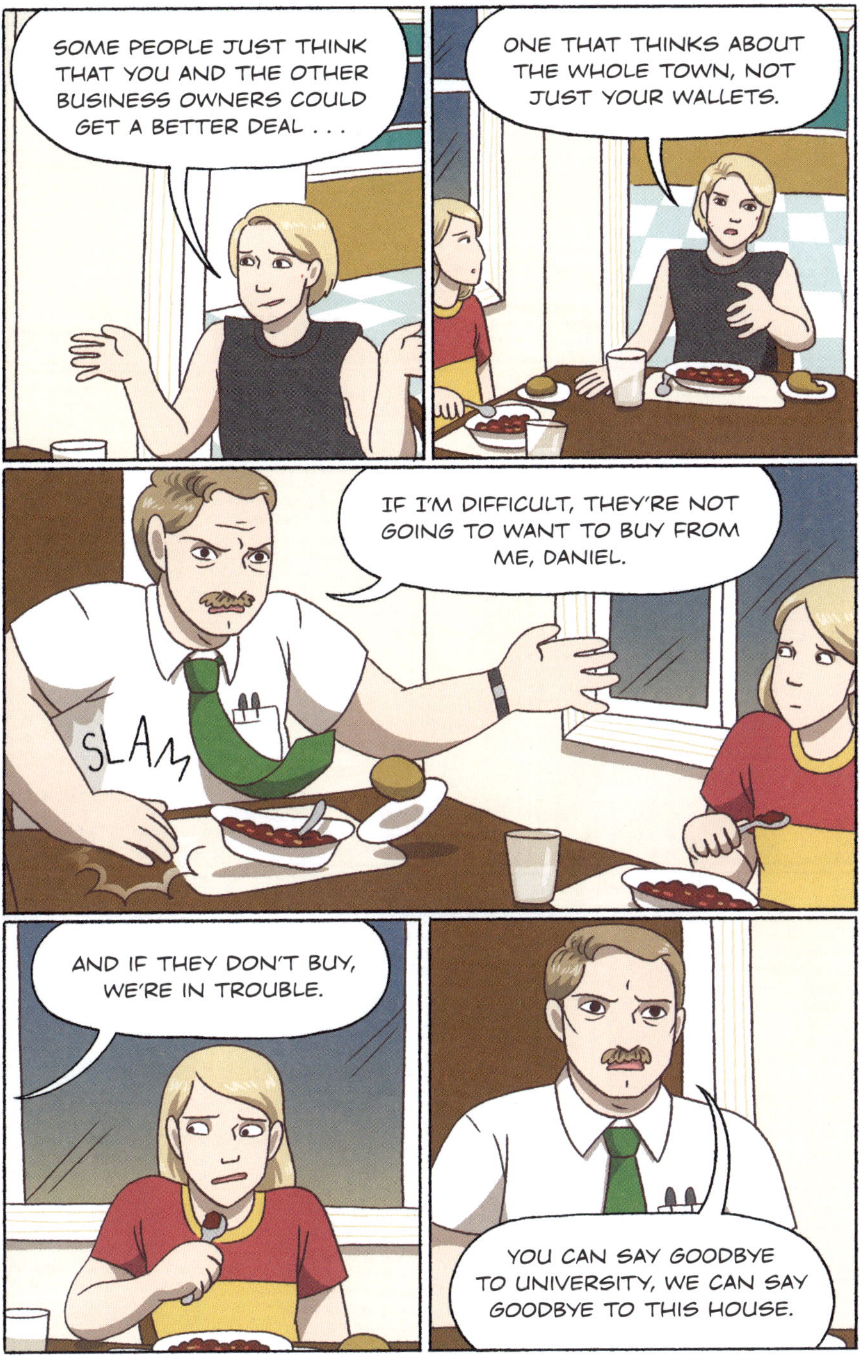
SOME PEOPLE JUST THINK THAT YOU AND THE OTHER BUSINESS OWNERS COULD GET A BETTER DEAL . . .
ONE THAT THINKS ABOUT THE WHOLE TOWN, NOT JUST YOUR WALLETS.
IF I'M DIFFICULT, THEY'RE NOT GOING TO WANT TO BUY FROM ME, DANIEL.
SLAM
AND IF THEY DON'T BUY, WE'RE IN TROUBLE.
YOU CAN SAY GOODBYE TO UNIVERSITY, WE CAN SAY GOODBYE TO THIS HOUSE.

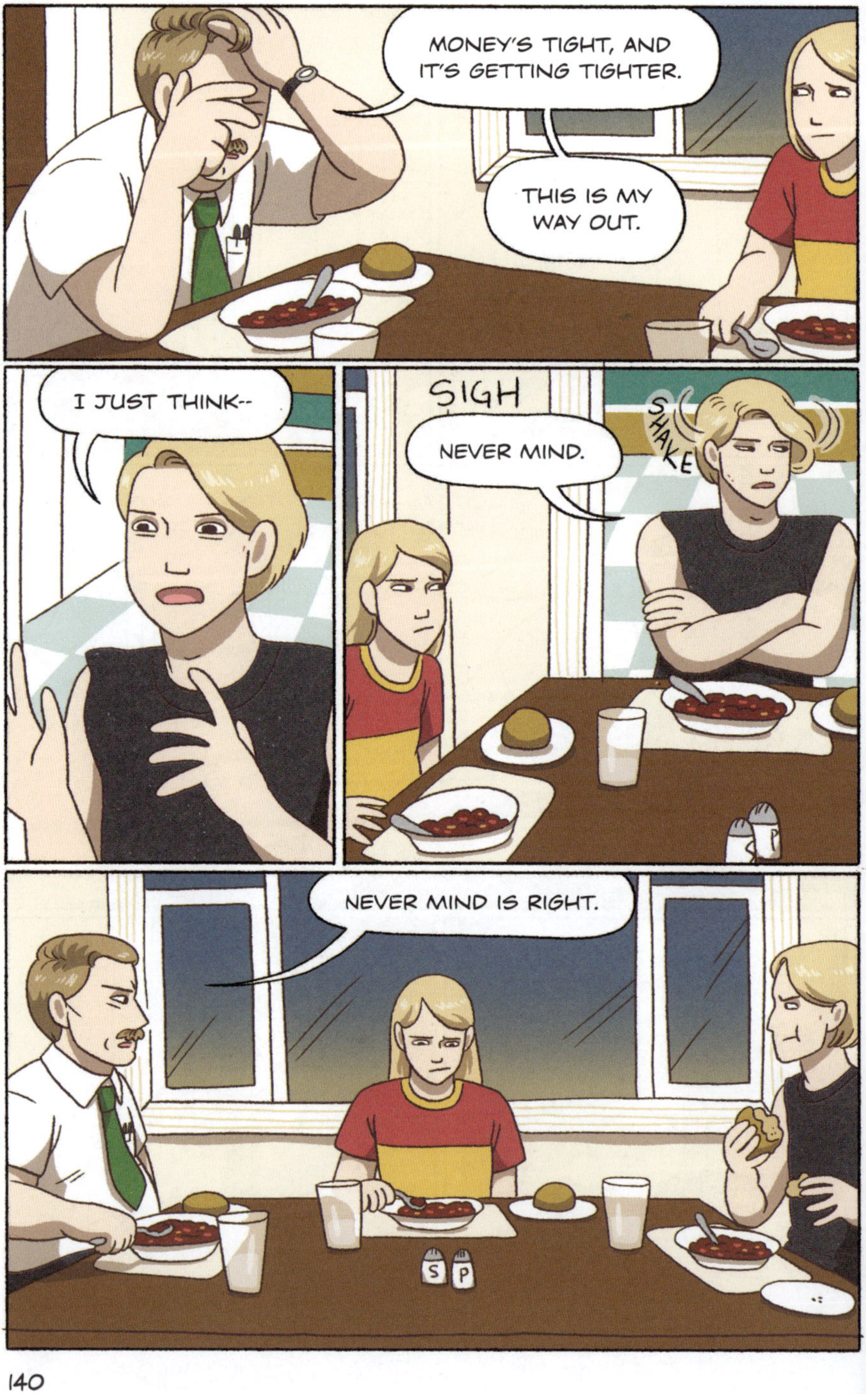
MONEY'S TIGHT, AND IT'S GETTING TIGHTER.
THIS IS MY WAY OUT.
I JUST THINK--
SIGH
NEVER MIND.
SHAKE
NEVER MIND IS RIGHT.
S
P

Dear Katia,

That sounds like an amazing night! I can't believe you got your first kiss at camp!

I've been getting to help out a bit with the carousel. Mostly just small stuff. Dad and Daniel are always working.

Love,

Lucy

CHAPTER 4

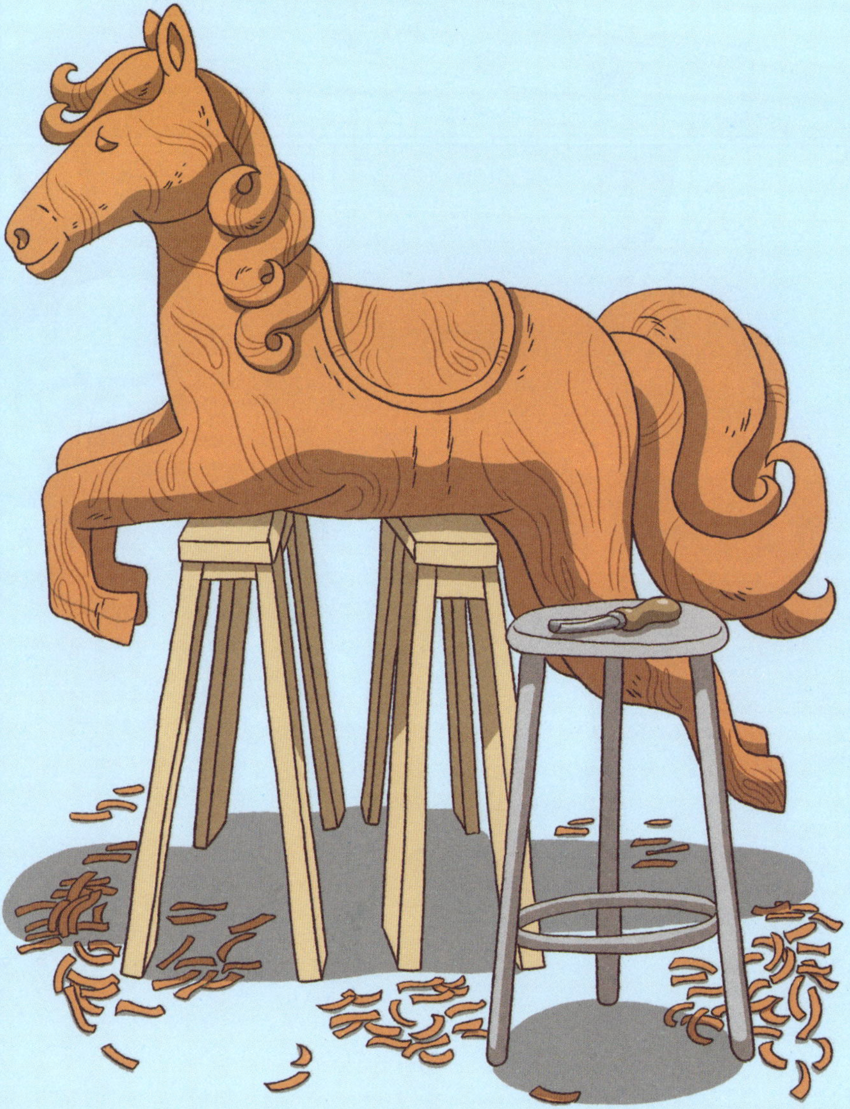

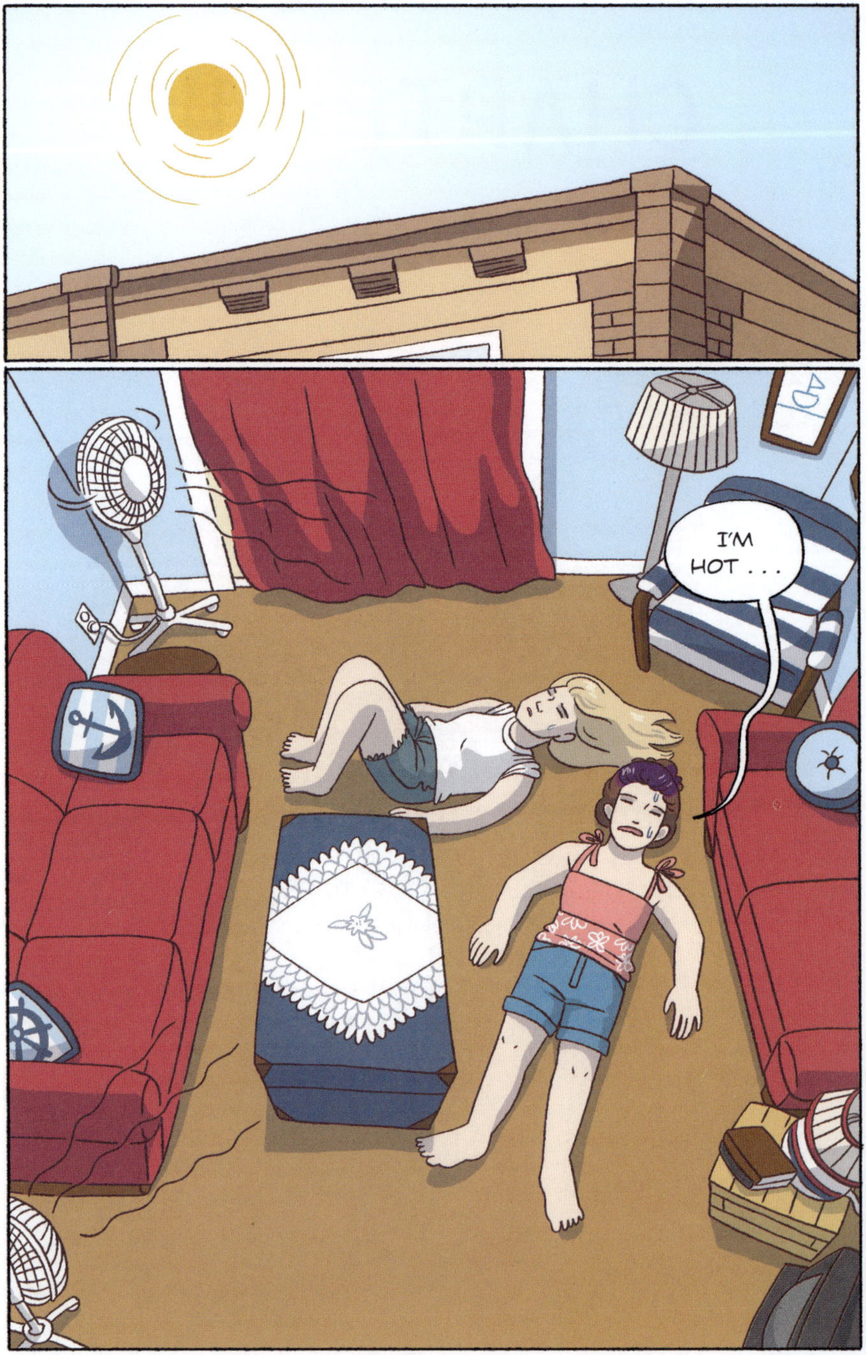
I'M HOT . . .

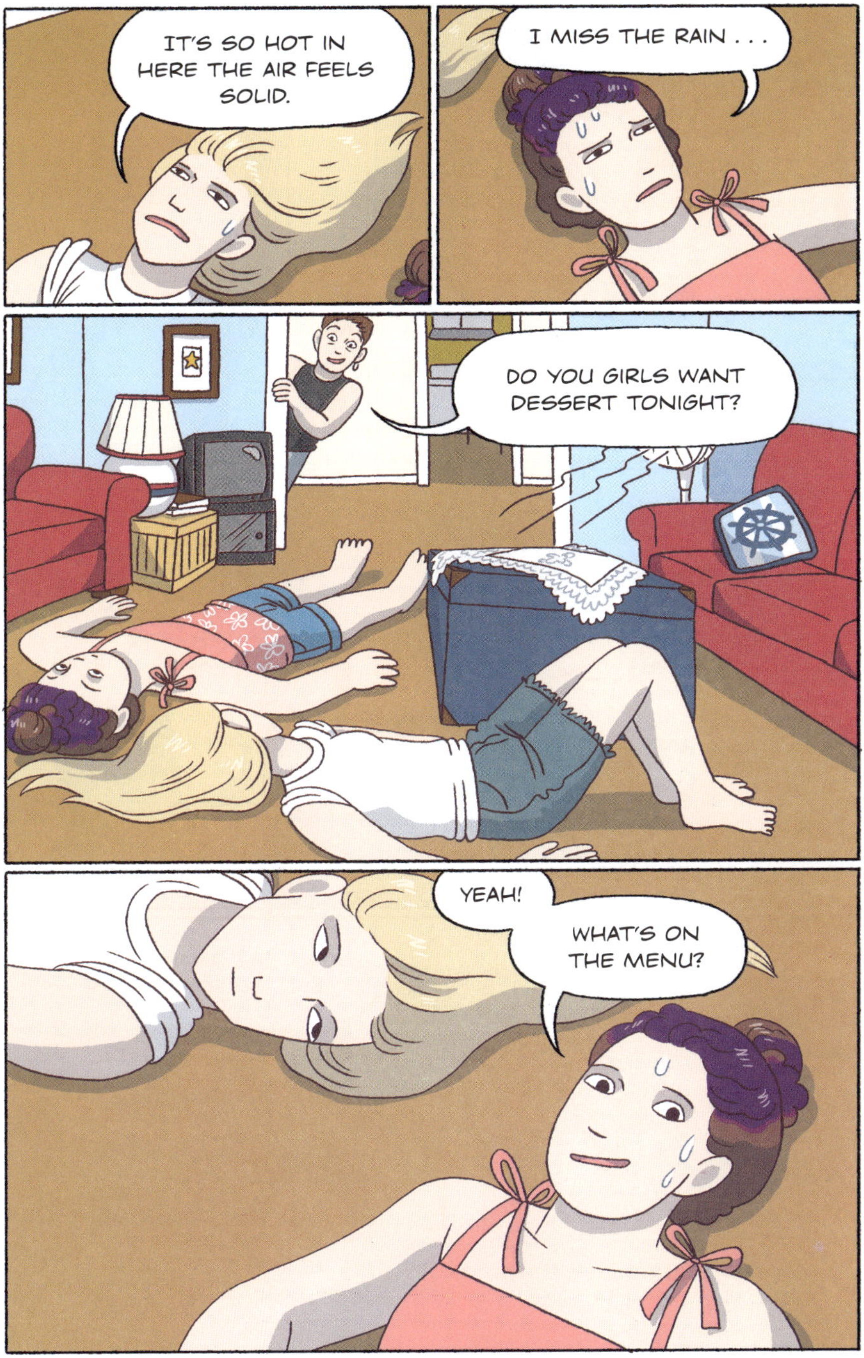

IT'S SO HOT IN HERE THE AIR FEELS SOLID.
I MISS THE RAIN . . .
DO YOU GIRLS WANT DESSERT TONIGHT?
YEAH!
WHAT'S ON THE MENU?

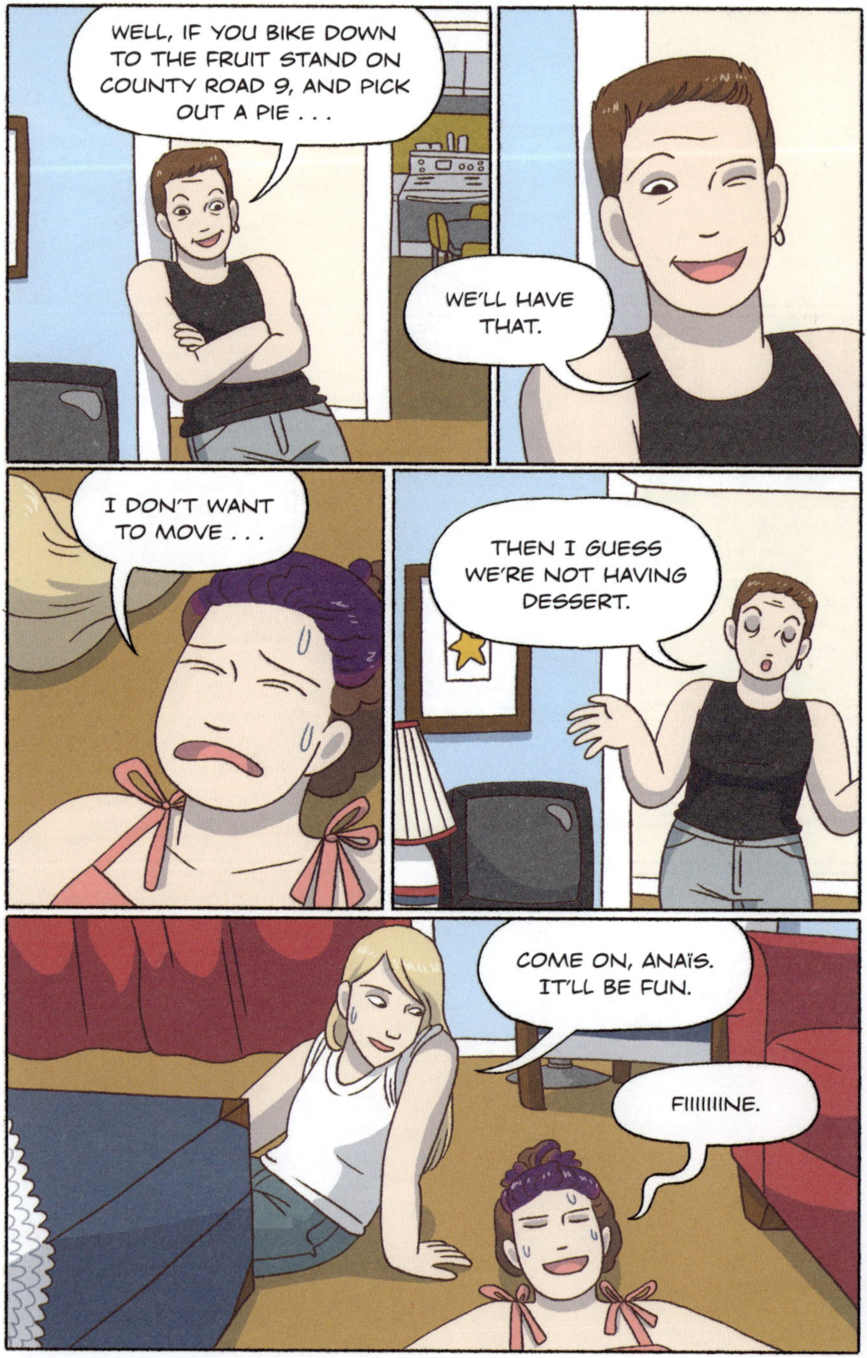
WELL, IF YOU BIKE DOWN TO THE FRUIT STAND ON COUNTY ROAD 9, AND PICK OUT A PIE . . .
WE'LL HAVE THAT.
I DON'T WANT TO MOVE . . .
THEN I GUESS WE'RE NOT HAVING DESSERT.
COME ON, ANAÏS. IT'LL BE FUN.
FIIIIIIINE.

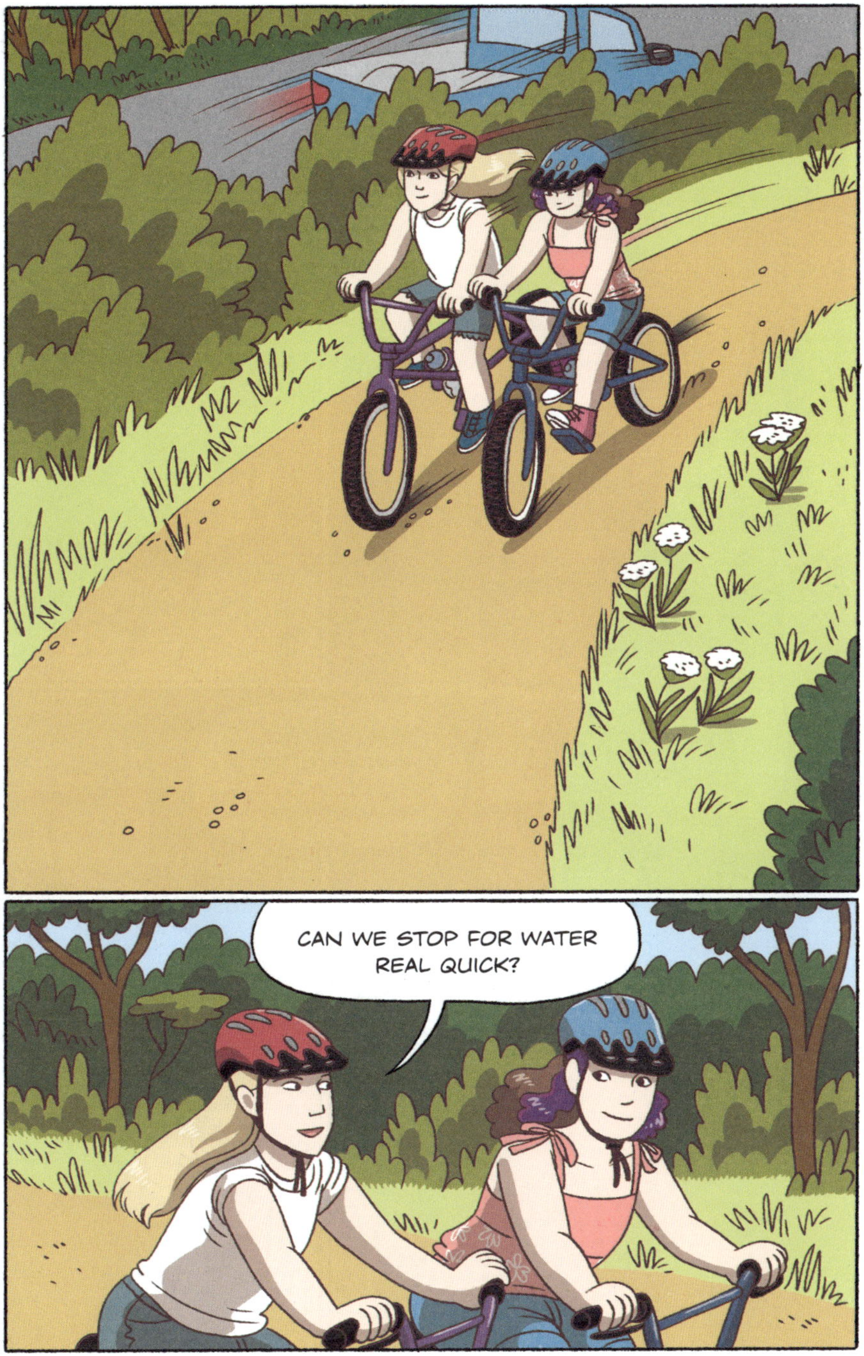
CAN WE STOP FOR WATER REAL QUICK?

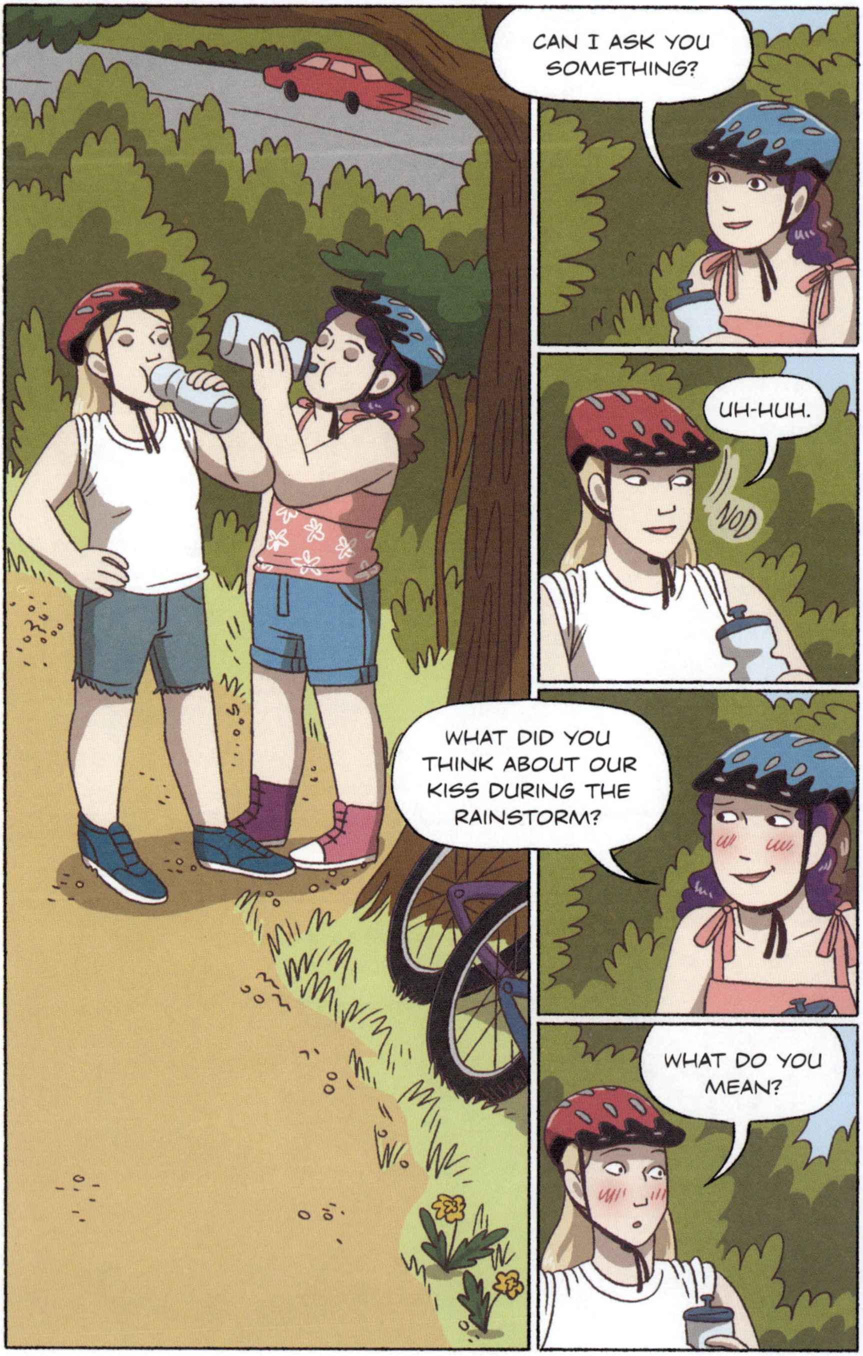
CAN I ASK YOU SOMETHING?
UH-HUH.
NOD
WHAT DID YOU THINK ABOUT OUR KISS DURING THE RAINSTORM?
WHAT DO YOU MEAN?

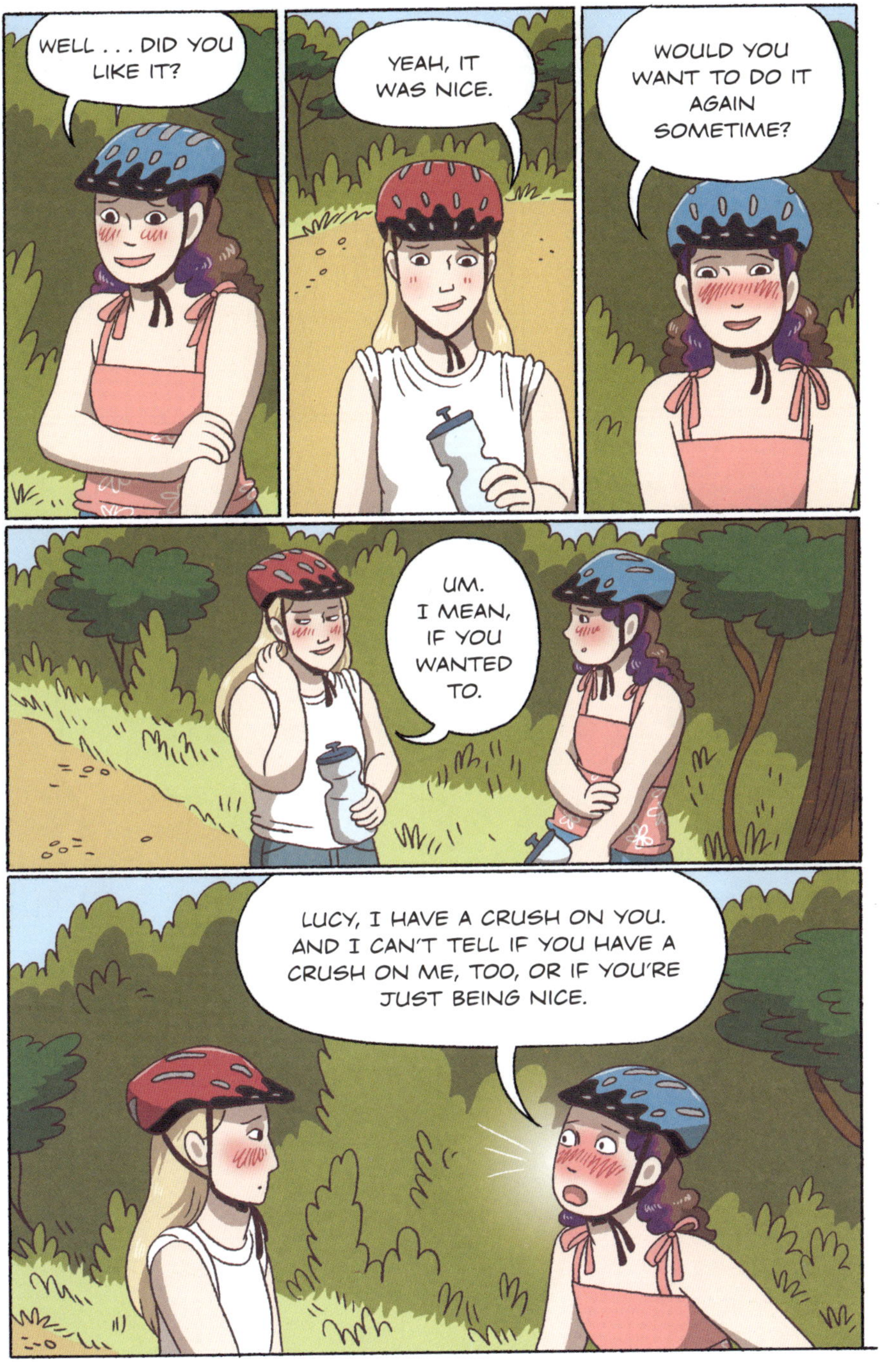
WELL . . . DID YOU LIKE IT?
YEAH, IT WAS NICE.
WOULD YOU WANT TO DO IT AGAIN SOMETIME?
UM. I MEAN, IF YOU WANTED TO.
LUCY, I HAVE A CRUSH ON YOU. AND I CAN'T TELL IF YOU HAVE A CRUSH ON ME, TOO, OR IF YOU'RE JUST BEING NICE.

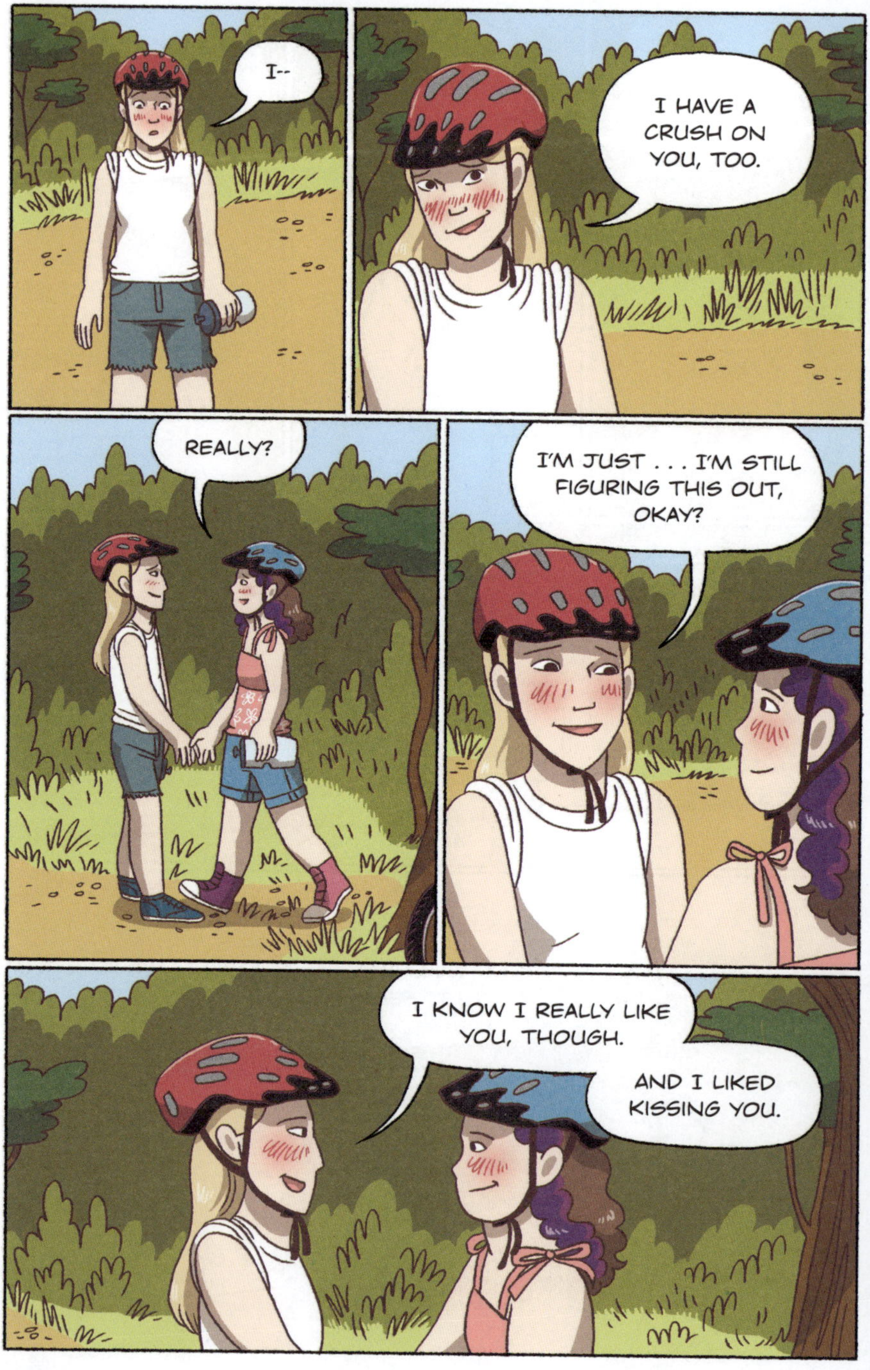
I--
I HAVE A CRUSH ON YOU, TOO.
REALLY?
I'M JUST . . . I'M STILL FIGURING THIS OUT, OKAY?
I KNOW I REALLY LIKE YOU, THOUGH.
AND I LIKED KISSING YOU.

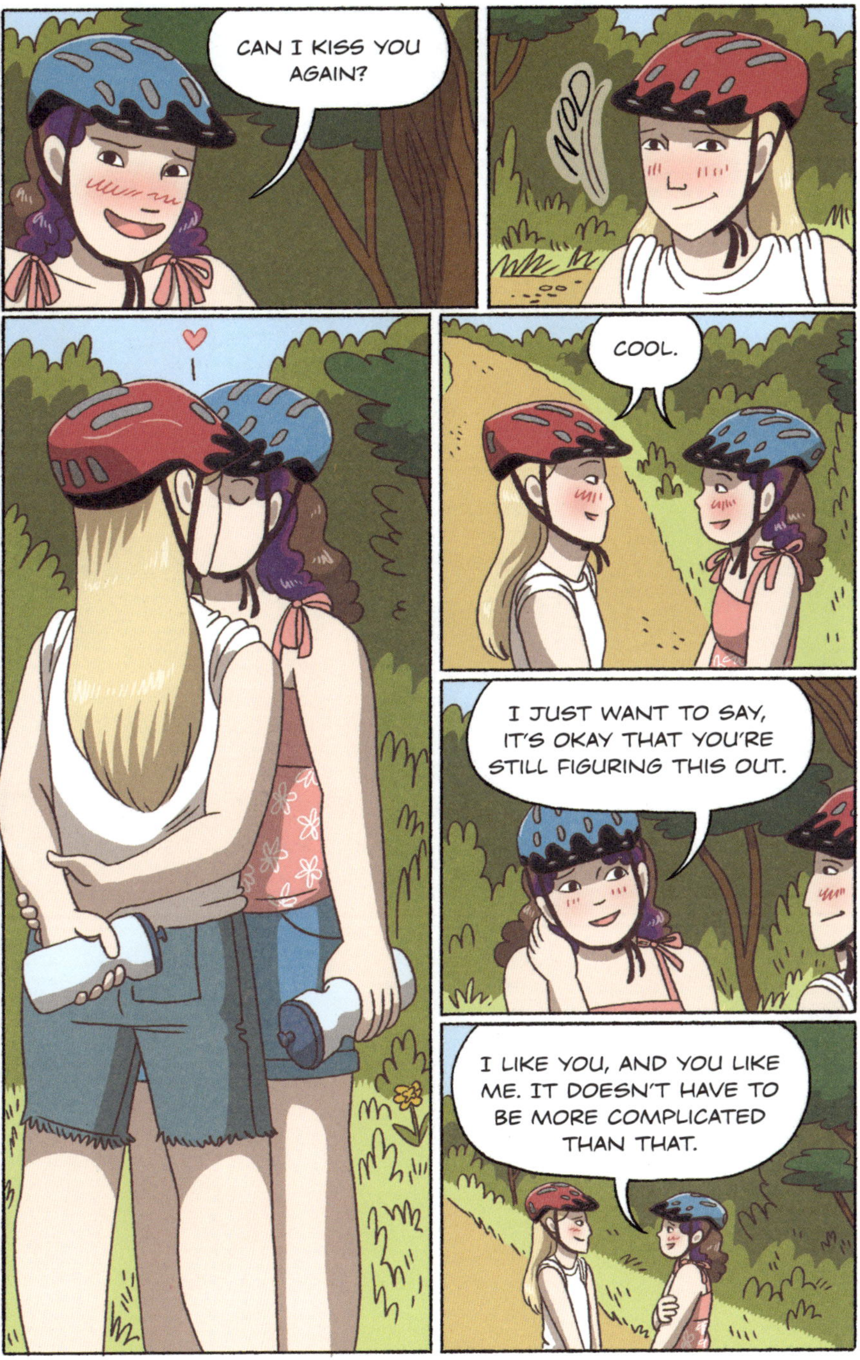
CAN I KISS YOU AGAIN?
NOD
COOL.
I JUST WANT TO SAY, IT'S OKAY THAT YOU'RE STILL FIGURING THIS OUT.
I LIKE YOU, AND YOU LIKE ME. IT DOESN'T HAVE TO BE MORE COMPLICATED THAN THAT.

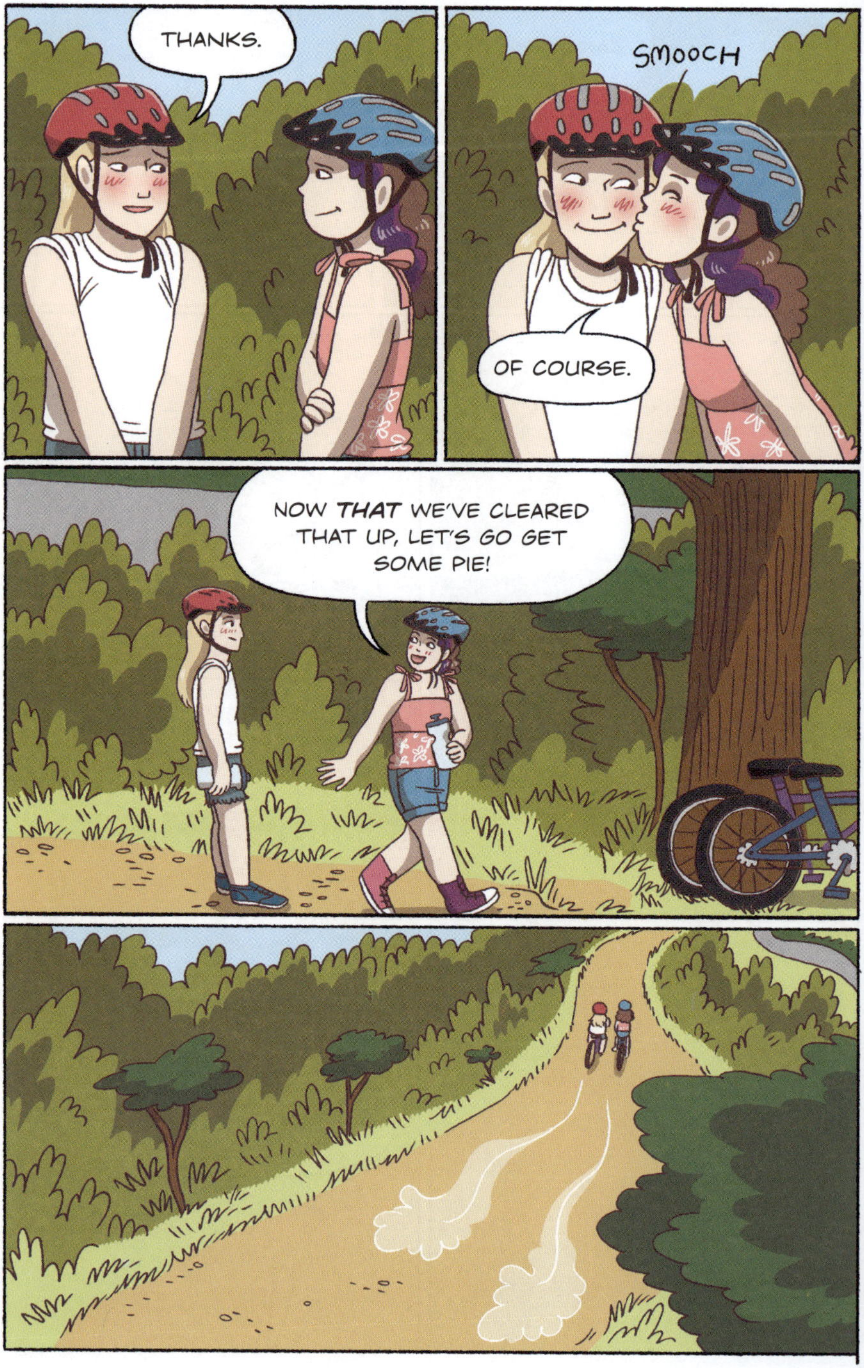
THANKS.
SMOOCH
OF COURSE.
NOW *THAT* WE'VE CLEARED THAT UP, LET'S GO GET SOME PIE!

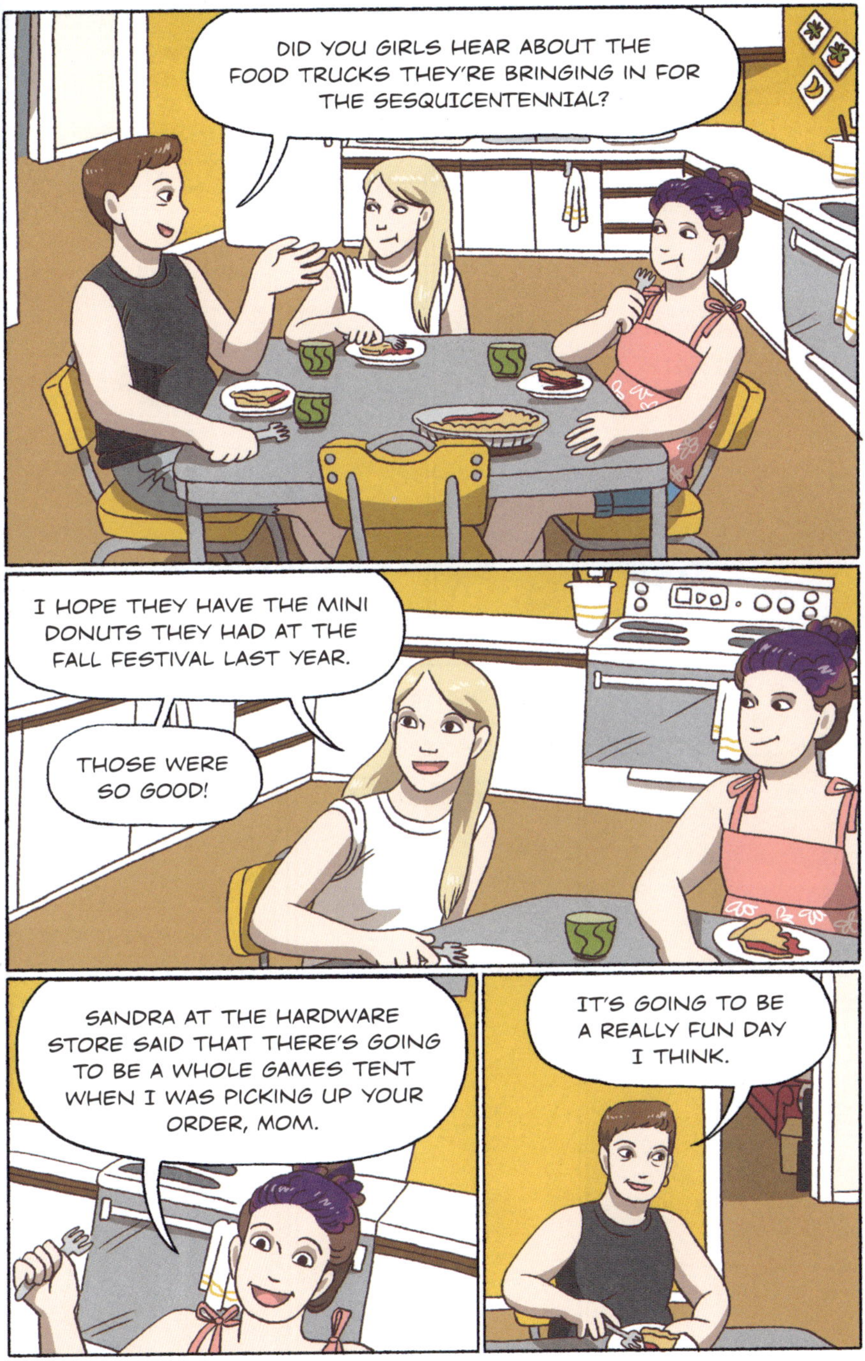
DID YOU GIRLS HEAR ABOUT THE FOOD TRUCKS THEY'RE BRINGING IN FOR THE SESQUICENTENNIAL?
I HOPE THEY HAVE THE MINI DONUTS THEY HAD AT THE FALL FESTIVAL LAST YEAR.
THOSE WERE SO GOOD!
SANDRA AT THE HARDWARE STORE SAID THAT THERE'S GOING TO BE A WHOLE GAMES TENT WHEN I WAS PICKING UP YOUR ORDER, MOM.
IT'S GOING TO BE A REALLY FUN DAY I THINK.

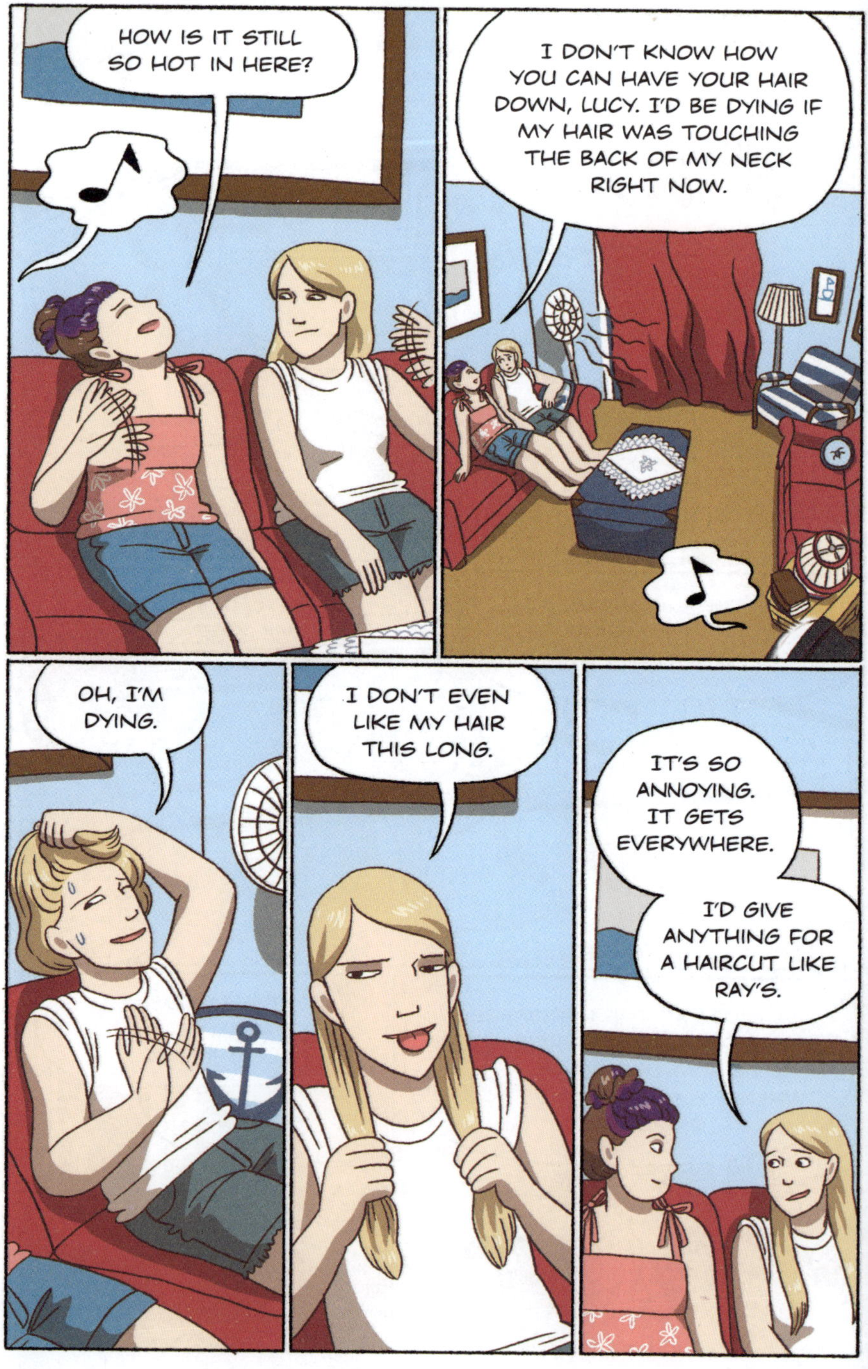
HOW IS IT STILL SO HOT IN HERE?
I DON'T KNOW HOW YOU CAN HAVE YOUR HAIR DOWN, LUCY. I'D BE DYING IF MY HAIR WAS TOUCHING THE BACK OF MY NECK RIGHT NOW.
OH, I'M DYING.
I DON'T EVEN LIKE MY HAIR THIS LONG.
IT'S SO ANNOYING. IT GETS EVERYWHERE.
I'D GIVE ANYTHING FOR A HAIRCUT LIKE RAY'S.

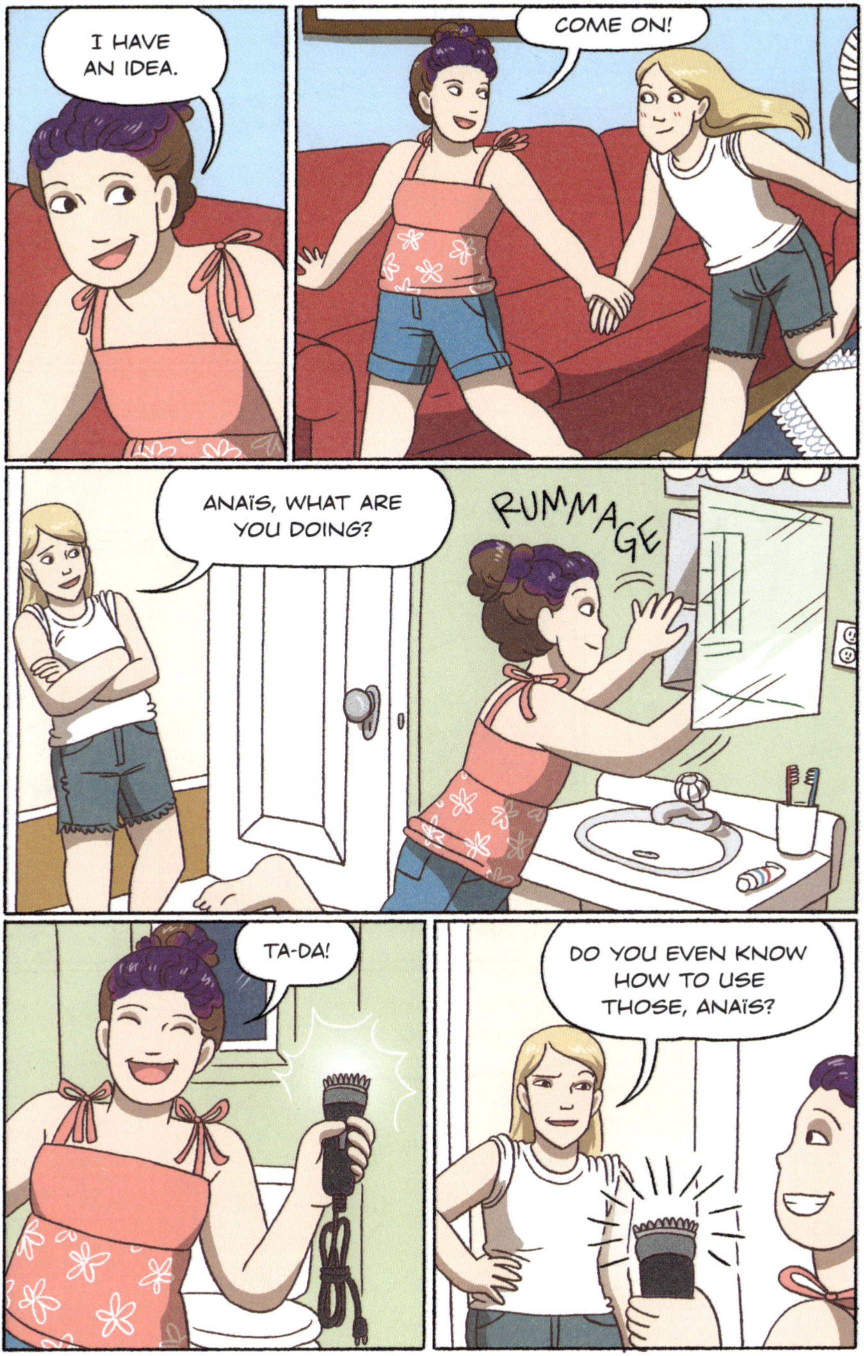
I HAVE AN IDEA.
COME ON!
ANAÏS, WHAT ARE YOU DOING?
RUMMAGE
TA-DA!
DO YOU EVEN KNOW HOW TO USE THOSE, ANAÏS?

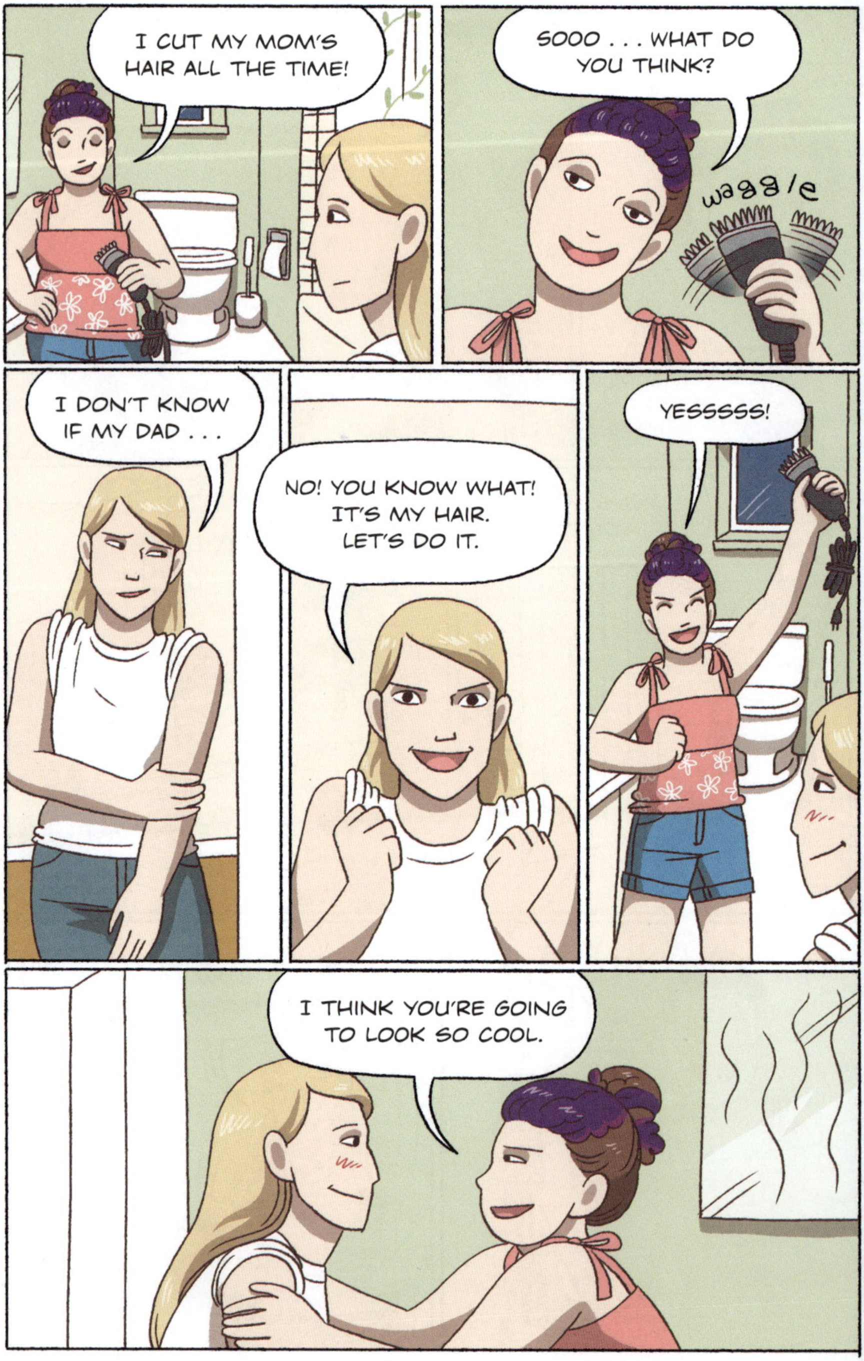
I CUT MY MOM'S HAIR ALL THE TIME!
SOOO . . . WHAT DO YOU THINK?
waggle
I DON'T KNOW IF MY DAD . . .
NO! YOU KNOW WHAT! IT'S MY HAIR. LET'S DO IT.
YESSSSS!
I THINK YOU'RE GOING TO LOOK SO COOL.

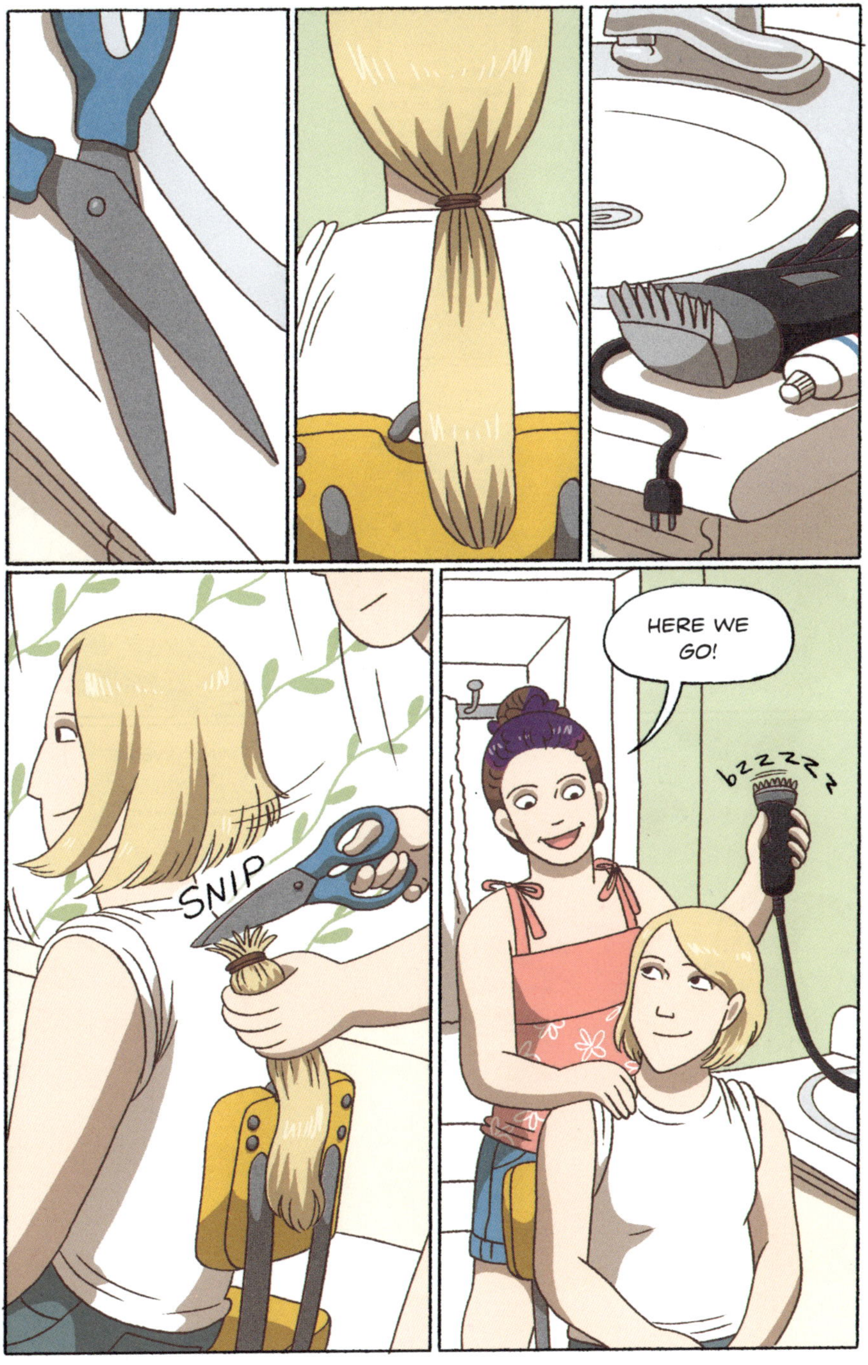
SNIP
HERE WE GO!
bzzzzzz

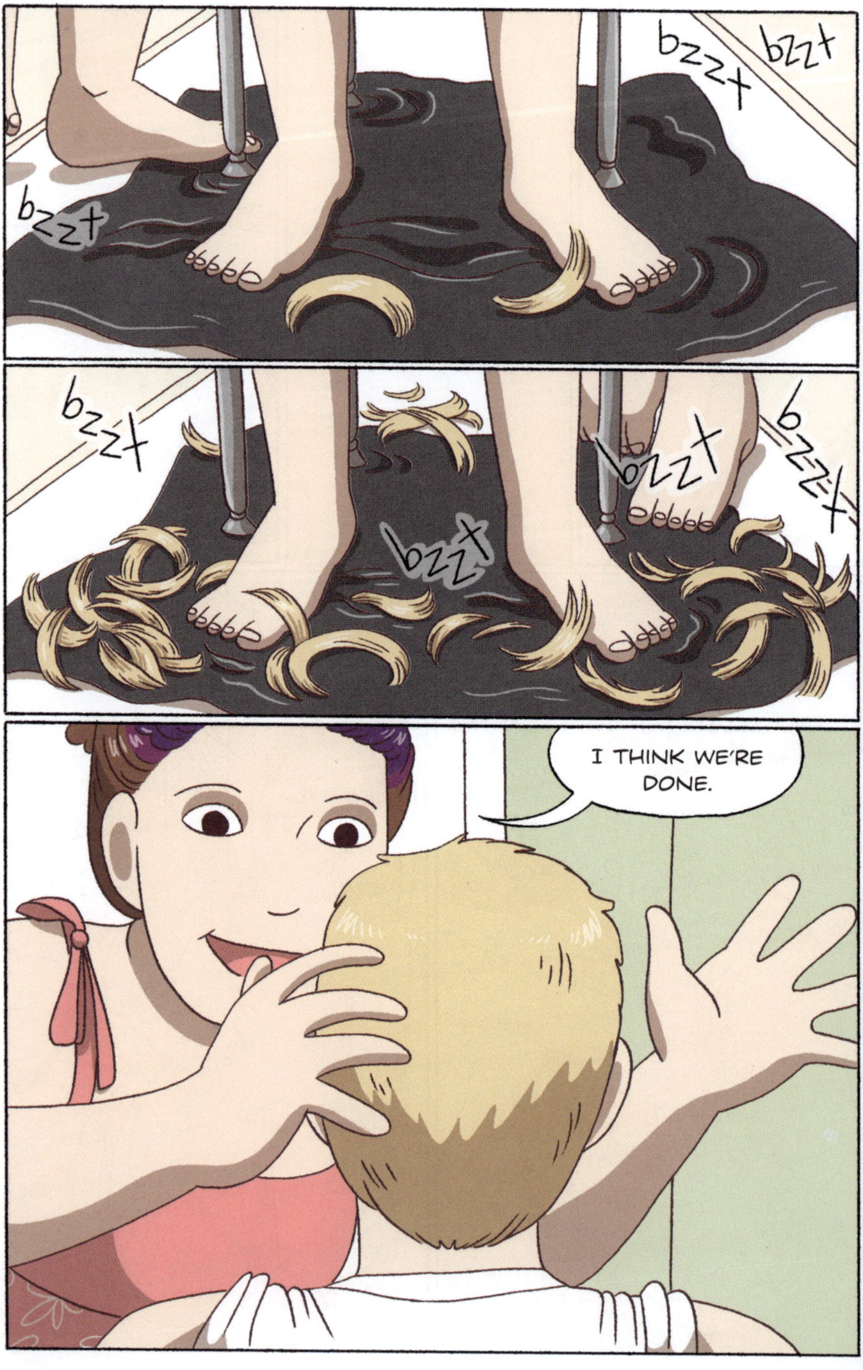
bzzt
bzzt
bzzt
bzzt
bzzt
bzzt
bzzt
I THINK WE'RE DONE.

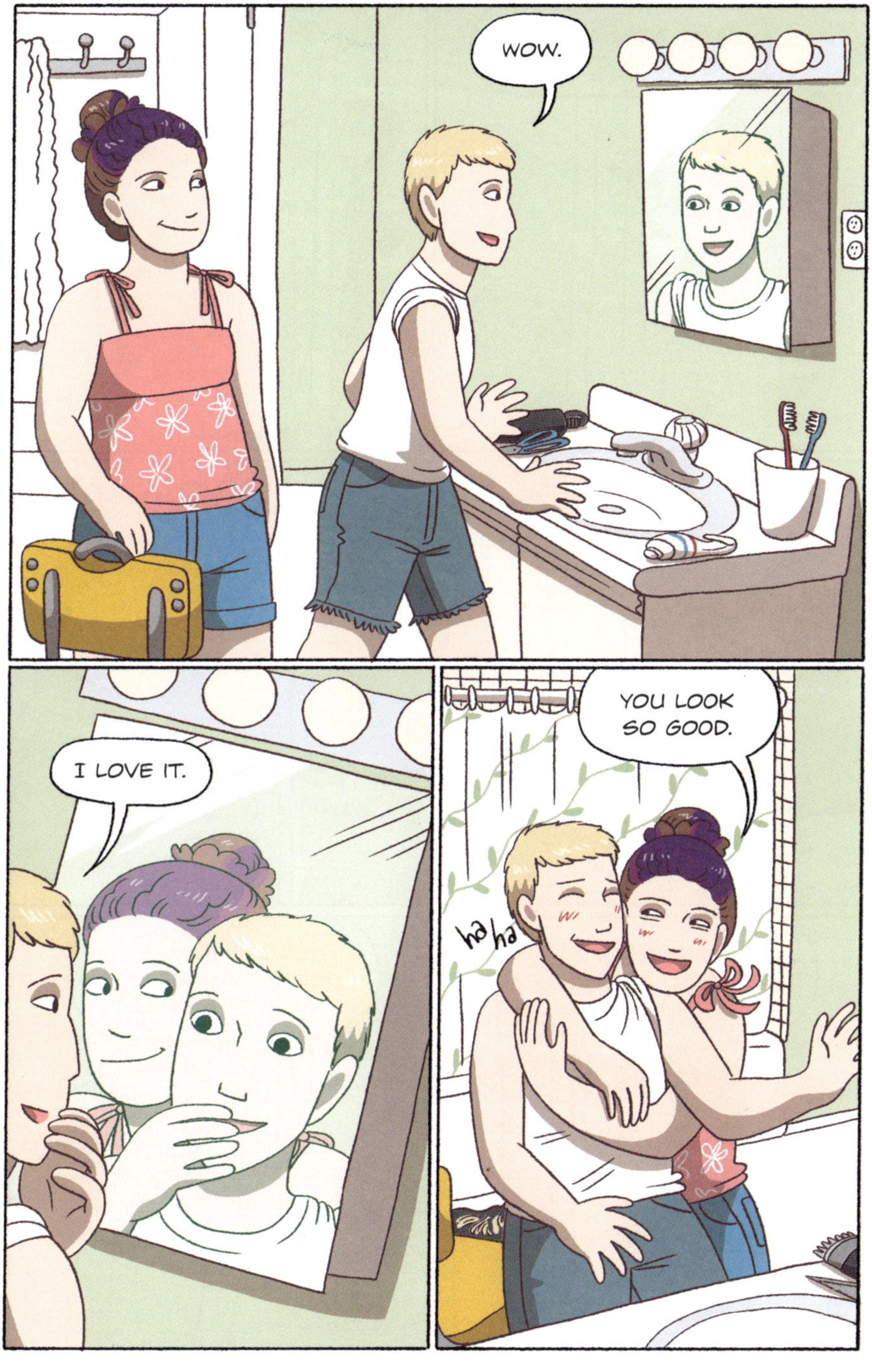
WOW.
I LOVE IT.
YOU LOOK SO GOOD.
ha ha

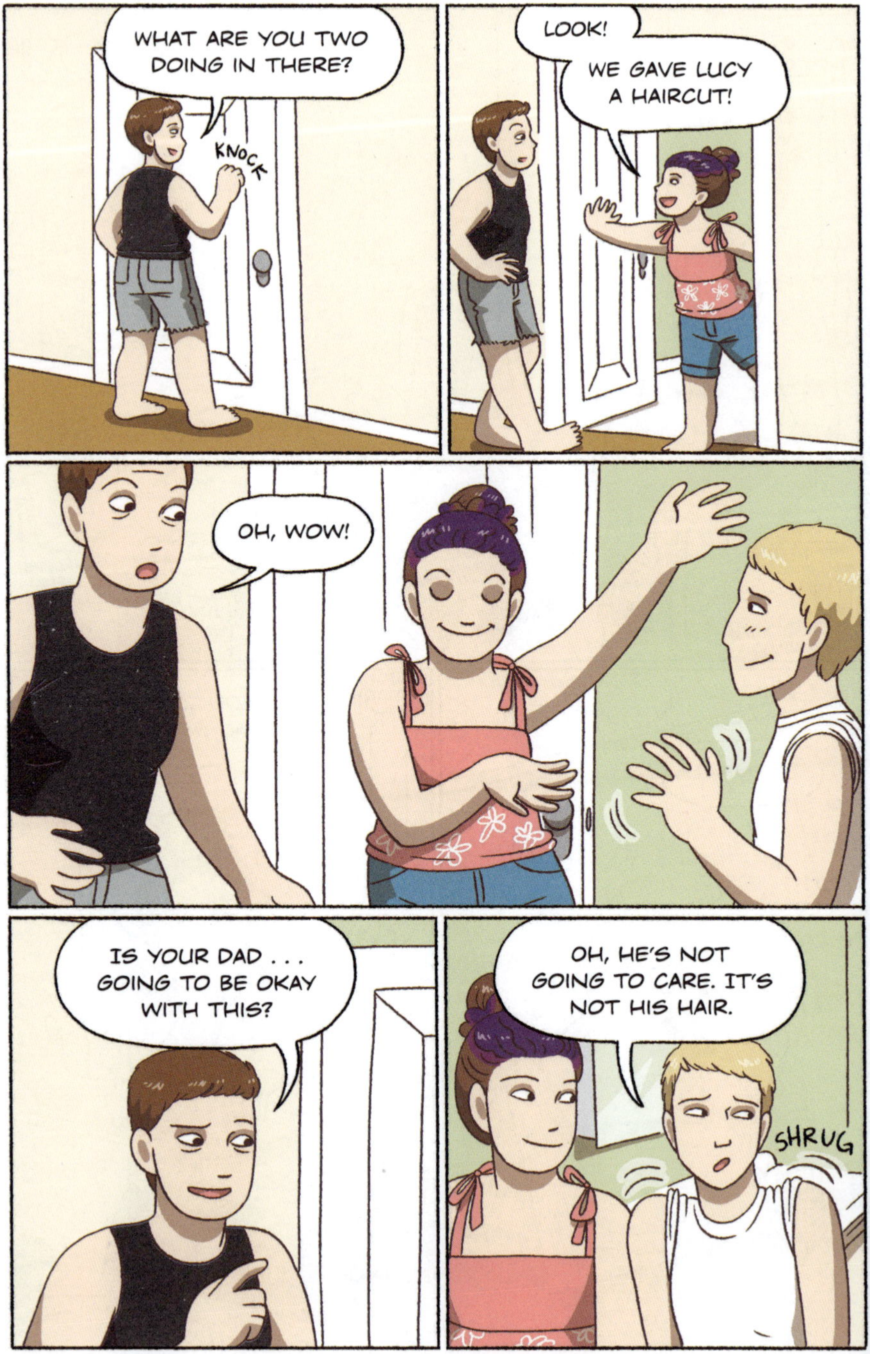
WHAT ARE YOU TWO DOING IN THERE?
KNOCK
LOOK!
WE GAVE LUCY A HAIRCUT!
OH, WOW!
IS YOUR DAD . . . GOING TO BE OKAY WITH THIS?
OH, HE'S NOT GOING TO CARE. IT'S NOT HIS HAIR.
SHRUG

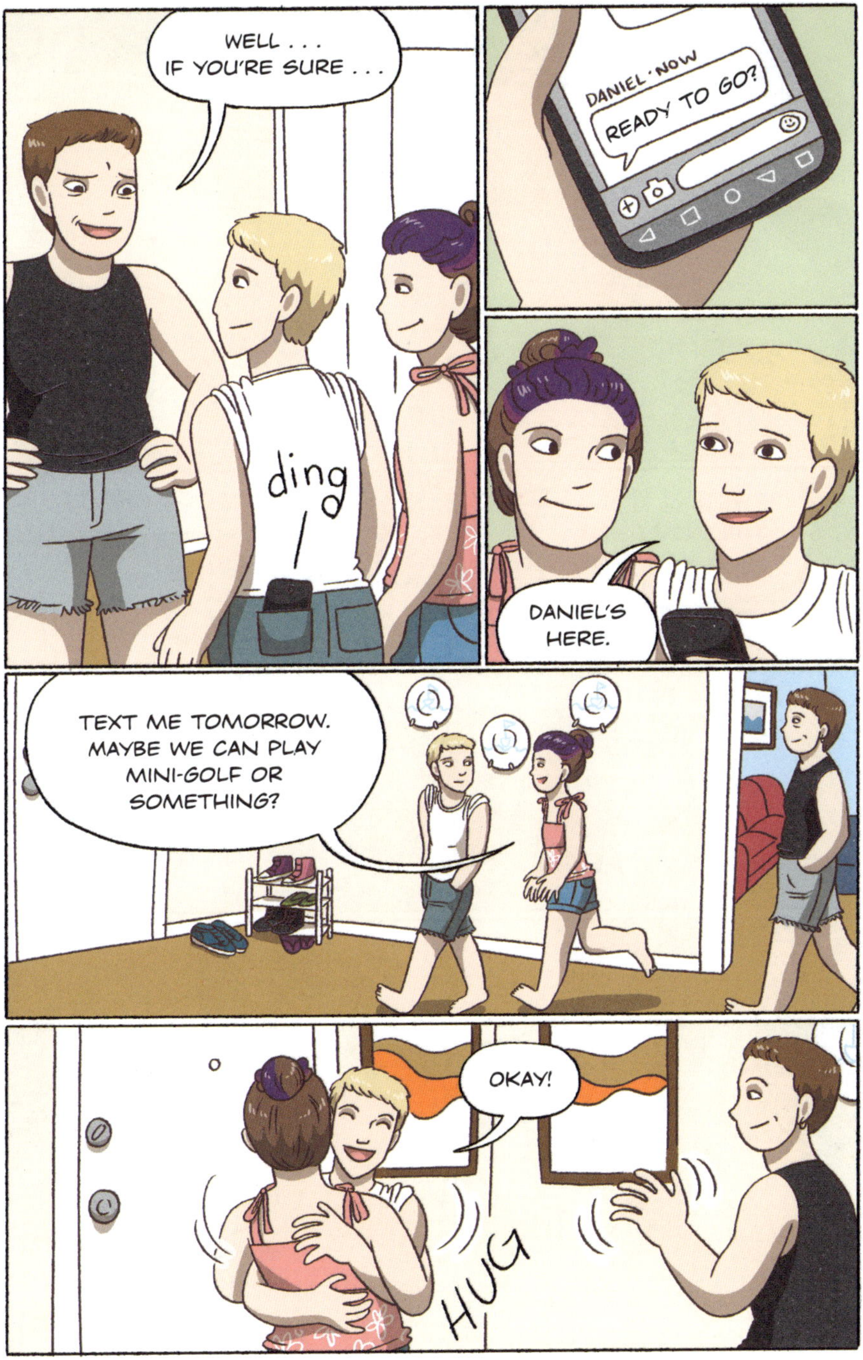
WELL . . . IF YOU'RE SURE . . .
ding
DANIEL · NOW
READY TO GO?
DANIEL'S HERE.
TEXT ME TOMORROW. MAYBE WE CAN PLAY MINI-GOLF OR SOMETHING?
OKAY!
HUG

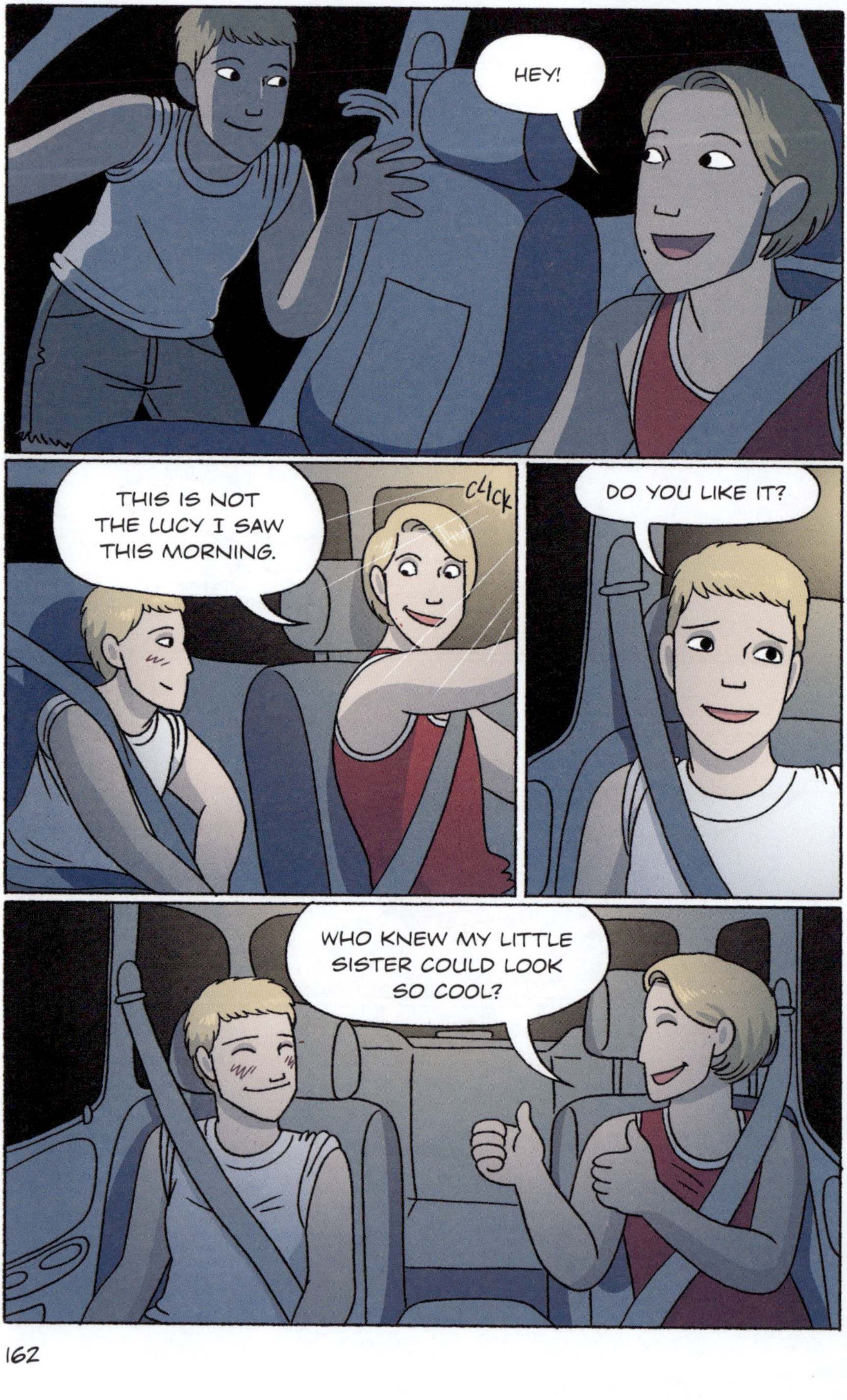
HEY!
THIS IS NOT THE LUCY I SAW THIS MORNING.
CLICK
DO YOU LIKE IT?
WHO KNEW MY LITTLE SISTER COULD LOOK SO COOL?

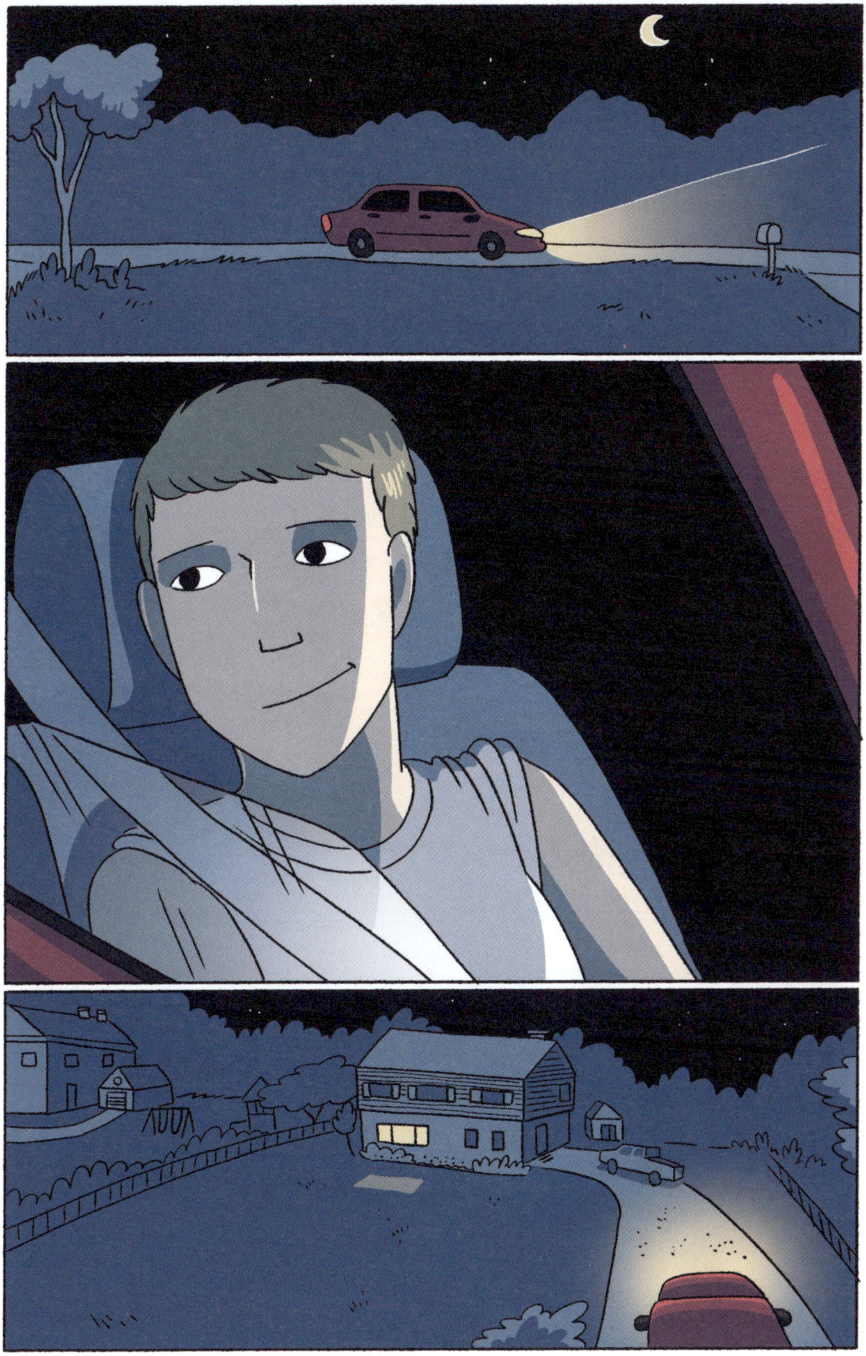

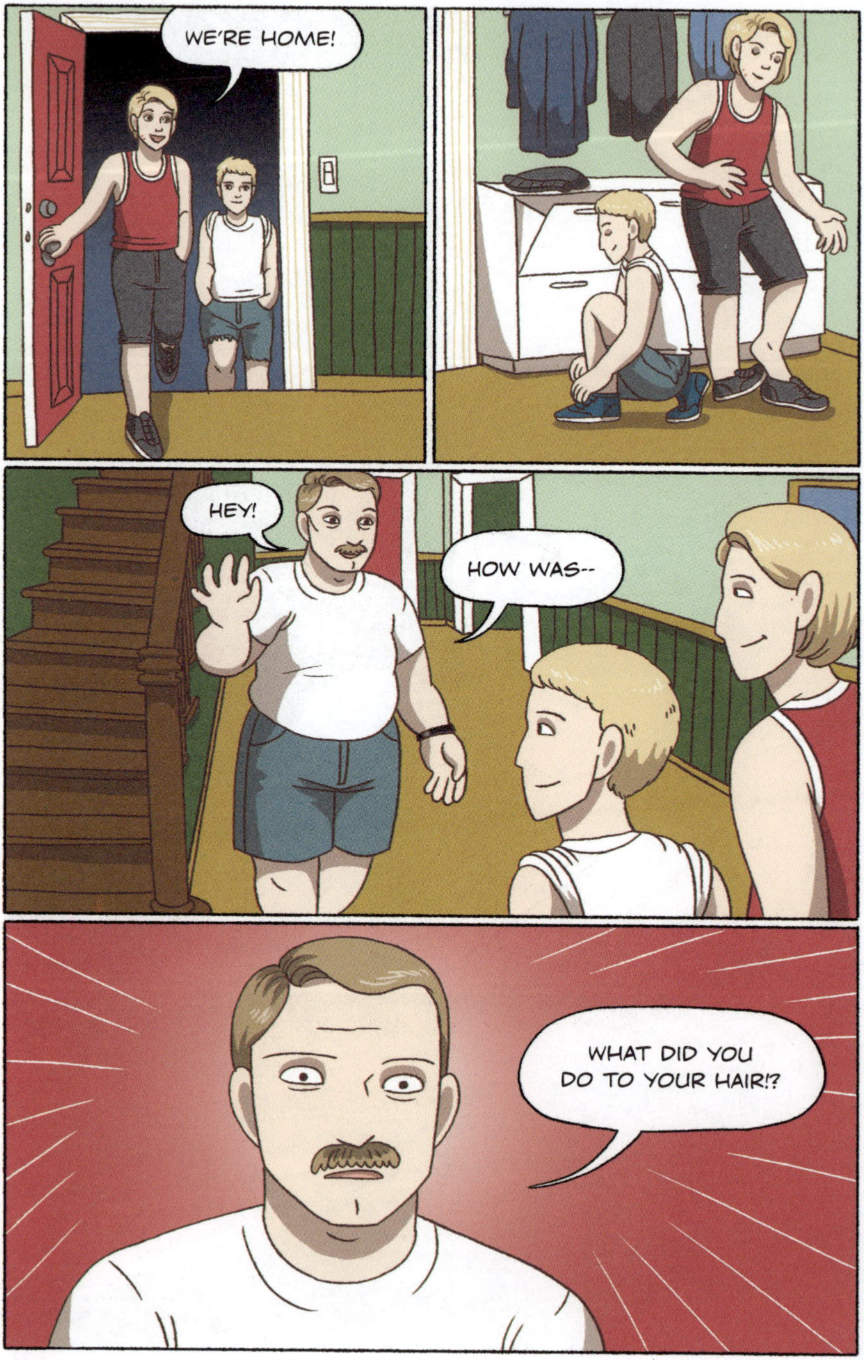
WE'RE HOME!
HEY!
HOW WAS--
WHAT DID YOU DO TO YOUR HAIR!?

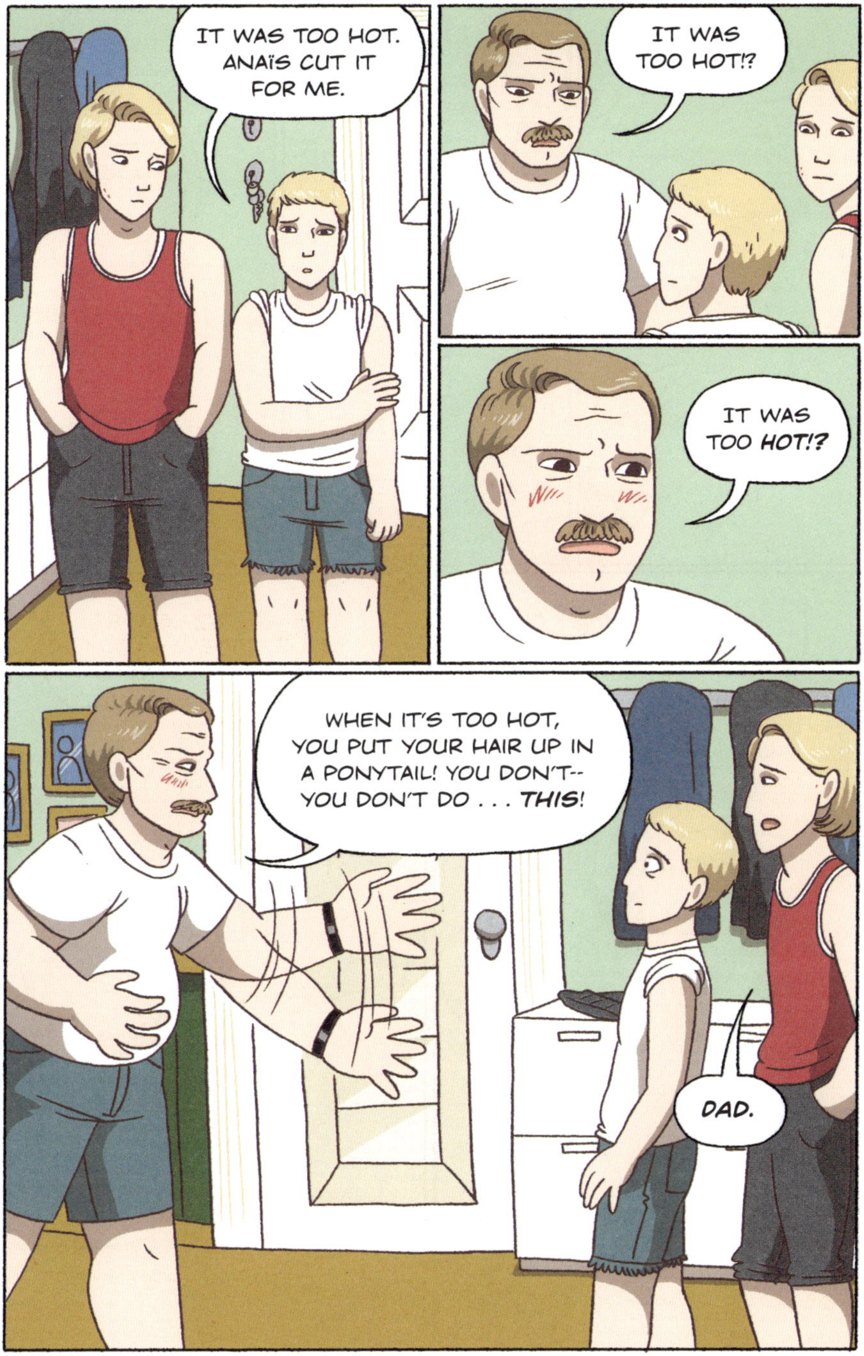
IT WAS TOO HOT. ANAÏS CUT IT FOR ME.
IT WAS TOO HOT!?
IT WAS TOO **HOT!?**
WHEN IT'S TOO HOT, YOU PUT YOUR HAIR UP IN A PONYTAIL! YOU DON'T-- YOU DON'T DO . . . **THIS**!
DAD.

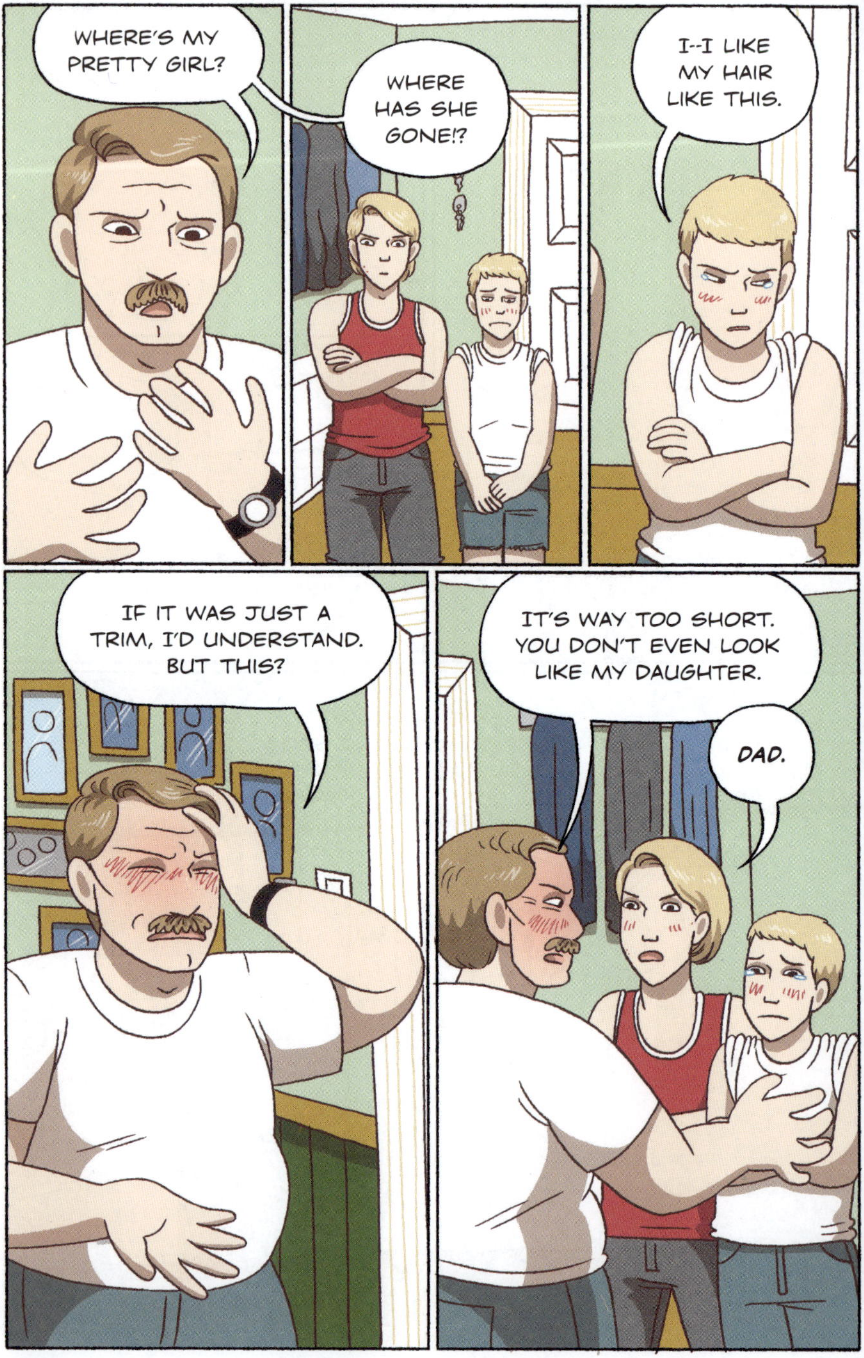
WHERE'S MY PRETTY GIRL?
WHERE HAS SHE GONE!?
I--I LIKE MY HAIR LIKE THIS.
IF IT WAS JUST A TRIM, I'D UNDERSTAND. BUT THIS?
IT'S WAY TOO SHORT. YOU DON'T EVEN LOOK LIKE MY DAUGHTER.
DAD.

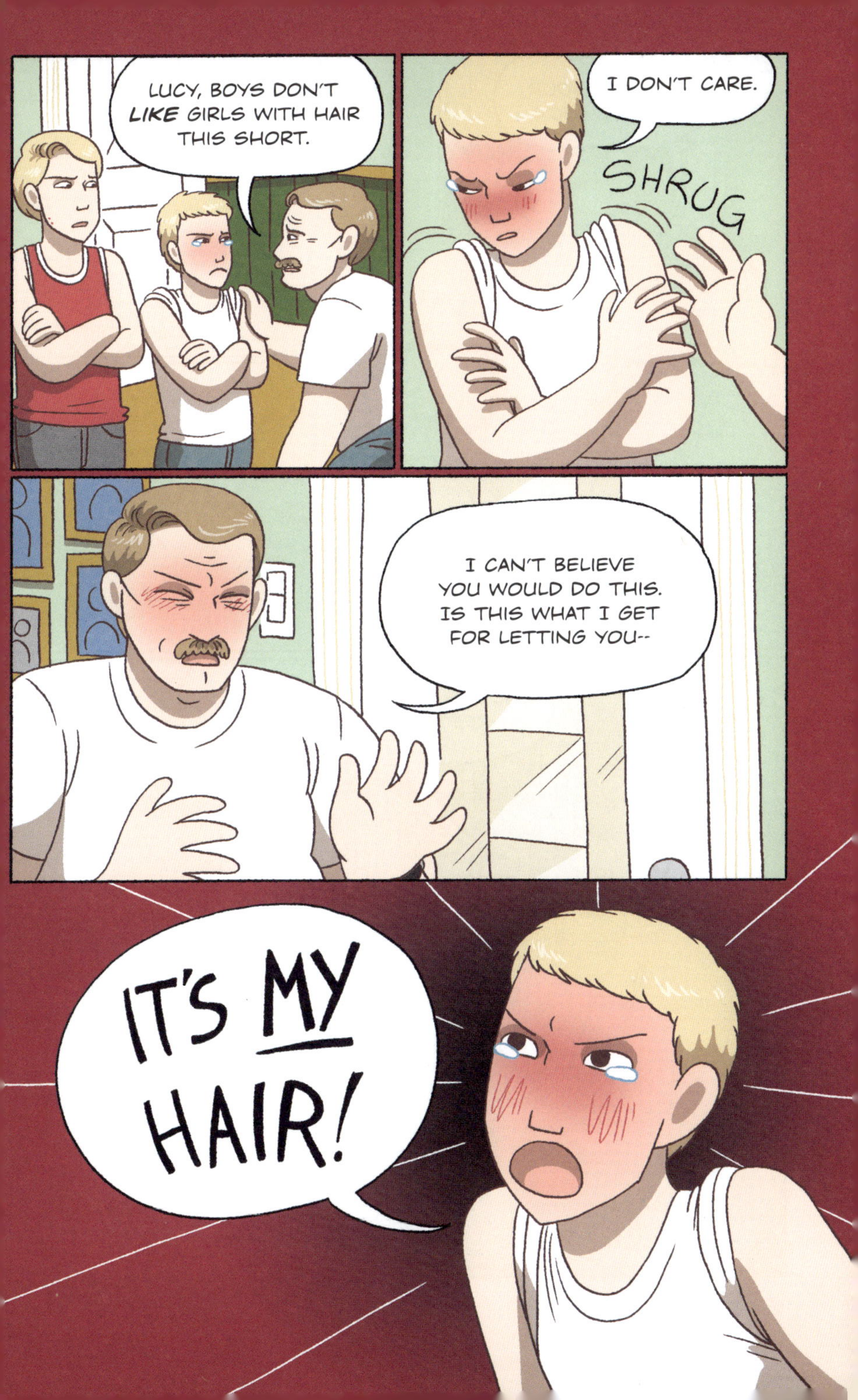
LUCY, BOYS DON'T LIKE GIRLS WITH HAIR THIS SHORT.
I DON'T CARE.
SHRUG
I CAN'T BELIEVE YOU WOULD DO THIS. IS THIS WHAT I GET FOR LETTING YOU--
IT'S MY HAIR!

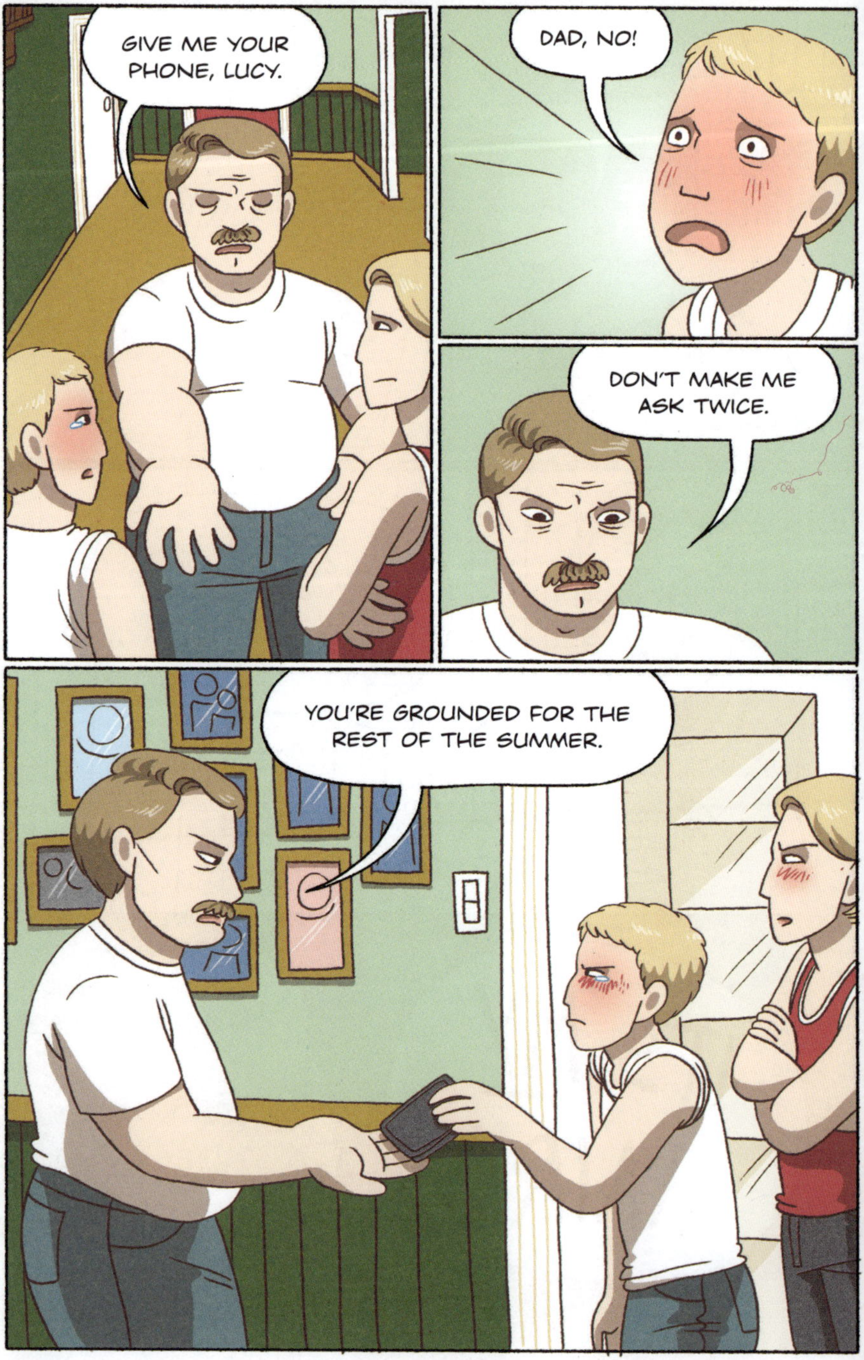
GIVE ME YOUR PHONE, LUCY.
DAD, NO!
DON'T MAKE ME ASK TWICE.
YOU'RE GROUNDED FOR THE REST OF THE SUMMER.

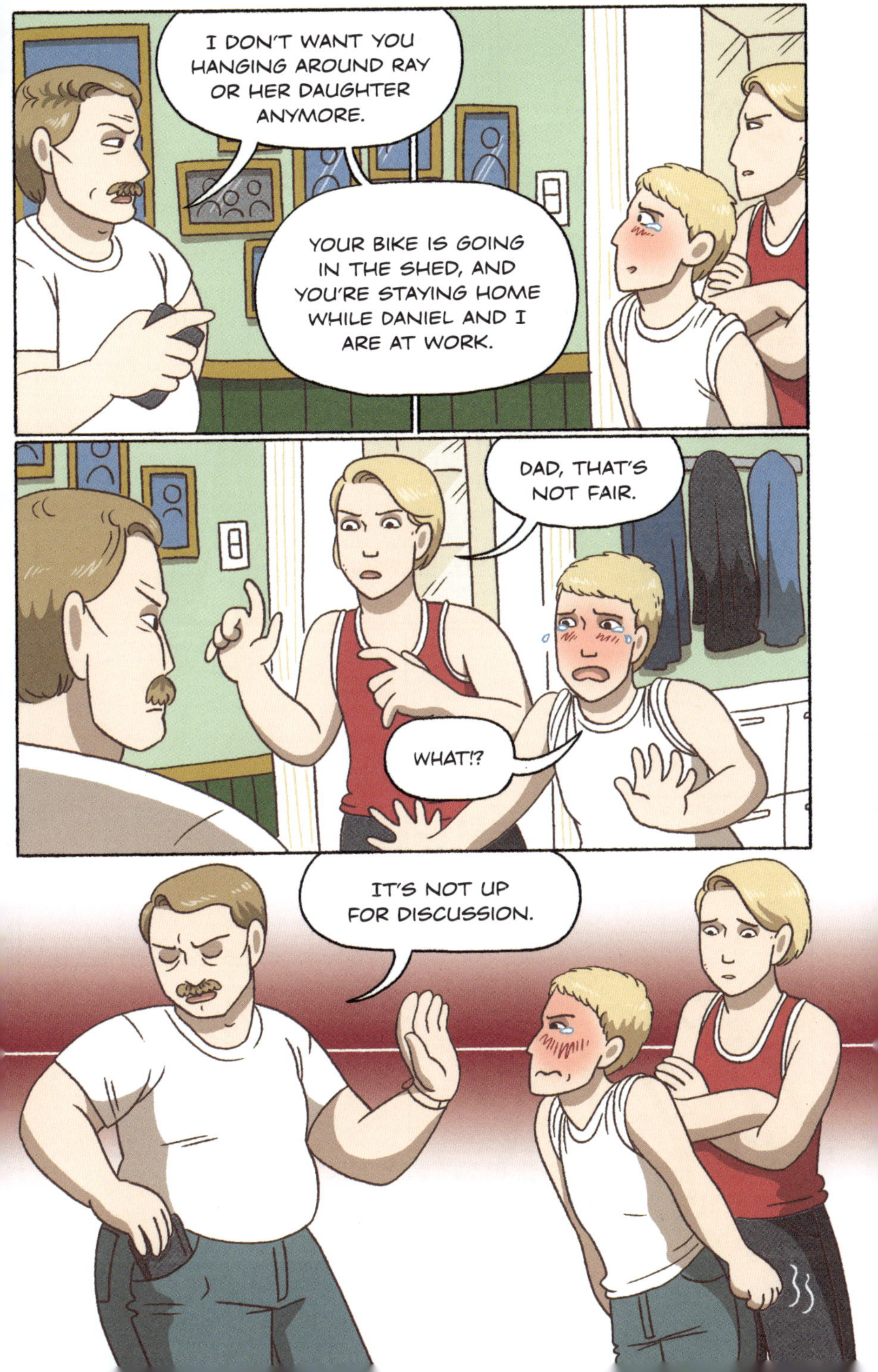
I DON'T WANT YOU HANGING AROUND RAY OR HER DAUGHTER ANYMORE.
YOUR BIKE IS GOING IN THE SHED, AND YOU'RE STAYING HOME WHILE DANIEL AND I ARE AT WORK.
DAD, THAT'S NOT FAIR.
WHAT!?
IT'S NOT UP FOR DISCUSSION.

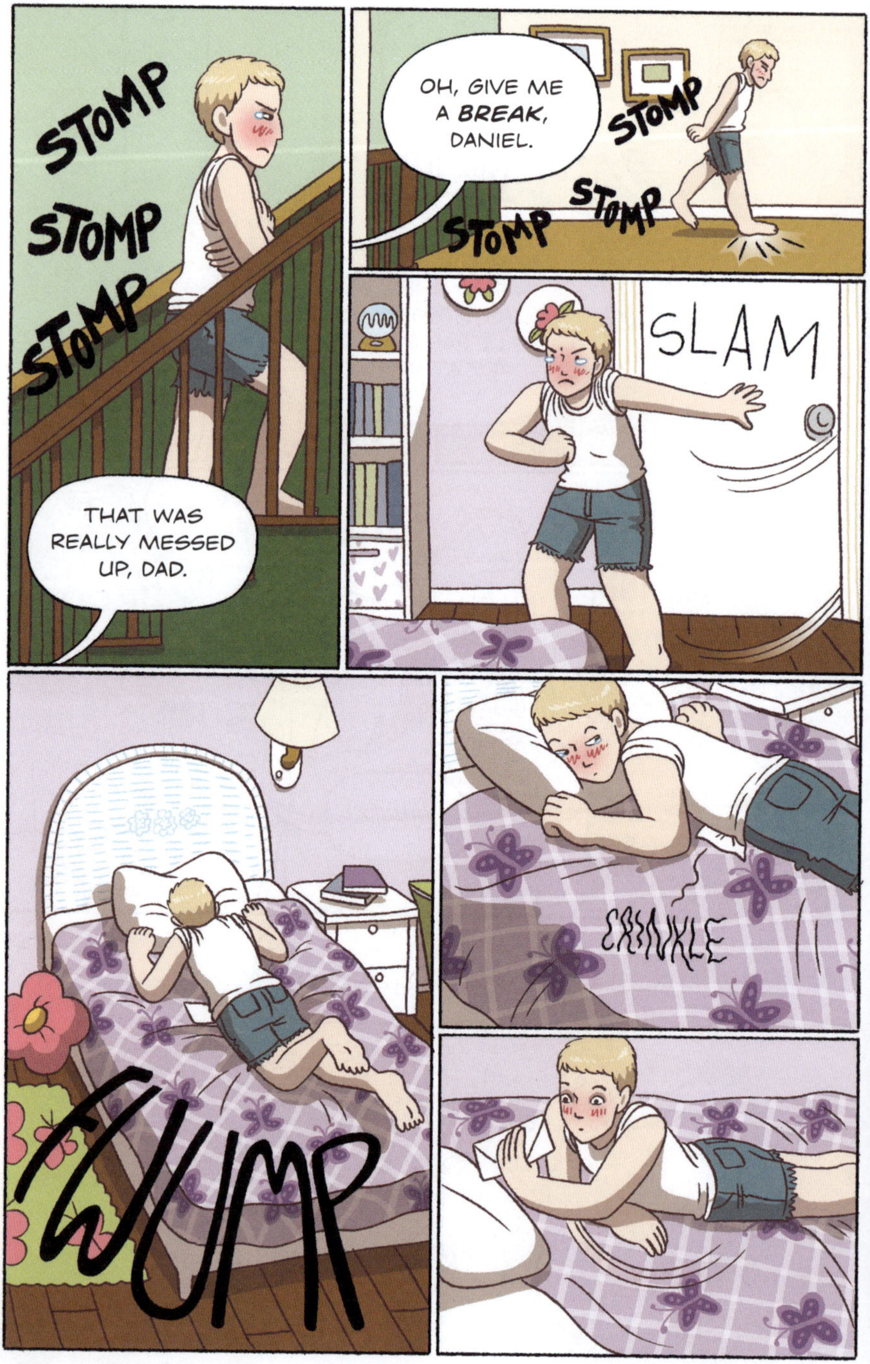
STOMP
STOMP
STOMP
THAT WAS REALLY MESSED UP, DAD.
OH, GIVE ME A **BREAK**, DANIEL.
STOMP
STOMP
STOMP
SLAM
FWUMP
CRINKLE

Dear Lucy,

Callum is officially my camp boyfriend. The secret got out because Talia caught us kissing behind the arts and crafts cabin before dinner. At first I was super embarrassed, but it turns out the other girls are totally jealous. None of them have camp boyfriends. Callum sits with me and holds my hand during campfire now.

This week we're having the Intra-Camp Olympics! There are five categories, and each cabin chooses someone to compete in them. I'm going to be teaming up with Jessica to do the canoe races. We practiced during our lake time today, and together we were the fastest in our cabin. We've already decided that we don't mind if we don't win gold, but we have to at least beat the Oak Cabin. I might be dating Callum now, but I haven't forgotten the ghost prank!

We have to plan out a performance for the opening ceremonies. Rachel is on the dance team at her school and she's been choreographing a whole routine for us. It's going to be SO cool! I'll show you how it goes when I get home.

Write to me soon!

Katia

    P.S. Beth taught us all a new
    friendship bracelet pattern.
    I made one for you.

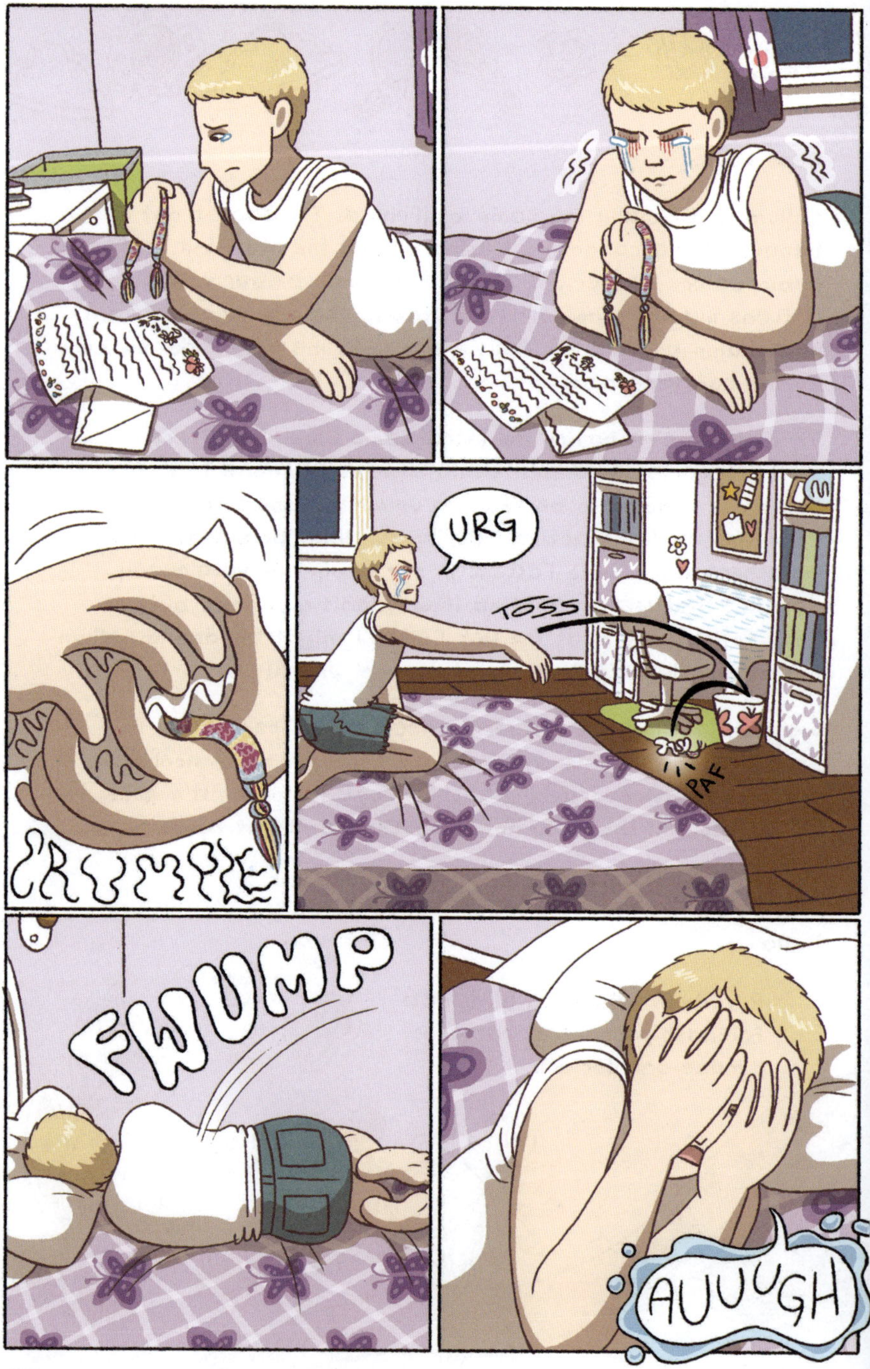
CRUMPLE
URG
TOSS
PAF
FWUMP
AUUUGH

~~Dear Katia,~~
~~Everything is terrible~~

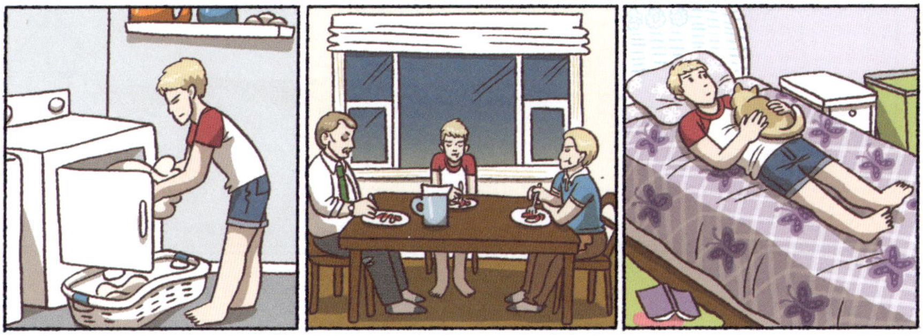

~~Dear Katia,~~
~~I don't know how to start this letter because everything is bad here. I cut my hair and my dad grounded me.~~

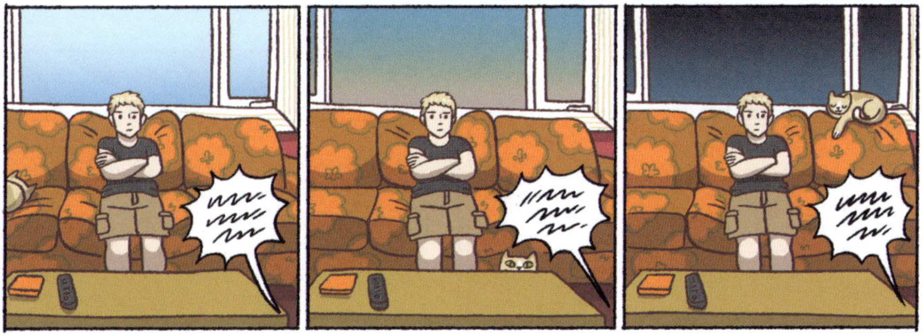

~~Dear Katia,~~
~~Things are bad. I have so much to tell you and I don't know how to start because I don't know what you're going to think about it. I cut my hair. I kissed a girl. I think I'm~~

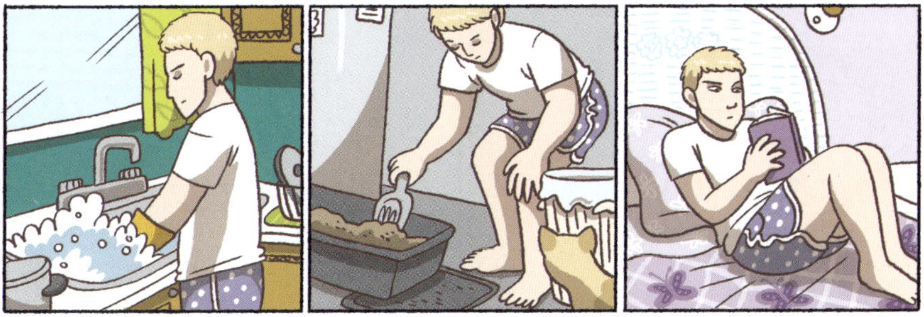

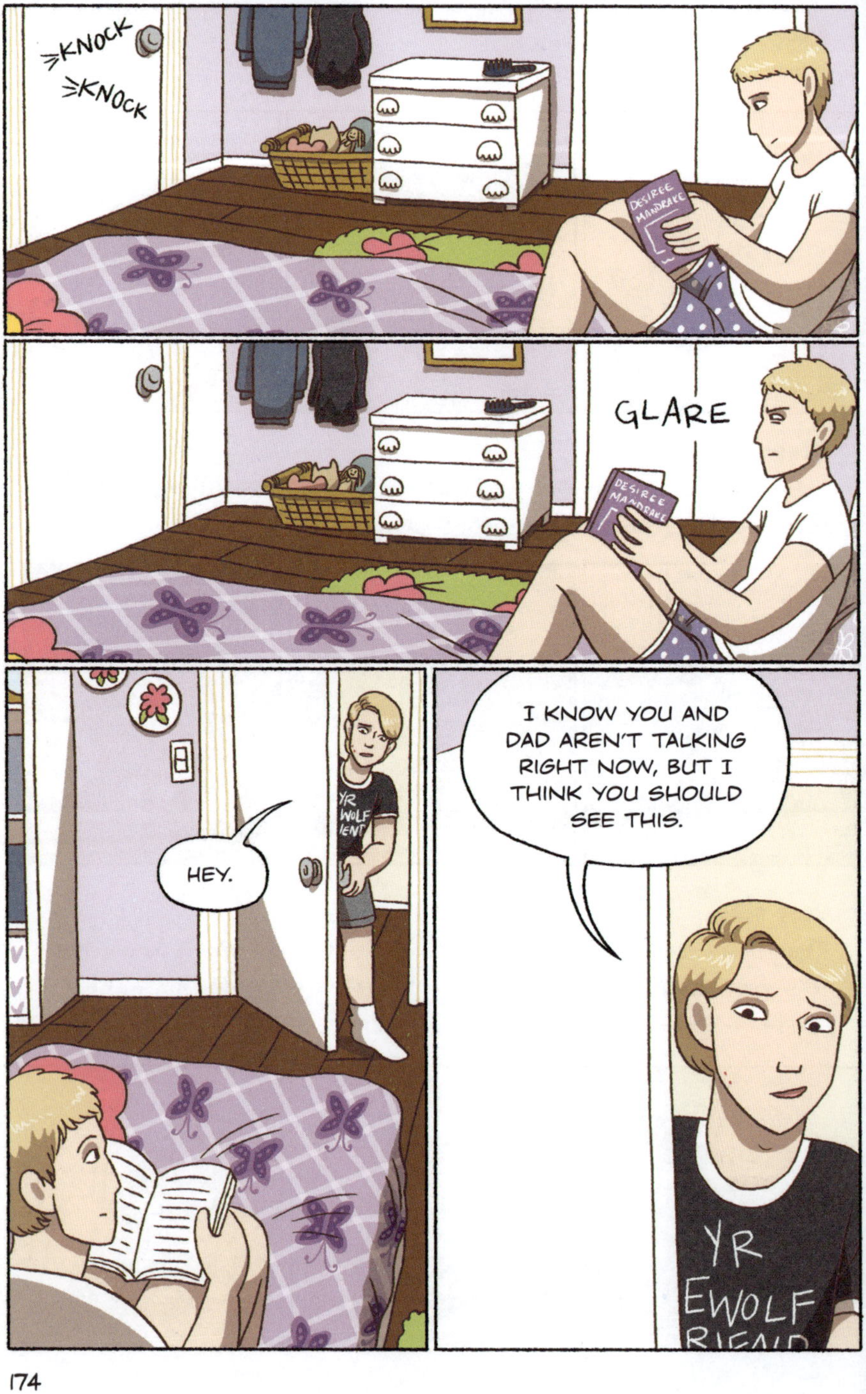
KNOCK
KNOCK
DESIREE MANDRAKE
GLARE
DESIREE MANDRAKE
HEY.
I KNOW YOU AND DAD AREN'T TALKING RIGHT NOW, BUT I THINK YOU SHOULD SEE THIS.
YR EWOLF

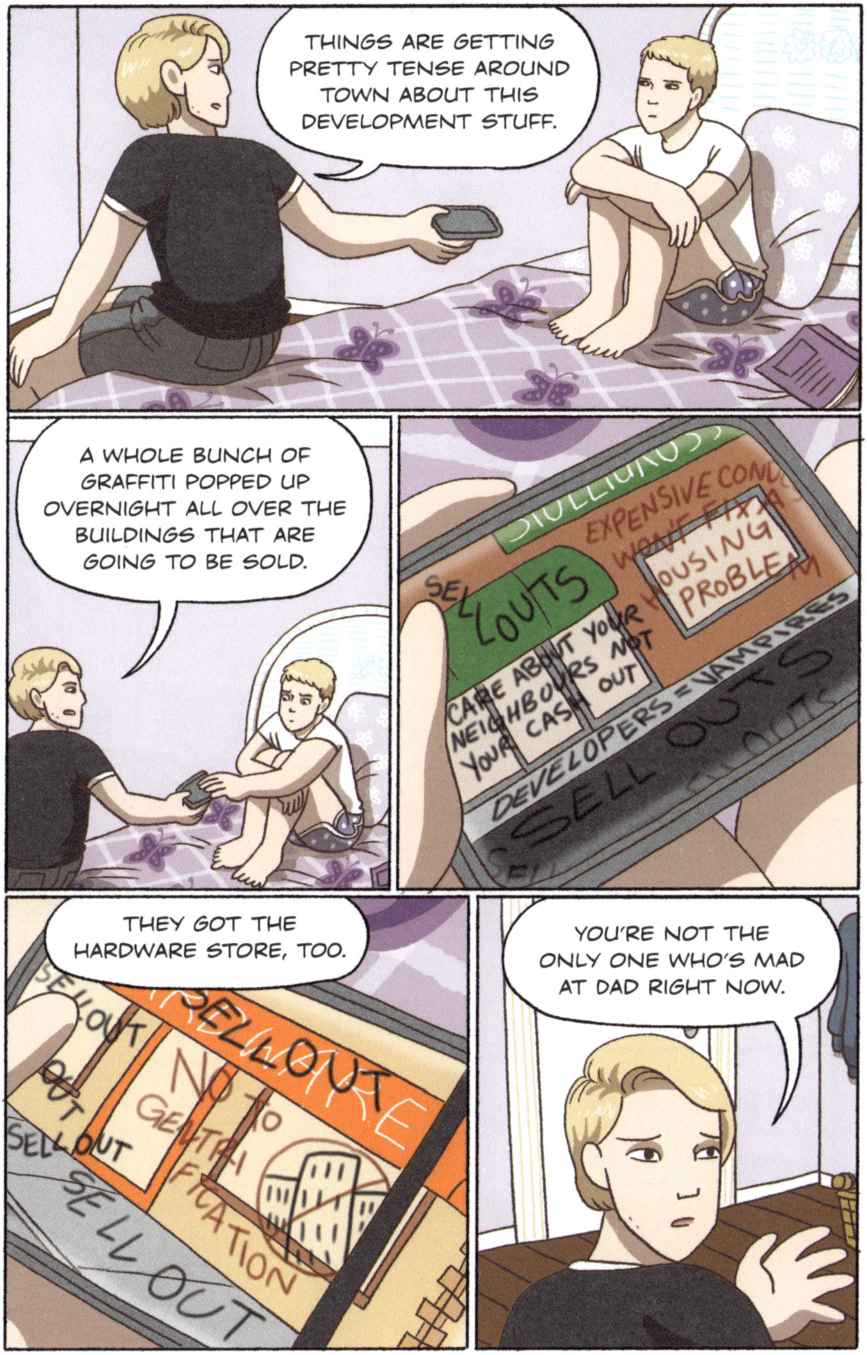
THINGS ARE GETTING PRETTY TENSE AROUND TOWN ABOUT THIS DEVELOPMENT STUFF.
A WHOLE BUNCH OF GRAFFITI POPPED UP OVERNIGHT ALL OVER THE BUILDINGS THAT ARE GOING TO BE SOLD.
SELLOUTS
HOUSING PROBLEM
CARE ABOUT YOUR NEIGHBOURS NOT YOUR CASH OUT
DEVELOPERS = VAMPIRES
SELL OUTS
THEY GOT THE HARDWARE STORE, TOO.
SELLOUT
NO TO GENTRIFICATION
SELL OUT
YOU'RE NOT THE ONLY ONE WHO'S MAD AT DAD RIGHT NOW.

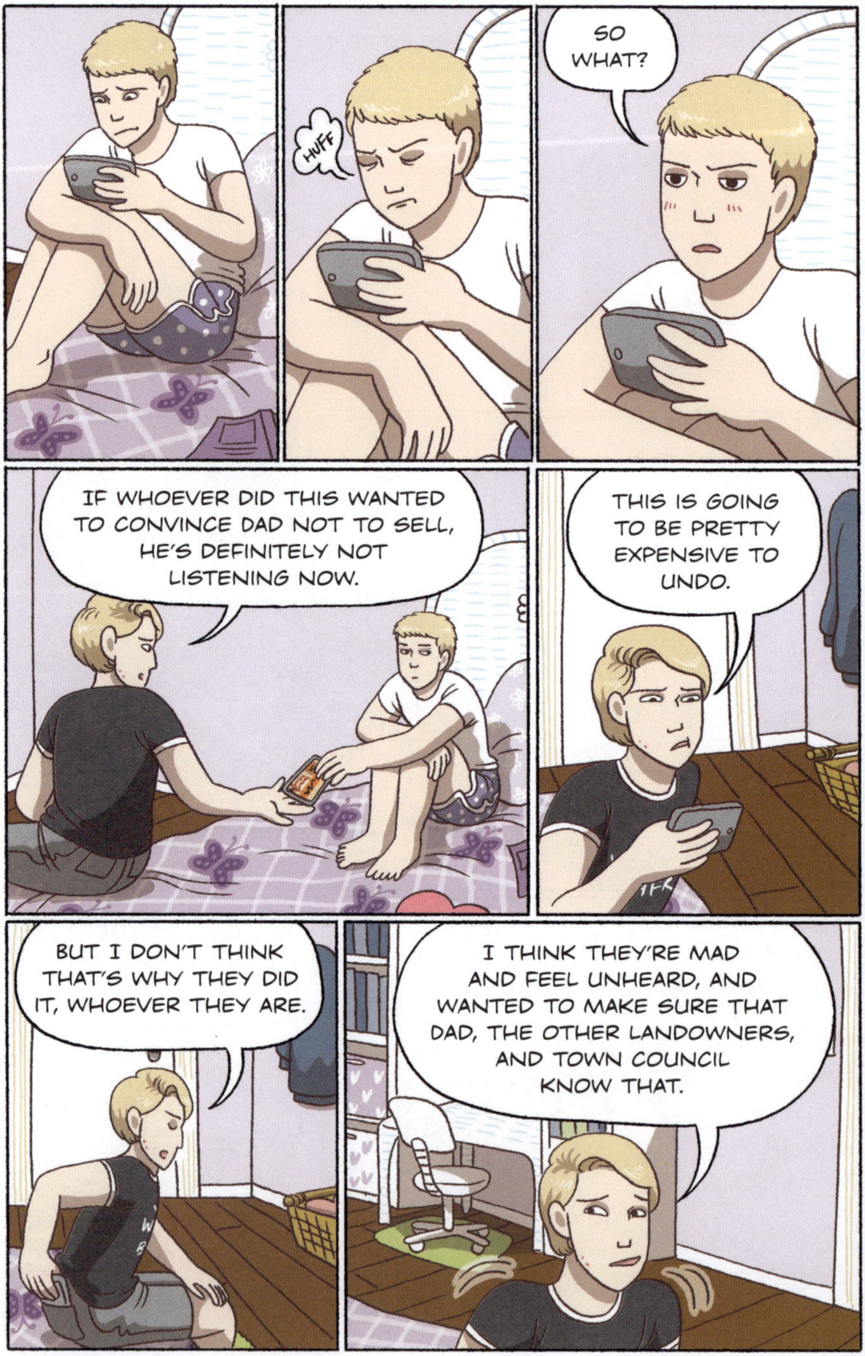
HUFF
SO WHAT?
IF WHOEVER DID THIS WANTED TO CONVINCE DAD NOT TO SELL, HE'S DEFINITELY NOT LISTENING NOW.
THIS IS GOING TO BE PRETTY EXPENSIVE TO UNDO.
BUT I DON'T THINK THAT'S WHY THEY DID IT, WHOEVER THEY ARE.
I THINK THEY'RE MAD AND FEEL UNHEARD, AND WANTED TO MAKE SURE THAT DAD, THE OTHER LANDOWNERS, AND TOWN COUNCIL KNOW THAT.

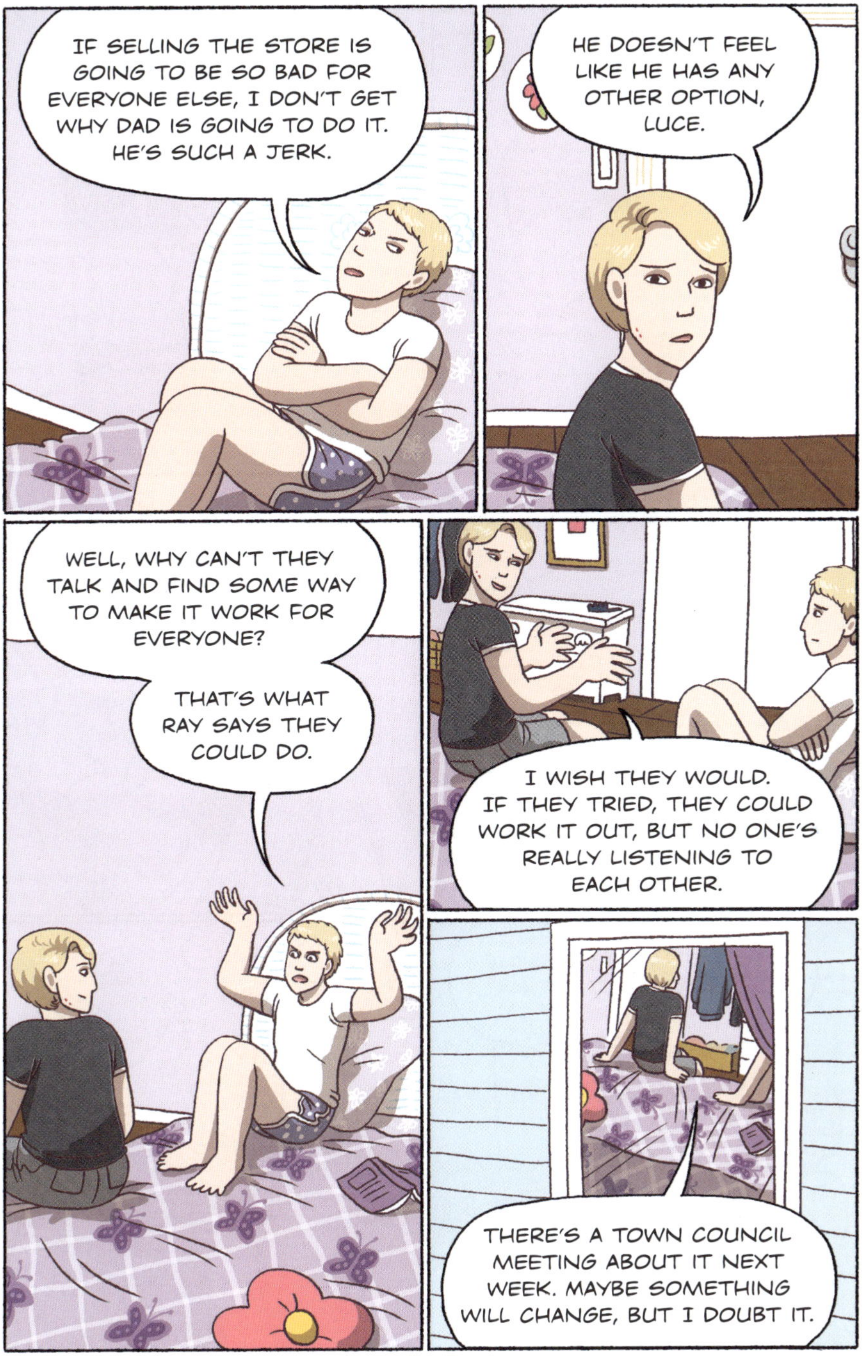
IF SELLING THE STORE IS GOING TO BE SO BAD FOR EVERYONE ELSE, I DON'T GET WHY DAD IS GOING TO DO IT. HE'S SUCH A JERK.
HE DOESN'T FEEL LIKE HE HAS ANY OTHER OPTION, LUCE.
WELL, WHY CAN'T THEY TALK AND FIND SOME WAY TO MAKE IT WORK FOR EVERYONE?
THAT'S WHAT RAY SAYS THEY COULD DO.
I WISH THEY WOULD. IF THEY TRIED, THEY COULD WORK IT OUT, BUT NO ONE'S REALLY LISTENING TO EACH OTHER.
THERE'S A TOWN COUNCIL MEETING ABOUT IT NEXT WEEK. MAYBE SOMETHING WILL CHANGE, BUT I DOUBT IT.

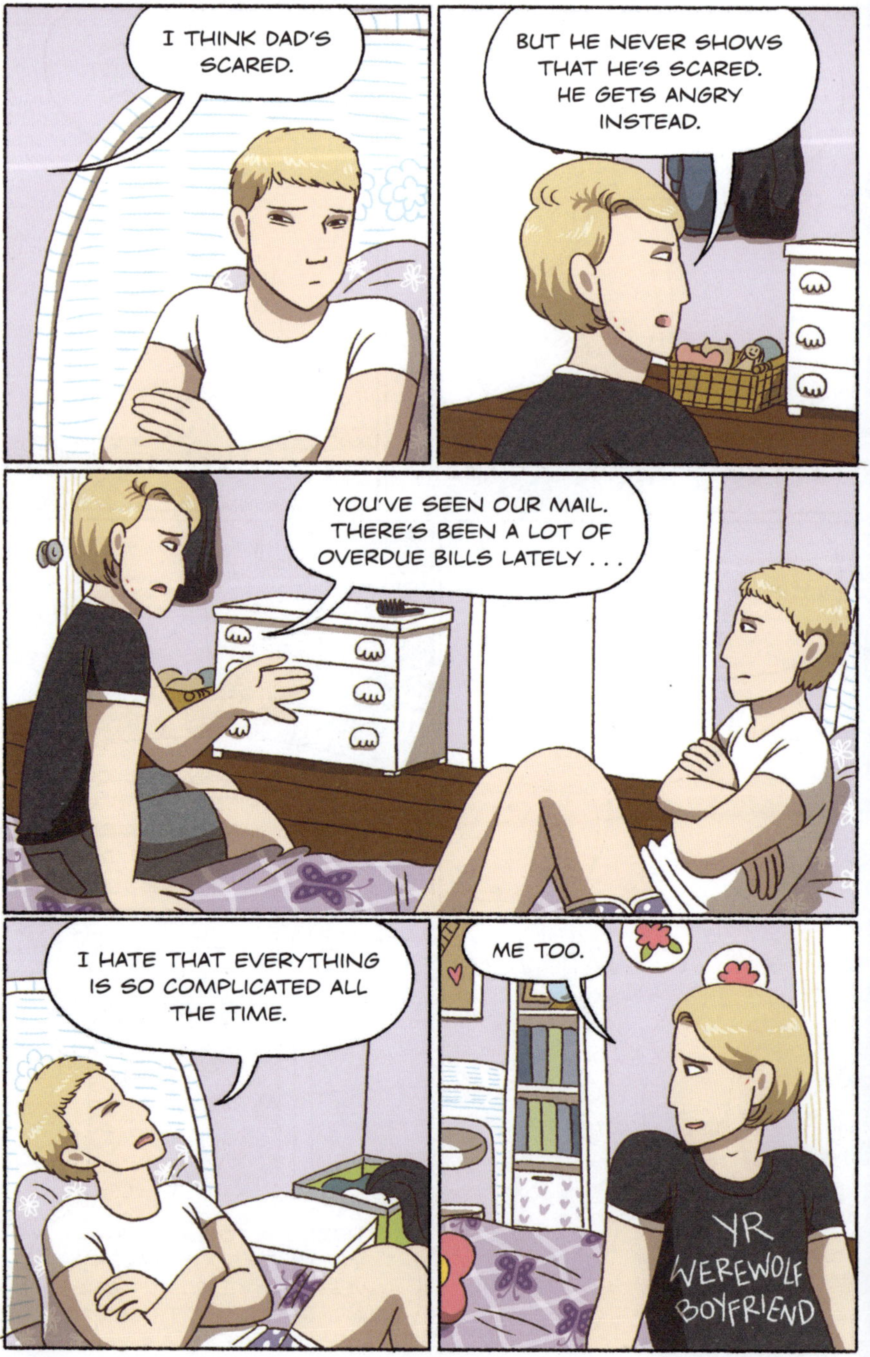
I THINK DAD'S SCARED.
BUT HE NEVER SHOWS THAT HE'S SCARED. HE GETS ANGRY INSTEAD.
YOU'VE SEEN OUR MAIL. THERE'S BEEN A LOT OF OVERDUE BILLS LATELY . . .
I HATE THAT EVERYTHING IS SO COMPLICATED ALL THE TIME.
ME TOO.
YR WEREWOLF BOYFRIEND

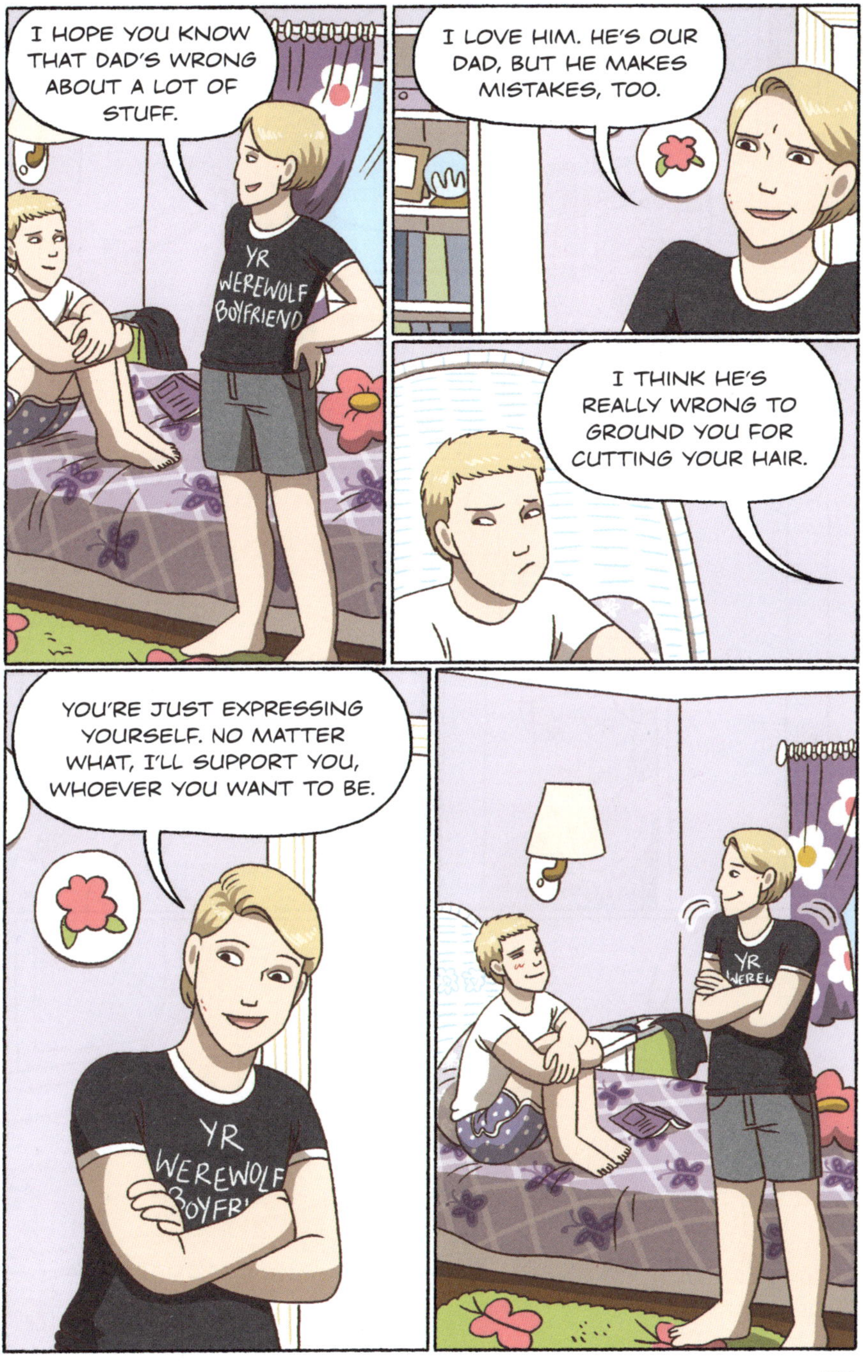
I HOPE YOU KNOW THAT DAD'S WRONG ABOUT A LOT OF STUFF.
YR WEREWOLF BOYFRIEND
I LOVE HIM. HE'S OUR DAD, BUT HE MAKES MISTAKES, TOO.
I THINK HE'S REALLY WRONG TO GROUND YOU FOR CUTTING YOUR HAIR.
YOU'RE JUST EXPRESSING YOURSELF. NO MATTER WHAT, I'LL SUPPORT YOU, WHOEVER YOU WANT TO BE.

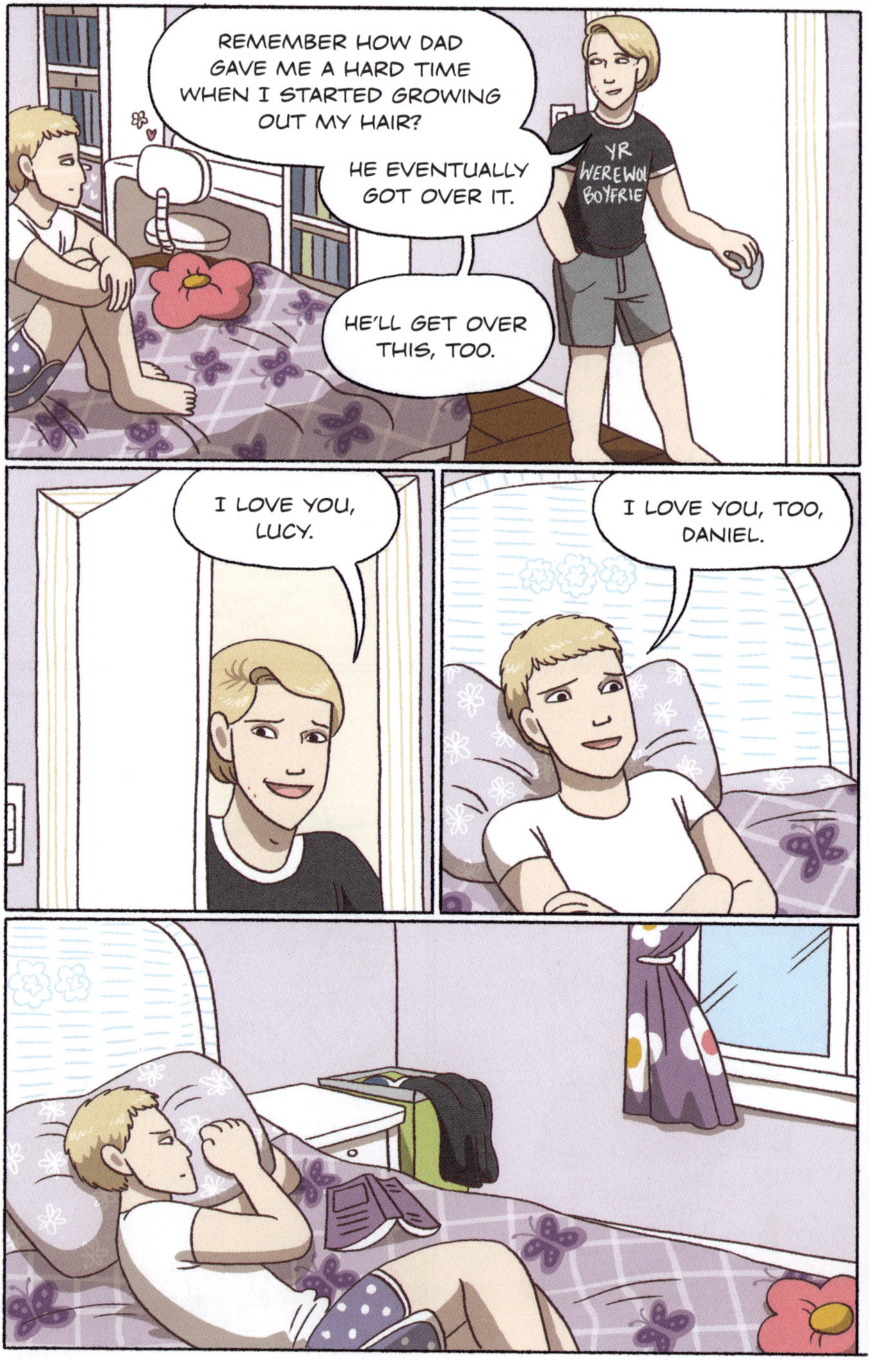
REMEMBER HOW DAD GAVE ME A HARD TIME WHEN I STARTED GROWING OUT MY HAIR?
HE EVENTUALLY GOT OVER IT.
HE'LL GET OVER THIS, TOO.
YR WEREWOL BOYFRIE
I LOVE YOU, LUCY.
I LOVE YOU, TOO, DANIEL.

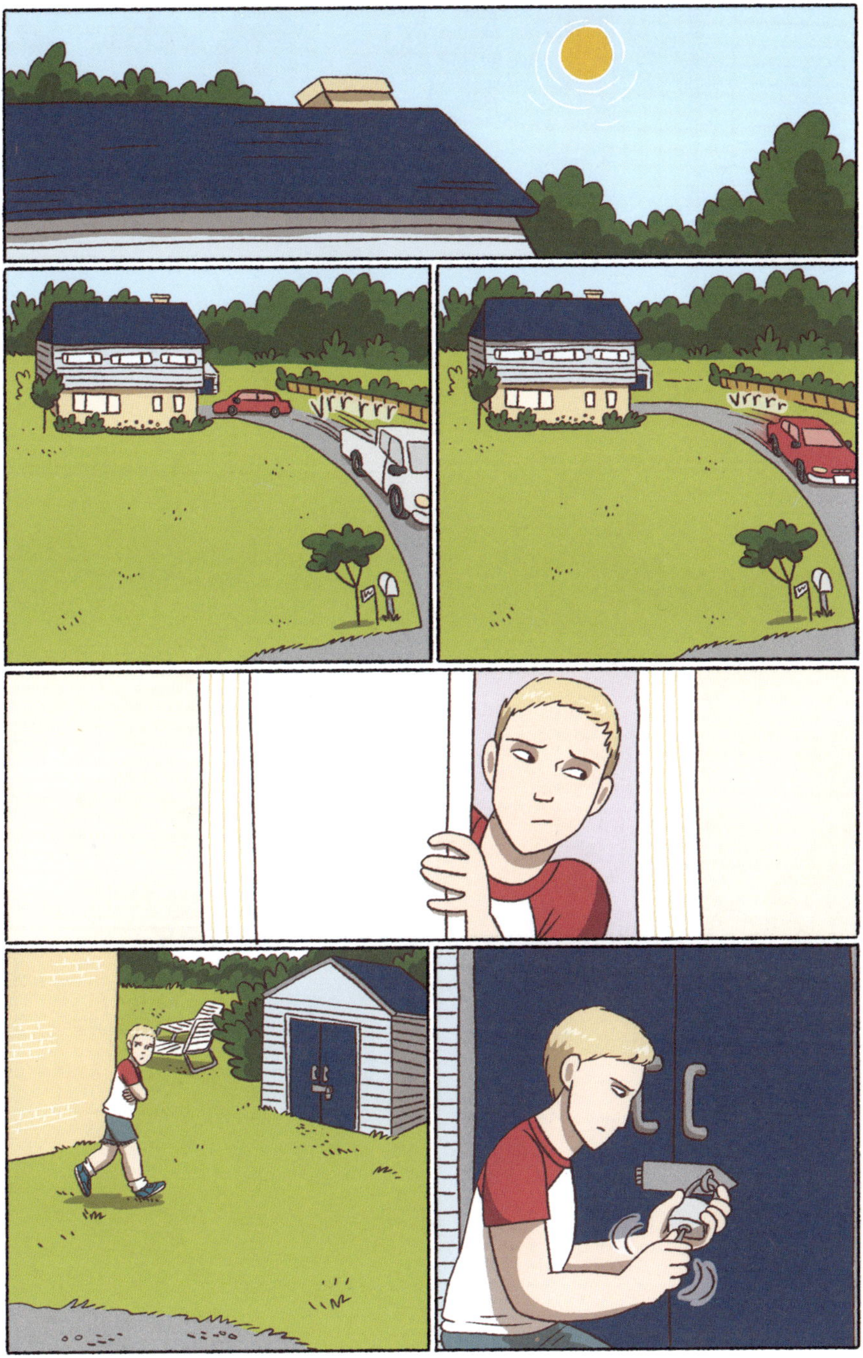
Vrrrrr
Vrrrr

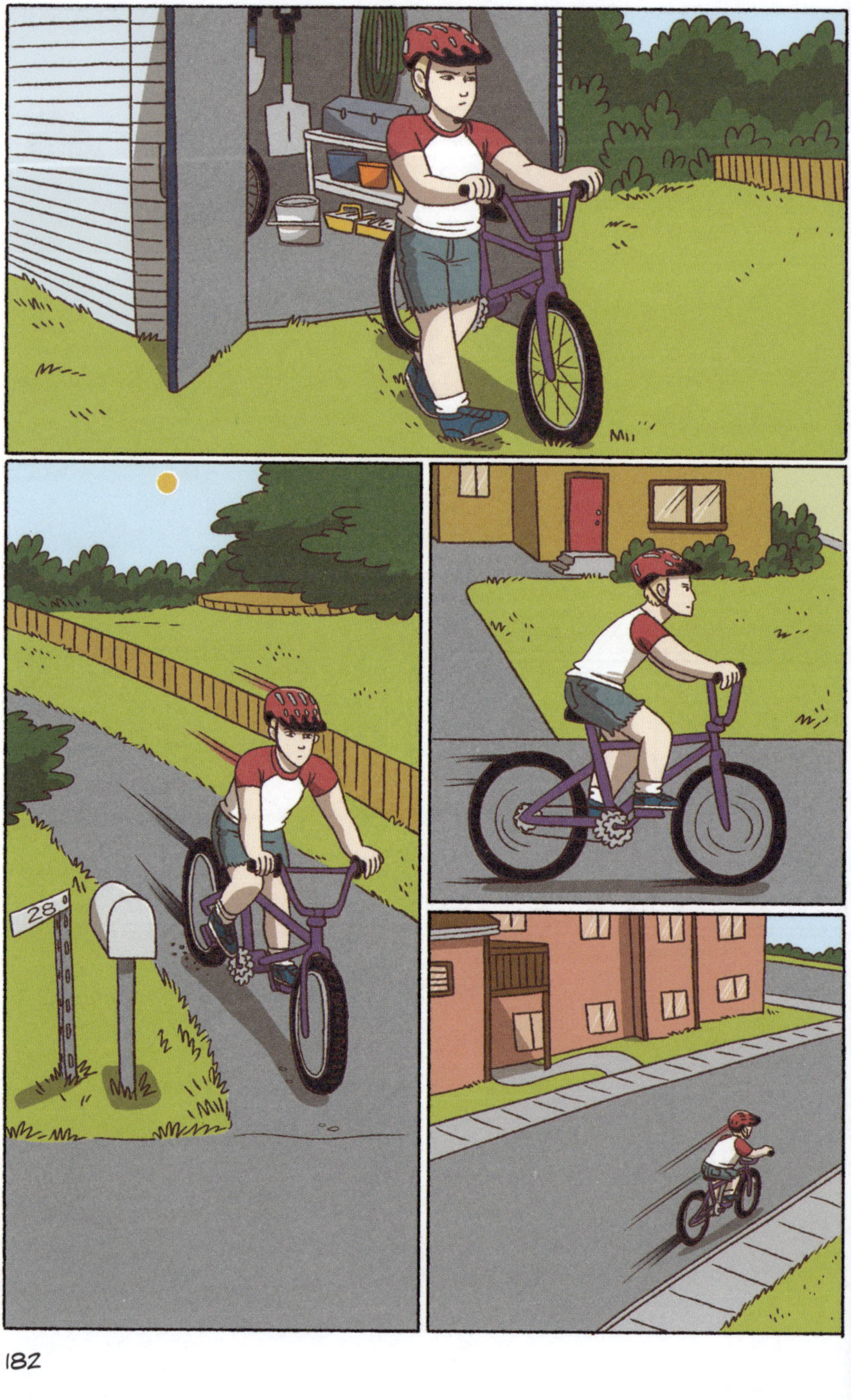
28

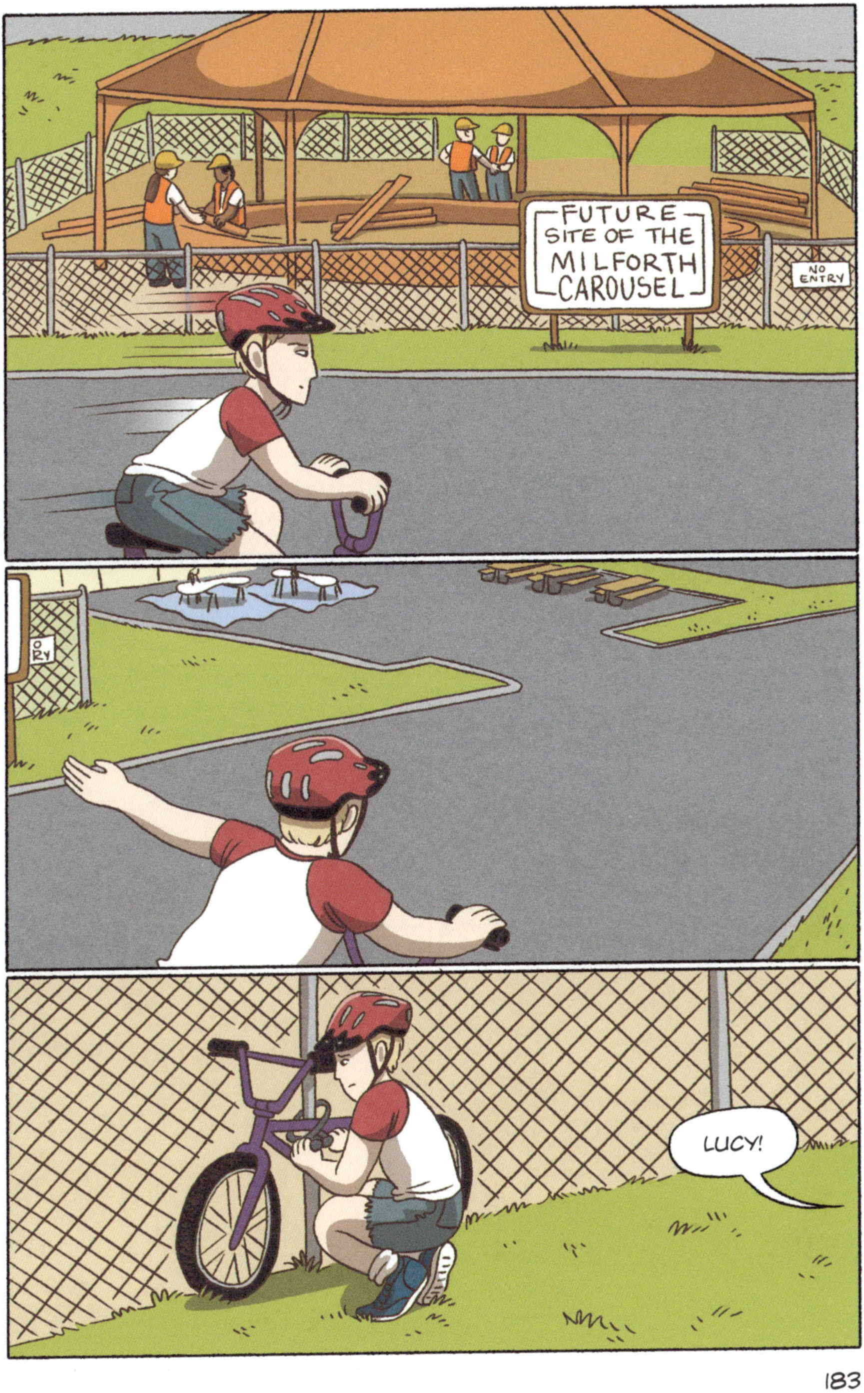
FUTURE SITE OF THE MILFORTH CAROUSEL
NO ENTRY
LUCY!

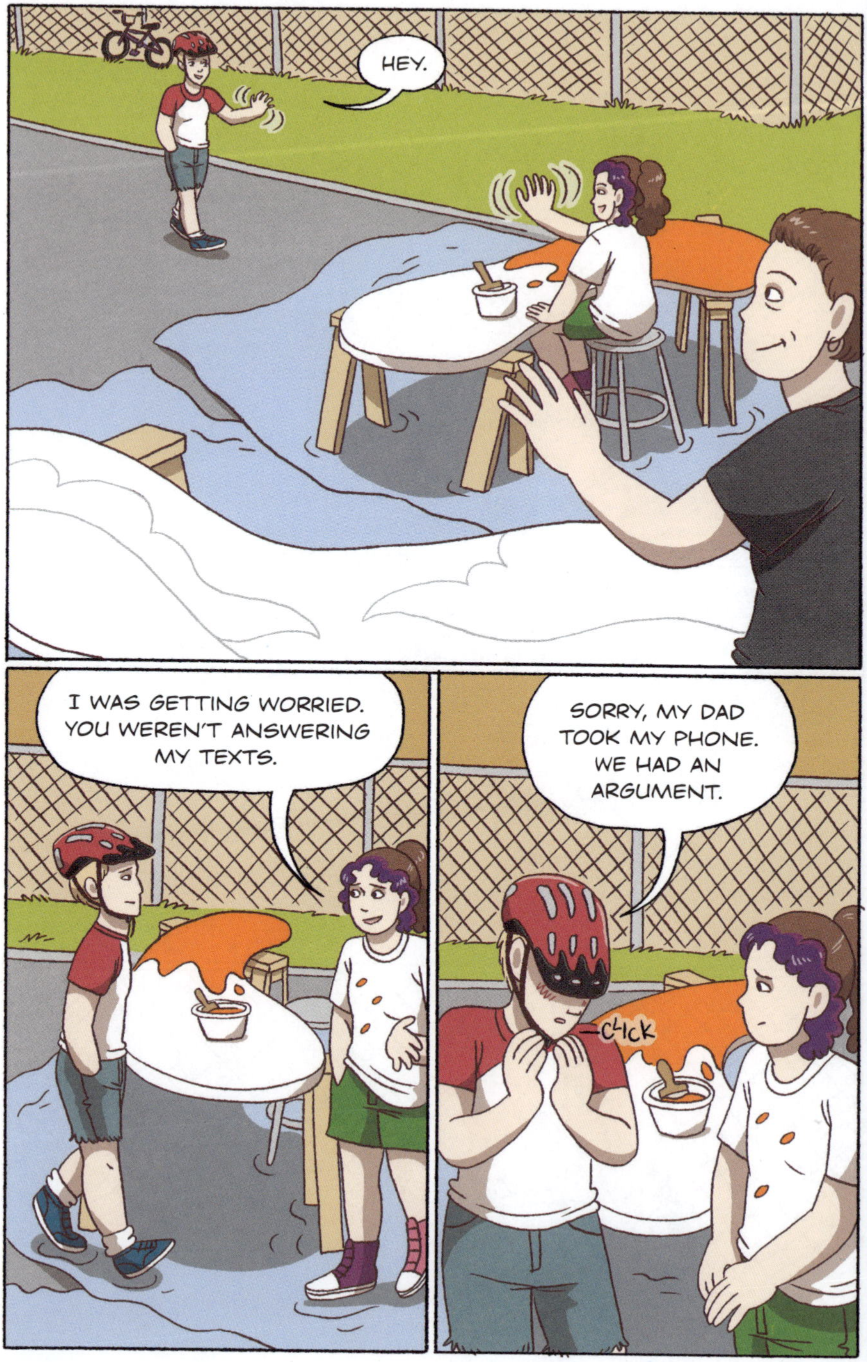
HEY.
I WAS GETTING WORRIED. YOU WEREN'T ANSWERING MY TEXTS.
SORRY, MY DAD TOOK MY PHONE. WE HAD AN ARGUMENT.
CLICK

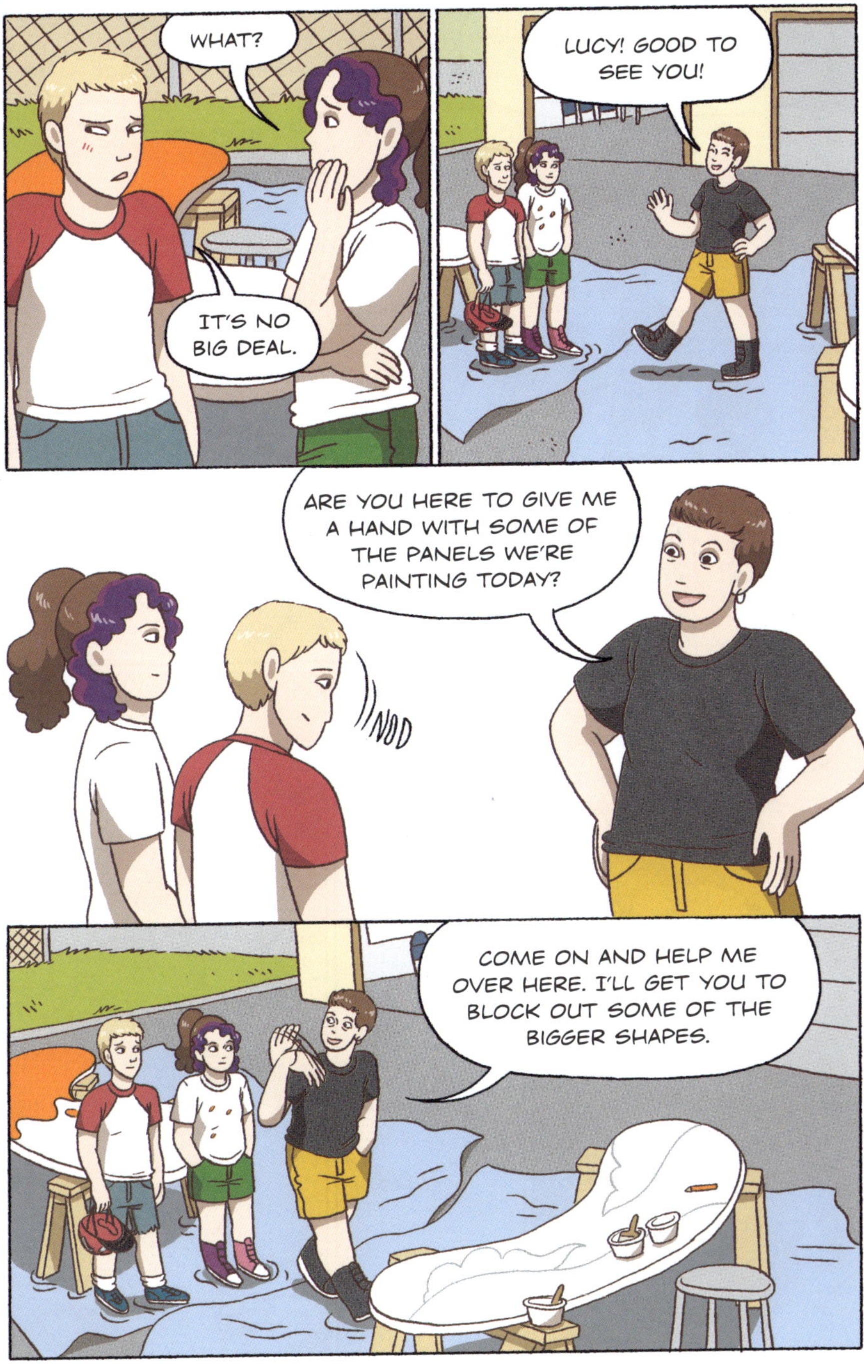
WHAT?
IT'S NO BIG DEAL.
LUCY! GOOD TO SEE YOU!
ARE YOU HERE TO GIVE ME A HAND WITH SOME OF THE PANELS WE'RE PAINTING TODAY?
NOD
COME ON AND HELP ME OVER HERE. I'LL GET YOU TO BLOCK OUT SOME OF THE BIGGER SHAPES.

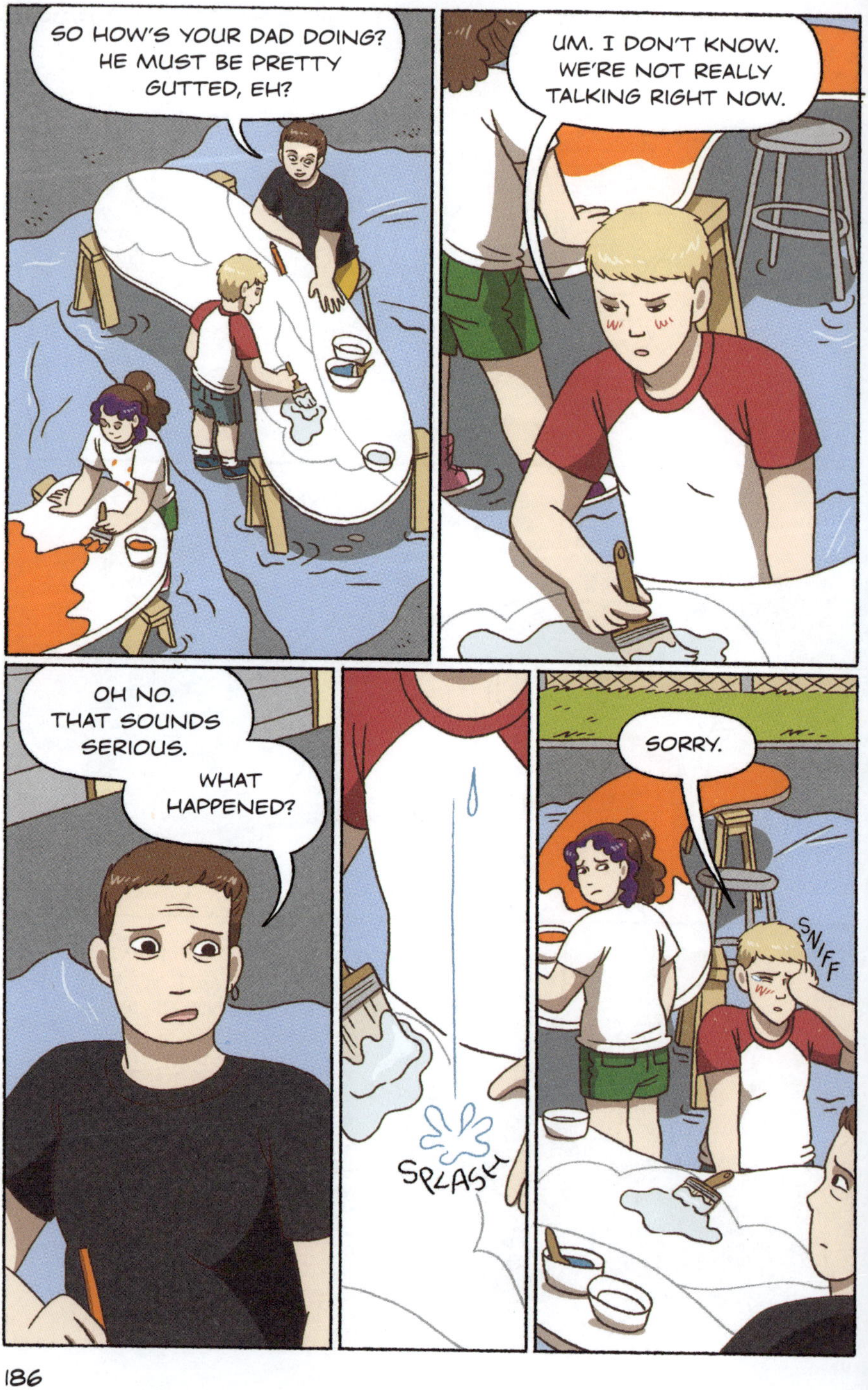
SO HOW'S YOUR DAD DOING? HE MUST BE PRETTY GUTTED, EH?
UM. I DON'T KNOW. WE'RE NOT REALLY TALKING RIGHT NOW.
OH NO. THAT SOUNDS SERIOUS.
WHAT HAPPENED?
SPLASH
SORRY.
SNIFF

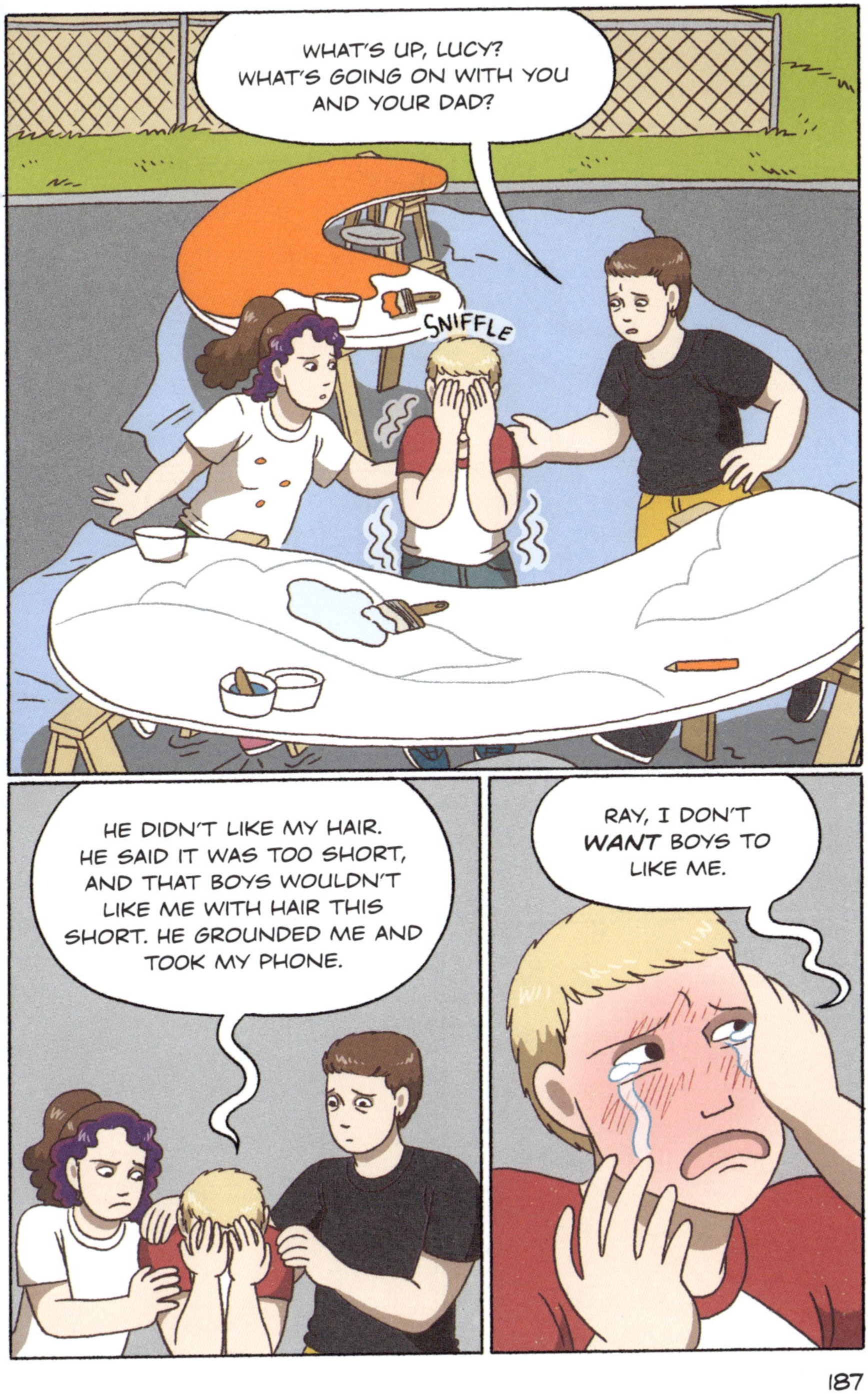
WHAT'S UP, LUCY? WHAT'S GOING ON WITH YOU AND YOUR DAD?
SNIFFLE
HE DIDN'T LIKE MY HAIR. HE SAID IT WAS TOO SHORT, AND THAT BOYS WOULDN'T LIKE ME WITH HAIR THIS SHORT. HE GROUNDED ME AND TOOK MY PHONE.
RAY, I DON'T *WANT* BOYS TO LIKE ME.

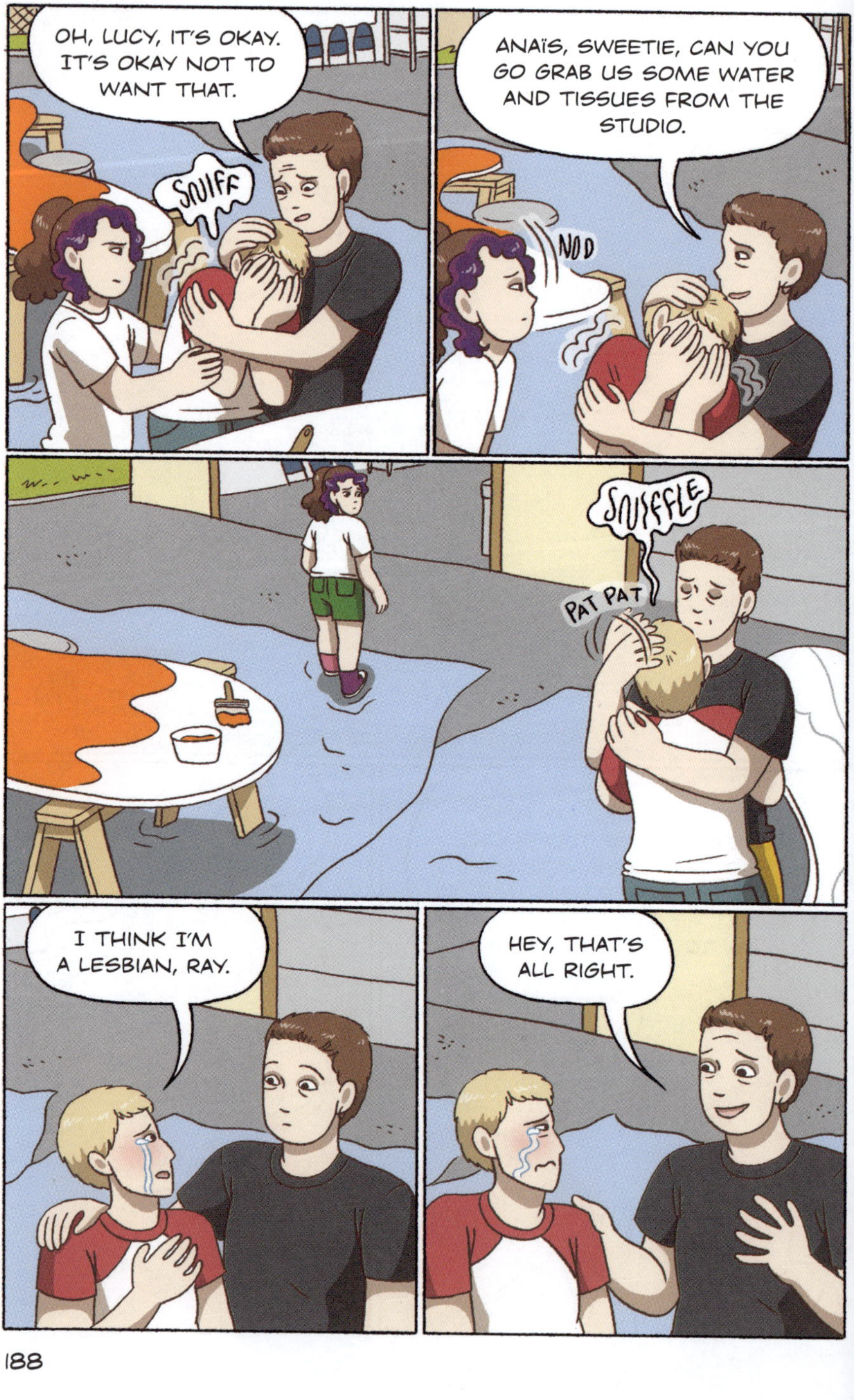
OH, LUCY, IT'S OKAY. IT'S OKAY NOT TO WANT THAT.
SNIFF
ANAÏS, SWEETIE, CAN YOU GO GRAB US SOME WATER AND TISSUES FROM THE STUDIO.
NOD
SNIFFLE
PAT PAT
I THINK I'M A LESBIAN, RAY.
HEY, THAT'S ALL RIGHT.

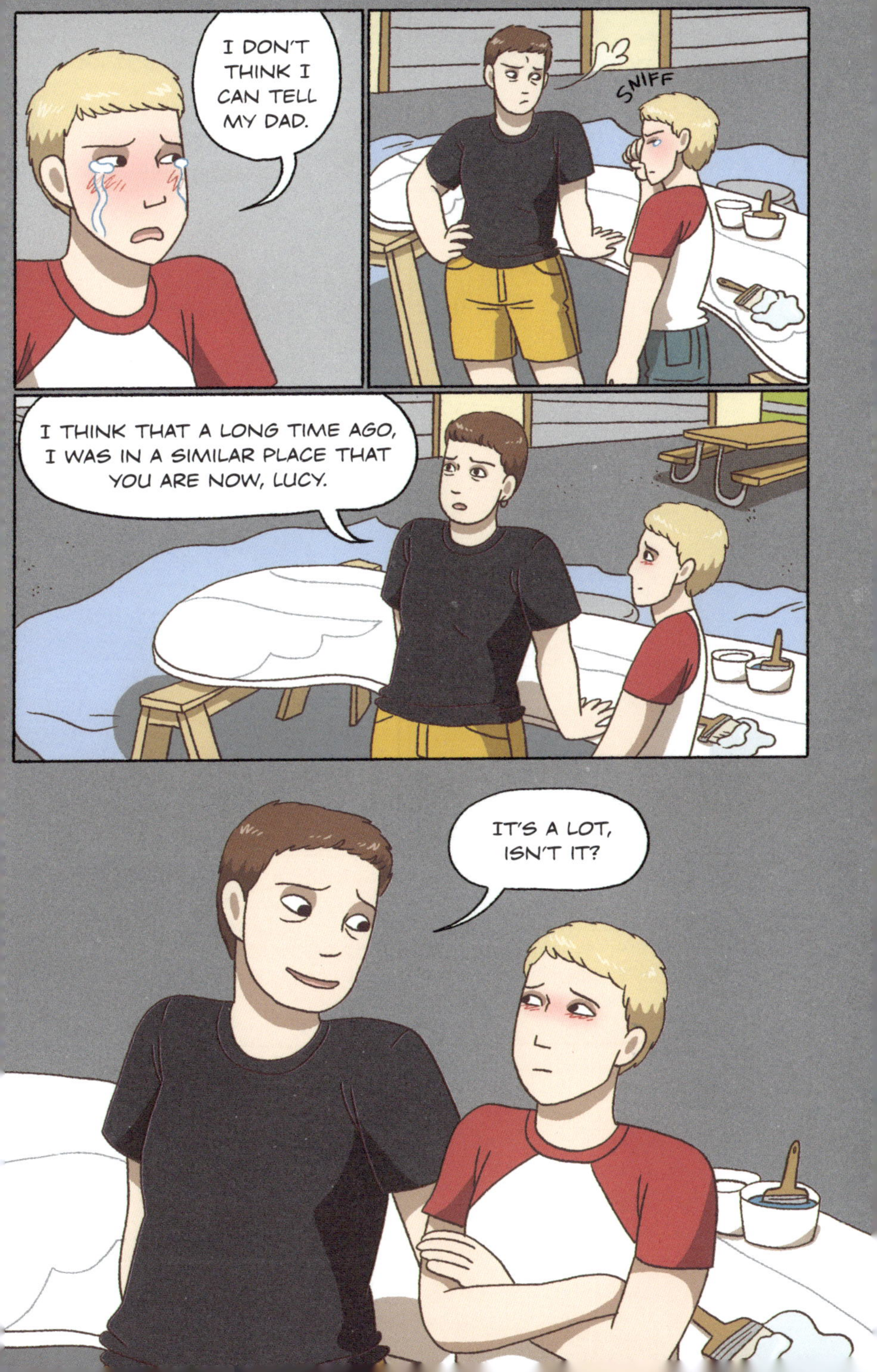
I DON'T THINK I CAN TELL MY DAD.
SNIFF
I THINK THAT A LONG TIME AGO, I WAS IN A SIMILAR PLACE THAT YOU ARE NOW, LUCY.
IT'S A LOT, ISN'T IT?

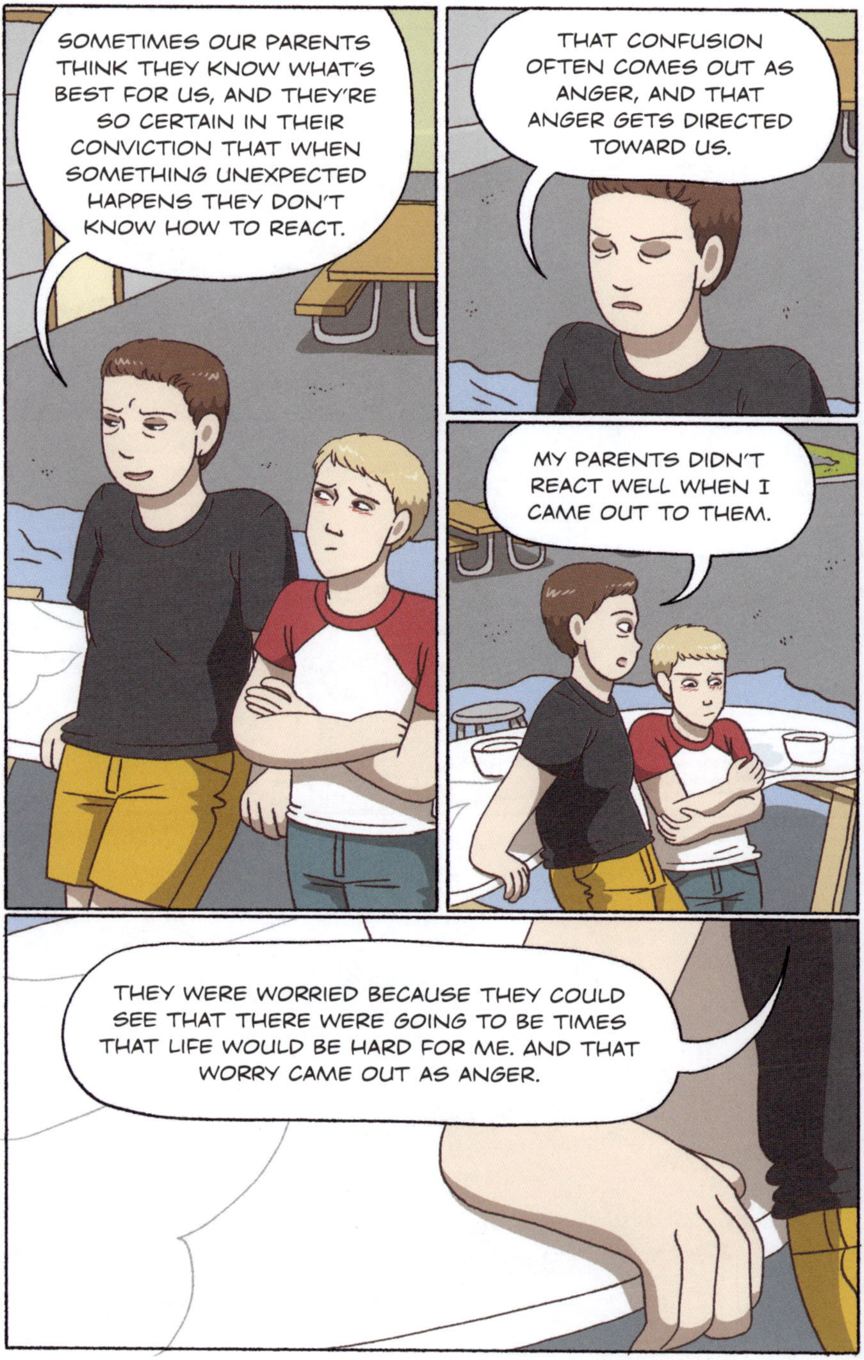
SOMETIMES OUR PARENTS THINK THEY KNOW WHAT'S BEST FOR US, AND THEY'RE SO CERTAIN IN THEIR CONVICTION THAT WHEN SOMETHING UNEXPECTED HAPPENS THEY DON'T KNOW HOW TO REACT.
THAT CONFUSION OFTEN COMES OUT AS ANGER, AND THAT ANGER GETS DIRECTED TOWARD US.
MY PARENTS DIDN'T REACT WELL WHEN I CAME OUT TO THEM.
THEY WERE WORRIED BECAUSE THEY COULD SEE THAT THERE WERE GOING TO BE TIMES THAT LIFE WOULD BE HARD FOR ME. AND THAT WORRY CAME OUT AS ANGER.

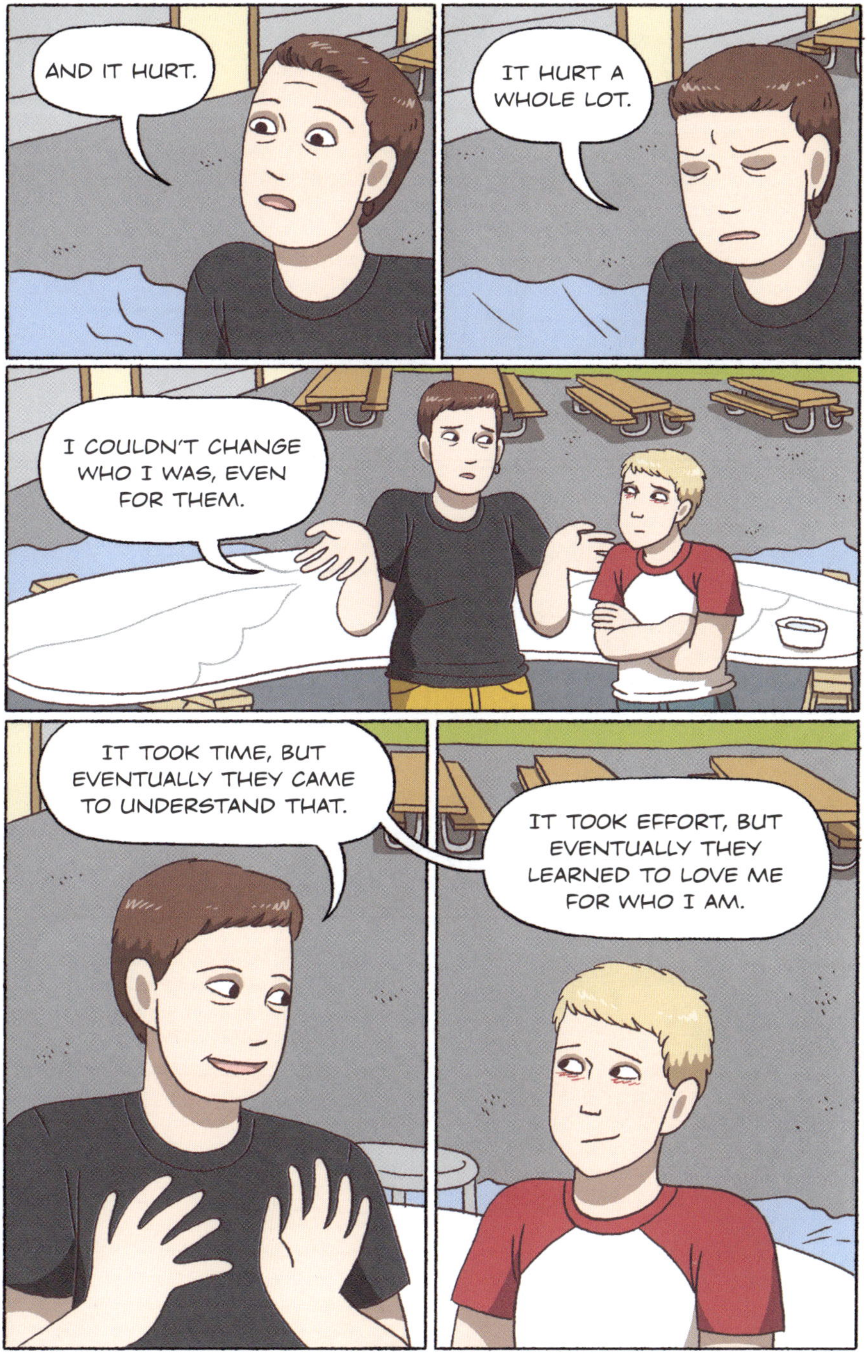
AND IT HURT.
IT HURT A WHOLE LOT.
I COULDN'T CHANGE WHO I WAS, EVEN FOR THEM.
IT TOOK TIME, BUT EVENTUALLY THEY CAME TO UNDERSTAND THAT.
IT TOOK EFFORT, BUT EVENTUALLY THEY LEARNED TO LOVE ME FOR WHO I AM.

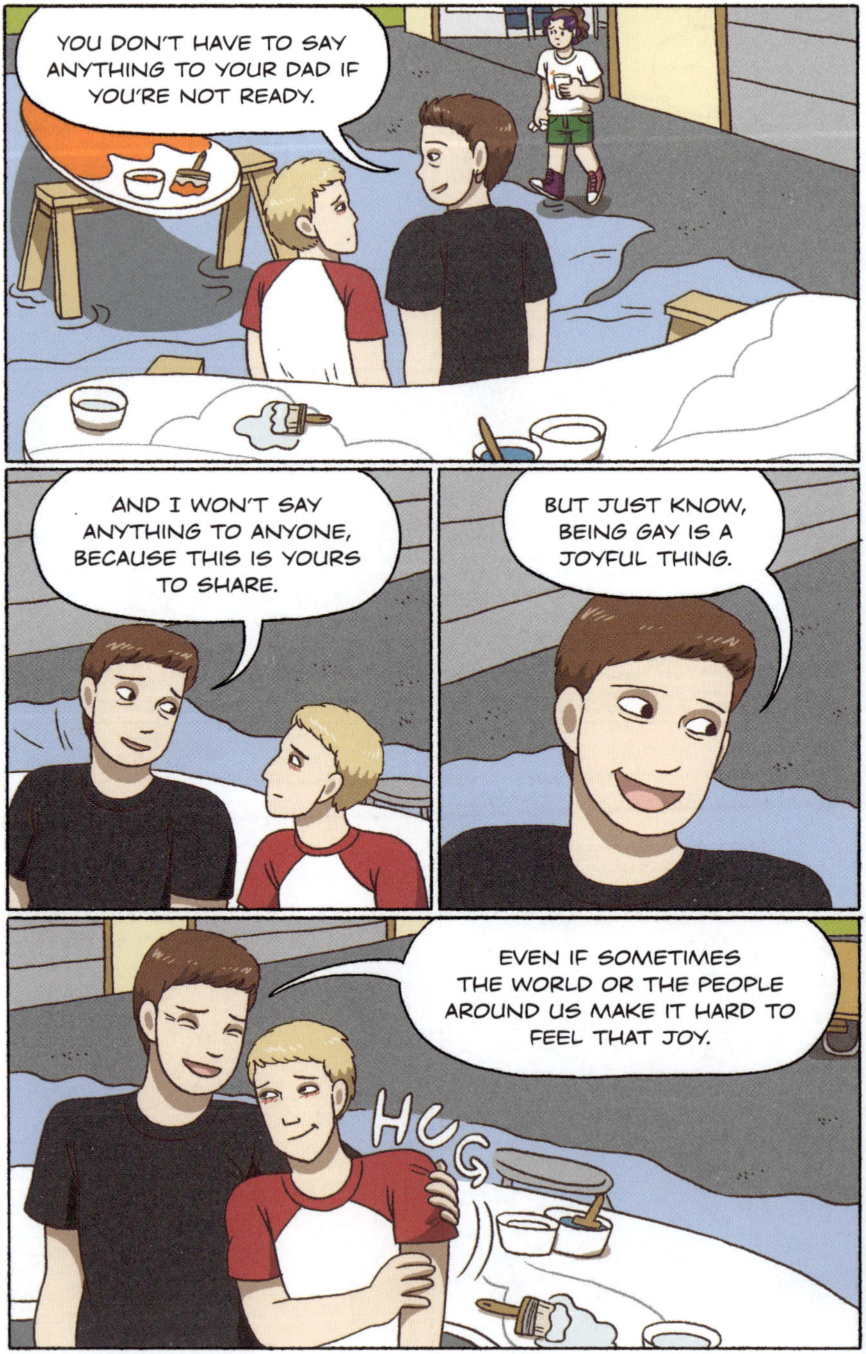
YOU DON'T HAVE TO SAY ANYTHING TO YOUR DAD IF YOU'RE NOT READY.
AND I WON'T SAY ANYTHING TO ANYONE, BECAUSE THIS IS YOURS TO SHARE.
BUT JUST KNOW, BEING GAY IS A JOYFUL THING.
EVEN IF SOMETIMES THE WORLD OR THE PEOPLE AROUND US MAKE IT HARD TO FEEL THAT JOY.
HUG

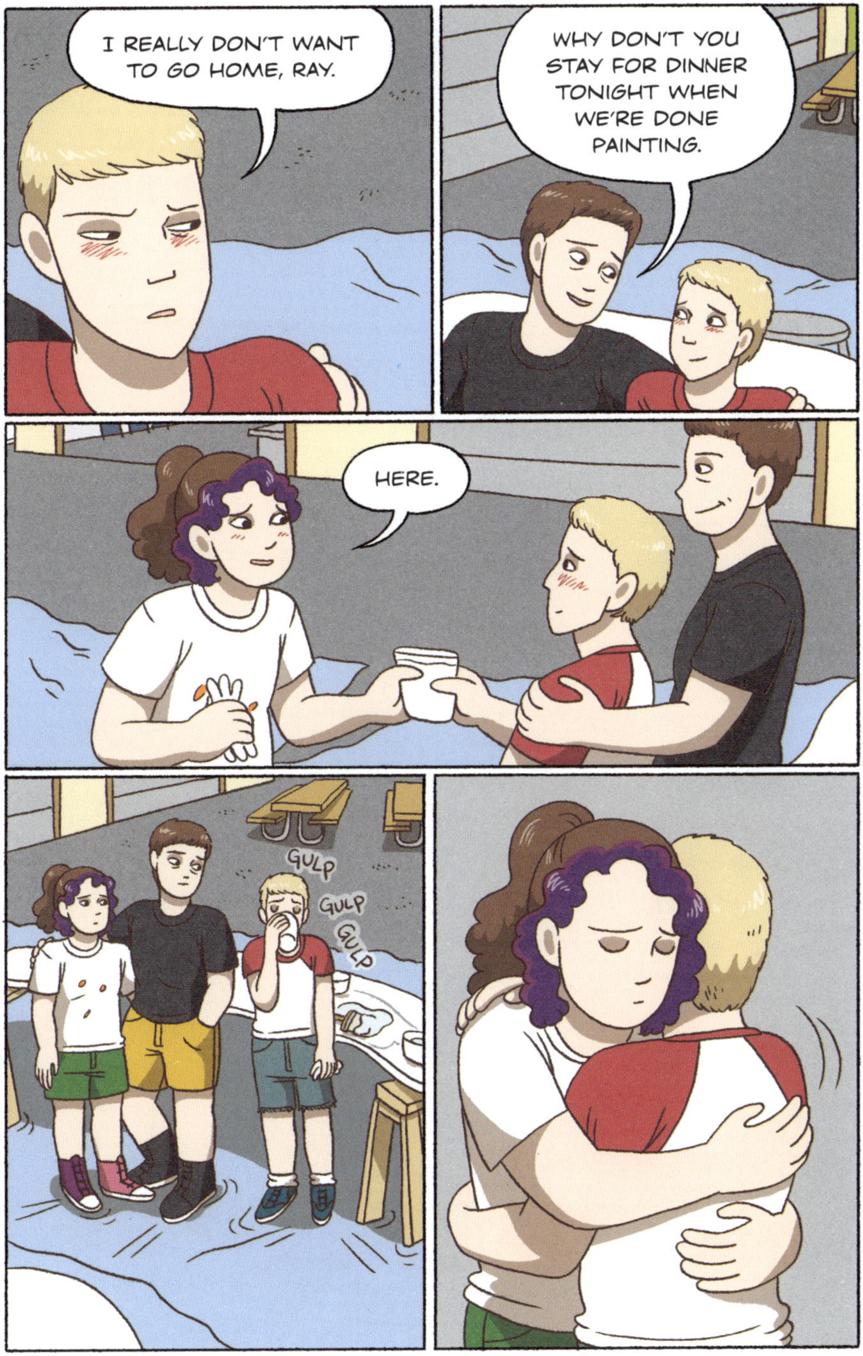
I REALLY DON'T WANT TO GO HOME, RAY.
WHY DON'T YOU STAY FOR DINNER TONIGHT WHEN WE'RE DONE PAINTING.
HERE.
GULP
GULP
GULP

CHAPTER 5

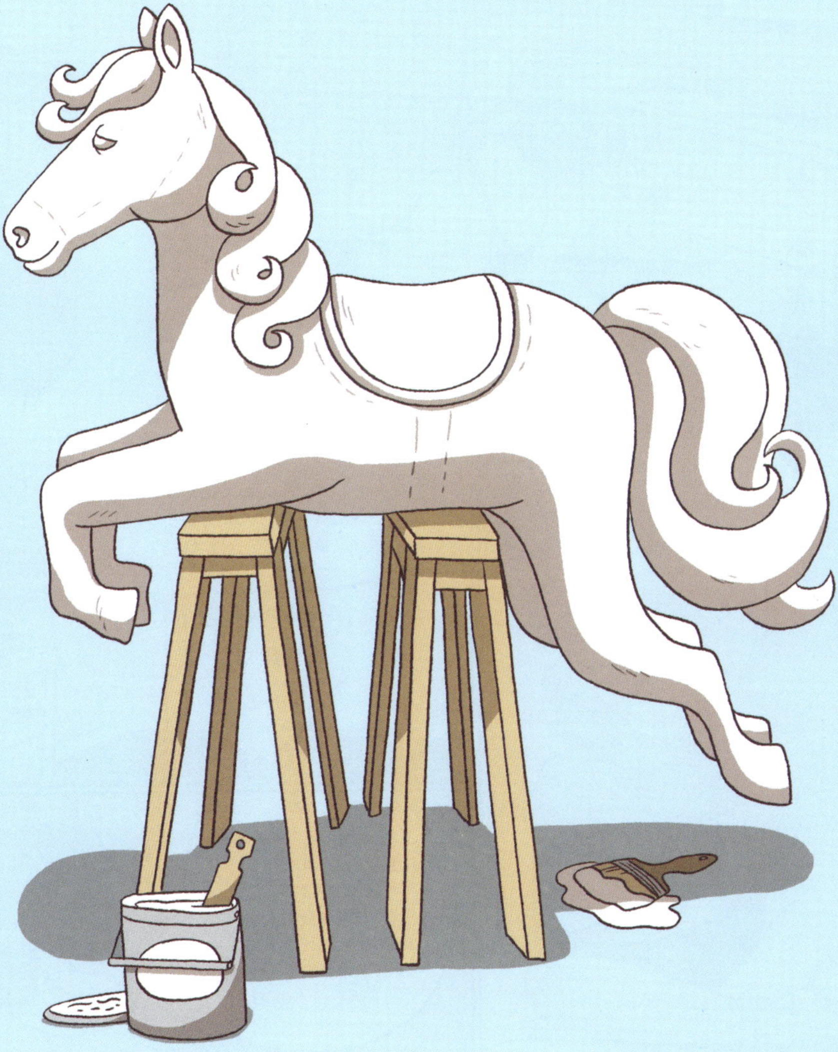

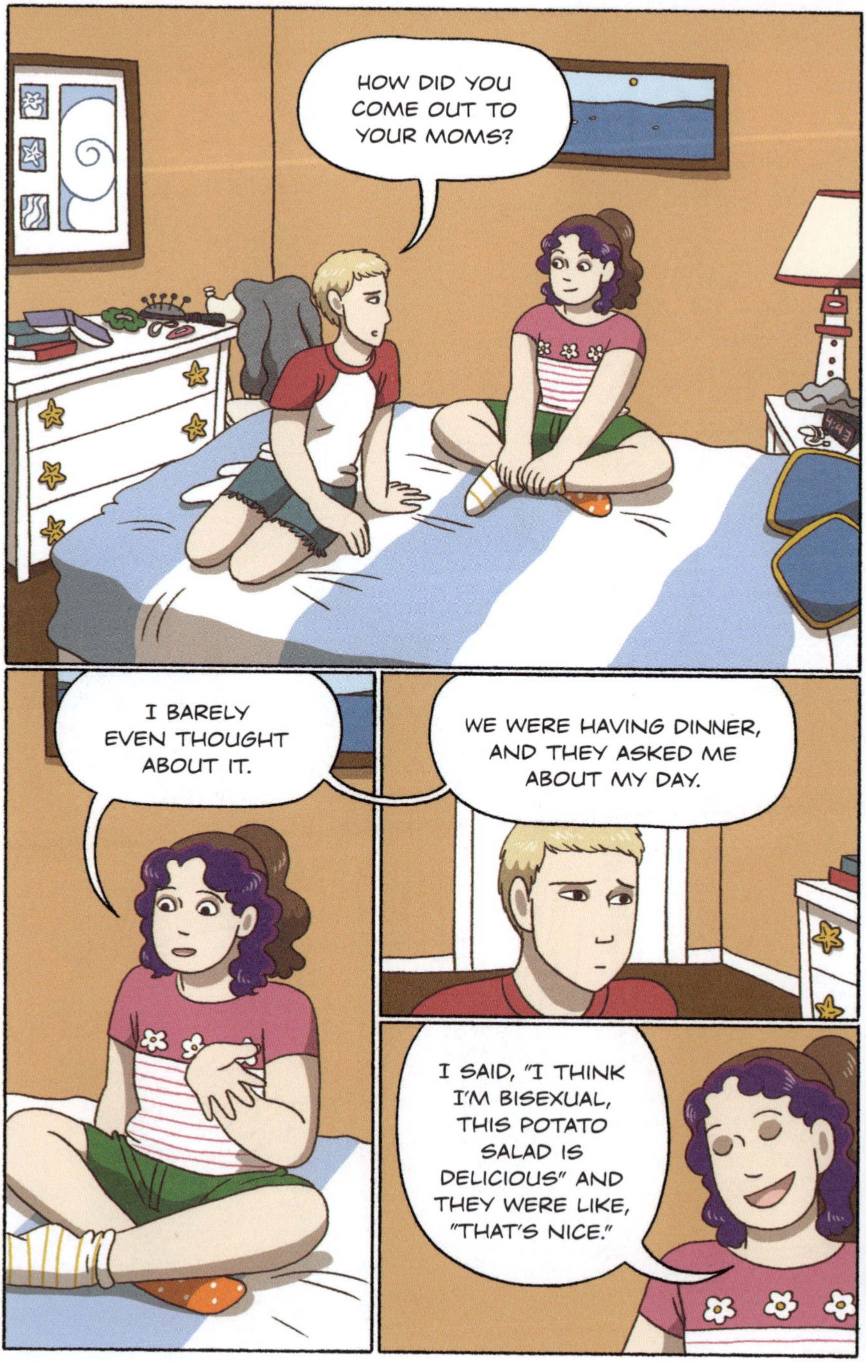
HOW DID YOU COME OUT TO YOUR MOMS?
I BARELY EVEN THOUGHT ABOUT IT.
WE WERE HAVING DINNER, AND THEY ASKED ME ABOUT MY DAY.
I SAID, "I THINK I'M BISEXUAL, THIS POTATO SALAD IS DELICIOUS" AND THEY WERE LIKE, "THAT'S NICE."

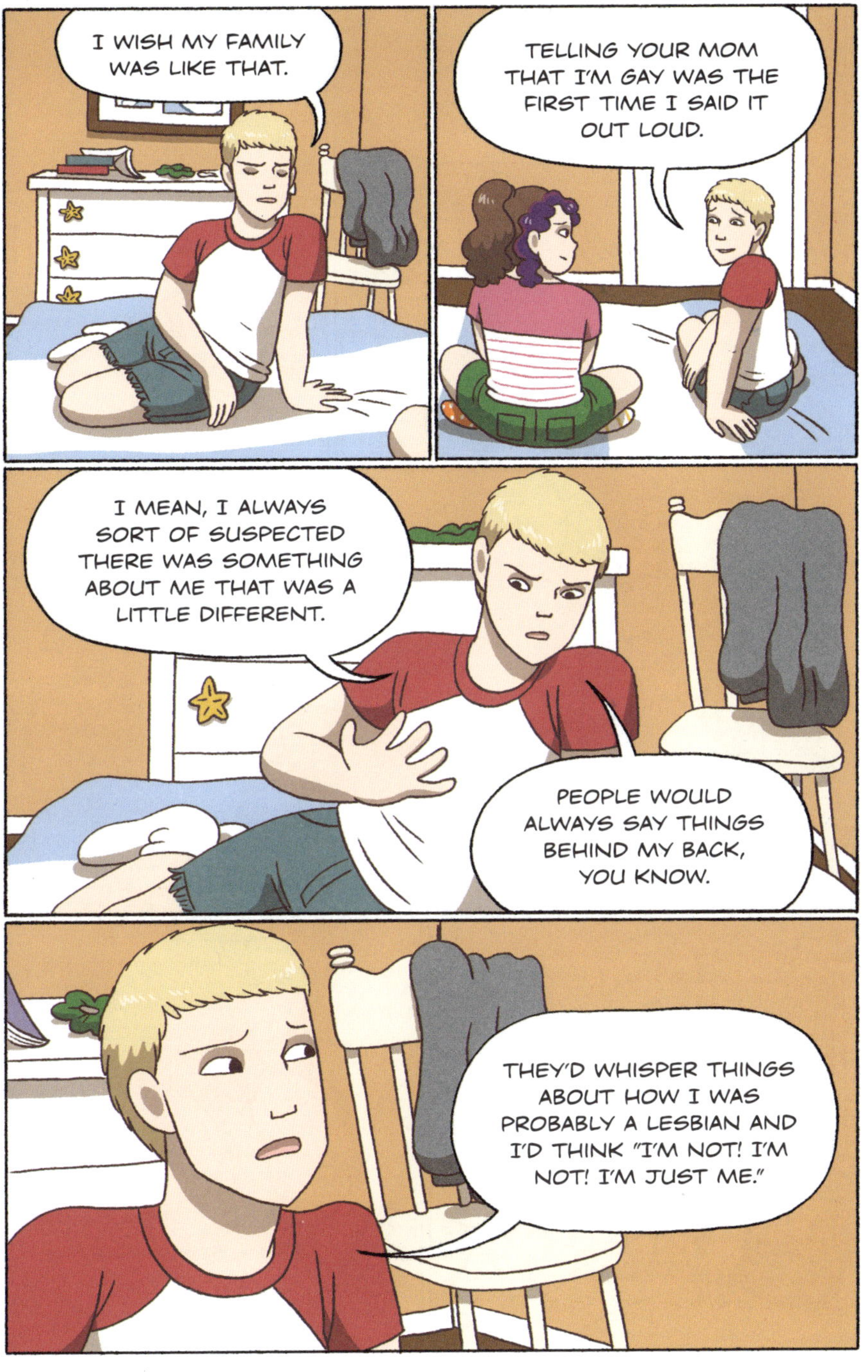
I WISH MY FAMILY WAS LIKE THAT.
TELLING YOUR MOM THAT I'M GAY WAS THE FIRST TIME I SAID IT OUT LOUD.
I MEAN, I ALWAYS SORT OF SUSPECTED THERE WAS SOMETHING ABOUT ME THAT WAS A LITTLE DIFFERENT.
PEOPLE WOULD ALWAYS SAY THINGS BEHIND MY BACK, YOU KNOW.
THEY'D WHISPER THINGS ABOUT HOW I WAS PROBABLY A LESBIAN AND I'D THINK "I'M NOT! I'M NOT! I'M JUST ME."

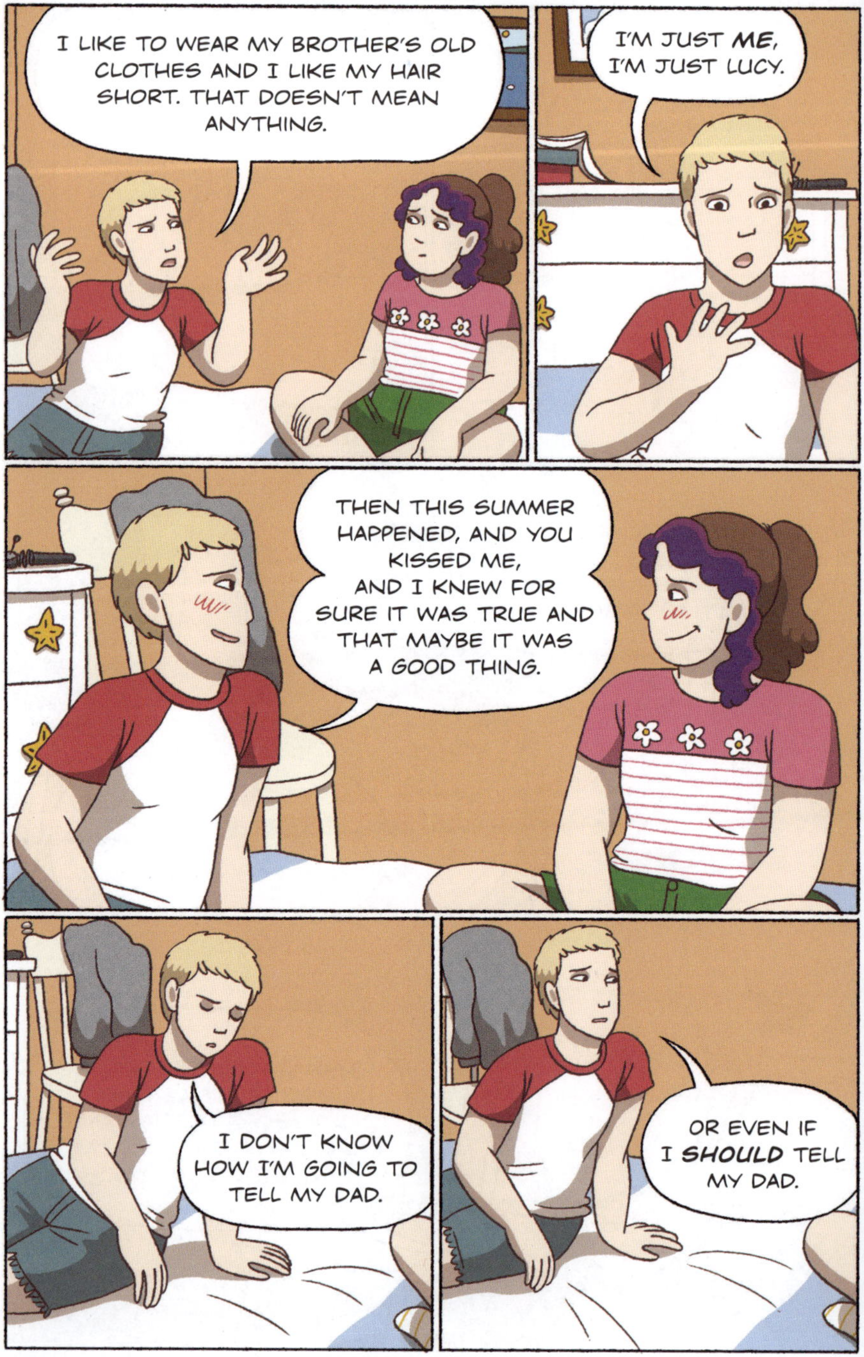
I LIKE TO WEAR MY BROTHER'S OLD CLOTHES AND I LIKE MY HAIR SHORT. THAT DOESN'T MEAN ANYTHING.
I'M JUST **ME**, I'M JUST LUCY.
THEN THIS SUMMER HAPPENED, AND YOU KISSED ME, AND I KNEW FOR SURE IT WAS TRUE AND THAT MAYBE IT WAS A GOOD THING.
I DON'T KNOW HOW I'M GOING TO TELL MY DAD.
OR EVEN IF I **SHOULD** TELL MY DAD.

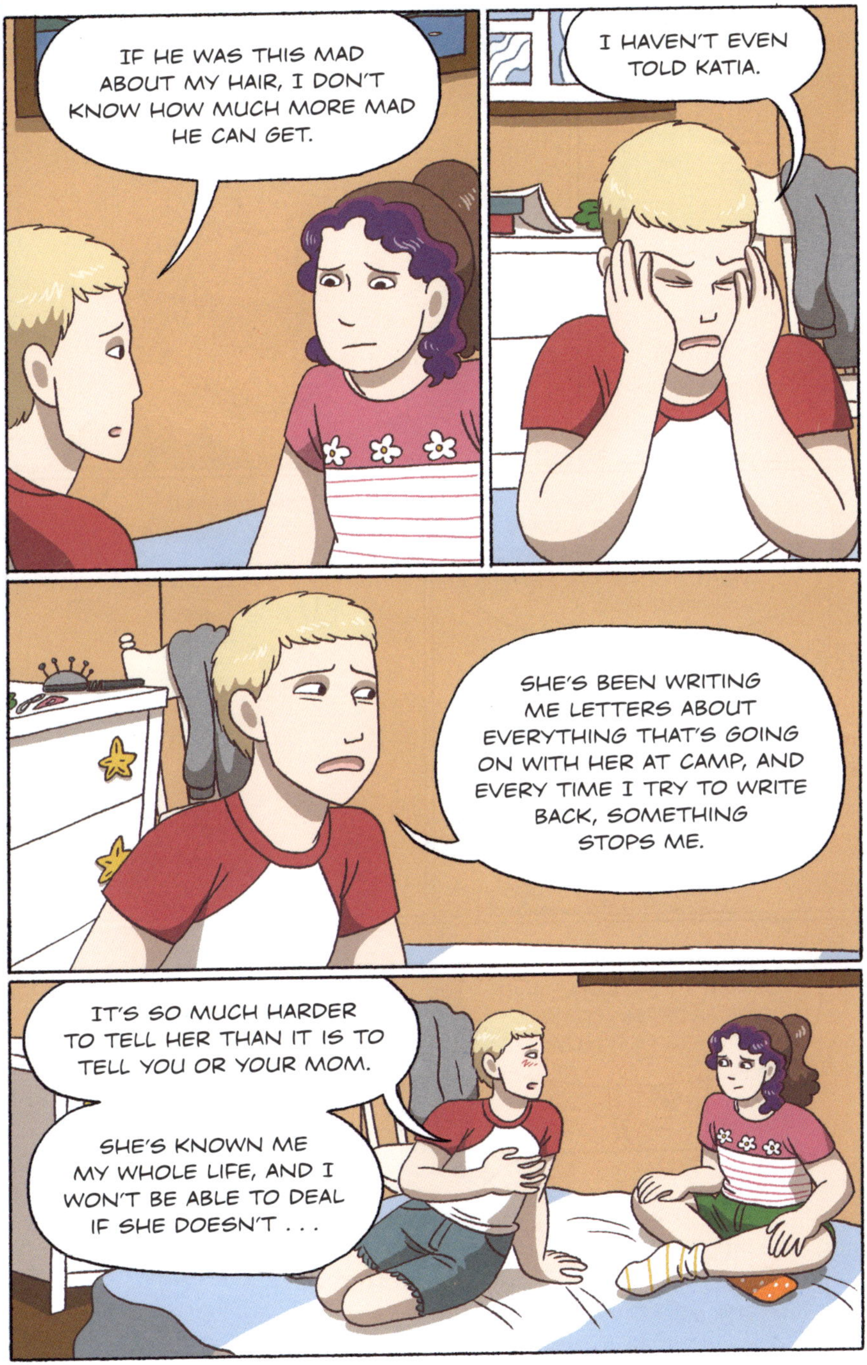
IF HE WAS THIS MAD ABOUT MY HAIR, I DON'T KNOW HOW MUCH MORE MAD HE CAN GET.
I HAVEN'T EVEN TOLD KATIA.
SHE'S BEEN WRITING ME LETTERS ABOUT EVERYTHING THAT'S GOING ON WITH HER AT CAMP, AND EVERY TIME I TRY TO WRITE BACK, SOMETHING STOPS ME.
IT'S SO MUCH HARDER TO TELL HER THAN IT IS TO TELL YOU OR YOUR MOM.
SHE'S KNOWN ME MY WHOLE LIFE, AND I WON'T BE ABLE TO DEAL IF SHE DOESN'T . . .

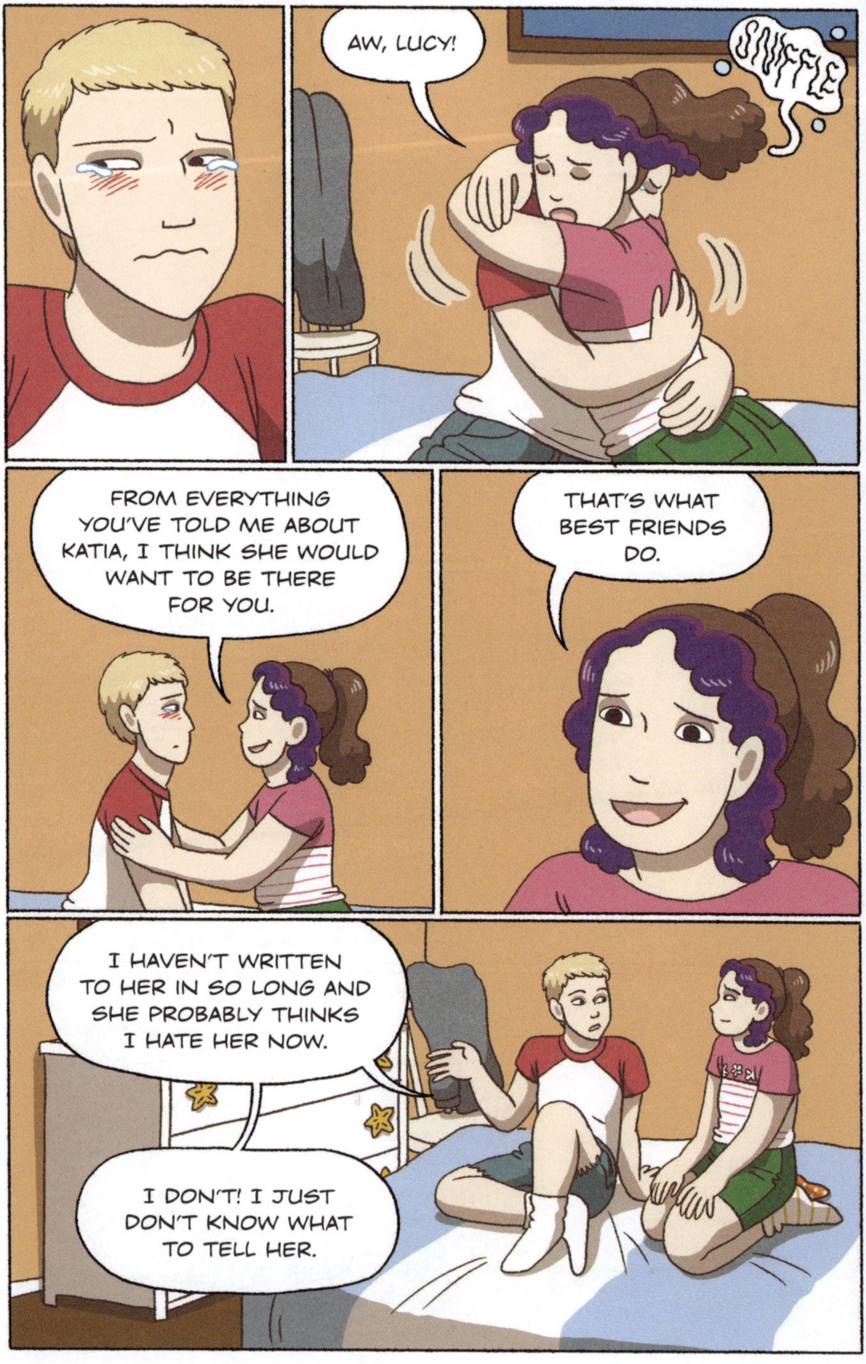
AW, LUCY!
SNIFFLE
FROM EVERYTHING YOU'VE TOLD ME ABOUT KATIA, I THINK SHE WOULD WANT TO BE THERE FOR YOU.
THAT'S WHAT BEST FRIENDS DO.
I HAVEN'T WRITTEN TO HER IN SO LONG AND SHE PROBABLY THINKS I HATE HER NOW.
I DON'T! I JUST DON'T KNOW WHAT TO TELL HER.

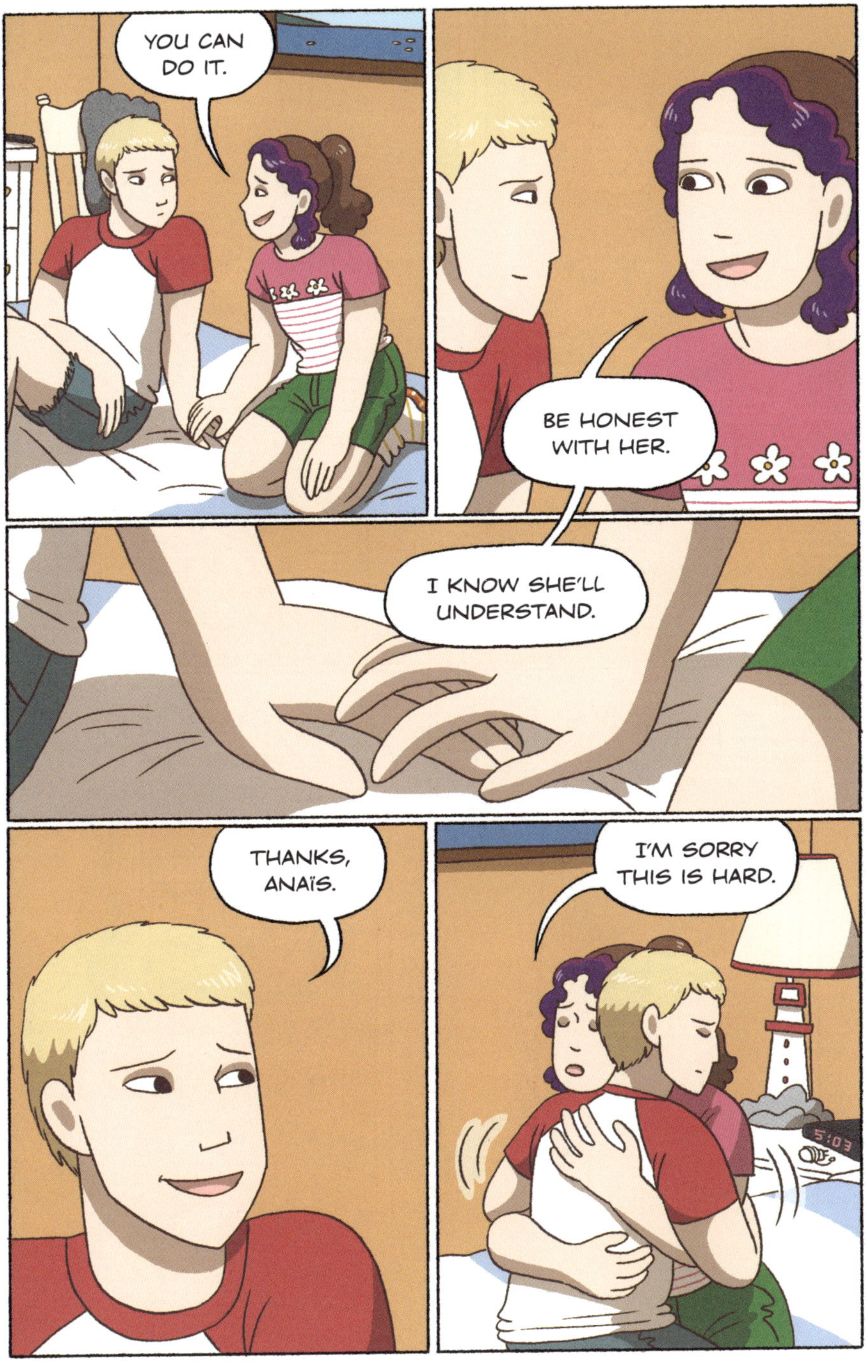
YOU CAN DO IT.
BE HONEST WITH HER.
I KNOW SHE'LL UNDERSTAND.
THANKS, ANAÏS.
I'M SORRY THIS IS HARD.

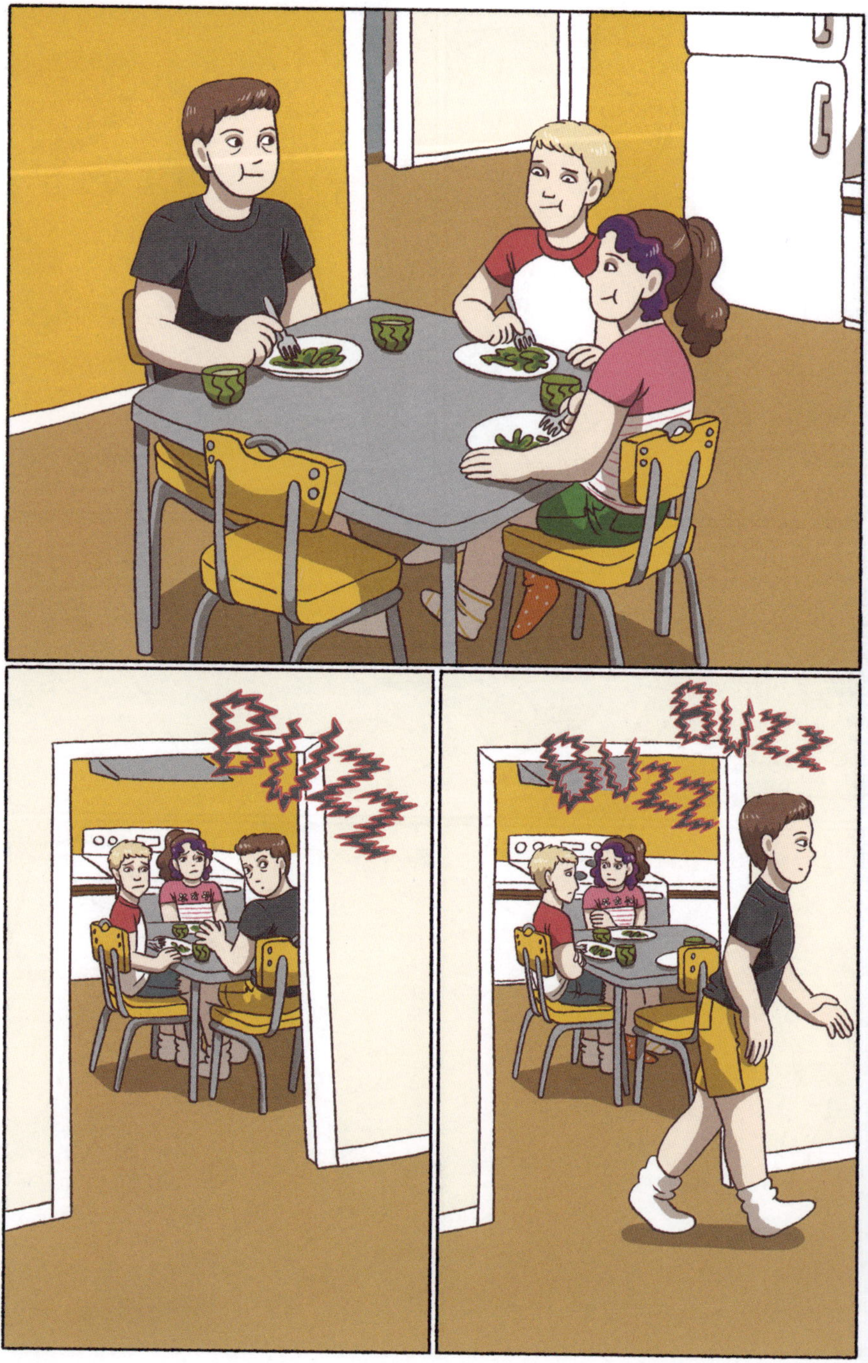
BUZZ
BUZZ
BUZZ

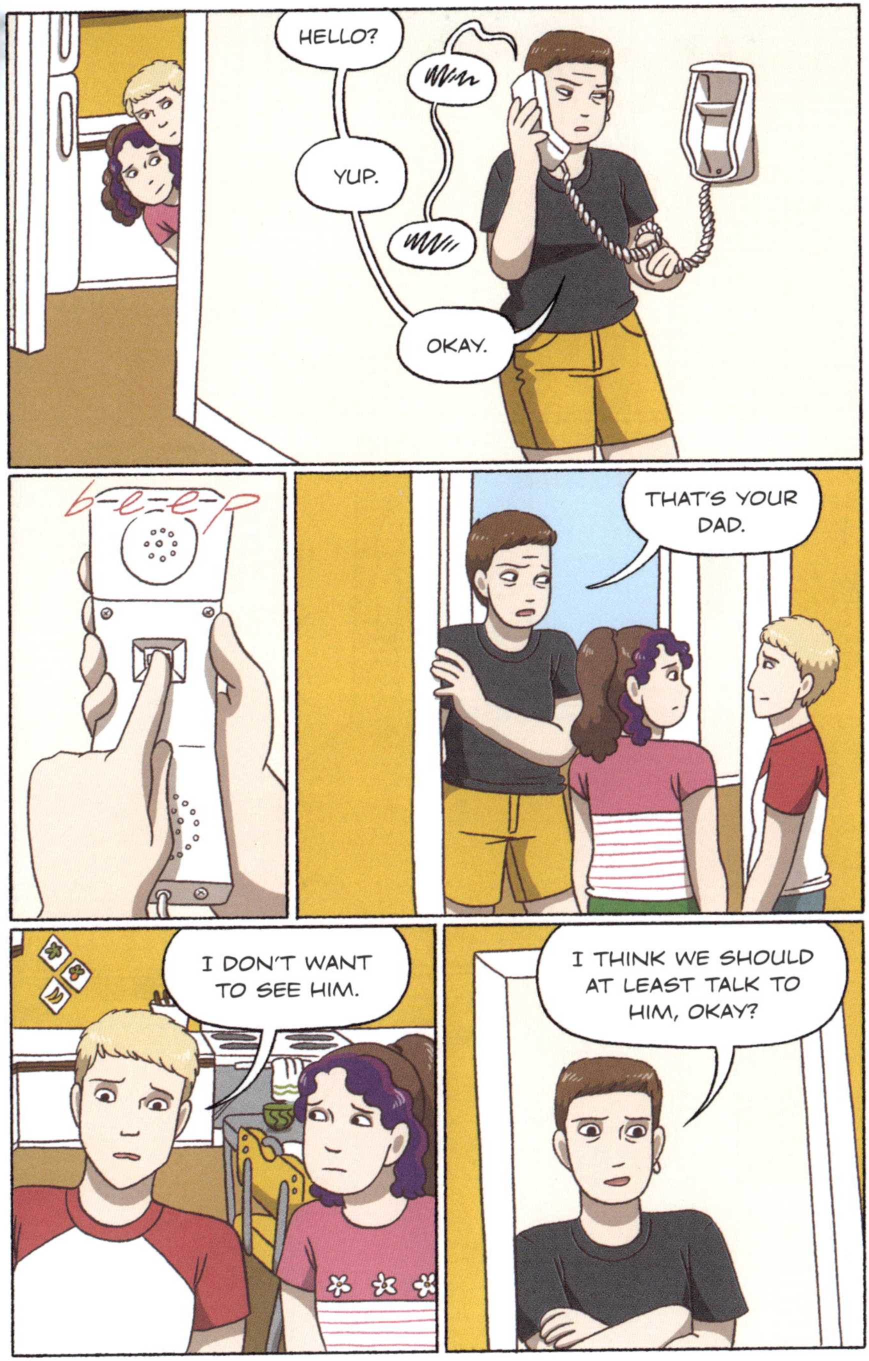
HELLO?
YUP.
OKAY.
b-l-l-p
THAT'S YOUR DAD.
I DON'T WANT TO SEE HIM.
I THINK WE SHOULD AT LEAST TALK TO HIM, OKAY?

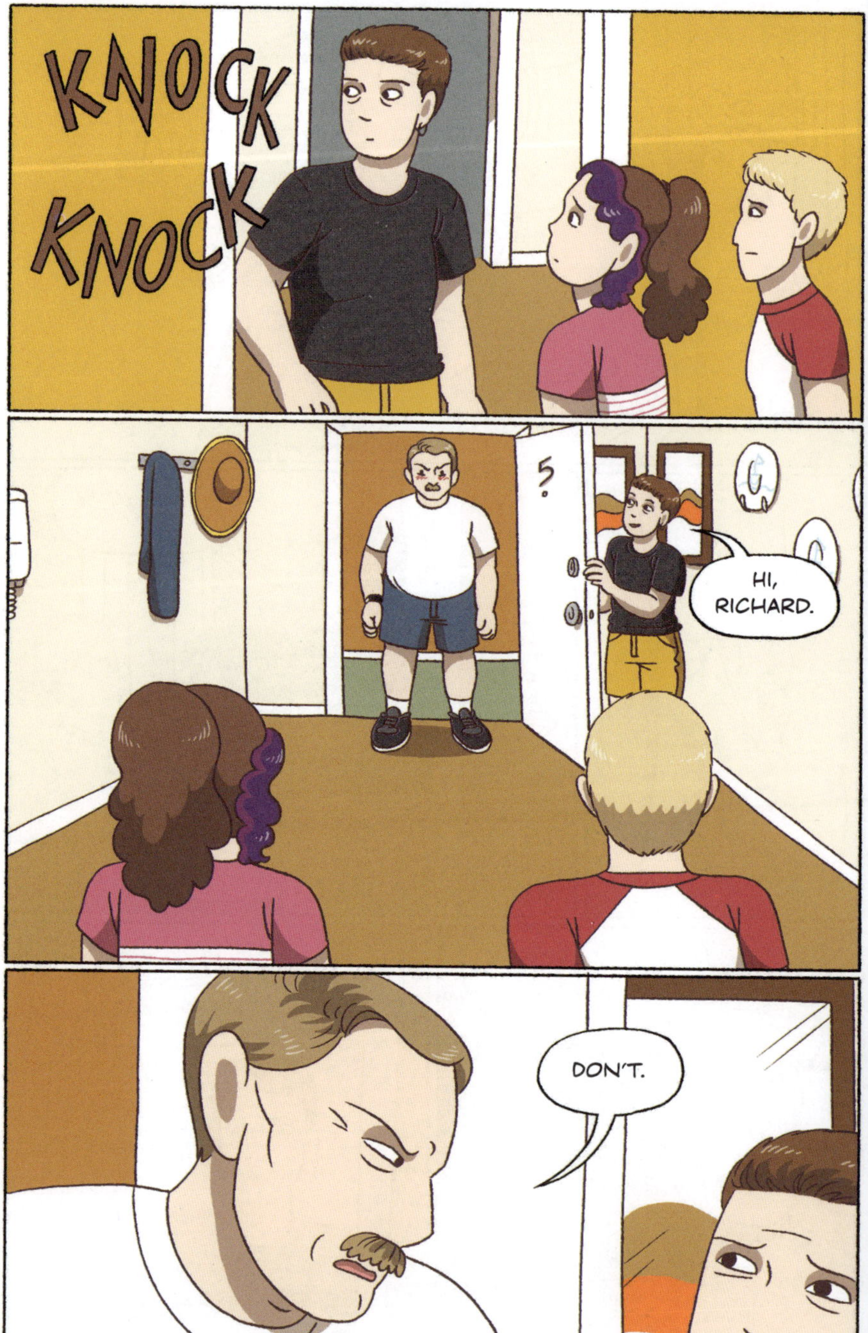
KNOCK
KNOCK
HI, RICHARD.
DON'T.

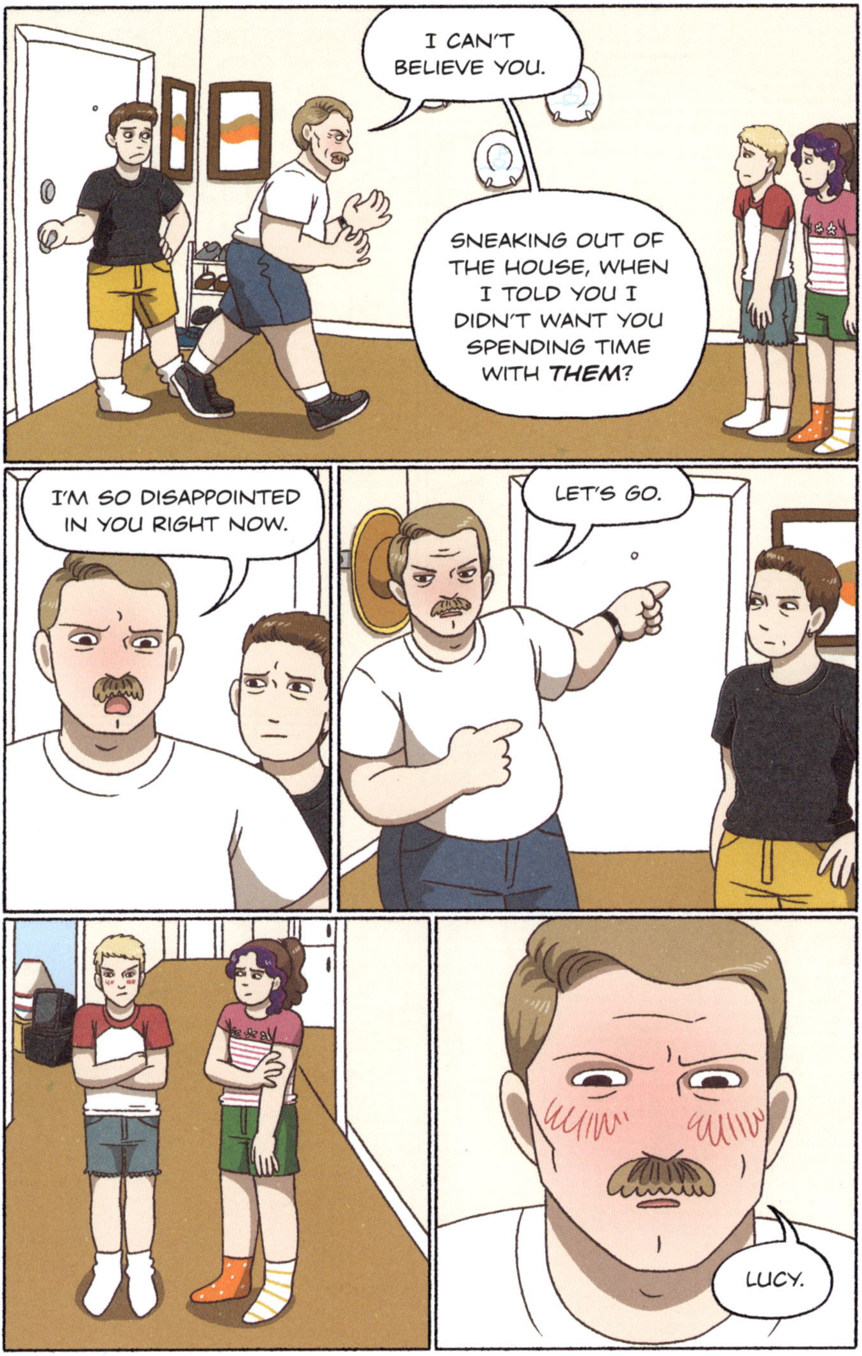
I CAN'T BELIEVE YOU.
SNEAKING OUT OF THE HOUSE, WHEN I TOLD YOU I DIDN'T WANT YOU SPENDING TIME WITH ***THEM***?
I'M SO DISAPPOINTED IN YOU RIGHT NOW.
LET'S GO.
LUCY.

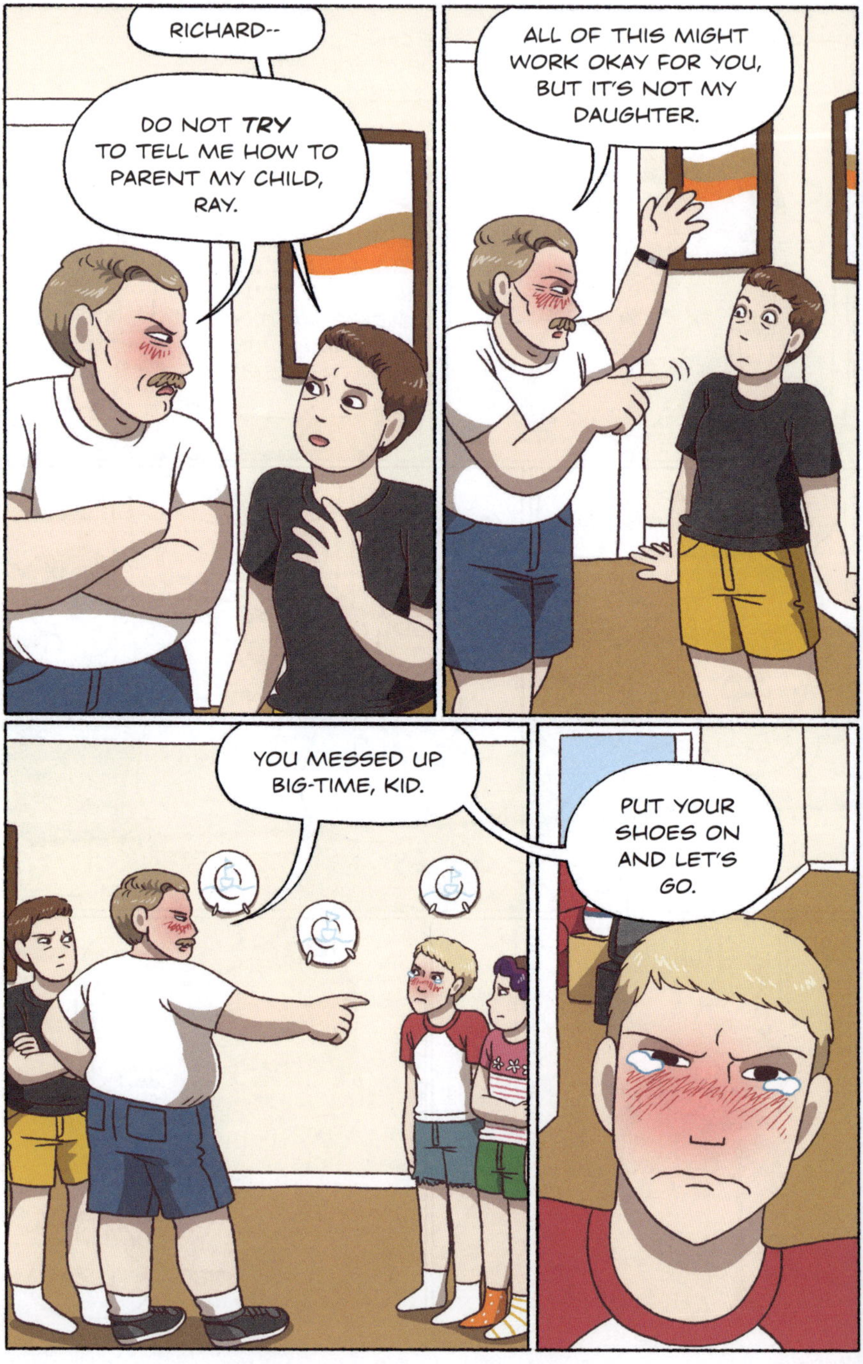
RICHARD--
DO NOT **TRY** TO TELL ME HOW TO PARENT MY CHILD, RAY.
ALL OF THIS MIGHT WORK OKAY FOR YOU, BUT IT'S NOT MY DAUGHTER.
YOU MESSED UP BIG-TIME, KID.
PUT YOUR SHOES ON AND LET'S GO.

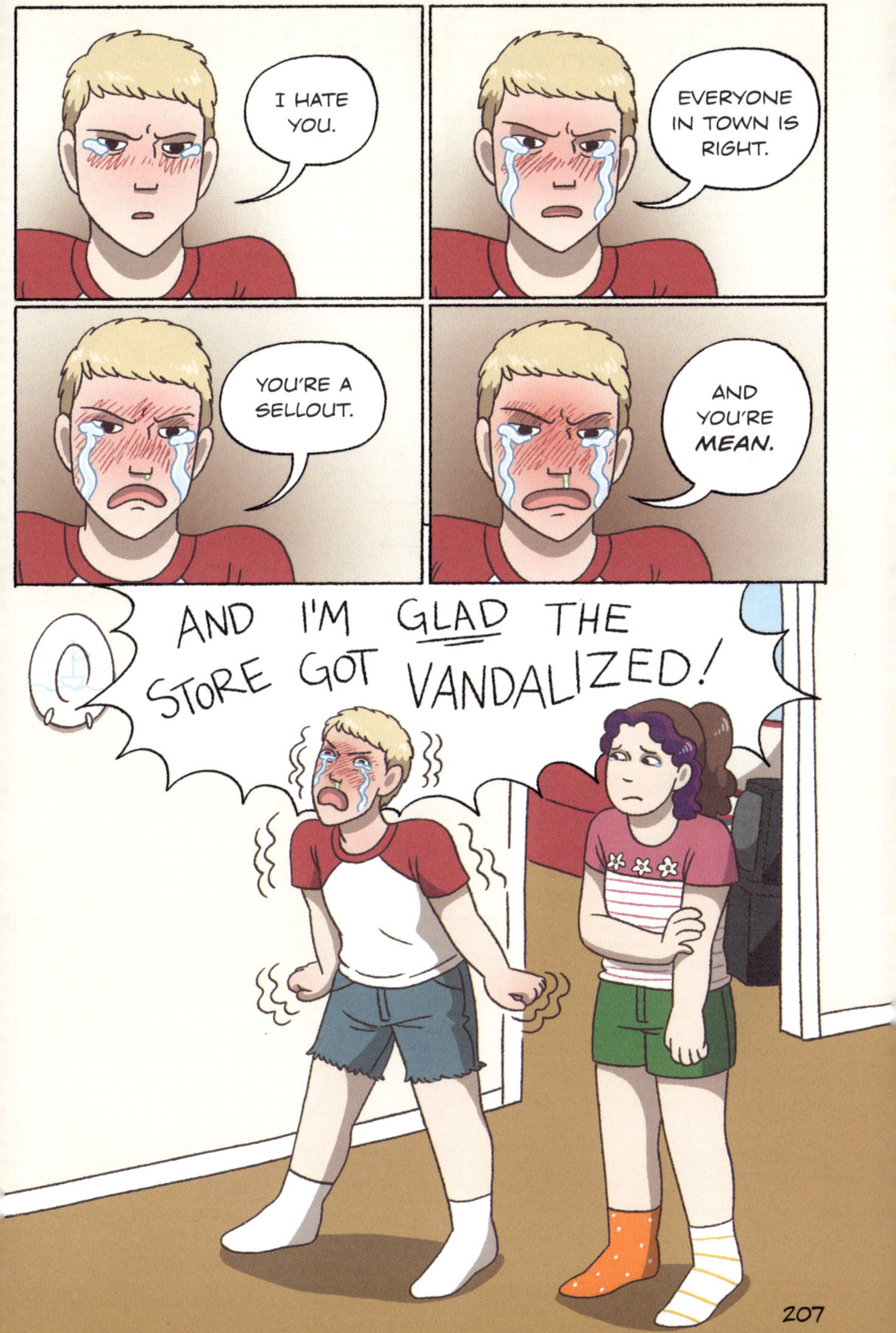
I HATE YOU.
EVERYONE IN TOWN IS RIGHT.
YOU'RE A SELLOUT.
AND YOU'RE MEAN.
AND I'M GLAD THE STORE GOT VANDALIZED!

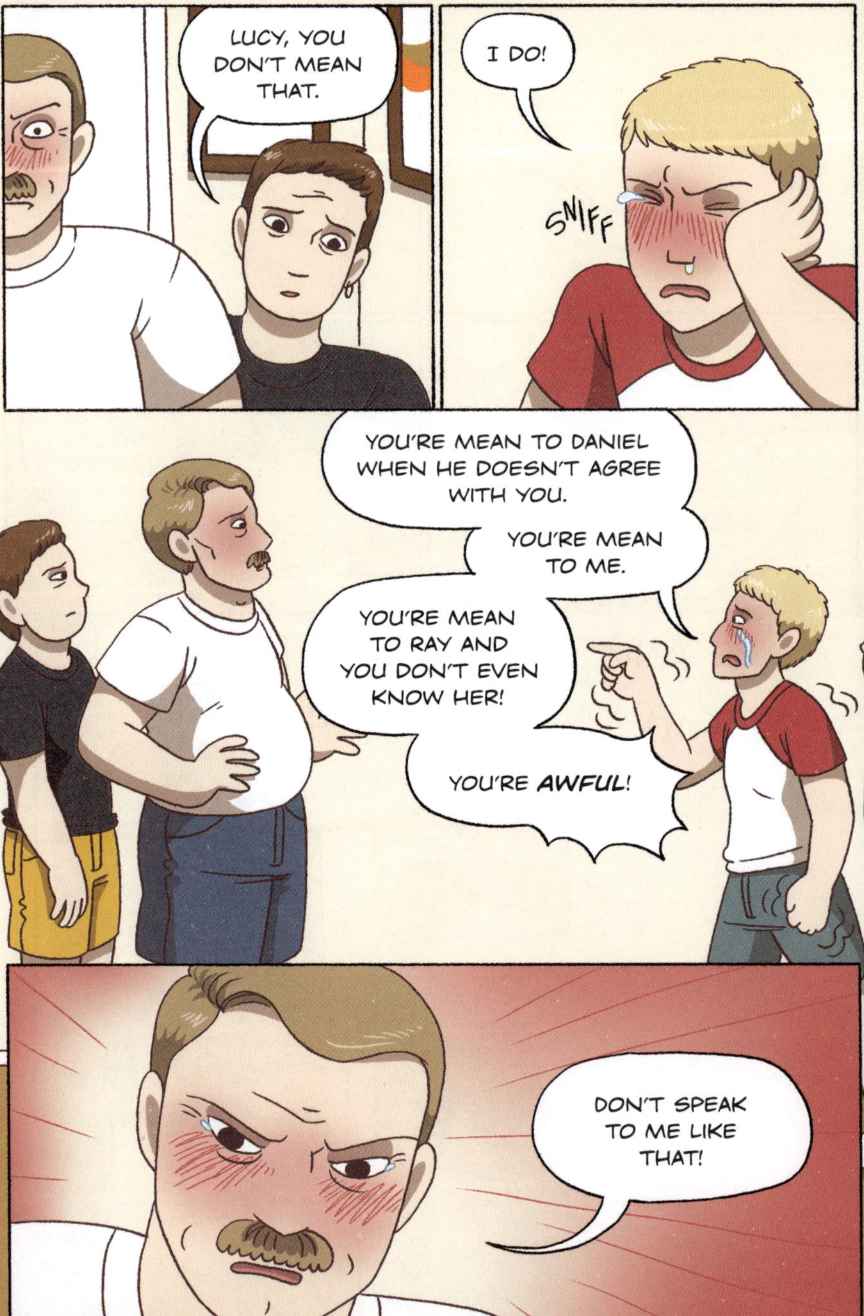
LUCY, YOU DON'T MEAN THAT.
I DO!
SNIFF
YOU'RE MEAN TO DANIEL WHEN HE DOESN'T AGREE WITH YOU.
YOU'RE MEAN TO ME.
YOU'RE MEAN TO RAY AND YOU DON'T EVEN KNOW HER!
YOU'RE **AWFUL**!
DON'T SPEAK TO ME LIKE THAT!

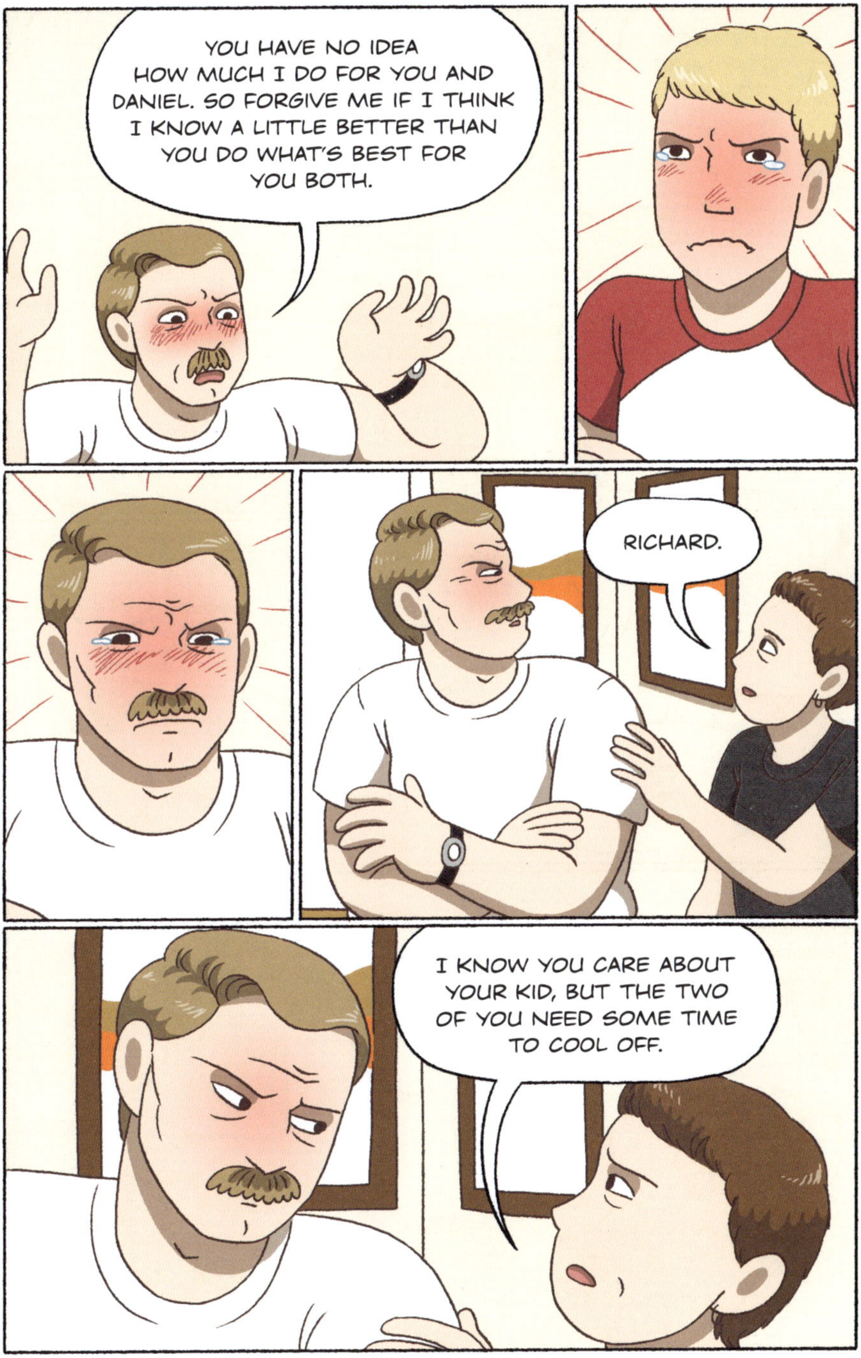
YOU HAVE NO IDEA HOW MUCH I DO FOR YOU AND DANIEL. SO FORGIVE ME IF I THINK I KNOW A LITTLE BETTER THAN YOU DO WHAT'S BEST FOR YOU BOTH.
RICHARD.
I KNOW YOU CARE ABOUT YOUR KID, BUT THE TWO OF YOU NEED SOME TIME TO COOL OFF.

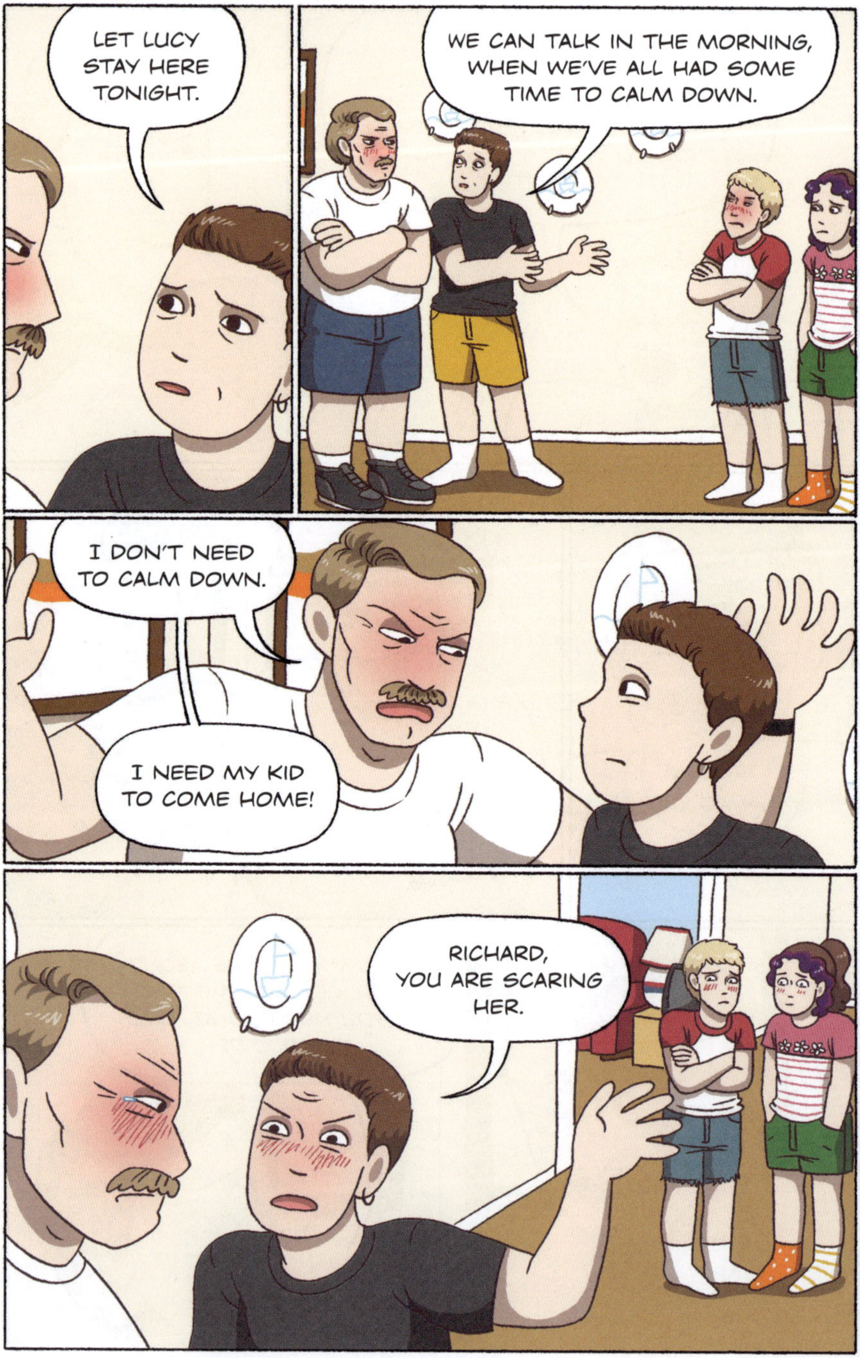
LET LUCY STAY HERE TONIGHT.
WE CAN TALK IN THE MORNING, WHEN WE'VE ALL HAD SOME TIME TO CALM DOWN.
I DON'T NEED TO CALM DOWN.
I NEED MY KID TO COME HOME!
RICHARD, YOU ARE SCARING HER.

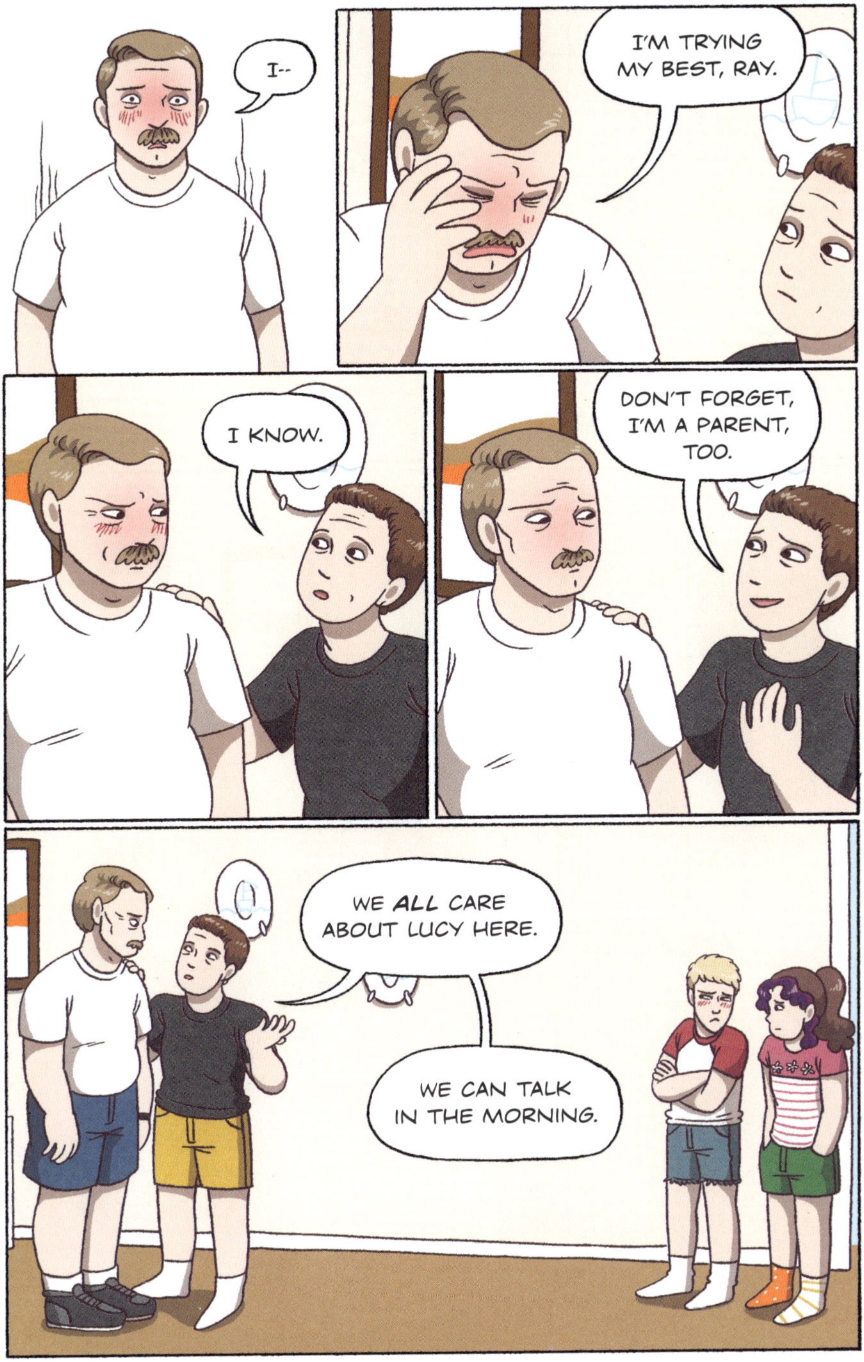
I--
I'M TRYING MY BEST, RAY.
I KNOW.
DON'T FORGET, I'M A PARENT, TOO.
WE ALL CARE ABOUT LUCY HERE.
WE CAN TALK IN THE MORNING.

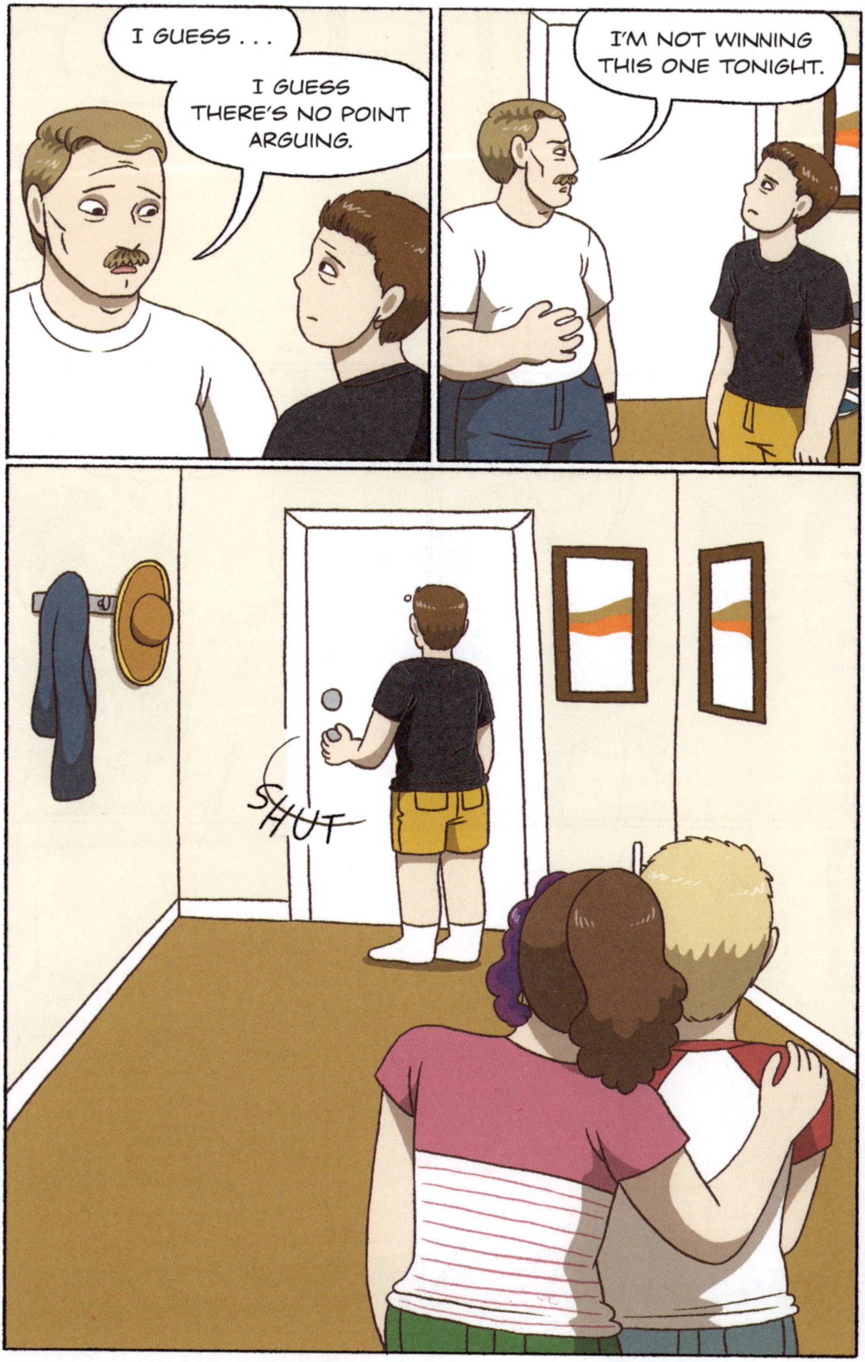
I GUESS . . .
I GUESS THERE'S NO POINT ARGUING.
I'M NOT WINNING THIS ONE TONIGHT.
SHUT

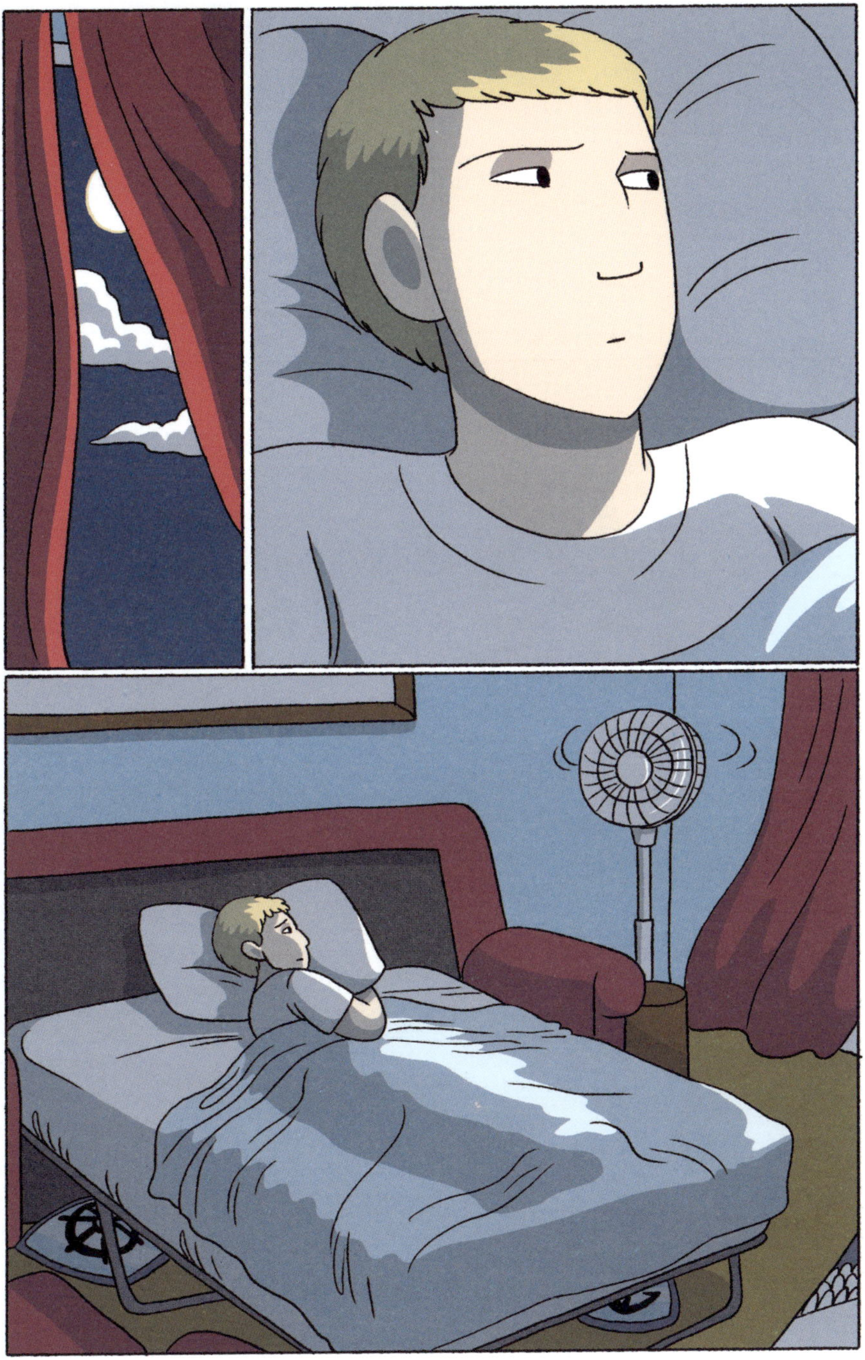

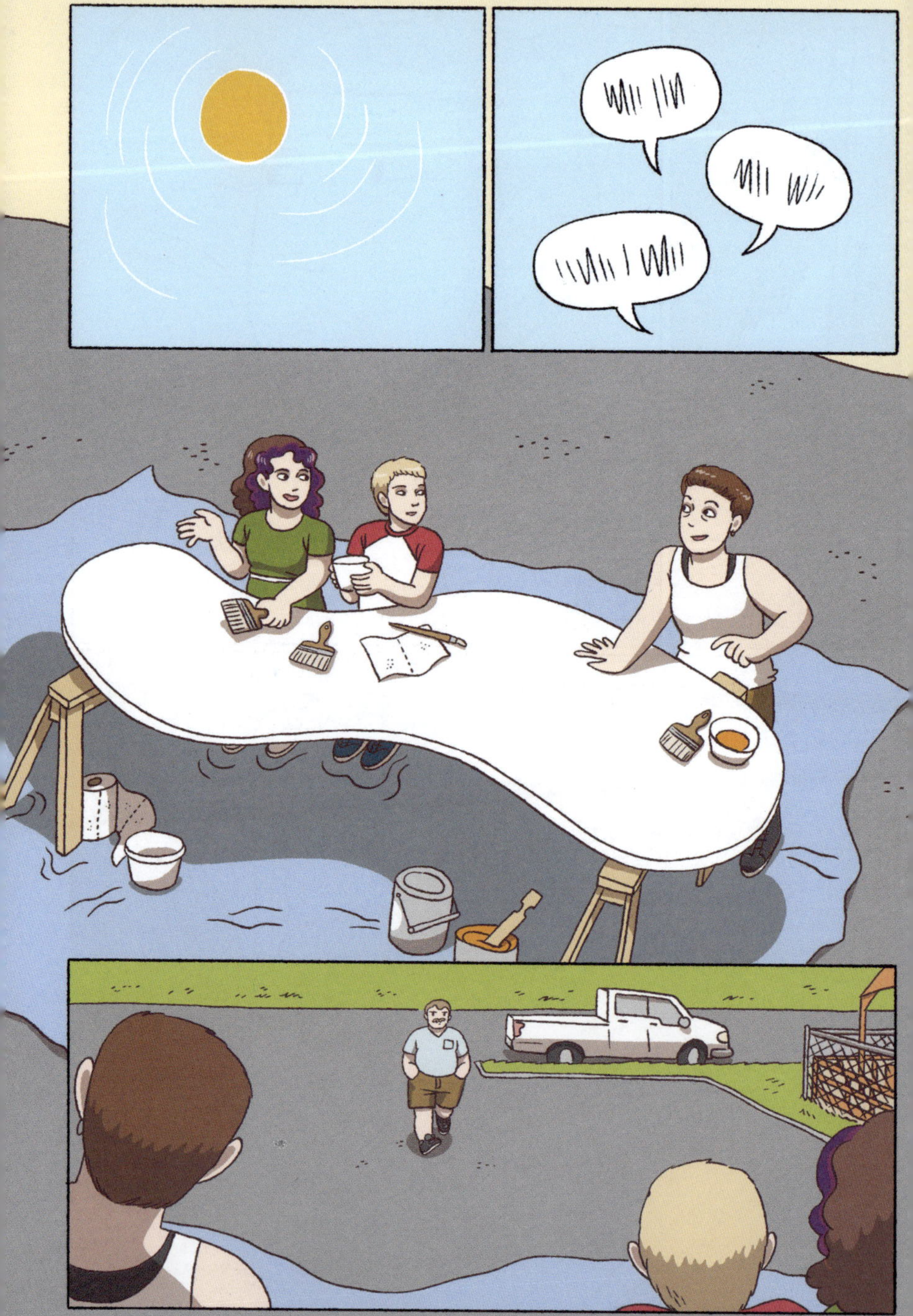

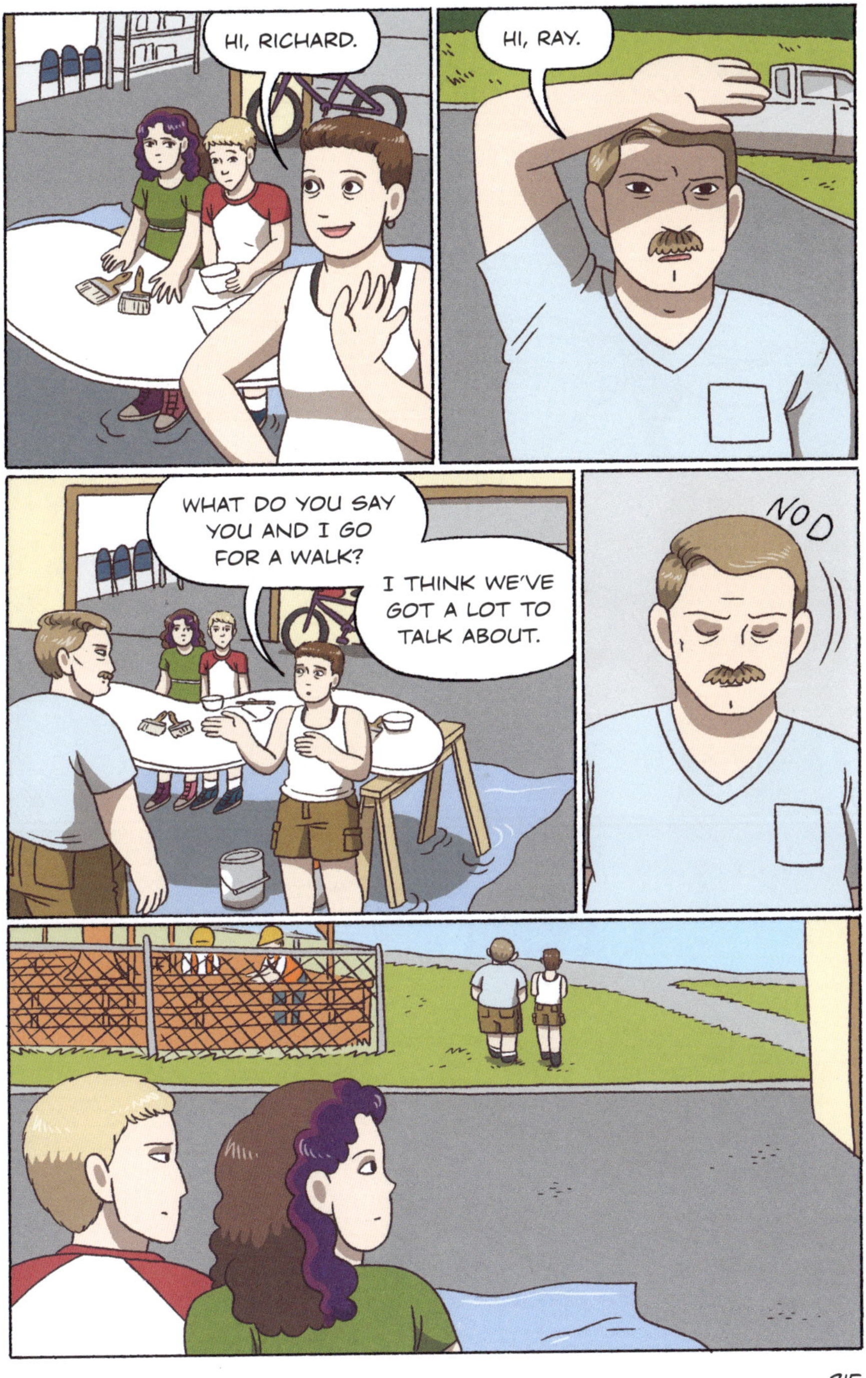
HI, RICHARD.
HI, RAY.
WHAT DO YOU SAY YOU AND I GO FOR A WALK?
I THINK WE'VE GOT A LOT TO TALK ABOUT.
NOD

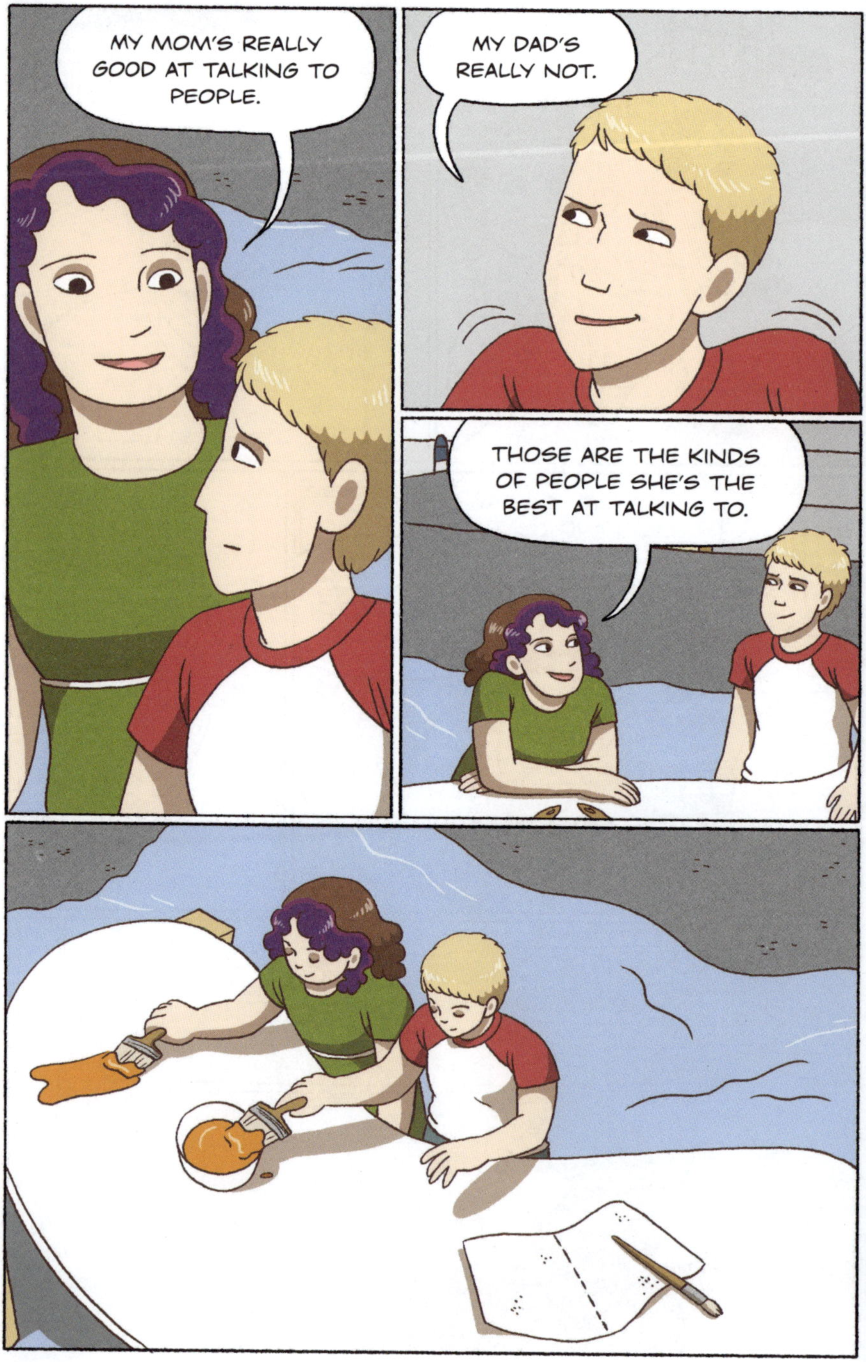
MY MOM'S REALLY GOOD AT TALKING TO PEOPLE.
MY DAD'S REALLY NOT.
THOSE ARE THE KINDS OF PEOPLE SHE'S THE BEST AT TALKING TO.

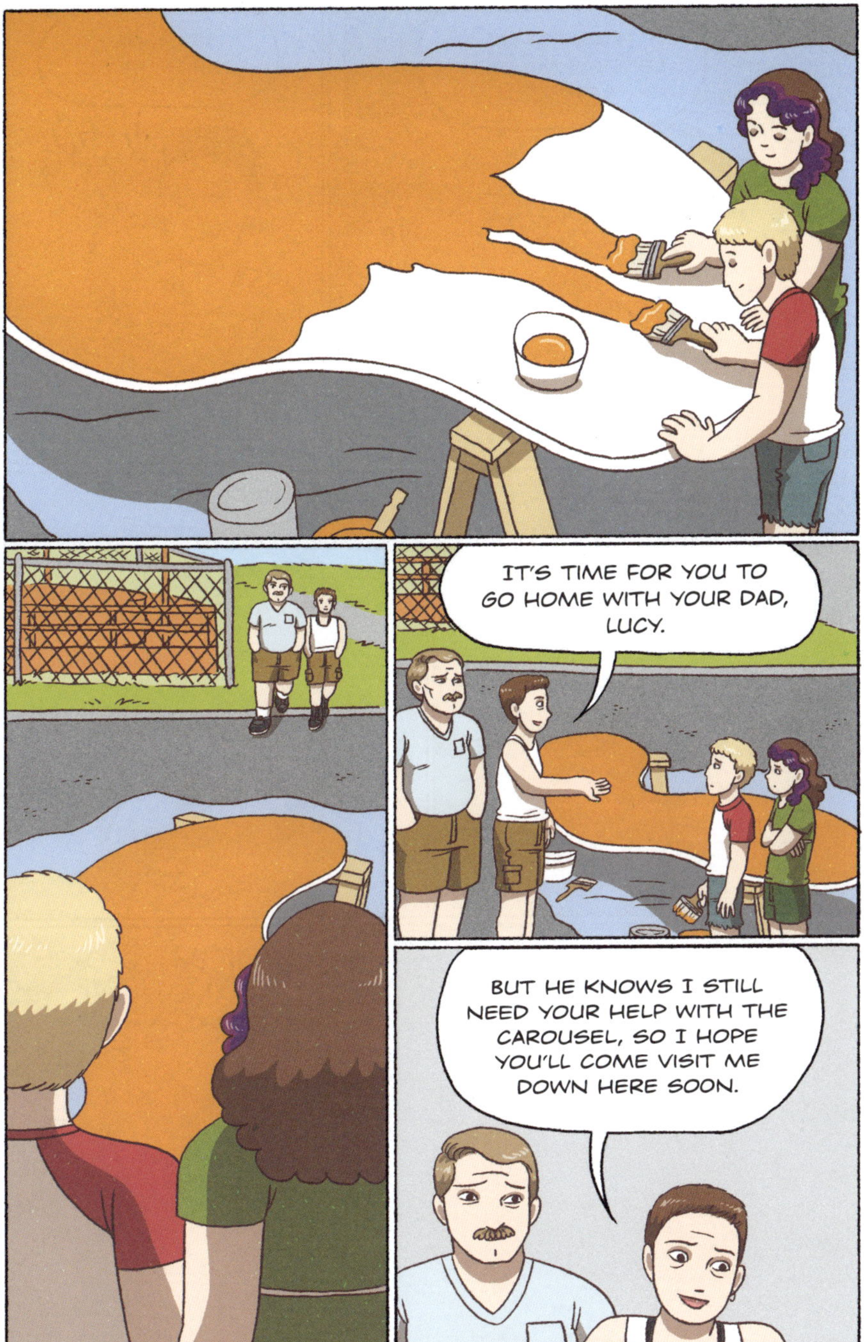
IT'S TIME FOR YOU TO GO HOME WITH YOUR DAD, LUCY.
BUT HE KNOWS I STILL NEED YOUR HELP WITH THE CAROUSEL, SO I HOPE YOU'LL COME VISIT ME DOWN HERE SOON.

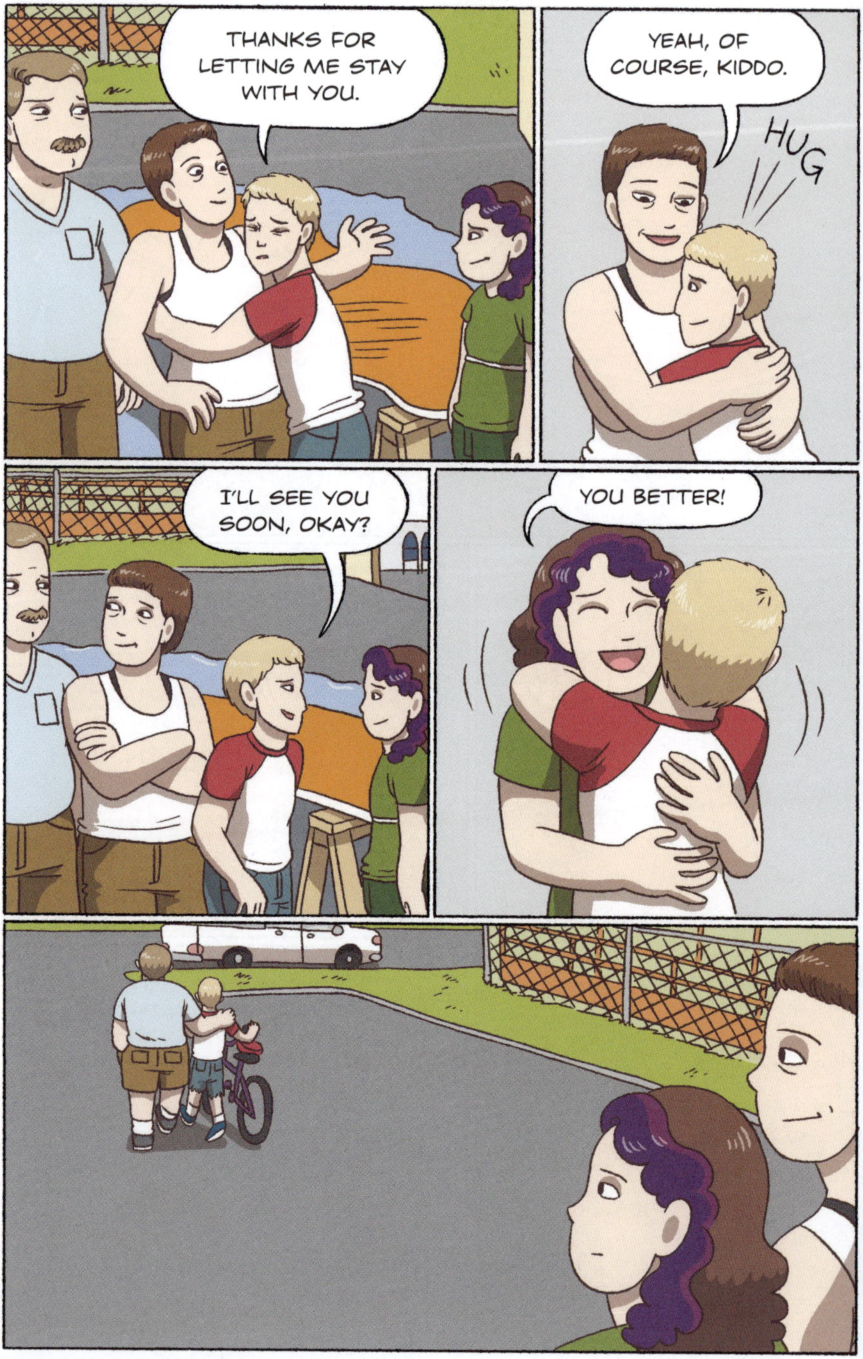
THANKS FOR LETTING ME STAY WITH YOU.
YEAH, OF COURSE, KIDDO.
HUG
I'LL SEE YOU SOON, OKAY?
YOU BETTER!

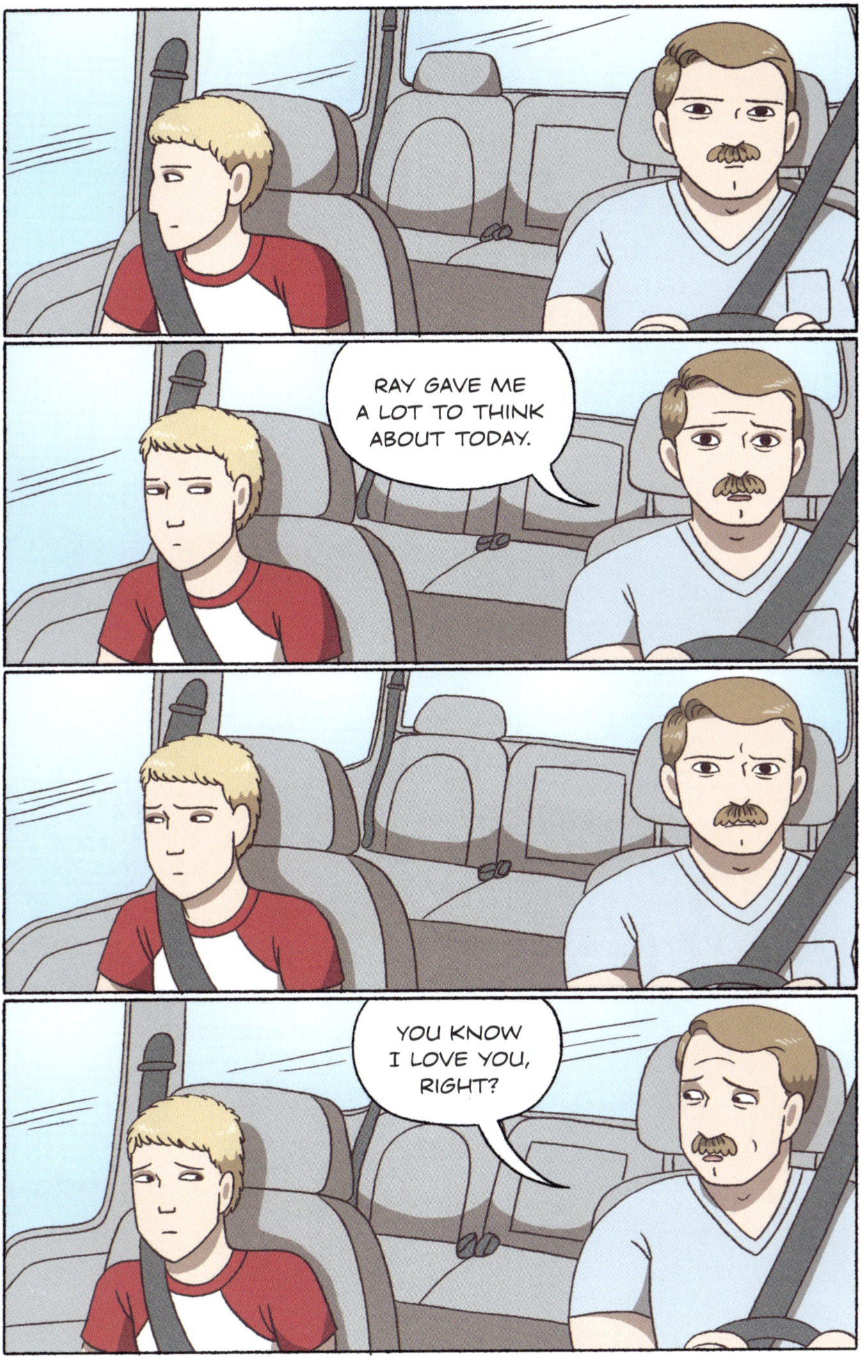
RAY GAVE ME
A LOT TO THINK
ABOUT TODAY.
YOU KNOW
I LOVE YOU,
RIGHT?

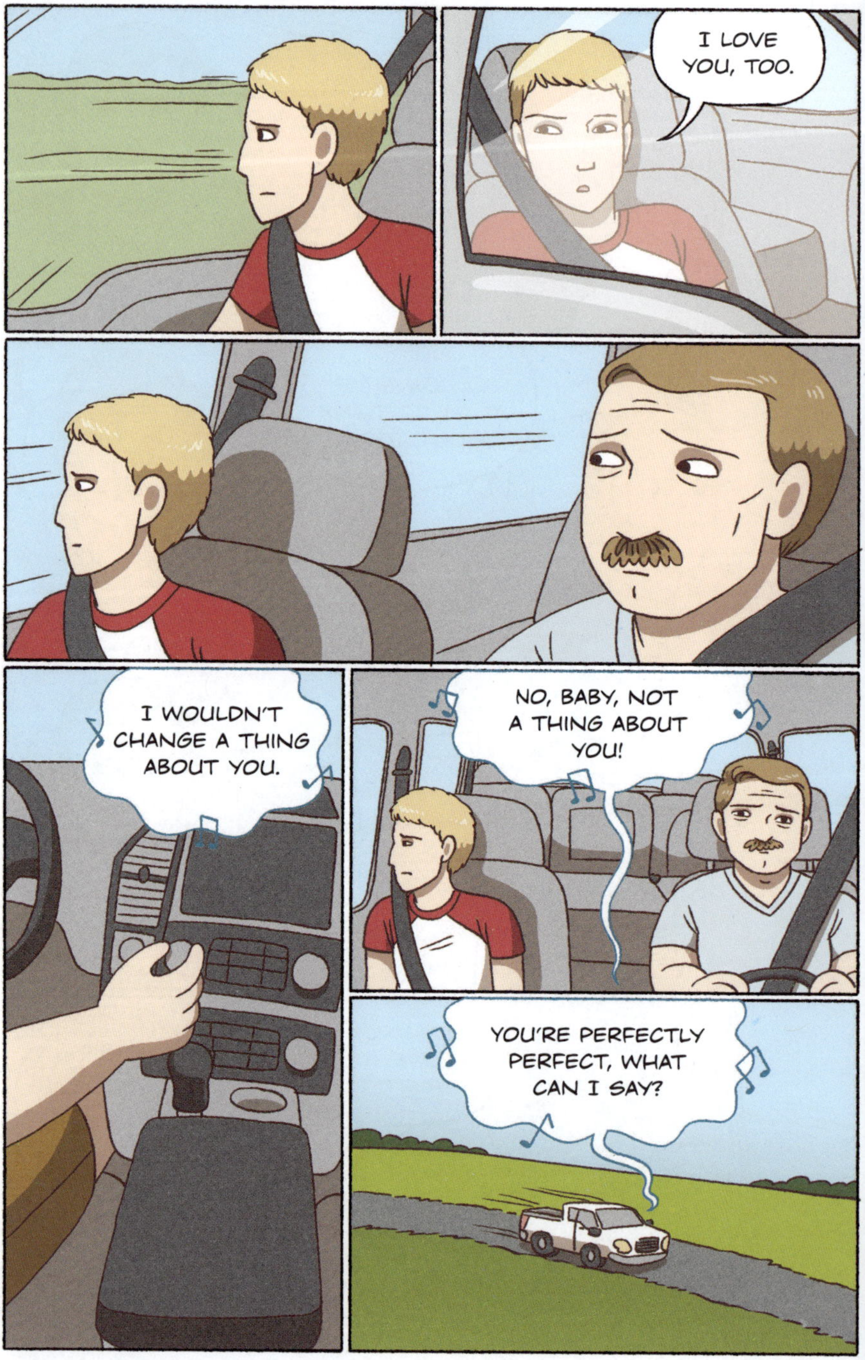
I LOVE YOU, TOO.
I WOULDN'T CHANGE A THING ABOUT YOU.
NO, BABY, NOT A THING ABOUT YOU!
YOU'RE PERFECTLY PERFECT, WHAT CAN I SAY?

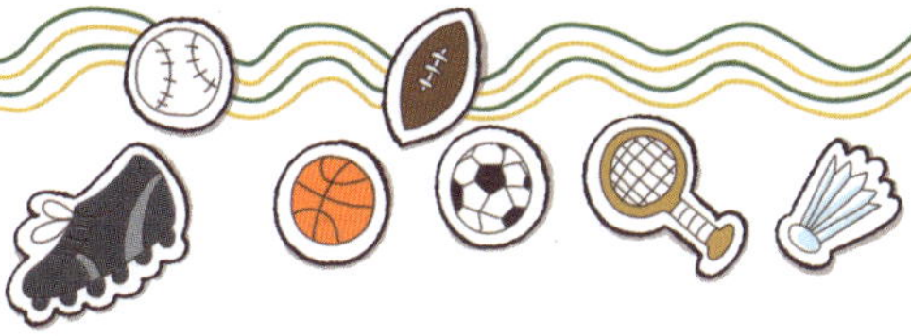

Dear Lucy,

We did it!!!!! Okay, so we didn't win gold, but we still beat the Oak Cabin boys at the Intra-Camp Olympics. We placed second (thanks to all the girls going ALL OUT at every event) and they didn't even place in the top FIVE. How's that for payback on the ghost prank!!?

Callum was weirdly mad about it. I think I might break up with him. It's been fun having a camp boyfriend, but if he can't be happy for me when I win, I don't know that he's worth it.

What's going on with you???? I'm worried maybe some letters got lost in the mail? I feel like I haven't heard from you in AGES. How's your dad? How's Daniel? Are you still hanging out with that girl from Toronto? Tell me everything!!!

Missing you loads,

Your BFFAEAEAE

KATIA

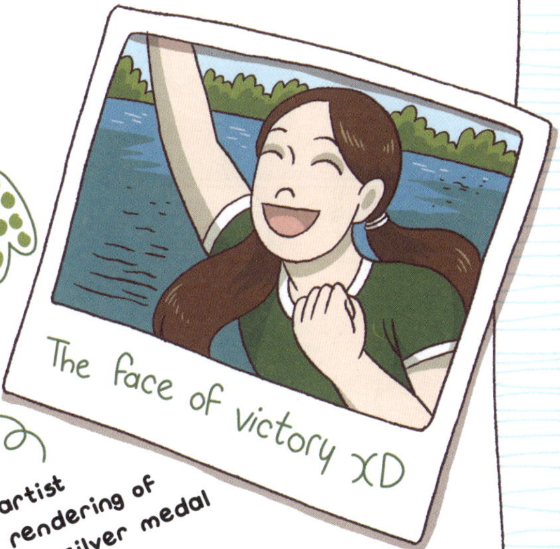

The face of victory XD

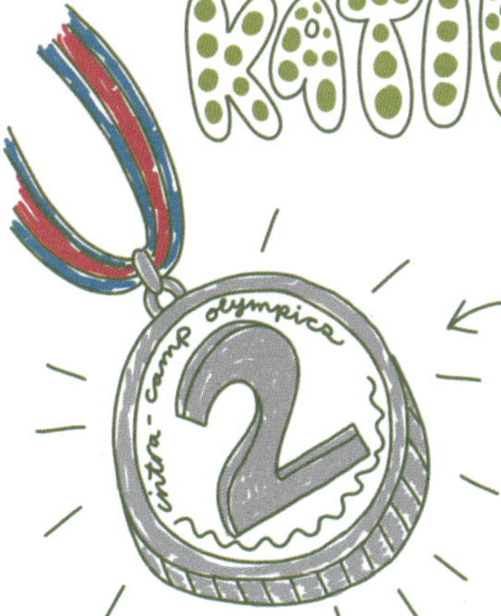
intra-camp olympics
2

artist rendering of my silver medal

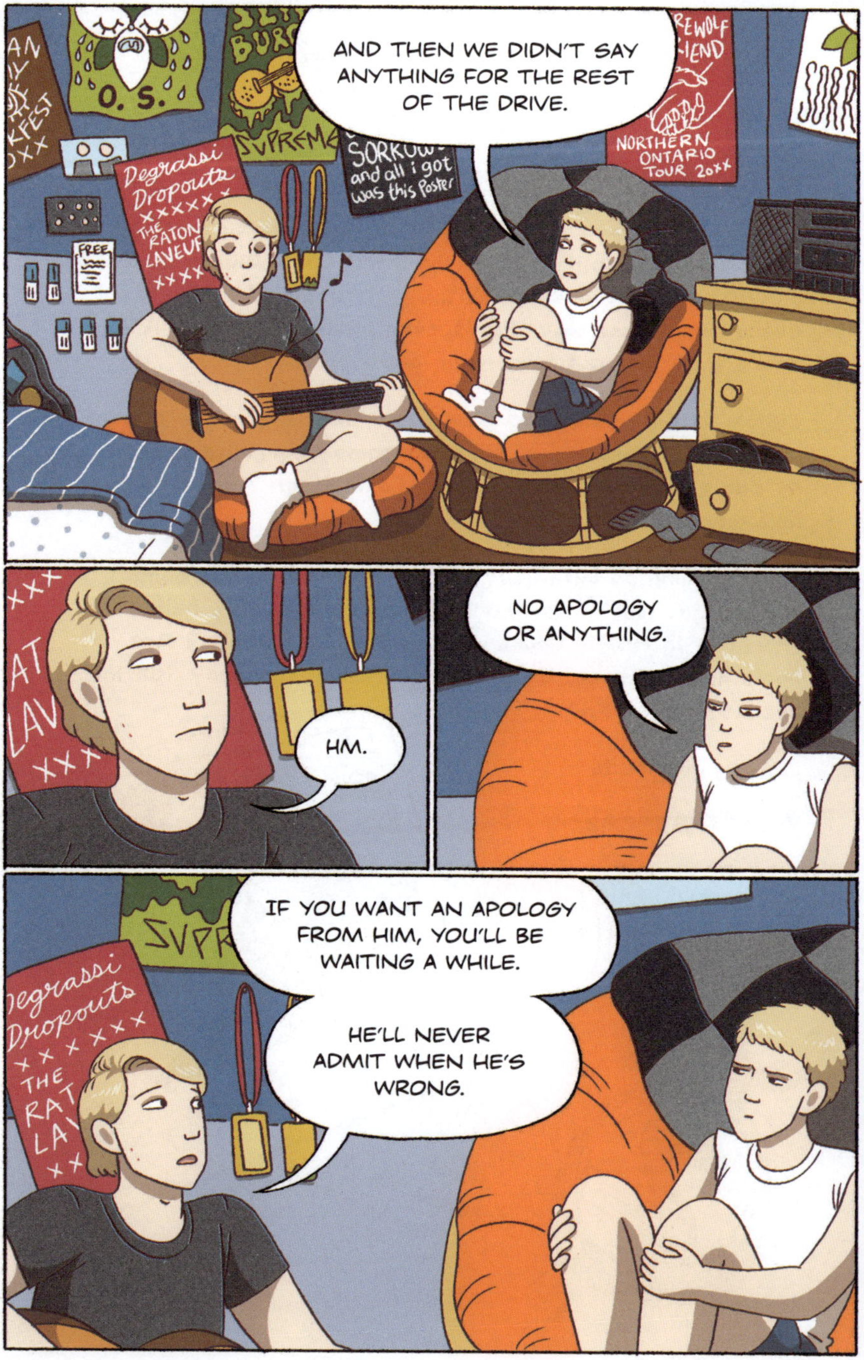
Degrassi Dropouts
THE RATON LAVEUR
and all i got was this poster
NORTHERN ONTARIO TOUR 20XX
AND THEN WE DIDN'T SAY ANYTHING FOR THE REST OF THE DRIVE.
HM.
NO APOLOGY OR ANYTHING.
IF YOU WANT AN APOLOGY FROM HIM, YOU'LL BE WAITING A WHILE.
HE'LL NEVER ADMIT WHEN HE'S WRONG.

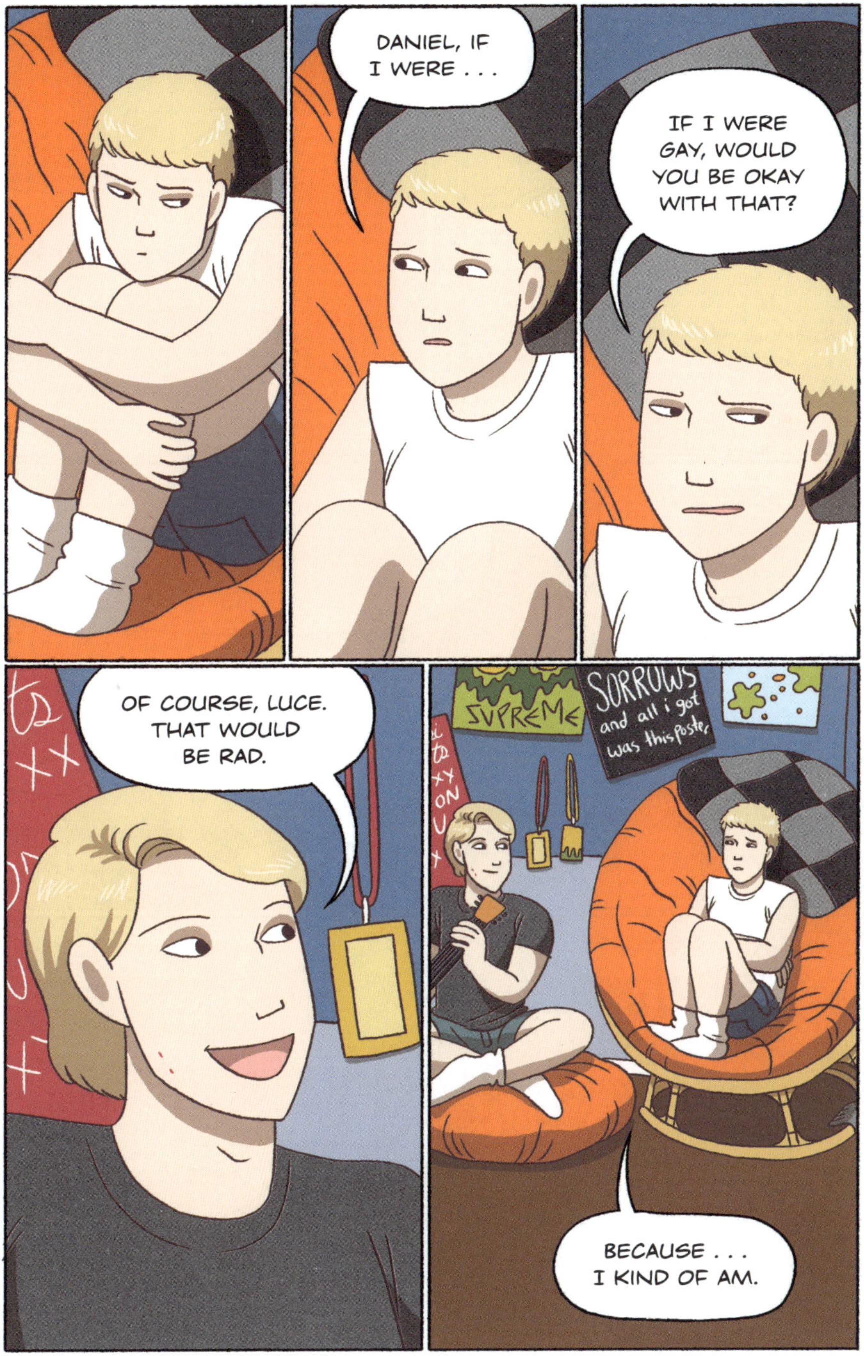
DANIEL, IF I WERE . . .
IF I WERE GAY, WOULD YOU BE OKAY WITH THAT?
OF COURSE, LUCE. THAT WOULD BE RAD.
SUPREME
SORROWS and all i got was this poster
BECAUSE . . . I KIND OF AM.

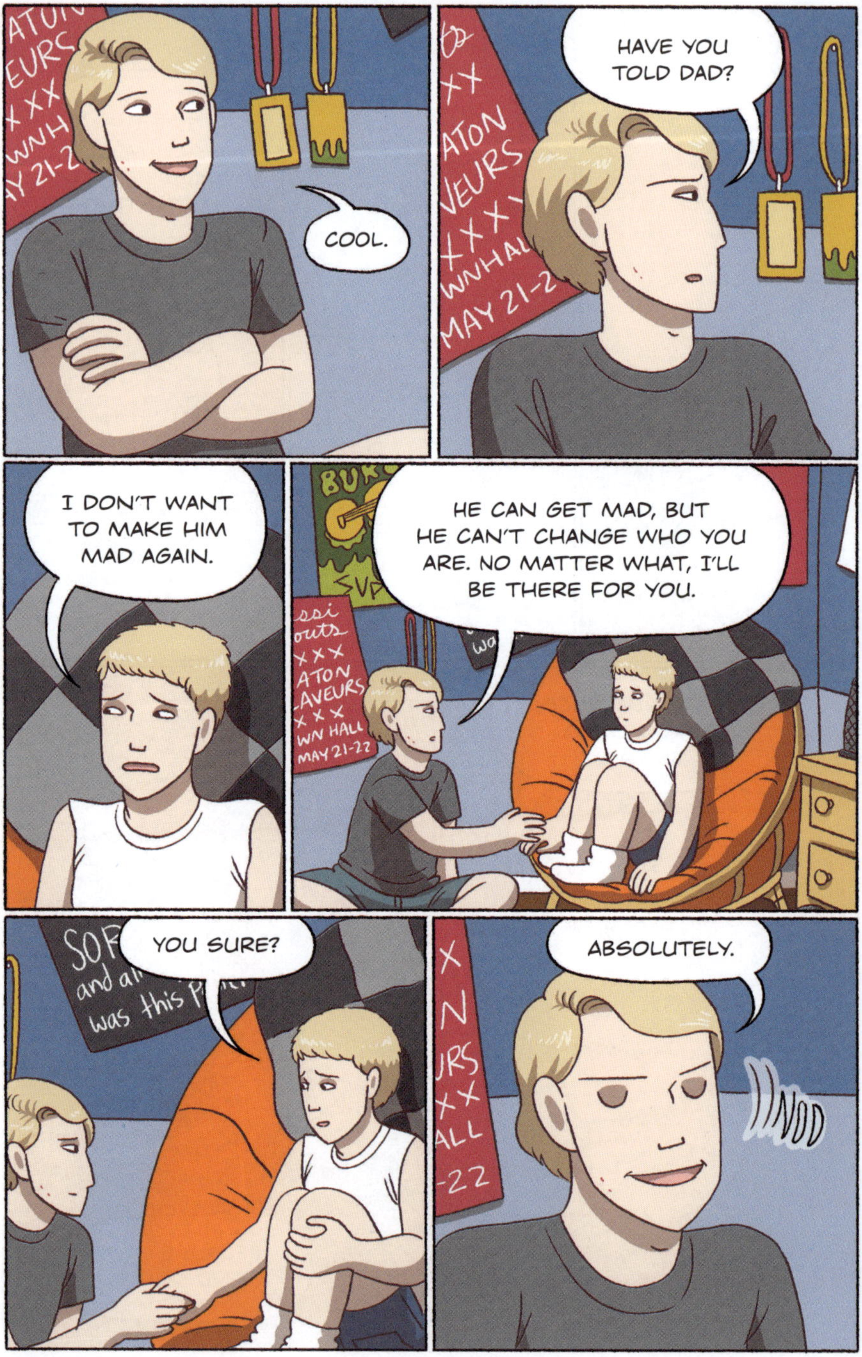
COOL.
HAVE YOU TOLD DAD?
I DON'T WANT TO MAKE HIM MAD AGAIN.
HE CAN GET MAD, BUT HE CAN'T CHANGE WHO YOU ARE. NO MATTER WHAT, I'LL BE THERE FOR YOU.
YOU SURE?
ABSOLUTELY.
NOD

Dear Katia,

I'm sorry. No letters got lost. I've just been bad at writing.

So much has happened this summer (and is still happening) that every time I tried to write, the words wouldn't come out how I wanted them to. So I just kind of gave up.

I've been figuring out some things about myself. It's been weird, and kind of hard, but I think also kind of good. I've been hanging out with Anaïs a lot (that's the girl from Toronto), and she's amazing. I think you guys would be friends if you ever got the chance to meet. She's nice, and smart, and the coolest person I've ever met (except for you, of course). She's bi, and her mom's gay, and meeting them felt like... all those times that I didn't quite fit in... they started to make sense.

GAH. I'm writing in circles trying to figure out how to tell you the simplest thing. I just hope you're still my best friend after you read this.

~~I'm bretty sure~~ I'm gay

I'm gay. Or a lesbian. Or whatever word you want to use. I haven't told anyone yet except you and Daniel. Daniel says he always kind of suspected (and he's being really cool about it).

Oh, and of course Ray and Anaïs know.

There was a big storm a few weeks ago. Anaïs was hanging out at my place. We were talking about first kisses (because you told me about yours) and it just kind of happened. We kissed and it was so so so nice. She told me later she had a crush on me, and I knew I liked her back.

I haven't told my dad about any of this, but I think he kind of knows. I let Anaïs cut my hair super short and he got so mad. I think because he thinks it makes me look more like a lesbian or something? And he doesn't like that. But that's what I am, so why is it bad that I look like it? I don't know, he's so confusing sometimes. We had a horrible, horrible argument, and I stayed over at Ray and Anaïs's for a night afterward. Everything still feels weird, though. I can't pretend it's all normal now! I'm angry at him for blowing up at me over my short hair. I wish he would apologize or something. Daniel says he probably won't though. I don't know what to do.

I'm sorry this letter is so long. I'm sorry I stopped writing. I miss you a lot.

Love,

Lucy

CHAPTER 6

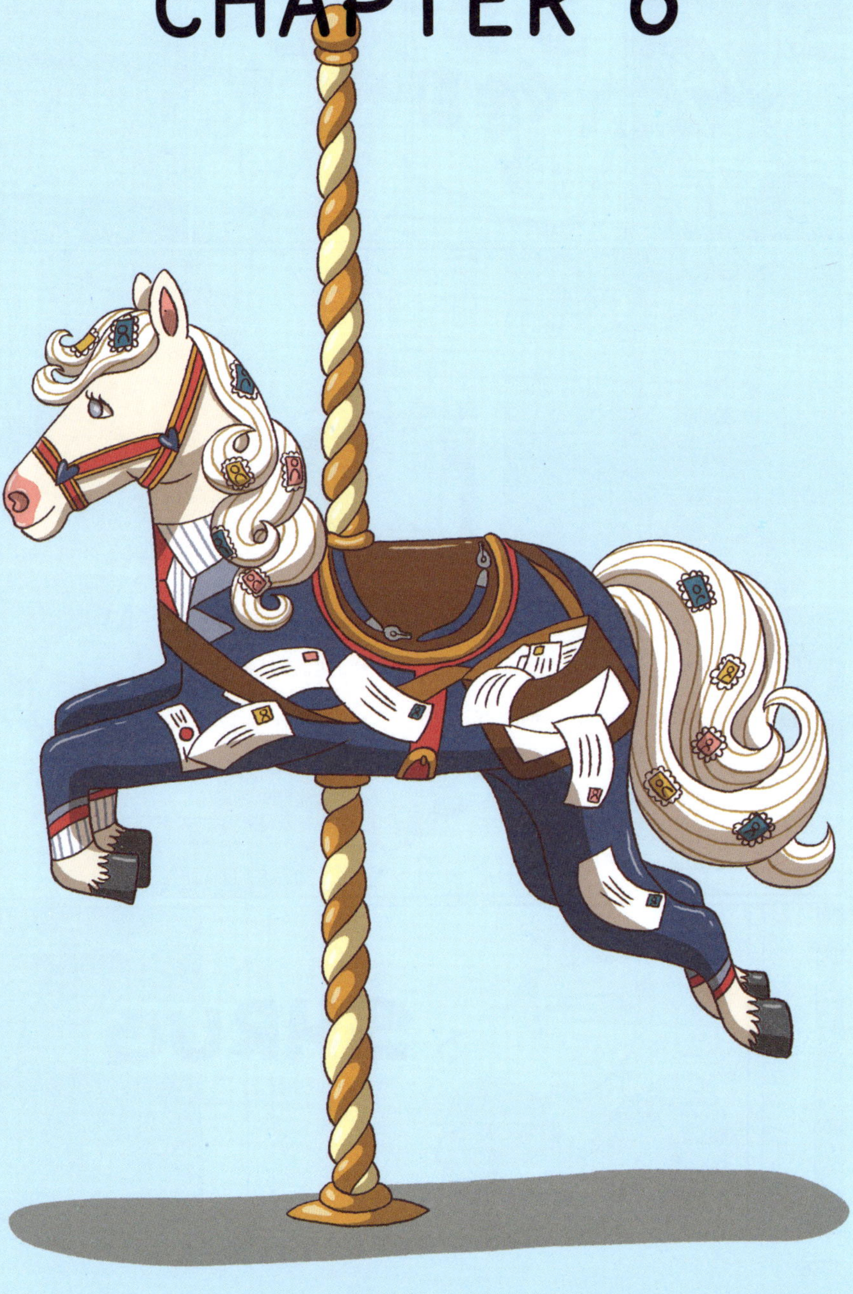

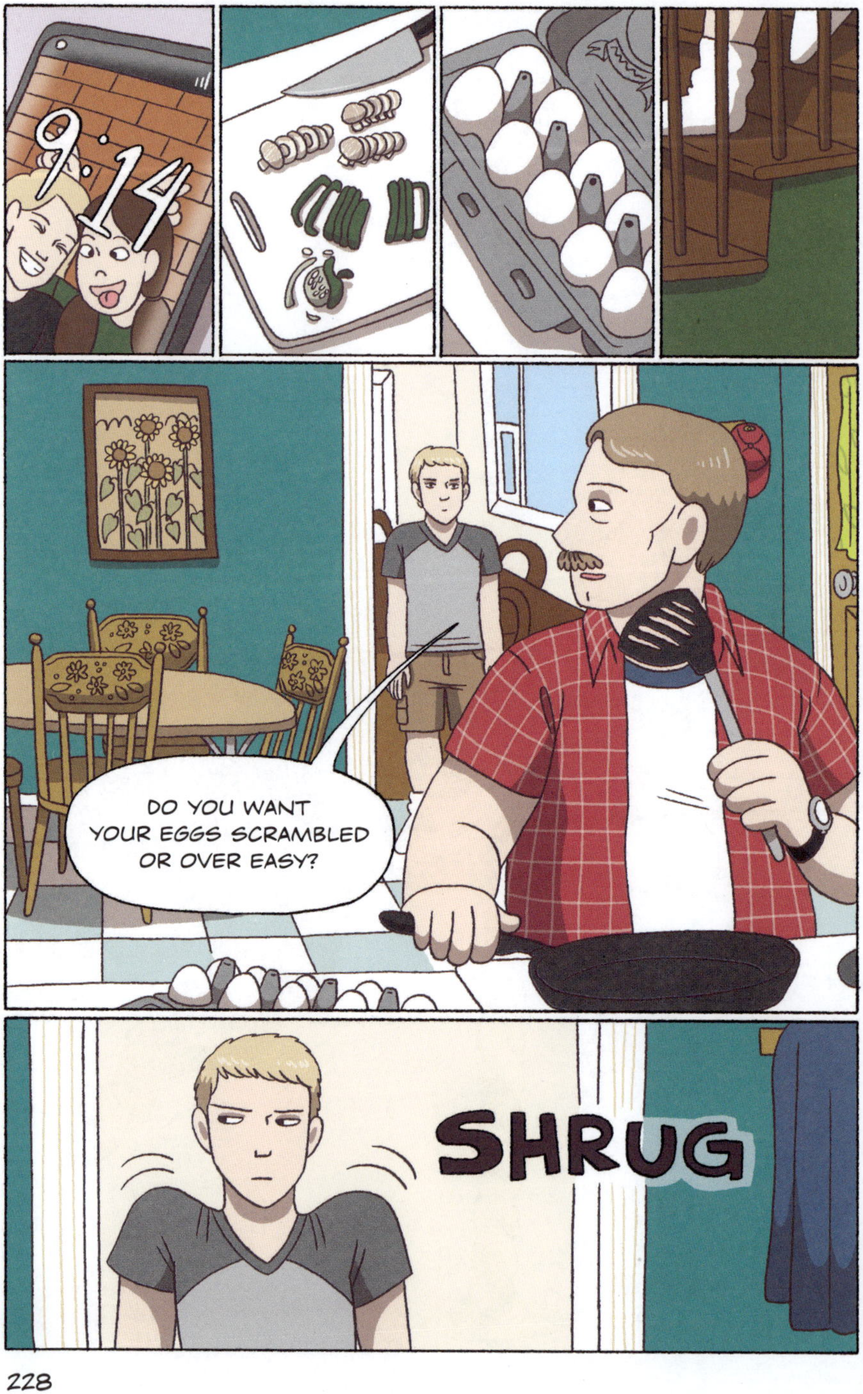
9:14
DO YOU WANT YOUR EGGS SCRAMBLED OR OVER EASY?
SHRUG

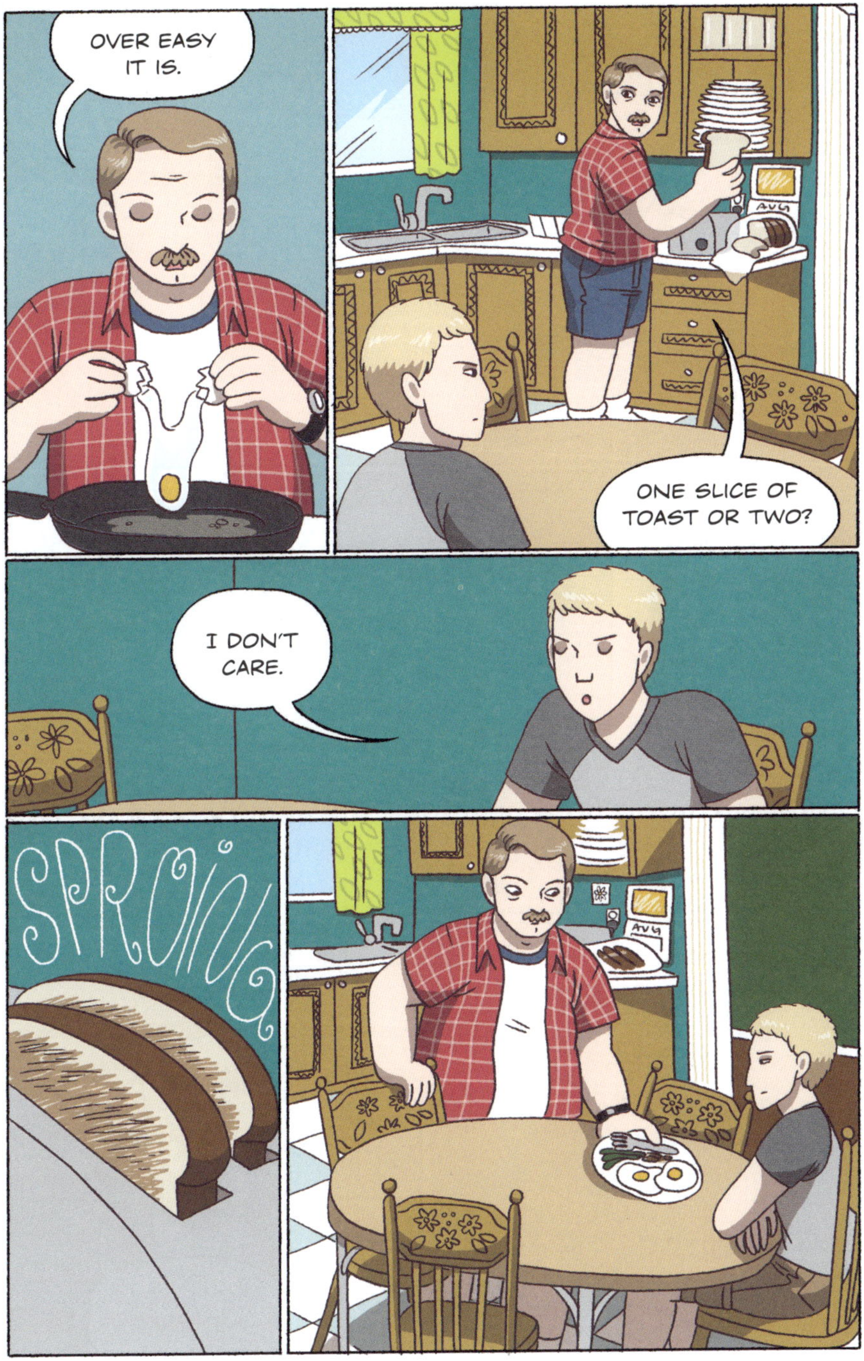
OVER EASY IT IS.
ONE SLICE OF TOAST OR TWO?
AVG
I DON'T CARE.
SPROING
AVG

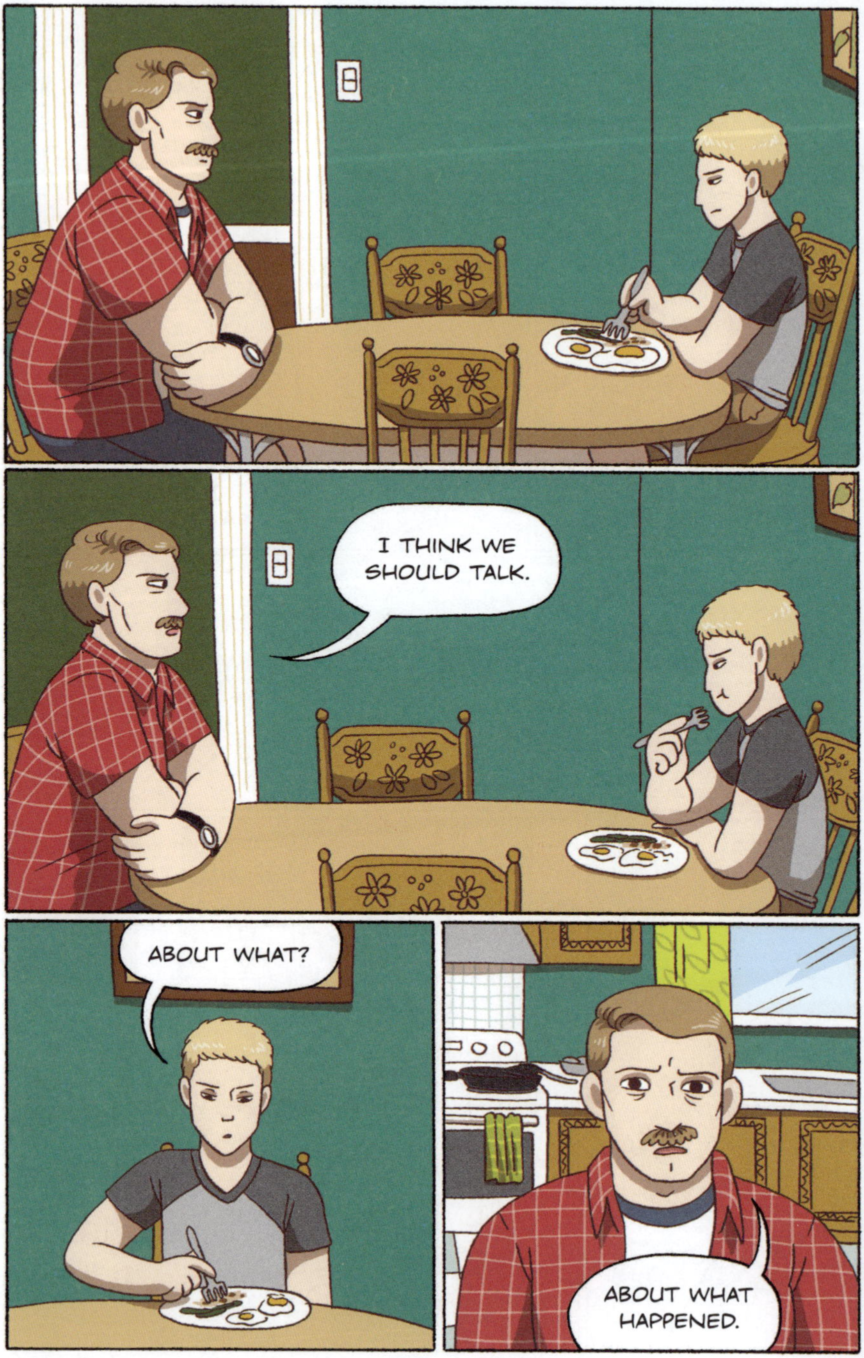
I THINK WE SHOULD TALK.
ABOUT WHAT?
ABOUT WHAT HAPPENED.

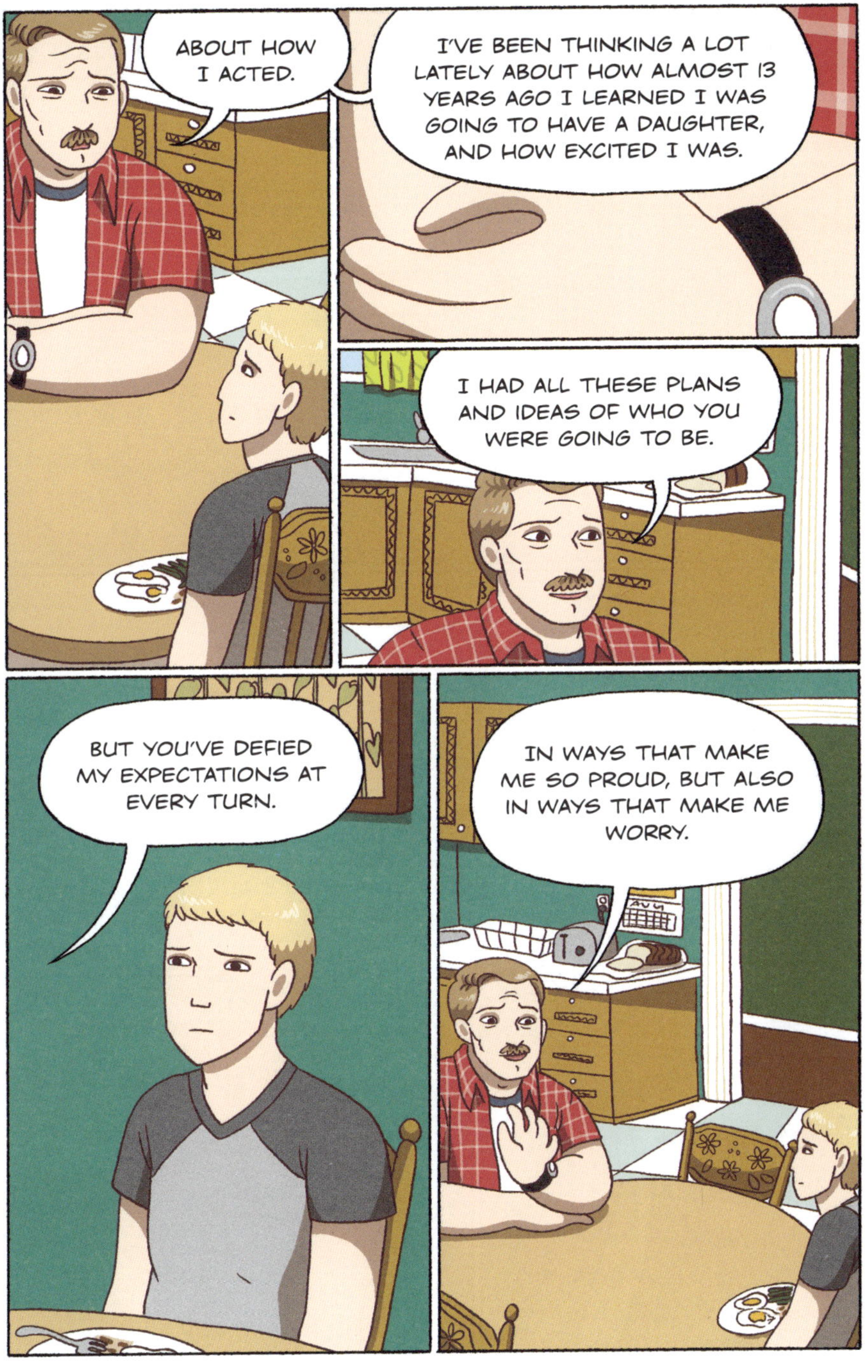
ABOUT HOW I ACTED.
I'VE BEEN THINKING A LOT LATELY ABOUT HOW ALMOST 13 YEARS AGO I LEARNED I WAS GOING TO HAVE A DAUGHTER, AND HOW EXCITED I WAS.
I HAD ALL THESE PLANS AND IDEAS OF WHO YOU WERE GOING TO BE.
BUT YOU'VE DEFIED MY EXPECTATIONS AT EVERY TURN.
IN WAYS THAT MAKE ME SO PROUD, BUT ALSO IN WAYS THAT MAKE ME WORRY.

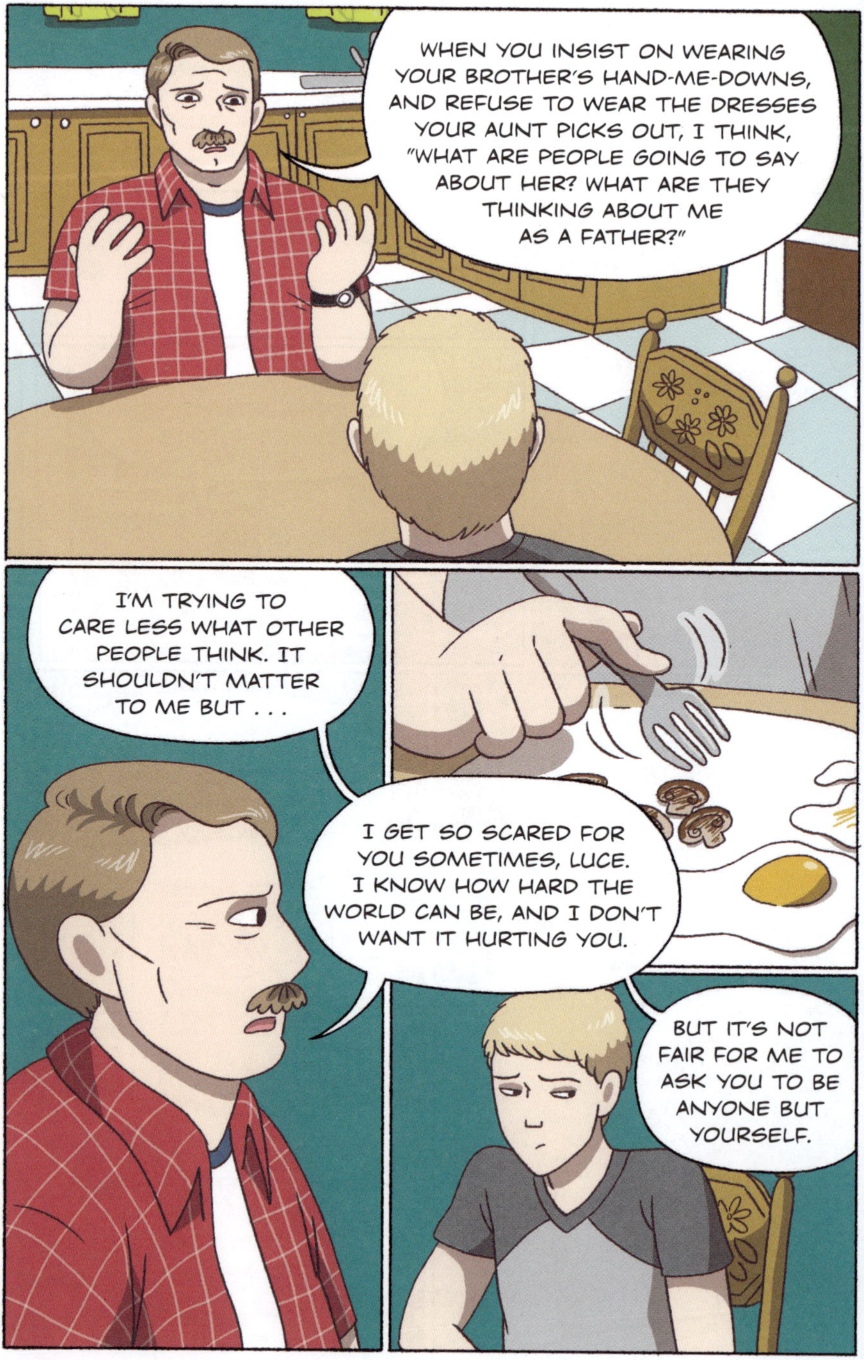
WHEN YOU INSIST ON WEARING YOUR BROTHER'S HAND-ME-DOWNS, AND REFUSE TO WEAR THE DRESSES YOUR AUNT PICKS OUT, I THINK, "WHAT ARE PEOPLE GOING TO SAY ABOUT HER? WHAT ARE THEY THINKING ABOUT ME AS A FATHER?"
I'M TRYING TO CARE LESS WHAT OTHER PEOPLE THINK. IT SHOULDN'T MATTER TO ME BUT . . .
I GET SO SCARED FOR YOU SOMETIMES, LUCE. I KNOW HOW HARD THE WORLD CAN BE, AND I DON'T WANT IT HURTING YOU.
BUT IT'S NOT FAIR FOR ME TO ASK YOU TO BE ANYONE BUT YOURSELF.

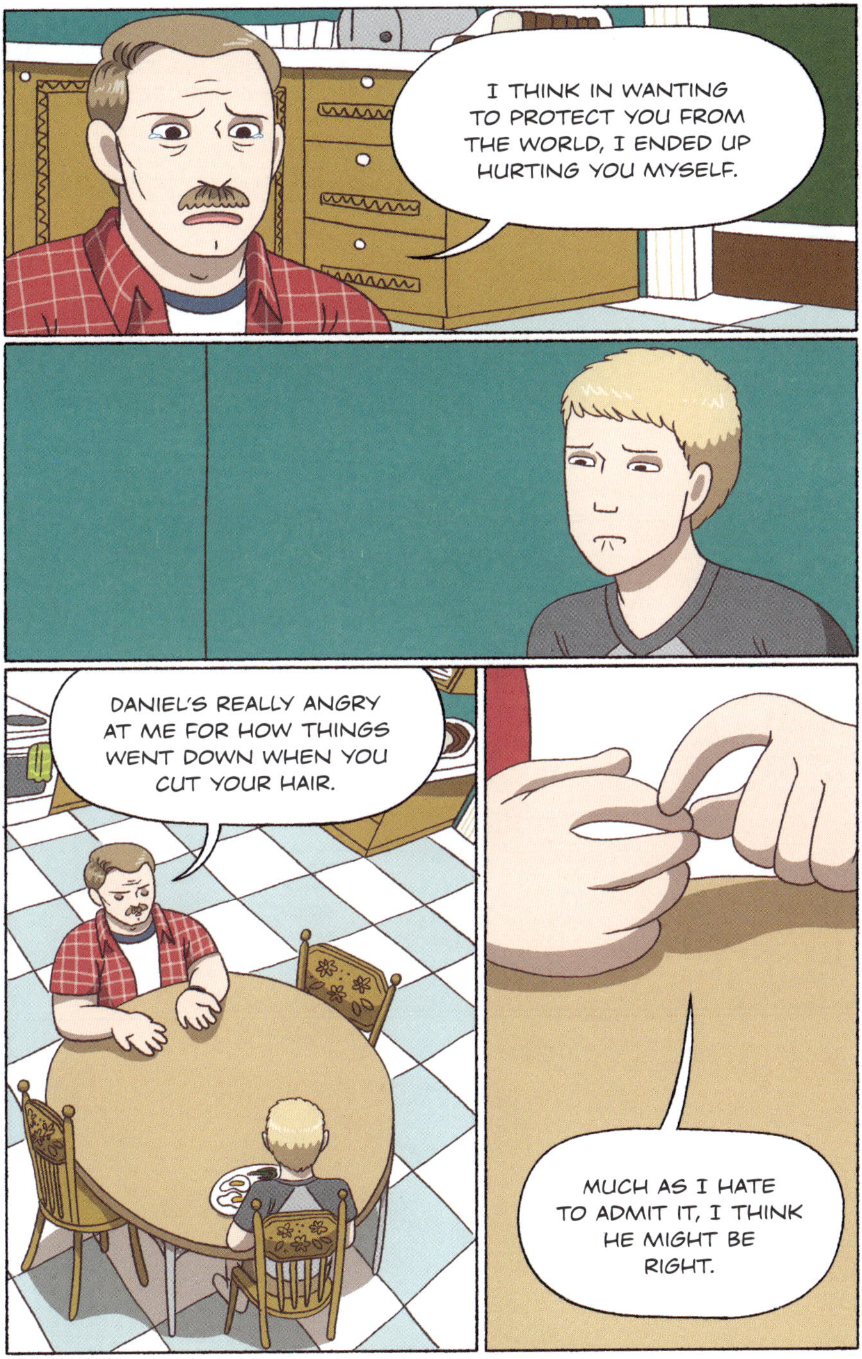
I THINK IN WANTING TO PROTECT YOU FROM THE WORLD, I ENDED UP HURTING YOU MYSELF.
DANIEL'S REALLY ANGRY AT ME FOR HOW THINGS WENT DOWN WHEN YOU CUT YOUR HAIR.
MUCH AS I HATE TO ADMIT IT, I THINK HE MIGHT BE RIGHT.

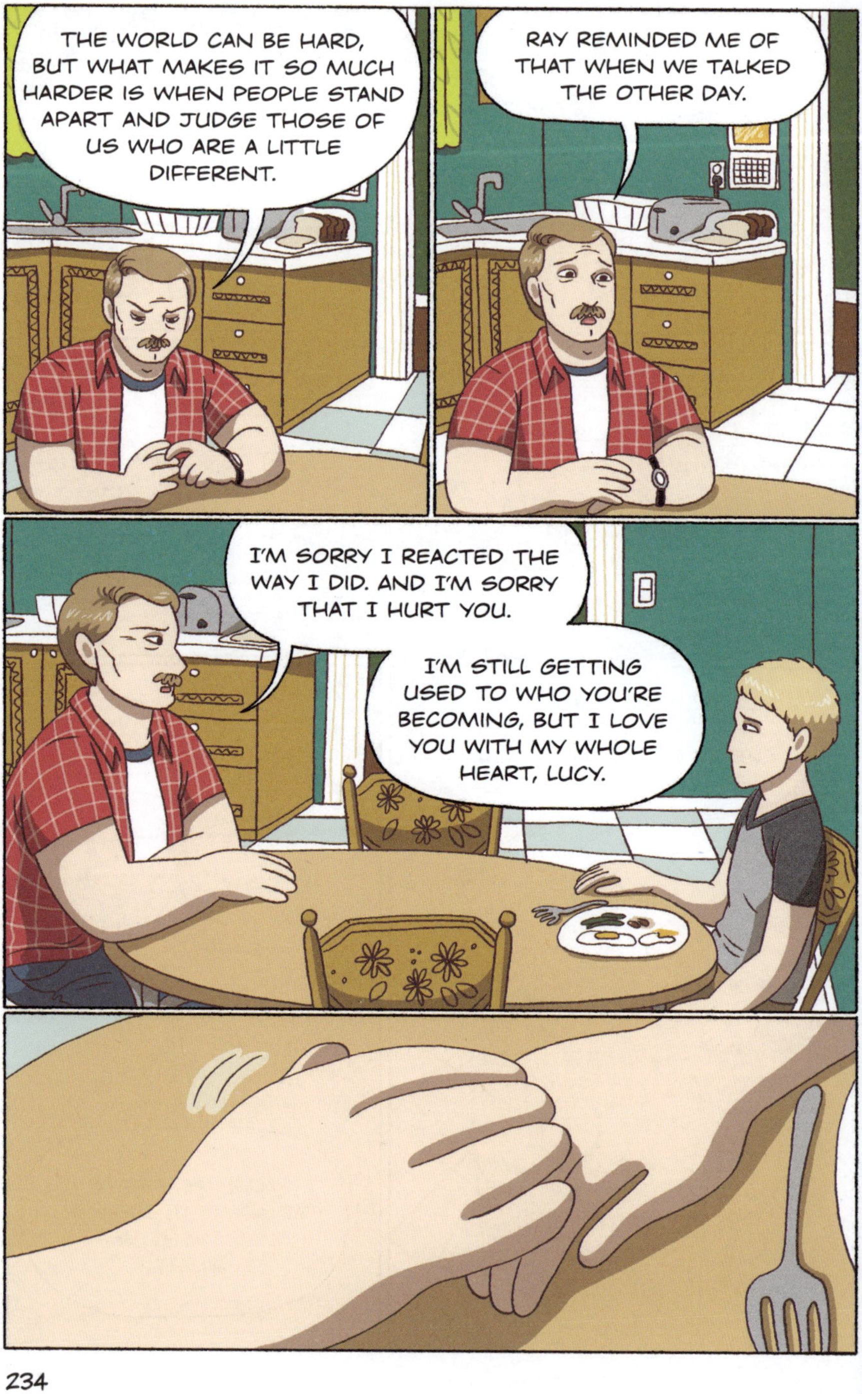
THE WORLD CAN BE HARD, BUT WHAT MAKES IT SO MUCH HARDER IS WHEN PEOPLE STAND APART AND JUDGE THOSE OF US WHO ARE A LITTLE DIFFERENT.
RAY REMINDED ME OF THAT WHEN WE TALKED THE OTHER DAY.
I'M SORRY I REACTED THE WAY I DID. AND I'M SORRY THAT I HURT YOU.
I'M STILL GETTING USED TO WHO YOU'RE BECOMING, BUT I LOVE YOU WITH MY WHOLE HEART, LUCY.

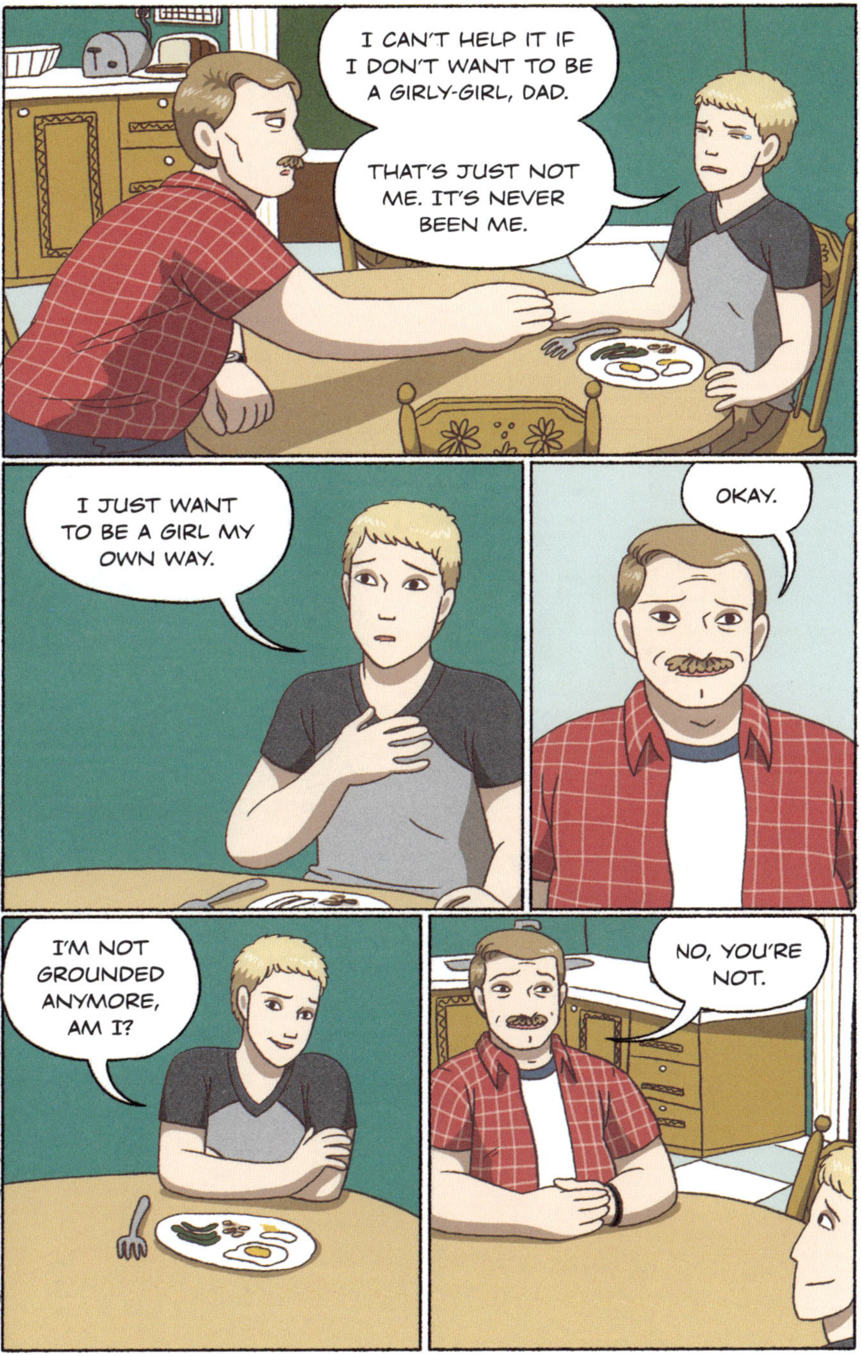
I CAN'T HELP IT IF I DON'T WANT TO BE A GIRLY-GIRL, DAD.
THAT'S JUST NOT ME. IT'S NEVER BEEN ME.
I JUST WANT TO BE A GIRL MY OWN WAY.
OKAY.
I'M NOT GROUNDED ANYMORE, AM I?
NO, YOU'RE NOT.

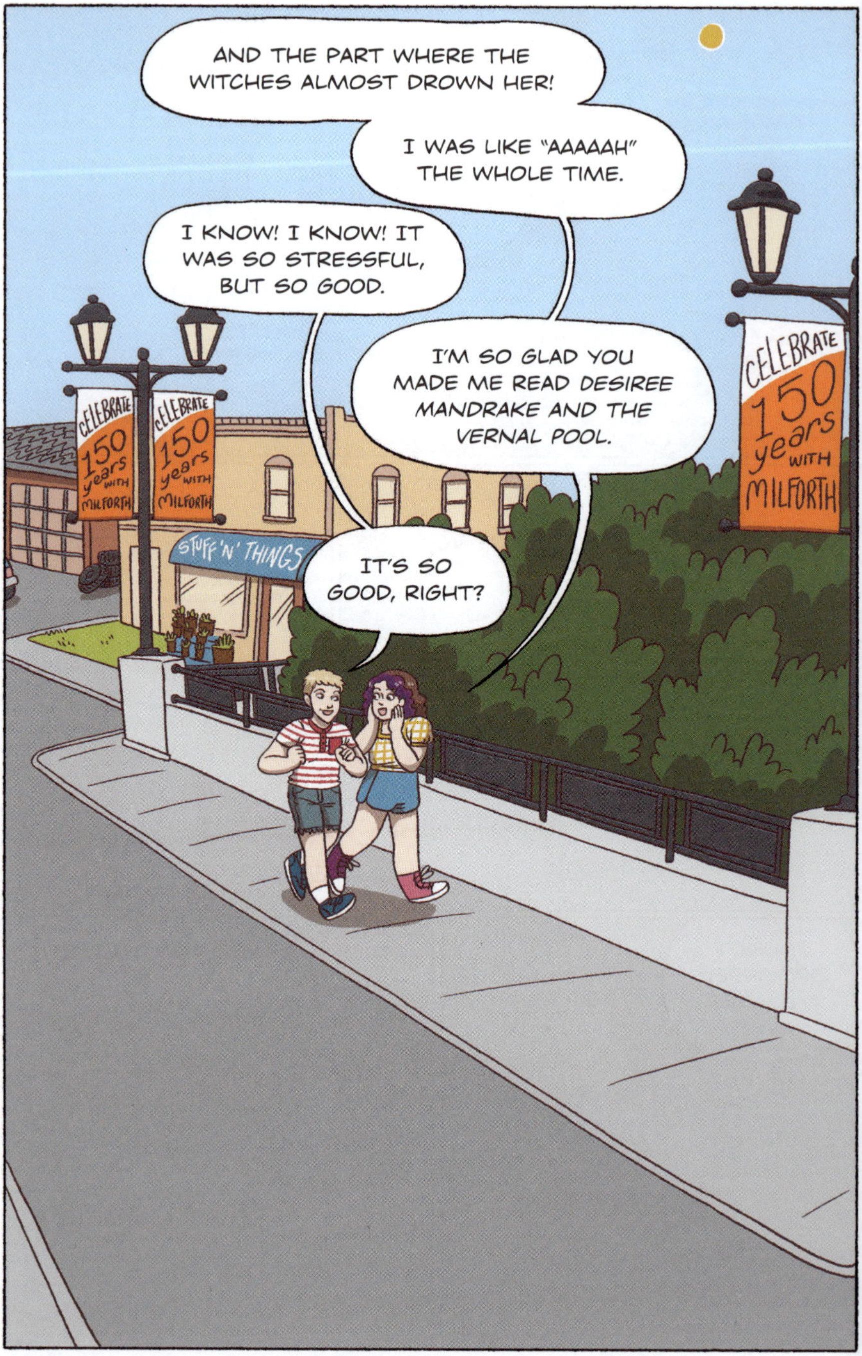
AND THE PART WHERE THE WITCHES ALMOST DROWN HER!
I WAS LIKE "AAAAAH" THE WHOLE TIME.
I KNOW! I KNOW! IT WAS SO STRESSFUL, BUT SO GOOD.
I'M SO GLAD YOU MADE ME READ DESIREE MANDRAKE AND THE VERNAL POOL.
IT'S SO GOOD, RIGHT?
CELEBRATE 150 years WITH MILFORTH
CELEBRATE 150 years WITH MILFORTH
CELEBRATE 150 years WITH MILFORTH
STUFF 'N' THINGS

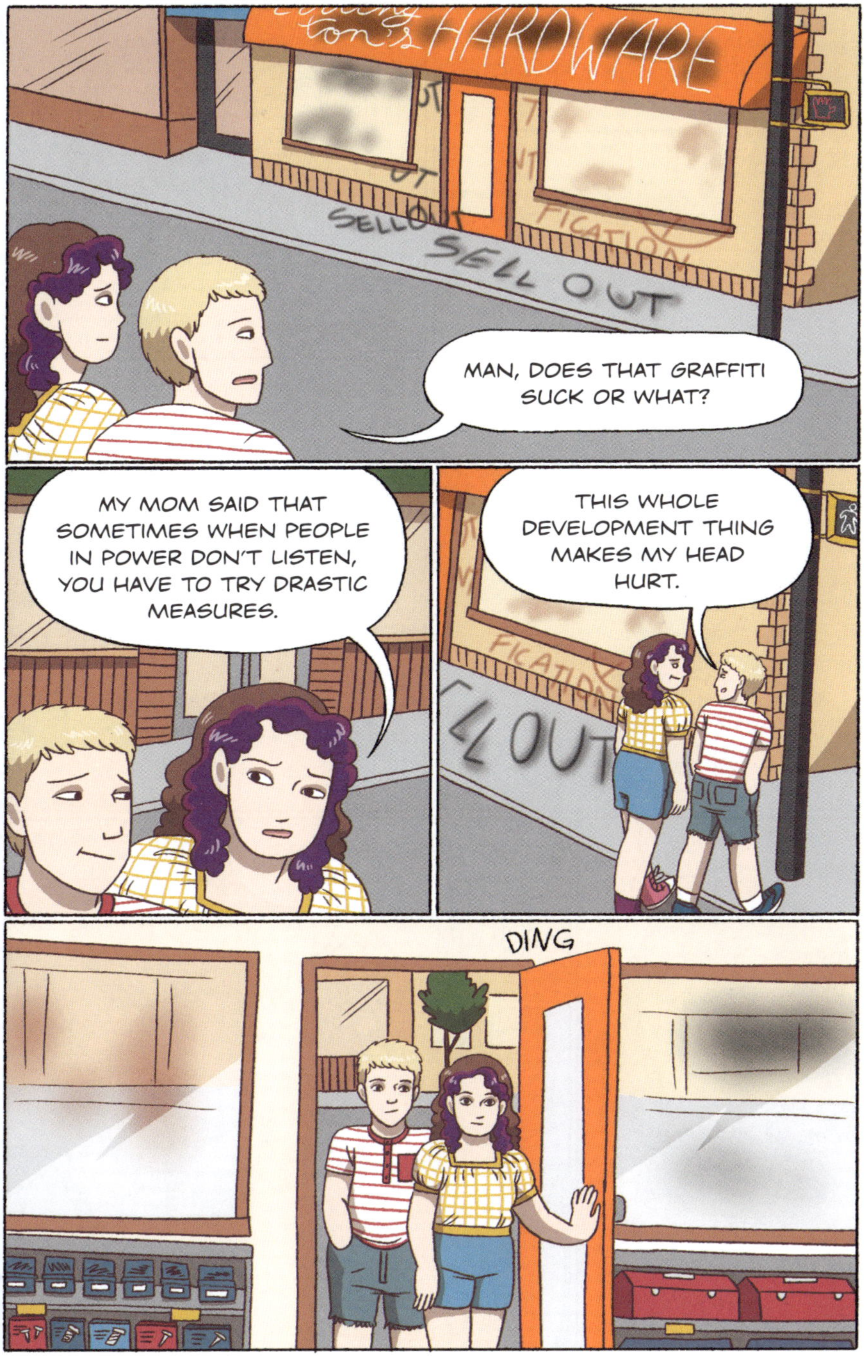
HARDWARE
SELLOUT
SELL OUT
MAN, DOES THAT GRAFFITI SUCK OR WHAT?
MY MOM SAID THAT SOMETIMES WHEN PEOPLE IN POWER DON'T LISTEN, YOU HAVE TO TRY DRASTIC MEASURES.
THIS WHOLE DEVELOPMENT THING MAKES MY HEAD HURT.
DING

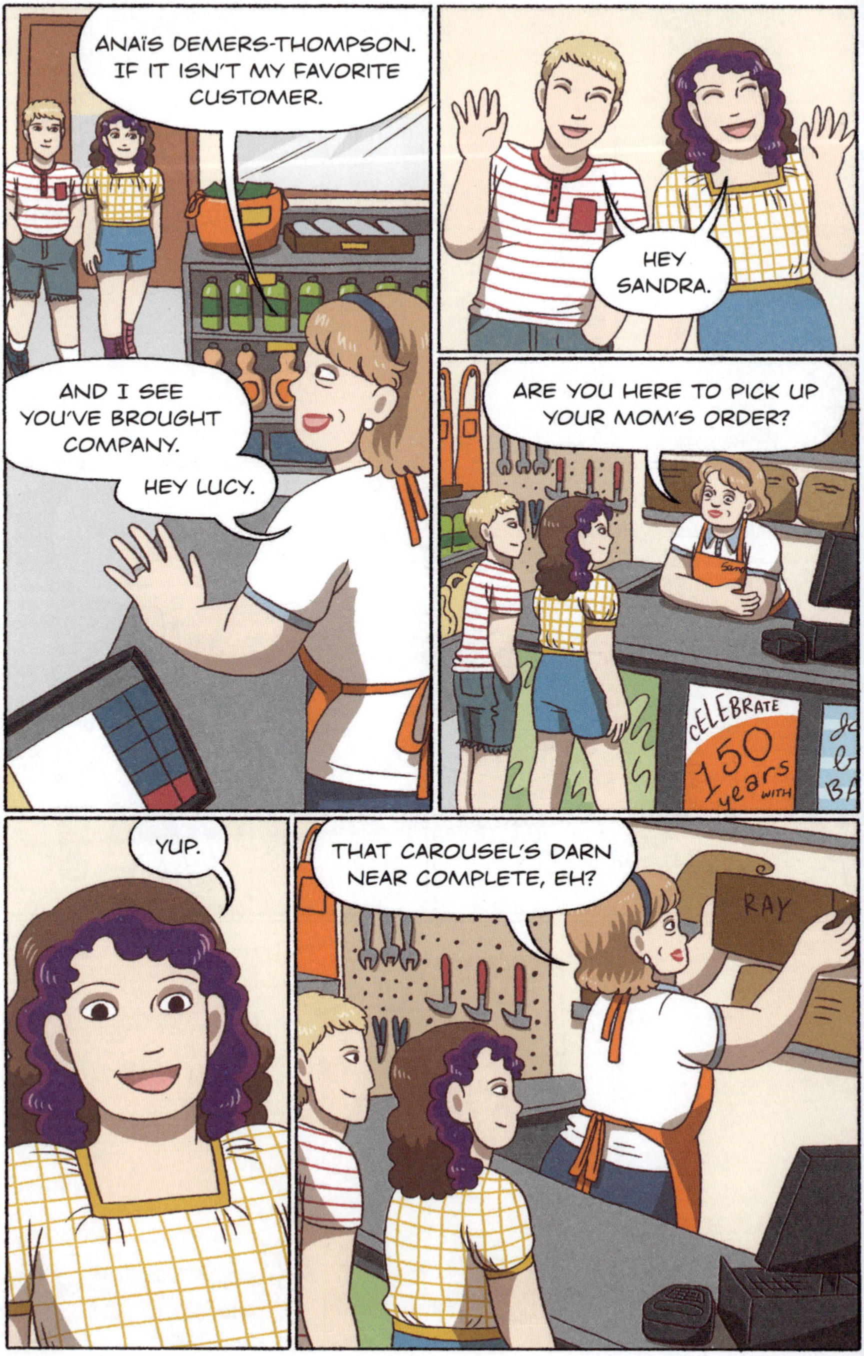
ANAÏS DEMERS-THOMPSON. IF IT ISN'T MY FAVORITE CUSTOMER.
HEY SANDRA.
AND I SEE YOU'VE BROUGHT COMPANY.
HEY LUCY.
ARE YOU HERE TO PICK UP YOUR MOM'S ORDER?
CELEBRATE 150 YEARS WITH
YUP.
THAT CAROUSEL'S DARN NEAR COMPLETE, EH?
RAY

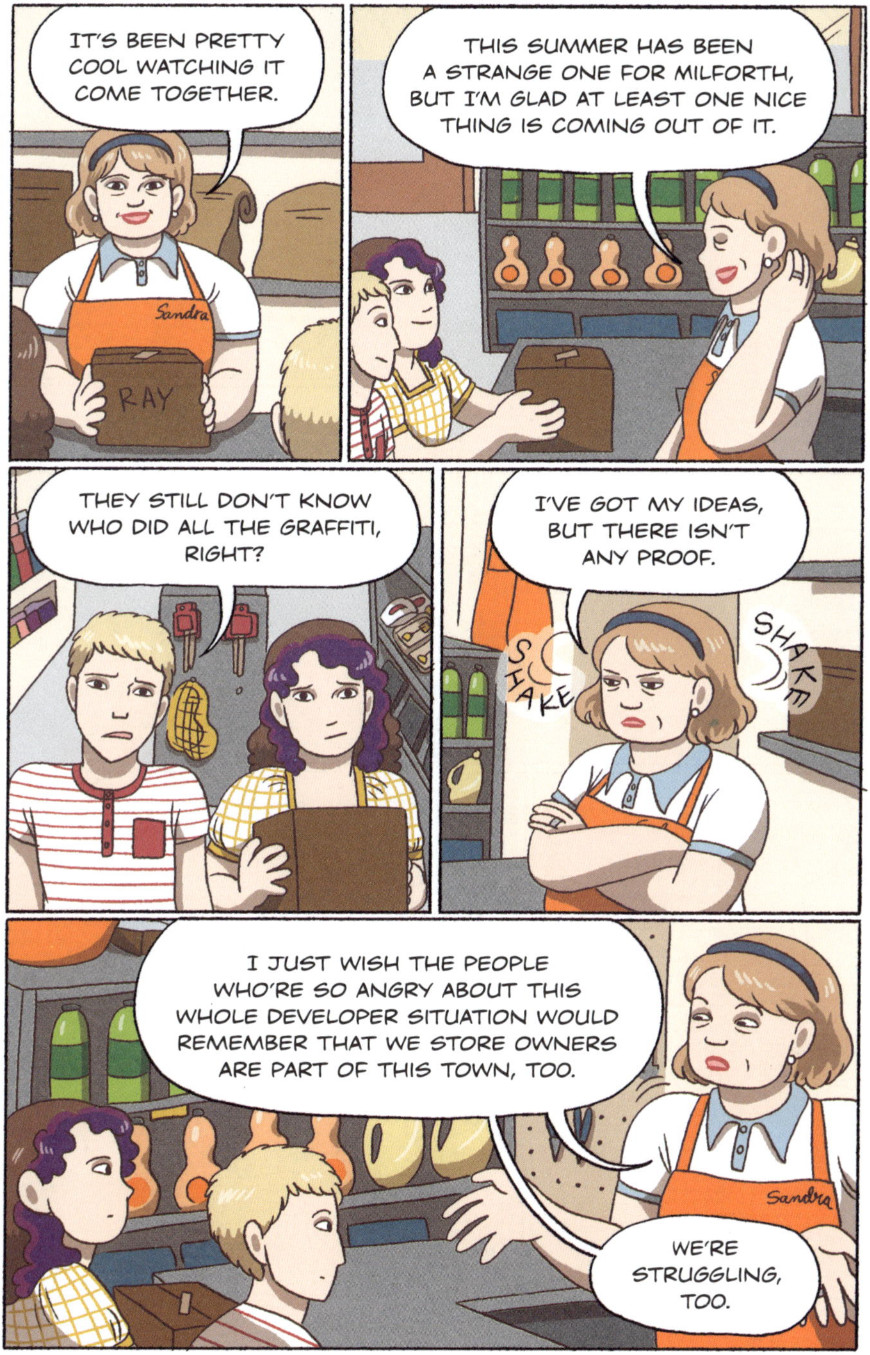
IT'S BEEN PRETTY COOL WATCHING IT COME TOGETHER.
RAY
THIS SUMMER HAS BEEN A STRANGE ONE FOR MILFORTH, BUT I'M GLAD AT LEAST ONE NICE THING IS COMING OUT OF IT.
THEY STILL DON'T KNOW WHO DID ALL THE GRAFFITI, RIGHT?
I'VE GOT MY IDEAS, BUT THERE ISN'T ANY PROOF.
SHAKE
SHAKE
I JUST WISH THE PEOPLE WHO'RE SO ANGRY ABOUT THIS WHOLE DEVELOPER SITUATION WOULD REMEMBER THAT WE STORE OWNERS ARE PART OF THIS TOWN, TOO.
WE'RE STRUGGLING, TOO.

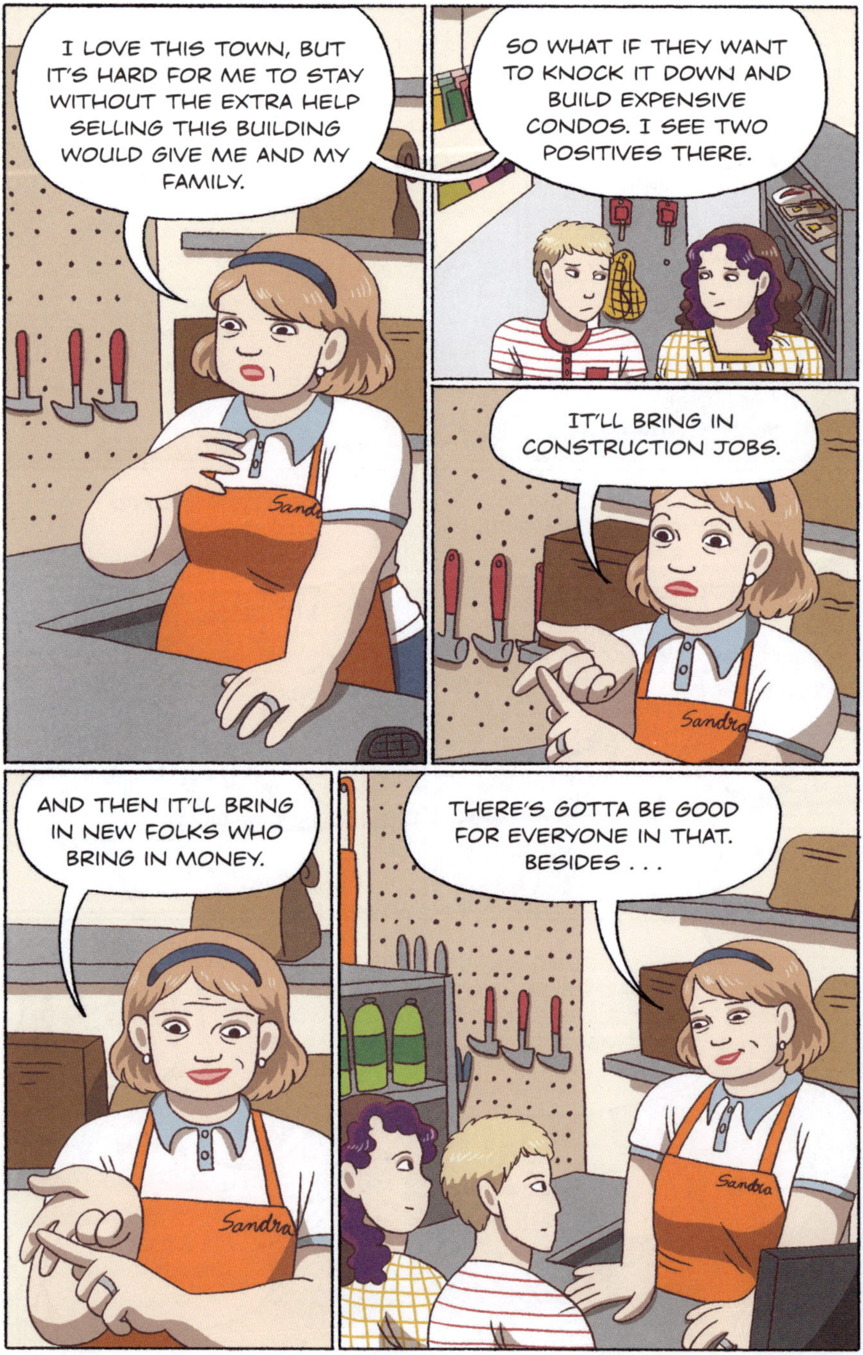
I LOVE THIS TOWN, BUT IT'S HARD FOR ME TO STAY WITHOUT THE EXTRA HELP SELLING THIS BUILDING WOULD GIVE ME AND MY FAMILY.
SO WHAT IF THEY WANT TO KNOCK IT DOWN AND BUILD EXPENSIVE CONDOS. I SEE TWO POSITIVES THERE.
IT'LL BRING IN CONSTRUCTION JOBS.
AND THEN IT'LL BRING IN NEW FOLKS WHO BRING IN MONEY.
THERE'S GOTTA BE GOOD FOR EVERYONE IN THAT. BESIDES . . .

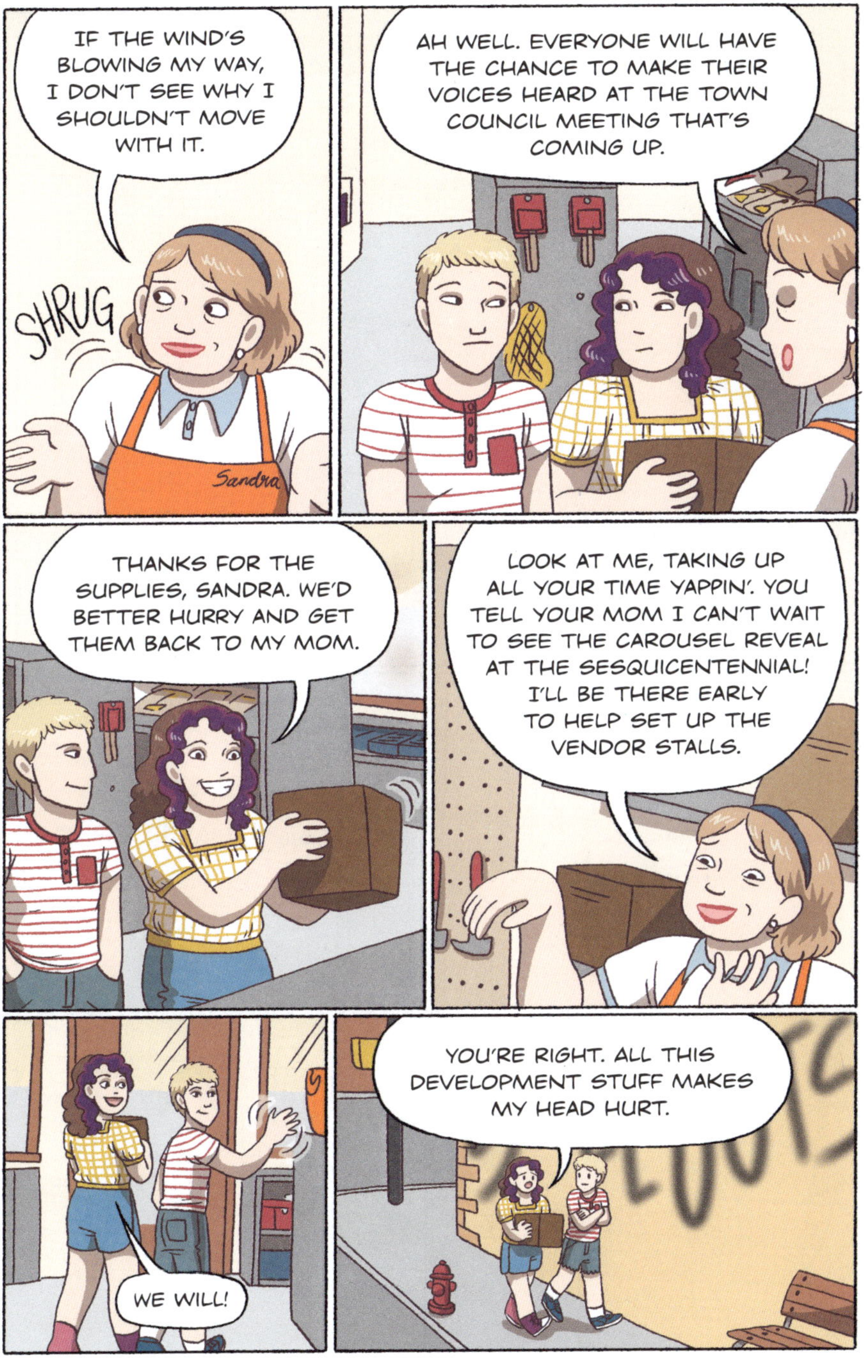
IF THE WIND'S BLOWING MY WAY, I DON'T SEE WHY I SHOULDN'T MOVE WITH IT.
SHRUG
Sandra
AH WELL. EVERYONE WILL HAVE THE CHANCE TO MAKE THEIR VOICES HEARD AT THE TOWN COUNCIL MEETING THAT'S COMING UP.
THANKS FOR THE SUPPLIES, SANDRA. WE'D BETTER HURRY AND GET THEM BACK TO MY MOM.
LOOK AT ME, TAKING UP ALL YOUR TIME YAPPIN'. YOU TELL YOUR MOM I CAN'T WAIT TO SEE THE CAROUSEL REVEAL AT THE SESQUICENTENNIAL! I'LL BE THERE EARLY TO HELP SET UP THE VENDOR STALLS.
WE WILL!
YOU'RE RIGHT. ALL THIS DEVELOPMENT STUFF MAKES MY HEAD HURT.

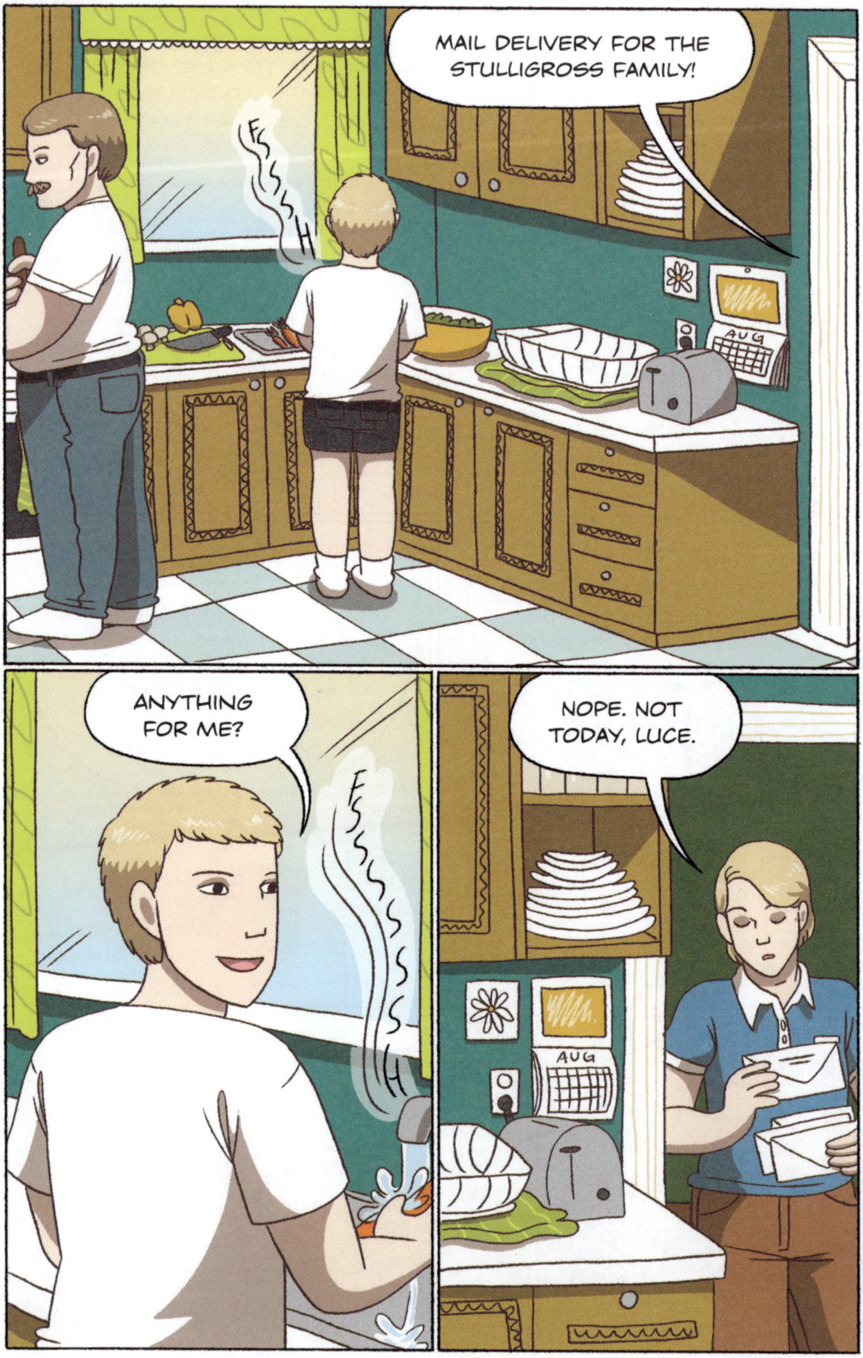
FSSSSH
MAIL DELIVERY FOR THE STULLIGROSS FAMILY!
AUG
ANYTHING FOR ME?
FSSSSSSSH
NOPE. NOT TODAY, LUCE.
AUG

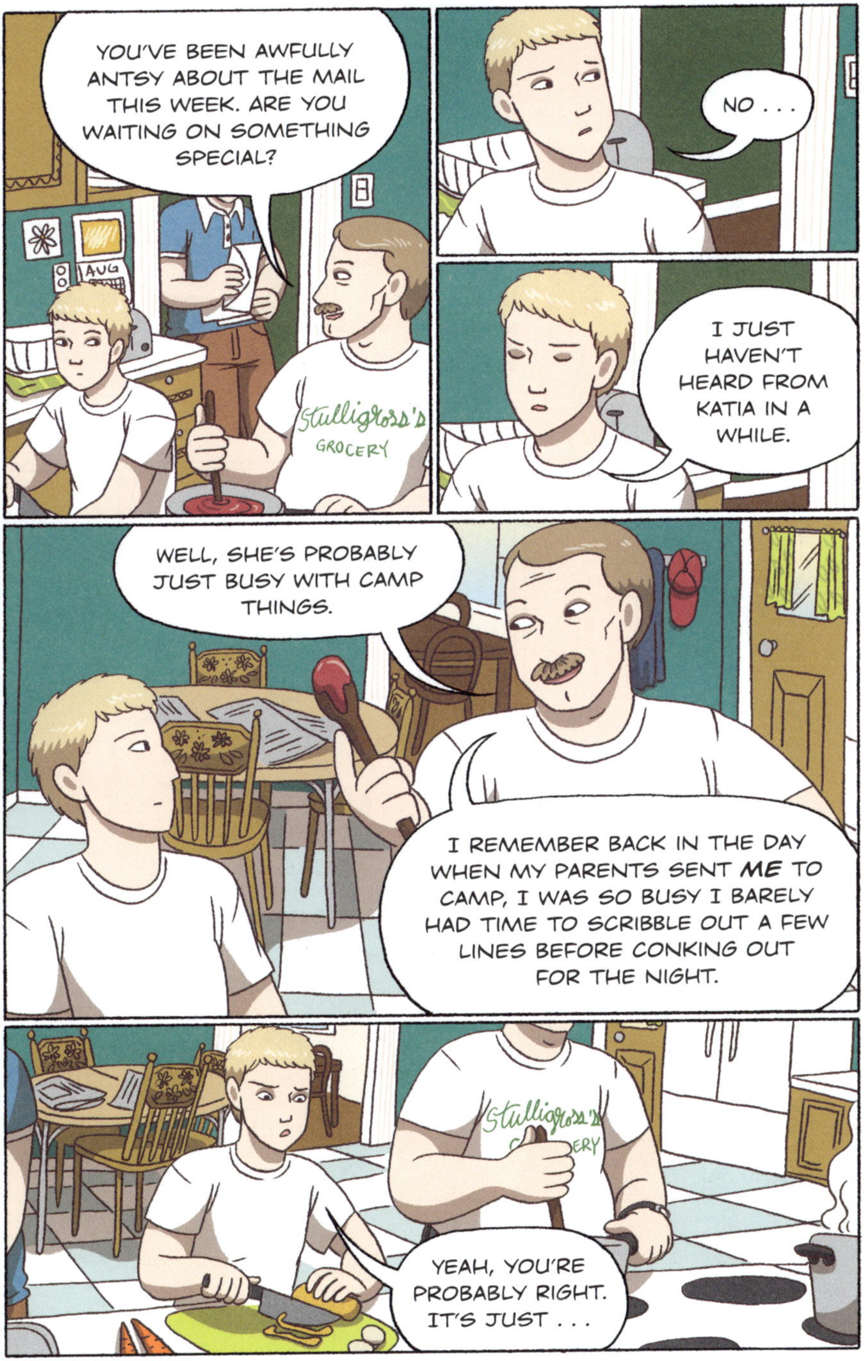
YOU'VE BEEN AWFULLY ANTSY ABOUT THE MAIL THIS WEEK. ARE YOU WAITING ON SOMETHING SPECIAL?
AUG
STULLIGROSS'S GROCERY
NO . . .
I JUST HAVEN'T HEARD FROM KATIA IN A WHILE.
WELL, SHE'S PROBABLY JUST BUSY WITH CAMP THINGS.
I REMEMBER BACK IN THE DAY WHEN MY PARENTS SENT *ME* TO CAMP, I WAS SO BUSY I BARELY HAD TIME TO SCRIBBLE OUT A FEW LINES BEFORE CONKING OUT FOR THE NIGHT.
YEAH, YOU'RE PROBABLY RIGHT. IT'S JUST . . .

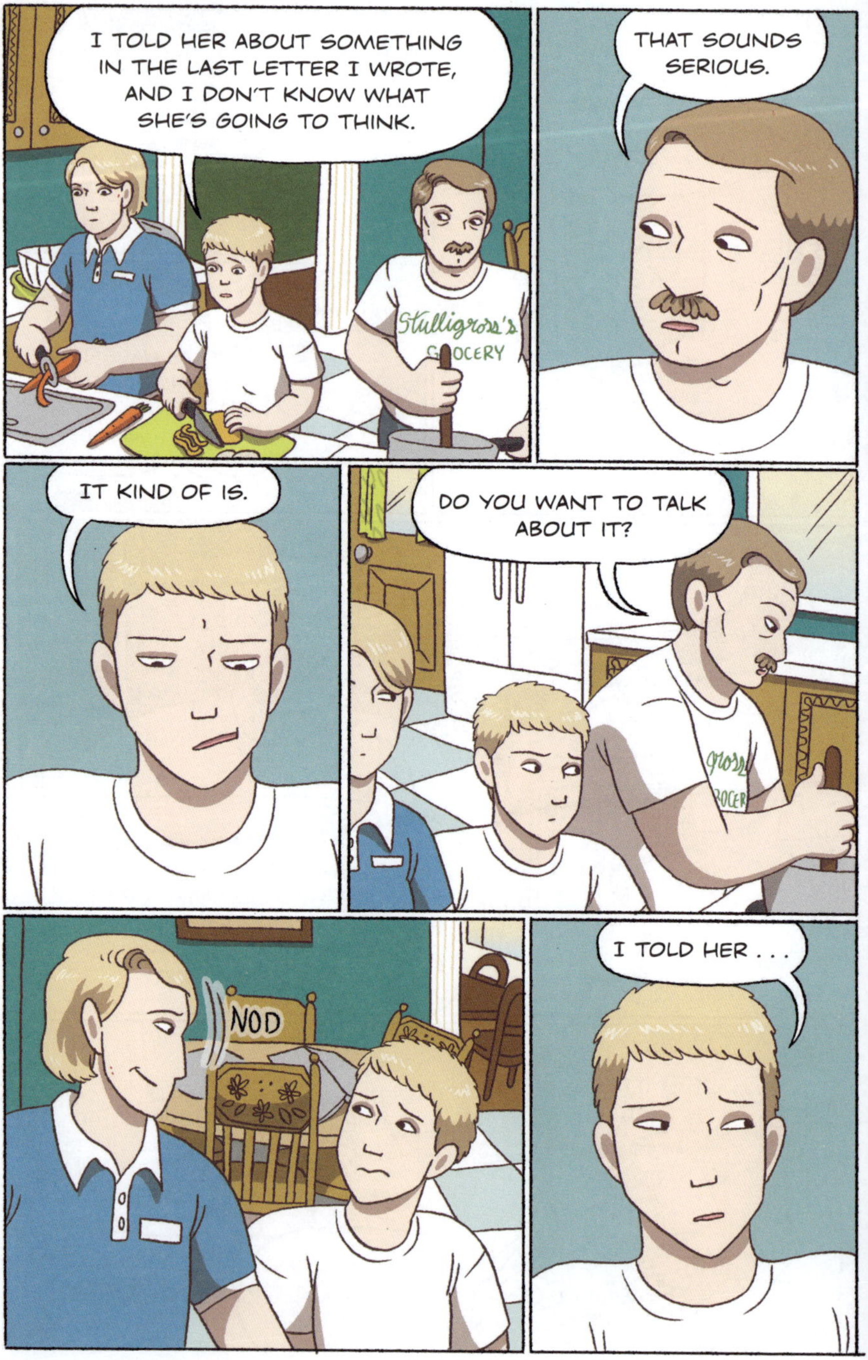
I TOLD HER ABOUT SOMETHING IN THE LAST LETTER I WROTE, AND I DON'T KNOW WHAT SHE'S GOING TO THINK.
Stulligross's GROCERY
THAT SOUNDS SERIOUS.
IT KIND OF IS.
DO YOU WANT TO TALK ABOUT IT?
NOD
I TOLD HER . . .

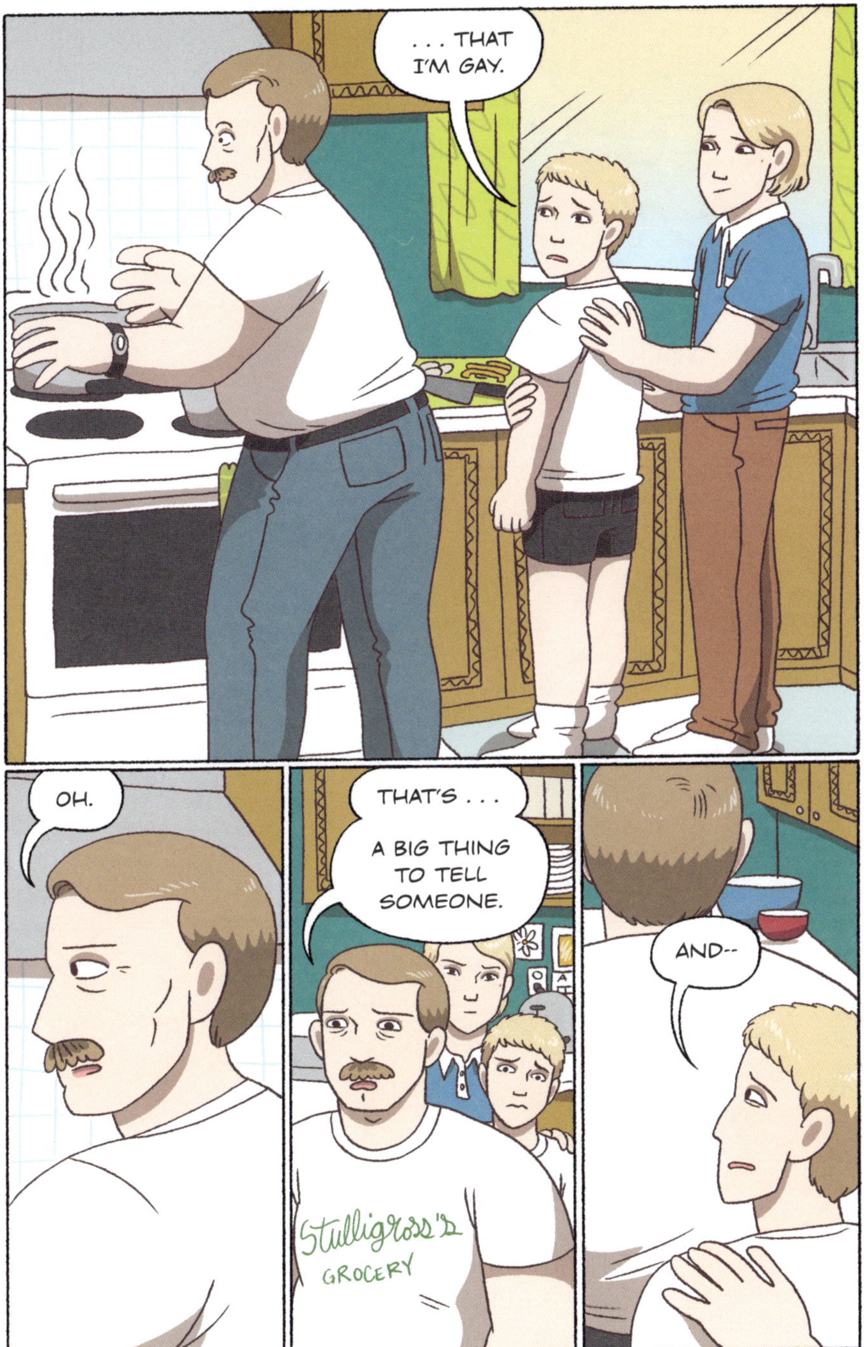

. . . THAT I'M GAY.
OH.
THAT'S . . .
A BIG THING TO TELL SOMEONE.
Stulligross's
GROCERY
AND--

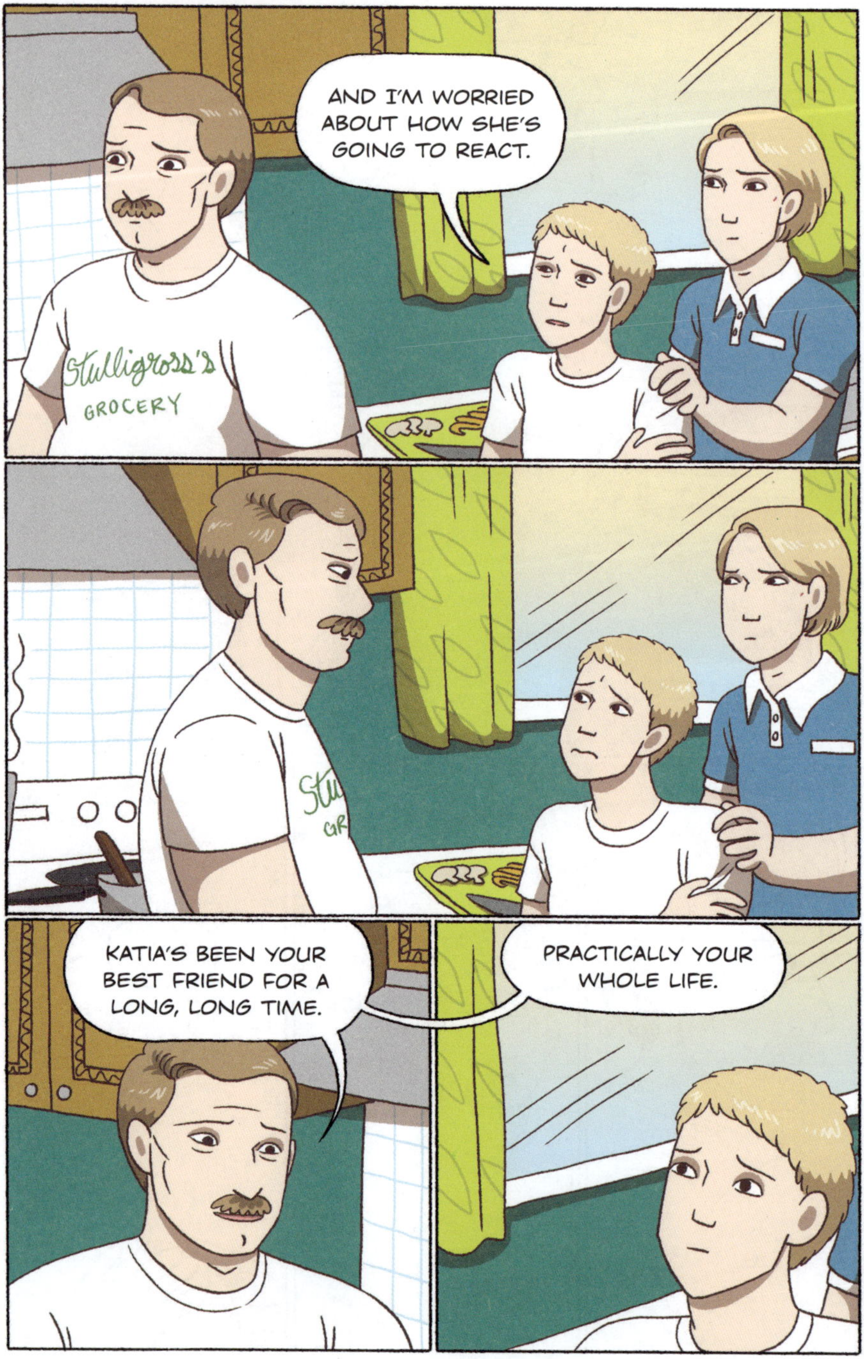
AND I'M WORRIED ABOUT HOW SHE'S GOING TO REACT.
Stulligross's GROCERY
KATIA'S BEEN YOUR BEST FRIEND FOR A LONG, LONG TIME.
PRACTICALLY YOUR WHOLE LIFE.

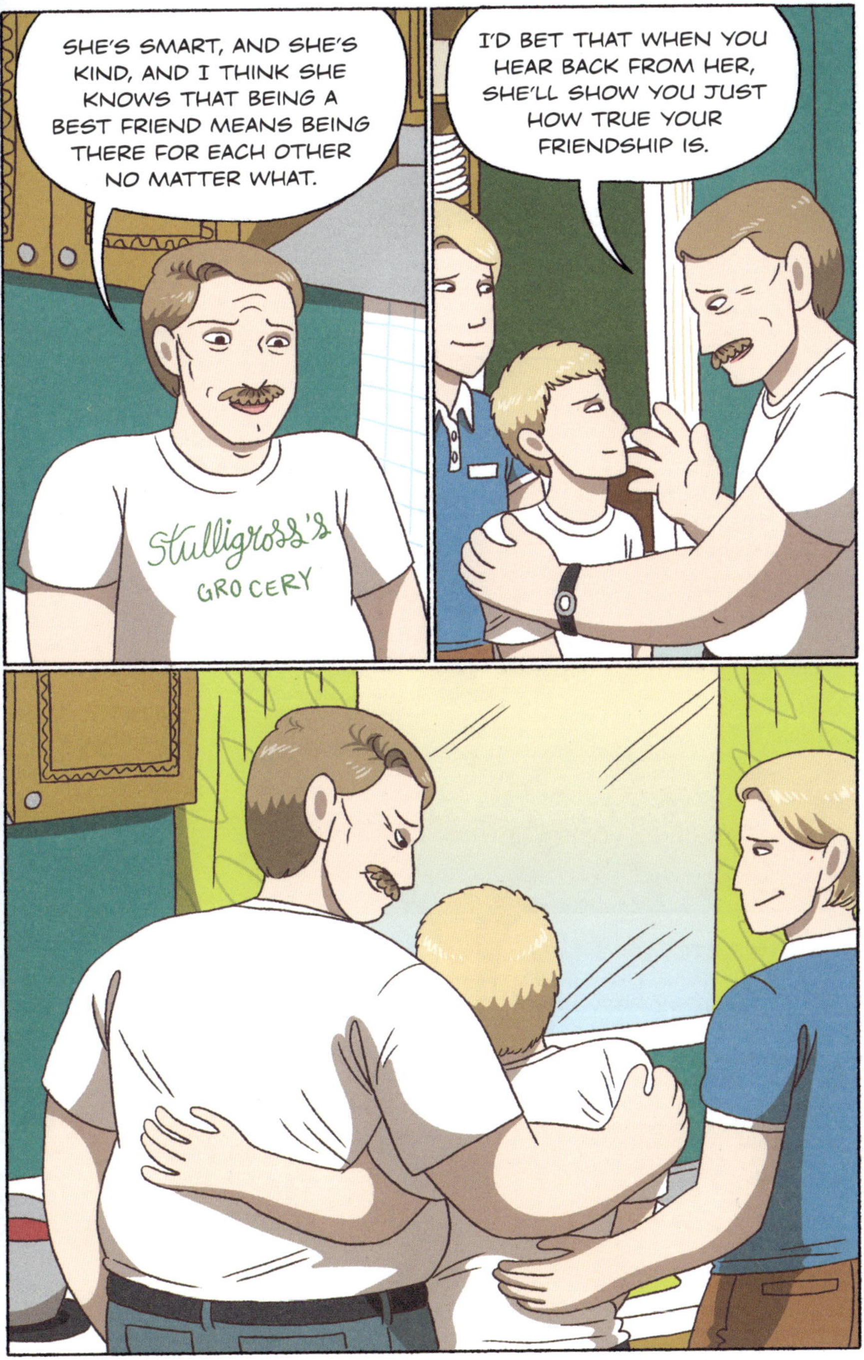
SHE'S SMART, AND SHE'S KIND, AND I THINK SHE KNOWS THAT BEING A BEST FRIEND MEANS BEING THERE FOR EACH OTHER NO MATTER WHAT.
Stulligross's GROCERY
I'D BET THAT WHEN YOU HEAR BACK FROM HER, SHE'LL SHOW YOU JUST HOW TRUE YOUR FRIENDSHIP IS.

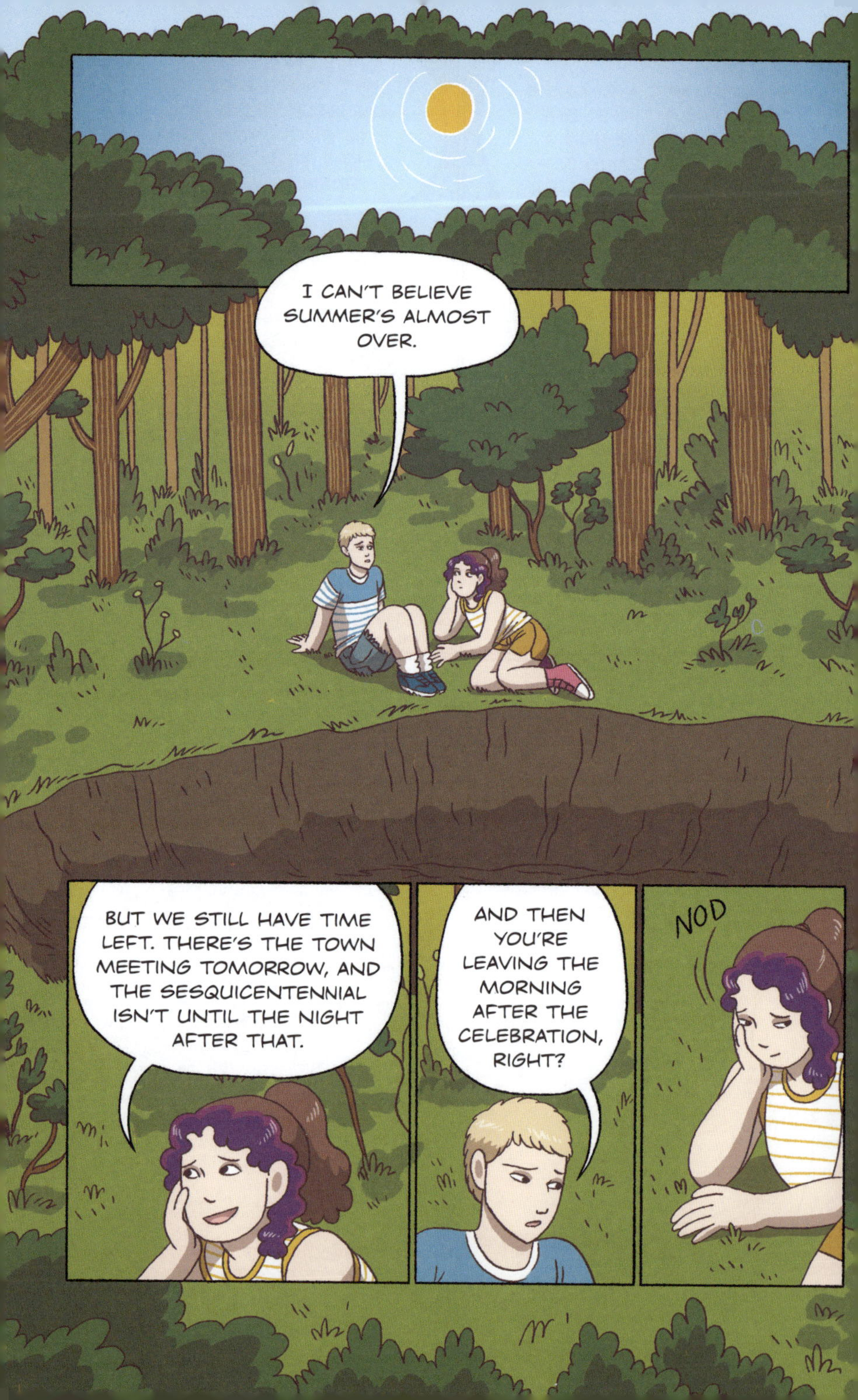
I CAN'T BELIEVE SUMMER'S ALMOST OVER.
BUT WE STILL HAVE TIME LEFT. THERE'S THE TOWN MEETING TOMORROW, AND THE SESQUICENTENNIAL ISN'T UNTIL THE NIGHT AFTER THAT.
AND THEN YOU'RE LEAVING THE MORNING AFTER THE CELEBRATION, RIGHT?
NOD

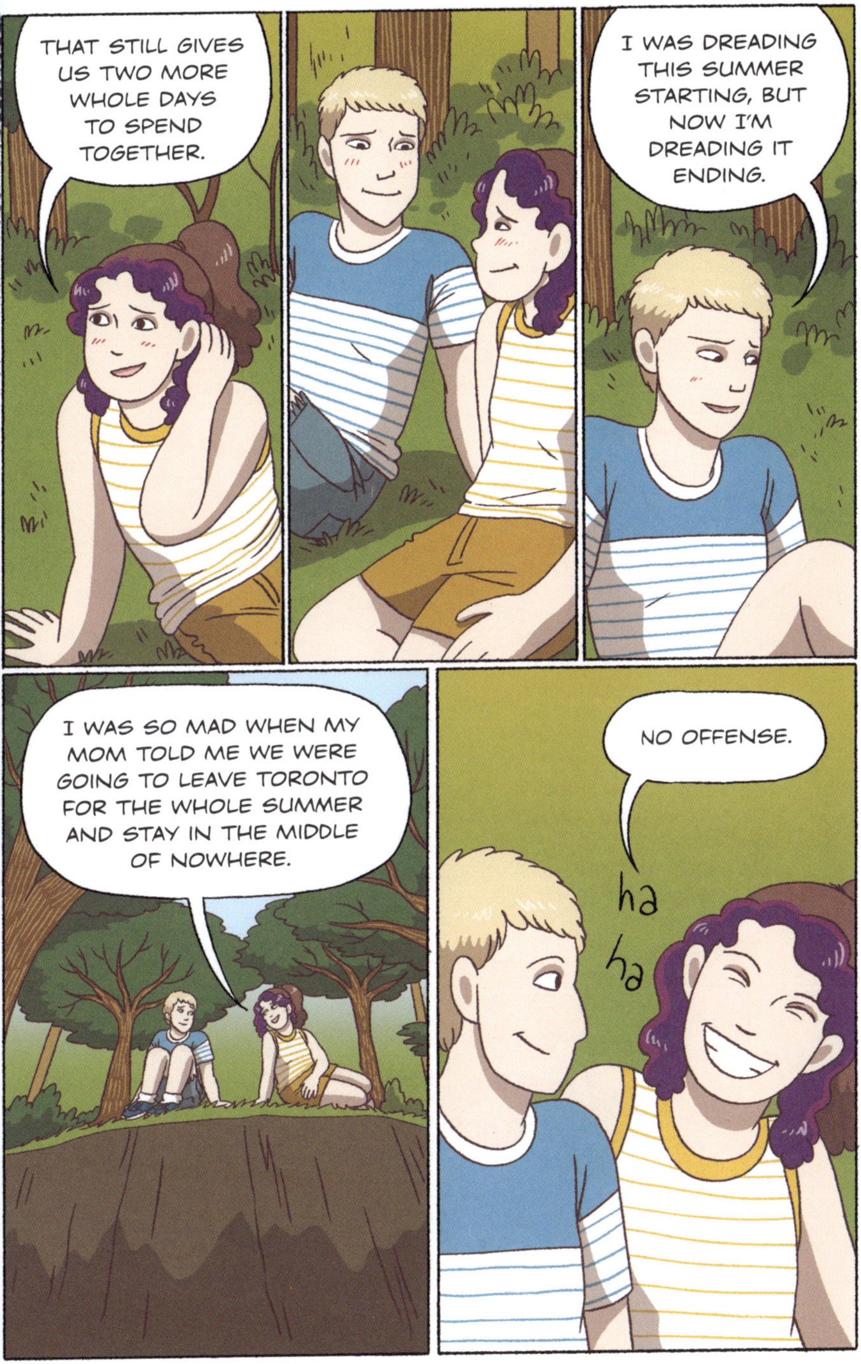
THAT STILL GIVES US TWO MORE WHOLE DAYS TO SPEND TOGETHER.
I WAS DREADING THIS SUMMER STARTING, BUT NOW I'M DREADING IT ENDING.
I WAS SO MAD WHEN MY MOM TOLD ME WE WERE GOING TO LEAVE TORONTO FOR THE WHOLE SUMMER AND STAY IN THE MIDDLE OF NOWHERE.
NO OFFENSE.
ha ha

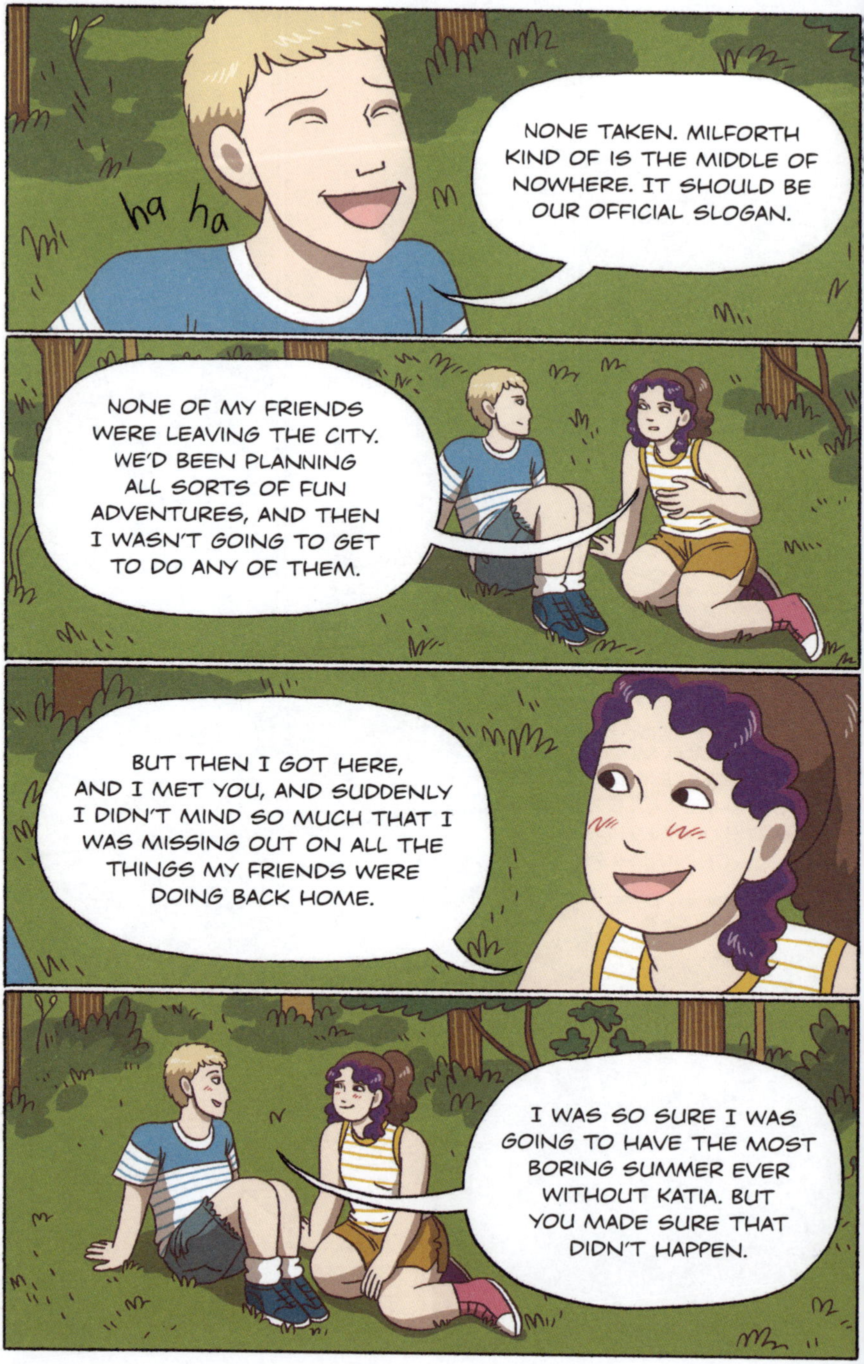
ha ha
NONE TAKEN. MILFORTH KIND OF IS THE MIDDLE OF NOWHERE. IT SHOULD BE OUR OFFICIAL SLOGAN.
NONE OF MY FRIENDS WERE LEAVING THE CITY. WE'D BEEN PLANNING ALL SORTS OF FUN ADVENTURES, AND THEN I WASN'T GOING TO GET TO DO ANY OF THEM.
BUT THEN I GOT HERE, AND I MET YOU, AND SUDDENLY I DIDN'T MIND SO MUCH THAT I WAS MISSING OUT ON ALL THE THINGS MY FRIENDS WERE DOING BACK HOME.
I WAS SO SURE I WAS GOING TO HAVE THE MOST BORING SUMMER EVER WITHOUT KATIA. BUT YOU MADE SURE THAT DIDN'T HAPPEN.

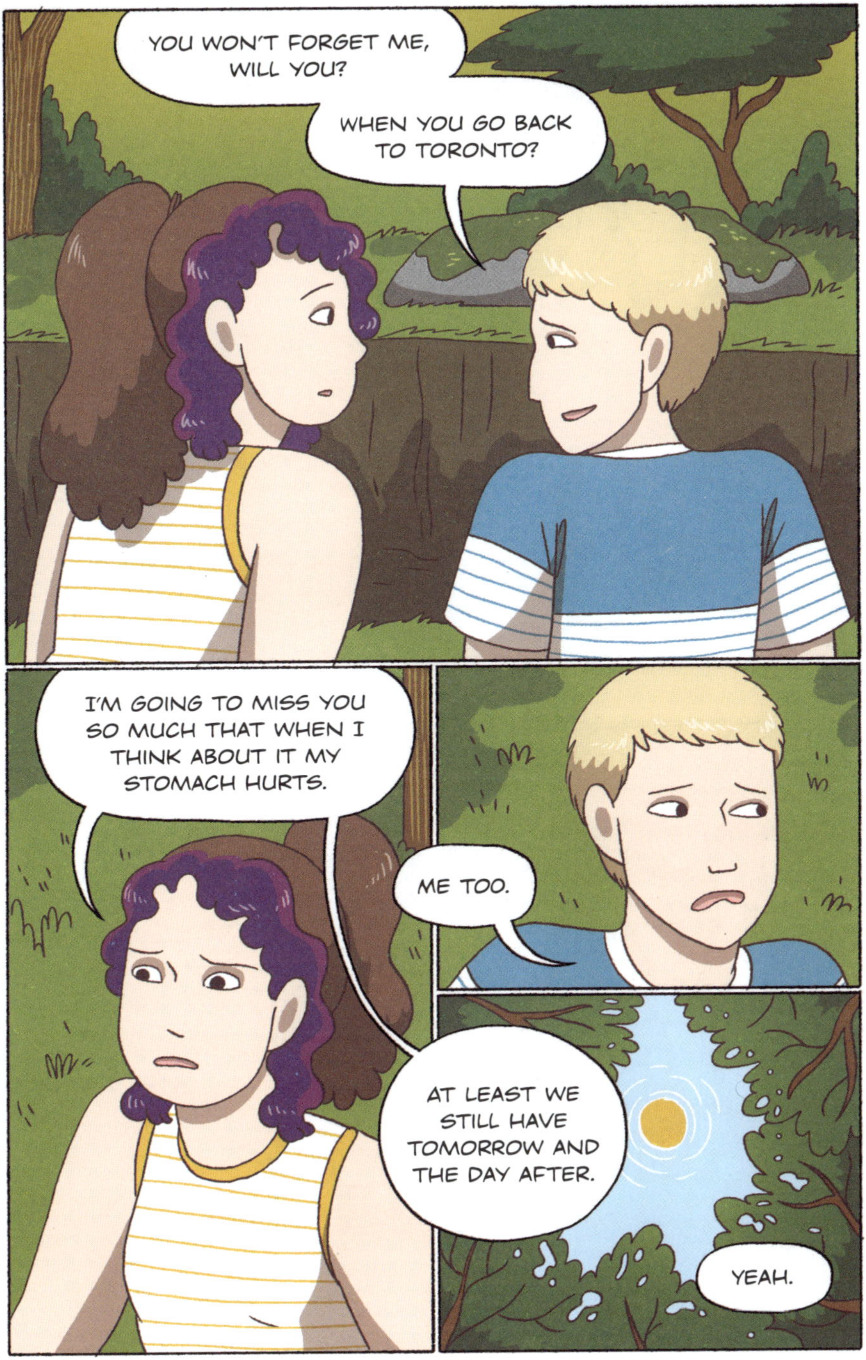
YOU WON'T FORGET ME, WILL YOU?
WHEN YOU GO BACK TO TORONTO?
I'M GOING TO MISS YOU SO MUCH THAT WHEN I THINK ABOUT IT MY STOMACH HURTS.
ME TOO.
AT LEAST WE STILL HAVE TOMORROW AND THE DAY AFTER.
YEAH.

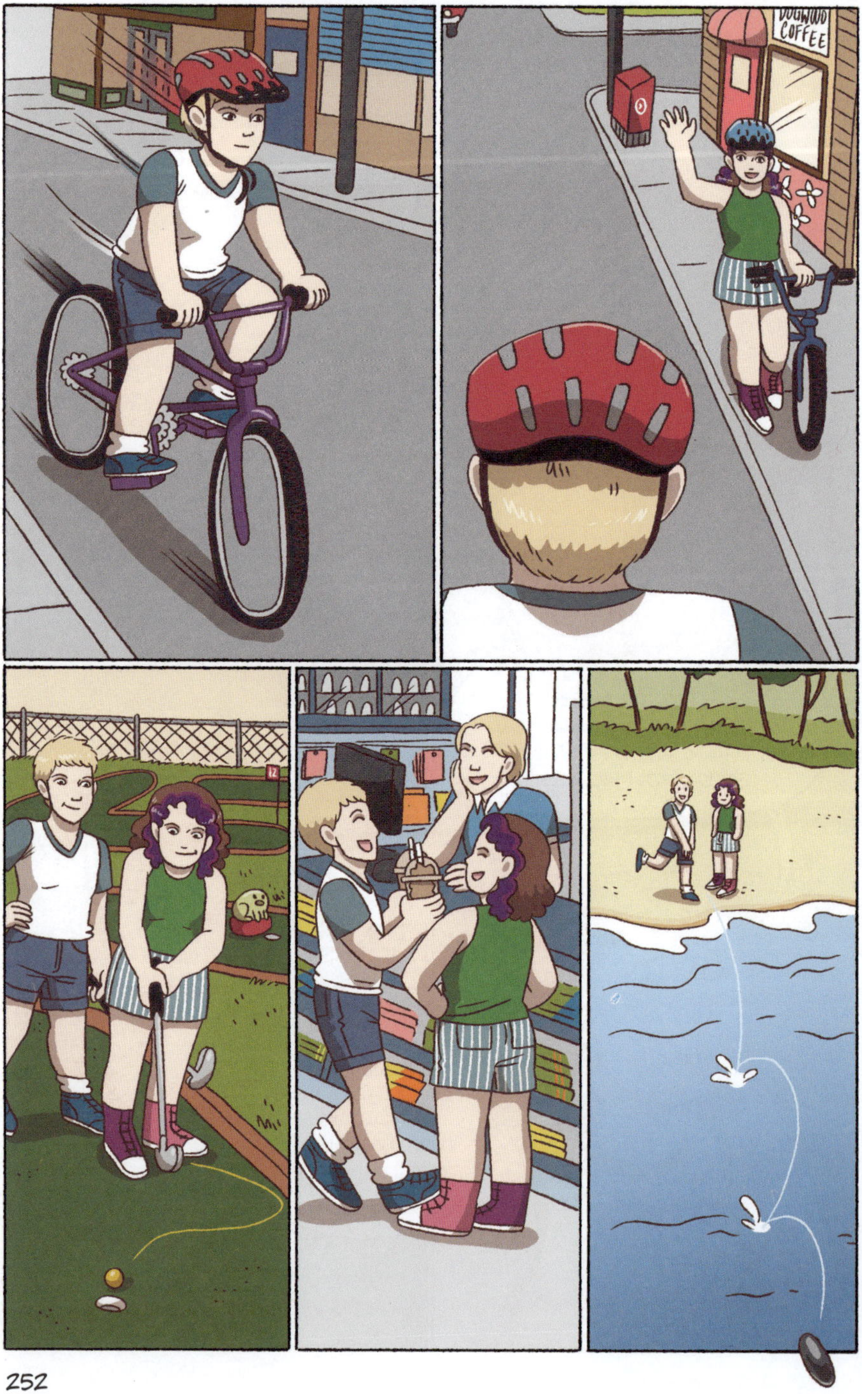
COFFEE

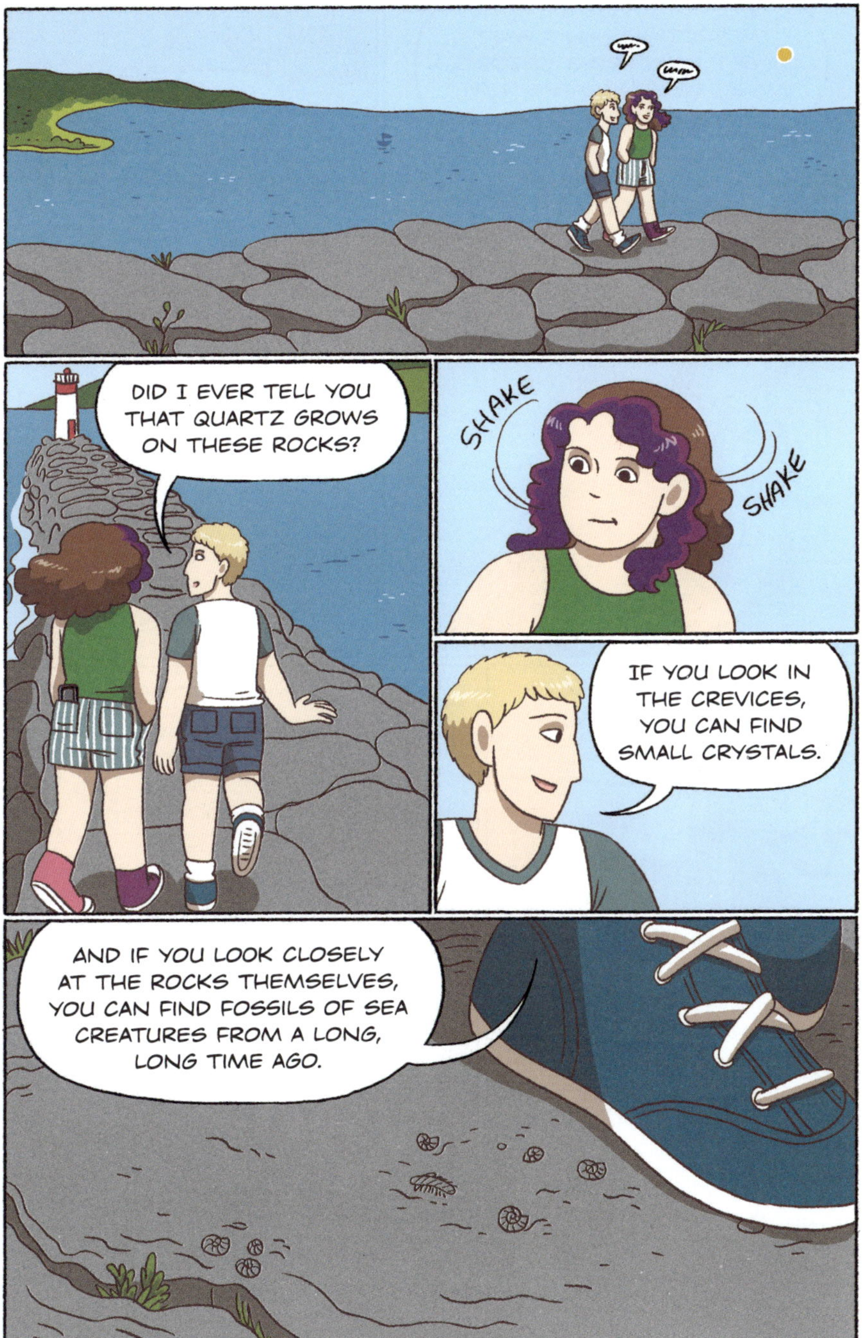
DID I EVER TELL YOU THAT QUARTZ GROWS ON THESE ROCKS?
SHAKE
SHAKE
IF YOU LOOK IN THE CREVICES, YOU CAN FIND SMALL CRYSTALS.
AND IF YOU LOOK CLOSELY AT THE ROCKS THEMSELVES, YOU CAN FIND FOSSILS OF SEA CREATURES FROM A LONG, LONG TIME AGO.

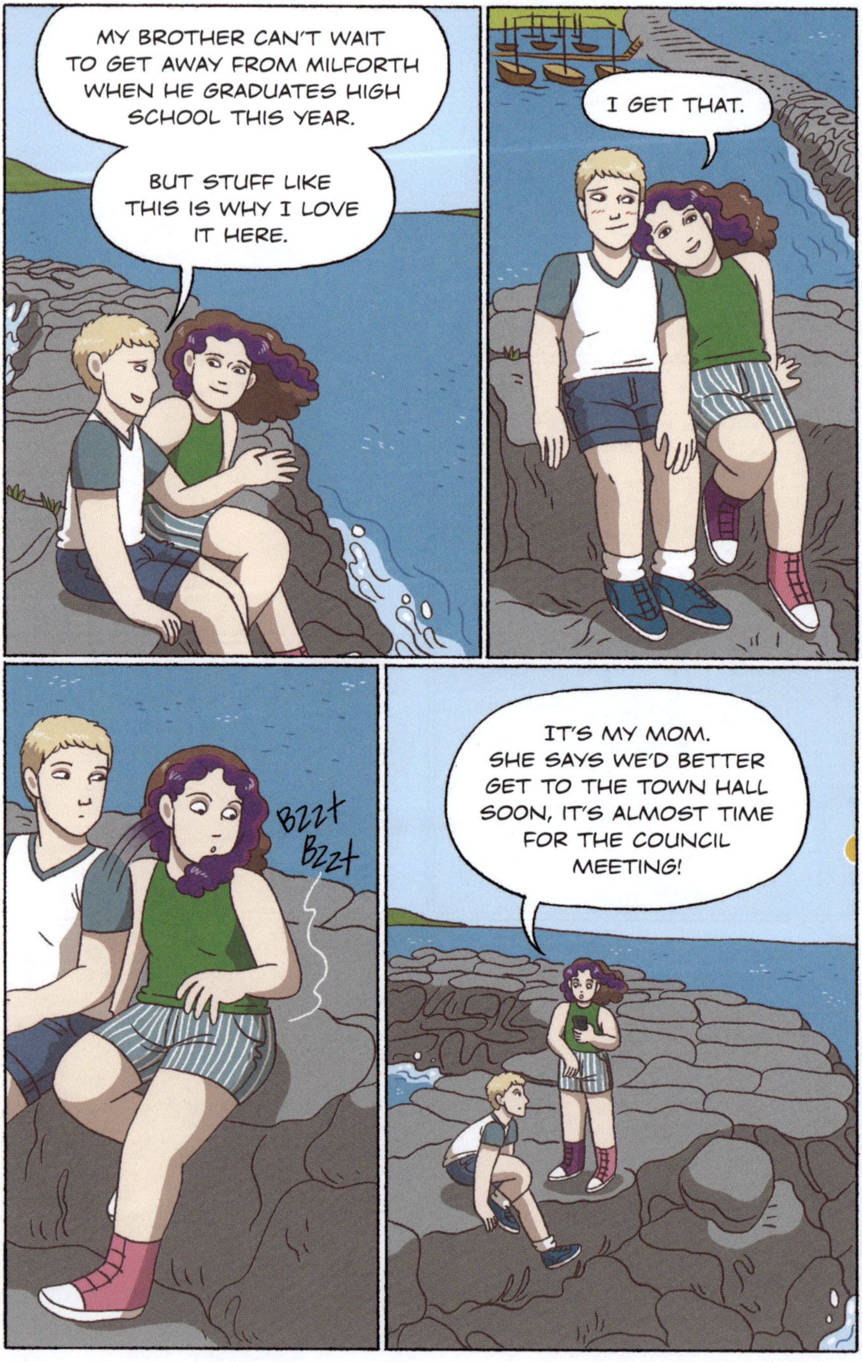
MY BROTHER CAN'T WAIT TO GET AWAY FROM MILFORTH WHEN HE GRADUATES HIGH SCHOOL THIS YEAR.
BUT STUFF LIKE THIS IS WHY I LOVE IT HERE.
I GET THAT.
BZZT BZZT
IT'S MY MOM. SHE SAYS WE'D BETTER GET TO THE TOWN HALL SOON, IT'S ALMOST TIME FOR THE COUNCIL MEETING!

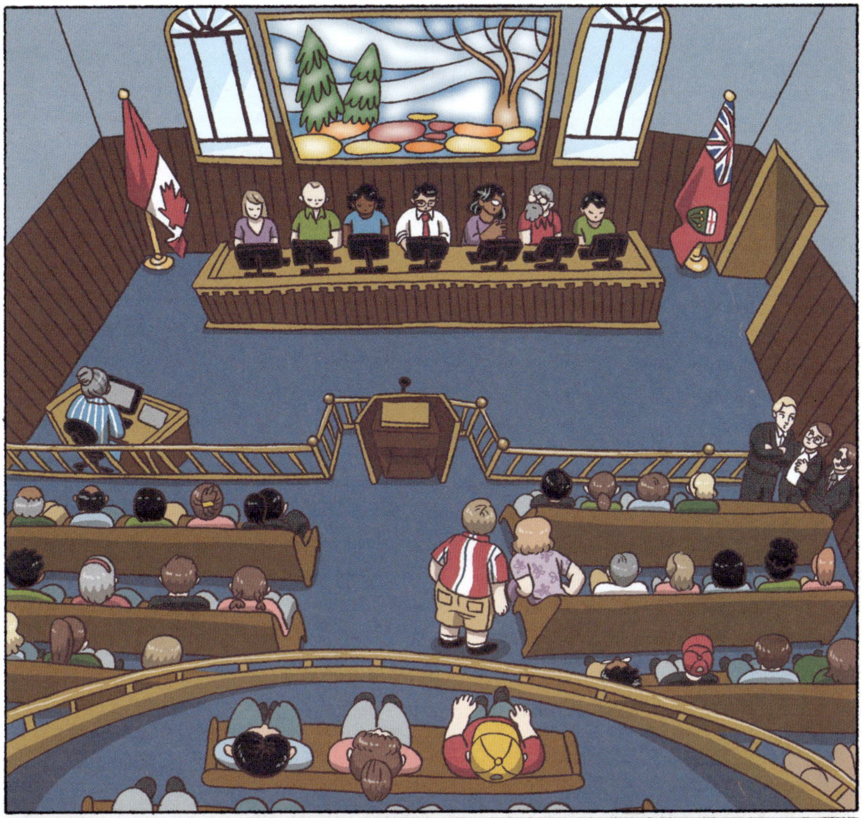

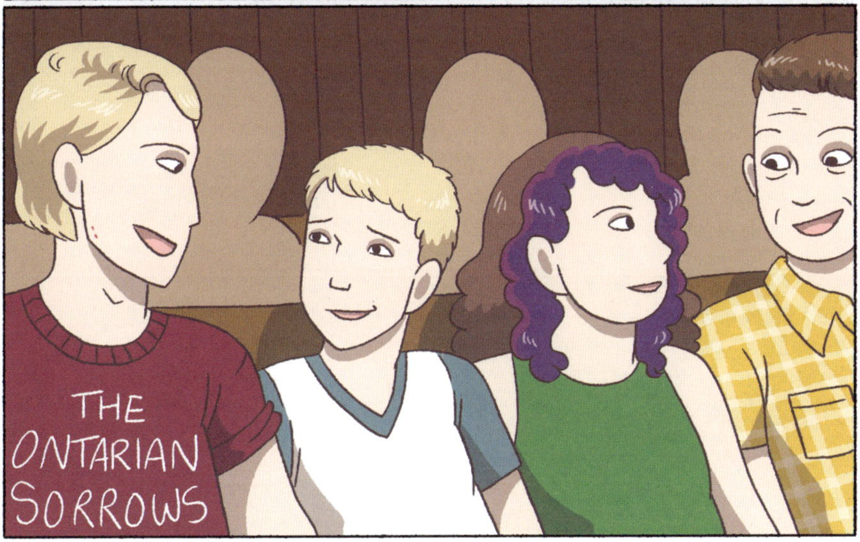
THE ONTARIAN SORROWS

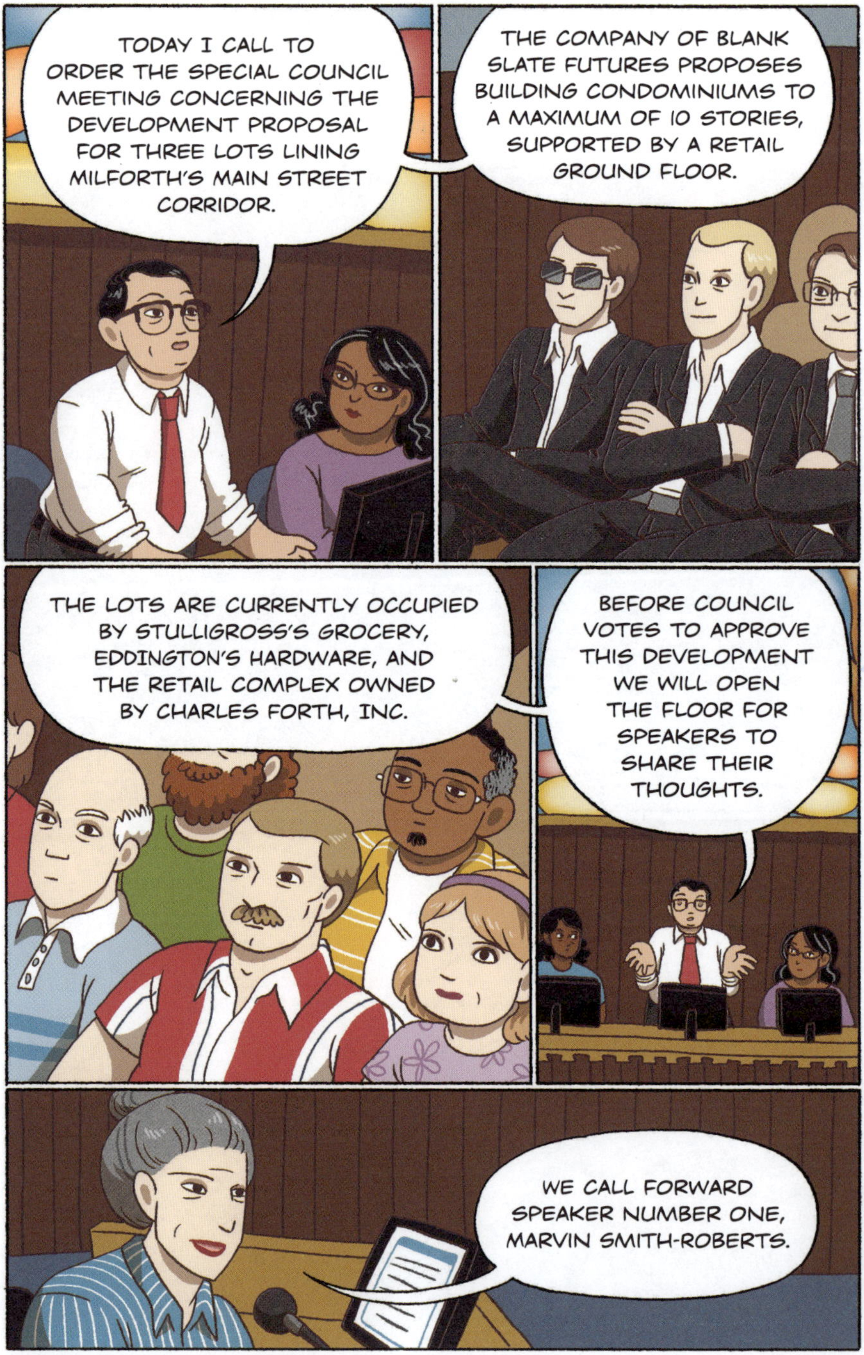
TODAY I CALL TO ORDER THE SPECIAL COUNCIL MEETING CONCERNING THE DEVELOPMENT PROPOSAL FOR THREE LOTS LINING MILFORTH'S MAIN STREET CORRIDOR.
THE COMPANY OF BLANK SLATE FUTURES PROPOSES BUILDING CONDOMINIUMS TO A MAXIMUM OF 10 STORIES, SUPPORTED BY A RETAIL GROUND FLOOR.
THE LOTS ARE CURRENTLY OCCUPIED BY STULLIGROSS'S GROCERY, EDDINGTON'S HARDWARE, AND THE RETAIL COMPLEX OWNED BY CHARLES FORTH, INC.
BEFORE COUNCIL VOTES TO APPROVE THIS DEVELOPMENT WE WILL OPEN THE FLOOR FOR SPEAKERS TO SHARE THEIR THOUGHTS.
WE CALL FORWARD SPEAKER NUMBER ONE, MARVIN SMITH-ROBERTS.

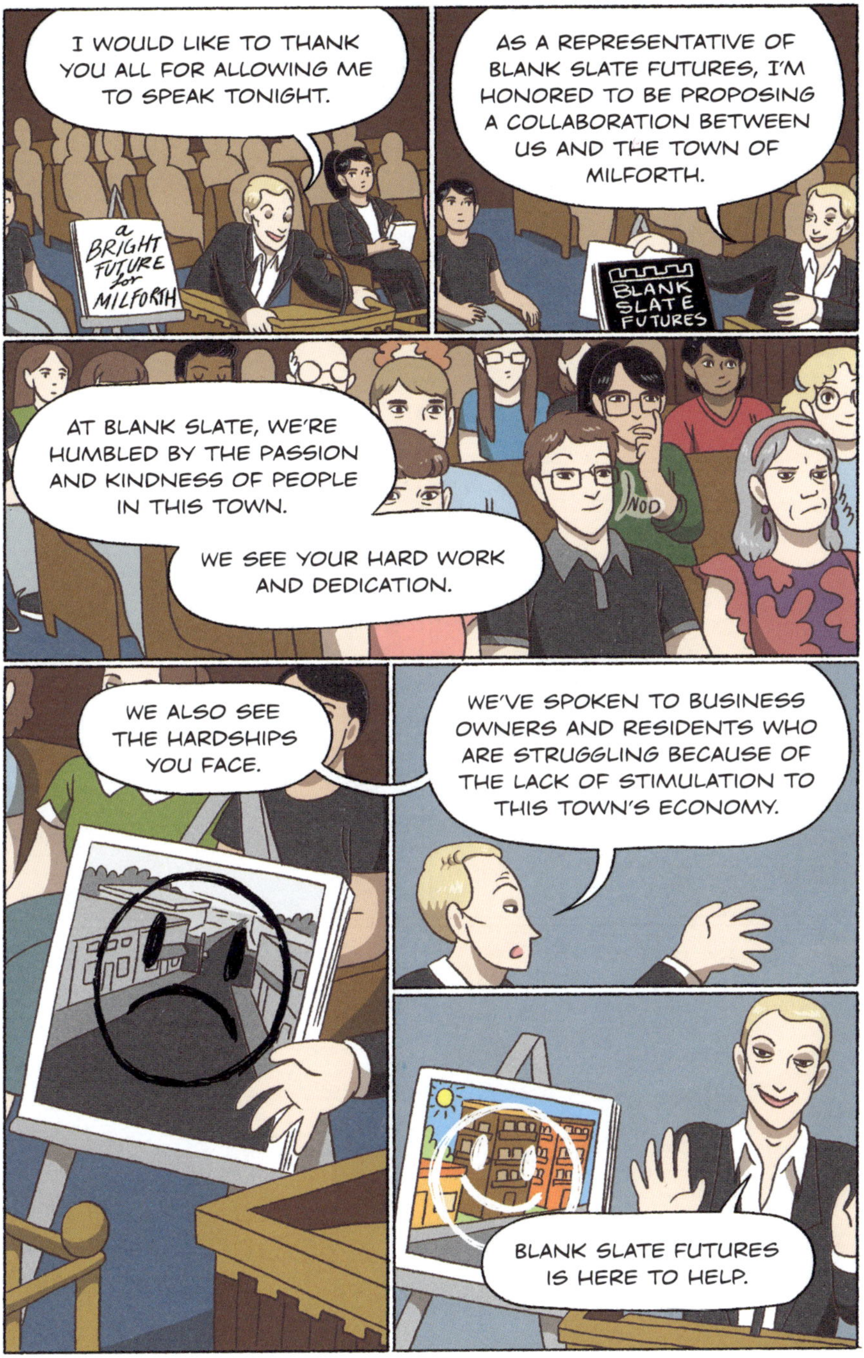
I WOULD LIKE TO THANK YOU ALL FOR ALLOWING ME TO SPEAK TONIGHT.
a BRIGHT FUTURE for MILFORTH
AS A REPRESENTATIVE OF BLANK SLATE FUTURES, I'M HONORED TO BE PROPOSING A COLLABORATION BETWEEN US AND THE TOWN OF MILFORTH.
BLANK SLATE FUTURES
AT BLANK SLATE, WE'RE HUMBLED BY THE PASSION AND KINDNESS OF PEOPLE IN THIS TOWN.
WE SEE YOUR HARD WORK AND DEDICATION.
NOD
WE ALSO SEE THE HARDSHIPS YOU FACE.
WE'VE SPOKEN TO BUSINESS OWNERS AND RESIDENTS WHO ARE STRUGGLING BECAUSE OF THE LACK OF STIMULATION TO THIS TOWN'S ECONOMY.
BLANK SLATE FUTURES IS HERE TO HELP.

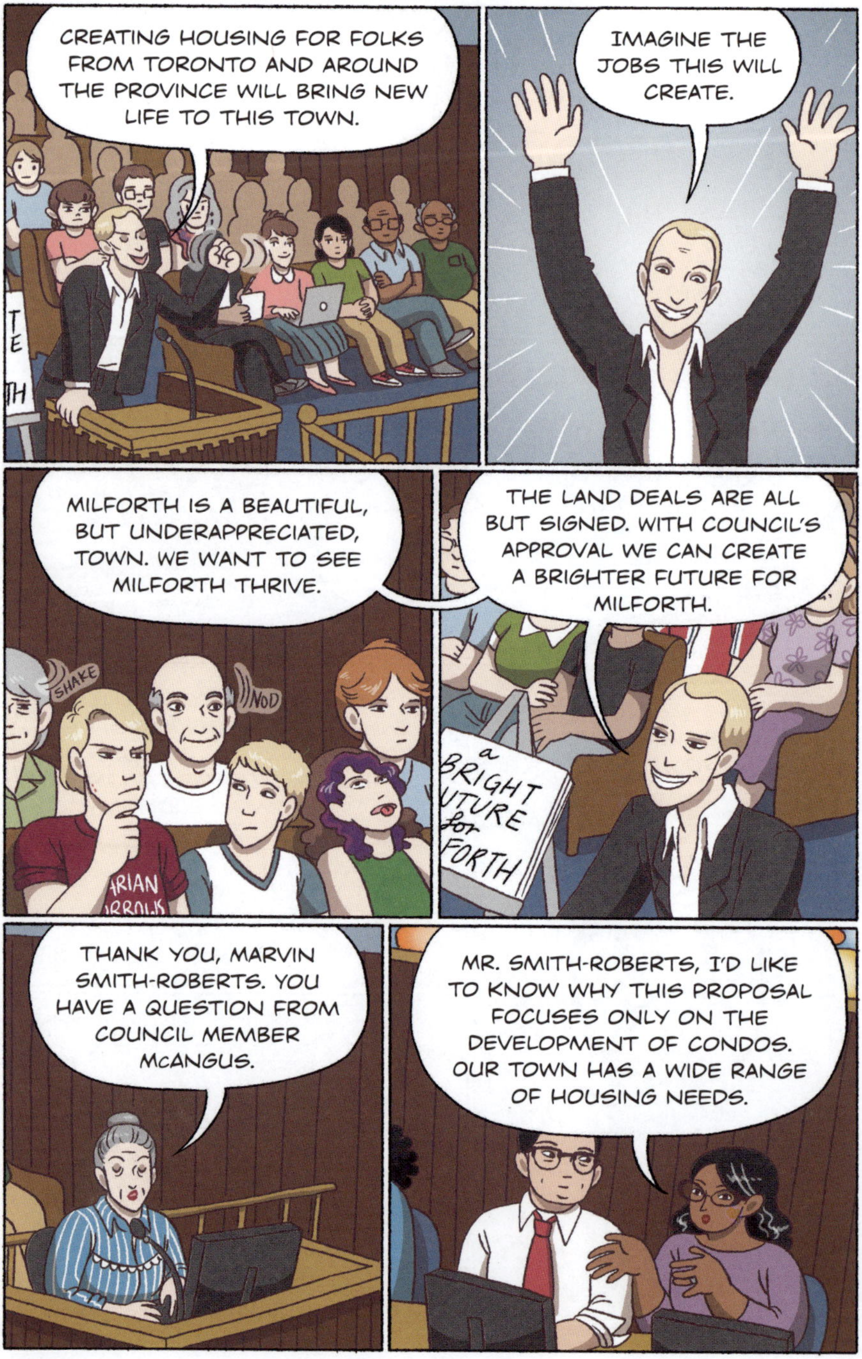

CREATING HOUSING FOR FOLKS FROM TORONTO AND AROUND THE PROVINCE WILL BRING NEW LIFE TO THIS TOWN.
IMAGINE THE JOBS THIS WILL CREATE.
MILFORTH IS A BEAUTIFUL, BUT UNDERAPPRECIATED, TOWN. WE WANT TO SEE MILFORTH THRIVE.
SHAKE
NOD
THE LAND DEALS ARE ALL BUT SIGNED. WITH COUNCIL'S APPROVAL WE CAN CREATE A BRIGHTER FUTURE FOR MILFORTH.
a BRIGHT UTURE for FORTH
THANK YOU, MARVIN SMITH-ROBERTS. YOU HAVE A QUESTION FROM COUNCIL MEMBER McANGUS.
MR. SMITH-ROBERTS, I'D LIKE TO KNOW WHY THIS PROPOSAL FOCUSES ONLY ON THE DEVELOPMENT OF CONDOS. OUR TOWN HAS A WIDE RANGE OF HOUSING NEEDS.

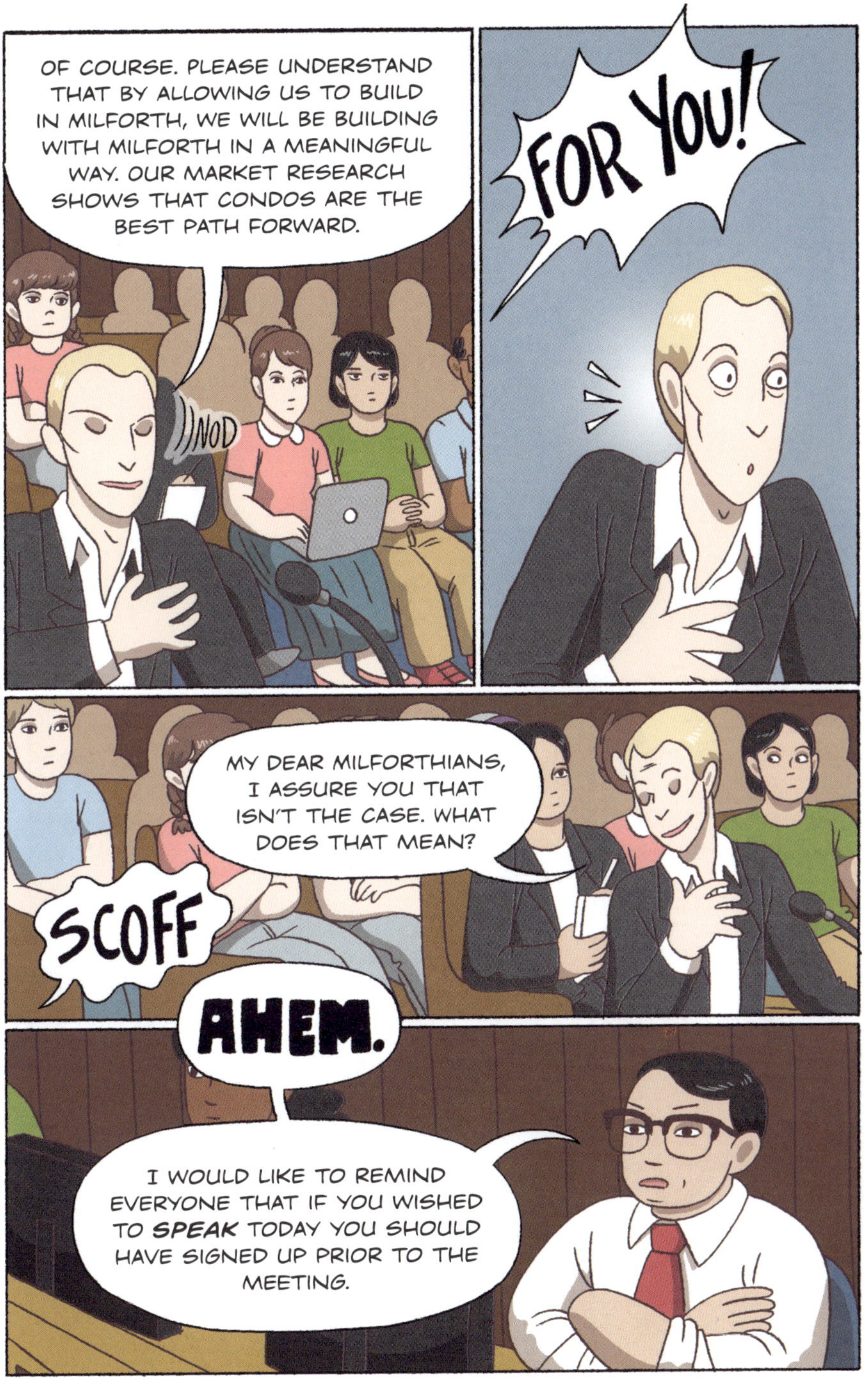
OF COURSE. PLEASE UNDERSTAND THAT BY ALLOWING US TO BUILD IN MILFORTH, WE WILL BE BUILDING WITH MILFORTH IN A MEANINGFUL WAY. OUR MARKET RESEARCH SHOWS THAT CONDOS ARE THE BEST PATH FORWARD.
NOD
FOR YOU!
MY DEAR MILFORTHIANS, I ASSURE YOU THAT ISN'T THE CASE. WHAT DOES THAT MEAN?
SCOFF
AHEM.
I WOULD LIKE TO REMIND EVERYONE THAT IF YOU WISHED TO ***SPEAK*** TODAY YOU SHOULD HAVE SIGNED UP PRIOR TO THE MEETING.

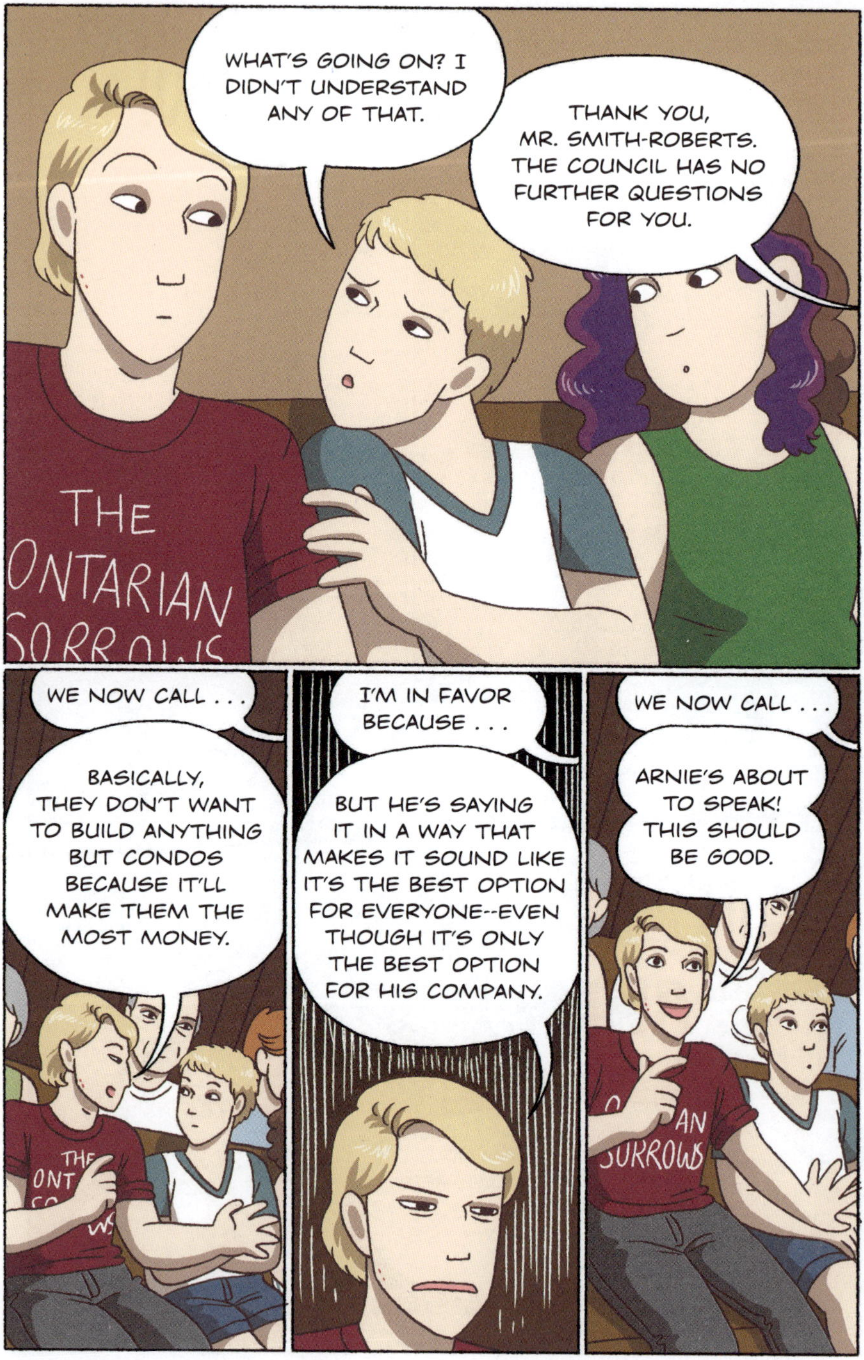
WHAT'S GOING ON? I DIDN'T UNDERSTAND ANY OF THAT.
THANK YOU, MR. SMITH-ROBERTS. THE COUNCIL HAS NO FURTHER QUESTIONS FOR YOU.
THE ONTARIAN SORROWS
WE NOW CALL . . .
BASICALLY, THEY DON'T WANT TO BUILD ANYTHING BUT CONDOS BECAUSE IT'LL MAKE THEM THE MOST MONEY.
I'M IN FAVOR BECAUSE . . .
BUT HE'S SAYING IT IN A WAY THAT MAKES IT SOUND LIKE IT'S THE BEST OPTION FOR EVERYONE--EVEN THOUGH IT'S ONLY THE BEST OPTION FOR HIS COMPANY.
WE NOW CALL . . .
ARNIE'S ABOUT TO SPEAK! THIS SHOULD BE GOOD.

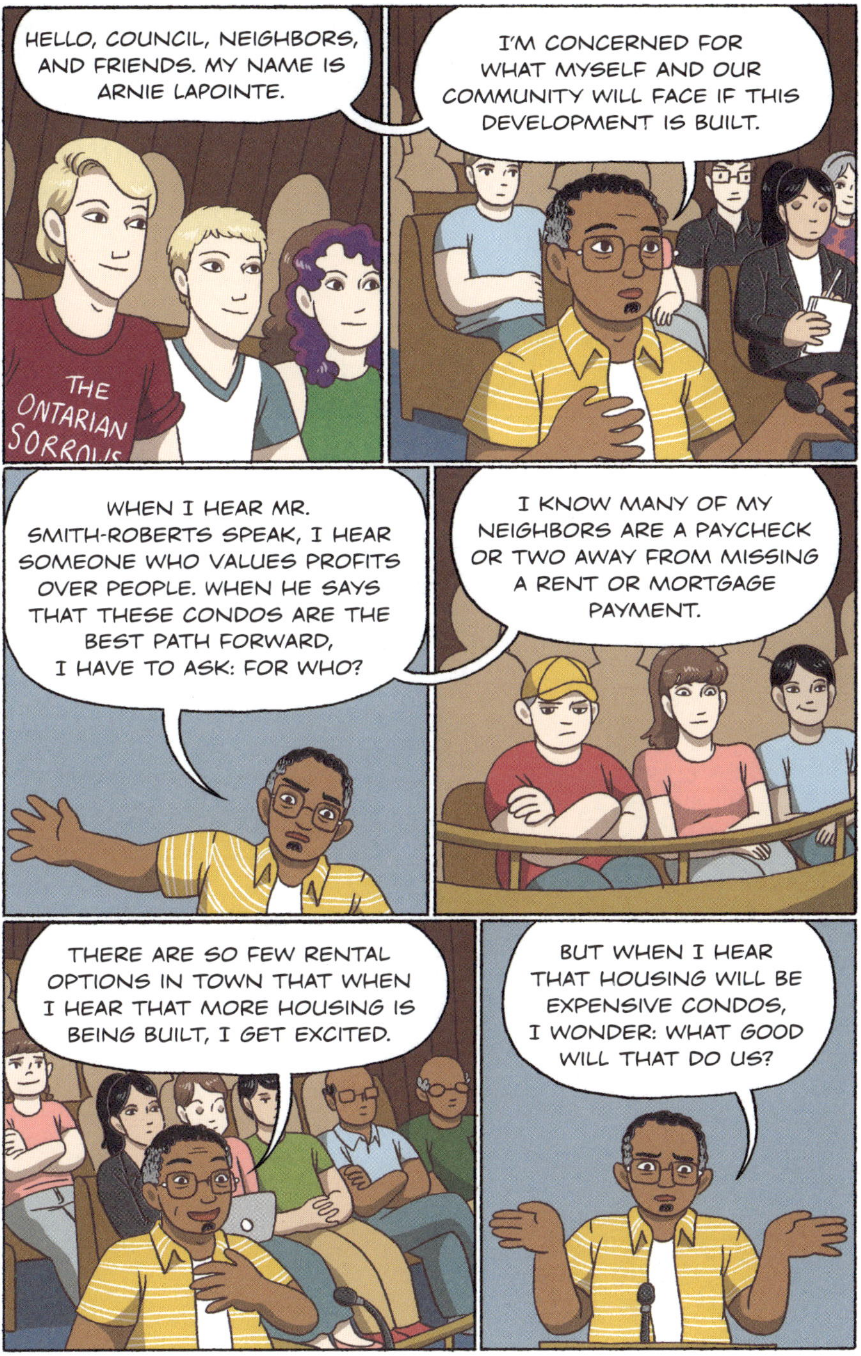
HELLO, COUNCIL, NEIGHBORS, AND FRIENDS. MY NAME IS ARNIE LAPOINTE.
THE ONTARIAN SORROWS
I'M CONCERNED FOR WHAT MYSELF AND OUR COMMUNITY WILL FACE IF THIS DEVELOPMENT IS BUILT.
WHEN I HEAR MR. SMITH-ROBERTS SPEAK, I HEAR SOMEONE WHO VALUES PROFITS OVER PEOPLE. WHEN HE SAYS THAT THESE CONDOS ARE THE BEST PATH FORWARD, I HAVE TO ASK: FOR WHO?
I KNOW MANY OF MY NEIGHBORS ARE A PAYCHECK OR TWO AWAY FROM MISSING A RENT OR MORTGAGE PAYMENT.
THERE ARE SO FEW RENTAL OPTIONS IN TOWN THAT WHEN I HEAR THAT MORE HOUSING IS BEING BUILT, I GET EXCITED.
BUT WHEN I HEAR THAT HOUSING WILL BE EXPENSIVE CONDOS, I WONDER: WHAT GOOD WILL THAT DO US?

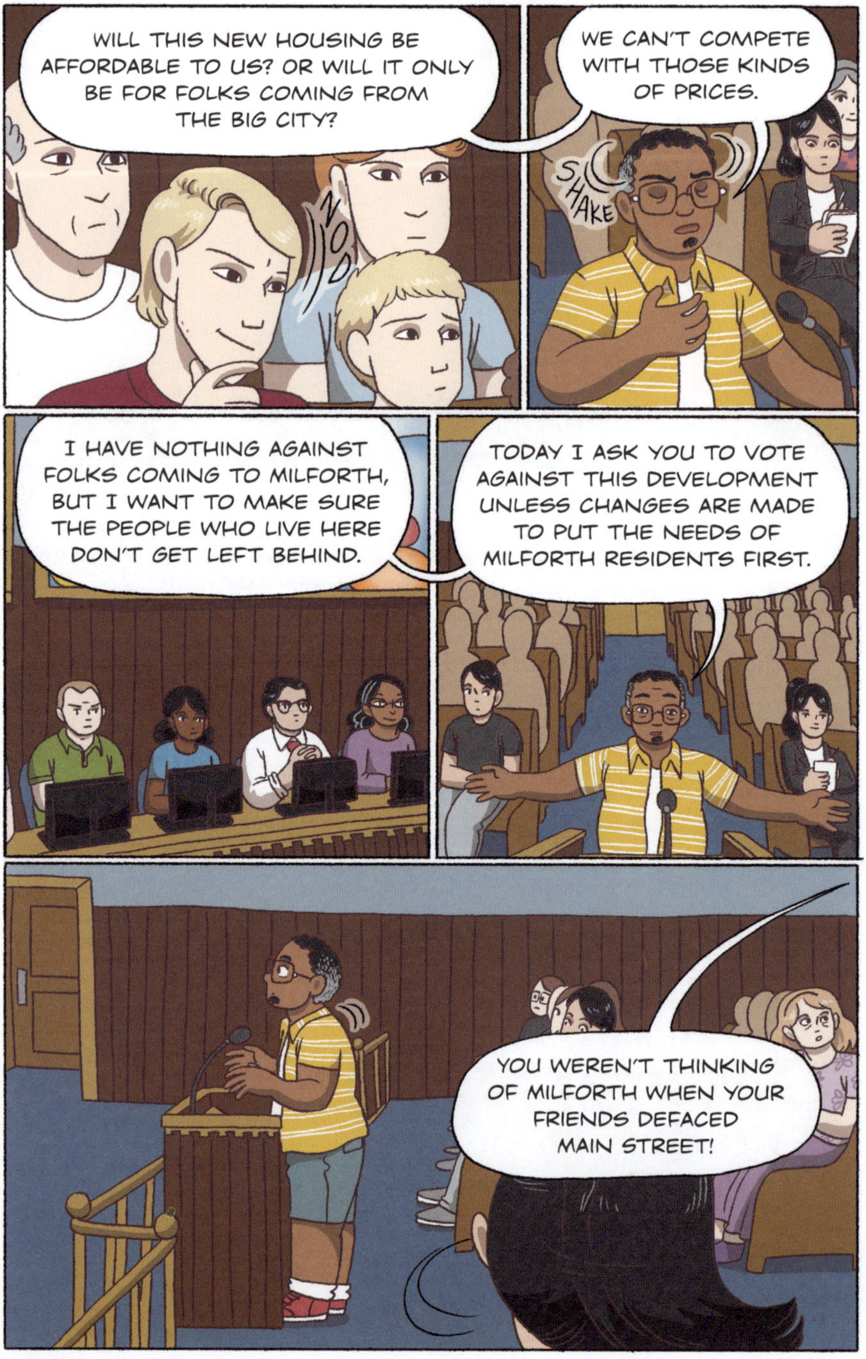
WILL THIS NEW HOUSING BE AFFORDABLE TO US? OR WILL IT ONLY BE FOR FOLKS COMING FROM THE BIG CITY?
NOD
WE CAN'T COMPETE WITH THOSE KINDS OF PRICES.
SHAKE
I HAVE NOTHING AGAINST FOLKS COMING TO MILFORTH, BUT I WANT TO MAKE SURE THE PEOPLE WHO LIVE HERE DON'T GET LEFT BEHIND.
TODAY I ASK YOU TO VOTE AGAINST THIS DEVELOPMENT UNLESS CHANGES ARE MADE TO PUT THE NEEDS OF MILFORTH RESIDENTS FIRST.
YOU WEREN'T THINKING OF MILFORTH WHEN YOUR FRIENDS DEFACED MAIN STREET!

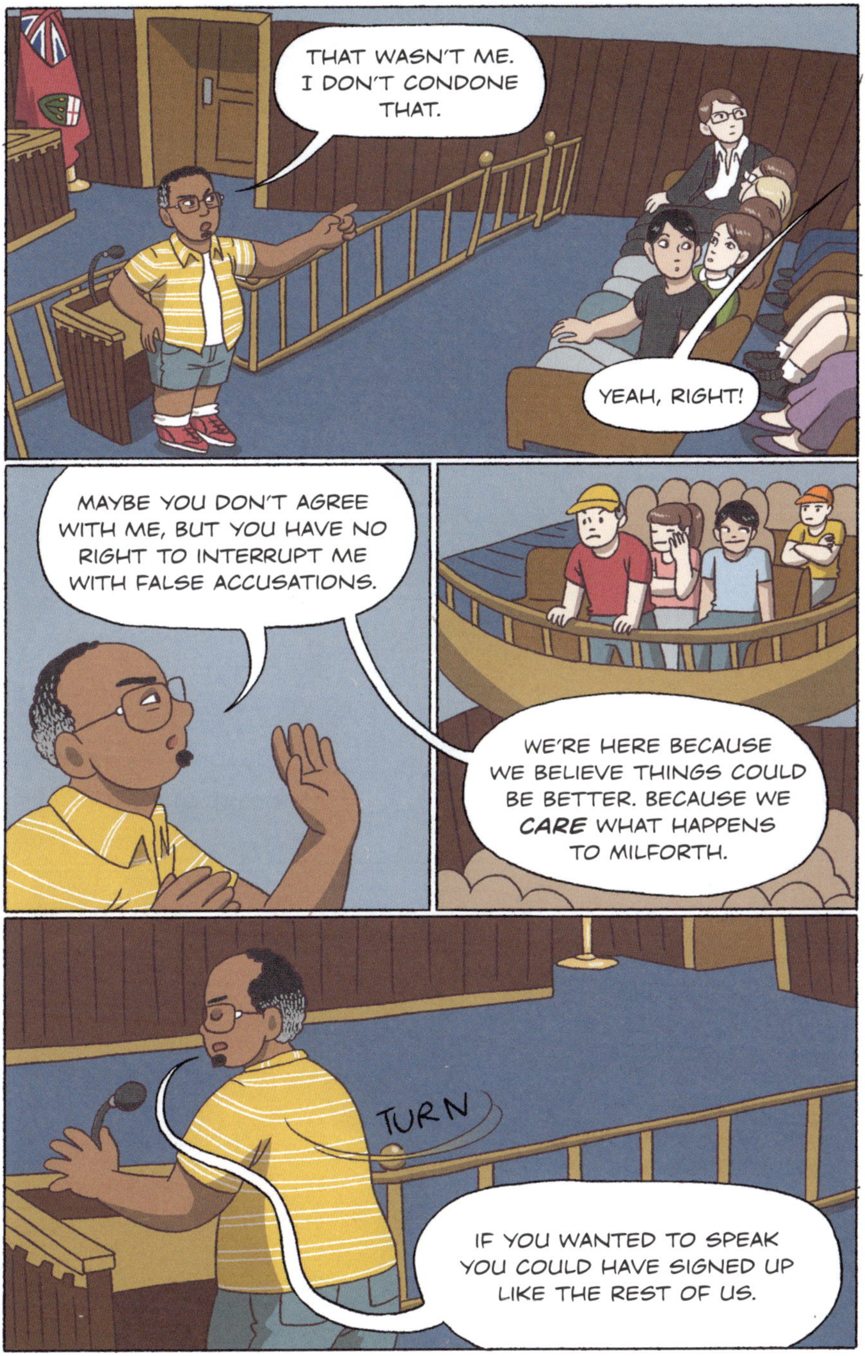
THAT WASN'T ME. I DON'T CONDONE THAT.
YEAH, RIGHT!
MAYBE YOU DON'T AGREE WITH ME, BUT YOU HAVE NO RIGHT TO INTERRUPT ME WITH FALSE ACCUSATIONS.
WE'RE HERE BECAUSE WE BELIEVE THINGS COULD BE BETTER. BECAUSE WE *CARE* WHAT HAPPENS TO MILFORTH.
TURN
IF YOU WANTED TO SPEAK YOU COULD HAVE SIGNED UP LIKE THE REST OF US.

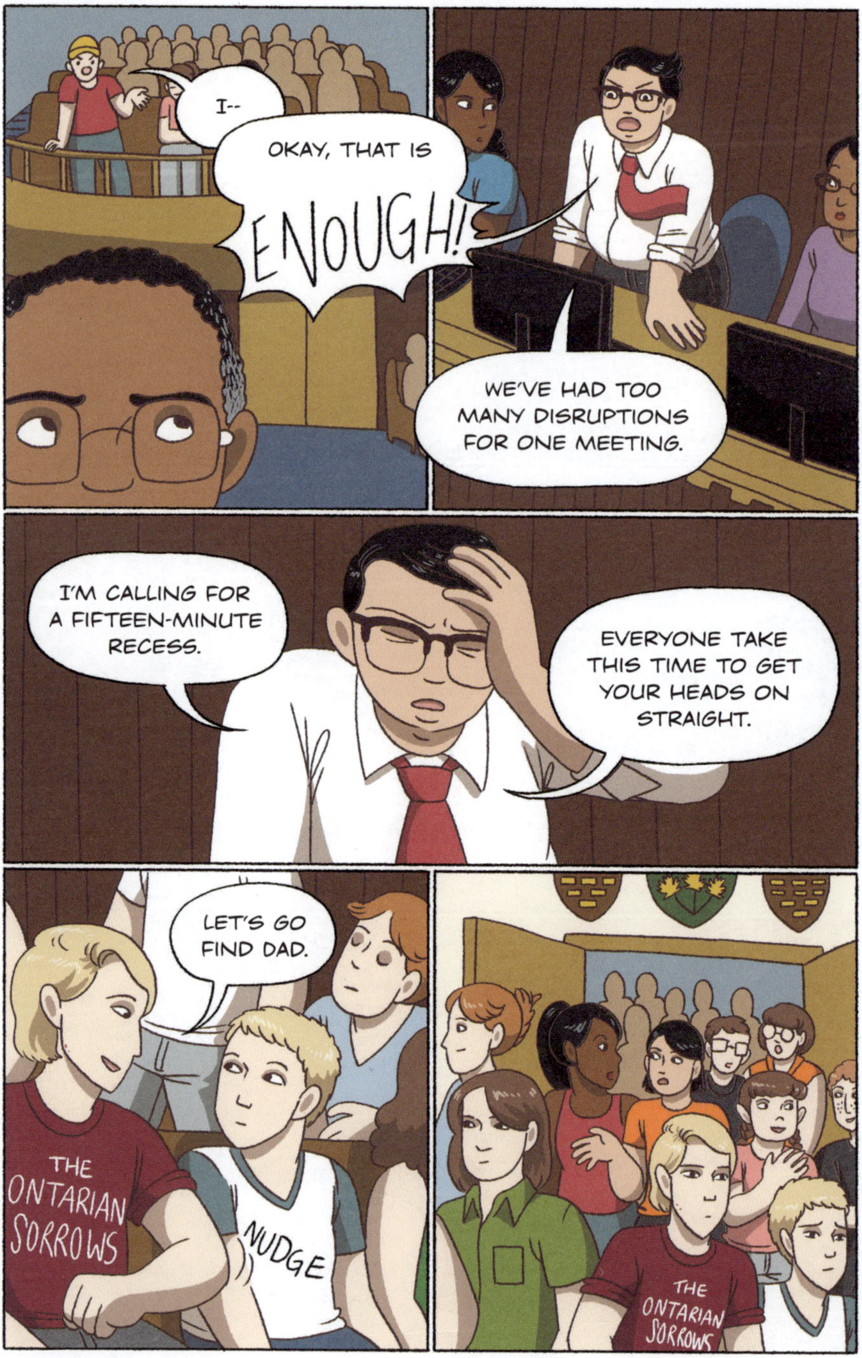
I--
OKAY, THAT IS
ENOUGH!
WE'VE HAD TOO MANY DISRUPTIONS FOR ONE MEETING.
I'M CALLING FOR A FIFTEEN-MINUTE RECESS.
EVERYONE TAKE THIS TIME TO GET YOUR HEADS ON STRAIGHT.
LET'S GO FIND DAD.
THE ONTARIAN SORROWS
NUDGE
THE ONTARIAN SORROWS

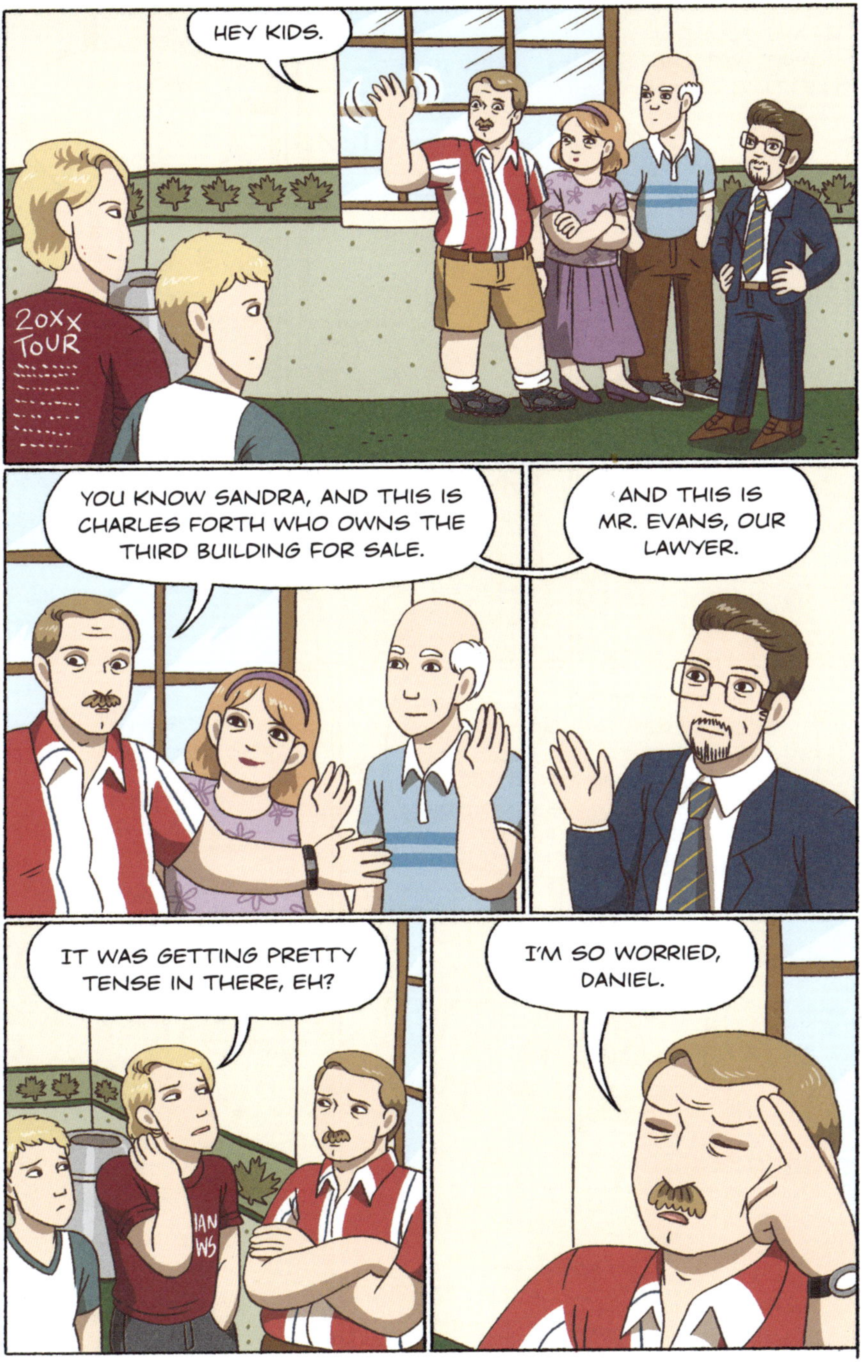

HEY KIDS.
2OXX TOUR
YOU KNOW SANDRA, AND THIS IS CHARLES FORTH WHO OWNS THE THIRD BUILDING FOR SALE.
AND THIS IS MR. EVANS, OUR LAWYER.
IT WAS GETTING PRETTY TENSE IN THERE, EH?
I'M SO WORRIED, DANIEL.

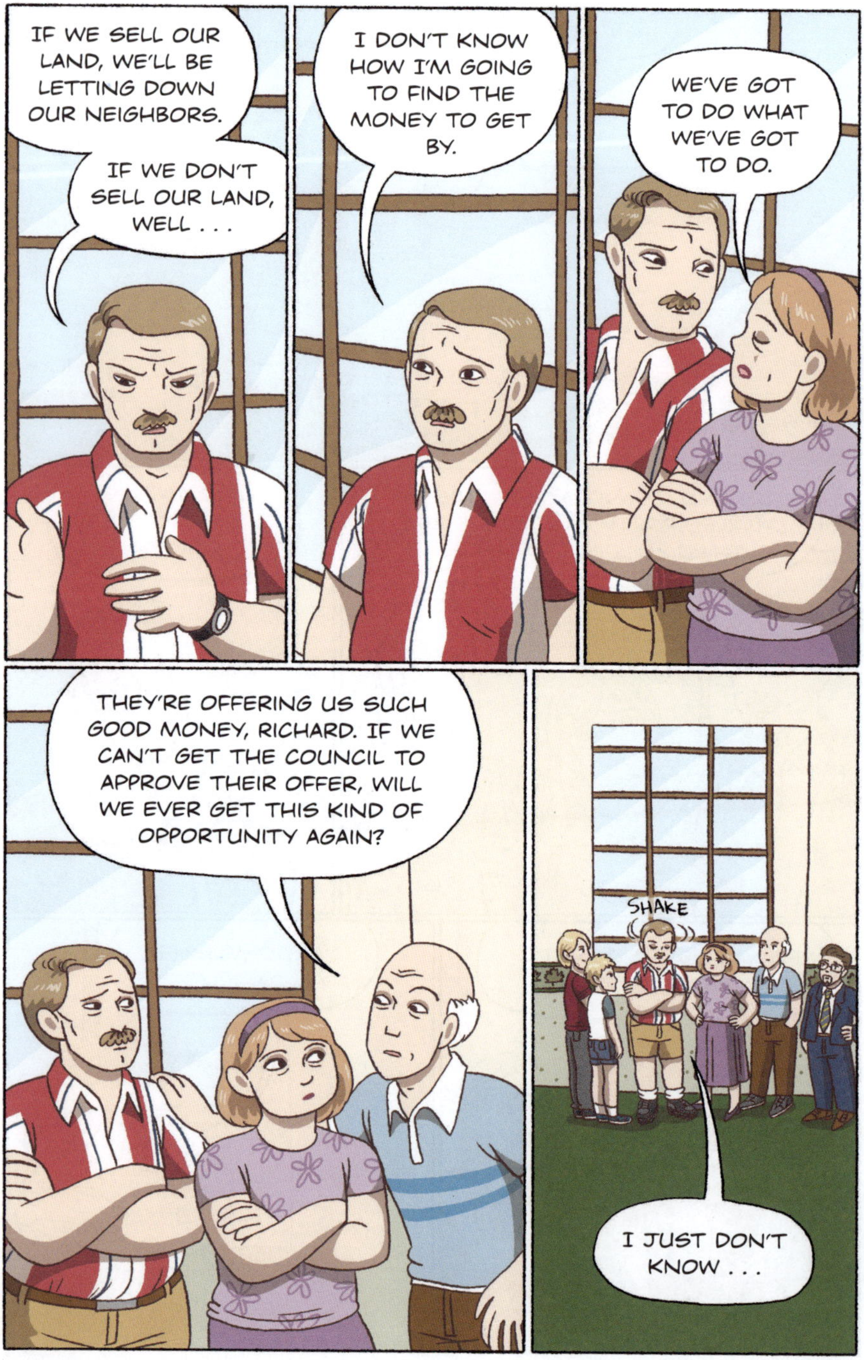
IF WE SELL OUR LAND, WE'LL BE LETTING DOWN OUR NEIGHBORS.
IF WE DON'T SELL OUR LAND, WELL . . .
I DON'T KNOW HOW I'M GOING TO FIND THE MONEY TO GET BY.
WE'VE GOT TO DO WHAT WE'VE GOT TO DO.
THEY'RE OFFERING US SUCH GOOD MONEY, RICHARD. IF WE CAN'T GET THE COUNCIL TO APPROVE THEIR OFFER, WILL WE EVER GET THIS KIND OF OPPORTUNITY AGAIN?
SHAKE
I JUST DON'T KNOW . . .

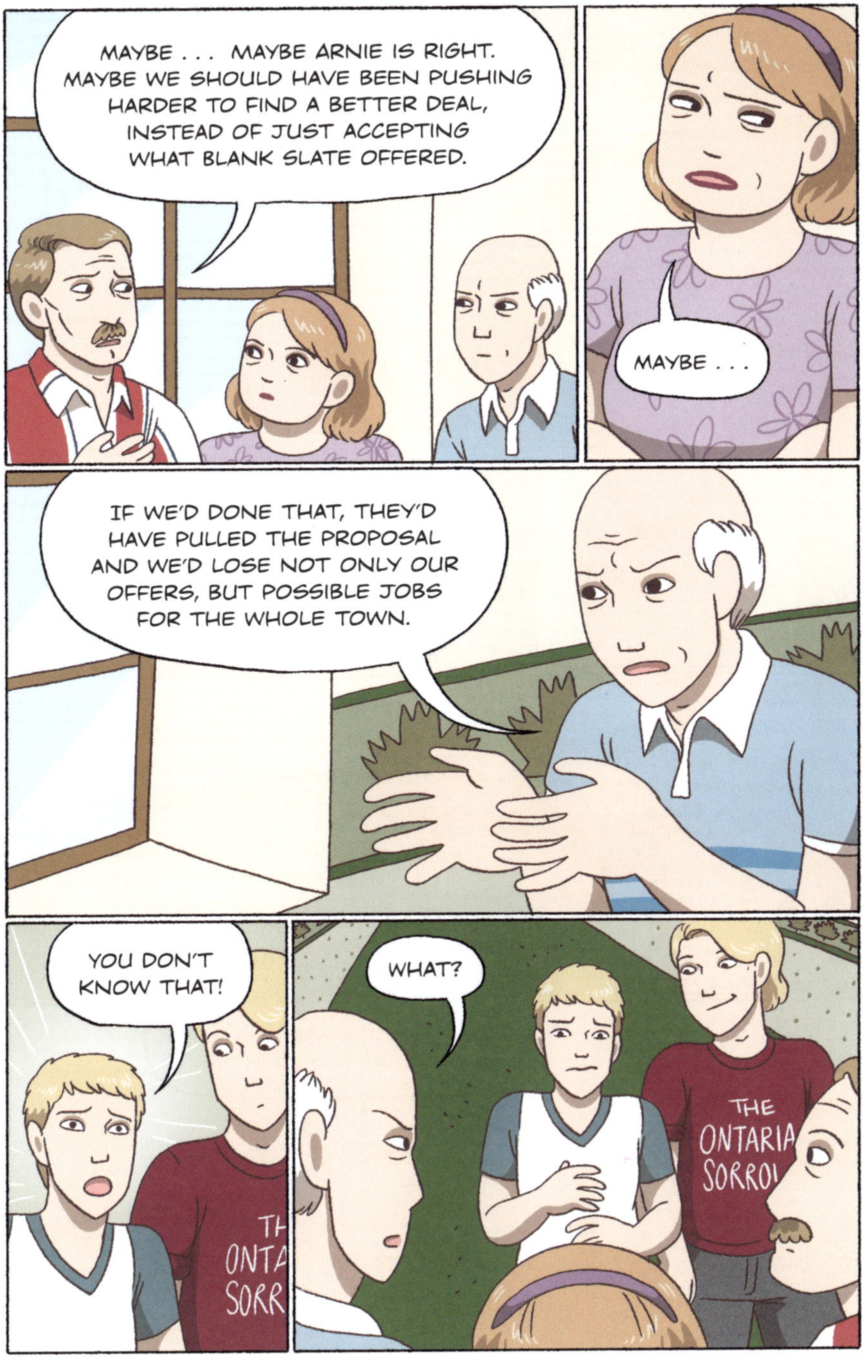
MAYBE . . . MAYBE ARNIE IS RIGHT. MAYBE WE SHOULD HAVE BEEN PUSHING HARDER TO FIND A BETTER DEAL, INSTEAD OF JUST ACCEPTING WHAT BLANK SLATE OFFERED.
MAYBE . . .
IF WE'D DONE THAT, THEY'D HAVE PULLED THE PROPOSAL AND WE'D LOSE NOT ONLY OUR OFFERS, BUT POSSIBLE JOBS FOR THE WHOLE TOWN.
YOU DON'T KNOW THAT!
THE ONTA SORR
WHAT?
THE ONTARIA SORRO

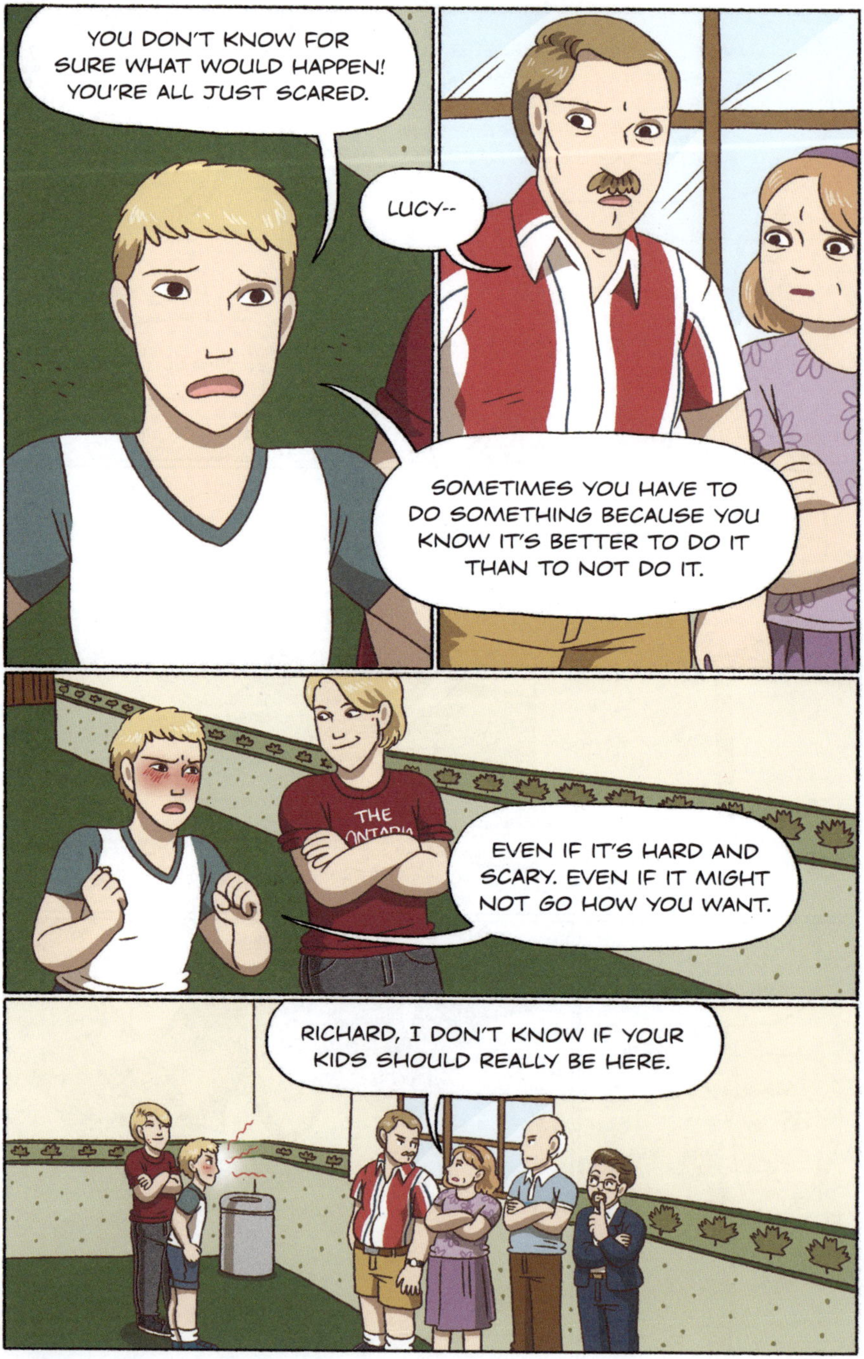
YOU DON'T KNOW FOR SURE WHAT WOULD HAPPEN! YOU'RE ALL JUST SCARED.
LUCY--
SOMETIMES YOU HAVE TO DO SOMETHING BECAUSE YOU KNOW IT'S BETTER TO DO IT THAN TO NOT DO IT.
THE
EVEN IF IT'S HARD AND SCARY. EVEN IF IT MIGHT NOT GO HOW YOU WANT.
RICHARD, I DON'T KNOW IF YOUR KIDS SHOULD REALLY BE HERE.

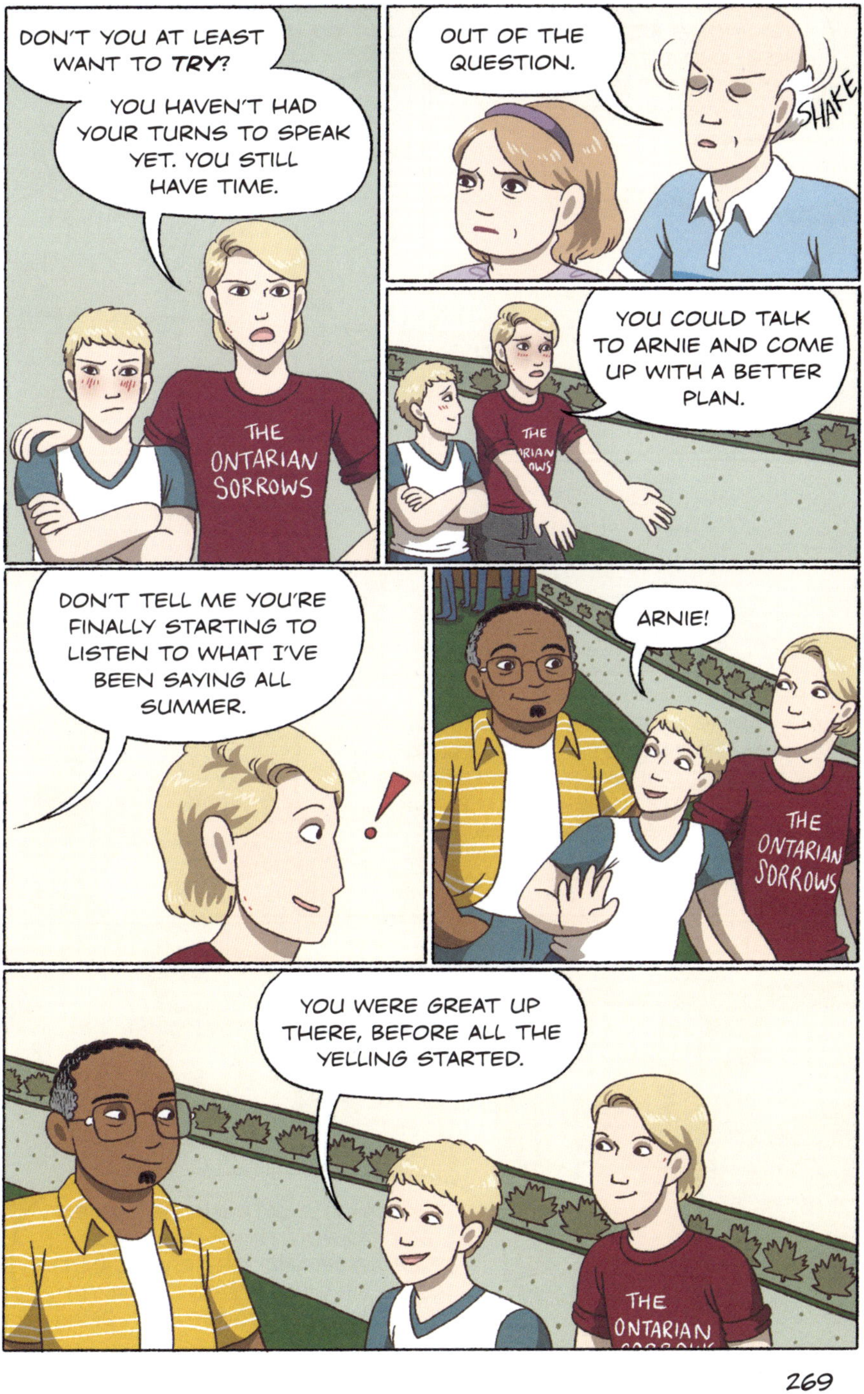
DON'T YOU AT LEAST WANT TO TRY?
YOU HAVEN'T HAD YOUR TURNS TO SPEAK YET. YOU STILL HAVE TIME.
THE ONTARIAN SORROWS
OUT OF THE QUESTION.
SHAKE
YOU COULD TALK TO ARNIE AND COME UP WITH A BETTER PLAN.
DON'T TELL ME YOU'RE FINALLY STARTING TO LISTEN TO WHAT I'VE BEEN SAYING ALL SUMMER.
!
ARNIE!
THE ONTARIAN SORROWS
YOU WERE GREAT UP THERE, BEFORE ALL THE YELLING STARTED.

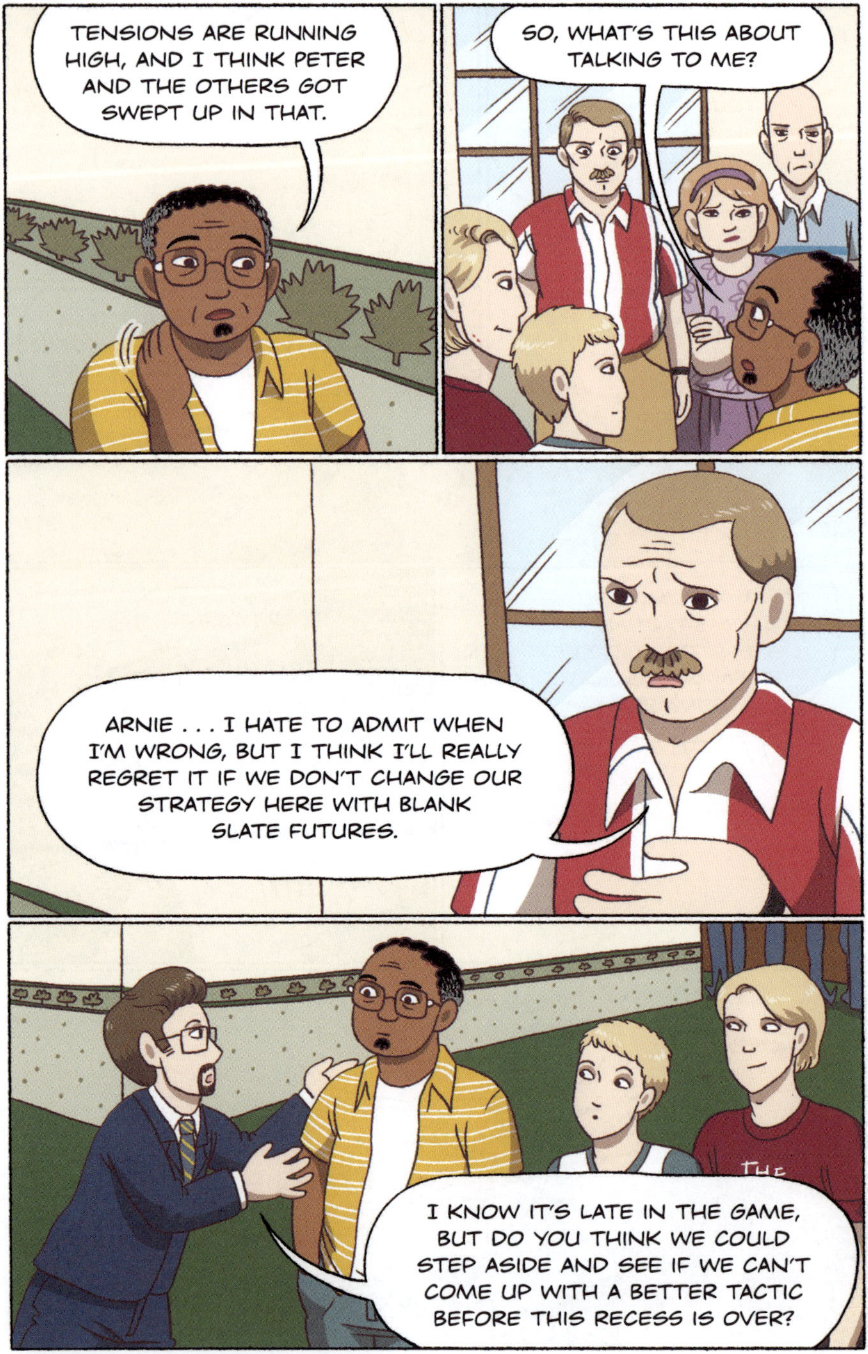
TENSIONS ARE RUNNING HIGH, AND I THINK PETER AND THE OTHERS GOT SWEPT UP IN THAT.
SO, WHAT'S THIS ABOUT TALKING TO ME?
ARNIE . . . I HATE TO ADMIT WHEN I'M WRONG, BUT I THINK I'LL REALLY REGRET IT IF WE DON'T CHANGE OUR STRATEGY HERE WITH BLANK SLATE FUTURES.
I KNOW IT'S LATE IN THE GAME, BUT DO YOU THINK WE COULD STEP ASIDE AND SEE IF WE CAN'T COME UP WITH A BETTER TACTIC BEFORE THIS RECESS IS OVER?

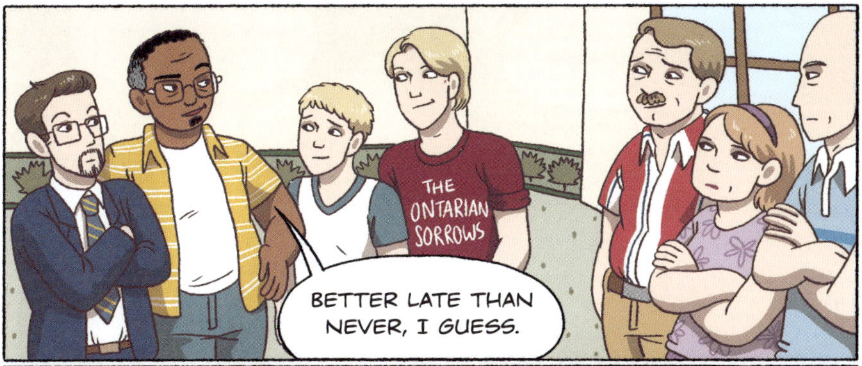
THE ONTARIAN SORROWS
BETTER LATE THAN NEVER, I GUESS.

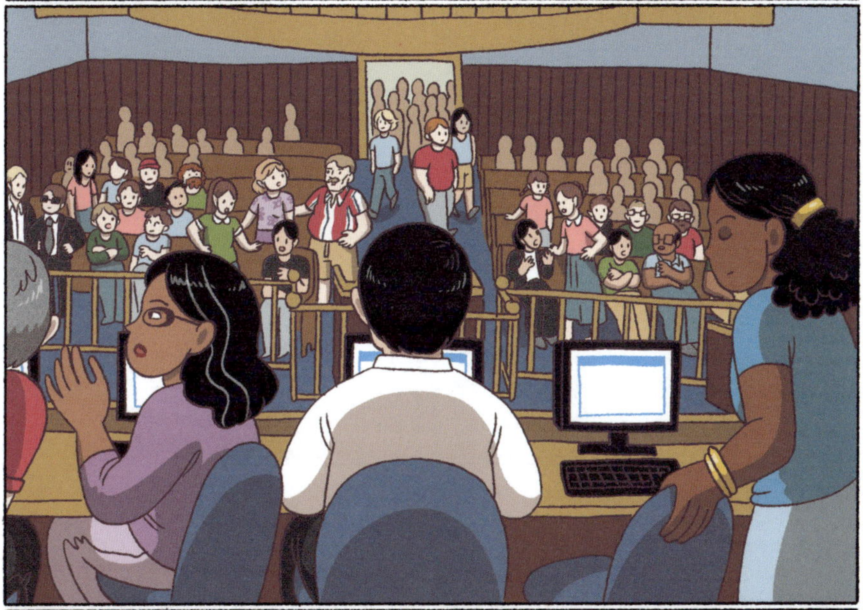

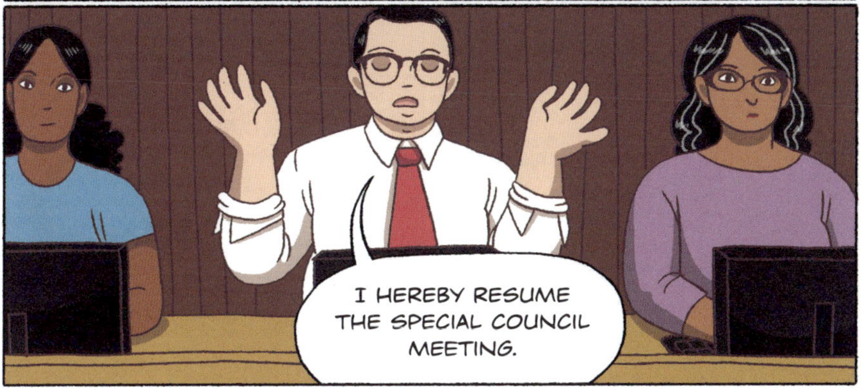
I HEREBY RESUME THE SPECIAL COUNCIL MEETING.

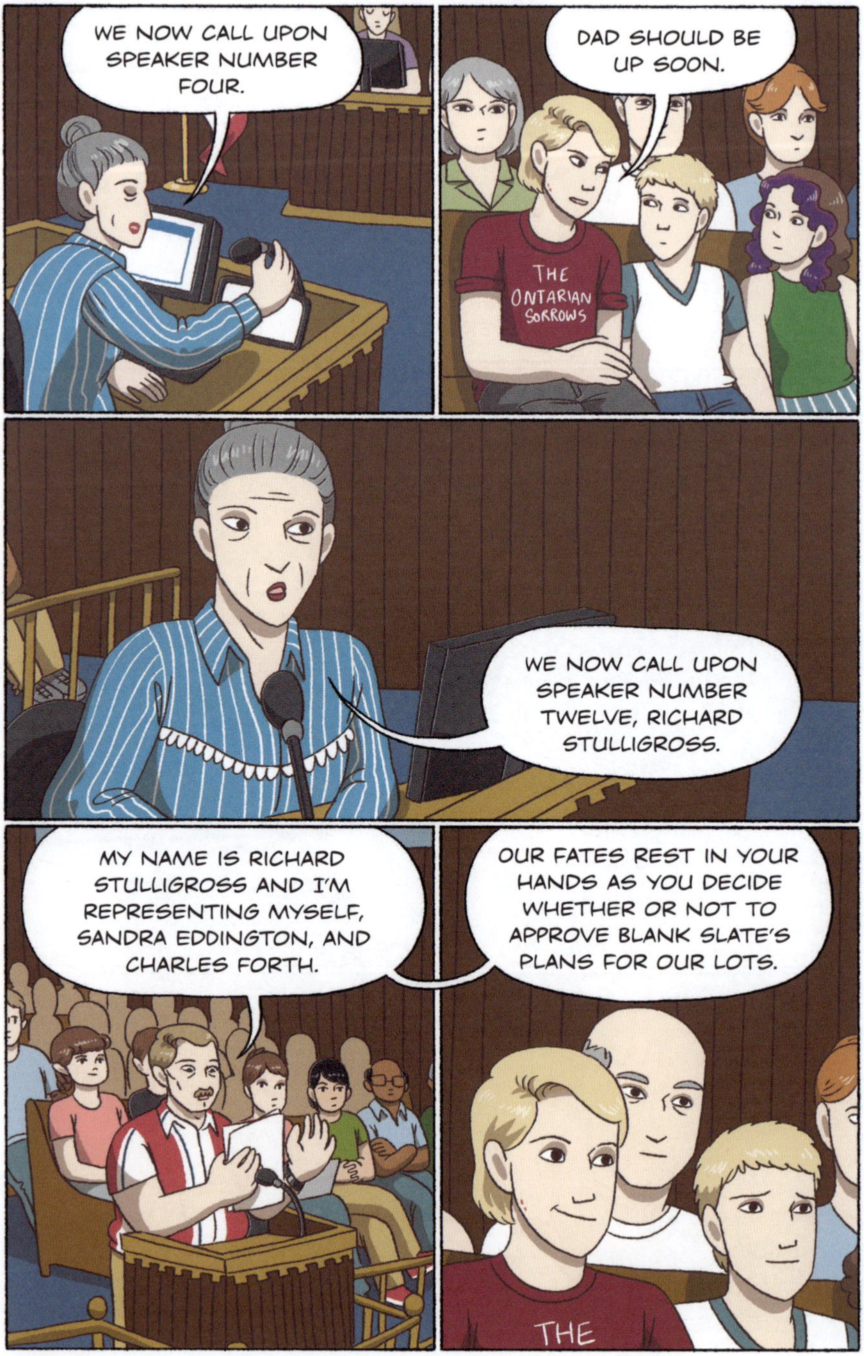
WE NOW CALL UPON SPEAKER NUMBER FOUR.
DAD SHOULD BE UP SOON.
THE ONTARIAN SORROWS
WE NOW CALL UPON SPEAKER NUMBER TWELVE, RICHARD STULLIGROSS.
MY NAME IS RICHARD STULLIGROSS AND I'M REPRESENTING MYSELF, SANDRA EDDINGTON, AND CHARLES FORTH.
OUR FATES REST IN YOUR HANDS AS YOU DECIDE WHETHER OR NOT TO APPROVE BLANK SLATE'S PLANS FOR OUR LOTS.
THE

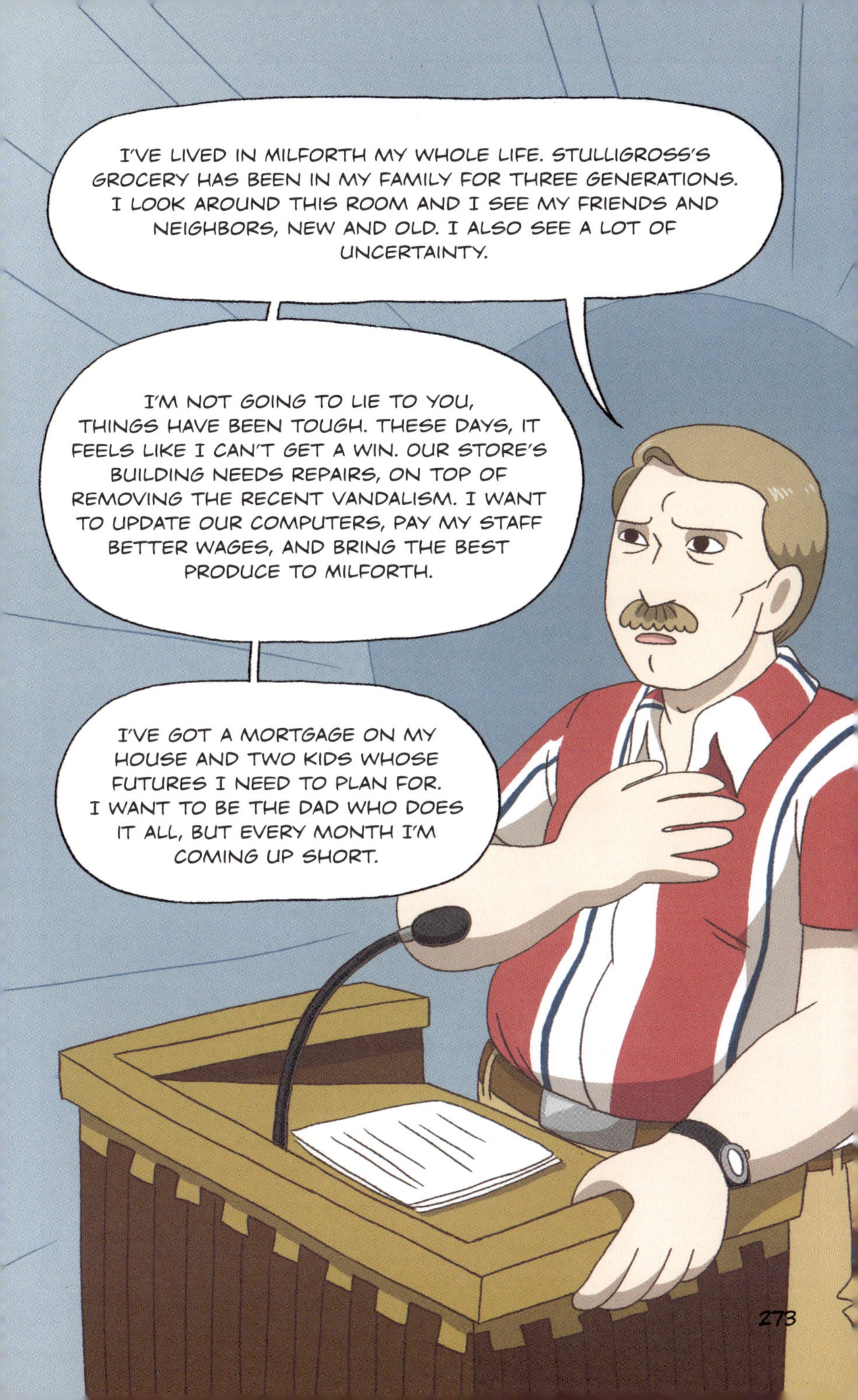
I'VE LIVED IN MILFORTH MY WHOLE LIFE. STULLIGROSS'S GROCERY HAS BEEN IN MY FAMILY FOR THREE GENERATIONS. I LOOK AROUND THIS ROOM AND I SEE MY FRIENDS AND NEIGHBORS, NEW AND OLD. I ALSO SEE A LOT OF UNCERTAINTY.
I'M NOT GOING TO LIE TO YOU, THINGS HAVE BEEN TOUGH. THESE DAYS, IT FEELS LIKE I CAN'T GET A WIN. OUR STORE'S BUILDING NEEDS REPAIRS, ON TOP OF REMOVING THE RECENT VANDALISM. I WANT TO UPDATE OUR COMPUTERS, PAY MY STAFF BETTER WAGES, AND BRING THE BEST PRODUCE TO MILFORTH.
I'VE GOT A MORTGAGE ON MY HOUSE AND TWO KIDS WHOSE FUTURES I NEED TO PLAN FOR. I WANT TO BE THE DAD WHO DOES IT ALL, BUT EVERY MONTH I'M COMING UP SHORT.

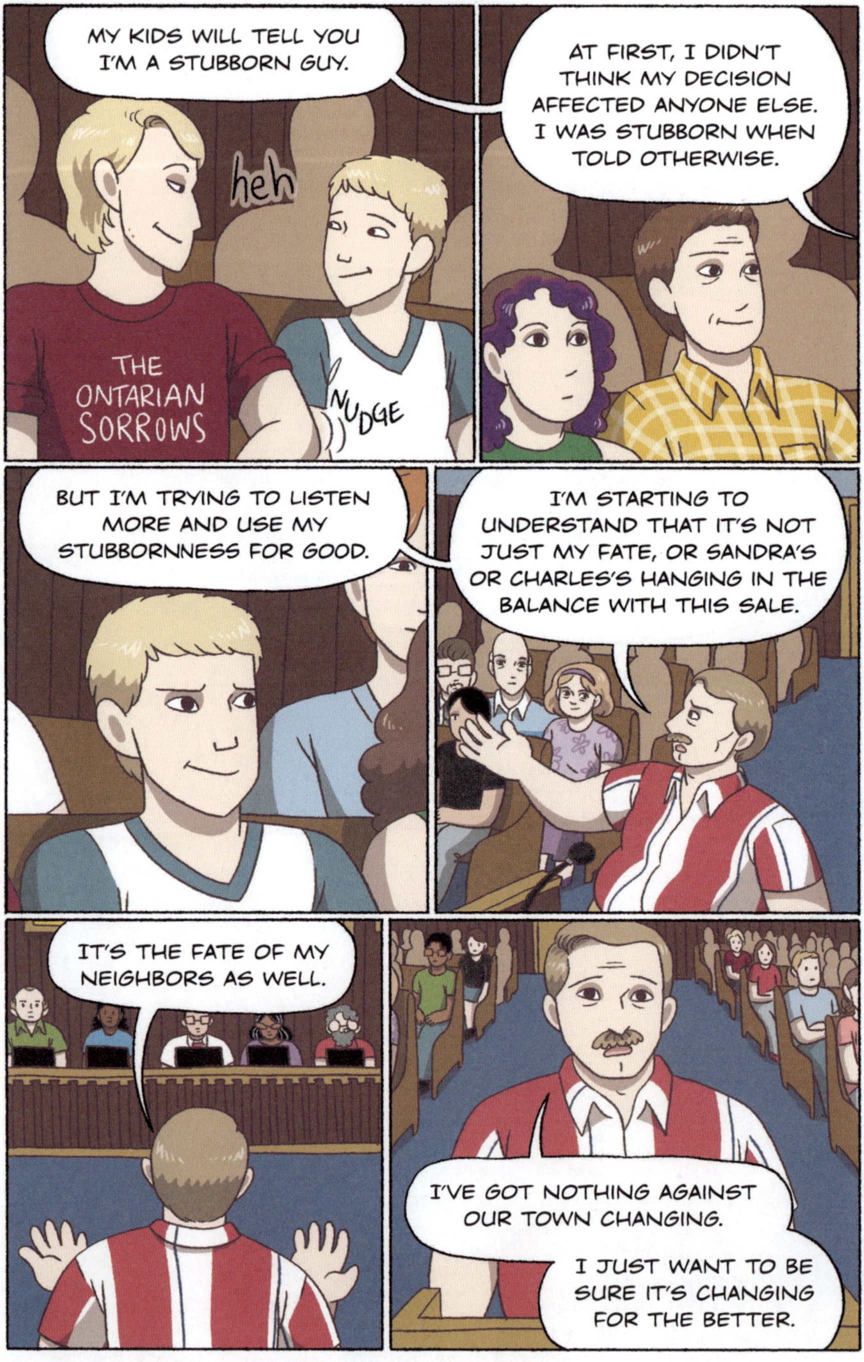
MY KIDS WILL TELL YOU I'M A STUBBORN GUY.
heh
THE ONTARIAN SORROWS
NUDGE
AT FIRST, I DIDN'T THINK MY DECISION AFFECTED ANYONE ELSE. I WAS STUBBORN WHEN TOLD OTHERWISE.
BUT I'M TRYING TO LISTEN MORE AND USE MY STUBBORNNESS FOR GOOD.
I'M STARTING TO UNDERSTAND THAT IT'S NOT JUST MY FATE, OR SANDRA'S OR CHARLES'S HANGING IN THE BALANCE WITH THIS SALE.
IT'S THE FATE OF MY NEIGHBORS AS WELL.
I'VE GOT NOTHING AGAINST OUR TOWN CHANGING.
I JUST WANT TO BE SURE IT'S CHANGING FOR THE BETTER.

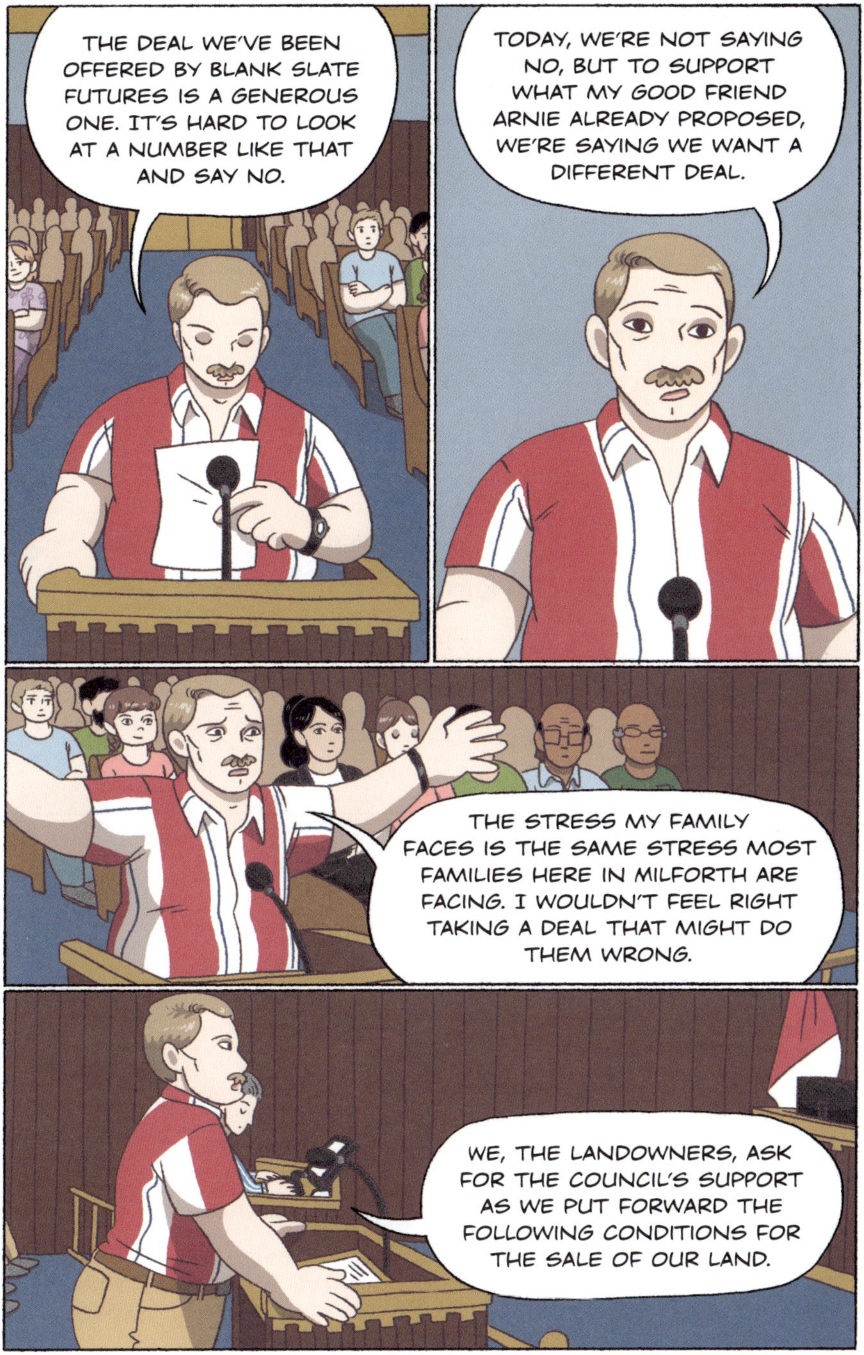
THE DEAL WE'VE BEEN OFFERED BY BLANK SLATE FUTURES IS A GENEROUS ONE. IT'S HARD TO LOOK AT A NUMBER LIKE THAT AND SAY NO.
TODAY, WE'RE NOT SAYING NO, BUT TO SUPPORT WHAT MY GOOD FRIEND ARNIE ALREADY PROPOSED, WE'RE SAYING WE WANT A DIFFERENT DEAL.
THE STRESS MY FAMILY FACES IS THE SAME STRESS MOST FAMILIES HERE IN MILFORTH ARE FACING. I WOULDN'T FEEL RIGHT TAKING A DEAL THAT MIGHT DO THEM WRONG.
WE, THE LANDOWNERS, ASK FOR THE COUNCIL'S SUPPORT AS WE PUT FORWARD THE FOLLOWING CONDITIONS FOR THE SALE OF OUR LAND.

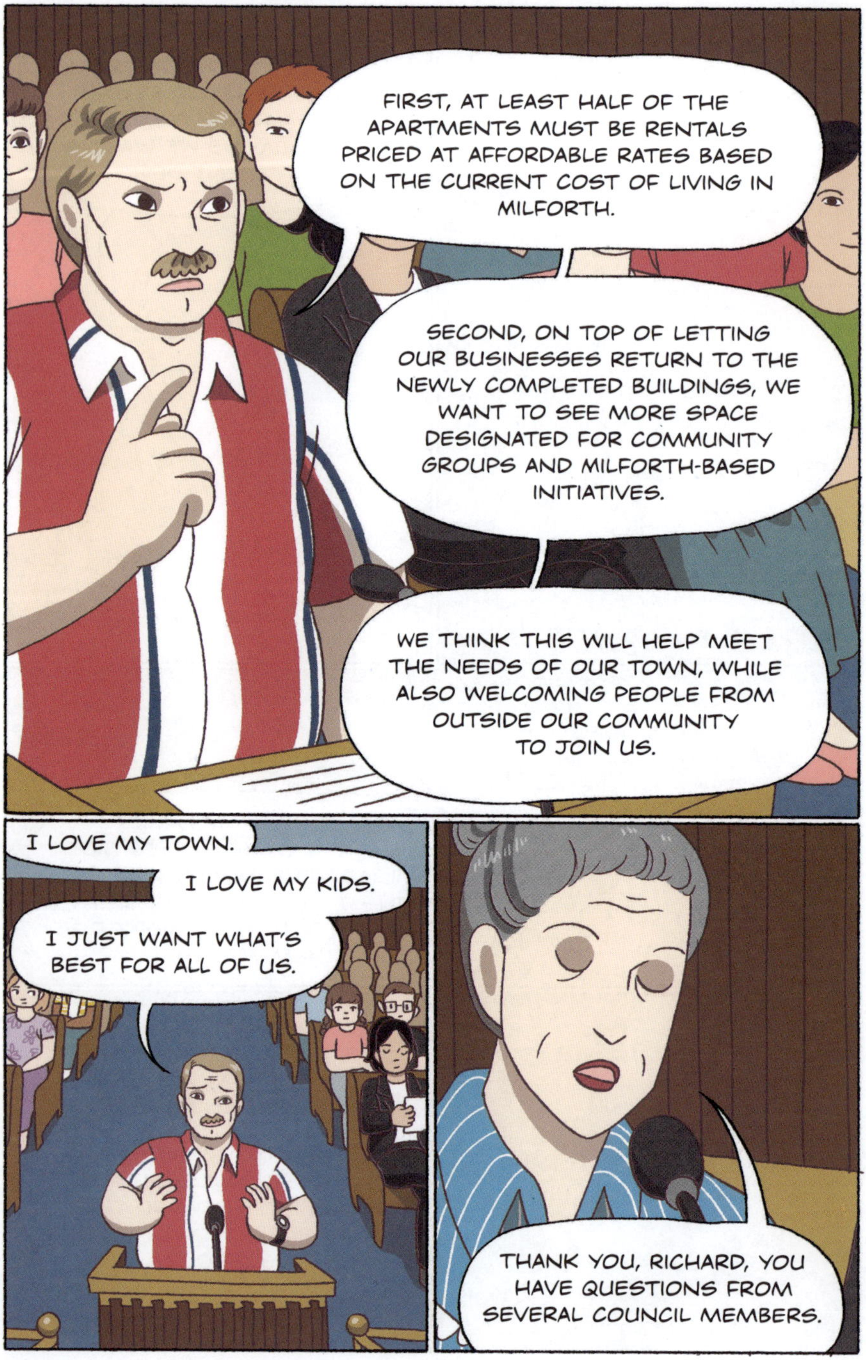
FIRST, AT LEAST HALF OF THE APARTMENTS MUST BE RENTALS PRICED AT AFFORDABLE RATES BASED ON THE CURRENT COST OF LIVING IN MILFORTH.
SECOND, ON TOP OF LETTING OUR BUSINESSES RETURN TO THE NEWLY COMPLETED BUILDINGS, WE WANT TO SEE MORE SPACE DESIGNATED FOR COMMUNITY GROUPS AND MILFORTH-BASED INITIATIVES.
WE THINK THIS WILL HELP MEET THE NEEDS OF OUR TOWN, WHILE ALSO WELCOMING PEOPLE FROM OUTSIDE OUR COMMUNITY TO JOIN US.
I LOVE MY TOWN.
I LOVE MY KIDS.
I JUST WANT WHAT'S BEST FOR ALL OF US.
THANK YOU, RICHARD, YOU HAVE QUESTIONS FROM SEVERAL COUNCIL MEMBERS.

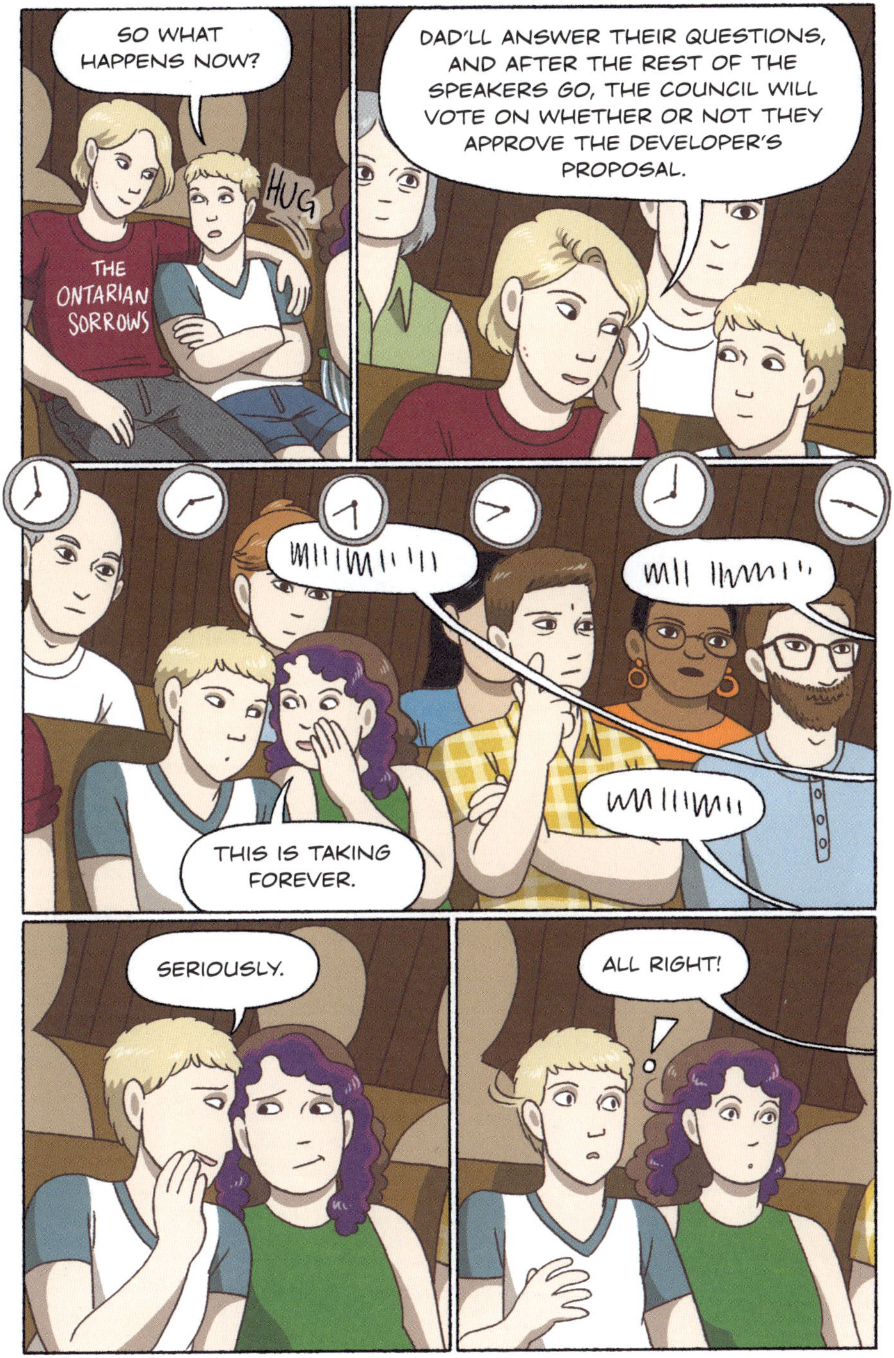
SO WHAT HAPPENS NOW?
HUG
THE ONTARIAN SORROWS
DAD'LL ANSWER THEIR QUESTIONS, AND AFTER THE REST OF THE SPEAKERS GO, THE COUNCIL WILL VOTE ON WHETHER OR NOT THEY APPROVE THE DEVELOPER'S PROPOSAL.
THIS IS TAKING FOREVER.
SERIOUSLY.
ALL RIGHT!
!

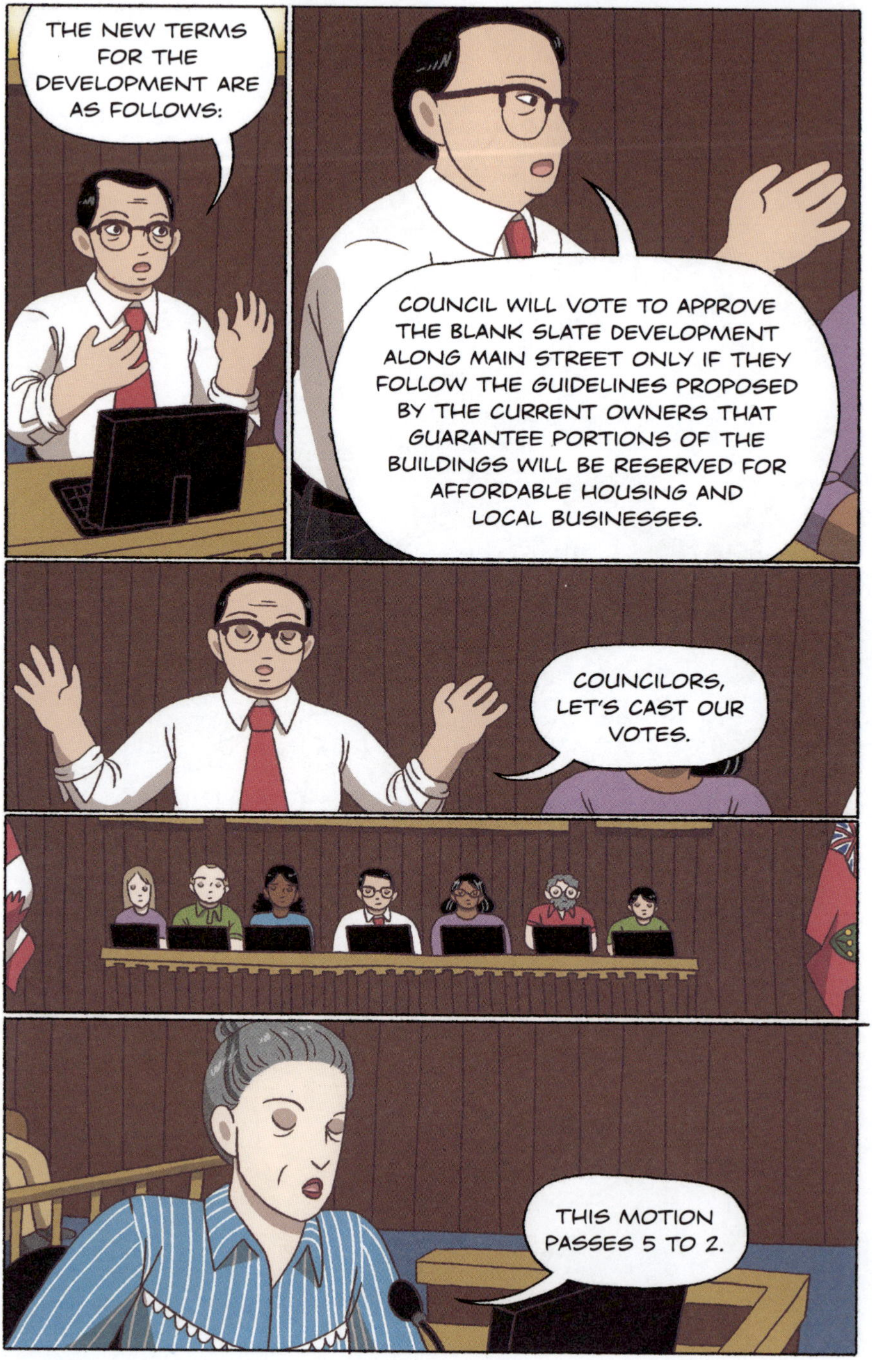
THE NEW TERMS FOR THE DEVELOPMENT ARE AS FOLLOWS:
COUNCIL WILL VOTE TO APPROVE THE BLANK SLATE DEVELOPMENT ALONG MAIN STREET ONLY IF THEY FOLLOW THE GUIDELINES PROPOSED BY THE CURRENT OWNERS THAT GUARANTEE PORTIONS OF THE BUILDINGS WILL BE RESERVED FOR AFFORDABLE HOUSING AND LOCAL BUSINESSES.
COUNCILORS, LET'S CAST OUR VOTES.
THIS MOTION PASSES 5 TO 2.

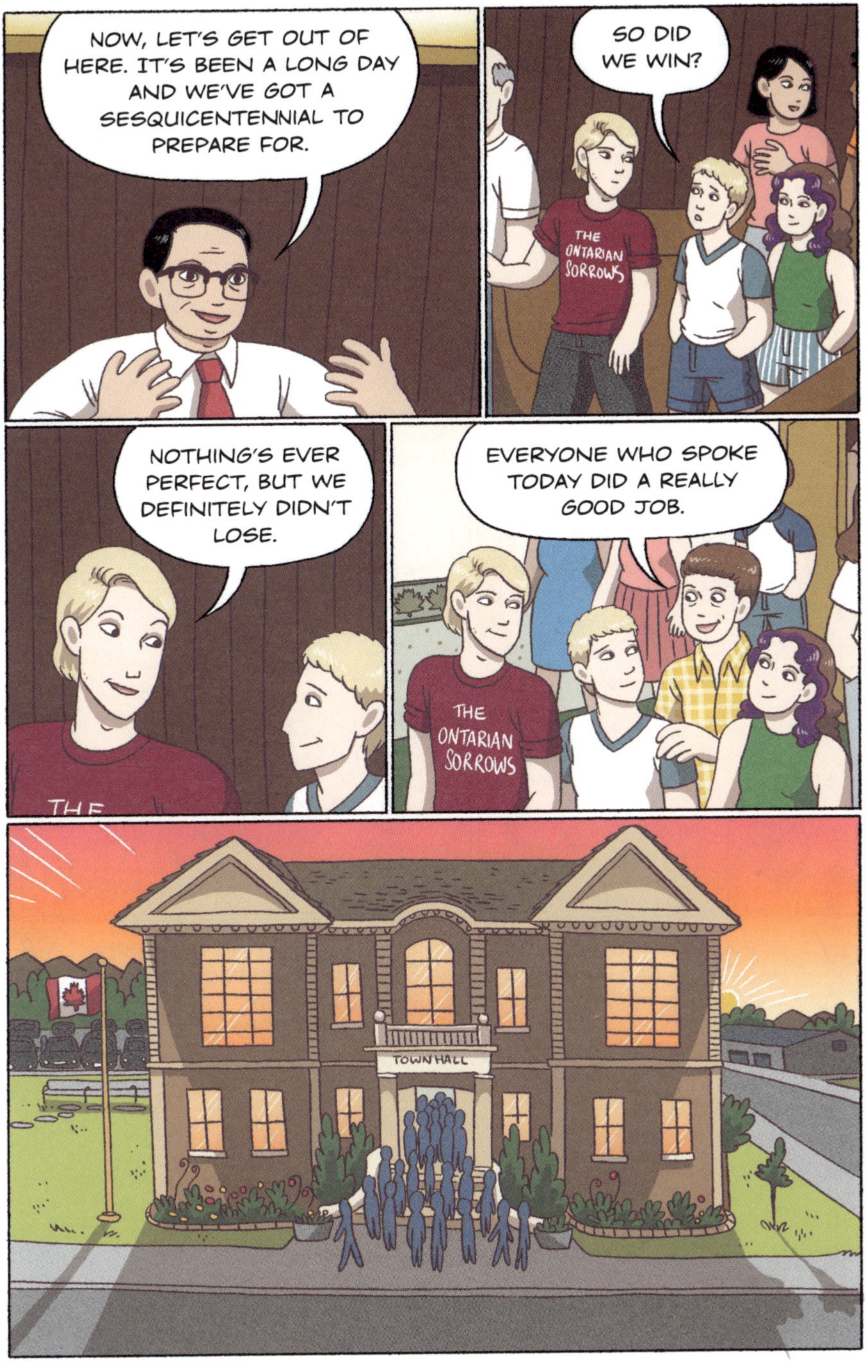
NOW, LET'S GET OUT OF HERE. IT'S BEEN A LONG DAY AND WE'VE GOT A SESQUICENTENNIAL TO PREPARE FOR.
SO DID WE WIN?
THE ONTARIAN SORROWS
NOTHING'S EVER PERFECT, BUT WE DEFINITELY DIDN'T LOSE.
EVERYONE WHO SPOKE TODAY DID A REALLY GOOD JOB.
THE ONTARIAN SORROWS
TOWN HALL

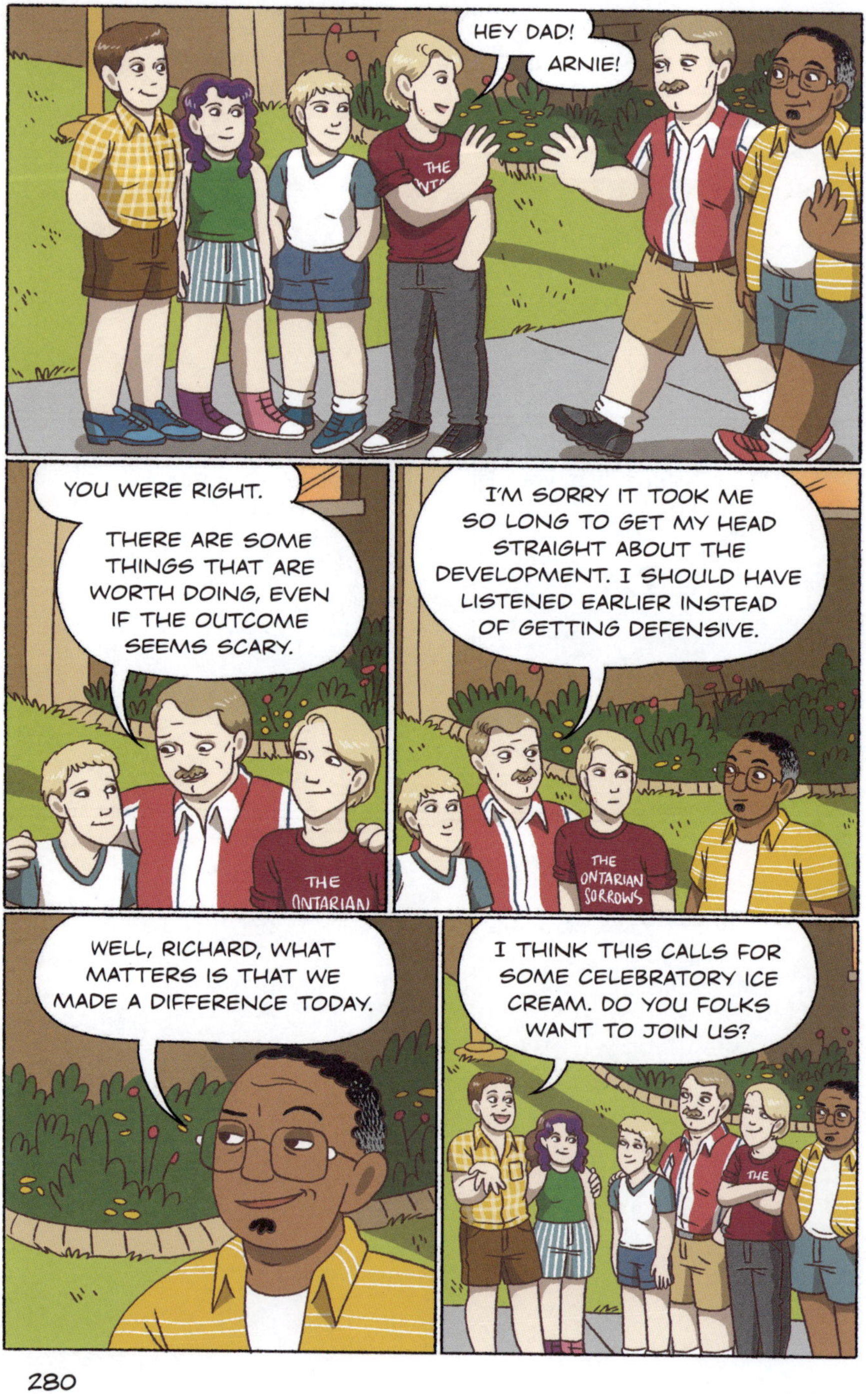
HEY DAD!
ARNIE!
THE ONTA
YOU WERE RIGHT.
THERE ARE SOME THINGS THAT ARE WORTH DOING, EVEN IF THE OUTCOME SEEMS SCARY.
THE ONTARIAN
I'M SORRY IT TOOK ME SO LONG TO GET MY HEAD STRAIGHT ABOUT THE DEVELOPMENT. I SHOULD HAVE LISTENED EARLIER INSTEAD OF GETTING DEFENSIVE.
THE ONTARIAN SORROWS
WELL, RICHARD, WHAT MATTERS IS THAT WE MADE A DIFFERENCE TODAY.
I THINK THIS CALLS FOR SOME CELEBRATORY ICE CREAM. DO YOU FOLKS WANT TO JOIN US?
THE

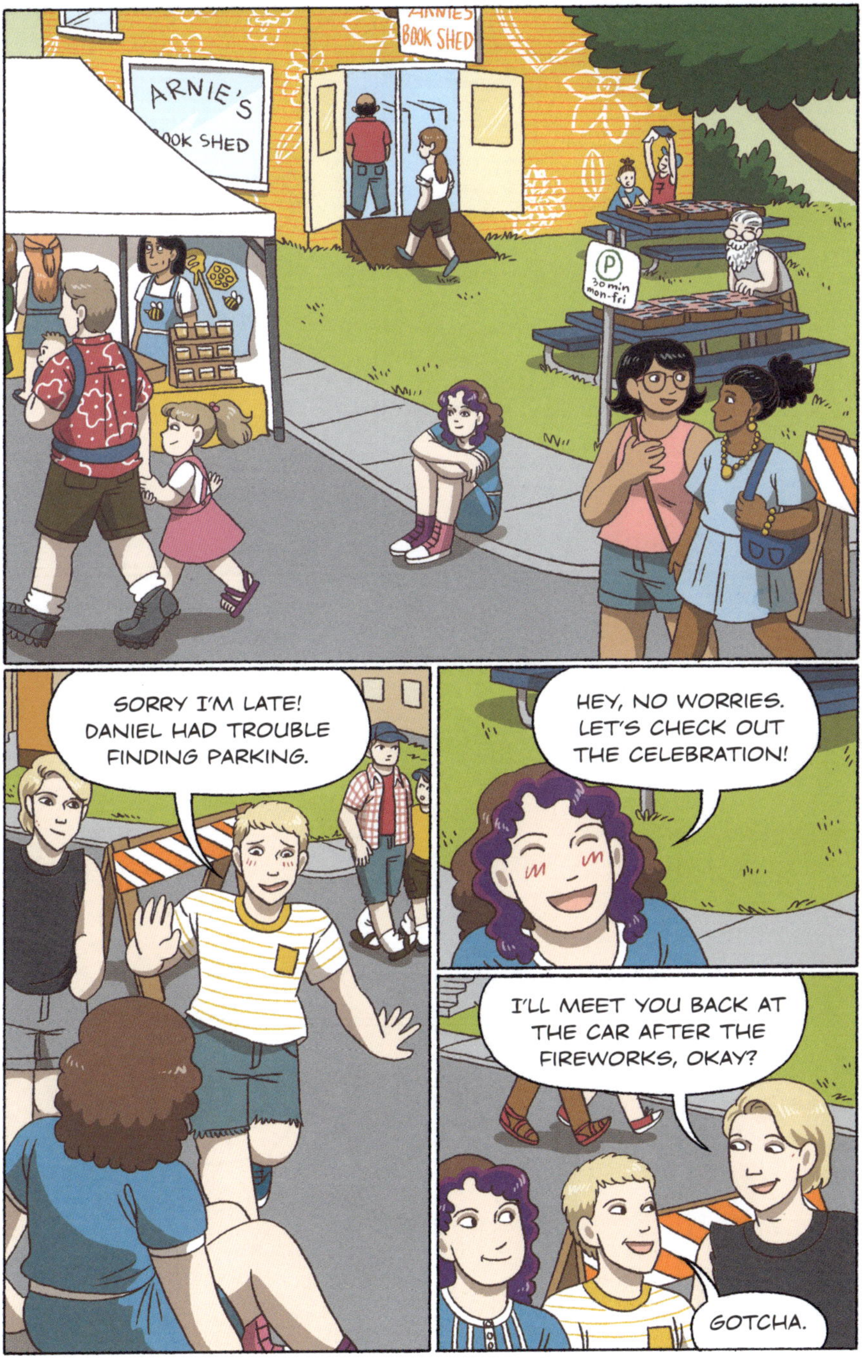
ARNIE'S BOOK SHED
ARNIE'S
BOOK SHED
30 min
mon-fri
SORRY I'M LATE! DANIEL HAD TROUBLE FINDING PARKING.
HEY, NO WORRIES. LET'S CHECK OUT THE CELEBRATION!
I'LL MEET YOU BACK AT THE CAR AFTER THE FIREWORKS, OKAY?
GOTCHA.

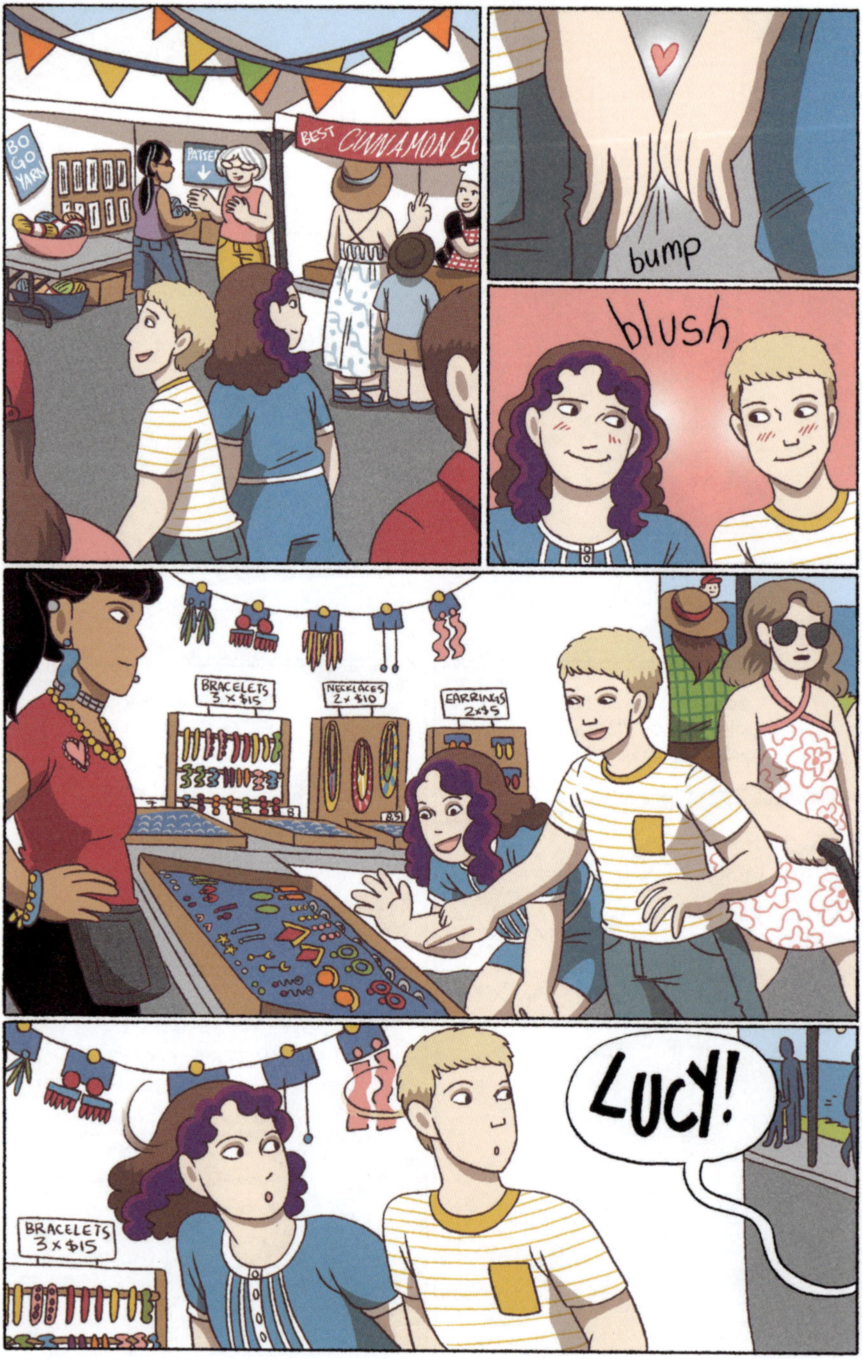
BO GO YARN
PATSEL
BEST CINNAMON BU
bump
blush
BRACELETS 3 x $15
NECKLACES 2 x $10
EARRINGS 2x$5
BRACELETS 3 x $15
LUCY!

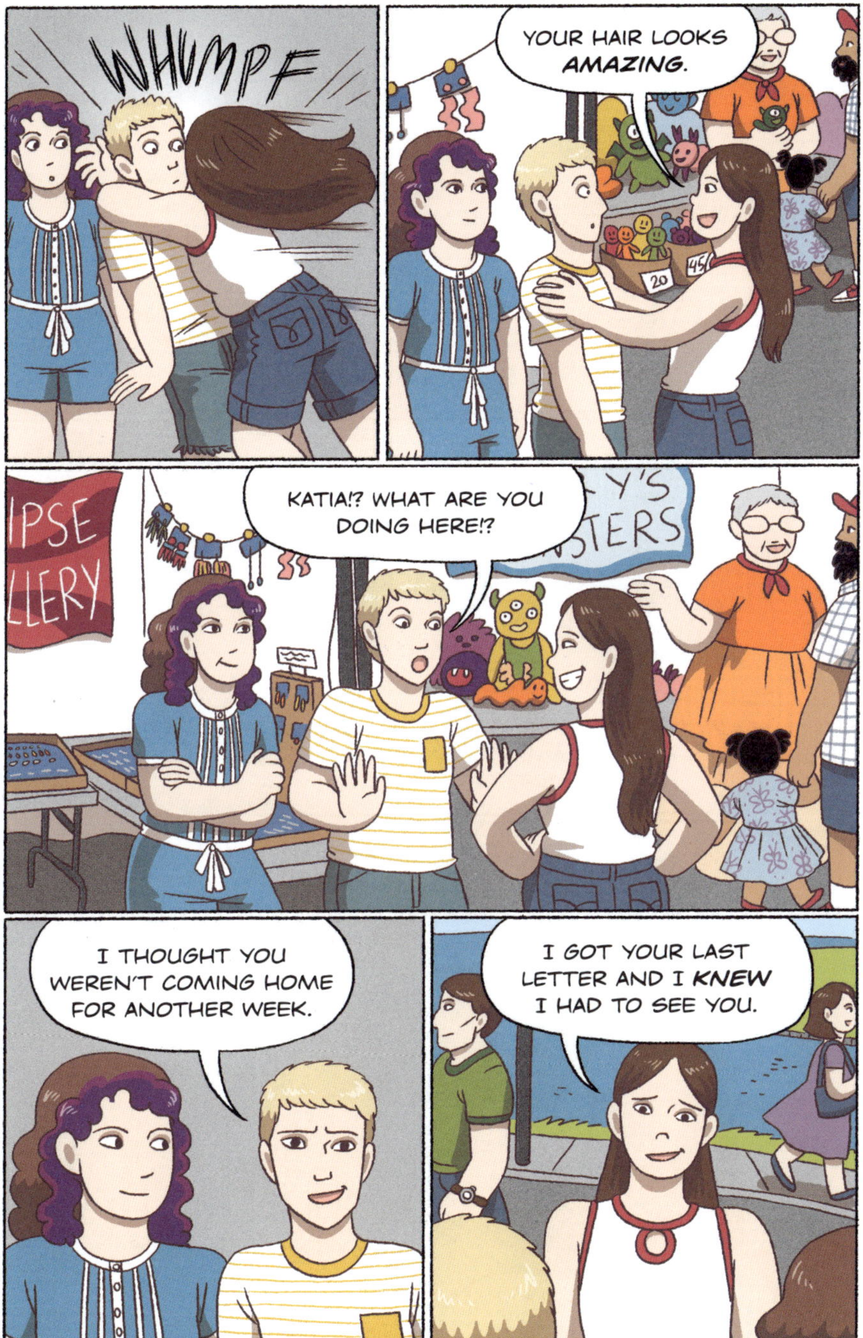
WHUMPF
YOUR HAIR LOOKS AMAZING.
20
45
KATIA!? WHAT ARE YOU DOING HERE!?
I THOUGHT YOU WEREN'T COMING HOME FOR ANOTHER WEEK.
I GOT YOUR LAST LETTER AND I KNEW I HAD TO SEE YOU.

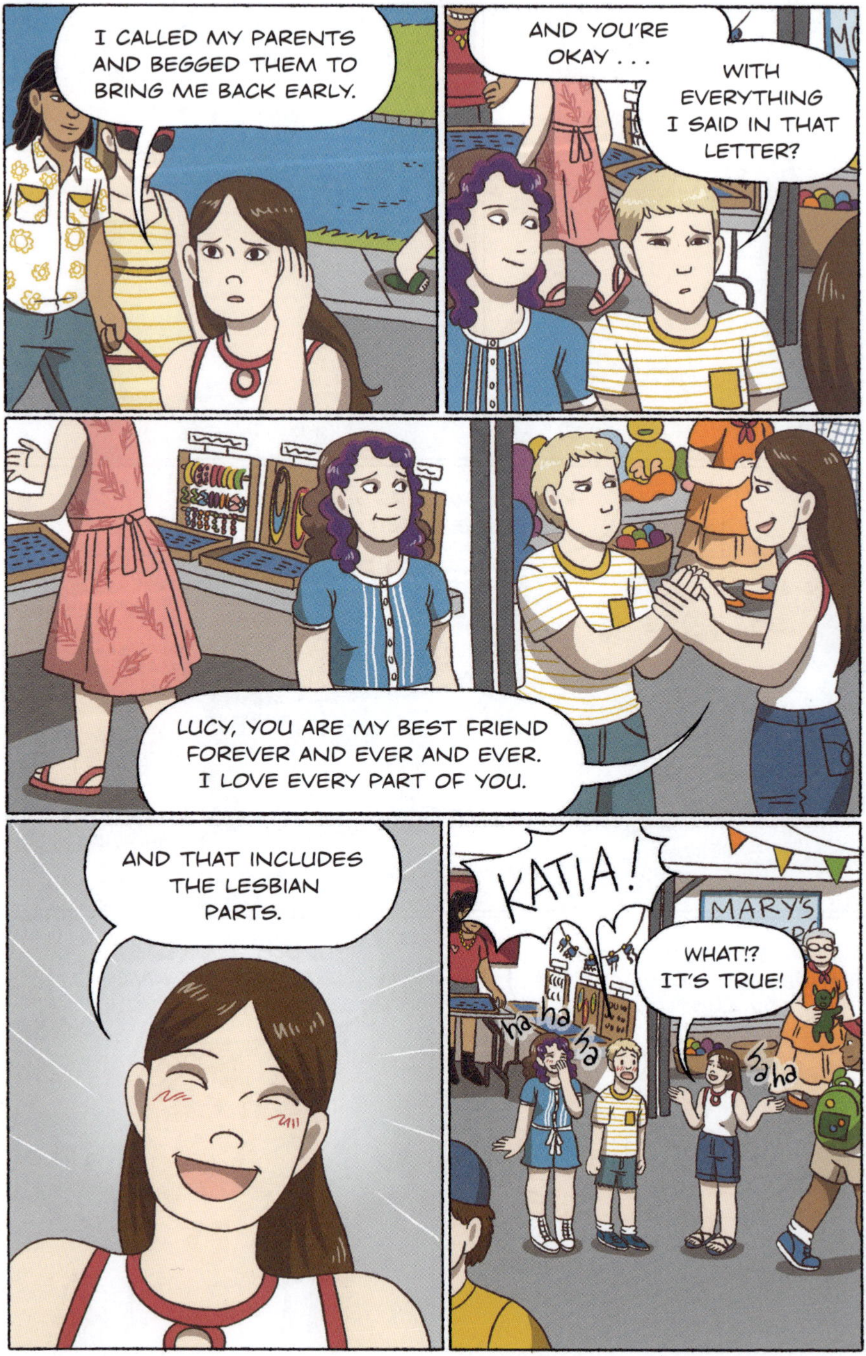
I CALLED MY PARENTS AND BEGGED THEM TO BRING ME BACK EARLY.
AND YOU'RE OKAY . . .
WITH EVERYTHING I SAID IN THAT LETTER?
LUCY, YOU ARE MY BEST FRIEND FOREVER AND EVER AND EVER. I LOVE EVERY PART OF YOU.
AND THAT INCLUDES THE LESBIAN PARTS.
KATIA!
MARY'S
WHAT!? IT'S TRUE!
ha ha ha
haha

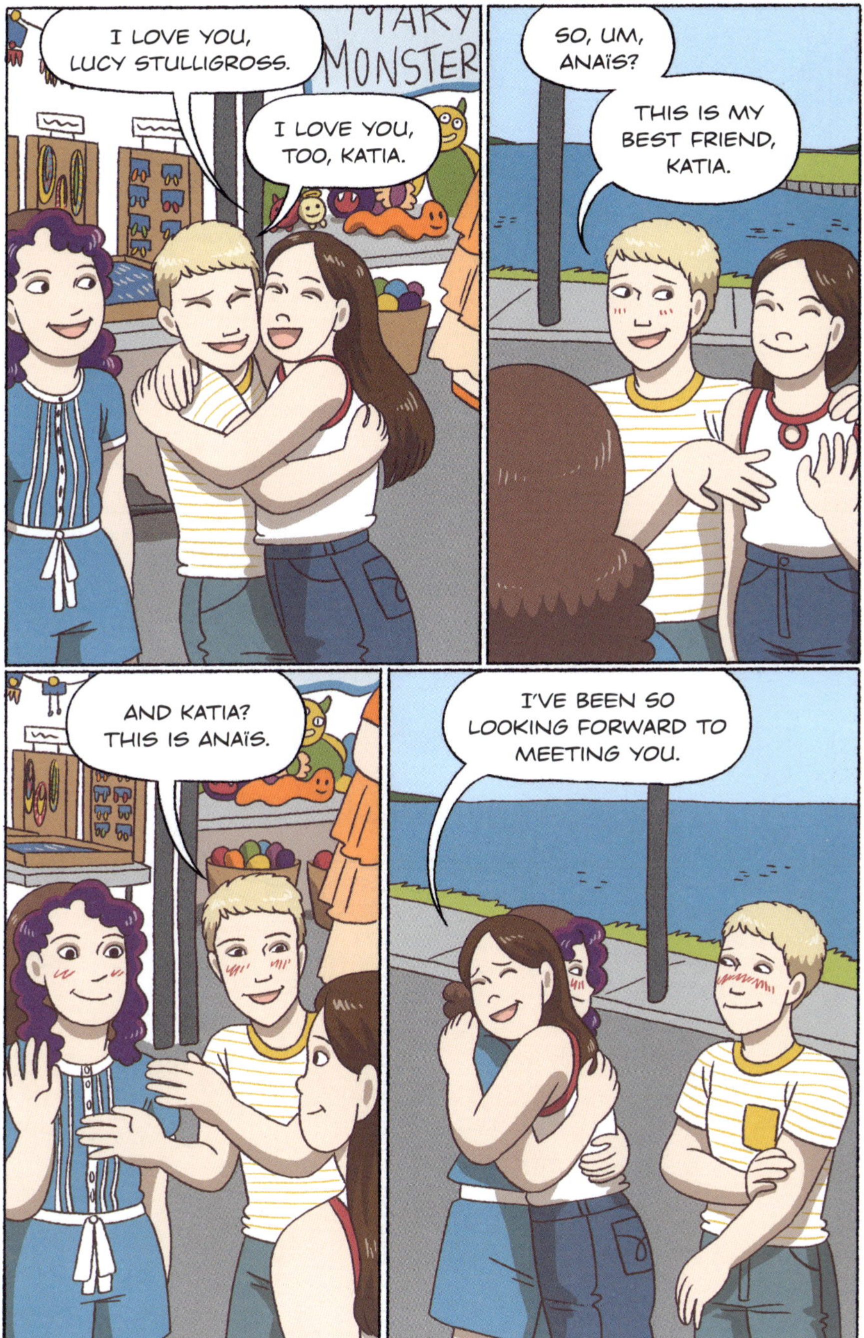
MARY MONSTER
I LOVE YOU, LUCY STULLIGROSS.
I LOVE YOU, TOO, KATIA.
SO, UM, ANAÏS?
THIS IS MY BEST FRIEND, KATIA.
AND KATIA? THIS IS ANAÏS.
I'VE BEEN SO LOOKING FORWARD TO MEETING YOU.

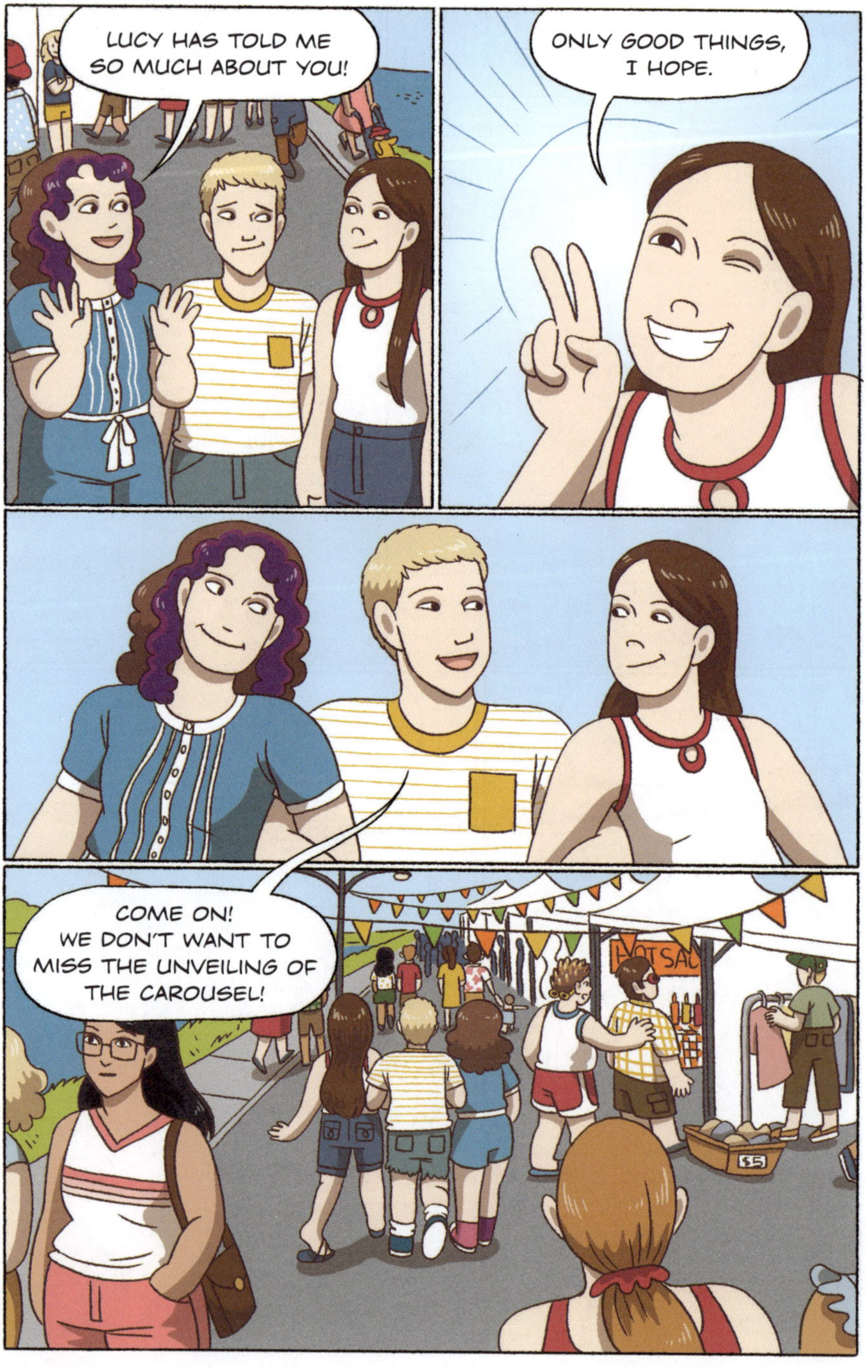
LUCY HAS TOLD ME SO MUCH ABOUT YOU!
ONLY GOOD THINGS, I HOPE.
COME ON! WE DON'T WANT TO MISS THE UNVEILING OF THE CAROUSEL!
$5

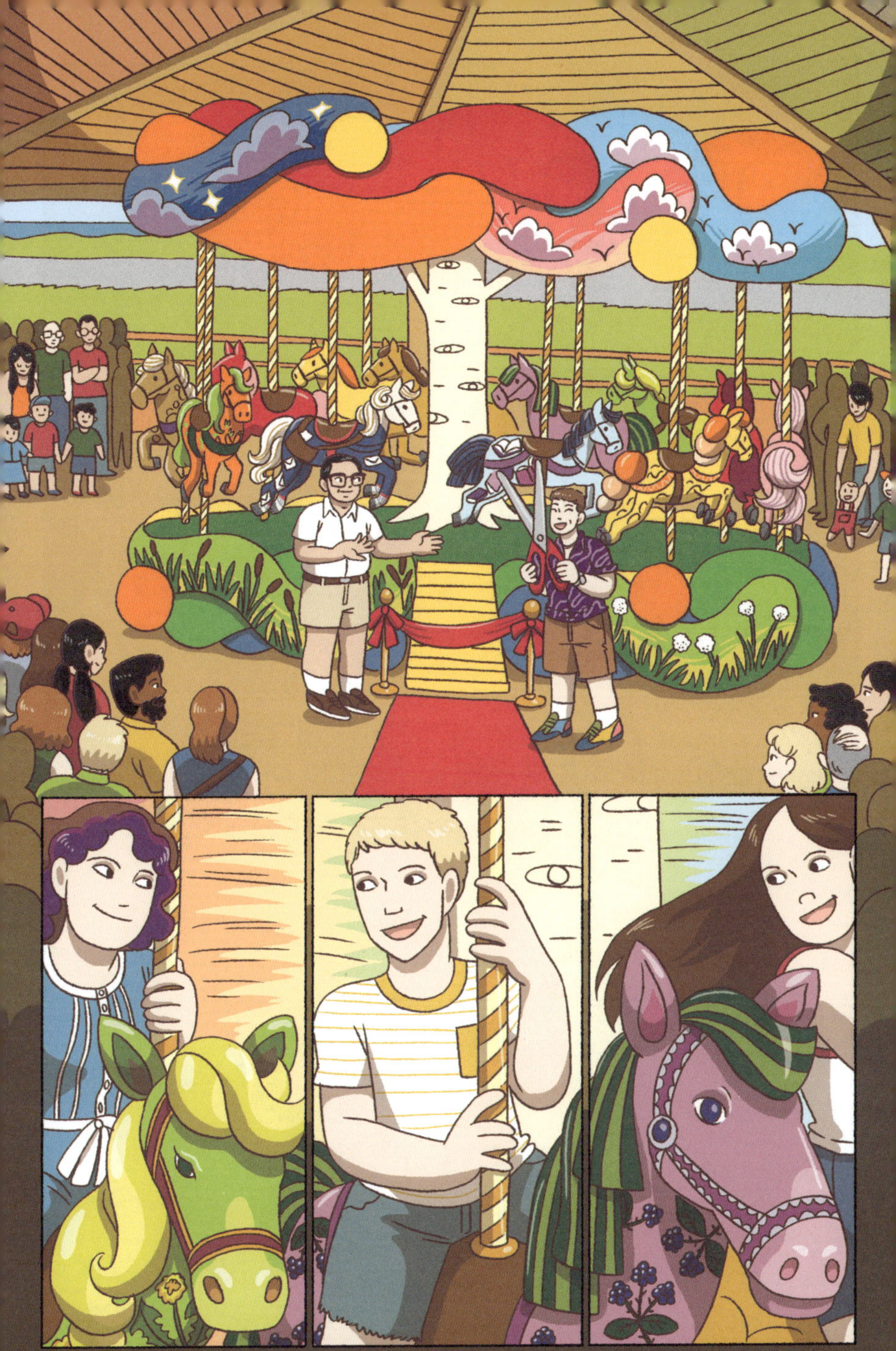

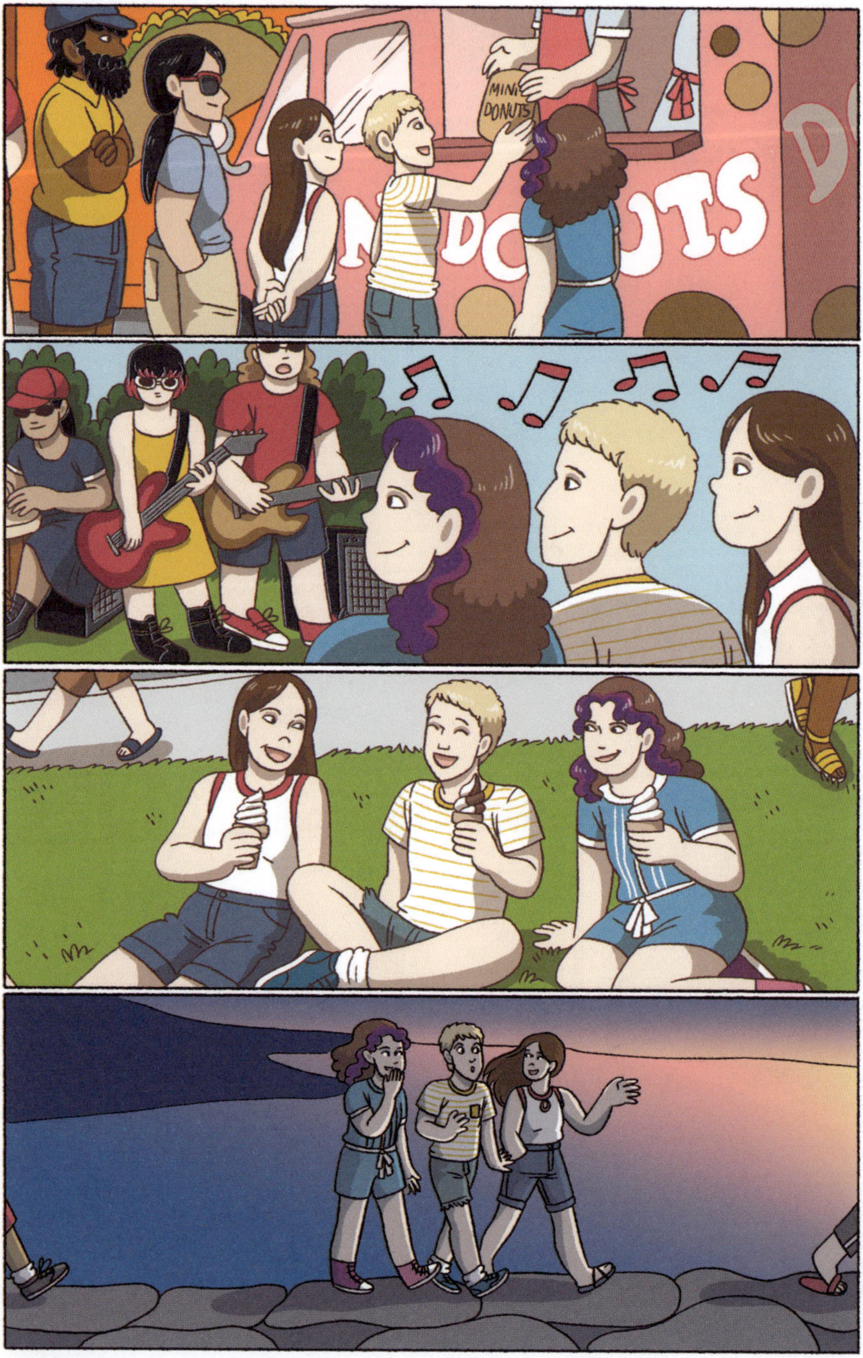
MINI DONUTS

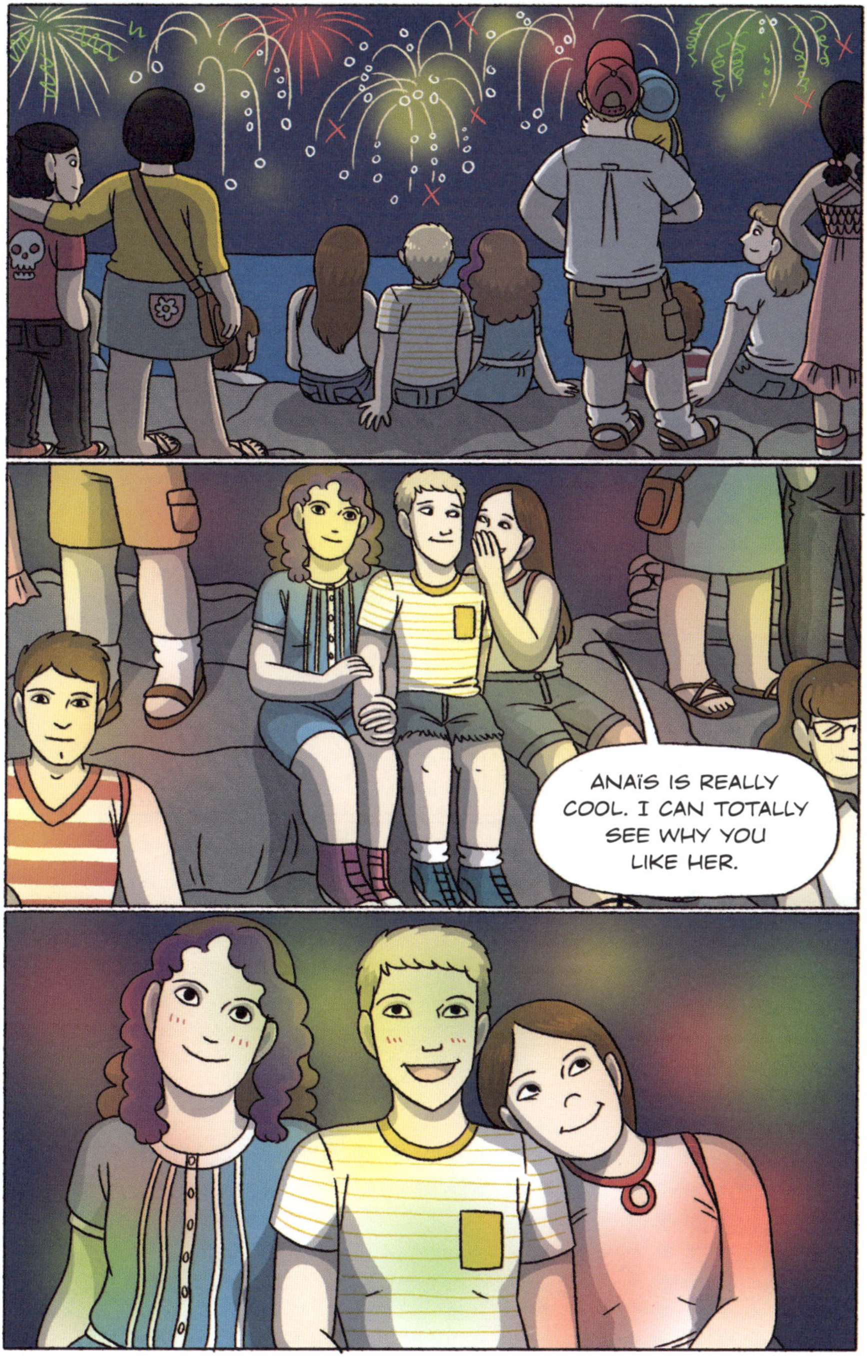
ANAÏS IS REALLY COOL. I CAN TOTALLY SEE WHY YOU LIKE HER.

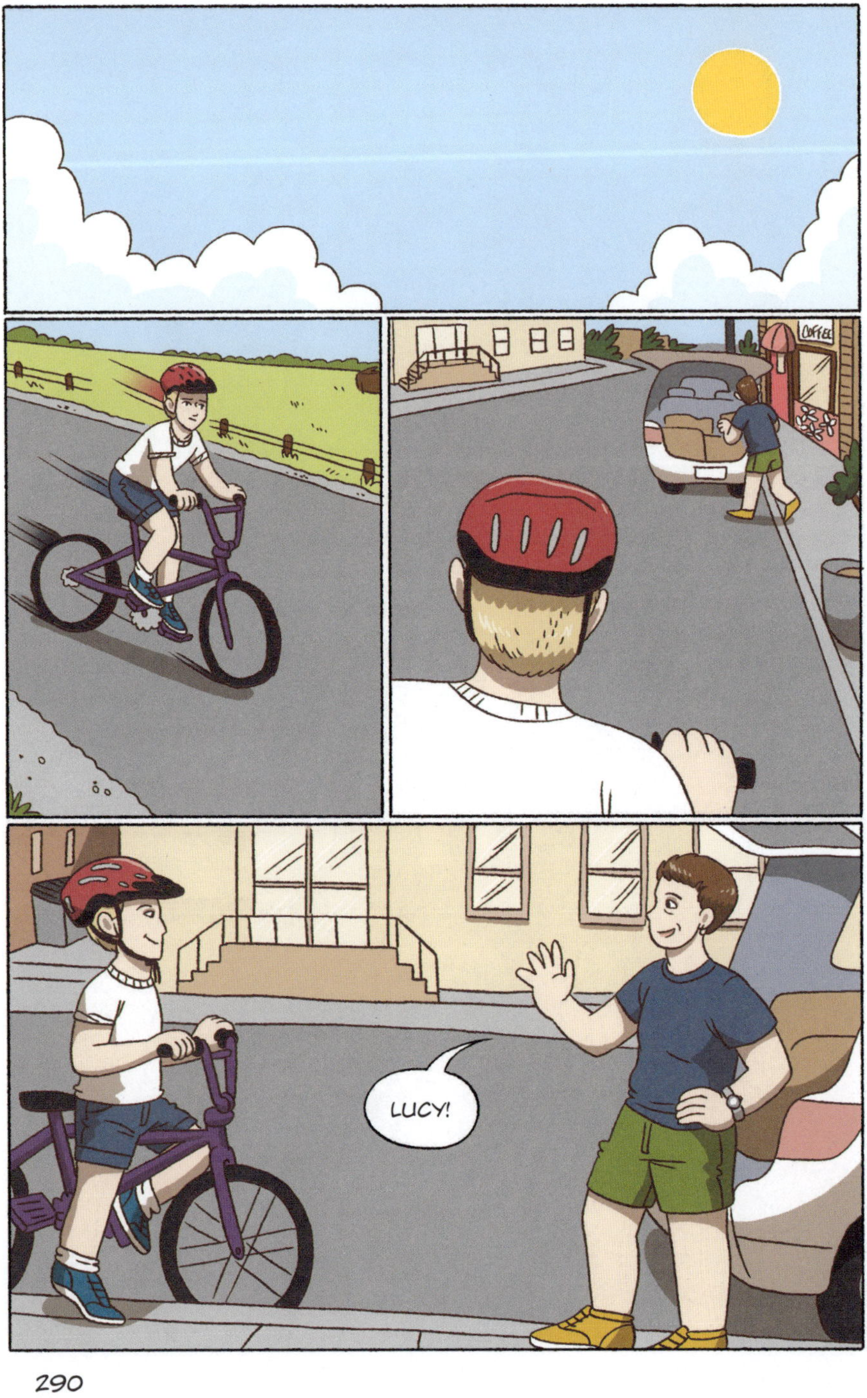
COFFEE
LUCY!

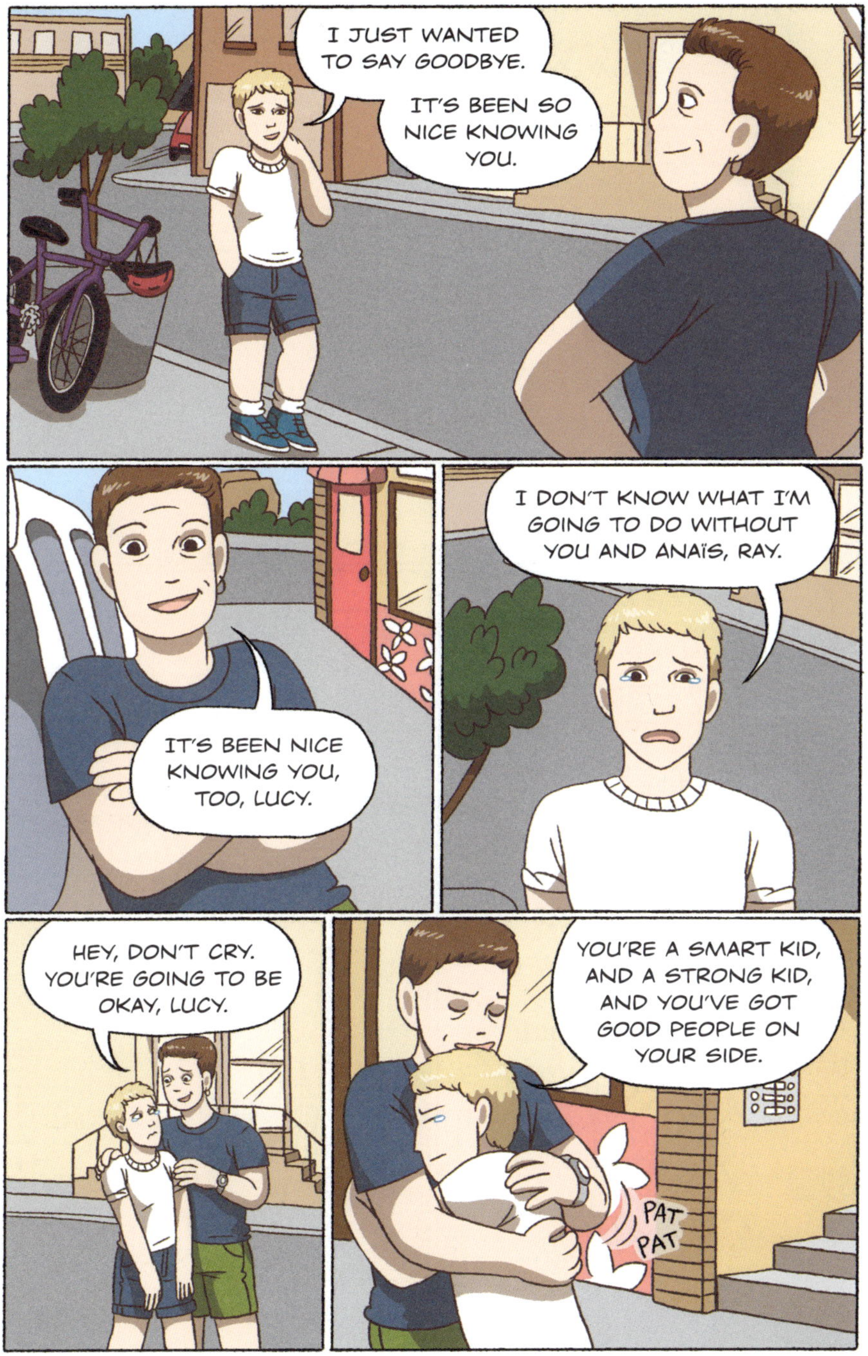
I JUST WANTED TO SAY GOODBYE.
IT'S BEEN SO NICE KNOWING YOU.
IT'S BEEN NICE KNOWING YOU, TOO, LUCY.
I DON'T KNOW WHAT I'M GOING TO DO WITHOUT YOU AND ANAÏS, RAY.
HEY, DON'T CRY. YOU'RE GOING TO BE OKAY, LUCY.
YOU'RE A SMART KID, AND A STRONG KID, AND YOU'VE GOT GOOD PEOPLE ON YOUR SIDE.
PAT PAT

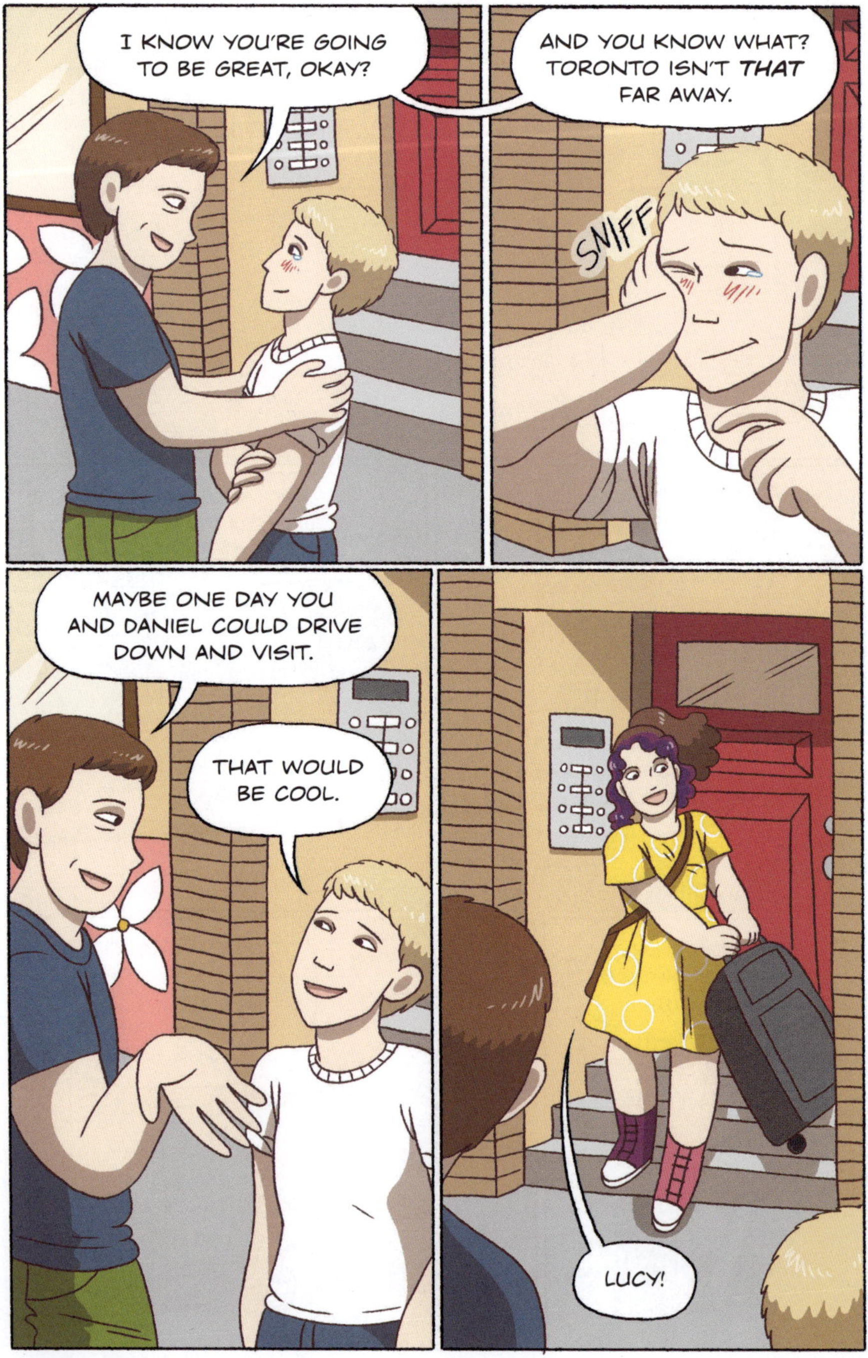
I KNOW YOU'RE GOING TO BE GREAT, OKAY?
AND YOU KNOW WHAT? TORONTO ISN'T ***THAT*** FAR AWAY.
SNIFF
MAYBE ONE DAY YOU AND DANIEL COULD DRIVE DOWN AND VISIT.
THAT WOULD BE COOL.
LUCY!

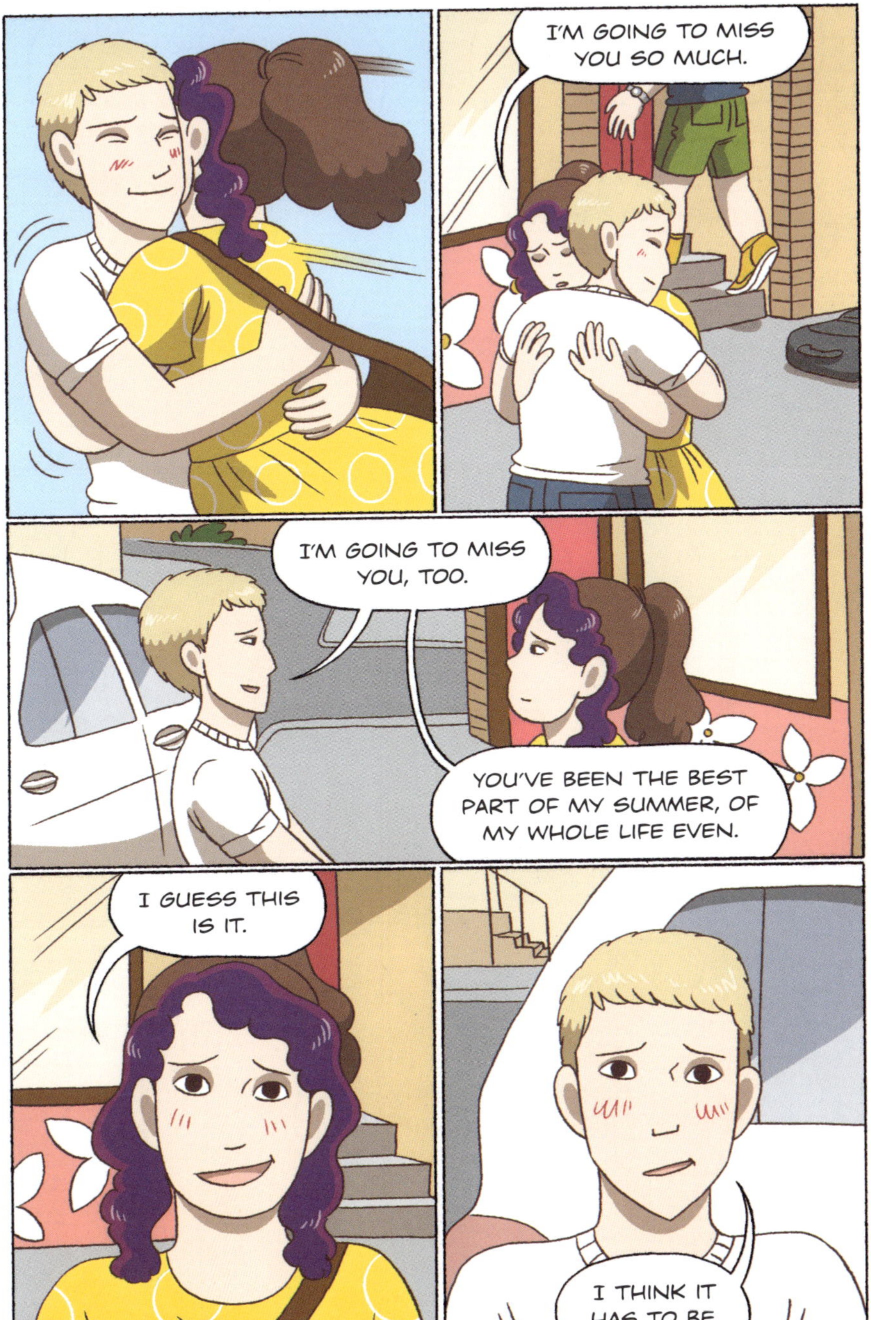
I'M GOING TO MISS YOU SO MUCH.
I'M GOING TO MISS YOU, TOO.
YOU'VE BEEN THE BEST PART OF MY SUMMER, OF MY WHOLE LIFE EVEN.
I GUESS THIS IS IT.
I THINK IT HAS TO BE.

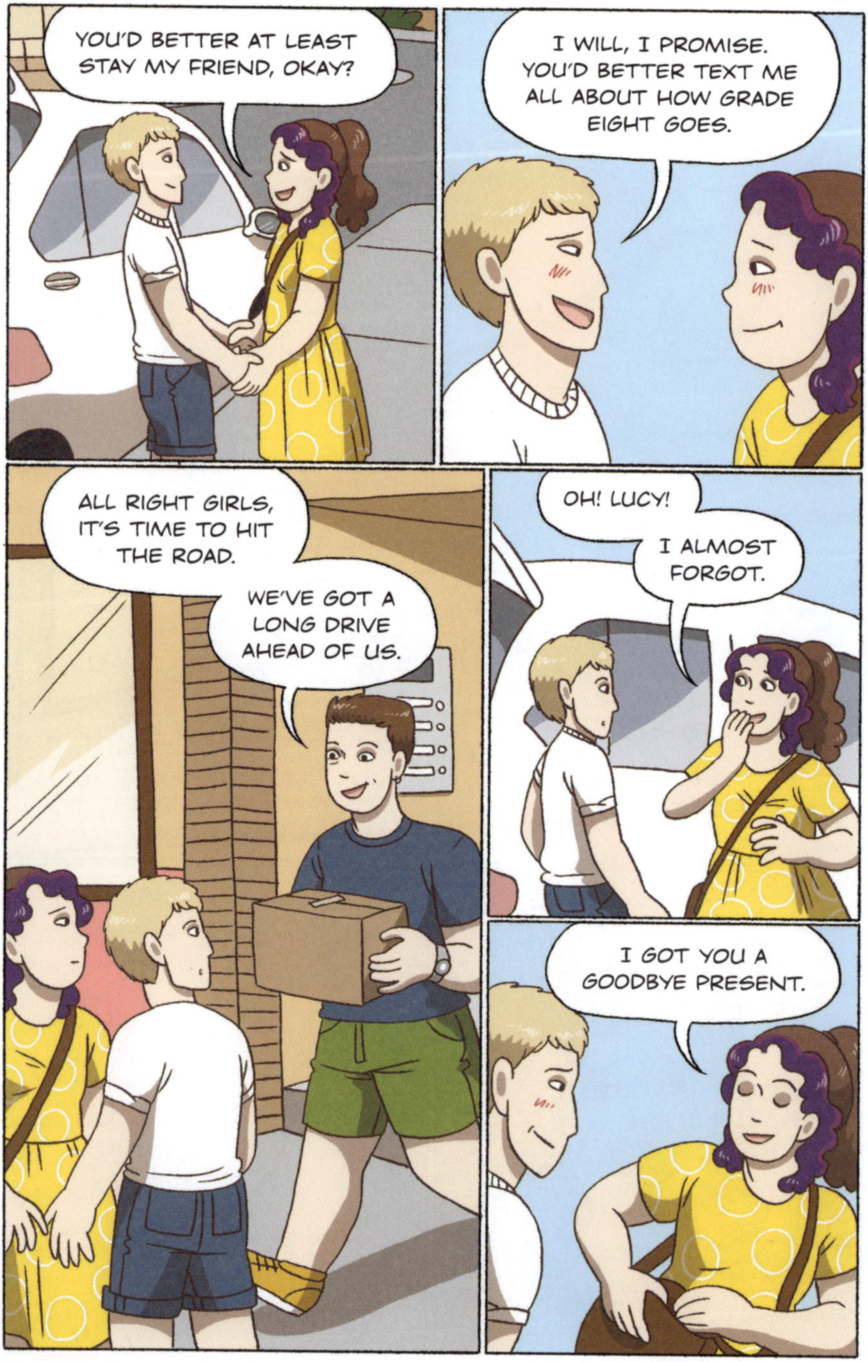
YOU'D BETTER AT LEAST STAY MY FRIEND, OKAY?
I WILL, I PROMISE. YOU'D BETTER TEXT ME ALL ABOUT HOW GRADE EIGHT GOES.
ALL RIGHT GIRLS, IT'S TIME TO HIT THE ROAD.
WE'VE GOT A LONG DRIVE AHEAD OF US.
OH! LUCY!
I ALMOST FORGOT.
I GOT YOU A GOODBYE PRESENT.

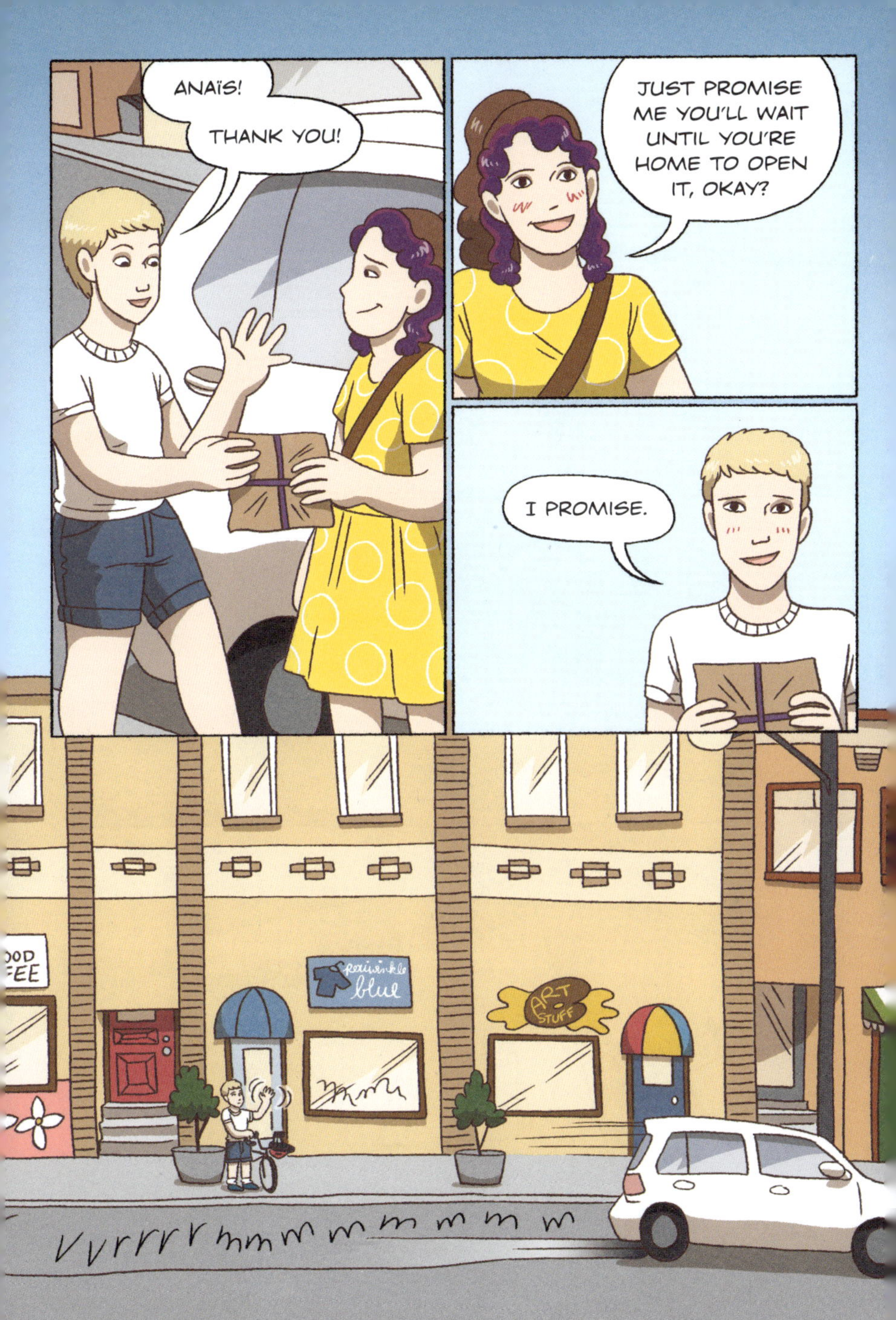
ANAÏS!
THANK YOU!
JUST PROMISE ME YOU'LL WAIT UNTIL YOU'RE HOME TO OPEN IT, OKAY?
I PROMISE.
periwinkle blue
ART STUFF
VVRRRRRMMMMMMMMMM

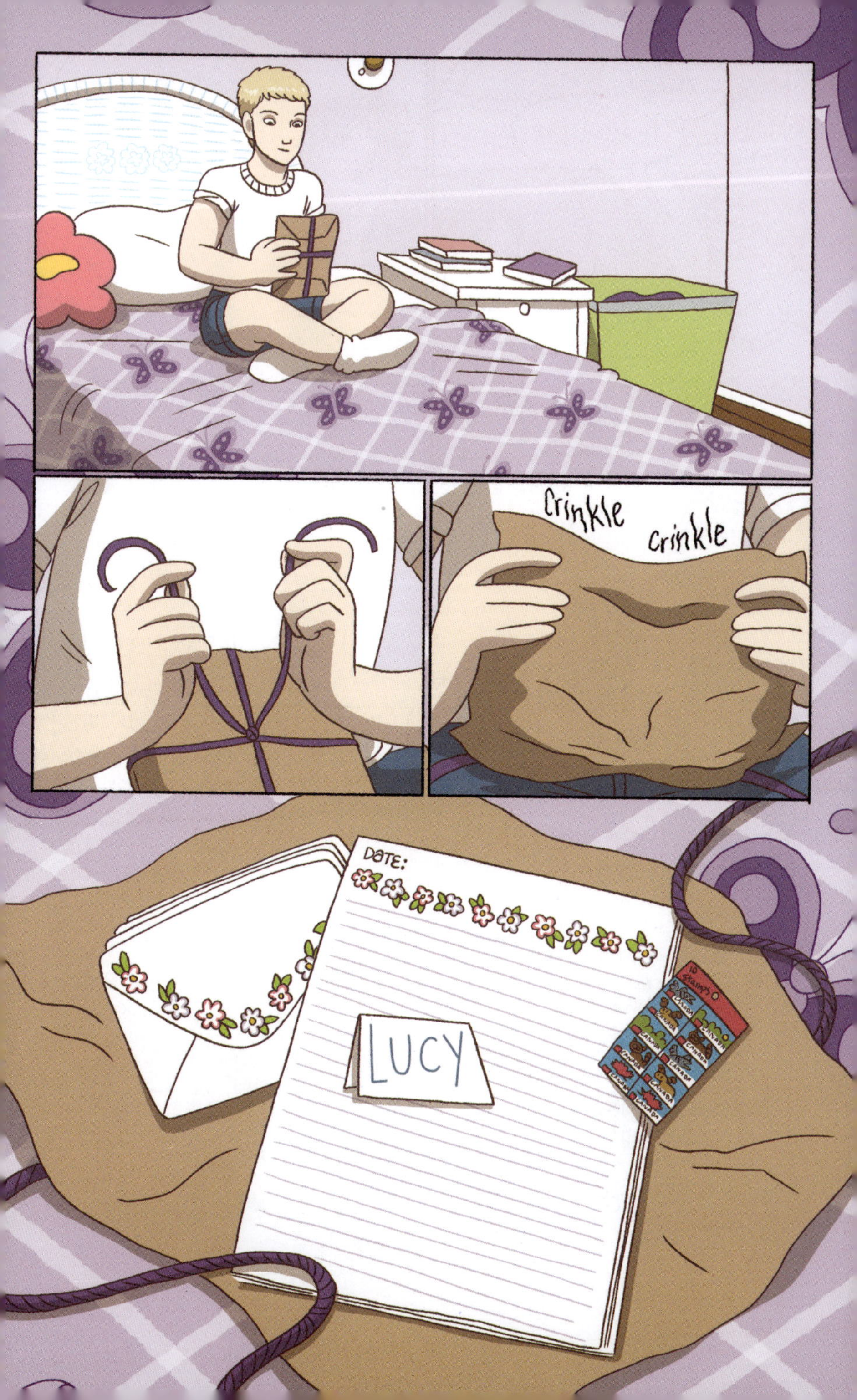
crinkle
crinkle
DATE:
LUCY
10 stamps
CANADA

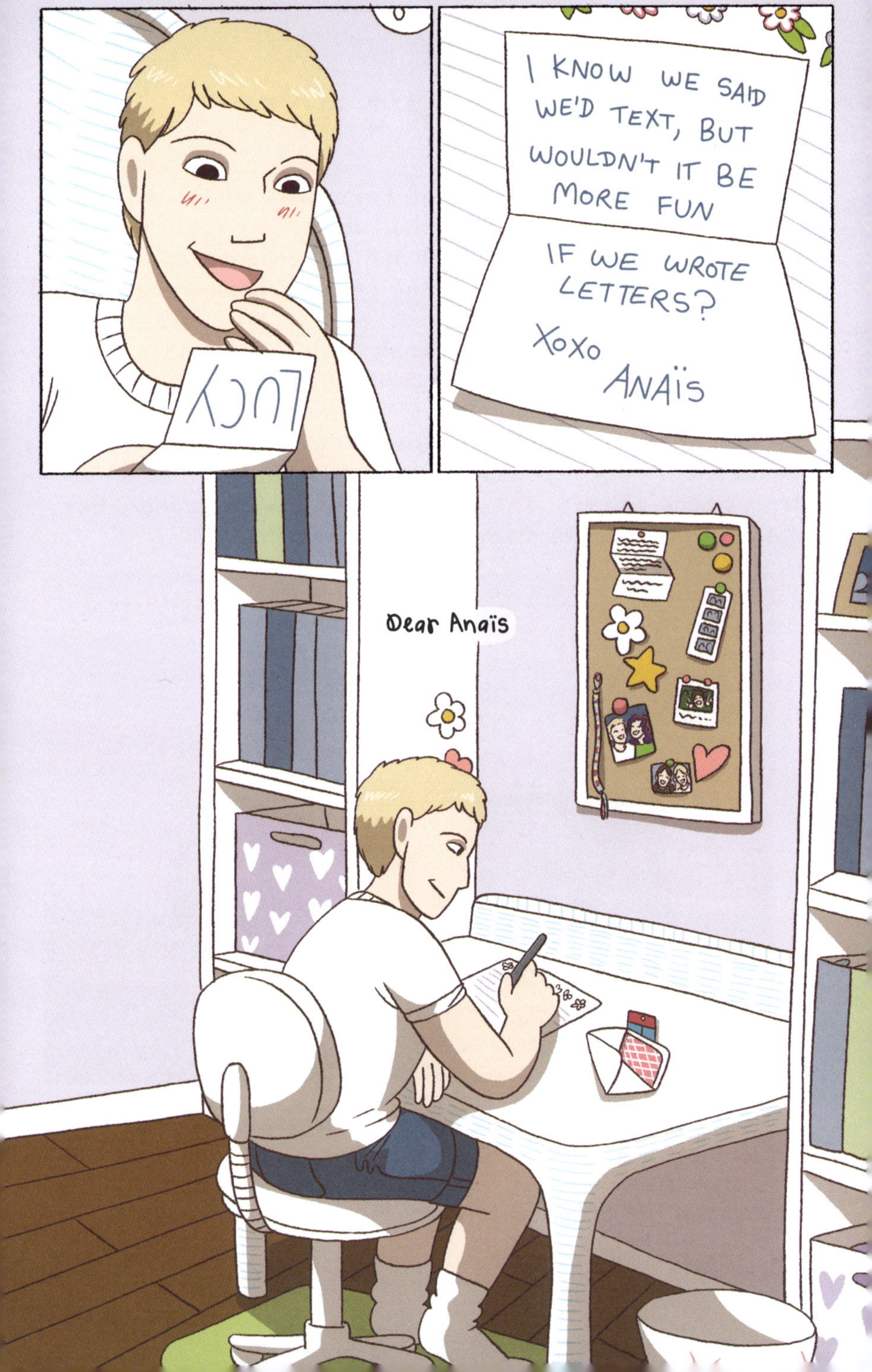
LUCY
I KNOW WE SAID WE'D TEXT, BUT WOULDN'T IT BE MORE FUN
IF WE WROTE LETTERS?
XOXO
ANAÏS
Dear Anaïs

AUTHOR'S NOTE

Milforth is not a real place, and I'm a very different person from Lucy. But both Milforth and Lucy sprang forth from my memories of being twelve with the sun on my face and the wind in my hair, biking along the endless ribbons of road that unfurl across rural Ontario.

I grew up in Toronto, like Anaïs. But I spent many summers and weekends several hours outside the city at a one-hundred-year-old farmhouse my family affectionately called "the Farm." My parents were married for a long time before they had kids. Sometime during that time, they bought the Farm as an escape from hectic city life. They sold it when I was fourteen, but many of my favorite memories happened there.

My parents love to cycle, and they shared that love with me and my sibling. In the summer, we would look at a map of the county surrounding the Farm. We'd choose a point on it and spend the day biking to a small town that usually wasn't

more than an intersection and a corner store. There are few feelings I love more than soaring along a rural road, listening to the bugs buzz in the fields, watching as the hot concrete shimmers with watery mirages ahead of me.

The Farm was full of adventures. When I was really little, my dad would load me and my sibling into a big yellow wheelbarrow and take us to explore the fields and forests. The neighbors baled the hay in our fields, and when we were older, we'd climb on the bales to fly kites. The Farm was perched on a particularly windy hill—so windy, in fact, that it was in tornado territory. The woods behind the house were encircled with raspberry

patches. There were many nearby lakes to go swimming in, and we'd hunt for fossils on the rocky beaches. We'd visit estate sales and markets to look at books and antiques (this is where I developed my love of used books—which I passed on to Lucy).

I could write about a million words about how much I loved the years we spent at the Farm. I could tell you about the gravestone in the woods, or the fox skeleton in the barn. I could tell you about all the nights the power went out in the winter and we had to sleep by the woodstove, or about the wild strawberries that grew in the lawn. But that would have to be a whole other book. Instead, I hope that when you read Lucy's story, you can feel some of the fun, the freedom, and the love of being a kid with a bike, and a whole summer of possibilities ahead of you.